Praise for

TALES OF PROTECTION

"As readers, we relax into the author's skillful hands, allowing his luminous writing to carry us, and the tale, along. . . . So wooed are we by Hansen's abilities to take us to new worlds that we . . . giv(e) ourselves over instead to the joy of remarkable storytelling." —*Los Angeles Times*

"A virtuosic, allegorical romp through history that offers some of the most beguiling storytelling in recent years." —*Seattle Times*

"[Hansen] fills each tale with compelling human details and unifies them with resounding charm." —*San Francisco Chronicle*

"Bulges with all the wonderfully strange, arcane information of centuries ago—how to read nautical charts, interpret rock formations, create aquamarine paint or gild a detail on a fresco." —*Newsday*

"Drunk with magic realism, miracles and meaningful coincidence . . . Beautiful and compelling." —*Time Out New York*

"Imprints itself on the mind like a Technicolor dream: beautiful, ethereal, just beyond the grasp of reason." —*The San Diego Union-Tribune*

"Some works of fiction are hypnotic, possessing—almost beyond our ken. . . . One such novel was last year's profoundly moving *Austerlitz*. . . . Another is *Possession*. . . . Now there is *Tales of Protection*, a monumental examination of coincidence and synchronicity." —*The Memphis Commercial Appeal*

"Dramatizes a moment when a life is changed radically and forever because of a phenomenon we call coincidence." —*The Star-Ledger* (Newark)

"A beautiful and charismatically written novel."
—*The Long Beach Union* (CA)

TALES

OF

PROTECTION

A Harvest Book • *Harcourt, Inc.*

ORLANDO   AUSTIN   NEW YORK

SAN DIEGO   TORONTO   LONDON

TALES

OF

PROTECTION

ERIK FOSNES HANSEN

Translated from the Norwegian by Nadia Christensen

Requests for permission to make copies of any part of the work should be
mailed to the following address: Permissions Department, Harcourt, Inc.,
6277 Sea Harbor Drive, Orlando, Florida 32887-6777.

www.HarcourtBooks.com

First published by Farrar, Straus and Giroux

The translator wishes to thank O. C. Hognander, Jr., for his valuable
editorial advice, especially regarding nautical terminology.

Library of Congress Cataloging-in-Publication Data
available upon request
ISBN 0-15-602794-1

Text set in Janson
Designed by Gretchen Achilles

Printed in the United States of America
First Harvest edition 2003

A C E G I K J H F D B

CONTENTS

TALES

OF

PROTECTION

PROLOGUE IN HEAVEN AND ON EARTH

Life is a bird. At four o'clock the temperature was 12 degrees Celsius. Already an hour before sunrise the birds in the trees around the fields began to sing, first carefully like small drops of sound in the air, then with uninhibited song. The light rose to the delicate sound of life, white membranes appeared on the surface of things. Leaves and grass glistened.

Earth's huge mass turned round, with inalterable power and speed; the planet's daily terminator, boundary line of the morning, came rushing from the east. The sun rose slowly in the sky. The temperature rose one and a half degrees. Suddenly flowers and trees were surrounded by an invisible cloud of pollen. If we'd had other eyes we could have seen these clouds like golden swirls around the crown of every flower, every catkin. As the temperature rose two degrees more, the soil began to surrender moisture, which rose into the air as invisible vapor. Every cell in the plants and ground surface breathed out moisture, leaves and blades of grass stretched imperceptibly, the birds sang, and around the plants' small nebulae of fragrance and pollen the insects began working with busy drilling sounds.

If we had eyes that could see the invisible, indeed, if one stood on the steps outside the vestibule of the little white wooden church and looked across the meadows and fields, one would sense at least some of the phenomena that occurred this early summer morning. But no one is standing there.

Apparently no one sees all this, no one is fully aware of what is happening here today, at this spot on Earth, by the little church, here where our story will begin. In the hazel-tree grove over by the stone fence a snout beetle is busily occupied, but if we ask her, she simply sniffs a few times and looks at us in bewilderment. Nearby we meet a hedgehog, who regretfully blames his eyes and general lack of an overview, and promptly lies down to sleep. But high in the air two swifts scurry about among many others. Their names are Kri and Kry, and their workday is already in full swing as they carry on their loud, shrieking conversations. So to begin somewhere, in order to get our story under way, we will interview Kri and Kry, who at this moment are flying the highest and have an overview.

Kri and Kry (busily): "We don't have time! We don't have time!"

Excuse me, I don't mean to disturb you, but what's happening here today?

Kri: "Oh, just the usual. Insects, and so forth. As for me, I live down there under the eaves of the church and have just become a father, so I'm rather busy. High up for food today. High up. Excuse me a moment—" (he swoops down suddenly) "—like that. A big one. A spider. The babies love them. They taste like—"

Kry: "I think he's wondering about something else, Kri." (aside) "He's so terribly proud of the babies. First time, and so forth."

A spider?

Kry: "Yes, didn't you know? Many spiders make their way high into the air. They use their web as a sail."

Kri: "Whee!" (swoops down abruptly again)

Kry: "Our task is to live in the air. We catch insects, and so forth. We soar on air currents and turn our undersides toward the sun, and so forth."

What kind of relationship do you have to the earth?

Kri (on his way up): "Are they still asking those questions?"

Kry: "A nonexistent relationship, I must say. Of course *we* see the rising moisture and notice temperature conditions down there, and so forth. They affect buoyancy, turbulence, thermology, and so forth. You see, newly plowed soil is black and moist and provides great buoyancy when the sun shines on it, as on a day like this. And of course we pay attention to the paths of insects in the air."

Kri: "Aha! Insects!"

Kry: "But otherwise we feel somewhat distant from the earth, to tell the truth. Our tasks are elsewhere. Air currents. Buoyancy zones above moist hollows in the ground, and so forth. It has to do with the shape of our wings. Maybe you'd be interested to hear a little about buoyancy, and so forth? A big city, for example, is filled with buoyancy zones and offers interesting aeronautical possibilities. It can be very challenging, one could say. Whereas other buoyancy zones, for example along a cliff-lined coast, can be dangerous. A friend from my youth, a storm petrel named Castro, poor fellow, perished a few years ago near Tenerife, close to the Pico de Teide volcano. Perhaps you know about the strong winds near the rock wall there? You don't? It's like a wind tunnel that occurs far up in the stratosphere. My friend was an adventurer, one could say, and so forth. Just like his father. Absolutely had to try; so the wind took him, one could say. Not until three weeks later did he come down, as a clump of ice."

Kri: "Ah yes, the southern migration. I'm already looking forward to more exotic food than these cabbage flies. Cardinal beetles. Banana flies, and so forth. Egypt's cicadas. Delicacies."

Kry (ignoring him): "In ancient Egypt, people didn't believe that swallows migrated south in the fall, but thought they dug themselves into the Nile's mud and sludge and went into hibernation, and so forth. A disgusting thought for a swallow. We swifts can sleep in flight, don't need to land. Do you know, our relative flight speed across a stretch of open sea can be as fast as—"

Thank you, thank you, very interesting. But to draw Kri into the conversation a little more, what's happening down there today?

Kri (stops on his way down): "Excuse me, what did you say? Well, there's a dead man lying down there staring. That's quite usual, for that matter. Happens regularly. Our babies are already used to it. Then the people dressed in black come and stand outside our home and weep for a while, and so forth, before they drive away in those—those—things. Excuse me."

Kry (slightly offended): "I thought he was more interested in what *we* were doing, but it was just a dead man. Yes, as always, human beings are

5

most concerned with themselves. They don't know the swallow's joy in the air, and so forth. But yes, that's right, they brought him yesterday evening, along with a great many flowers."

So he's been lying there all night?

Kry: "All night. But let me tell you more about thermology above stretches of open sea. You see, just above the crests of waves, when the wind blows, it creates a—"

Kri (interrupts his colleague): "Please forgive Kry. The elder's wisdom of life. Flying knowledge, and so forth. It's true that they brought him yesterday. Excuse me."

Was anyone with him?

Kri: "No one except the young girl."

Did she cry?

Kri: "She cried. And so forth."

⚓

It is still dark inside the church. From the ceiling, in the center section where the choir and nave meet, hangs the church's votive ship, a model of a seventeenth-century Danish frigate complete with rigging and armament, painstakingly made. The church lies near the sea, and the congregation hung up *Ulrik Christian's Rescue* on Easter Sunday 1721. Tonight the ship is decorated with black mourning crepe, which hangs from its crossbeams along with the golden lion ensigns. It sways slowly in the darkness. The bowsprit is turned toward the east (toward the altar and the rising sun), and it sails through the night and into the morning as it has done for a hundred thousand nights.

The church is dark. A heavy, sweet scent of flowers fills the air.

Outside, everything that happens each morning is happening; here inside nothing happens. Life is a bird. And you are the branch that sways back and forth.

⚓

Now the girl enters the church, opens the instrument case, seats herself with the cello supported between her thighs, and begins to play.

The old man lay in his coffin and thought all this and saw everything he hadn't seen before. To be dead was unlike anything he had experienced. He reminisced quietly in the darkness; the darkness was like lukewarm, liberating water after a long, long workday. Let himself sink into the tub and smile, ahh! He touched the old femur fracture; odd how different it was when pain didn't shoot through his thigh and far up his back with the slightest movement. Strange he hadn't thought about how stubborn and angry it had made him. But this gentle darkness was a blessing, ahh! It took away all his anger, all his annoyance. Ahh, to feel pain after pain disappear. Through the darkness the dead man could see everything the living can't see. Somehow he seemed to be inside and outside at the same time, inside the coffin and in everything outside it. He was inside and outside time, and that was something quite new. He could see everything at once. *He* could see the colors shimmering around birds' wings, the insects' airy golden streets; *he* could see the swirls that moisture and pollen and ethereal secretions created around each flower in the fields; from here he could see the sun rise and the earth turn, and he could see the girl's face in the blue dawn light out there; he could hear the music she played; but above all, and this was something quite new, something utterly remarkable and unlike anything he had ever experienced: he could hear the music behind the music, not what was in the air sending vibrations to the stone floor and timbers, to his coffin lid, but the original, the intended music, the music behind the music (and perhaps that was best, for usually she didn't play very well). It was utterly, wonderfully strange, and unlike anything else. Yes. He had to smile. And the smile became a light in the good darkness where he was rocking slowly. It was unlike anything he had experienced, and he had experienced much, oh yes, much, much. He saw the girl's face out there in the music, yet not just her face but also the reality (behind), and he smiled again (smiling was completely different now) and thought, oh yes, ahh, if I'd been young, as young as I feel right now, and was out there with you (or in there—odd, how little difference there suddenly is between in and out, ahh!), if I'd been out there with you, been young and strong and tanned and sinewy, then I'd have taken your arm and run out with you, out across the fields, taken you deep down into mining tunnels, or up into the mountains to see the sun rise. I'd have (ahh!) shown you the whole world, the world that once was mine, that I ruled like a god, where I was a boy and a young man, and like a hunter I wrung from the earth everything it could give me of secrets and riches—and I'd have smelled you (the dead old man was no longer ashamed to think such things), sniffed you, savored you, and smiled at you. I'd have watched the day dawn with you.

And suddenly he realized that he would miss the world greatly, and he nearly began to weep, but it wasn't weeping (it was completely different now, everything, ahh, was different); it was something else.

Her face—

Grief, he thought, *grief about everything that is.*

But he knew that this condition would not last, that it was an intermediate state, that he soon would leave. But for a while, for a short time yet, he would linger here, then he would leave with the rushing sound of light and humming insects. A little longer. As he had stripped away everything else, almost like articles of clothing, he would also strip away the memories. Everything he remembered. And he remembered much more than his own life. This morning he could remember almost *everything.*

And here she stops playing her chaconne, puts down the bow and the instrument, goes into the sacristy. It has grown light in the church while she played, the day has arrived, and our story can

PART ONE

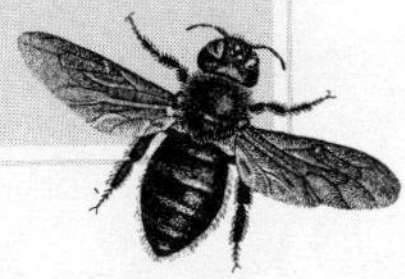

ONE

*Tantus amor florum et generandi gloria mellis.**

VIRGIL, *Georgics, IV*

begin. The old man was finally dead, and he had a splendid funeral. No expense was spared. The church was decorated with flowers from the altar rail all the way to the vestibule; floral wreaths had arrived from far and near, from business connections and competitors, from Lloyd's of London, from the government and the industrial association. The royal palace had sent a garland. And since the old man had also held his protective hand over a few painters, memorial wreaths had come from them, as well as from the artists' association. The family was represented by large and small floral arrangements, of course; there were wreaths from the Greek and Japanese embassies, and from several giant foreign corporations. A casual glance at the floral splendor in the old church would make one think the old man had been much loved, but there was scarcely a greeting from a single friend, because he'd had no friends. At least not in recent years. He had grown very old, and most of the few friends from his youth had crept under their coffin lids long before he did. In a sense, the old man had probably helped to drive his friends into an early grave with his difficult, nagging

---

*So great is their love for the flowers,
so great their pride over the honey they create.*

11

ways and his everlasting whims, follies, ideas, and attacks of rage that had caused those closest to him agonizing moments and long, wakeful nights. He had been one of those people who seem to absorb the strength of others, and perhaps that was why he had grown so old. He had also been miserly. For the last thirty years he'd had no close friends at all, so it was a lonesome man who lay in the oak coffin up there by the altar; respected, of course, for his power and glory, but lonely. People bowed before the casket when they came in, bowed for the mining company, for the shipping company equities and the art collection, bowed for the fruit imports and large stockholdings in the paper industry, but no one bowed for a friend. His wife had died early, and he had no living children; however, a long string of nephews, nieces, grandnephews, third cousins, and an endless number of more distant shoots on the family tree were now gathered expectantly in the three front rows of pews. It was a rare family gathering. None of them had been particularly close to him. And despite all the beautiful memorial tributes, and despite the preacher's arduously prepared sermon—he shone like a grief-stricken orange from the pulpit—nobody had really known him. With the possible exception of one person. And that possibility was what everyone feared.

Cheerful white sunlight streamed through the windows as the preacher spoke, the floral arrangements glowed in pastel spring colors and put the entire congregation in a festive mood somehow. Even the organ music in a minor key could not destroy the impression of something beautiful, something *proper*, here within these white wooden walls. For the expectant family the only fly in the ointment was the girl sitting there, somewhat hidden in the third row.

Now and then they stole sidelong glances at her; yes, she looked sad, but not *too* sad. For the most part she sat staring down at her blue corduroy skirt. It looked homemade. "Too bad she has long arms," whispered Aunt Gussi to Aunt Ella, who promptly began busily looking in the hymnbook. That Gussi—she could never restrain herself. But what if it was true, about the tattooing? At least they hadn't seen the much-discussed ring in her nose, the ring Peder always called the enfant terrible ring, whatever he meant by that. But it probably could be removed for solemn occasions.

"As we bid farewell today," said the preacher. Uncle Christian sat in a dark suit in the middle of the front row, squeezed in next to his brother

Peder. Company manager Christian Bolt had a good grasp of the firm's day-to-day operation, and everyone assumed that *he* . . . Yes. It must be he. He was not at all sure himself. He stole a quick furtive glance at the girl sitting back there with downcast eyes. He saw only her hair, not her face. God knows what the old man might have come up with. *That* would certainly be a feather in Peder's cap. The thought did not make Christian Bolt very happy. And he suspected the old man might have come up with a little of everything just to annoy him, Christian. The brothers were in their fifties and were like two peas in a pod—as businessmen often are. Peder, the younger of the two, was assistant manager and had the least to do, so he was always suntanned. Christian looked at his brother's brown hand resting on the pew beside his own pale one; he felt tired and overworked, and in moments like this he sensed he was moving too quickly toward the Great Beyond. He just didn't want Peder to think he had missed out on anything. The workday in the old tyrant's service had been much too long; the old man had never wanted to die, let alone give away anything. God knows what he might have come up with. He stole another quick furtive glance at the girl.

"But Death is a friend," the preacher intoned, "who releases and opens." The sermon dragged on, and the audience began staring up into the air. A strange custom, thought Aunt Gussi, to hang a boat under the ceiling. Outside was the early summer day, bright and enticing, and lawyer Holst had already set a meeting for that evening at the old man's estate. There was much to divert attention from the sermon that day.

Despite discretion and the duty not to divulge confidential matters, the family knew the old man had been to town just once in the past year, when he had gone to the lawyer's office. Suddenly he had stood in the doorway of the venerable office on the third floor; he had climbed all the steps alone and had created an infernal commotion because the secretary did not immediately recognize him but, on the contrary, asked if he had an appointment; and also because lawyer Holst, who did not have extrasensory perception and so could not anticipate the old man's unexpected arrival, was out of the office. The old man was like a comet, a truly unpredictable one that usually stayed in distant invisible celestial spheres and only showed itself near Earth once in a blue moon. The lawyer was tracked down with the help of a mobile phone; he was in an important bankruptcy meeting at the bank, but when he heard who was in the waiting room at his office he turned pale and trembled so violently the mahogany table reverberated and instant coffee could not alleviate his shaking. Lawyer Holst left the failing bank at once and reached his office fourteen minutes later, a personal record for that distance. Then the old man disappeared into the lawyer's office and stayed there a long time. The lawyer had requested the folder containing his will, and Andersen, the old man's jack-of-all-trades, had to witness something or other along with a secretary. Then Andersen drove the old man home. And that was the last time the testator was seen in town. It was disturbing.

The preacher had much to say about the old man's long adventurous life, from the time he mined gold in Africa as a young geologist in the thirties and survived both malaria and murder attempts, to the mysterious and dubious years when he was said to have worked with rubber and rashness in the Far East and to have discovered a revolutionary new distillation method that made him even richer, until he resurfaced again in London during the war, where he attracted attention by turning up at lunch with King Haakon at Foliejon Park in January dressed in a tropical suit and sandals. The preacher had to slide over what happened after the war; he did not mention that the old man liked to shatter glasses at board meetings and that he sent his exhausted brothers to an early grave. Instead, the preacher said a few words about his support for art. After the old man moved to the family residence at Ekelund his appearances in the capital city grew increasingly rare, but he still held the business in a firm grip and regularly called the family to Ekelund to take them to task. This was also the period when he got his research notion, and when the senile old alchemist enthusiastically poured money into crazy projects, from nuclear physics to zoology and horticulture, and filled Ekelund with strange animals and things—until he disappeared entirely into great and lofty loneliness and his isolation became complete. The family gnashed their teeth. The preacher said nothing about this either.

During the final decades of his life, he had been almost inaccessible; he buried himself in his studies and his sumptuous estate with his art, his garden, and his bees.

With one exception, however. In the very last year of his life the old black sheep had had company in his tyrannical loneliness, from the family's black lamb, a slightly peripheral grandniece. Lea. Months went by before the family heard that Lea lived at Ekelund, helped the old man with the garden and beehives, and also assisted Andersen in the house. For that matter, it was just like old Bolt to shower his love on precisely her. It was very disturbing. She had been sweet as a child, they recalled, serious, mature for her age, and somewhat remote, with black ribbons in her hair—always black ribbons; her widowed mother put them on the child. But then came the difficult years, and the black ribbons disappeared irretrievably. Lea probably resembled her mother. Or maybe she simply resembled her granduncle. In any case: somehow or other these two family rejects, the old man and the young girl, had met each other. The family cast stolen glances toward the slight figure in the third row, while the preacher talked and talked, about the resurrection and the life; her face was tilted down toward her lap the whole time and was almost hidden by all the blond hair. They shuddered at the unpleasant thought of the past year's symbiosis between those two out there at Ekelund. God only knew what it might lead to.

The family thought about all of this.

"And the peace of God," the pastor quoted, "that passeth all understanding, shall keep your hearts and your minds."

But Lea, sitting there in the third row, thought about the silent trip in the ambulance and about the old man's face, helpless and frightened as a baby's. His hands fumbling for hers. The tires singing, singing in the wet spring night. And the strange feeling of *time*, of an eternity of time, the feeling that nothing was urgent where they were driving. She remembered the oddly reassuring look he gave her when they arrived at the hospital, friendly and resigned at the same time, while she gently stroked his hair. His hair was clammy with cold sweat. She had never touched it before. She thought about what he had whispered before they came with their tubes and everything suddenly began happening so quickly again and his eyes seemed to fill with smoke. As Lea sat looking down at her skirt, she told herself that he was the only person in the family who had acted *real* toward her, even until the last evening.

"Brothers!" quoted the pastor, "I do not consider that I have made it my own; but one thing I do: forgetting what lies behind and straining forward to what lies ahead, I press on toward the goal."

In her mind, Lea saw her uncle; from beneath his white mustache he sent her a gruff, uncertain laugh as she opened one of his beehives for the first time, her hands numb with fear—as if he wondered whether she was good for anything at all. Sitting there, Lea did not know if she had been good for anything.

Was she good for anything?

"I wonder," he answered her from far away in the sunlight of that day, "how bees can know, even before the day begins, that precisely today the red clover will bloom, and fly toward it, while the next morning *know* that today it's the heather's turn, and set out in a completely different direction. How can all these small insects *simultaneously* know, without a brain, without knowing anything, that today they should visit *this* meadow, and tomorrow *that* one?"

The bees buzzed around them, numbed and sleepy; the air was pungent with smoke and beeswax. The sight of tens of thousands of creeping insects had an unpleasant effect on Lea, it made her scalp prickle, but the old man's face was serene behind fine-meshed black netting. "On the whole," he said, as he carefully put down the smoke blower, "it's a question of knowing without knowing."

"Knowing without knowing?" she had to ask.

"And wanting without wanting. If you want something too intensely, things fall apart in your hands. You start to doubt everything. As soon as you let go, everything comes *to* you. Then you *know*, without knowing."

"Is that true in business too, Uncle?" she asked in a slightly mocking tone, which she immediately regretted, but he was not offended.

"In business too. Here, hold this for a while." He gave her the smoke blower. Slowly and carefully he lifted out a dripping golden honeycomb. "Actually, it applies to everything one does," he grunted, "or it ought to apply. To everything. Careful now, you've got to move slowly, or they get irritable. Like me."

But Lea also remembered the very first day, when she had stood outside the big house in the rain and rung the bell, without wanting anything at all, without knowing how she had gotten there, almost without knowing who she was.

"And who are *you*?" he barked. He towered in the doorway, tall and thin and terrible, with white hair and rubber boots. The depths of his eyes glittered with old age and primitive rage as he scrutinized her. "Well?" he snarled, when she had introduced herself. He looked disapprovingly at her backpack and wet clothing. "You can't stay here. Nobody is welcome here. Andersen will drive you to the train." And how should she reply to that? Ever since she was a child she had heard how awful he was, how impossible and stingy and hostile toward the family; she had heard all the stories about the strange things he did, heard that he sent family members a bill for each minute it took to read the letters they sent him, heard all the whispered suggestions about nursing homes and a legal declaration of incompetence; but an old man who cared for ten beehives and a park with a greenhouse all on his own did not let himself be declared incompetent so easily. When Lea met the old man she was terrified and did not know what to say. She did not know anything, was just soaking wet. So she said nothing. The old man gave her a hasty look, turned on his heel, and disappeared into the house. She noticed that he limped. He shut the door firmly behind him.

As she sat on the front steps looking out across the coarse gravel driveway, the tears had come. She clung to her backpack, clutched it as if it were an old traveling companion who had seen and understood everything. When the door opened behind her, she thought it was this Andersen who was going to drive her out into the world again, send her out into the breakers from which she had just struggled ashore. But it was the old man, and he said:

"All right. It's getting late. There are no more trains tonight. I'm a bad host. Do you want to come inside?" He did not apologize; that would not be like him. But he said: "We have a room, if you'll take what you get. Until tomorrow," he growled. Then two strong hands arrived, Andersen's, and helped her to her feet. She remembered almost nothing from the trip to the second floor, just a few glimpses of dark furniture and a tapestry hanging in the stairwell, along with the look the old man sent her from below as he watched her being shown upstairs to bed. He looked a little worried. A little. Then she remembered the cool sheets and sleep that came like a gentle kiss; in a final whiplash of wakefulness she thought: Just so he doesn't call home. Then she slept. When she woke, she had slept half a day and a whole night. Bees tapped gently on the windowpane, sunshine filled the room. Outside, the world was green and light. For a moment she felt completely calm; she jumped out of bed, peered outside. There lay the garden with all the flowers, the garden she had heard so many stories about, and there, down there in the corner, something brown padded around on two feet, a pair of wise old eyes met hers, frightened. Then the eyes disappeared behind some raspberry bushes and were seen no more. So it was true after all, everything in the stories she had heard.

She stood there in a T-shirt and underpants. Her clothes lay on the chair by the bed, her backpack was beside the chair. It was a simple, old-fashioned room, with a washbasin and chamberpot. The furniture was old and dark, the white sheets and pillowcase were starched, the coverlet had a damask pattern. On the walls hung only a small watercolor of a young woman reading. Lea thought she recognized the style, but the picture was unsigned. On the table was a tray covered with a white doily, and on the doily, a plate with four open-faced sandwiches, two caraway cheese and two liverwurst, as well as a pitcher of milk. From a thermos of coffee came a slight gurgling sound. For the moment she was almost happy, everything was easy and light and peaceful. She ate and looked out at all the bees.

He hadn't called home.

Earth sprinkled on the coffin lid. Lea listened. She wondered whether he had stood looking at her while she slept, if by secretly watching her he had learned everything he needed to know from her night face, from the childish underwater movements sleep gives us, from expressions and gestures she was unaware of. Was that when he chose her? Had he known everything? Had he stood by her bed and said those things about coincidences? Lea listened. Far away she heard the preacher pronounce the benediction, nearby she heard the old man lean over her sleeping face and whisper into the room (she heard both things simultaneously), and she realized that he had been her friend.

"The Lord bless you and keep you"—*You can stay here for a while after all*—"The Lord make His face shine upon you and be gracious unto you"—*Coincidences, ah yes, that's surely what brought you here*—"The Lord lift up His countenance upon you and give you peace"—*One mustn't scorn coincidences*. But she would not cry, not now.

The funeral was over and the old man would be cremated, so there was no graveside ceremony. The guests left the church solemnly and with proper formality, but by then Lea had rushed ahead and was already outside. Andersen stood waiting for her with the Bentley; she had not asked him to do that, but there he stood, erect and silent as always, and somehow not fully present, with his chauffeur's cap under his left arm and his right hand on the passenger door. For a moment she thought she would keep running—run farther, farther across crunching gravel paths, as she had done once before—but she obediently leaned over and got into the car, disappeared from the sight of those on the church steps, aunts and uncles and cousins, who squinted curiously toward the light and toward her. Andersen slammed the car door and they drove off.

TWO

Pastor Sørensen made a final round through the parlors at Ekelund and shook hands. My sincere condolences. My sincere condolences. The family was distracted by the paintings and furniture; it was interesting to be here, most of them had never set foot inside the house. Now and then they pulled themselves together and lowered their voices, but then a new shriek arose and they all craned their necks to see another expensive painting, and still another, and a Chippendale chest of drawers and one more sideboard. The pastor felt uneasy at the sight of this flock of flamingos in black. They shook his hand absentmindedly, said good-bye, and thanked him for the sermon, and then their faces disappeared into the furnishings again. Waitresses hovered around with drinks and small sandwiches. The parquet floor creaked, the air smelled of good cigars. The pastor looked around, there was one other person he wanted to bid good-bye. Because when he thought about the funeral that morning—no, to tell the truth *that* wasn't what he was really thinking about. He looked around at the bereaved family and suddenly regretted his egotistical efforts with the sermon. At his age he shouldn't let himself be duped by the deceased's wallet, but he probably couldn't help it. No, he was thinking about the hours just before the funeral; he had been sitting in the sacristy, enthusiastically polishing the sermon, when music began coming from within the church. He hadn't known anyone was there.

He had gone over to the sacristy door, peeked out, seen her sitting there playing, next to the casket. For a moment he considered going out to say something to her, but instinct stopped him. This is a farewell, he suddenly realized. It's best that I leave. So he quietly withdrew to his office.

There was still plenty of time to finish his preparations. The smell of flowers pervaded even his office, ethereal oils and pollen sated the air. He polished his sermon, polished his glasses, thought about smoking a forbidden cigarette, but the flower fragrance was all he needed. The whole time he heard the cello music from the sanctuary. The girl played freely now; it was no longer Bach, just in the style of Bach, just strokes of broken chords. Listening to them almost made him dizzy. Outside the sun had risen completely and the morning light was crystalline. Then there was a long silence, until he heard the sound of the clasps on the cello case. She came into the sacristy, saw him, stopped short.

"Very beautiful," said Pastor Sørensen. "Are you going to play at the funeral?"

She blushed, shook her head. Then she disappeared out the door.

After a while he went into the sanctuary. She was sitting far back in the church, near the transept. He went over to her. She looked down at her hands and seemed a little indifferent. He could not tell if she had been crying, but it was still almost two hours until the ceremony, and the pastor felt strangely eager for company.

"May I show you the church?" he asked.

They stood in the bell tower, the swallows flew in and out under the eaves with cries in their throats. She let her hand glide over the huge bronze bell. It was smooth and cool, yet seemed porous.

"There's something written here," she said.

"That's right," said the pastor. "It's an old bell. Can you read what it says?"

She leaned over in the semidarkness.

"Yes," she said, "but I don't know what it means."

"Read it, and I'll translate."

"Deum laudo: Vivos voco: Mortuos plango: Fulgara frango."

"It's an old bell. That's Latin."

"Is it a rhyme?"

"This is what the bell says. It says: I praise God, I call to the living, I sorrow over the dead, I tame the lightning."

"Aha. Tame the lightning?"

"Benjamin Franklin discovered the lightning rod by flying a kite in a thunderstorm and letting the lightning go to the ground. The church strongly protested such newfangled ideas because for thousands of years it had been the custom that man tamed the lightning and calmed Nature by ringing the church bells, continually, as long as the thunderstorm lasted. This in spite of the fact that many sextons and vergers lost their lives holding the end of the rope when lightning found the big bronze bells in the tower."

"Aha," she said again.

"It's an old bell and an old church."

"I don't believe in God," she said. "Quite the opposite."

"Well, well."

"And now you'll start to pray for me, I guess."

"Certainly. Every evening."

"Thank you for showing me around."

"Thank you for the music. The funeral guests will probably arrive soon."

"They probably will. I'd better go back to my seat."

"Down there in the middle?"

"Yes."

"Why so far away from the coffin?"

"Oh. All the people. Maybe I shouldn't be here at all, but I thought: The hell with them."

"Hrumm."

"Pardon me."

"I know the old man was in good spirits during his last months."

"That's what people say."

"Surely he'd have wanted you up next to the casket."

"Probably. But now he's not here to nag anymore."

"De mortuis nil nisi bonum."

"Oh? What does that mean?"

"One shouldn't say bad things about the dead."

"But one should say good things?"

"No."

"Actually, one can say as little as possible."

"Yes."

"One can leave the sorrow to the bells."

This is what Pastor Sørensen thought about. Yes, there she was. Lea stood in the library, where the fewest people were, talking with one of her aunts, a rosy woman in her fifties; she seemed relieved when the pastor came and interrupted the conversation.

"Well, hello, Pastor," said the rosy woman.

"My sincere condolences," said Pastor Sørensen, taking her hand as he had learned; he lifted it slightly toward his face. The rosy woman left. From behind she was completely black.

Lea nodded to him.

"I think you forgot your cello in the sacristy," he said.

"That doesn't matter," she said, "it doesn't belong to me."

"It doesn't?"

"No—" She sounded a little uncertain. "It was his, like everything else. He bought it for me."

"Then he'd surely have wanted you to keep it."

"It really doesn't matter," she said.

The pastor stood there not quite knowing what to say.

"There's so little one can keep," he said, and heard at once how stupid that sounded.

She smiled a little.

"It must be fun to be a pastor," she said. "And to come *out* so much among people."

The pastor quickly collected himself.

"Yes. But the most fun of all is to be able to leave sometimes."

She gave him a satisfied look.

"Please knock on the door," he said, "if you come by to pick up the instrument."

"I don't think I'll do that," she said, "but thank you anyway."

❧

Trembling silence prevailed in the large, old-fashioned study, "the office," as it was called there in the house. The family looked around with an uncomfortable feeling, their earlier enthusiasm was gone, the hour of truth had come. Their eyes took in everything in the room; the stained-glass octagon in the ceiling depicting craftsmen's guilds from the Middle Ages, the oil paintings, some worth a fortune, a Braque, a Cézanne, a Munch—a magnificent Munch—and eight small Zorn nudes frivolously placed right behind the desk chair, so anyone who had the misfortune of sitting in the visitor's chair must have felt quite schizophrenic seeing Wilhelm Bolt's bulldog aspect in the desk chair and the smiling invitations right behind him. The women had always seemed to laugh contemptuously at the poor visitors who sat there perspiring; their alluring, mocking smiles said: You can't have us, we're Wilhelm Bolt's harem—*the women had always been on Wilhelm Bolt's side!* There was no sense to it.

There were large notebooks on the shelves behind the desk, crystals in showcases, a big old microscope on a table in the corner, a gilt leather pad on the desk.

Sitting there with his papers in front of him, lawyer Holst leaned forward now. He cleared his throat, pushed his glasses to the tip of his nose, and began.

"It was the testator's wish that all who are remembered in his will should gather in his home immediately after the funeral to hear the will read. As you all know, he distributed a significant part of his fortune to his legal heirs during the last years before he died. However, he still retained 51 percent of the shares in Bolt Holdings, Inc., in addition to his Ekelund residence and its contents, as well as a number of other assets. The shares represent not only the estate's greatest financial value, but also the controlling interest in Bolt Holdings, Inc."

Many of the family's lesser personages were already a little lost, but the lawyer doggedly went on.

"The testator wished the equity holdings with voting rights in the company to constitute a block. So some months before his death he asked me to establish Ambrosia Holdings, Inc., a holding company with stock valued at 910,000 kroner. His 51 percent of Bolt Holdings has been placed in Ambrosia, which now controls Bolt Holdings."

Peder and Christian nodded approvingly from their seats in the front row. This sounded excellent and wise. However, many family members began to feel transported to the morning's soporific sermon; it did not make things better that everyone had drunk white wine. One cousin suddenly yawned loudly.

"At the same time as the new company was established," continued the lawyer with a sharp glance at the sleepy man, "a new will was drawn up. It is dated February 21st of this year, and reads as follows:

" 'My Last Will and Testament. All previous wills are hereby nullified. I, Wilhelm Jeremias Bolt, born April 10, 1912, who am without heirs and inherited my wife's estate, declare as my final wish that at my death my property shall be divided thus:

" 'My nephew Christian Bolt shall inherit 300 shares of Ambrosia, Inc., each with a face value of 1,000 kroner. My nephew Peder Bolt shall inherit 200 shares, my niece Gussi Fricke née Bolt shall inherit 150 shares, my niece Ella Bolt likewise 150 shares . . .' "

A sigh of relief went through the group, because everyone understood this; they almost applauded. On the whole it was a proper will, correct and pleasing, and just what one could have expected of a sane person. It was a long document and reading it took a long time, for there were many securities to distribute. As there should be. Christian Bolt stretched in his chair as contentedly as a board chairman, Ella and Gussi began to breathe normally, the lawyer kept intoning new percentages and sums, everything according to customary practice. The family cast sidelong glances at Lea, who sat at the edge of a dining room chair and kept looking down. It was impossible to say if she seemed disappointed. But what had she expected anyway? As Aunt Ella had said to her earlier that afternoon, after one too many glasses of white wine:

"My dear Lea, you've lived out here for a few months, and he got old and all that, and well, maybe he had changed. Maybe he was nice to *you*. But that doesn't mean you have any idea . . . one shouldn't speak ill of the dead, but . . ."

"De mortuis nil nihisi bene," said Lea. "That's how you say it in Latin, I believe."

"Yes, my dear, but you didn't *know* him. Absolutely not. You have *no idea* how he *could* be. How he sent a van that time in '67, yes, of course, that was before you were born, but he *sent* a van, a *moving van*, and *took away* the dining room set he had loaned me three months earlier when we moved to Ris. We were sitting at the table."

"Maybe he needed it," said Lea a little uncertainly.

"My dear, it wasn't *this* dining room furniture, it was a much cheaper set. He'd had it in his apartment in town on Gyldenlovesgate, the place he never used anymore. And do you see it here? Oh no, it's probably sold. In any case, *we* never saw it again. He couldn't give anyone *anything*. Not *anything*. Yes, I know he gave to those artists, but after all, they didn't *belong*. *They* didn't have to be on their toes for him. But *we* had to. As Peder always says: Blood is thicker than turpentine."

"What did you do then, without dining room furniture?"

"Well, we could hardly write to him and complain! When we discreetly asked if he was going to keep the dining room set, we got a bill for the moving van, along with a letter that was so—so— Oh hello, Pastor." She set her face into more serious creases when the pastor materialized.

What had Lea really expected? She sat there on the dining room chair, appearing fairly indifferent to everything; the family almost felt a little sorry for her as the securities and stockholdings were distributed. She looked up, gazed out the window, seemed not to be listening.

Lea was not listening. In fact she was thinking about death, even if it was a funeral.

How did Lea look at death? At the sight of all the guests she felt a great emptiness. What was it about death? She always felt an emptiness like this at funerals. Death, that's what repeats itself. Death, that's what repeats itself. It is the cold hard bunch of keys that jangle in your pocket, that will open the doors of all your days, again and again the brass keys glide in and out of notched lock slits. Death is the innumerable snips of kitchen scissors, knives and forks clinking in the silverware drawer; it is the old-fashioned alarm clock ringing on thousands of mornings. It is the glasses you take off and fold up, take off and fold up, over and over again, it is everything that repeats itself, it is thousands of ordinary things floating in a black, colorless darkness, clanking like chains. Death is everything that repeats itself. Lea had thought about this quite a bit; at each of the three funerals she had attended, this empty metallic feeling had come over her. Death is the sound of the reflector in the camera's shutter mechanism, it is ten thousand exposures of a random street scene or an empty park. That was how Lea saw death, and she had some experience of it now. Certainly others had more experience, the old man, for example, but she had never been able to talk with him about it. Not like that. But he had *known* something about it, and that was one reason it had been good to be near him. In his irritable loneliness, at the microscope, bent over crystals, or eating in the dining room with all his paintings, he gave the impression that he knew about things you couldn't talk about. He was like cold clinking metal. Like coins. He was like coins toward everyone. That's how he had been toward her the first day. That's how he was almost all the time. Like Lea herself. Like she had been for a long time, almost always. Like she would always be from now on, or wished she would always be. They suited each other well.

But there was something else too. It was the cautious solemnity in his hands when he lifted the frames from the beehives, searched for and found a queen bee, planted a tulip bulb. And he taught her. Then for a moment the two of them, together, seemed to escape what repeats itself. As time passed, the moments had borne fruit in the old man. He suddenly smelled of very old aftershave. He appeared in a tie for dinner; he had a flower in his buttonhole, sent Andersen upstairs to her room with fresh orchids every other day. He held out the chair for her, let her go first through doorways, old as he was. It was a game they played. He knew that himself and didn't talk about it either; they never talked about it. He smiled sardonically when he held the door for her. The only thing he ever said was one morning when he tramped into the greenhouse, obviously pleased; Lea was working with some cuttings. He nodded briefly and immediately got very busy with a case of tulip bulbs, sorted and sorted, but seemed preoccupied. Lea had to stop her work and look at him. He appeared a little intoxicated. He fussed with the bulbs for a long time, then he said: "I telephoned the chief magistrate's office today." He held up a bulb and scrutinized it carefully, like an amateur actor in *Hamlet*. "There's no reason a granduncle can't marry his grandniece. Just wanted to investigate that." He glanced up from the bulb, like a goldsmith from his jewelry, and gave her a look filled with fun and adventure. "Just to make sure, I mean." With that he busied himself with the tulip bulbs again. Lea swallowed.

This was *another* side of death, a side she did *not* like to be reminded of. Everything during the past year had actually concerned death. They had probably both known that. The trip in the ambulance that night was just the final end. Lea did not like to think about that. Lea only wanted to think about what repeats itself. She did not want to think about how she had to swallow in the greenhouse, about moments when she felt warm and surrounded with admiration, moments when he buzzed around her like a swarm of bees, wound golden threads around her. His had been an infatuation from another time, noble and dignified and refined. It did her good to be with him. Precisely because he had experience with what repeats itself, because he could be like cold clinking silver, because there was so much they did not need to talk about—this made her melt. And she let him be infatuated. It didn't matter. He would die soon. At night she sometimes dreamed that she lay beside him, perfectly still, watching him in a deep sleep. Sometimes this dream flowed into the Dream, the dream about the other one, but that did not bother her. When they took walks together on the estate, she gave him her hand, which grew small and warm in his. "You're my walking stick today, my dear," he might say. Often that was the only thing he said on such walks. She never thought about the city. It was like a deep sleep. Dog roses grew in thickets around the house. The days passed peacefully. In the evenings she watched from her window as bright beams from the lighthouse cut through the darkness down by the sea, again and again. She heard the whistling buoy breathe with the sea breeze; it lay with its old sorrow somewhere far out among white breakers. The sound stayed with her into her sleep, into her dreams and her breathing.

That's how it had been. It had been a grace period. From now on she would always be like clinking metal.

" 'Finally,' " read lawyer Holst, " 'finally, my grandniece Lea Bolt shall inherit one—one—share of stock, with a face value of 1,000 kroner, in Ambrosia Holdings, Inc.' " Lea heard her name mentioned and looked up in confusion.

" 'Ekelund Foundation, which is established at the same time as this will, shall inherit the Ekelund estate, manor number 1, farm number 2, with its entire inventory, together with 10,000,000 kroner from my bank deposits for upkeep of the estate.' "

The lawyer paused for a moment, pushed his glasses all the way up to the bridge of his nose, and looked at the group. Then he continued:

" 'My grandniece Lea Bolt shall use my property as her own as long as she wishes, except that she cannot dispose of it. When she no longer wishes to use the property, or when she dies, the income from the property shall go toward educating the descendants of my nephews and nieces.' "

Suddenly there was a silence so profound that no one really heard the lawyer continue reading about bank deposits and cash, even though it was all very nice; some went to those closest, primarily to Christian, some was wisely put aside in funds for regular distribution to more distant shoots on the family tree. The family first regained its senses when the lawyer came to the parting shot.

" 'It is my wish that the assets in Ambrosia Holdings, Inc., shall be kept together as much as possible and be directed in the spirit I have directed them. Therefore, I have formed the company with two classes of shares, A shares and B shares. The shares are comparable, except that only the class-A share, which goes to my grandniece Lea Bolt, has voting privileges. Stock trades that surpass the face value of the stock can be paid only if the owner of the class-A share . . .' " But this was too much for the more commercially gifted family members, several were already on their feet; Lea looked at them in bewilderment.

"Signed, Wilhelm Jeremias Bolt. And it further states: 'The undersigned, supreme court attorney Bjørn Wexelsen and caretaker Viktor Andersen, are summoned as witnesses to the issuance of the present Will and Testament. We confirm that we both were present when Wilhelm Jeremias Bolt signed the will. Likewise, we affirm that he was in full possession of his mind and faculties and that the will was read to him slowly and clearly before he signed it. We are both over eighteen years of age.' "

"Who the hell would have believed it," said Uncle Christian; his face was as white as a summer cloud.

"What does this mean?" asked Aunt Gussi, who had also risen from her chair.

Lea stood abruptly, looked at the lawyer in bewilderment. Then she quickly left the room.

"What does this mean?" Aunt Gussi asked again, a little louder.

"It means you'll have to postpone the dining room furniture again," said Peder caustically. Then he laughed a little. "This is what you were afraid of, isn't it, Christian?"

"He couldn't restrain himself," said Christian.

The gathering broke up quickly. Cars accelerated furiously in the gravel outside. Some of the more indifferent male cousins wandered around a while longer and downed a few drops from tall glasses, a couple of them gazed after Lea with drunken hopefulness; then they too were hurried out the door by Andersen.

Lawyer Holst searched worriedly for Lea, he looked for her in the library and in her room. Her room was empty. It was light and silent.

"Damn," said the lawyer.

Andersen stood in the doorway behind him.

"Miss Bolt has gone out," he said.

The lawyer turned, examined him with polite jurist eyes.

"And you knew this too, Andersen," he said.

"Yes," said Andersen. "But if I may be so bold: so did you, Mr. Holst."

"I assumed she had been informed. But no one told her."

"No," said Andersen. "That would have been contrary to Mr. Bolt's explicit instructions."

"Doesn't it bother you?" asked the lawyer.

Andersen seemed to bob to the surface for a moment and said: "I have no opinion about that."

The lawyer pondered this for a moment.

"Gone out, you say?"

"Yes," said Andersen, "she rushed out the door. I don't know where she is."

THREE

Lea sat in Jacob's little house at the far end of the garden, chatted with him and comforted him a little, because Jacob had been beside himself the whole week since the old man's death. He just moped around, picked at his feet, ate hardly anything, did not show even the slightest interest in peony buds; normally Jacob liked to pick the round hard buds off the stalks and play ball with them. It was too bad for the peonies but fun for Jacob, although strictly forbidden. But he would not do even that.

The morning after the old man died the little house had been empty, and when Lea returned from the hospital late that morning she had found Jacob sitting by the greenhouse in silent despair. He had not eaten, just drunk a little water.

Things had continued like that. Yesterday and today he had been completely impossible, with preparations for the reception and all the strange people suddenly walking around his domain, so Andersen had needed to lock him in his little house.

"You mustn't take it so hard, Jacob," said Lea, patting the back of his head. "It's the way life goes."

But the ape just hung his head, did not raise his eyes.

"Besides, you're just an animal, and animals can't grieve; that's scientifically known."

Jacob lifted his head slightly, sent her a reproachful glance.

"All right, all right," said Lea, "but you've got to eat something anyway. You can have little open-faced sandwiches with brie and an olive and lots of lovely toothpicks."

Jacob sighed and did not say anything. Lea grew silent too. It was always nice to sit in here with Jacob, it was warm and dry and clean and attractive, with yellow straw in the corner where Jacob slept. He had all his treasures here, the red-and-yellow ball, the coconut shells, the big drum, the rattle, the mirror in which he liked to look at himself. He could look in the mirror for hours, especially if Lea was there and occasionally peeked into the mirror at him. Then he usually smiled and chattered contentedly, and ruffled her hair, because he thought it was lovely to see their faces together in the mirror. But now he simply sat there. After a while he rose heavily, shuffled over to his corner, and lay down.

"Now you're being impolite, Jacob," said Lea, but Jacob was beyond customary human practices today.

"Maybe *I* might need somebody to talk with too," she said gently. He did not respond, but she saw that it hit home. "I guess you probably miss the walks with him." Jacob remained silent, but clearly agreed.

"You two were alike."

The ape turned, looked at her appreciatively.

"Equally obstinate and odd, both of you."

Jacob seemed about to disagree, when Andersen appeared in the doorway.

"Excuse me if I'm disturbing you," he said carefully, "but the lawyer just left. He wanted to talk with you."

"I see."

"I took the liberty of telling him that I didn't know where you were. Even though I thought you were here."

"Uh-huh." She looked down. "Thank you."

Andersen contained himself for a while. Then he said: "How is he?"

"He still won't eat," said Lea. "Just sits and mopes."

"That's not good."

"We'd better try bamboo shoots again."

"Very well, Miss Bolt."

"Or maybe he'd like some apples. Don't we still have a basket of last year's Gravensteins?"

"Yes, I think so, Miss Bolt."

"Tell me, am I to be kept a prisoner here on the estate forever? Is that the idea?"

"No," said Andersen. "That was not mentioned in the will."

"And the other things?"

"I was to greet you from Mr. Holst and say that if you require advice and guidance, he is at your disposal."

"Yes, but what does all this mean? Does it mean I own everything?"

Andersen thought about this.

"No," he said. "But you control it."

"Control?"

"Yes."

"Everything? The house and the business and—"

"Yes. Just as Mr. Bolt did."

Lea bit her lips together and noticed that the tears she had held back all day were now about to overwhelm her.

"But that's crazy," she exclaimed. "*Me!* It's completely absurd!"

"I can't imagine so," said Andersen. "Mr. Bolt rarely did anything without a definite reason."

"And what would that reason be?"

Andersen emptied Jacob's water dish into the sink and refilled it with fresh water from the faucet.

"What would that reason be?" Lea repeated.

"It . . . ," said Andersen, "it will perhaps become clear when you see the whole situation. Little by little. I really don't know."

Lea was about to say something, something harsh, but Andersen forestalled her.

"Do you wish to eat at seven this evening as usual?"

She closed her mouth around what she had intended to say. Andersen stood before her, gray-haired and deferential.

"Yes, thank you," she said in a small voice.

"I'll get the apples right away. I'll order more bamboo shoots tomorrow morning."

"Good," she said.

Andersen kept standing there.

"That will be all," she said.

She looked at Jacob over in the corner. Do you remember when I came here, the first day, she said. I saw you and the old man together, you were taking a walk. I remember that, said Jacob. I was quite beside myself that day, said Lea. I realized that, said Jacob. You probably miss those walks, said Lea. I do, said Jacob.

She had seen them from her window, as she stood in her T-shirt and underwear looking out at the morning, her first morning at Ekelund. They were strolling in the garden, the old man ahead with his walking stick and behind him padded his brown friend, sniffing good-naturedly. Now and then they paused by beds and perennials, and the old man took out his calendar and crossed off and made notations for each plant while leaning heavily on the ape's shoulder. Sometimes he spoke to the ape, gestured with his free hand, discussed a special plant's case with the same worried look as when one discusses the welfare of a problem child. From her window Lea could not hear what the old man said, but the ape appeared to agree with him for the most part. Once in a while they stopped by a particularly successful bush, then the old man beamed, smiled, and enthusiastically gave the ape an absentminded clap on the shoulder. Each time the ape stood at his master's side, loyal and serious, looking thoughtfully at the marvel. By one of the tulip beds the old man took small garden shears from a pocket in his dark suit and cut a pretty little bouquet, which he handed to Jacob with a shy, friendly gesture; he patted the ape's shoulder again as Jacob sniffed the flowers contentedly. Then they walked on through the garden, the two lonely old fellows. Now and then Jacob ate a tulip.

Lunch was at two in the afternoon. And Lea, who had heard quite a bit about the old man's crazy insistence on punctuality, was in the dining room at exactly five minutes to two, wearing the only skirt in her backpack and her nicest shirt. She could not do anything about her shoes; all she had were the tennis shoes she was wearing, and they were still damp. When she entered the room she found herself standing alone by the long table, which was set at one end. The elegant table service gleamed on the white linen tablecloth. She particularly noticed the goblets; they were different from any Lea had ever seen, slender and light, with a tall stem and a delicate spiral pattern around the edge of the glass. Their simple abstract form seemed almost functionalistic. Still, she had the impression they were older than they appeared, somehow they seemed covered with a fine mist of time. The carafes on the table were created by the same masterful hand. The serving platters were of heavy hammered silver, the porcelain delicate and elegant; she guessed they were middle-European, but knew too little about such things. However, she quickly forgot the table setting when she began looking around the dining room. It was a large room, the table could certainly seat twenty people, and on the walls hung paintings, *many* paintings, each more magnificent than the last, masterpieces from many lands, primarily from more recent epochs, expressionists and a few surrealists, but also some German romantics. Lea, who until now had stood nicely behind her chair waiting for the old man like a well-bred person, tore herself away from the table and began gliding toward the pictures. Slowly, solemnly, she walked around the room, from painting to painting, as if deeply moved, hypnotized, absorbing colors and hues. The large glass doors were open slightly, and sunlight and warm afternoon air entered the room from the garden, played with the sheer white curtains, drew strange green-and-gold impressions on the walls and ceiling. Lea *glided*, from a wonderful Cézanne to a tiny little Franz Marc, and was just about to step back to admire it from a distance when a scraping mechanical sound from the piece of furniture in the corner startled her; it sounded like an elderly cyclist was imprisoned there. Then tinkling bells were heard, like bells during mass in a church in a southern country. Now for the first time she saw the clock; no, not a *clock*, it was a *universe*; a tall cabinet made of fine dark wood, with spiraling columns and filigreed carvings, with a face and geometric symbols, with planet orbits, clock weights, figures, bells. Now the whole zodiac began to move around a silver globe, while figures representing all the workers' guilds announced their arrival one by one in a little opening in the cabinet. It must be very, very old and absolutely priceless; it *worked* after all. Delighted as a child over a music box, she ran to the cabinet and stood there wide-eyed; here came the silversmith and the painter, the weaver and the carpenter, the miner and the sailor, the glassblower, the watchmaker . . . they bowed to her and displayed their small gifts, lifted their arms holding tools and equipment, bowed again. And she laughed, as the cabinet's bells played a little melody, a strange, slightly melancholy tune, almost like an old refrain. She had never heard the melody before, but it went straight into her and forced her to hum along, while the craftsmen and farmers strolled about with the wandering stars and constellations.

Then the clock struck two, the figures and celestial objects stopped moving, and the doors in the small openings closed.

It was two o'clock. The room grew very quiet. She was startled when a strong voice behind her suddenly began to sing, the same melody the clock had just played, the first part of the refrain:

We bring our gifts while the day counts the hours
A house is built in heaven when life is past . . .

The old man stood behind her.

"Excuse me," she said, "I got so absorbed." He smiled a little.

"I'm glad you like the world clock," he said, with a trace of embarrassment. "It's very old. Please sit down." She hesitated a moment, but decided he would manage his chair and his walking stick alone. He seated himself stiffly, pulled the napkin out of the napkin ring.

The table was set for just the two of them; obviously the ape Jacob did not take part in the meals. Andersen served. They ate in silence.

First came a chicken consommé with green peas, followed by lumpfish with finely chopped almonds, potatoes, and glazed carrots, then salad and a piece of chèvre. They concluded with fruit. With the lumpfish they drank wine from one of the slender carafes; she guessed it was Sancerre. She tried to catch his eye several times during the meal, but he was obviously used to eating alone, in silence, and concentrated completely on the food. He ate slowly and deliberately, chewed every bite. After every seventh forkful he raised his napkin to his mouth, wiped his lips briefly and purposefully. Then he continued eating, precisely, methodically. Andersen glided in and out with the plates, poured wine into the glasses. When they got to the cheese, the old man raised his glass to her and sent her a searching look.

"I hope it tasted good," he said politely.

"Yes, thank you." She raised her glass uncertainly.

"You're welcome. It's a long time since I had human companionship here other than Jacob. And Andersen, of course." It sounded as if Andersen did not fall entirely into the category of human companionship.

She did not quite know what to say. She looked at the glass she held in her hand.

"One of my treasures," he said. "Venice, very old."

"Everything here is old."

"Everything, my dear. Including me." She was touched. It was a long time since anyone had called her my dear.

"They say that—"

"Yes?"

"No, it wasn't anything."

"I see," he smiled gruffly. "I *know* they need to say *something* about me. *What* they say I can only *suspect*. But you've had a good upbringing and don't want to hurt me by telling me."

She looked down.

"I suspect," he went on, just as gruffly, "they think that they know quite a bit about my mental condition, that my way of life goes beyond eccentricity, and that my daily existence is hardly characterized by silver platters and Venetian glass. One would think," he said bitterly, "that I was one of those senile, slovenly old people who are disoriented and no longer can knot a tie. This . . . wishful thinking, if I may say so, is founded on the happy expectation of some day being able—to find *themselves* in these rooms, along with a diligent notary, awaiting the probate court's ruling." He paused dramatically. "And now they've probably—*sent* you here, to *investigate*."

Silence followed this proclamation.

"*Well?*" he said ominously. "Am I going to be declared incompetent?"

She stared down at the napkin in her lap. The world clock ticked.

"*Hmm?*" he growled. "Am I close to death?"

She looked at him abruptly. Everything she had been through the past days rose in her as rage, and all at once it poured out of her.

"No," she said angrily, "you're shamelessly alive. *You* are alive, *you*, an old man, while—*you* are alive, yes, that's certain. With Venetian glass and

German masters and everything. Paintings that—no one has seen. That no one will ever see. They will never be shown to anyone. No one is here with me to see them. No one is here with me. Does that make any sense?"

The world clock ticked. She heard the train wheels turning, turning, footsteps on gravel, sounds from a weary organist.

She had rushed from the darkness and fragrant flowers in the chapel, out into the rain and wetness, did not look back. Four more minutes, she thought, it takes four minutes before the flames are turned on; gravel crunched beneath her feet as she ran across the cemetery, four minutes, four times sixty is two hundred and forty, two hundred and forty seconds. Two hundred and forty seconds left, two hundred and thirty-nine, step, two hundred and thirty-eight, step, step, thirty-seven, step, thirty-six, step, thirty-five, step, he still exists, step,

    his body still exists, step
    white in the coffin bed, step
    two hundred and thirty-three, step,
    it's still soft, step
    it's still tough, step
    his hand still exists, step
    has not become fire, step
    there are still traces, step
    of the look in his eye, step
    two hundred and twenty-six, step
    he is still here, step
    everything still exists.

Is there no end to this graveyard? It goes on and on, like an eternal wet greensward, she counts the seconds, step, step, she herself stands still, the cemetery runs past her. Gravestones glistening with rain reflect the trees and sky, the writing on the stones becomes meaningless and strange in these heavenly reflections that repeat the great sorrow of the sky and trees. Names, dates, moving farewells—it all becomes incomprehensible, like Cyrillic letters, all of it, *Here lies our beloved Ship Owner August Christian Frederik Enevold Christensen born 5.6.1863, died 5.7.1939. "God resurrected him when He released the pangs of death."* What does that mean? she wonders, step, step, it might as well be Chinese, *resurrected him when He released the pangs of death* had once been a person, he was Ship Owner and Beloved. Now his name is a mirror for leaves and clouds, barely visible anymore. *Here sleeps our child Anna Frederika 4.13.1933–12.25.1940. "For Heaven belongs to such a one."* It can't be seen, can't be deciphered, it's just a child now turned to dust; but then she has to stop, because her eye falls on *Our beloved Butcher Ole Johan Lamb* and she understands the Cyrillic writing immediately, but it's too much, she bursts out laughing and turns toward him to show him Butcher Lamb. They have often walked like that in cemeteries, in many towns, looking at gravestones, the two of them together; humorous inscriptions, touching inscriptions, and grotesque inscriptions, but Butcher Lamb takes the prize. She turns toward him and laughs. Laughs into the empty air. Then she runs farther, the minutes are gone, now he's lying in the oven, in the fire, now he's gone, together with Ole Johan Lamb and Anna Frederika, *9845666 Air Force Sergeant Reginald Barke (aged 19) Royal Air Force. "His command is eternal life." Died for peace and freedom.* We've walked here, she thinks, I've often walked here in the morning with silver on my lips, coming from him and the night. Now I'll never do it again. And everything, the cemetery, the gravestones, the crosses and small doves, trees and gravel path, rain and air, everything runs past her. The cemetery never ends. Behind a tree she finds the front door at home, she runs up the stairs and from the window of her small apartment can just glimpse the crematorium's chimney through the treetops, she snatches the clothing and objects that happen to be hanging on the tree's branches, with her backpack over one shoulder she runs past geranium beds and British soldiers' graves, between the white crosses in the liberation soldiers' corner she sees the train arriving at the platform, and she clears herself a path through the forest of tombstones and names, leaps onto the train at the last moment, the whistle blows, the cars give a jolt, and the train rolls away with her, out of the cemetery, takes her away from all the dead, great and small, away from the smoke rising from the crematorium and the aunts in Persian lambskin coats who smell of flowers and are still standing in the square wondering where she went.

Instead of her steps, she now hears the clacking of the train's wheels. It is traveling south, toward Salzburg and Verona and maybe even farther, far away from rain and smoke. But already after a few stations everything becomes unbearable again, she keeps asking the conductor and the other passengers if it's not too warm in the car, they shake their heads in surprise, then look at her sympathetically. They are on the point of offering condolences. As time goes on, she realizes she won't get to Verona with this train. At some random station she sees a white truck on the platform; written on the truck are the words SET YOUR CLOCK BACK TODAY. She can't imagine what these meaningless words are advertising, but she finds them strangely moving. She looks at the small gray Norwegian town with no sign of intelligent life lying outside the windows. Verona, she thinks. "Set your clock back today," she reads; and suddenly it's so warm that she grabs her backpack and rushes from the train just as the conductor blows the whistle. He stares at her in surprise as she tumbles onto the platform, for a moment he seems about to go over and express concern for her, but then he remembers the train, looks perplexed, waves the green flag. "All aboard," he shouts, and watches her struggling to her knees; he swings on board and the doors close. The motor is running in the white truck, it is already starting to drive away. She gets to her feet, takes a few tentative steps after it. "Set your clock back today." Then, realizing she will not reach it, she gives up. So here she stands, no train, no ride, not a soul to be seen anywhere, and the rain has stopped for only a short time. But look: the white truck stops at the station exit, remains in gear and drones a little. Without a second thought, Lea musters the last of her energy and races over to the truck, jumps in front of the windshield, and waves a white thumb in the driver's face.

"Hey, what are you doing?" he calls out the window.

"Can I get a lift?"

"Well . . ." He hesitates a little. "That depends on where you want to go." The driver is quite young and fat.

"Where I want to go?"

"Yes. Where are you headed?"

She is about to say Verona, but stops herself.

"I don't know," she says.

At that the driver smiles, but it's not a nasty smile, so she's not afraid.

"I see," he says. "Maybe you don't know where you are either?"

"No," she says, which is true. "I was—thrown off the train."

The driver gives her an understanding look, as if he knows what it means to be thrown off the train in this life.

"Well, hop in, then," he says. "I can always drive you a little way."

She scrambles in. Set your clock back today. The truck smells like flowers.

"I'm headed south," he says. "A few kilometers at least. Is that all right?"

She nods.

"But I have things to deliver along the way. Just so you know."

First they drive slowly through the ugly little railroad town. Once or twice the truck stops at one of the small gray cement houses, as gray as the sky and fjord. The driver jumps out quickly and gets his wares, whatever they are, from the back of the truck; she really doesn't care. She sits there dully staring out at the empty streets. She still does not know where she is and makes no particular effort to know either, has never been very good in geography. Just outside the town, near the church, the driver makes yet another stop. He obviously has a larger delivery there, because he is out of the truck for a long time. Lea thinks she probably should have helped him, since he's so nice and is giving her a lift and everything, but she can't bring herself to do it, just gives him a wan smile as he fastens his seat belt. He probably realizes that she isn't her usual self, even if he doesn't know her, because he nods reassuringly at her again and smiles his smile, so friendly and uncomplicated. An uncomplicated person, thinks Lea, how nice. A driver. Maybe a craftsman. The simple uncomplicated person puts on a cassette with a violin concerto by Locatelli, drives on through rainy weather and fjord wind; he whistles a little, increases his speed, drives surely and comfortably, knows the truck. All of a sudden she feels so *well*. The fat young driver, his truck and Locatelli and this morning hour, the rain, the fields and meadows, the fjord below—they all go together somehow. He probably drives here every day and helps young girls in need. He should have been driving a red sports car, riding a white steed, she thinks, she should have convinced him to run away with her to Verona, or at least to Frederikshavn. For a moment she imagines he is slim and tall and blond, and the music is rock 'n' roll, but she stops herself, he's better the way he is, where he is, right now, in his white truck with the strange words on it.

Set your clock back today. What could he be delivering? She has to ask after all.

"What do you have in the back?"

"Heh!" he says. "Can't you smell? Flowers. Flowers and fertilizer. I'm a gardener. Henry's Nursery, that's me."

"Oh." She says no more.

"I'm delivering greetings and funeral wreaths and things like that."

"Can a person make a living at that?" she asks, just to have something to say.

"No, not in such a small place. But I sell garden tools and fertilizer and chemicals to gardeners, and that amounts to quite a bit. Now we're going up here, for example, to the estate, to deliver extra-fine fertilizer for orchids."

"The estate," she says quietly, and looks at the landscape. They have left the main road and are driving up a tree-lined avenue.

"Old Bolt, who owns the Ekelund estate, has a big garden and his own little nursery too. I deliver all sorts of things to him, seeds and bulbs alike. Fabulous flowers he cultivates. High quality. Never seen the like. To be perfectly honest, I'm glad he does it just as a hobby. You could say that if I, Henry's Nursery, have an ordinary plant school, then Bolt has a whole university. Oxford, at least. No, there wouldn't be many flowers sold at Henry's Nursery if Bolt sold flowers. I think I'm the only one in town that's been allowed to see them. Except for Andersen, of course. And the animal."

"The animal," she repeats, and says no more.

"Yes, well, he has . . . he is . . . well . . . a strange one, old Bolt. You see, he is . . . look, we're here now." They drive into a large yard, stop in front of the main building, which is big and white and a little dilapidated. "I'll just go in with some boxes now," says the driver, "and then I'll drive you farther down toward the highway." He smiles at her again, disappears out of the truck. She watches him in the side mirror, yes, he is carrying a box from the truck; a middle-aged man wearing overalls comes out of the house, greets the driver briefly. Then together they bring in boxes from the back of the truck, some six or seven in all. When they have finished, estate owner Bolt comes out on the steps with his walking stick, panama hat, and rubber boots; the fat young driver, who is also a gardener and named

Henry, goes up to the old man on the steps, greets him politely, bows a little too deeply, like an apprentice to a master. She looks at Bolt, he is very old now, a little stooped, but still supple around the eyes and mouth, she can see that, even at this distance.

Henry's face is flushed when he slides into the driver's seat again.

"That was Bolt," he says proudly.

She smiles, but does not reply.

At the end of the avenue, she stops him.

"Henry," she says, "it's terribly nice of you, really, that you'll drive me all the way down to the main highway, but it's fine if you let me off here."

"Oh, but . . ."

"Honestly. I want to walk a little. I need some air. Just tell me which direction to take. The weather is better now too."

At that moment, raindrops begin pounding loudly on the front windshield.

"Tell me," he begins anxiously, "is something wrong?"

"It's nothing to worry about. It's been a hard day. I need some air. The smell of the flowers is so strong. It's a personal matter, Henry. Honestly."

Now he gets really worried.

"But are you sure that—that I shouldn't drive you to . . ." He looks as if he could imagine driving her to a reputable kennel, but she shakes her head firmly and smiles at him as confidently as she can.

"Honestly," she says, "everything is just fine."

Was he a little offended? In a few brief words he explains which road she should take, then he lets her out, says a quick good-bye, and drives away. She looks at the white truck, sees again the advertising on the side; it's amazing, she has to look twice: BUY YOUR FLOWERS TODAY.

That's what it actually says: Buy your flowers today.

When the truck is well out of sight, she turns and walks back up the tree-lined avenue. She stands in the rain looking at the white house for a long time, so long that her teeth begin chattering. There is no one to be seen in the yard; she goes right to the front door and rings the bell. The man in overalls opens the door; he is obviously the man named Andersen.

"Yes?" he says slowly and formally, and examines her somewhat disapprovingly, from top to toe, with her backpack and everything.

"Hello," she says, suddenly a little frightened. Maybe he'll go and get a rifle. I didn't think of that.

"Yes?"

"Hello. I'd like to speak with Uncle Wilhelm."

"Hmmm?"

"Uncle Wilhelm. My granduncle. My name is Lea Bolt."

⟡

The old man gazed at her thoughtfully. She sat holding the fruit knife tensely, her face pale. Had she shouted?

"You're welcome," he said.

⟡

Lea sat alone in the dining room. The world clock had just played its melody. It was nine o'clock. On the table in front of her was a plate with the remains of her supper. It surprised her that she had eaten well; she hadn't noticed that she was hungry. But she hadn't noticed what she had eaten either.

Andersen had set her usual place. The silver bell was on the other side of the table, where the old man usually sat. She looked at it, irresolute. Then she leaned across the table, picked up the bell, rang it.

Andersen stood in the doorway. She looked at him a little uncertainly.

"I've finished eating, thank you."

He cleared the table without a word. Set your clock back today. So now the old man was dead and could not come up with any new ideas. He had been sitting here at the table in the evening, right across from her, when suddenly he had clutched his shoulder and bent forward, and his heart had failed.

"I've put the coffee in the library. I'll leave now, if you don't wish anything further."

"No, thank you," she said. "You must be tired."

"Yes," said Andersen formally, "it's been a long day. Good night." She heard him go out the kitchen door, heard his footsteps disappear toward the annex where he slept.

The house was completely quiet. The old man had lain on the floor here, she had tried to talk to him, but he was unconscious the whole time.

She went into the library, poured coffee. The room was utterly silent. She sat for a while, took a book from the shelf, tried to read. Then she rose, went to the window. An evening breeze rustled the trees in the garden. Far out in the twilight she heard the whistling buoy.

❧

And we who see Lea standing there, alone in the big house, we send her a kind thought as she stands looking out. Outside in the garden evening has fallen. The lighthouses are being lit along the coast; she can see their lights come on, one after another. The garden rustles, snails lay their silver stripes on the leaves, a hedgehog family is out walking. The bees are asleep in their warm hives. Jacob sits in his little house in the garden; he is lonely.

How are you, Jacob?

Not good.

You didn't eat?

No. Didn't.

Don't you want to talk about it?

No. Don't-don't.

What are you thinking about, Jacob? Tell me.

Don't know. Don't. Thinking about when she came here. The first days. Didn't like it, didn't, must admit that. Suddenly another person was here besides the old man.

You're forgetting Andersen.

Yes, and him too, of course. Frightened her the first time we met. The old man had taken her into the garden; think they had eaten together. This is Jacob, he said. Started leaping and howling, and she got frightened. Didn't like that she came, didn't.

But you changed your mind, didn't you?

Do you hear the trees rustling outside? Like that sound a lot.

But you soon changed your mind, didn't you?

This is Jacob, said the old man. Shouldn't he really have been named Esau? she asked. To say something like that! The old man laughed, and said something incomprehensible. Usually he never did that. Never. When

45

she first came, her face was very white. She wasn't here, even though she was here. She didn't look at Jacob. Nothing existed for her. We animals notice things like that. Jacob notices things like that. Was mean to her. She sat on the bench by the greenhouse one day. Tried to scratch her. She just cried and went away. Away. She didn't talk to anyone. Didn't. The trees outside are rustling.

Aren't you hungry?

Not hungry. She was white and far away. Thought she was evil. Looked like she was dead. The old man got worried. Usually he never was. Never. She did nothing. None of all the things she did later. Slept a lot. Think the old man thought about her a lot.

You were jealous?

Envious, yes. Suddenly she was the one who walked in the garden with the old man. He talked with her. Didn't like it. Didn't-didn't.

But you soon thought differently.

The meals got better. As she grew into the life here. Much better, to be honest. Thanks to her. But we animals take longer to get used to things than you do. Went for walks together, all three of us. The old man couldn't do much anymore, but she would come into the house here and sit and talk for a long time. Told me many things. It was very nice. Nice.

So in the end you liked each other.

In the end, yes. But still it's very different now, with just her. Am very sad. The old man has been here so long, and she just a little while. Don't know if she'll stay. Maybe she won't stay. Maybe she'll go away. The old man is gone. Don't understand why he's gone. Listen to the trees.

❧

"I'm sorry if Jacob frightened you. He's not used to strangers."

"I was startled," she said. Jacob kept hopping up and down, and tried to grab her with his long brown hairy arm.

"No, Jacob," said the old man, gesturing angrily with his walking stick. "Shame on you! Can't you see we have a guest?"

"Shouldn't he really have been named Esau?"

"Why?" The ape jumped up and down and let out a few angry cries.

"Wouldn't that have been more appropriate for a furry fellow?" She tried to smile.

"Who has sold his birthright, you mean? Hmm. Hmmhmm. That's not a stupid idea. Not stupid at all." He smiled gruffly. "Are you absolutely sure the two of us are related?"

"Yes, Uncle. My father was your nephew Axel."

"I hardly remember him."

"Neither do I."

"I don't remember any of them. Not any. Don't want to."

She looked at him.

"I think I'll go and pack now, so I can catch the evening train."

"Yes," was the brusque reply from under the mustache.

"Take care, then, and thanks for the dinner, Uncle Wilhelm. Good-bye, Jacob!" The ape seemed visibly relieved because she appeared to be leaving. "And thank you for letting me sleep here last night. I didn't know where I was and had no place to go."

"Good-bye," said the old man.

She began walking toward the house.

"It's odd that you should end up right here," he said behind her.

"Yes," she said, half turning around. "Coincidences are strange sometimes."

"Yes!" he said.

"You're not so bad, Uncle," she said. "Not as bad as they say."

He kept standing there, leaning on his cane.

She went up to her room, packed her backpack carefully; her clothes had dried. She saw that her hands were shaking a little, saw that she had hastily taken along the strangest things when she left home: a mateless sock, winter underwear, a toothbrush glass, a shaving kit. His shaving kit. She sits there with it in her hands and notices she is trembling. She had thought: He's forgotten his shaving things again. That's what she had thought. He's forgotten it, I need to take it in my backpack. She looks at the two silvery metal cylinders, one for the brush, the other for the shaving soap; they look like two salt shakers. It's a practical travel shaving kit, it had been quite expensive, and he was ridiculously proud of it, but nonetheless he usually forgot it. His voice on a southern summer morning: *You can al-*

ways tell a man by his shaving gear. Idiot, she said, that's not how you can tell a man. *It's not?* he said, and came over to her with his face covered with lather. Now she sits holding the two cylinders against her face, she screws together the shaving brush, sniffs it, lets it glide over her skin and lips, senses his smell so powerfully it gives her a jolt, feels dried lather like wax against her cheek. I've got to stop this, she thinks. She unscrews the brush, pulls it into the cylinder; the shiny surface is spotted with soap scum, with fingerprints. She puts the shaving gear in its bag, the little leather sack where it belongs. Her hands are trembling.

Andersen suddenly stands beside her, and she gives a start.

"Tell me, do you always sneak up on people?"

"No," he says. "I'm sorry, that was not my intention. Mr. Bolt asked me to inquire whether you would consider having supper with him this evening."

"Thank you very much," she says, "but I don't think so. I should get on my way. I need to get on my way."

"In that case, Mr. Bolt asks whether you need a ride to the train station."

"That would be nice."

"There is a train in one hour. Mr. Bolt asks further whether you need money."

"No, thank you," she says firmly. "I don't think so."

"Mr. Bolt asks in case—"

"Goddamn it, just leave me in *peace!*" she screams.

He leaves without a word. She sits hunched over her backpack. After a while she hears the old man's heavy footsteps crossing the floor.

"You shouldn't leave when you feel like this," he says.

"I know," she says.

"You can stay until you feel better. For the time being."

"Thank you," she mumbles. "For the time being."

❧

So I didn't leave then. Just stayed and stayed. Wonder if you ever realized what was going on with me. Or if you knew as little about me as I knew about you. You never asked. I never told you. Couldn't. There was so much we never talked about. Best that way. Wonder if you realized.

Lea looked around the room, at all the books lined up stiffly in the bookcases, the expensive vases on the bric-a-brac shelves on either side of the double doors, the dark easy chairs, the brass ashtrays, the corner cupboard. Behind the cracked white marble woman's head in the bookcase stood a forgotten wineglass from the afternoon. I wonder if you ever realized.

And somewhere far away, silently, from within all the old objects around her, something seemed to reply.

FOUR

That was how Lea came to the old man with her sorrow and stayed, as spring slowly passed and summer came, without her really noticing. Everything in the house ran like clockwork, and Lea, who already early in life had sent her clockworks into retirement, thought it was a harsh regimen at first. The meals were eaten at the stroke of seven, two, and seven o'clock. Her uncle always ate in silence, methodically, and afterward exchanged a few words with her about the weather, about some perennials he planned to look at, maybe about the ape's welfare. Then he disappeared, went off to his daily tasks. He was always busy. He didn't subscribe to a newspaper, and his only radio loomed in the living room as a monument to the fifties' view of the future as something made of fine wood with yellow knobs. Although he had a phonograph, she never played records on it. Didn't touch the piano either. During the day she saw him working in the garden with Andersen, she saw them in beekeeping outfits as they disappeared through the hedge on their way to the meadow where the beehives stood. She never went down there because all the buzzing around the white boxes was too much for her, it made her nervous. The third day she had unwittingly gotten too close, and had run away so fast her whole body gasped; the air had been black with bees. Long after she had hidden in her room she seemed

50

to hear the buzzing, and the room's white walls became spotted with blue before her eyes.

At first, she just walked around. The days flowed into each other, like a flicker of light. She slept a great deal. Didn't notice much. If she met him on one of her walks, he didn't exchange many words with her because he was busy. Never asked. After supper she liked to sit alone in the library and read, read without knowing what she read, while he disappeared into his office, which was in the next room. He always left the door open, and clearly made a point of doing so—to be courteous. He always politely said good morning, good day, good evening, and good night. But aside from that, his considerateness did not go much beyond leaving the door open between them. Nonetheless, she no longer felt that she was in the way or unwelcome. He let her be as she was, by herself, left alone. She wanted to be left alone. He also wanted to be left alone. He sat in his office bent over large record books that he wrote in, completely absorbed. He could sit there until late at night, needed little sleep, and always appeared for breakfast at seven o'clock in fine fettle. Andersen drove to the post office regularly, where he picked up thick envelopes, whole packages bearing colorful postage stamps, which he placed on the old man's desk. Her uncle found them there in the evening when he sat down to work and opened them; once, from a distance, she had seen the contents of such a package—stacks of written pages, some typewritten, others in different handwriting and colors. They looked like letters, without envelopes. With the help of a magnifying glass and eyeglasses, and puffing on a big black diabolical cigar, the old man paged contentedly through the papers, constantly making notes in the record books; now and then he chuckled a bit over a page, held it up in front of him toward the light like a rare object, admired it. Then he continued writing in the large notebook. There were many such record books in the office, thirty or forty at least. All neatly marked with numbers and letter codes. She had the impression that the old man corresponded with the entire world. But this could not be the case, because he never answered any of these letters, if they even *were* letters, except for a few small, lightweight airmail envelopes that Andersen took to the post office in town once a week, along with the week's domestic business correspondence. When her uncle was finished with a package of written pages, Andersen always stood beside him ready to take the pages and file them. Even though he was so tired at the end of each day that he swayed on his feet; she could clearly see that. Andersen was responsible for taking care of everything at Ekelund. Her uncle gave mysterious instructions for each sheet of paper—C45, he mumbled, half aloud, A12b, H30—and Andersen put the pages into large binders.

One evening, after nearly a month had passed, and he was sitting like that behind his record books, the telephone on his desk rang.

Lea, who had been lost in a book, without reading, looked up in surprise. It was the first time the telephone had rung the whole time she had been there. The old man looked at the black Bakelite instrument as if it were a poisonous spider that suddenly had landed among the papers on his desk. He visibly gathered his courage, then picked up the receiver.

"Bolt!" he shouted.

. . .

"No!"

. . .

"And who's that, if I may ask?"

. . .

"Oh, I see. Yes, yes. In any case, *I* haven't seen her."

. . .

"Yes, I understand. But it doesn't matter to me what you might have thought."

. . .

"Do what you want, confound it. I've got nothing to do with it."

. . .

"And why should it interest me if you find her?"

. . .

"You're wasting your efforts, believing things like that about me. Good-bye."

He sent her a long, fiendish look after he put down the receiver. Then he disappeared into his papers again.

Lea put the book away, stood up, walked over to the door. She had sat there reading, had read and read the same sentence over and over again, for nearly a month. Now suddenly she felt that she had awakened. She knocked on the door frame.

"Yes!" he growled, clearly annoyed at having been disturbed twice in a row. She kept standing at the threshold, leaned into the room.

"Excuse me," she said, and what should she say next? "Can I help you with anything?" she asked.

"What? Help with anything?"

"Yes, I see Andersen—"

"What about Andersen?"

"I just thought that—"

"What did you just think?"

"I thought maybe I could—"

"Yes, *out* with it, girl!"

"Andersen is very tired after his day's work, and I thought I could take the office duties off his hands."

"But you can't do that," he said crossly.

"I can both read and write," she informed him.

"Is that so?" He looked up at her, somewhat more gently disposed. "Well, well. But," he gestured toward all the binders and record books, "this is my great task," he said. "My life's work. I've been working on it—ever since—for a long time."

Suddenly he seemed a little proud.

"And Andersen, you see, he's my—scientific assistant. He knows the system. It's very complicated." He shut the record book, stood up. "It wouldn't be an effective use of time to teach it to you. A scholarly work as large as this takes time. And time—that's become precious to me."

At that moment the world clock began to play its melody in the dining room.

"So—he's worn out, you say? I hadn't noticed that."

"But he is," she said sullenly.

"Yes, yes, perhaps. Well, well, so you've noticed that." He scrutinized her, went over and took her arm, led her into the library again. "Well, if you really want to make yourself a bit useful, now that you're here," he said, "and relieve poor Andersen, then it's better that you help with the garden and the beehives during the day, instead of loafing around. There's plenty to keep you busy."

They sat down.

"But the scientific work," she said with curiosity.

"So Andersen is worn out? That's odd. Well, well. He's not getting . . . younger, either, I guess." He stretched out his bad leg. Suddenly he looked at her with great delight.

"I said you weren't here."

She looked down.

"They didn't believe it, of course. They just wanted to let me know." He laughed.

She had to laugh a little too. Her face felt unaccustomed to that.

"So *now* they're looking for me," she said ironically. He ignored her comment.

"Well, well," he said. "We can call it an incognito recreational stay."

"Ha," she said. She expected he would ask now, but he didn't ask, never asked. Didn't say she had to call home. Offered no advice, no opinion. Didn't seem to be especially interested in reasons and motives. In this he was different from almost everyone else she had met.

Instead he said: "So here we sit, then, the two outcasts." He rose, went to the corner cupboard, poured himself something in a large brandy glass. He fumbled in his pockets for his cigar case, she stood up and was about to go into the office to get it, but he waved her away. "No, not in there," he said; then he shuffled in and got the cigars himself. He sat down with difficulty, stretched out his leg again, raised his glass, sniffed down into it.

"I tell you, there's a great deal of re-creation in the mere atmosphere of a glass of brandy like this. But what am I thinking of—wouldn't you like a glass too?"

"Yes, thank you."

He started to get up from the chair again, but this time she forestalled him. He let it happen.

"Re-creation, yes," he said, as she went to the cupboard to fill a glass. "That means to restore. No, no, don't take from the fancy bottle, take from the little ugly one. That's the best."

"This one?" She held up a dark bottle with no label.

"Yes, that's right."

A dark brown fluid ran thickly into the glass. She corked the bottle, sat down with him, they raised their glasses to each other.

A stream of warmth and light rose from her abdomen to her head.

"Well?" he smiled.

"—powerful!" she said, when she caught her breath again.

"That's a Madeira from the West Indies," he said, "from 1828, if I remember correctly. Just taste that, it was made when Goethe was still alive, and Beethoven had died only the year before."

She drank some more. A sunny landscape rose in her, she seemed to see hands, brown hands, in the sunlight, green leaves, a yellow beach, a blue sea.

"Since then it's been drawn again and again, about every twenty years, so it would keep. Quite unique, isn't it?"

"It tastes absolutely pure," she said, "and yet heavy."

"Yes," he said, "you can truly talk about restoring something when you drink an elixir like that." He leaned back, suddenly seemed very young, very dreamy. "Eighteen twenty-eight—tastes like a good year for people," he said. "No chemicals in the alcoholic beverages, no pollution in the grapes." He sighed. "Besides, it's good for the thighbone. Best medicine to be found."

"But the scientific work, Uncle," she prodded again.

"Hush. Not now," he said. "Maybe I'll tell you about that sometime later. If you want to be involved in scientific work, you must first—do you have an education?"

"No," she said.

"Are you stupid?"

"No," she said.

"Well, anyway, scientific work starts with concrete things, you see. With what's close to the earth."

She looked at him uncertainly.

"It starts in the garden," he said. "On the shelf over there you'll find a large book of etchings in a folio format." She stood up. "On the top shelf. There, yes. Take it down. Careful, damn it! That's older than the Madeira we're drinking."

She carried the treasure carefully over to the table.

He opened it. The large, brittle pages held text and copperplate engravings. The plates depicted bees, or parts of them, in sections, and were drawn in perfect detail.

"Can you speak French?" he asked.

"A little," she said. "I'm better in German and Italian."

"Well, that's something," he said. "Yes indeed. Then you'll learn French while you read this book. Aren't the pictures extraordinary?"

She nodded.

"This is the great Huber," he said. "Franz, or François, Huber. His letters to the insect researcher Charles Bonnet, *Les Nouvelles Observations sur les Abeilles*—New Observations About Bees. Published first in 1789. The second part didn't come until a quarter of a century later. An inexhaustible treasure for a bee researcher. Inexhaustible. This folio edition contains both parts, and was published a little later, with illustrations. Of course they're not by Huber. Of course not!"

"Should I read this, Uncle?"

"Yes, certainly."

"But I'm no good in natural science."

"I see. The great François Huber was born in Geneva in 1750," the old man continued stubbornly. "While still a young boy he became *blind*."

"Blind?"

"At most, he could sense a glimmer of light at midday. He never saw a honeycomb in his life, far less a bee, to say nothing of the even smaller parts that you see pictured here, the claw joints in a bee's foot and the antenna cleaners in a worker bee's foot, the stinger, the mandibles, the honey bladders, the rectum bladder, and so forth. It's very small, as you see. Still, Huber became one of the greatest—if not the greatest—bee researchers the world has seen. His blindness saved him from less important things; and 1789 was, as I said, a good year for him, unlike many other people."

"But—but how did he do that?"

"It's a very beautiful story. With the help of a faithful lifelong servant—François Burnens, if I remember correctly, who became his eyes and hands, who made the observations for him and with him, and described them to him—Huber could devote his whole life and his keen analytical and systematic mind to research about bees. Even though his eyes were poorly suited to natural science. It was Réaumur's writings about bees that caught Huber's interest, and with the help of his servant Burnens he began to conduct experiments. Through the veil of his dead eyes, his thoughts managed to break through yet another veil into the mysterious invisible laws that protect nature, into the deepest secrets in the beehive. As another great writer about the life of bees has expressed it: There is hardly a more moving and instructive tale of human suffering and triumph than the history of the patient collaboration between François Huber and his servant François Burnens. It teaches us that we must never, under any circumstances, renounce the desire for truth and the search for truth."

"Never," she said, obediently.

"The etchings came later, of course."

"Yes," she said.

"Even though subsequent research has made great leaps forward, no one has been able to disprove or refute any of blind Huber's main observations. They are still the basis for our knowledge about bees today."

She looked at the thick book.

"He's a captivating writer besides. You must read it carefully, it's a valuable edition," he said. "Take good notes. There's a French dictionary in the bookcase. I'll have Andersen get a beekeeper's suit for you; then one day we'll go and say hello to the bee colony together, and see if your lessons have made any impact. That is, if you still want to *relieve* Andersen."

"Yes," she said, and thought: Thirty days in prison are like thirty years for an Indian.

"If you're going to stay here, it's really time you start to make yourself useful," he said.

"Yes," she agreed.

"You're absolutely right," he said. "It's really time. Now that you've gotten used to this place, I'm glad you finally want to assert yourself a little more. Not just sit and read and walk around in a daze. So we'll see what you're made of. Cheers. It's really not a moment too soon."

❧

Esteemed Sir!

I have noticed that the removal of one antenna does not exert any visible influence on the instincts of the queen, the worker bees, or the drones. If I cut off a small part of the antenna, they do not lose the ability to find things, which they demonstrated by being in the hive and performing their usual work. Their behavior when deprived of both antennae cannot be attributed to pain, but to the impossibility of

57

adapting themselves among, and communicating with, other members of the colony.

⚬✣

Summer came while Lea read. The bees hummed in their hives, crept along her arms, up the net in front of her face; she was numb with fear at first.

"If a young worker bee hasn't been out before," said the old man, "it's completely helpless if we move it just a couple of meters from its hive. It doesn't know where its home is. First the young bees must whir around the opening of the hive a little, in a small cloud, with their heads turned toward the entrance. We call it the foreplay. Then little by little they learn where their home is, and can set out on longer trips."

Summer came. Lea read. "They orient themselves with the help of their sense of smell," her uncle told her, "and above all, their eyesight; they can clearly distinguish among white, yellow, blue, and violet, but they're color blind when it comes to grass-green and bright red. On the other hand, they can see all the ultraviolet that our eyes can't perceive, so they can distinguish between colors we confuse, such as zinc-white and lead-white."

Summer came. Every morning Lea got up and read. Obediently. She was dead tired, but forced herself to get up. Concentrated on the written words. Later she went to the beehives with her uncle. Slowly her anxiety lost its hold. He taught her to see the differences among the small cells for the worker-bee progeny, the larger cells for the drones, and the largest for the queen larvae. He showed her how the bees returned with clumps of pollen on their feet, he showed her how they fed the young and the queen, he showed her the big, stupid drones, whose only task was to mate with the queen.

⚬✣

Esteemed Sir!
It is established that queens continue to be barren, even in a seraglio of drones, when one keeps them imprisoned in the hives. This led me

to the conjecture that queen bees cannot be inseminated in their dwellings, but only in the open air. I will now give you an exact account of the experiment we performed on June 29, 1789. We stationed ourselves outside a hive whose virgin queen was five days old. It was eleven o'clock in the morning, the sun had been shining since early morning, and the air was hot. We enlarged the entrance of the hive we wanted to observe, and turned our entire attention toward the bees that emerged from it. First came the drones, who flew away immediately as soon as we had freed them. Shortly afterward the young queen appeared in the hive entrance, but did not fly away at once. We saw how she remained on the alighting board for some moments, and stroked the back of her body with her rear legs, while the workers and drones that went in and out paid no attention to her, seemed unaware of her at all. Finally she flew away. When she was a meter or so from the hive, she turned around and approached the hive again, as if to take precise note of the hive entrance—out of prudence, one would think—and thereafter moved away and flew in horizontal circles about two to three meters above the ground. We now made the hive entrance smaller, so she could not return unnoticed, and then positioned ourselves at the center of the circles that the queen was tracing, in order to be able to watch her movements and behavior more easily. But she did not remain long in this favorable position; soon afterward, she flew away swiftly and disappeared from our field of vision. We then positioned ourselves in front of the hive, and after seven minutes saw the young queen fly back and alight by the hive entrance. We held her to examine her, but saw no outward sign of insemination. We let her go into the hive, where she remained for a quarter of an hour. Then she came out again, flew up, looked carefully at the hive and then disappeared high into the air. This time she was gone for all of twenty-seven minutes. When she returned and sank to the alighting board, she was in quite a different condition; the hindmost part of her body was covered with a white material that had become thick and hard, her sex organ was half open, and we could clearly see that her interior, including the ovary, was filled with the same white material. It exactly resembled, in both consistency and color, the fluid which fills a drone's seminal vesicle.

We enclosed the queen in the hive, and after two days it was evident that she had become fertile. She was clearly fatter and, moreover, had already laid nearly one hundred eggs in worker cells.

⌀

Lea stumbled through the old book. Slowly she saw the chaos of the tens of thousands of creeping bees that studded the honeycombs become a comprehensible whole, or at least almost. Two of the hives were purely observation hives, where the bees' daily life could be observed through glass.

"Bees are deaf," the old man explained. "It's odd when you consider that they make so many different buzzing sounds. But maybe they sense the vibrations all the same. Maybe they make sounds *we* can't perceive. Also, they *sense time* in a different way than we do. If you feed them at a certain time each day, they come to get food at the same time day in and day out. Look there. They're talking with each other now." A migrating bee stood on the alighting board wriggling back and forth in a sort of dance. The bees around it paid close attention to the dance.

"That bee has found a source of honey. Now it's telling the others about the place and the kind of flower. Had it found a source of pollen, the dance would have been completely different."

"By wriggling like that?"

"Mmm. I wonder what it's saying."

"It must be impossible to translate."

"I'm not so sure about that. I think it's very factual. Everything that's beautiful and wonderful and poetic is at the same time very factual. *The wind is coming toward you from the northwest. Your wings must beat fast. Fly up toward the great warm light. Take the heart side of the great light. Fly past the apple tree that has shed its blossoms. Fly past the field clover and the melilot, the willow herb, and the two linden trees, go behind the linden trees, in the shadow of the linden trees the wild raspberry bushes are blooming. There. Now. Follow me.* I think the bee is saying something like that, in translation. But I think it's expressing this in some sort of number language. In numbers and sequences and rhythm."

Suddenly the swarm of bees that had been watching the dancing bee flew away.

"Well, well," he said. "Here I am, an old man, teaching you about the bees and the flowers." He chuckled beneath his hat. Gave her a cheerfully stern look: "You know what such things can lead to."

"Aha," she said.

"Now I'm going to teach you to clip the queen's wings."

"Clip her wings?"

"The hive is full, do you see that? The bees are at their best and richest now in June, the honey is glistening, they're fully supplied. Then they want to swarm. The old queen lays new queen larvae, and after that she flies out with almost the entire colony to establish a new state. In the worst case, they might disappear entirely. So we clip the queen's wings. When she flies outside, she falls to the ground. Then we can sweep the swarm back into the old hive."

The queen stood in a circle of workers. They bowed respectfully to her, they fanned her with their wings to cool her and showed every sign of veneration. The queen herself seemed a little slow and listless. Without further ado, the old man picked up the monarch, who was somewhat longer and larger than the other bees, held her between his thumb and index finger, took out a scissors. It was sad to watch, Lea thought. But the queen did not seem to be bothered by losing her wings. When he put her back, her subjects continued their exercises in subjugation, undisturbed.

"Later, after they have swarmed, they hatch a new queen, who kills her predecessor. The same way bees kill other bees that have a *foreign smell*, those who mistakenly enter the wrong hive. They're merciless, in all their harmony."

"Harmony, you say. It sounds like the primeval picture of a fascist state."

"Hmmm. There's really nothing simpler, or more foolish, than to draw cheap parallels and analogies between nature and human society. One must be very careful about doing that without thorough knowledge of the subject. I'm not sure that one automatically gains wisdom from the ant. Writers have praised the bees and their system, its order, equilibrium, and harmony. Yes, yes—the writers, you know, they're writers. But a writer would scarcely last five minutes as a bee before his days were ended."

Lea laughed.

"On the other hand, you can see the whole bee colony as one organism, in which the bees are single cells and repel foreign substances, just as the human body does. A similar process occurs with certain amoebae. They can live as a large colony of happy, greedy single amoebae, but the moment a danger threatens, they unite, create something that resembles one organism with a center and a periphery, create an inside and an outside, develop different biological priorities; some become sex cells, some become motion organs, and this entire cell society moves away to more favorable living conditions, dissolves, once again becomes single amoebae."

"And how do they make—what would you call it—the decision?"

"Bravo. That's a very interesting question. How, at what point, do they decide to form an entity? They send each other electrochemical signals, to be sure, but that doesn't really explain anything. It's as if there were a greater will behind it. How do the bees *know* it's time to swarm? How do they realize the hive is so rich, so full of abundance, that it's time to divide themselves, let the old queen leave with tens of thousands of bees and form a new colony? They do it only in abundant years, not in lean years. The individual bee can't know it, can't 'decide' it, nor the queen either, because she's probably more stupid than the rest. They *all* know it. What *will* lies behind it all? That's interesting. But a bother for the beekeeper, because one has to run around and climb trees and sweep the swarm from the place the queen and all the bees have settled, and then install them in an empty hive. So we try to prevent them from swarming naturally."

From then on, Lea's tasks included finding the queen in hives that were ready to swarm and clipping her wings; but she didn't always have the heart to do it, as she stood there with the swarm's great mother looking so tiny between the tips of her fingers. Instead she prayed a silent prayer that her bees would not swarm that summer, and released the queen, unclipped, into the hive again.

She was gradually allowed to do other things too, scrape honeycombs, extract honey, inspect the brood nests. She learned to get stung too—*to take* the stings. The first time she got stung, she did not fully realize what had happened. A bee had gotten into her sleeve, and suddenly her whole underarm hurt. She stiffened, felt sick, began fumbling feverishly with the arm of her jacket. "Did you get stung?" the old man asked, utterly calm. She nodded. "Don't start waving your arms. Don't drop anything. Just stand there calmly, and finish what you're doing. It's not dangerous, and it goes away fast. A potato, Andersen, damn it, a potato!" Andersen hurried off, while they carefully finished their work. Then he came running back with a peeled potato, which he rubbed on the beesting. The swelling went down, she did not utter a word of complaint. The old man looked at her approvingly. "Today you've taken a big step forward in your training in scientific methodology," he said. Later she did not really mind getting stung, in a way it seemed to wake her up a bit; with each sting she felt she came to her senses more, and she was no longer so tired in the morning.

There were many other books on the shelves about bees, and about botany and zoology, and she grew calm and clearheaded from reading them. One morning she dreamed that the old man gave her a sailboat, and that she sailed alone to another coast, although she had always been afraid of the sea. But in the dream she was not afraid, felt only delight that the boat carried her.

In the evenings the old man sat with his record books, working serenely.

Several weeks passed in this way. She looked around Ekelund, began to undertake expeditions of discovery in the rooms and on the property. Slowly she learned to know the estate, the small garden pavilion, the orchard, the greenhouse, the empty stable, the sheds, and the row of cement foundation walls next to Jacob's little house. The park, large and empty and slightly overgrown. And inside the main house, all the paintings, the books, the furniture. It was an old house, the central part had been built in the beginning of the eighteenth century, and the wings were added later. On the first floor the rooms were lined up in rows, the library and office faced the yard and had a view toward the fjord, while the dining room and the other rooms faced the sea. Several of the rooms were dusty and somewhat empty; they clearly were not in use. The atmosphere was a little like a museum. There were paintings and furniture from the early eighteenth century, chests of drawers and small boxes, rococo chairs too old to sit on, candelabra, antlers on the wall, a genuine stuffed bear, portraits in gold frames, stern men in wigs, dreamy women in graceful empire-waist gowns, children with blond hair and blue eyes. They looked at her from all the walls. Now and then it seemed she could recognize an expression, a look; for instance, a little nineteenth-century boy in a velvet suit seemed to glance at her, and she thought of her father. But for the most part they were strangers, forgotten, long departed, meaningless to her. She tried to imagine her own picture hanging among them, equally departed. That was not so difficult. They belonged together. They were family after all.

Once children had scampered through the rooms here. It was hard to determine the boundary between the old days and now. Her uncle and all his things were, in a way, a continuation of the old days. And, Lea thought, there was only a short time between the old man and the little boy in velvet—an hour, a striking of the clock, a glance into the room. Maybe she was a child at Ekelund herself now. One in the line of Bolts.

On the mansard floor of the west wing a whole row of closed rooms were used purely for storage, room after room. She was not allowed to go into them. "Parts of my collections are there," said the old man, somewhat proud and embarrassed at the same time. "Terribly unsystematic, I'm afraid. Awfully messy in there. It's Andersen's fault. He hasn't cleaned there for years. Oh well. You may take just a peek, if you want to. Nothing . . . dangerous in there." And she went from object to object; lifted bedsheets, peeked in cupboards and drawers. It reminded her of stealing into the untidy attic as a child, the only difference was the type of objects. This was the untidy attic of a prince from *The Thousand and One Nights*. There were ship models and figures of saints, procession masks and musical instruments from the old man's time in the Orient, carved wooden figures from Africa, Egyptian hippopotamuses, a small menagerie of stuffed animals. An entire corner cabinet contained only glass; seventeenth-century Dutch glass, Nøstetangen goblets etched with battle scenes and shipwrecks; there were vases from Bohemia and Schleswig, and a large set of the Venetian glasses with their pure, simple form and inlaid twisted white threads. "It's not called *threads*," the old man had said at the dinner table, "it's called *a reticello*." Yes, of course. "Everything is *called* something, Lea." Yes, of course.

In the next room was a cupboard containing crocks of dried chemical preparations, a chest of drawers filled with unusable Bunsen burners, chemical-distilling equipment, and old petri dishes; she guessed this was the remains of her uncle's revolutionary rubber distillation. More fascinating were several showcases filled with stones and crystals from his geology studies before the war, all a bit dusty, with yellowed cards and labels written in her uncle's handwriting, youthful handwriting, now faded. They appeared somewhat forgotten, although it was a lovely collection: a marvelous rock crystal, a piece of gneiss sprinkled with perfectly formed garnets, a large yellow beryl, a rather large piece of silver with threadlike ramifications taken directly from the vein, likewise a somewhat smaller piece of gold right from the mountain, and even more remarkable, a box containing a tiny, perfectly round piece of gold. It was mounted in an old iron frame. No other minerals or stones in the collection were cut or polished. Two large glass cabinets in the same room held a collection of antique microscopes; she suspected they must be invaluable, but they seemed as neglected as the crystals and everything else in these rooms. One microscope had an ocular tube of dark wood, ebony or boxwood, with ivory and guaiacum shims; it appeared to be the oldest. The rest were all brass. But they too must be very old, judging from the spiraled engravings on the objects: "Johann Michael Milchmeyer Uhrmacher und Opticus in Frackfurrt 1738," "Dollond LONDON," "Jones's Most Improved Compound Microscope," "Plössl in Wien," "Powell & Leland No. 1"; but also newer, recognizable names: "Gebr. Seibert," "Carl Zeiss, Jena." Thomas.

Thomas. "When one holds it before one's eye and looks through it at a drop of water from the pond, one sees more than a thousand marvelous creatures, which one otherwise never sees in the water, but they are there, and that is true. It looks almost like a plate filled with shrimp leaping amongst each other, and they are so greedy, they tear off each other's arms and legs, hind ends and edges, and yet they are happy and satisfied in their way."

Thomas, she thought, you wouldn't have been interested in the goblets with the sharp etchings (sharp as knives) or the crystals (opaque forms), but you would have liked the microscopes (you liked such things, *constructed* things, things with parts that can be unscrewed from each other), and you would have brought up Hans Christian Andersen's drop of water. Or Søren Kierkegaard's lorgnette. How did he put it? To see God with a lorgnette? No, how did he put it?

"It is innocent and beautiful and moving that the Lover looks adoringly at the Beloved, but it is pretentious to look at her through a lorgnette. And therefore the natural scientist uses a microscope as the dandy does a pince-nez, except the scientist focuses the microscope toward God." "*In the end all depravity will come from the natural scientists.* Many admirers believe that when investigations are made under the microscope, they are scientifically serious . . . It is quite in order that a man both naïvely and profoundly says: I cannot see with the naked eye how consciousness comes into existence. But that a man puts a microscope before his eye and then looks and looks and looks—and still cannot see it: this is comical. And it is especially ridiculous that this is supposed to be serious."

She looked up both quotations in the library and read them to her uncle at the supper table that evening with a certain enjoyment; she laughed as she read, but the old man simply barked a brief, disdainful laughter. Well, well, she thought.

"Didn't Kierkegaard wear glasses?" he growled. "He should have thought about that before he wrote those words. Most likely he was wearing his glasses in order to write his nonsense. A microscope is just a very strong eyeglass lens." She did not answer, did not think. "Had it been up to that sort of reactionary, we'd still be using crystals in a leather mask before our eyes. Like the yellow beryl in my collection. Did you know that, by the way?" She did not answer, did not think. "Eyeglasses are made from beryl. Everything is *called* something, Lea." Yes, yes. The corners of her eyes were stinging, and she thanked him for the meal. He did not notice anything. That night she lay half awake, could not really sleep, could not really rest, wanted to leave. Outside, the buoy whistled. I'm almost completely awake now, she thought. I'm awake and clearheaded and calm. Still, I'm more restless than before. It's more painful than before, because it's a cold, sharp wakefulness, sharp-edged as a lens. Outside, the buoy whistled.

Imagine the fjord without any markers, without spar buoys and buoys, without lighthouses. Imagine the coast as it *was*. Beneath the gleaming, smooth blue surface are underwater reefs and shallows; only someone who knows the waters can sail without markers. The fjord glistens, a myriad of tiny points and strips of bright light appear and disappear, swiftly, like vibrations. Buoys and spar buoys loom like dark pointing fingers in all that light. Imagine if nobody knew where the reefs were. Thomas. In a toolshed she found a boy's old bicycle that she oiled and repaired somewhat, so she could go off on her own. She bicycled a few times out to the tall lighthouse on the headland, but it was locked. It was as white as marble. When the fishing boats came in, she thought, and saw this lighthouse, then they knew they were home, even if they were still many miles at sea. Then they knew that an eye saw them. Now the eye was closed. Sometimes she went swimming, but did not enjoy it, because when she swam out and turned around, the beach looked so empty. It was better to just ride around on the bicycle, because the exercise took away some of the loneliness. Sometimes she slept in a small two-wheeled cart in the midday sun, while white clouds rushed across the blue heights overhead. Swallows shrieked in the air above her. The sorrow was like a cat's paw: now soft and gentle, now with its claws extended.

They were four at Ekelund. The ape Jacob gradually became a friend. At first they maintained a sort of armed neutrality. She brought food to him, talked to him a little while he sat down to eat. Jacob pretended not to see her, turned his face away, ate in lofty silence. Now and then she made an observation, about the weather, about what they had been doing that day; Jacob just looked at her without interest, as at a guest who has stayed too long. That's how it was at first. Jacob was even less interested than the old man had been. All things considered, Lea thought it was a straightforward and undemanding attitude. One day as she was sitting in the little house, she said: "When I was little, I had a father."

Jacob chewed an apple, gave her a quick glance, kept on chewing.

"Nobody remembers him any longer, except me. Do you want to hear about him?"

Jacob did not answer, but seemed to shrug his shoulders, as if it made no difference to him.

"He was my friend," Lea continued uncertainly. She thought Jacob looked a little more interested. So she told about her father. Afterward she cried.

"He was with me and around me. He lifted me high into the clouds and I danced on his shoulders. He sang for me and I sat on his lap and saw his hands flow over the piano keys. He had long, white, slender, slightly nervous hands. But in his arms it was safe and filled with singing. He always sang. I wanted to just sit with his arms around me at night when I couldn't sleep. It helped to just sit with him, it was paradise. He was tireless. His voice was strong and sure, everything in him kept time with the song: his legs, the rocking of his arms, his hand patting my head, his breath, his heart. I was a star, no, I was a comet, with a long shining tail, speeding joyfully toward the singing sun. I danced on his shoulders."

Afterward she cried. Jacob ambled over to her, patted her arm hesitantly. Offered her an apple.

"You're nice, Jacob," she said.

Jacob nodded.

"Do you think," she began, "since you know Ekelund . . ." Jacob looked at her kindly. "Maybe I can stay here a while longer?"

Jacob said nothing.

"Sometimes I want to leave. Just go away from here."

Jacob thought about this. He'd had a good life at Ekelund, had always been here. Only now and then, when the treetops rustled especially strongly at night, or in cold winter weather, a wave of longing went through him, a longing to go away. He said nothing, looked down.

"But I don't know where I'd go," she continued. "I don't know how things would go. I don't know what would happen to me."

Jacob said nothing.

"It's sort of strange that I'm here, isn't it?"

Jacob nodded, almost imperceptibly.

That's how she slowly became friends with Jacob. It was more difficult with the fourth resident on the estate. On the lower floor, in the blue old-fashioned kitchen, Andersen ruled. There he had his small desk, under the big unused signal board for the masters' bells. In the old days there must have been many servants, now he was alone. Alone with the bags and boxes, receipts, lists of things to remember. Andersen sat there at his desk, and when he wasn't sitting there, he went about busily, was everywhere, yet never seemed in a hurry. The lightbulbs were changed, the lawn raked, the flowers watered, a windowpane replaced in the greenhouse, the ovens blacked, the world clock wound, the windows in the parlor facing the garden closed in the evening, the breakfast laid out, lunches and suppers prepared, wine bottles brought to room temperature; always exquisite food. A mushroom omelet, open-faced roast beef sandwiches, a steak, a honey-glazed saddle of lamb; he pickled and preserved and pressed fresh juices. He was always there. The old man hardly ever needed to ring the little bell or call for him, it was as if he could read thoughts, as if he had antennae in all the Ekelund rooms and on the whole estate. For when the old man needed help with something or wanted to give Andersen a message and looked up, somewhat preoccupied, with a squinting, slightly searching glance—well, where the devil is he?—then Andersen always *was* there. Within fifteen seconds at most he stood there silently, with a friendly half-lowered gaze, to hear the old man's wishes and inquiries—although *demands* was probably the correct word. But Andersen never grumbled; rather, he seemed to regard each new task as a pleasant challenge. Without being asked, Lea began to carry in groceries from the car, put them in the refrigerator and pantry, investigate food supplies, write lists for bee-smoking equipment they needed, feed Jacob, clip bushes, clean bathrooms. Andersen never *said* he appreciated the help, but he did not object either. Utterly correct, speaking always in the third person plural, well dressed, up early, late to bed, never a friend visiting, never a day off—but he was not at all like a butler. Rather, he seemed like some sort of priest, a proper priest of the old-fashioned type with a calling and a ruffled collar, or perhaps like a patient blacksmith with limitless strength, or perhaps like a researcher bent over his microscope, obsessed with his task. How old could he be? Judging from his appearance, perhaps in his late fifties, but there was something about him that made Lea think he was as old as Ekelund itself. That he had always been there, that he had always walked through the rooms and wound the clocks. Lea was a little afraid of him. He was neither irritable nor cross, he just *was*. He never *said* anything. He accepted everything. That frightened Lea. His face had a stiff, taciturn expression, with an ironic half smile at the corners of his mouth. Once a week people from the cleaning service came, every fourteen days Henry's Nursery arrived to help with larger tasks in the garden, and Andersen led the work like Napoleon at Austerlitz. Lea noticed that others were a bit afraid of him too, everyone except the old man. When she went into the small town with Andersen to help him carry groceries and pick up the mail, she noticed how people in the stores and on the street became a little different when they arrived. Andersen wore his chauffeur's uniform. When the shopping was finished, she always treated him to an ice cream; they sat on the wharf and ate in silence. She never managed to ask him about anything, other than utterly concrete things. He was like gray rainy weather, deep and impenetrable, in the middle of the hot sun. Lea noticed that people stared at her too, as she walked with Andersen, as if some of the strangeness about him infected her as well. Whenever she saw Henry's Nursery again, either at Ekelund or in town, she greeted him, but he stared too; she had become a stranger to him. Then she felt the paw lightly scraping in her breast. Not much longer now, then everyone would know. She ducked a little as they rounded each corner, as if someone stood there waiting for her.

Then came June 28.

"Are you nervous about something, Miss Bolt?" Andersen suddenly asked that morning. They were sitting on the wharf together and she had just thrown the rest of her ice cream to the gulls. It struck her that it was the first time he had asked her a direct question.

"No," she said.

"We are having a fine summer," he said. "It's good that you are helping in the garden."

"Yes," she said. "Thank you."

"We could not have managed it alone much longer. You know, Bolt is no young man. He's got that thigh, it's an injury from his youth. In recent years he has begun to notice it again. The wounds reopen when one gets old."

"Mmm."

"I am speaking from experience," said Andersen. She looked at him. But he did not meet her gaze. "You do not need to be afraid, Miss Bolt. Once one is allowed to stay at Ekelund, one does not have to leave."

"One doesn't?"

"That's how it is. I speak from experience. Mr. Bolt relies on you. In the fall there will be a great deal of fruit in the garden. He is unable to climb a ladder anymore, you know. His heart. I am not so young either."

"Have you been at Ekelund a long time?"

"A very long time. Mr. Bolt relies on you now. You came to Ekelund by a very remarkable coincidence. Mr. Bolt attaches great importance to the nature of coincidences. You can depend on him. You need not be uneasy."

"Yes, but I *am* uneasy."

Andersen ate the rest of his ice cream, looked at her, smiled slightly. It was merely the shadow of a smile, and she wasn't sure if she had seen him smile that way before. His eyes narrowed, became almost friendly. It struck her again, as it would often strike her later, that she didn't know anything about him, that he was a stranger, that he had no points of contact, to time or place, that he was far away.

"Thank you for the ice cream," he said. "We must go and get food for Jacob."

Esteemed Sir!

On the 28th the queen had not yet finished laying eggs. But her body had become very thin, and she began to be restless. Her movements grew more lively, but she still examined the cells, as if she was going to lay eggs in them. Sometimes she also thrust half of her body down into them, but then quickly withdrew it again without having laid an egg. Once she laid an egg in a cell without pushing very deeply into it, but the egg proved to be improperly fastened; it did not have one end on the bottom of the cell, but hung from one of the six-sided edges. During her activities the queen made no audible sound, nor did we hear anything other than the usual humming of the bees. The queen slipped past the bees she met on her way. Sometimes the bees she met stood still, as if to watch the queen, or struck out at her vehemently, knocked her with their heads and crept onto her back. The queen then continued with some of her workers on her back; none of them gave her honey to eat, she had to take honey herself from the open cells she found along her way. The bees no longer formed a lane or regular circles around her. Those she had initially set in motion by her wandering followed along with her; as she passed other bees that had remained in the honeycombs until now, they too were set in motion. The path the queen had taken could be recognized by the commotion she had caused everywhere, a commotion that did not die down. Soon she had visited every part of the hive and started a general uproar. If a corner remained where the bees were still calm, the restless ones promptly came by and planted the unrest there too. The queen no longer laid eggs in the cells, but let the eggs fall; the bees stopped caring about the young bees, they all rushed about in confusion; those who returned to the hive were drawn into this storm of movement as well and grew very agitated, without thinking about cleaning off the balls of flower dust they were carrying on their legs. Finally all the bees rushed toward the exit at once, and the queen with them.

⁂

Lea stands at the window. The house is completely quiet. The old man is dead, and far away. Yet he is nearby. She hears the wind blowing. She hears the rushing sound of the bees as they hurry through the hive after their queen.

"We, the bees, bear witness: We are happy! We have a queen! Our dark dwelling is flowing with honey and sweetness. There is only abundance and satiety. We are waiting. We are waiting for the right hour. The cells for May honey are still wide open and fragrant. It is warm in the hive. A swarm of ten thousand create a cooling wind. Another throng cares for our forty thousand offspring lying pale as wax in the warm depths where they have just hatched. And in the deepest, most sacred place in the hive our twelve princesses are asleep, wrapped in their shrouds; they are waiting for their hour, waiting for one of them to awaken to life and become our new mother. For days we have waited. For days we have hummed loudly and happily, but the right hour did not arrive. And now it is happening. Suddenly we know it. Our wings know it, and our antennae know it. We all know it. We can feel it in us and around us. Now we are the happiest. Outside is the light. Now the great movement is coming."

⁂

June 28. She sat in Jacob's house. I had another friend, you know, Jacob. I danced on his hands and his male organ; he had strong, clever hands that could take everything apart. They were white too. His hands, I mean. I wanted only to be with him. He took me apart, he put me back together again. Put me back together again after everything went to pieces. I whirred like a coffee mill, ground fine aromatic powder, ready to brew. He was clever with his hands, he made me function. At last I danced again. I was a flying coffee mill, traveling through the universe, with a long tail of delicious foam, twelve grams of coffee is subjected to a pressure of nine bar, the result is an espresso, delightful foam, a dancing coffee mill–comet foam, warm foam. I'm sorry that everything has to end, that sooner or later everything leaves, that all comets lose their tails. It's over, but it *shouldn't* be over. I don't want to go back where I was, I want to keep traveling in space, to be put back together, new and shiny as silver, shiny as a sports car, a coffee mill–comet convertible, fly up high. Why was he taken from me? Why do I have to remember all this? I don't want to remember.

✌

The odd thing was that Lea was not frightened when the swarm of bees settled on her head. Not at first. She immediately understood what was happening; she was walking through the garden, after leaving Jacob's house, when the swarm landed. At first she was completely coolheaded, stopped short, and closed her eyes tightly. What was happening seemed to be happening far away, in another country. She stood absolutely still. The terror did not come until later. The bees were on her head, covered her hair. They were like a huge clump of warm, buzzing life. Outside her eyelids it grew completely dark, for the bees crept onto her eyes and covered them, as well as her ears and nose. She stood absolutely still and breathed carefully through her mouth, through her lips, through clenched front teeth. She thought: I must stand absolutely still. I must not move. I must not laugh. I must not move before someone finds me. It could take an hour or the whole day, but I must not move. Her hands kept wanting to go up to her head to brush away the bees, but she said to them: Stay still, hands. And her hands obeyed, for a little while. She noticed how the intense sound of the bees and the lack of visual sensations made her a little dizzy, but she said: Body, keep standing. Her legs trembled, and her knees and stomach felt weak, but she told her legs that they must stand straight. The whole time her body wanted to do something other than she did, and that felt strange. But she kept standing, the bees slowly calmed down on her head and upper body. Soon she was far away, soon she had floated to a distant place and scarcely noticed how at regular intervals she commanded her body to hold its own. It was an impulse that came almost automatically. She herself was somewhere else in the darkness, a warm, golden, rocking place. A place with bright ochre houses and strong sunlight, and she saw his face, glistening with grease in the sunlight; he straightened up from the engine casing and smiled at her, as if he understood everything and forgave everything. *Help me, my darling, help me*, she whispered behind her teeth. At that moment his image disappeared, and she almost lost her breath. Then she floated away again, this time farther back, now she saw a misty schoolyard, the figure in front of her appeared only as a shadow. *You can have me*, she heard her own voice say, provocatively, scornfully. *You can take me. I can suck you too, you'd probably like that.* The shadow towered before her. *Please*, she said, pleadingly now, *you can do whatever you want, as long as you don't tell anyone. I'm good at it.* A bee stung her neck, and she came to herself again, was present behind her eyelids and teeth again, and felt afraid, more afraid than she had ever been, because she happened to think about the artery and nerves in her neck. If I faint now, she thought, they will kill me. The bees. They think I have a foreign smell. They crept and crawled on her, buzzed contentedly, probably thought she was a good tree in which to establish their new colony. It was as if they had swarmed on her forever. She noticed that she was about to lose her balance again, forced herself to stay erect. And suddenly it seemed to her that this was just a repetition of something, that she had undergone this before; she thought about what she had done as a child, when she wanted to escape the bad thing, then she had just closed her eyes and said kare kare kare, ma ma ma, without a sound; she had floated away and let everything happen to her, and she had survived, because she had a golden place far behind her eyelids that no one knew about, behind kare kare kare, ma ma ma, where she was alone and nothing could reach her. Now, inside the swarm of bees, she found her way back there. It would be all right, as long as they did not sting.

> *Kare kare kare, do not let them sting,*
> *Ma ma ma, do not let me fall,*
> *Kare kare kare, let the buzzing sing,*
> *Ma ma ma, I can kill them all.*

She had forgotten what the garden looked like and where the trees grew, where the house stood and if there was a house. But she did not forget to tell her body at regular intervals, when it had to be reminded, that it should take everything very calmly. She herself was another person entirely, and she was many places simultaneously. *I can kill them all.* Within her, everything grew quiet and light, totally white with light, and suddenly she remembered everything, everything that had happened, everything she hadn't wanted to think about the past months, everything she hadn't wanted to remember the last three years . . .

. . . And she didn't know whether she had stood for five minutes or for five hours, but suddenly, in the white light, she heard a voice, warm and very near, and very tender, and it was the most beautiful thing she had ever heard and almost made her cry. It seemed very noble, very polite and proper, and it said something she thought she recognized. It had already repeated the words many times when she came up to the surface in herself again; suddenly she could feel her lips and all the creeping bees, and the voice said carefully:

"Lea. Lea. Good girl. Stand absolutely still. It will be over soon." She realized it was her uncle's voice, but it sounded different through all the bees. Slowly she began to sense things outside herself again, she noticed movement and rustling, and her uncle's voice which said: "Remember what I've said about bees that are swarming. They're not angry. They're happy. But they can become frightened. Now we mustn't frighten them. Stand completely still. My goodness, how good you are at standing still. It will soon be over." Also these words reminded her of something from long ago, something she had heard before, but her uncle meant it only in a good and proper way. She felt the tears wanting to come. She stood still. The whole time he puttered around her, encouraged her, said kind words to her. "You were about to fall when I found you, you were swaying a little, but now you won't fall. You'll never fall again. See. Here comes Andersen with a brush and pail, and now it will soon be over. Listen to me, Lea. Stand absolutely still. Don't move until I tell you to, because we've got to get them all. Don't move even if you get stung a little. Andersen brought a whole sack of potatoes along."

Then she felt careful touches of the bee brush against her head, against the bees on her head, it was as if she had a thick, living armor outside her cranium, a conqueror's helmet of bees, and the touch of the brush felt distant and numb somehow. She got stung regularly. But soon she realized he had come closer, and he asked her to lean her head, carefully, to the left. It took a while before her neck would obey, because she had almost forgotten how to lean her head, but finally she remembered. And then she noticed that she could breathe through her nose again, the buzzing grew fainter and suddenly sounded enclosed, then she felt a couple of fingers carefully remove stragglers from her hair and neck, and gently lift the neckband of her T-shirt and the waistband of her jeans. He did not say excuse me, but she noticed that his fingers said excuse me. He had fingers that could ask forgiveness. Then his voice said: "You can open your eyes now. You did very well."

Far away she glimpsed his face, behind the black mesh beekeeper netting, his eyes smiled toward her as blue and relieved as those of a young boy who has put a baby bird back in the nest. She cast her eyes around the garden. Everything looked different. He looked different, and Andersen looked different. The trees—they seemed very strange, almost unrecognizable. To say nothing of the sky. It was best not to mention the sky. The sky seemed very odd. Just the color of it. She took a few steps, and it felt strange to walk. Then she fainted, and awoke after they were in the house. Still she managed to climb the stairs on her own. But at the top she felt faint again.

Even after the doctor had been there and given her the world's biggest injection of antihistamine, yes, for a long while afterward, she continued to have the feeling that everything was different than before and almost unrecognizable. She had remembered everything, there within the bees, and for a long time could move freely among all her memories without it having any effect on her. She was no longer restless, and she was not afraid. She felt utterly young, younger than any child. For three days after the swarm of bees settled on her, she lay in bed. When she came down to supper the third evening, the table was laid especially elegantly and tall slender candles burned in all the candlesticks. The old man stood waiting for her, wearing a dark dinner jacket and a bow tie. A small package lay on her plate. It contained a necklace of fine, embellished silver, with three green inlaid stones, two small and one large.

"Very old," said her uncle. "Beryl. Norwegian stones."

She stood with the necklace in her hands; the stones were like balls of green star fire between her fingers. Everything was different. She put it on quickly, before he could help her.

"It becomes you," he said.

"Thank you," she whispered.

"If you want to see in the mirror, I'll ask Andersen to wait with the food."

"Yes, please," she whispered, and slipped out of the room, up the stairs, into the large old-fashioned bathroom. She stood for a while looking at the necklace around her neck, exactly where her skin met her white T-shirt. She had not looked at herself in the mirror since the bees. Her face was different. Sterner. Sterner, and yet more open. Everything was different. The only correct thing was that the necklace hung there so out of place on the white cotton. It fit with her face now. Only after a while did she see the blue dress hanging on the cupboard door; the shoes stood beside it.

She came down to the dining room again, did not say anything. He held the chair out for her. The dress rustled as she sat down.

"Skol," he said, and raised his glass. "It's good to have you on your feet again. I must say you frightened me."

"Thank you," she said, still just as softly. "Thank you very much."

"I hope you aren't offended that I took the liberty. I was a little tired of—what's it called—jeans, and men's white T-shirts." She blushed, could not help giggling a little, and looked down.

"Yes, yes," he said. "Whatever you call it. But I admit—yes, I admit the jewelry looked very nice on you in your T-shirt too. I must admit that. Skol."

"You're out of your mind," she said. The room seemed to expand around her, and she saw reflections of the facets of the precious stones on all the walls, on her hands, on him; or maybe it was just that everything was different. She felt as if she were constantly falling, but without being afraid.

"It's good to have you on your feet again," he said. "You must never do such a thing again."

Then autumn and winter came.

❧

She walks from object to object in the rooms where he is no longer. There is his magnifying glass, there the microscope where he taught her to analyze crystals. In the hall hangs the panama hat and pith helmet, along with

77

the rifles and machetes and the unforgettable megaphone, the old man's chief social resource.

The old man's social life was very sporadic and eccentric, and limited to his quarterly visits from parish youths. It always happened the same way, and in September Lea took part in such a session for the first time.

One evening as Lea sat reading and the old man was bent over his work, they heard shouts and automobile engines in the yard. She looked up in bewilderment and rose from her chair, but the old man was already at the window. Out in the yard were two cars full of hooting and howling boys. An Amazon and a Buick. "Hell," said the old man, and closed the curtain. At the same time, Andersen entered the room.

"We're besieged," said the old man. A tinkling of broken beer bottles could be heard out in the yard. "It's the revolutionaries; they've come to storm the estate. Andersen," he said, "you know what you have to do." Andersen disappeared. Lea peered out from behind the curtains. The cars had now started driving round and round in a war dance in the yard. "Lea," said the old man, drawing her away from the window, "you come with me." He seemed fired up. "They come about once every four months," he said. "It's no problem to get through the gate."

Andersen suddenly stood there holding two rifles and a few boxes of cartridges.

"Can you use a rifle?" barked the old man.

"No," said Lea, and gulped.

"Hmm. You'll have to give us a hand," he said. "You take the Mauser, Andersen, and I'll take the elephant rifle. Turn off all the lights!"

He gave Lea an impatient look.

"Well, don't just *stand* there. *Turn off all the lights!*" he growled. "We need the *element of surprise*." Obediently she went through the rooms, from lamp to lamp.

"Uncle Wilhelm," she said uncertainly as she stood over by the sconce, "shouldn't we call the police?" He looked at her in horror.

"The *police!*" he exclaimed in disgust. He knelt by a window, fingered the hasp. "With my own two hands I've defended myself all these years, against worse bands of thieves than these infants, and I should call the police—the royal Norwegian police—for a bagatelle like this? Nonsense . . .

Andersen, open the window, you cover the back! Lea, you keep an eye out from the bay window."

He shoved up his own window with the rifle stock, cleared his throat, stopped. "The megaphone!" he said bitterly. "Andersen, you're losing it, damn you, where's the megaphone?!" Andersen put down the rifle, diligently hurried into the hall, returned with the megaphone. It was camouflage colored. The old man put it to his mouth and leaned out the window.

"Listen, you trash!" he thundered. Great jubilation from the gang in the cars. "This is the estate owner, Bolt, speaking! You're on private property. You've got sixty seconds to leave, otherwise we open fire!"

"*Yaaah!*" shouted the wild Indian voices out there, full of anticipation.

"This is the only warning you'll get! We'll shoot with live ammunition! Sixty seconds! Fifty-nine, fifty-eight, fifty—"

Out in the dark they took over the counting: "Fifty-seven! Fifty-six! Fifty-five!—"

The old man put down the megaphone, stretched with satisfaction.

"Do you remember the attack on Cape Libelle, Andersen?"

Andersen chuckled contentedly at his position, took aim.

"That was a different story," said the old man, half to Lea, half to himself. "We held off thirty men who came to burn up everything, and there were only four of us."

"Thirty-seven! Thirty-six! Thirty-five!—" came the loud, happy roar from out in the darkness; the group had turned off the headlights now.

"Or the band of thieves in Borneo," he said dreamily. "That time we could easily have become the dinner menu. But it was actually pretty simple. The mangrove swamps were easy to fight in."

"Twenty-two! Twenty-one!—"

"It was very different with the Japanese in Sumatra," whinnied the old man excitedly. "The attack on Dai-Na. They were like horseflies with wartime authority."

"Seventeen! Sixteen! Fifteen!—"

"And Miss Lea here wants me to call the police because of a swarm of *moths*, ha!" He cocked the rifle.

"Three! Two! One! *Yaaaaah!*"

"*Moths!*" shrieked the old man into the megaphone. "You were warned!" The next instant he fired off a salvo that rattled the windows and glass. Over in the corner, Lea ducked instinctively. Great jubilation out there.

"*Yaah!* Aim lower, Bolt! Aim lower!"

Andersen fired his weapon too, whereupon terrible cracks and bangs were heard outside; one of the attackers had brought a shotgun, they were also throwing stones and shooting caps.

"Wonderful," Bolt mumbled, firing again. On fiery steeds the Indians rode toward the fort, wild and shrieking, their faces covered with terrifying war paint, their bare chests gleaming in the prairie night. A couple of them were quite good-looking, Lea thought.

"Cartridges here!" shouted the old blue-jacket, and Lea crept across the floor with the box. The Commandant loaded, aimed, fired—calmly, almost cheerfully. "War!" he shouted. "We'll never surrender." Waves of Indians approached with loud war cries, but each time they were driven back by new salvos from the blue-jackets.

"Cartridges, Miss Lea, please," Andersen said mildly.

A Molotov cocktail flew through a window.

"Cartridges here!" howled the old man. Lea crawled as if possessed. Glass tinkled, and fine slivers sprinkled down her back. "Damn rifle!" he growled. "We should have had automatic weapons. Are you wounded?" he asked her. She shook her head. "If I should fall," he said solemnly, "you take command." Glass tinkled again. "You scum!" he screamed out the window before firing off a new volley.

The attackers began to withdraw with feathers flying. A new Molotov cocktail came through the window. The Union flag fluttered amid a shower of arrows and thundering canon.

"Camel shit!" shouted the old man. Andersen chuckled, fired again after the retreating men. The Indians leaped off their horses, and got into the cars with a stream of jubilant shouts and swearwords in the local Indian dialect.

"We'll be back!" "Just wait!" "Don't give up, you old devil!" A final Molotov sailed in the window but, like the previous ones, contained only beer.

"Sissies!" shouted the Commandant. "Come back and fight!"

"Next time we'll take the girl from you, old man!" someone yelled outside. "She can ride on my gear stick!" Bolt blasted off two shots in rapid succession, they heard some headlights shatter, and the mood became remarkably subdued. Car doors slammed in fear, gravel crunched, the boys disappeared, first the Buick, then the Amazon. "Victory!" shouted the old man, and fired a victory salute.

A few minutes later, a police car drove into the yard and firm sheriff footsteps were heard heading toward the front door. The old man got to his feet and went around turning on lights. Andersen rectified the damage, wiped beer from the carpet. Lea sat in a corner, quite shaken by the unusual social conventions with the local youth.

"Get up," the old man said brusquely. "Where's my cane—aww, what the hell." Limberly and quickly he walked into the library, rifle in hand, and poured three glasses of whiskey to the brim. The doorbell rang.

"Sheriff Bødtker," Andersen announced. "As usual."

Sheriff Bødtker appeared at the door to the library about two seconds later.

"Well, good evening, Sheriff," said Bolt enthusiastically, and took a sip of whiskey. "This is certainly a surprise. What are you doing here at this hour?"

"Listen here, Mr. Bolt," the sheriff began.

"A little highball, perhaps? Andersen!"

"No thanks, I'm on duty, and—"

"A stiff brandy for the sheriff too," the old man said courteously. "Please sit down, Sheriff. What can I do for you?" Andersen brought the drink.

"This can't continue, Bolt. You must understand that," the sheriff said steadily. "There's been a ruckus here again tonight."

"Ruckus?" said the old man, and opened the rifle barrel. "There hasn't been any ruckus here. Has there been a ruckus here, Andersen?"

"No," said Andersen, as he swept up pieces of glass.

"There, you hear," said the old man, emptying cartridges from the rifle. "At most, a little hunt. We shot a few moths to tatters."

"On the way up here I met the usual gang in their cars," said Bødtker. "A couple of headlights were gone, I could see, and one rear window."

"Was it you who got the rear window, Andersen?"

"Yes!" Andersen boomed.

"You were certainly lucky with that shot. Well done! I didn't even notice it. Bad taste in cars, for that matter. Don't you want your brandy, Sheriff?"

"If this continues, I'll have to confiscate your rifles, sir."

"Go ahead. There are more where they came from." He held out his rifle magnanimously. Instead of taking it, the sheriff picked up the brandy glass, and smiled.

"Or I might have to arrest you."

"Arrest *me*? Don't talk nonsense. Skol."

"Skol. It's *dangerous*, you know. Won't you stop it? The police really have other things to do than deal with this every couple of months."

"Exactly what I just said to Lea. Lea, this is Sheriff Bødtker." Lea shook his hand.

"Good evening," said the sheriff. "And who is the new face in the safari?"

"This is my new mistress," said Bolt with relish. "We're living in wild and dangerous immorality. She's scarcely more than a minor, Sheriff."

"I see. Well, it was nice to meet you."

"Likewise," said Lea.

"Aren't you going to arrest me for that?" the old man said in disappointment. "A moral conduct case would have been exciting after the hunt."

"Unfortunately," said Bødtker, "I don't think there's any punishable relationship here."

"I bought her in the white slave trade," said the old man lasciviously, and began polishing the rifle barrel with his handkerchief.

"Do you have a receipt for that?" asked the sheriff.

"No, just think, I didn't ask for one."

"Then, unfortunately, there's little I can do."

"Too bad."

"Lea—was that your name?"

"Yes," she nodded. "Lea Bolt."

"Lea Bolt . . ." said the sheriff thoughtfully.

"*Damn!*" the old man whispered to her savagely. "We're *married*," he said loudly.

"Congratulations. Do you know that you've been reported missing, Lea?"

"Nonsense," said the old man. "She's not missed by anyone. She's *here*, after all, in her *home*."

"This is getting more and more serious," said the sheriff. "Attempted murder, disturbing the peace, white slave trade, moral misconduct, kidnapping . . ."

"Yes!" exclaimed the old man enthusiastically. "Andersen, go and get my toothbrush."

"I think we'll let it go with a warning this time," said the sheriff, and drained his glass. "Lea, you must telephone home."

"No," said Lea.

"Hmm," said the sheriff. "Hmm, hmm. I see. Well. Thanks for the drink, Bolt. But don't do this anymore. It's *dangerous*. Someone could get hurt."

"Won't you have another little one, Sheriff? So I can tell you about my hunting trips to Africa and Borneo?"

"No, thanks. Another time."

"I'm a very good shot," said Bolt. "I've never killed anyone without intending to do so."

"That's encouraging," said the sheriff. "Thanks for the visit, sir." He put on his cap, sent Lea a meaningful glance. "*Call us* next time, *before* you take up weapons."

"Write that down, Andersen! You know, Sheriff, my memory has gotten so poor in my old age."

"I've said the same thing to you for ten years now."

"Well, there you see. Good-bye now!"

"Good-bye," the sheriff said, and left.

The old man settled himself comfortably in a chair, leaned back, took another sip of brandy. "Fine fellow, that Bødtker. He's polite too. It's nice that he drops in now and then. Come on, drink up now! We've got to celebrate the victory!" Andersen picked up his glass, Lea picked up hers, still slightly shaken.

"Skol!" said the old man. "Skol to a marvelous evening!"

"Skol!" said Andersen, unusually loudly and cheerfully. He positively grinned. Lea stared wide-eyed at the two men. It was the first time she had seen Andersen take a drink.

"A marvelous evening," said the old man again. "And here's to you, Lea, my little okapi, and your baptism by fire. Skol to you! Didn't she do a good job, Andersen?"

"A splendid job," Andersen said emphatically. "You were splendid, Miss Lea."

"And do you *remember* how the Japanese were impaled on the palisades that time, Andersen? That was certainly lively," said the old man dreamily.

Suddenly Lea said: "Maybe someone should see to Jacob."

"Yes, of course! What am I thinking of! He usually gets flustered by the gunshots. Andersen?"

"No, no," said Lea moodily. "I'll go. I need a little fresh air after all the smoke."

"Yes, cordite can make your nose sting," said the old man. "It's odd that the smell didn't give us away to the sheriff. Skol, Andersen."

Lea left them behind, disappeared into the soft autumn darkness. An impaled Japanese hung in the big plum tree. Perhaps he would hang there all winter.

&

Lea stands by the desk. Opens drawers, searches carefully. Eyeglasses, a magnifying glass, ivory letter opener, old invitation cards from Alvøen in an unopened box, envelopes, stamps. One of the drawers in the solid piece of furniture is locked. The top drawer. She looks in the other drawers for the key, but does not find it. So she gives up, turns out the lamp, goes into the library.

FIVE

Someone said her name. She was far away, in sunlight and the humming of bees. Her name again, like a bell echoing, like a bell echoing against a pale yellow wall. The paved street. Children running through the narrow passages, quickly, noisily. The heat. The little brown town on the hill. A face in the sunlight.

"Miss Bolt."

She opened her eyes. Andersen shook her shoulder carefully.

"I think you slept in the chair last night."

"Hmm," she said, and stretched. "I want to sleep a little more." She wanted to go back to her dream and the sunlight.

"I'm sorry, but the lawyer is on the telephone."

"Oh," she said. "Can't you ask him to call back in a year."

"Unfortunately," said Andersen, "there is business to attend to."

Lea stood up, suddenly wide awake.

"Besides, Jacob is worse."

"He still won't eat?"

"No."

"Is he drinking?"

"Yes. A little."

"I see. We'll see to him after breakfast." Andersen nodded.

"You can take the telephone in the office."

She rubbed her face, stepped over the threshold into the office, seated herself unhesitatingly in the old man's chair, picked up the telephone.

"Bolt!" she barked into the receiver.

❧

Conversation on a December morning:

"You must remember that one generally loses money by owning stock. Stock prices need to at least keep pace with the rise in the cost of living in order for one to benefit at all from owning stock."

"I really don't want to know this." It was one of the hundreds of conversations they'd had about finances, the only area in which the old man had been unable to awaken Lea's interest.

"It's been better in recent years, but in the sixties it was bad. Especially the stock of Norwegian companies."

"I see." She yawned pointedly, stirred her tea.

"Never depend on market analysts or other such prophets. Their predictions are no more likely to hit the bull's eye than are cocksure tips on horses from the suspicious types one meets outside a racetrack. If you don't know anything about horses—"

"Uncle—"

"—you ought not to play the horses. If you don't know enough about companies and about financial record keeping, you also ought to stay away from stockholdings. The most important—"

"Uncle—"

"—the most important thing is to look at the write-offs in the accounts, and in order to understand something about that, you need to compare accounts, from company to company. Far too many people go into the market without a thorough knowledge of the business behind their stocks. If you hold steel stocks, you need to know enough about steel. You need to know something about the ore stratum, so you don't end up with what we call 'number mines.' Likewise, if you have rubber stocks, you need to know enough about rubber. You need to know the difference between rubber and rubber. You must be able to predict the market demand. I think about the poor old fogey who bought two huge boatloads of rubber gut for what he believed to be a bargain price. That stuff, by and large, can only be used as a laxative. Heh, heh, you could say that he—"

"Uncle Wilhelm. We're having *breakfast*."

"You must learn to *smell* when there's something wrong with the accounts. And be careful about companies with frequent leadership changes. That's never good. The best investment you can make is to put money into real estate. As long as the market isn't feverish. But on the whole, business is a system of balances, the theoreticians insist. If the balance collapses, due to some crisis, market mechanisms will quickly move the system toward a new balance. If demand for a product is lower than the supply, prices will fall, producers will reduce the supply, consumer demand will rise as a result, and thereby a new balance will—"

"Uncle! I'm *really* not interested in this."

"Things went to hell with rubber, you know, when artificial rubber came. But I kept my stocks, because I knew that sooner or later the caoutchouc market would go up again."

"You're always like that. You count money everywhere."

He suddenly grew silent. Outside the windows, light fluffy snowflakes were falling. It was early winter. She continued.

"You act that way even with the *bees*. You like to figure out how you're going to make each hive produce a larger yield. I've seen you. Bee colonies get combined and divided, and queens get put to death indiscriminately. And all autumn long you sat figuring out the price per kilo of honey."

"Yes, but I never sell any of it to Honey Central," he added stubbornly, turning ominously red above his collar.

"That's not the *point*!" she said.

"Everything costs money," he said irritably. "I think it's interesting."

"All right," she said, "we'll leave it at that."

"No, you *must* learn this, Lea. The *really* interesting part comes when you've learned the basic theoretical principles. But you never let me get that far. The interesting part is when the systems deviate greatly from predictions, when they do *not* calm down, but are in an inexplicable crisis. But first you need to understand the basic principles. I've used the beekeeping business to explain this to you many times. What are variable expenses?"

"I don't know. I really don't know."

"You know from beekeeping. It's sugar for winter feeding, for example. Then, what's net gain?"

"Uncle, you and the rest of the family understand this so much better than I do."

"Hah," he said. "The rest of the family don't come here. Listen now. Net gain is income from the product minus the variable expenses. Net gain must take into account *fixed* expenses, like depreciation and maintenance and interest payments, and also allow for earnings for the work."

"Greed," she said, "and desire for money have ruined the world. You should have chopped down the rubber trees over there in the East while you still had them and planted oil palms instead; then people would have had a little cooking fat. But no. Profit. Yield. Face value. I get sick just from *hearing* all these words."

"You can't deny," he said with repressed anger, "that the profit motive is the most powerful driving force in society. Why does the worker work? Because he wants to earn money. Why does the merchant sell? Because he—"

"I *can't stand* to listen. I've heard this lesson all my life. How *can* you go straight from the beehives and all that teeming life out there, or from the snowflakes, which you stand and look at under the magnifying glass on the veranda—"

"Snowflakes!" he said offended. "You must be crazy."

"I've seen you. You stand out in the yard in the morning looking at snowflakes on your mitten. You seem absolutely enthralled."

"I'm not senile after all."

"You have the magnifying glass in your pocket. And then you go inside and sit down and calculate how—how much you've earned since yesterday, for all I know. What makes you think you have a *right* to that? I know what you're like, all of you. You, and all the others."

"This is the most impudent . . ." he said furiously. "Get out."

She stormed out of the dining room, up the stairs, took her backpack from the closet, began to pack. But there wasn't really room for all the clothes and objects. Like a madwoman, she began separating out everything he had given her since she arrived: toilet articles, dresses, work clothes, writing materials, sketch pad, music, things—fast! His, all of it. Bought and paid for. She had stayed here like some paid companion for more than half a year, withering. A wall decoration, that's what she had been. She rushed out of the house. But got no farther than the entrance gate before she stopped, looked across the empty white fields, and turned around. He stood in the entry waiting for her, leaning on his cane. He did not say a word.

"I'm sorry," she said, looking down.

"Snowflakes are very interesting," he sighed in resignation. "I started with geology. I haven't told you about crystals."

"No," she said, and smiled a little.

"We ought to look at crystals together under the microscope."

"Yes," she said.

"They are . . . very beautiful lying on my mitten. Haven't you noticed that?"

"Yes," she said. "A long time ago."

"Very beautiful. They're visible for only a moment. Then they melt. I can watch that again and again."

❧

But the lawyer did not want to talk about business. At least not in the usual sense.

"This is a matter that I should have discussed with you after reading the will at Ekelund yesterday," said lawyer Holst. "But I couldn't find you. I guess you were indisposed."

"I was indis— Yes."

"I understand. Well, it's a detail that wasn't mentioned in the will, but which is evidently related."

"Yes?"

"The Ekelund Foundation controls another foundation, but I've never really understood what it is." He paused. When Lea said nothing, he continued. "It's called SERIA. Does that word mean anything to you?"

"No," said Lea. "Seria?"

"It's probably one of Bolt's many—" He searched for polite words.

"Crazy ideas?"

"Hmm, well, he was involved with many things which could not strictly be called business activities, and which at the same time were a little too extensive and . . . unusual . . . to be regarded purely as hobbies. The bees and the orchids, for example; earlier he was also very taken up with exotic animals. Didn't he still have an ape?"

"Jacob."

"Yes, of course. He used to have a complete menagerie. The entire garden was full. When people from the Animal Protection League came, he threatened them with an elephant rifle. The marmot in particular really bothered the neighbors. It never slept. He got involved with many other things too. But this SERIA is a little unclear." He paused. "During the past twenty years SERIA's activities have increased substantially, and it's been our job to handle many of the administrative details; among other things, we've made payments of various kinds, fixed and variable, to a wide variety of sources."

"What kind of activities are we talking about, can you tell that by the amounts? I mean, by the recipients and so forth?"

"I don't know," said the lawyer, "it's not clear what the payments were for. One could imagine it was some sort of charity—"

So then I was mistaken about him, thought Lea.

"But—" said the lawyer. His voice seemed to be left hanging in the air.

"But—?" said Lea.

"It concerns rather large amounts. For example, a semiannual contribution went to an institution called ANCA in New York."

"Oh?"

"It was a very large amount."

"Yes? And what is ANCA?"

"To be honest, I've never known what it was. But it's not purely a matter of a contribution; it's always been different sums in payment of a bill. 'For services rendered.' But the bill has given no indication of the kind of services rendered."

"I see," said Lea, gathering her wits. "I assume that this sum—"

"It's taken from the SERIA Foundation, which is controlled by the Ekelund Foundation, which you now manage. I've taken the liberty of investigating the nature of ANCA's activities, because I assumed you would want to know what the money is actually being spent for."

"To tell the truth, I haven't thought much about any of this."

"I realize that, but the situation is what it is. At least for the moment.

And you're the one who must decide to what extent the payments will continue in the future. Therefore, I've made some inquiries. Quite simply, ANCA is an American clippings agency."

For a moment there was silence.

"A clippings agency?" Lea said in bewilderment.

"Argus, in fact. An agency that watches newspapers and other media, and collects articles and reportage on the basis of key words or a specific theme."

"I don't understand," said Lea. "What would he do with that?"

"As far as that goes, it's quite usual if you want to keep track of a particular subject," said the lawyer. "For example, if you want to get hold of everything that is reported about your firm, or if you want to collect all the printed analyses of a segment of the market. Coffee prices, for instance. But—" Again his voice was left hanging.

"But?" she prodded him.

"But this was a very large sum. There's no explanation for that."

"How much?"

"The total for last year was almost thirteen thousand American dollars."

"Thirteen thousand," she said. "So that's a lot?"

"It's expensive to use Argus," said the lawyer, "but not *that* expensive. We're talking about more than eighty thousand kroner. In addition—" She heard him shuffling through papers. "In addition, there are several equally strange bills, from several different countries, which probably total well over 250,000 kroner annually."

She let out an involuntary humming sound.

"That's a great deal of money," said the lawyer. "In the case of individual accounts and fixed contributions, I've managed to identify the type of activity. There are several clipping agencies in other countries, a couple of doctors, and even a few university institutes here and there. And probably strangest of all, a couple of detective agencies. The contributions, if you can call them that, vary from tens of thousands down to a couple of thousand kroner. And I thought maybe you knew—"

"No," she said. "I don't know anything about this. Detective agencies?"

"Yes," he said. "I've wondered about these payments for many years.

But I couldn't ask *him*, of course. Also, every year a contribution still goes to this Myriatidis."

"Myria what?"

"Myriatidis. Oh, that's right. It was long before your time. Maybe you haven't heard about Myriatidis."

"Who—or what—is that?"

"*That* is a Greek atomic physicist. I think. Everyone thinks. Nobody knows. He lived at Ekelund for a while many, many years ago. Before my time too. You ought to ask someone in the family if they can tell you more about him; he was employed in the company for a while. He was going to equip the shipping company's tankers with atomic power. Instead he moved in at Ekelund, where he gave Bolt private tutoring in atomic physics. He also had an office in town, with a secretary. There he helped himself to both the cash box and the secretary; it turned into a very interesting case for the authorities. But it was before my time, as I said."

"Uh-uh."

"Also, two letters of a more personal nature have arrived. One from a certain George Drake, Esquire, in London—I recognize the name, he has received a fixed small sum each year, about a thousand kroner. It's a long letter of condolence expressing his sympathy concerning the old man's death, and at the same time he expresses the hope that someone will carry on the SERIA Institute in his spirit—"

"Institute?"

"Precisely. The SERIA Institute. And if that is the case, he asks that I convey his condolences and his wish that the new leader of . . . the institute . . . will contact him to resume the support."

Lea said nothing.

"Tell me," said the lawyer, "can you make any sense out of all this?"

"No," she said.

"Likewise, Dr. Michael Schleierhüter from the psychology department at the university in Heidelberg has written to me wondering if the correspondence will continue, now that Doctor Bolt is dead."

"Doctor Bolt?"

"Yes. He *was* a doctor. In geology. At any rate, he would have been a doctor in Germany. Most people become that in the German language if they have so much as seen a university canteen. In any case, he also wants to be in contact with the doctor's successor."

"That would be me then," said Lea worriedly.

"Yes. Of course, I'll have to pay everything that appears to be simply a bill, but I don't know what I should do about the quarterly contributions to individuals, and so forth."

"How do they know that he died?"

"Our office sent out a notice to all his contacts as a matter of routine."

"And who are all these people?"

"I have no idea. That's what I hoped *you* knew."

"I don't," said Lea, "as I said before." She sat thinking. Her eyes glided along the record books and binders on the bookshelves.

"Detective agencies. University institutes. Myriatidis. It doesn't fit together," the lawyer said somewhat crossly. It sounded as though this had irritated him for many years.

"No," she agreed.

"Actually, I'm waiting for instructions as to what I should do. That's your responsibility, I'm afraid."

"I realize that," Lea sighed. "What would you advise me to do?"

"I can write a somewhat vague letter on your behalf asking them to contact you, and saying that you aren't completely clear about their relationship to the old man, and that they should describe it, and that you would like to take a closer look at the possibility of continuing the support. Something like that."

"Do that," said Lea somewhat dejectedly.

"Maybe you can find some answers at Ekelund," suggested the lawyer.

"Maybe," said Lea. "Myriasidis, was that his name?"

"Myria*ti*dis."

"How are things otherwise?"

"I'm afraid that—well, the family doesn't take it very well, you know. Your Uncle Christian is thinking about quitting. He's obviously very offended. It would be terrible if he quit."

"It's not my fault after all, none of this," said Lea, and heard that something happened to her voice.

"Well, no," said the lawyer. "But he doesn't know that. You could risk becoming chairman of the board now, Lea."

She just sat looking straight ahead.

"I realize this has come on you unexpectedly," said the lawyer, "and if you wish, I can certainly try to calm them down. But then I must have instructions from you. And it would probably also help if you had a talk with your Uncle Christian." Lea gripped the telephone receiver tightly, suddenly felt tears in her eyes.

"I never wanted anything to do with all this," she said quietly. "I can't do it. I don't understand these things. Don't want to."

"No," said the lawyer. "But that's how it is."

Jacob wasn't well at all this morning. He lay on his back, breathing weakly and slowly. His eyes were closed, but a narrow yellow strip of his eyeball was visible. His breathing gurgled a little with slime. He seemed very old. Lea tried to liven him up, shook him, cajoled him, but to no avail.

It smelled different in here today, and Lea was taken aback. Then she realized it smelled like death. It was as if something was present in the little house, something large and distant and silent, unmistakable. Lea became desperate.

"Are you going to die—you too, now—without giving me a further explanation," she said, almost furiously. "What's the *meaning* of this! What did he *mean*?"

The stern tone in her voice seemed to revive Jacob just a little; he barely opened his eyes, gave her a listless yellow look, lifted his head. Immediately she was there with the cup, forced sugar water into him. He took a sip, as if surprised that it was still possible to drink, as if he had forgotten how to do it.

"Jacob," she said, "I *know* how you feel, but I don't know how I'm going to help you. If you die too," she said savagely, "I don't know what I'll do."

Jacob sank back into his lethargy again, closed his eyes.

"The hell with him," said Lea. Andersen stood in the doorway.

"I've brought some fruit juice," he said. "Fruit juice and a few other things. I squeezed it myself." He held out a baby bottle filled with a thick fluid of indeterminate color. "My special blend," he said. "A so-called 'Tiger Tail.' My own recipe. Bolt gave it the name. I used to blend it for

Mr. Bolt and the others in Ceylon, when things were at their worst and nobody had time to eat. It contains a lot of energy and a lot of . . . Well, I didn't have *all* the ingredients, but I thought maybe Jacob . . ."

She nodded gratefully, lifted Jacob's head from the straw, and held it carefully while Andersen gently pushed the bottle between Jacob's dry, yellow teeth. She patted the ape's head reassuringly, hummed a little for him, softly and anxiously.

Are you sleeping, are you sleeping
Brother Jacob, Brother Jacob?
Morning bells are ringing,
Morning bells are ringing.

Jacob drank hesitantly, she heard the swallowing sounds in his throat. "Ding, ding, dong. Ding, ding, dong." He paused a little, waited, drank a bit more. When he had drunk two-thirds of the juice, he pushed the bottle away.

"Now we'll wait and see," said Andersen quietly. They sat in silence for a while. Now and then the ape opened his eyes; it seemed to Lea that his eyeballs were perhaps a little less yellow now, but his gaze was just as listless. The minutes passed. Lea gave Andersen a reflective look.

"I don't quite know how to say it . . . ," Lea began. "I have to ask you, Andersen: How are things with *you*, now that . . . Uncle Wilhelm is dead?"

"What? With me?" He looked quite astonished.

"Yes—if you'll stay here, if you want to continue in your job—if you . . . if you'll stay, I mean."

"I understand. Yes, of course I'll stay, if you wish, Miss Bolt. It's my duty."

"I know so little about the practical things. I don't know anything about all this. So I must ask you what your salary is now, and if you want an increase."

"What?"

"Salary. Wages, I mean. Do you want a raise in your salary?"

"But my dear Miss Bolt, didn't you know?"

"Know?"

"Mr. Bolt thought it was sufficient that I had my board."

Now it was Lea's turn to look surprised. She was about to say "What?" too, but managed instead to say: "Board?"

"Board and room, of course. And clothes and other necessary expenses were covered."

"*How* long did you say you've been here?"

"I've always been satisfied with the arrangement, Miss Bolt."

This is slavery, thought Lea, but she said nothing.

"I've seen the work as a challenge in itself. I will be pleased to continue doing my tasks." He was once again like gray rainy weather, impenetrable. Maybe if I took him on a hunting trip, Lea thought, or if we got something to shoot at again.

She wanted to ask him, ask him about everything, but somehow couldn't. It was like talking to the rain. She pulled herself together, opened her mouth, cleared her throat. Then all at once Jacob moved, half rose, moaned. He looked toward the door, the half-open door, pleadingly.

The smell in his little house was the same, and you could still touch and feel the foreign presence like a foul breath.

"He can't stay in here," she suddenly declared, decisively, knowingly. "Or he'll die. Today. He needs to get out into the fresh air."

Andersen nodded solemnly. Then they helped each other get the ape to his feet.

"Where?" asked Andersen, breathing heavily.

"Down to the pond," said Lea. "He usually likes to sit there."

Supporting Jacob between them, they left the garden and went down through the park, on gravel walks and half-overgrown paths, past the old oak trees and somewhat neglected lawns and beds. She had always had the feeling that someone lived in the large empty park, because it had existed there alone so long. It was always strange to walk there by herself.

They sat Jacob on the little bench. Lea sat down beside him. Things seemed to brighten for him somewhat, now that he was out of his house.

"Here," said Andersen, handing her the bottle of Tiger Tail. "Try to give him a little more. I'll go and get more juice, as well as some fruit."

He left, his footsteps crunching among the trees.

They sat quietly on the bench. The ape seemed to be brooding about something, a mystery, a secret, as if he *knew* something, knew what the meaning had been, knew what the old man had been thinking, knew what he had left behind and intended. Or maybe Jacob only brooded over the great, ancient mystery of his species; the sorrowful amazement at still holding evolution's old-maid card; it's not an entirely easy matter to fall off the heap just a few million years before you could have reached the goal, could have helped build pyramids and solve third-degree equations, and must sit here eating raw bamboo shoots instead.

A dragonfly flew just above the water-lily pads in the pond, slowly, glittering like silver; Jacob's eyes followed it alertly for a little while, then he retreated back into himself.

"So here we sit," said Lea. "Lea and Jacob." Jacob did not say anything, but put his hand on her shoulder, cautiously. Something about the movement reminded her of a small child, something half conscious or unconscious. It was hard to say what he meant by that, if he meant anything at all. Her own hand was like a child's compared with Jacob's aged, wrinkled hand. The treetops rustled, there was the dragonfly again. Now it had a golden sheen. When I was little, thought Lea, there was a time when everything had voices and could talk to me. Everything, the insects in the air, the trees, the walls of buildings, the stars, and the soap bubbles in the washbasin. Wasn't that so? And now I can't even get an old ape to tell me what he knows, far less a wretched caretaker. The ape *can't* say anything, and Andersen *won't* say anything. Or maybe I'm just not able to ask. Maybe I'm about to be grown up, she thought. Maybe that's what it is. Suddenly she felt old, older than Jacob, but it was a different kind of age, an age that was old and young at the same time, like the age of water. It was the age of her *species* that she was feeling. Maybe there's something to what the old man said, she thought. Maybe people have actually been on the earth forever. "I've seen strange things," he had said one evening while looking at the crystals, "when we drilled and cut deep into the earth. Strange, inexplicable things and forms. I've seen a little of everything. Maybe humanity is the most ancient species of all, because it's always the youngest."

She closed her eyes. It seemed as if the water in the small pond rose, rose and filled the park, filled the whole world.

She opened her eyes. Two dragonflies were flying across the pond in the sunlight, one had attached itself to the other with the rear of its long, slender body; they were swarming. They flew in a perfect, slow, swaying rhythm, like one large insect with a double set of wings. Now and then they landed, rested, and then continued flying. As they flew, the female curved her lower body upward in the air, it met the male's, and they looked like a large gold ring hovering above the water.

But Jacob would not eat or drink anything more that day, and toward evening he was just as poorly again. He shivered, even though it was a warm evening, and they had to spread a lap robe over him.

Andersen sat with him for a while into the evening.

For the first time, she goes into the old man's bedroom.

It is quite different from what she imagined. There is none of the luxury that marks the rest of Ekelund. Bare, austere, like a monk's cell. The bed is an old iron bed, narrow, lonely. On the night table are a magnifying glass and a water carafe, nothing else. On the toiletry table, a comb, clothes brush, and a bottle of Kölnischwasser. There are no other objects in the room, except for an old cylindrical miner's lamp on the chest of drawers; the glass in the lamp is broken. In the drawers she finds only clothes and a small African box containing tie pins and cuff links, nothing else. One picture hangs on the wall, a photograph of a young woman with a small child in her arms; it's old, somewhat faded and unclear; the picture was taken in bright sunlight, and the most strongly lighted parts are now white as paper; the two figures' dark eyes squint toward the sun there in the picture frame. Lea does not recognize them. Aside from this, the room is empty, the walls white, the window white, the evening dark. There are no curtains, just a shade. The old man's feet are sticking out from under the bed, no, it's his slippers of course; his dressing gown has fallen from the clothes tree and is lying on the floor. She picks it up. She stands with it in her hand a few seconds, then hangs it up with a decisive movement.

☙

Finally, with an air of determination, she goes down to the library.

She sat and waited until Andersen had come in and said good night—there was still no change in Jacob, but he was asleep. After she heard Andersen disappear into the annex, she resolutely went over to the bookshelf, pulled out as many record books as she could, carried them to the desk, and dropped them with a thud. She sat down.

She sat at the desk with perhaps twenty record books in front of her, feeling a little dizzy. This is idiotic, she thought. Ha. There was no end to it. The books were neatly numbered, but the thought of starting with number one and working her way through to the twentieth (or whatever number it might be) almost nauseated her. I'll jump right into the middle instead, she thought (that's what she usually did with thick books), and get some idea of what he was doing.

She picked up a record book at random, opened it. The writing was clear and uniform, in black ink.

VII.3.45./n.prk.3.or. Oslo. Law student Niels Peter Knudsen on 3/15/89 is assigned to Reading Room seat #15 at the University library. At 3 PM he goes to the Solli Plass post office; draws #15 in the waiting line. His sister turns 15 the next day.

Aside from that, the page was empty. Strange. The next page had a longer paragraph:

1372.syn./medio August 1966, Paris, France. Partially confirmed. Student at the Sorbonne, Jean Morissaie, 22, meets a friend at his favorite café. His friend is drunk and talks about a girl he met in Marseilles during his vacation. While the friend is speaking, a young girl comes into the café. Morissaie exclaims confidently: "There she is! It must be she." His friend looks up; it *is* the girl from Marseilles, Miss Juliette Bellucci, who just happens to be in Paris. Jean Morissaie cannot explain later how he could know it was she, since his friend had not described Miss Bellucci in detail. But Morissaie married Miss Bellucci eight months later. He committed suicide in 1968 for no apparent reason.

Lea sat looking at the words, without understanding much. Nothing more was written about Jean Morissaie. She turned the page. There, in the same neat writing, she read:

1373.pk./June 3, 1965, New York City, New York, United States of America, confirmed. Sales agent William Partridge, 43, is going to take the elevator from the 46th to the 54th floor in a building on West 46th Street. Outside the elevator he gets an inexplicable anxiety attack, is unable to enter the elevator. The moment the elevator leaves, he feels ill, begins to rant and rave (he himself remembers little of this); those standing near him must calm him down. Immediately afterward, the elevator car plunges; all the occupants are killed. The same year, Partridge has a son (see note P XXVII 4667.a.v.f./.).

This is madness, she thought again. What in the world is this supposed to mean? On the next page was a funny story.

1855.dr.pk./4.27.1966, Copenhagen, Denmark. Confirmed by several (see note). Ole Jensen, mailman, 37 years old, dreamed that he received a bag of "King of Denmark" candies in the mail from his sister, who lives in Sweden and whom he has not seen for several years. Jensen thought it was a strange dream, and told several colleagues about it. The next day he delivers mail on his usual route; at Sct. Annae Plads number 3 he bumps into King Frederick IX on the stairway. His Majesty has been on a private visit in the building. Jensen apologizes profusely for not looking where he was going, the king is in a good humor and speaks pleasantly with him for a few minutes before he leaves (one source would have it that His Majesty jovially offered the mailman a "King of Denmark" candy, but that is unconfirmed). When he gets out on the street Jensen realizes that in his royal disconcertion he has completely forgotten to deliver the letters; he re-enters the building and delivers them. Back on the street again, he meets his sister, who has just come on the boat from Sweden. Without that delay he would not have met her there and then.

Lea put down the record book, still without any further understanding. Maybe the old man *was* crazy. She opened another book at random, and read:

1374.dr.kra./April 17, 1955, London, England, unconfirmed. John Swanyard, a dentist, is walking to work at Hanover Square. On the way he sees a road construction worker who at first glance bears a striking resemblance to his deceased father, who died in a car accident the previous year. Dr. Swanyard gets an emotional shock, feels ill, and has to sit down. The road construction workers come to his aid; the one whom the dentist thought resembled his father earnestly says to him: "Don't go to work today, my friend, take a walk in the park instead." Now, on closer inspection, there proves to be no likeness between the road construction worker and the dentist's father. Dr. Swanyard does not go to work, and takes a walk in the park instead. There he meets Miss Wilhelmina Dale, whom he later marries.

Lea put the book down. No, she thought, there's no meaning in this. What in the world had he been doing?

For a moment she considered going to get Andersen, but changed her mind. Then she began to search in all the books for some key to the system, an explanation. She looked for a code summary, an introduction, a tiny hint. She could see a pattern in the code, but it did not mean much to her. When she found nothing in the record books, she began searching the binders, which were filled with letters from all corners of the world as well as a great many newspaper clippings in several languages. After that, she began opening desk drawers.

One of them was still locked.

1376.c.A.(v?)/ultimo September 1977, Trollheimen, Norway. Confirmed by the two people involved. Chief engineer at NVE, Kolbjørn Kristensen, and student at NTH, Anne Marie Wiik, attempted to come down a mountain in heavy fog. At four different times they thought they heard people shout; they stood listening, shouted back, but got no answer. They began to question whether they had actually heard something, but the fifth time they were both certain that they heard people, because the voices were very close. According to Wiik, the voices shouted, "Wait, wait." They stop completely and keep shouting back and listening. No one answers. The fog lessens for a moment and Kristensen and Wiik suddenly see they are close to a cliff, which they would have walked off had they not stopped; they are standing about 3 meters from it. As far as they could determine, no one else was in the vicinity.

She slammed the book shut. She found no meaning in this. Thoroughly irritated, she stuffed all the books back on the shelves again. "No," she said aloud. For a moment she thought she could talk with Andersen, but no. No. This was enough. So it was better to do as she had thought—thought even long before the old man died, and thought in the days until the funeral and the unhappy reading of the will—that she would pack her things and leave, that it was high time now, that it had been time for quite a while. She had *thought*. But something had been missing. Each time she had pulled herself together to pack a little, look over things, think about what she should do now, everything turned gray and dull around her and in her. Leave, but to *what*? Nothing and no one was waiting for her outside Ekelund. She didn't long for anything or anyone, she longed for nothing and no one. If you take longing away from a person, action is gone too. So she hadn't been able to leave. But now, perhaps soon now, after having looked in the books, it was finally time. At any rate, it was impossible to stay here. He had been crazy, everyone knew that. These books were merely the proof. Pointless fragments of stories, true or untrue, stylistically terrible, some seeming to have some sort of meaning, others as empty as a blank page. Good night, she thought. Maybe she could take the cello with her anyway. After all, he had wanted to give her something; it was better that she ended up with something she had *use* for and *pleasure* from, rather than a dilapidated estate with a dying ape and an unsuccessful authorship in the form of a "research project." Furious, she went to bed. No, she thought before she fell asleep, I don't want to stay here any longer. For the first time in a long while she felt that she was ready, that she wanted to get out, away from here, that something was waiting for her out there, she wanted to travel on a train, breathe city air. Perhaps buy a painting. I don't want to be here any longer, she thought with angry satisfaction. He was crazy. I want to be somewhere else.

1377.d.sv./Vienna, Austria, August 3, 1957. Confirmed by those involved except for Dr. Ransmeyer. A married couple, Haakon and Else Knudsen, a medical doctor and college teacher from Kristiansand, Norway, are on vacation in Vienna for the first time after the war. One afternoon they talk about Dr. Knudsen's college friend from Linz, Heino Ransmeyer, whom they have not seen or been in contact with since before the war; they have not thought about Ransmeyer for many years. The same evening they go to the Burg Theater; in the vestibule they meet Ransmeyer and his wife, to the great pleasure of all four. It also turns out that the R. couple has reserved seats next to the Knudsens in the orchestra section. (Dr. Ransmeyer dies some months later of cancer. See note PXVII.183-1377.s.)

She spent the next two days packing. The ape grew steadily worse.

SIX

The night before Jacob's last day the old man is with the ape. In the main house, Lea is sleeping; the portraits and old clocks are sleeping; Andersen is asleep in the annex. But the old man is with Jacob. He is the way he has been for a while now, outside and inside at the same time. Jacob is very excited by the visit; he has thrown off the lap robe and is sitting up.

This can't go on much longer, Jacob. The days come and go. I'm starting to get uneasy. She's packing her suitcases. Things can't continue this way.

Jacob nods, still feeling a little weak.

She has to realize it *by herself*, Jacob.

Yes, says Jacob. She ought to realize it. But it's as if she doesn't want to.

I really thought she would realize it by herself. That was the plan. She's got to realize it by herself, if there's to be any meaning in it.

Jacob nods sadly. It's dark and cozy in the ape house, but he is not happy.

Yes I *know* it's lonesome, says the old man, but do you think it's any more fun for *me*?

That was a stupid thing to say, says Jacob quietly.

Yes, yes, says the old man, glossing over the ape's comment. But if there's to have been any meaning in all of it, she must realize it by herself. Discover it on her own. That's what I thought anyway. She, she is—that she came to Ekelund is, so to speak, the very proof, the final confirmation that I've been right all along. That all my work hasn't been in vain.

Jacob nods.

But now I don't know any longer.

Yes, says Jacob. One has to keep nudging her.

Bravo, says the old man, from inside and outside, you're right, Jacob. You know what you need to do.

Lea awakens, bewildered. There is someone in the room.

"Who *is* it?" she asks fearfully. It's completely dark, and she hears him breathing. With the fingers of sleep still clinging to her, she thinks it's the old man, she is almost sure of it, there is a faint odor of Kölnischwasser; he steals closer to the bed, she can dimly see his outline in the dark, no, it's *not* the old man, now the air suddenly reeks with terror, she is as frightened as a child, is about to scream. Then suddenly the air smells like silver; reassured, she stretches her arms toward Thomas. The lamp gets turned on. It's Jacob—Jacob, who stands there by her bed as quiet and polite as a mute servant.

"Jacob," she says, "how did *you* . . ."

But Jacob does not reply; he stretches out his hand very gravely. He is holding a small shiny object in his hand, between his thumb and forefinger, yes, Lea has to take another look, but that's right, his thumb and forefinger create a perfect closed circle, and where the circle ends, between the tips of his fingers, the ape holds a shiny object. It is a key.

He places it on her breast, bows, and turns away; at that moment the lamp is turned out, although it's probably not the lamp after all, because the light shimmers away, like a swarm of dragonflies. "Jacob," she says, but is overwhelmed by darkness and is inexplicably drawn back into sleep, sinks into the dreamless darkness.

She does not awaken until late in the day, dull-headed, not remembering anything, but knowing that something has happened. She puts on her clothes, just shorts and a T-shirt, runs out into the sunlit garden. Jacob is sitting in his house, Andersen is raking the lawn. Now she remembers.

"Andersen," she asks, "was Jacob out of his house last night?"

Andersen looks at her uncomprehendingly. Then he smiles.

"Miss Bolt," he says, "something unbelievable has happened!"

Jacob sits behind a closed door eating as if he had never done anything else; he stuffs bamboo shoots and apples into his mouth, holds them with his fingers like any other ape.

"He's eating again," says Andersen. "It's absolutely wonderful. I thought we would lose him today."

"Yes!" says Lea, and runs into the house again. It's a very hot day, and she is already sweating; is warm, ready, almost as if she desires a man, a boy, a sun-warmed lover. She runs up to her room, looks in the bed, searches among the bedclothes. Nothing. A little disappointed, she turns to leave. Something glitters on the rag rug by her foot; on the floor lies a key.

❧

Pregny, August 28, 1791

Esteemed Sir!

I had a hive which had five or six queen cells with cocoons in them at the same time; one was older than the others, and therefore hatched from the cell earlier. The young queen had scarcely been out of her cradle for ten minutes when she sought out the other, closed queen cells and violently threw herself onto the first of them; we saw how she tugged with her teeth at the enclosed cocoon's silk sheath, thrust her rear end down into the cell and made various movements with it, until finally she was able to give her rival a fatal stab with her stinger. Then she left this cell, and the bees that had been watching widened the opening and pulled out the corpse of a queen.

Now we wanted to see what would happen if two queens came out of their cells at the same time, and how one of them would lose her life. Our observation of this situation I find recorded in my journal entry of May 15, 1790. On that day, in one of the smallest hives, two queens emerged from their cells almost simultaneously. The moment they saw one another they rushed at each other furiously, ending in a position where each had her rival's antenna between her teeth; heads, breasts, and rear ends were pressed tight

106

against each other, and they had only to curve the backs of their bodies to penetrate each other with their stingers. But it did not seem to be the will of Nature that their battle should bring death to them both; one could be tempted to believe Nature had decreed the queens must separate immediately if there was any danger that such a thing could occur. Scarcely had the two rivals noticed the rear parts of their bodies touching each other than they tore themselves loose and pulled apart. I believe in this case one can easily guess Nature's purpose.

There must be only one queen in a hive; if another is born, or if an outside queen comes into the hive by accident, then one of them must die. It cannot be left up to the bees to carry out this judgment, because in a colony with so many individuals, one cannot always expect complete agreement; one group of bees could easily attack one queen, while another group attacked the other queen, leaving the hive without any queen at all. So the duel must be left to the queens themselves. However, since Nature will allow only one queen to fall victim in the fight, Nature has wisely arranged it so that when both queens' lives are in danger, the combatants are filled with intense fear and think only about escaping, not about using their stingers.

I am well aware that one can easily make mistakes when one wants to pursue every phenomenon to its ultimate cause, but in this case the purpose and the means seem to be so clear that I am not afraid to offer my hypothesis.

Several minutes after our two queens had parted their fear disappeared, and they sought each other out again. The stronger, or angrier, queen threw herself on her rival, got into the root of her wing, crawled onto her, lowered her rear end toward the other's hindmost rings, and easily penetrated her foe with her stinger; then she let go of the wing and withdrew her stinger. The conquered queen collapsed, helplessly dragged herself away; soon she lost her strength, and died a short time later.

If one robs a hive of its queen, the bees do not notice it immediately; they go on with their tasks, care for their young, and continue all their normal business with their usual calm. But after a few hours they become restless; the whole hive seems to be agitated,

107

one hears an odd whirring, the bees stop caring for the young, hurry excitedly back and forth across the honeycombs, and seem quite crazed; now for the first time they have noticed that their queen is no longer in their midst. But how can they notice this? How can the bees on one honeycomb know that the queen is not simply sitting on another honeycomb?

There is no doubt in my mind that it is awareness of the queen's absence which causes this restlessness among the workers. As soon as one returns her to the hive, they grow calm. The remarkable thing is that they literally appear to recognize her. If one puts in a new queen instead of the old one, they treat that queen as if they still had their own monarch: they grab her, surround her on all sides, and hold her prisoner in an impenetrable clump until she dies of hunger or is choked.

On the other hand, if one waits a day or so before replacing the old sovereign with a new one, she is received in a friendly manner and immediately acknowledged as the queen of the hive.

❧

It is autumn when he comes, cold yellow autumn; one afternoon he stands in the living room, unwashed, longhaired, wearing a yellow slicker. He seems frightened, hunted; his soul is nipping at his heels. His eyes are blue and distant, they look at her and ask.

The old man comes out of his office.

"So, here's a check for you," he growls.

The young man takes it, looks briefly at the old man, then back at Lea.

"I hope you get over the worst hump now."

"Wouldn't you rather buy a painting?" he asks faintly.

"No," says the old man. "I've stopped buying now. You can get money, but I can't buy. Others—can do that, when I'm gone."

"Are you sure you won't buy one?" he asks dully, looking at the floor.

"I'll never buy any more. So, get going now. You shouldn't come here and disturb me. You should stay in town or go to the mountains. Couldn't you have sent a letter? You can stay at the boardinghouse by the train station tonight. Andersen will drive you. Good-bye, now. And good luck. And don't drink so much tonight."

His look is like a sea of turpentine. He nods slightly to Lea. Involuntarily, she nods in return.

"Poor fellow," says her uncle when the man has left. "He's not very talented either."

She saw him a few more times that autumn. He sometimes hung around the Ekelund estate. She saw him at a distance, in the park, through the rows of trees, on the other side of the field, down by the gate. Always far away. He never saw her. He stood looking straight ahead, as if Ekelund's buildings were simply air to him. Each time she saw him she thought: "I can kill them all."

Later, he disappeared.

The bees forget their old queen when she has been gone for a day or so. I refrain from any hypothesis in that regard.

Up to this point my letter has only included descriptions of fights and tragedies. Perhaps in conclusion I should report some example of the beautiful and appealing art of industriousness. But in order to avoid having to return to stories of battles and murder, I want to report at once my observations of the drone battle.

As you know, all observers agree that at a certain time of the year the worker bees drive out the drones and kill them. Réaumur speaks about these executions as a terrible slaughter; he does not explicitly say that he has witnessed such a battle, but my observations correspond so precisely with his account that one must assume that such a battle has occurred before his eyes.

The bees generally get rid of the drones in July and August. During those months one sees the drones hunted down and chased out onto the alighting board, where they gather in tight clusters. Since at the same time one sees masses of dead drones lying in front of the hive, it seems certain that worker bees kill them with their stingers as soon as the persecution begins. Yet one does not see worker bees use this weapon in the honeycombs; there they are satisfied with hunting down the drones and driving them out. You say yourself, esteemed sir, in a new annotation to "Contemplations Upon Nature," that it seems the drones get crowded together into a corner of the hive and die of starvation there. This is a very plausible assumption, but it could also be possible that the bloodbath occurred inside the hive, without our being able to observe it, because the hive is dark inside, and therefore eludes the eye of the observer.

To settle this question, we got the idea of putting plates of glass under the alighting board the hives rest on and stationing ourselves under it, so we could see what was happening on the stage. This course of action proved very expedient. On July 4, 1787, we saw the bees begin the drone battle in six hives, all at the same time and under the same conditions. The plates of glass on the beehive stand were covered with bees that appeared very angry and attacked the drones the moment they came down to the bottom of the hive; they grabbed the drones by their feelers, legs, or wings, tumbled them about for a long time, and finally killed them with their stingers—which for the most part they aimed toward the openings between the drones' abdomen casings. The moment this terrible weapon struck the drones was the moment of their death; they stretched out their wings and gave up the ghost. But it seemed that the worker bees did not regard the drones as being as completely dead as they appeared to us, because they kept on sticking the drones and bored their stingers so deep that they often had trouble pulling them out again. They had to curl themselves into a circle to get their stingers out of the carcasses.

On the following days we assumed the same position to observe the hives, and we witnessed new murder scenes. During three whole hours we watched our bees continously killing drones. The previous day they had killed drones in their own hives, whereas this day they attacked the drones that had been driven from other hives and sought refuge in theirs. We also saw them tear out some drone larvae still lying in the cells, then greedily suck every bit of fluid from the larvae and drag them out of the hive. The following day there appeared to be no more drones in these hives.

These two observations seem conclusive to me; it is unmistakably clear that Nature has dictated that at a certain time of year the worker bees must kill the drones in their hives. But what means can Nature use to awaken their rage toward the drones? This is one of the questions. Meanwhile, I have made an observation that perhaps can help to solve the mystery someday. In hives without queens the bees never kill the drones; on the contrary, the drones find a safe place of refuge there, even during times when they are murdered mercilessly elsewhere, and one often finds great numbers of them there in January. They are also tolerated in hives which do not have a true so-called queen but still have bees that lay drone eggs, and likewise also in hives where the queens are only semifertile and only produce drones. In other words, drone battles are found only in hives where the queens are completely fertile, and always only after the swarming period is over.

Esteemed sir, please be assured of my very deepest respect, etc.

&

The cello arrived along with the snow. It snowed in all of Ekelund's rooms, the flakes lay on the picture frames and carpets, there was white on the armrests and bric-a-brac shelves. But when she played there was a melted circle around her. She had to play for an entire winter, keep the snow and cold at a distance. The bees have gone to sleep in their boxes; the hives look like small mounds under the snow. It's warm inside the hives, as warm as inside the cello. When she plays the snow melts around her.

One morning someone comes, and takes her from this place
One morning she stands silent, with a tense and frightened face
One morning she's exposed, a hanging there will be
One morning she is naked, and dead for all to see

"You have a visitor, Miss Bolt."

In the living room. The tall, slender figure in the corner by the window, the winter light from outside, the fluttering clothing, the long black hair. Lea felt like tearing out her own hair again.

"Mother."

"Lea. How *could* you?" Everything around Lea turns completely white as her mother speaks. Hadn't it snowed like that once before? One day when she had kicked and bitten as they dragged her down the stairs?

One morning someone comes, someone awakes instead
One morning the sun enters, is strong and warm and red
One morning she's eternal flame and flesh and breath
One morning she says to him: There isn't any death.

"Don't you want to talk to her?"

. . .

"Lea. Seriously. Aren't you going to . . ."

. . .

"Shall I tell her to leave?"

. . .

"What's wrong?"
"Help me, Uncle Wilhelm. Help me."

⌘

1399. Moscow, 1985. Thomas Arctander, a student with a government scholarship, rides on a bus through Moscow late one afternoon; begins talking with the driver. They are alone on the bus, and they start a conversation about literature. The driver stops the bus, and they continue the conversation, which becomes very pleasant and personal. Eventually they touch upon the Stalin period, on arbitrary imprisonments and prison camps. The driver relates his own family's story. His father, who worked in a factory at the end of the '40s, came to work fifteen minutes late one day. The *streetcar* had been delayed, but no excuses helped. He was condemned to a work camp for six months. His job was to float logs; it was in the spring. On one of the father's first days in the camp, the commander's little daughter falls into the water and disappears under a log. The father dives in and saves the girl. In gratitude, the commander offers him vocational training while in the camp. "Tell me what you want to be, and I'll arrange it for you." "I want to be a driver," replies the father. He is transferred to the police driving school and receives training as a heavy-transport driver. Once out of the camp he begins working in his new job. But late one night some months afterward he hits a little girl in the dark. She dies. He is sent to prison for a year and loses his driver's license. Out of prison again, he gets his old job back at the factory while waiting for his driver's license to be renewed. At the factory he meets a young woman; she had been the driver of the streetcar that, years earlier, was delayed fifteen minutes. They get married.

This is the story of how the bus driver's parents became his parents. (Thomas Arctander, *Conversations about Russia*, Oslo, 1991, pp. 177–80.)

∞

This evening she sits with the key. "You're to go into town, Andersen," she says to him. At first he refuses, but he has no choice.

"The working environment, you know, Andersen. Go out and have a really good time for a few hours."

He sets a lovely supper table and is about to leave. As he stands in the doorway, hesitating slightly, she goes over and hugs him. He stands perfectly still, unmoved, gives her a crooked smile.

"No. Don't be ironic, Miss Bolt. It doesn't suit you."

She laughs. He smiles and leaves.

Then she is alone in the house. Jacob is taking a nap in his house after a filling meal, but Lea does not sleep, she does not eat; once again she goes into the office, sits down in the old man's chair, lets her hands glide along the desk pad. The old man is by her side.

Listen, he says, aren't you going to pull yourself together soon?

Pull myself together?

Don't you remember what I whispered to you in the ambulance?

What did you mean, Uncle?

You're just pretending. I really don't have time for this. I can't make many such visits. I have to go other places.

Surely you have a little time.

Have you ever thought about what time really is?

Physics tells us that time and light are the same size; you tried to teach me that, Uncle.

Well, you've learned that much anyway. Yes, but what *is* it?

I think we've had this conversation once before.

You're quite right. We had this conversation in October, after your mother had come here to take you home. I was already quite ill. And she didn't exactly make me any better. Good thing we got her thrown out. It just shows that one can't be too careful in choosing one's parents.

That's very true.

You weren't in a good mood either, and threw out one of your usual youthful questions about *why* this and *why* that. Then we came to believe something about coincidences and destiny, you and I. Do you remember what I said?

Yes, you said that—

I said that both are, in fact, simply words for something we don't understand. Whether one calls it coincidence or fate is completely irrelevant, because the strange thing is *that anything even occurs*. That's the incredibly odd thing, isn't it? That anything even *is*. What *is* it? What *are* all the bees, the water, the air, you, I? That it *is*, when it could just as well *not* be. That time *passes* at all, when it could just as well *not* pass. That something *happens*, when it could just as well *not* happen.

And how do you see this now?

From my present perspective, I'm even more amazed.

Honestly, she says, what do you *mean* by leaving me all this? What is it supposed to be good for?

But there is no longer anyone beside her, just a gentleness in the air, like the memory of a smile. On the shelves are the record books, filled with numbers, weighty, waiting for her. She knew perfectly well, of course. In the ambulance he had whispered, as she stroked his hair: "The work, Lea, the work isn't finished."

In the locked desk drawer lay a manuscript. "Introduction and Scientific Preface," the title page said. It was quite thick, and handwritten, in the old man's fine, rather elaborate script. She opened it in the middle.

. . . So what is serialization? One can say that it is the opposite of causation. In his almost forgotten work *Das Gestz de Series* Paul Kammerer defines the concept:

"A 'series' manifests itself as a constant repetition or accumulation in time and space of the same or similar things and events, even if the individual events or things in the series, as far as one can determine through precise analysis, are not connected by the same active cause." This is Kammerer's definition of the "Series Law." Jung calls it "Synchronicity," and gives a similar definition in his essay on the principle of a-causal connection:

"Synchronicity is the merging in time of two or more causally unrelated events which have the same or similar meaning."

She stopped reading, skipped back in the manuscript.

Every event is in principle completely improbable. The very existence of the world is completely beyond what we could expect; indeed, the very fact that we are alive is an extreme eccentricity in the universe's ocean of molecular events.

She flipped past several pages.

. . . In other words, it is a matter of improbable coincidences. It is a matter of "strange things." Of apparently meaningful coalescences that have no causal connection.

Anyone who has sat at a card table will have noticed that good luck and bad luck seem to come in portions. Players will talk about "lucky" and "unlucky" days. Not only cardplayers, for that matter; we all think that way. And sometimes it is as if events really conspire against us. "Strange things" happen, things that defy the possibility of chance.

Let us first take a look at the concept of coincidence:

If one tosses a coin, and gets "heads" nineteen times in a row, most people will think the chance of getting "tails" the twentieth time must be very high. Nonetheless, the chance is still only fifty-

fifty that the twentieth time it will be "heads" again. In the course of a huge number of tosses, let's say about ten thousand, the number of "tails" and the number of "heads" will even out to about five thousand of each. This is called the Law of Large Numbers, and it is fundamental to figuring probabilities. Determining probabilities—using statistics and the possibility of chance—is the basis for nearly all human activity, from nuclear physics to sociology.

Nevertheless, we can speak with good reason about the paradox of coincidence. As we know, in playing roulette the ball can land on red or black, like the front or back of a coin. The longest series of continuous reds registered in Monte Carlo are twenty-eight on red. The twenty-seventh turn of the roulette wheel is causally independent of the twenty-eighth turn, which again is causally independent of the twenty-ninth turn of the wheel. There is always a fifty-fifty chance the red will win again. Still, over time it evens out. In other words, the paradox consists in the fact that mutually independent events seem to achieve a constancy.

During several summers, I counted beestings. Each time I or my assistant got stung, I noted it. In a usual summer we got between twelve and fifteen stings each. Never more, never fewer. In the end I could know with certainty how many stings I would get the next summer.

Another example is the number of dog bites in New York City. In 1955 an average of 75.3 instances of dog bites were reported to the health authorities per day. The next year the number was 73.6 per day. In 1957 it was 73.2. It was 75.5 in 1958 and 72.6 in 1959. The number is, as we see, fairly constant, just as with beestings. In other words, the number of dog bites for future years can be figured rather precisely. But each dog bite is causally independent of all the other roughly 75 dog bites that day. Each bite constitutes a separate event, a separate accident, a complicated series of circumstances and coincidences that occur in very different situations and have a very different impact on the individual's daily life. It could be a matter of an elderly hairdresser who has never been bitten by a dog before, and never will be again, but suddenly a furious shepherd visits her salon; or it could be a cultivated lapdog from the

Upper West Side that has never seen a mailman nor bitten a soul, but all of a sudden gets a divine inspiration to bite the maid. Suddenly these individuals are assigned to fill the gaps in the predictable statistics. One would think it impossible to reckon the number of so many complicated individual situations, but in fact it is not. It is noteworthy that situations that are unpredictable individually, *as a whole* show a stable average.

How then do New York's dogs *know* that they have filled the day's bite quota? How do the bees in the hive *know* that they have given me and my assistant enough stings for the summer? Or let us return to roulette. The roulette wheel has thirty-six numbers, eighteen red and eighteen black. It also has a thirty-seventh number, called "zero." If the wheel stops at "zero," the stakes all go to the house. This ensures the casino's profits. How does the roulette wheel "know" that on average it must stop on "zero" once in thirty-seven? The many small coincidences offset one another, it is said, and one thinks this explains something, but the paradox of coincidence is not thereby "understood." We base our actions on these consistencies, but we cannot fathom them. The most remarkable phenomenon is when they seem to occur in clusters. In other words, when they drastically depart from probabilities. But in principle, the most remarkable coincidence that occurs is no more remarkable than that everything else occurs. It is simply more peculiar than the other events, but not unexplainable.

Let us therefore approach serialization in another, more biographical manner. Events in my own life led me to an early awareness that different people seem to experience certain kinds of events. Some people always seem to be witnesses to serious accidents, while others go through life without seeing so much as a bicycle accident. Other people are constantly *having* accidents, always are sitting in the passenger seat in a collision, snow slides off the roof onto their heads, etc. Some constantly save lives. Others constantly *are* saved. Some people constantly win lotteries and bets, even though they never buy more lottery tickets than others, while others never win so much as a fruit basket. Some constantly miss out on chances, while others seem incredibly lucky. Some make out strangely well, or we say they have a "flair." There are many stories about scientists or artists working on a large project who suddenly, purely by coincidence, are bombarded with information and references that help them in the project; relevant references suddenly seem to pop up everywhere, unrequested and effortlessly—in lectures, correspondence, and conversations—in too great a concentration to be "probable."

One can say that these events, these coincidences, seem to accumulate beyond the possibility of chance.

She had to stop reading. She stood up. It was growing dark outside. The seventh night the old man was gone. She picked up the manuscript, glided into the library with it, began to read even before she plopped down into the chair.

Scientific theoreticians long maintained that a scientific explanation consists in its ability to formulate precise prognoses. A rigorous experimental situation is most often a linear or deterministic situation. But reality is otherwise, because the hundred thousand small coincidences and uncontrolled influences can have decisive importance in the outcome of a situation. Scientific predictions about how reality progresses can only be approximate and of limited validity. The newest research in this field functions with a "chaos coefficient." In this field of research, as in the field of quantum theory in physics, one speaks of Nature itself containing an ontological scope of freedom.

But what about situations in which reality goes beyond the probability of chance? The question then becomes whether there is a connection between this inexplicable accumulation of coincidences and the individual's life.

In the old days one spoke about "fate"; one was born under a lucky or an unlucky star. Today we no longer talk about fate, we talk about coincidence. The question is whether we really understand what we are saying.

It sounds more scientific to talk about coincidences. But in fact it explains little. Actually both words, "fate" and "coincidence," describe something we do not really understand, namely *that something even occurs.*

Lea stopped reading again, looked around the room. Everything seemed to have a bluish tone, every line had a blue edge, like the color deviation through a lens. She took a breath, continued reading.

. . . namely *that something even occurs.* This *that* is quite extraordinary. Since it could just as well, and just as probably, *not* occur. That the bees *are*, that water, stars, language *are*, when they could just as well *not* be, indeed, in all likelihood *should* not be. Or, to take something more down-to-earth: in our everyday life we walk across the street without being run down. If an accident occurs, we talk about a set of unfortunate circumstances. If we are miraculously saved, we say that coincidences, those thousand small related causes, were on our side. But this word "coincidence" expresses as little as the word "fate." An event occurs at the cost of everything that *could* have occurred. What about the myriad of equally probable series of events, which then remain theoretical? That we are always *rescued* from defeat and *survive* for a while yet? In every statistical study of the prognosis for survival for, let us say, one thousand incurably ill people whose maximum life expectancy following diagnosis should be no more than four years, there will always be two or three who are cured inexplicably and continue to live for fifty years, and who are quietly removed from the data, because otherwise they would utterly ruin the statistical curve—it would never reach zero.

It becomes especially interesting when the event not only contradicts the laws of probability to an extraordinary degree but also has a meaningful effect on us and seems to express itself in an almost frighteningly readable language. Often we see this as unconnected enjoyable or unpleasant experiences, because they do not have a realistic effect on us, they seem "contrived." If one presented them in a novel, the reader would dismiss them as unbelievable, even if they are ever so true, by saying: Such things don't really happen after all!

To repeat: in principle, every event is unlikely. The more it contradicts probability, the more it attracts attention. But thanks to the Law of Large Numbers, we can always explain *how* this event occurred as an eccentricity, far to the right or left on the Gaussian curve.

Science operates in limited, controlled situations, with statistics and a throw of the dice. Since numerous such eccentric, improbable separate events, unrepeatable in the laboratory, seem to be intimately connected to our significant biographical experience, we find ourselves forced to evaluate whether there are not reasonable grounds to ask about the *why* of these events.

The answer need not lead to a postulation of any form of divine providence. What we are trying to show is the existence of an underlying *something*, an active universal principle for life's coincidences, which manifests itself often with some people, more rarely with others.

Science can always explain, qua mathematical eccentricities, *that* and *how* a strange thing happens, but can it explain anything about the *why*? Can it even ask about the *why*?

Our universe is an ocean of single, chance molecular occurrences, where the Law of Large Numbers and the constancy of chance are endlessly active. Perhaps *other* powers are active in this sea too? Are there also sharks? Are there currents and energy fields we have been unable to map, because they cannot be duplicated in a scientific experiment?

To seek for a *why* is contrary to scientific method. Science has defined itself as unable to be concerned with such unreproducible situations.

How then to capture them, or become better acquainted with their character, without resorting to mysticism?

I myself have not cast dice; nor have I (like some pioneers) counted people who happened to walk past my bench in the park, or sat beside me on the streetcar, nor have I noted sex, clothing, and age. I have gathered *concrete* accounts, accounts of unusually great deviations from the normal—individual accounts of remarkable coincidences and gross improbabilities, stories of coincidences *that had a concrete and decisive effect on the life story of one or more people*.

I began with accounts I already knew about, investigated them, tried to verify them. Gradually I went further, pursued historical accounts. Later I also began to collect information through others. When I had done this for a while, it struck me that one should be able to observe such events with the aid of milestones, with the aid of a worldwide network of observation posts. This, I assumed, would be the only scientific method whereby one could maintain what science *cannot* maintain. I asked myself: Would not the totality of these observations constitute a proof? Would it not point toward a universal principle that works against the probabilities of chance, a principle that shows itself now and then, without warning, qua strange and improbable coincidences in the individual life?

I have been collecting these accounts for several decades. One day, when research on the theoretical basis for serialization has been carried further by people with greater insights into physics and mathematics than I, when serialization is recognized as a principle of natural law, on a par with the Law of Large Numbers, then my collected accounts perhaps may be useful.

I have no conclusions to draw at the moment, other than that the material suggests there is, in addition to causality, an a-causal principle at work in the universe which strives toward unity, edification. My observations of Nature suggest this too. I spent a long time studying forms of crystals and deviations within given patterns. Later I worked with leaves and moss, mold fungus and slime fungus. Where does the amoebae colony *get* its collective will? If unknown forces affect people, they must also affect other forms of life. To test this theory I started observing events in the lives of more highly developed animal species, but captivity made realistic observations impossible. So I began studying the life of bees instead. In a beehive one has a whole *world* available for observation.

Bees too must be affected by the same principles in Nature. I have observed individual events in the life of bees for many years, and plan to collect this material into a separate work, if time and strength allow.

As I see it, this is the area where we come closest to a new connection between a person's life and experiences on the one hand, and theoretical scientific perceptions on the other hand. In other words: my bold concept, and perhaps my misfortune, is that I glimpsed a bridge between humanity and science, between biography and universe, between subjective and objective perception.

The collected accounts fall into several categories: from the simplest of the simple, where only one or two parameters are coincidental and have no significance other than the obvious oddity, all the way to long, complicated accounts, where the coincidences are so numerous and have such a thorough effect on those implicated that their lives are changed forever.

In the odd, simpler category, for example, is Kammerer's Case #46, which occurred during the summer of 1906. Baroness Trautenburg, a spinster, born 1846, is injured by a falling tree. The same summer, in a completely different place, Baroness Riegershofen, a spinster, also born 1846, is injured by a falling tree. Four coincidences: Baroness, spinster, age, tree. Odd, but nothing more. A more entertaining account is Kammerer's Case #10, which deals with two young soldiers who were admitted, separately, to the military hospital in Katowitze, Bohemia, in 1915. They did not know each other. They both had pneumonia, both were born in Schlesien, both were nineteen years old, both had volunteered for the supply corps, and both were named Franz Richter. Six coincidences.

So one can ask: What happened when Franz Richter met Franz Richter? Did their meeting affect their lives, did they become friends forever, did they fall in love with the same woman? Did Franz Richter have anything to do with Franz Richter? Or did the coincidence become just an absurd and amusing story, like hundreds of thousands of similar stories that can be told at a tavern table or to one's grandchildren? And what about the many such accounts that border on ghost stories, where the coincidences are so numerous, and the subjective experience so strong, that one can only imagine how the event must have affected those who experienced it?

Drawing from the limited available literature in this field, I have tried to classify my case accounts by type and morphology: analog and homologue series, cyclical series, phase series, inverted series, pure and composite series, and so forth, even if the possibilities for classification are somewhat inadequate. It has been a time-consuming task, and it is far from finished.

The easiest task has been collecting the written accounts, through newspapers and magazines. On the other hand, it has proved time-consuming to verify each one with several written testimonies. Verbal accounts have been more difficult to get, but with the help of like-minded people in this country and abroad, and not least, a large financial contribution, I have been able to build a small network of reliable informants, who have systematically gathered oral accounts, which they or I have been able to confirm. This apparatus is still intact, waiting for someone who can utilize it.

What I have always sought are accounts that deviate from the normal to a great degree—where one or several people change course entirely, where those involved are led completely off track and end up in quite a different place than one would expect. There are many accounts of people escaping accidents or death through the intervention of improbable or inexplicable events. In short: events deeply affecting an individual's life have seemed the most significant to me.

A very few of these thousands of events are, in other words, my pearls, my jewels. They are the best of the accounts where sources and testimony are meticulously verified. Of these, some must be said to be the crown jewels. From among them I have made a sober selection; this is my lifework and what I leave behind of true value to humanity. But we must fear that the most precious, most remarkable of such events will never be written down in any chronicle, never be transmitted to us, other than as vague, mystical outlines of extraordinary happenings that once took place. This in spite of the fact that each and every person's life bears the traces, indeed, the circular effects, of such events.

Lea put down the papers. She looked at the record books on the shelves, went from one thing to the next. It was completely silent inside her.

There is a circle around Ekelund this evening. The sky slowly darkens. Someone is leaving. Perhaps she will leave too. She does not know what she will do. Perhaps she will go away. Perhaps she will stay. She is a profound memory. She is the world clock. The sky slowly darkens, the earth turns. It is summer again. The grass is completely dark now. Perhaps somewhere there is an answer as to why. Something brought her here, through all time. No one is with her any longer, but someone is here. Now she can almost remember everything, almost as it was when she was inside the bees, but even more: she can remember everything, even that which lies beyond her own experience. Everything that has happened. Thomas. We met each other and lost each other. Many things happened, over long periods of time, in order that the two of us should lose each other.

Outside, dusk has fallen. The fjord lies like a blue stripe. The whistling buoy has begun to breathe. Along the coast she dimly sees shimmering lights appear. Suddenly a beam of light slashes the sky, then another. Farther out the light blinks rhythmically, reliably. Now

PART

TWO

ONE

BRIEF OVERVIEW OF LIGHTHOUSE HISTORY

Enter Mariners, *wet.*
Mariners: *All lost! to prayers, to prayers! all lost!*
Boatswains: *What, must our mouths be cold?*

SHAKESPEARE, *The Tempest,* I.1.

the lights are lit. Imagine the coast as it was, without markers and lights. Yes, for that's how the coast was, like a dark animal with bared white teeth and foaming jaws that snapped in the night, without a single friendly flash to show the way. Only the stars shone. That's how the coast lay, unchanged for centuries, from the beginning of time. And anyone sailing in the darkness must sail like a storm swallow, by instinct and feeling. Now and then, on a stormy autumn night, perhaps a restless group on a small island goes up to a high ridge, a lookout knoll, or a sand dune. They stand there in all that darkness. Perhaps there is a father or a brother in that group, perhaps a wife holding a child's hand. They peer uneasily into the heavy sea spray. They are waiting for someone. Then perhaps they light a bonfire for the one or ones they await, and for a vessel sailing blindly somewhere out there. And perhaps their small bonfire saves the boat they are waiting for, perhaps a straining, searching eye sees the faint light in there, like a single dying glow in an oven's black opening, or perhaps the little group stands there waiting in vain. But the next morning the fire has burned out, and the next night the coast lies as dark as the land and forests within.

That's how the coast was. In other parts of the world proper lights were lit early, in real lighthouses, on the shores of the Bosporus or along the dangerous Strait of Messina, where Charybdis' swirling whirlpools meet Scilla's treacherous cliffs, or at Ostia and Ravenna, at Puetolis, on Capri and Yenişehir, or at the Roman outposts along the English Channel at Dover and Boulogne. And even much earlier, it is rumored, coasts in the southern part of the world were like magnificent necklaces at night, where the glittering stones in the chain were not only blazing towers but actual temples, where generations of priests served the gods of the sea and wind and stars, followed their movements, preserved navigation charts and coastal profile maps, pilot books and voyage descriptions, peripli and port entrance details, taught seamanship and navigation, and kept the fire lit day and night as hymns to the gods rang out. It is enough to mention one, the most splendid of them all: the lighthouse outside Alexandria, the Seventh Wonder of the ancient world, on the island of Pharos, *Phrah*, island of the sun god. Pharos gave its name to the word for lighthouse in many languages, and to the word for knowledge about lighthouses, *pharology*. The tower at Pharos was as high as a mountain, an incredible 173 meters, and its light could be seen a full day's sail from land. But all of this disappeared again, as did the Romans' lighthouses, and was forgotten. Dark times came, earthquakes and floods and plagues came, and people forgot how mankind built and took care of such towers. Once again, all the oceans lay surrounded by darkness. Along the coasts lived people ruled by minor chieftains, bandits, earls of Lade, and that sort of stockholders—people who no longer understand about lighthouse towers, and at most manage to light a kettle of coal and tar once in a while if the weather is exceptionally foul and if the lighthouse owner has remembered to buy fuel and happens to be sober that evening (this is the golden age of free competition). But at the same time, these are people who are just as likely to light fires purely as traps, lights at wrong places to lure ships to go aground where the coast is more dangerous (these are, as we said, the freest nights of free enterprise). On the beach, poor people stand waiting: hungry, greedy, like the breakers. Perhaps there will be a cargo of timber to salvage, perhaps barrels of herring. Because beach robbery is their privilege—this is the *only* privilege in their meager, windblown life as fishermen and tenant farmers. They can freely help themselves to whatever floats ashore onto the beach, living or dead, onto *their* beach, and they will get paid for what they salvage. They utilize this privilege for what it is worth. And in many places their evening prayer sounds like this one, from the Baltic:

> *God bless our fields and glades,*
> *Our young men and our maids.*
> *Give salt on the beach and fish in the net.*
> *Show the crab where the trap is set.*
> *God, let a large ship run aground on our reef tonight!*

Or like this one from the Scilly Isles:

> *We pray Thee, O Lord,*
> *not that wrecks should happen,*
> *but that if any wreck should happen,*
> *Thou wilt guide them into the Scilly Isles*
> *for the benefit of the inhabitants.*

Or like the girls on Tristan da Cunha who have no dowries:

> *Dear God send me a shipwreck, so I can get married!*

Yes, as long as it is not one's *own* brothers and fathers and sweethearts who lose their lives that night. Every shipwreck becomes a sinister celebration, a welcome contribution toward feeding oneself. And even if the ship they placed in danger carries nothing but manure, the sailors out there probably have a few shillings in their pockets if they get to shore and to the group waiting there, axes in hand, to kill them. No one asks about a lost schooner and a few drowned people more or less. They sink the corpses or bury them in a dead-man's cliff. The coast hides many corpses, and many wrecks, and no one counts them. It is not the sea the sailor most fears. It's the coasts. And not only because they are dark but because dark people live there. For many centuries it is like this. Only monks and hermits think of tending lighthouses on their own, out of Christian duty. For a long time monastery signal fires are all that light the coasts. Then perhaps a big landowner here and there is given lighthouse rights, and sets up a swinging lantern or a coal kettle at a high point; however, it is most often not the light that interests him but the heavy lighthouse toll he charges ships, and the coal kettles smoke more than they illuminate and go out when it rains. Eventually there are many such lighthouse speculators. The shipowners, however, are not at all interested in having too many lighthouses and lights along the coasts, except at the most dangerous places, because it is more profitable to figure on losing a cargo ship and a few souls once in a while than having to pay all those tiresome, meaningless lighthouse tolls in every harbor. These lighthouses are an unnecessary, expensive, newfangled luxury.

But now, in this century, the glorious glowing nineteenth century, now the lights are being lit in earnest. Although at first it goes slowly. In the beginning, toward the end of the century of revolution, while the new age is still only dawning in people, swinging lamps and lanterns, which are scarcely more than protected bonfires, are set up—blazing kettles hanging from the arm of a scale, or simple oil and codliver-oil lamps. Later, as the 1800s get under way, the pace picks up, in step with industry and technology. For now the engineers arrive. Small energetic eccentrics, with assignments and patents from all the newly created lighthouse commissions and lighthouse services in the coastal nations; men with stiff collars, field glasses in their inside pockets and algorithms in their hearts, brothers of the bridge builders and machine makers, captains in the engineer corps who know the formulas for determining the degree of iron fatigue just as well as they know Jesaias, Homer, and Shelley. Semipoets and bachelors, married to their duty. Eddystone? Impossible to build there, out in the middle of the ocean? Weather too rough to land boats at Grip and Fastnet Rock? Too bare on the Gjesling Islands? Too dangerous to live on Hestskjær? Too cold on New Year Island? Too inaccessible at L'Enfant Perdu? Nothing is impossible for such an engineer, a royally appointed government official no less. They are the new age's cathedral builders, but their edifices will not merely point like fingers toward heaven in warning, they must last through autumn storms and February hurricanes; they must stand in snow and ice, they must be built in remote places, on ground far out to sea that is scarcely more than a reef, where the construction workers stand in water up to their waists and masses of heavy spray wash over them day after day, where seawater fills the drill holes, where a sudden storm in

August can wash away an entire summer's work. And they must build with heavy granite, with ashlar blocks as big as horses and oak beams as thick as grown men. All of this must be transported out there and be hoisted into position and be put together into a single compact construction, while the salt water stings raw knuckles and sore feet. The engineer oversees the laborers like a hungry fish hawk as they toil away season after season. Slowly the lighthouse rises, slender, solid, built to withstand *everything*. And the people on the mainland look out at the lighthouse that guides ships and souls safely to harbor. The coast has become lighter. And then it happens anyway, the storm of the century sets in, a storm that lasts for a week, and when the weather finally clears, and people on the mainland automatically turn their uneasy gaze outward, out to the new lighthouse, there is nothing to see; where the lighthouse once stood, emptiness suddenly shimmers in the sea air, and the waves break over bare rock again. The lighthouse, the mighty and everlasting lighthouse, with its blocks and beams, and all those living in it, has been blown away like a feather, gone without a trace. Only a few twisted pieces of iron bristle from the rock. But when the tears are dried and people have gone from house to house and talked long and trembled over what happened, the engineer returns with his field glasses, his theodolite, and his tables, his blueprints and slide rules, with a little more repressed anger than before, lines have formed at his jowls, like knife scratches on his face, and it is simply a matter of starting over again. Drill even deeper, build with even heavier materials, wedge the stone even tighter together this time until, three seasons later, the lighthouse once again stands on the reef, white and comforting, in the sunlight. For how long? No one knows.

And now as the nineteenth century gains momentum, the little men, the engineer captains and inventors, work tirelessly. They travel incessantly to the most inaccessible small islands and reefs, and put them on their lists of dangerous waters and unbuilt lighthouses. Eventually there are a great many of these men, they get titles and uniforms, they become lighthouse directors, lighthouse inspectors, and lighthouse chemical engineers.

Slowly the coasts get lights. And the engineers' lighthouse lists are like litanies, a salvation litany, and the names are known on all the seas, among all who sail. If you follow the coastlines' intricate crooks and curves on the navigational charts, you find them, small black names printed in the middle of large colored circles and sections: Mull of Galloway, Stevns Klint, Helgoland, Dyrhólaey, and Eddystone Rocks; the ancient Coruña and Cape Finisterre; or Hoek van Schouwen, Vardø, Gotska Sandön, Utsira, and Bull Point; Great Ormes Head, Ceuta, and Dunnet Head; and in more distant waters shine names like Cape Reinga, Toi Misaki, New Year Island, and Cape of Good Hope. And every lighthouse has its specific task and its specific function. Farthest out in the open jaws of the sea lies the first front, the initial line of defense; the lighthouses out there must warn shipmasters that they are nearing a coast, islands, and underwater reefs. Then, when the initial dangers have been left well behind and the vessel nears land, the second line appears—the lighthouses and lanterns along the channel that indicate where the shipping lane lies. Finally, in the third line, are the lights that point the way in the seaward approach. Each of these lighthouses has its own particular position and characteristics, its own address; to make sure there is no danger of confusion and that they can be distinguished from one another even under the most difficult conditions, each address has its own specific light pattern, its sequence, rhythm, and color. For in their tireless efforts, the engineers have created an infinite number of different lamps since coal lighthouses were abandoned just a few decades ago; now flashing-light instruments, lightning-flash instruments, steady, alternating, and occulting lights, parabolic reflectors, sidereal instruments, sidereal-mirror instruments, and sector instruments prevail, all of different sizes and classifications. Some lighthouses are equipped with more than one light, with a pair of lamps placed one above the other; others have attached side lamps. In addition, there are the sound signals, foghorns and tocsins, which also have their own frequencies and characteristics. And along the coasts the number of lighthouses slowly increases to hundreds and thousands.

Things have gone quickly, every decade new improvements arrive, and the people by the sea begin to respect and honor and tip their hats to the strange little engineers and inventors who have made navigation safer and more exact. Within a relatively short time pharology has become a precise science. Only a few decades earlier the lamps in the lighthouses were nothing other than coal pans and tallow candles, or primitive flat-wick lard oil lamps, smoking and sooting, with a roughly hammered brass plate put up as a reflector. And these smoking oil lamps were in principle no different from the oil lamps the Romans had used, or the Egyptians and Babylonians—a dish of oil with a wick stuck into it, that's all. For thousands of years people have worked and read by the light of these miserable lamps, which give off a minimum of light for a maximum of smell. The flame gets its air supply only from outside the lamp; the oil is not fully utilized but gives off residue and smoke. It was in the light of such a lamp that Galileo ruined the last of his night vision as he wrote his forbidden manuscript about optics; and it was in the light of such a lamp, where the wick had to be trimmed every three minutes, that Descartes taught people to think clearly as he slowly froze to death in the Stockholm castle. But neither of those two giants came up with the idea of discovering a better work light. Only when their successors, the pedantic little engineers, begin to look at the problem of the all too faint lighthouse flames along the coasts do the lamps improve—also in homes and on streets, in workplaces, mines, and offices. In 1784 Argand constructs the Argand lamp, the first to utilize the oil completely. At last people have a lamp that really shines, a lamp that not only can be used in the lighthouses but expands the workday by many hours. Everyone knows the Argand lamp, soon it is found in every home. The wick is made like a tube or, more correctly, like a stocking; the flame is circular and gets its air supply from beneath—from outside and inside simultaneously. To create an even steadier and stronger airflow and make burning even more effective, the Argand lamp also has a tall cylindrical glass around the flame, which creates a chimney effect. In principle all oil-burning lighthouse lamps are Argand lamps, with a series of later modifications and improvements, not least because of access to the light cheap kerosene—paraffin—which, from the middle of the century, displaces the use of heavy sperm oil, rape oil, and lard oil.

In 1819 Augustin-Jean Fresnel, perhaps the greatest name in pharology's short history, constructed a lamp that could have up to five round wicks, one within the other; in other words, a quintuple lamp, something that gave a stronger and, most important, a more stable amount of light. The great Fresnel was originally a road construction engineer. When Napoleon returned from Elba, Fresnel was among the troops that tried in vain to keep the tyrant from returning. The attempt failed, as we know; and while France again lay on its back and fawned over the melancholy little Corsican conqueror in order to get at least a one-hundred-day encore, Fresnel was thrown into prison. It must have been a truly dark and wretched prison, because in his cell Fresnel began to think about the nature of light, and about the problem of diffraction, and decided to dedicate his life to optics. He became its foremost modern innovator and the father of modern lighthouse lamps.

But other engineers contributed to the development of lighthouses as well. There were many improvements in the years that followed; one could mention Fahrque's piston lamp, the so-called regulator lamp, which used an ingenious floating principle to provide an even flow of oil to the wicks and to reuse excess oil. Or we could mention Borda's rotating watch apparatus, first used at Dieppe in 1783. However, the most memorable day in the history of lighthouse technique still belongs unquestionably to the great Augustin-Jean Fresnel; on July 25, 1823, Fresnel's diotropic glass lens was put into use for the first time at the Cardouan lighthouse in France. The light-refracting lens, which sits like a hollow polished diamond around the flame, is constructed to refract light rays *both* vertically and horizontally and send them out as a collected bundle of light. With one stroke, all the old assertions about metal reflectors, mirrors, simple lenses, and prisms were completely outdated; here was a lens that greatly intensified the weakest flame and completely utilized the amount of light. Later, Fresnel created his fixed-light lens, which refracts the rays vertically and sends them out as a horizontal belt of light. Fresnel constructed both of these lenses in six different normal sizes, called orders, with focal distances from the sixth order's 150 centimeters all the way to 920 centimeters for the first order; this classification has been retained, so Fresnel's lenses are used virtually unchanged in all lighthouses to this day. Fresnel's last masterpiece, the catadioptric prism, placed in his diotropic lens, both reflects *and* refracts outward the light rays that strike it. To produce these crownglass monsters, in sizes which until then had been unthinkable, and cement together the individual parts of the glass mass with sufficient precision and clarity presented the glassworkers with great challenges. Among other things, one had to find a way to harden the glass and make it completely clear and transparent, without even a hint of blue, and without veins and bubbles. To achieve this task, Fresnel had the good fortune to have at his side one of the foremost opticians of his day, with the very appropriate name Soleil; Monsieur Soleil found the practical solutions to Fresnel's ideas. Within a very short time Fresnel and Soleil could deliver their lenses to lighthouses in coastal nations virtually all over the world.

But there is still room for improvement; lamps will be made even brighter and cheaper, using completely new techniques and dangerous new fuels, electric arc lamps and hazardous gas; lighthouse beams will be screened and colored in different sectors, to give characteristic light to different parts of the shipping lane. The engineers do not rest. They do their experiments in city laboratories, then travel from lighthouse to lighthouse to test their theories. There they are met with evident distrust from the lighthouse keepers and lighthouse officials—the lighthouse keepers are the only ones who do not tip their hats to them. For it is the lighthouse keepers who must live with the modern lamp glass, which cracks because of uneven cooling, or acetylene gas burners that explode in their hands; it is the lighthouse keepers who get blamed if the flame goes out or if the lens gets covered with soot, or the new blinking apparatus stops going around because the floater gets cut if the quicksilver mirror it rotates in is not level. No, the lighthouse keepers are far from enthusiastic when the engineers arrive with a boat full of their new discoveries and experiments and lay claim to the lighthouse keeper's place, time, and silence, stick their noses into his daily duties, and steal from his vital alertness. The lighthouse keeper wants to have peace and the fewest possible factors of uncertainty because he has to light the lights; it is his task to see that they are lit each evening and extinguished each morning, no matter the circumstances, no matter what.

Now the lighthouses are lit. Now, in this century. It is this century, the 1800s, that has lit lights along the coasts, that has made the most distant coastal lanes navigable also at night. One by one they are lit and remain; stormy night after stormy night the lighthouses shine, as clear and trusting as a child's soul shines through the body's sickness and fevers; the lighthouse casts its regular, reassuring beams across foaming stretches of ocean. Attention, says the light, it's dangerous to sail here, go outside. But that's not all the light tells. It also tells that in this tower, by this light, a pair of eyes is always on watch across the sea, day and night, no matter what the weather. Be it dead calm or storm. While the breakers pound like wet fists against the tower's walls, or whip all the way up to the light so the whole lighthouse shakes, so even the half-meter-thick granite blocks tremble like trees in the wind. There is always someone keeping watch out across the sea from the tower. And those who have sailed along the coast on a stormy night know that where the light shines there is also rescue, should an accident happen. Lighthouse folk live there, quiet and lonely people, sometimes two or four officials alone for weeks on a barren island, sometimes with their entire families, with goats and small farms, a whole life, on a patch of ground far out to sea. There they live, those who must look after the engineers' constructions and make sure they function day and night. Some used to be seamen, others are unpromoted officers or students, dreamers and men with hermit natures, unsuited to life ashore; some are addicted to drinking, others are dependability personified, some have found God out there, others long to be ashore the whole time and avoid their colleagues. At such a lighthouse the officers can carry out their duties for months at a time without exchanging a word because they have said to each other everything they had to say long ago; they polish lamp glass and remove condensate, they keep the lighthouse logbook and make meteorological observations in total silence and loathing—but when a vessel goes aground and fires off its distress flares, they know what they need to do; then they must go out into the storm together and try to shoot a rescue line to the disabled vessel, or set out to sea in the lighthouse rescue boat, despite wind and weather, and maneuver themselves through the breakers, if it is possible to row at all. They must do things that would have made any little engineer in his laboratory wet his pants with terror, and they must operate like one man; they must practice the precise, wordless craft of heroic rescue.

Because shipwreck and loss can still occur. Oh yes, shipwrecks still occur, despite all the lights that are lit, despite all the lamps and markers placed as warnings along Norden's coasts, by islands, underwater reefs, and skerries. Also this December morning in the Baltic—58°23'30'' north latitude, 19°11'45'' east latitude, if anyone cares to look on a chart, or 1°10' east, figured from Stockholm's Observatory, for anyone who prefers that— more specifically, December, 13, 1898.

TWO

GUESTS ON A GRAY MORNING

For this is the story of Josefa, and perhaps it begins here, this early December morning at Sandön Lighthouse Station. Or perhaps it begins later; perhaps the story of Josefa begins the following summer, when things went so badly with Aid, as the lighthouse folk called the poor half-mute lighthouse keeper Enberg, or perhaps it begins later the same winter, when her catechization went so poorly. Or perhaps when engineer Palm came to the island. Although perhaps the story of Josefa begins a dozen years earlier and even a few more years before that, already before she was born, before she had run the first barefoot steps in the fine white sand or jumped from pebble to pebble on the beach, before she had taken her walks on the island in the lee of Sandön's tall solemn pine trees and sung her songs, and before she had collected her treasury of shells and round stones, of amber and seagull eggs, of Roman coins, Carolingian silver, and Hanseatic pennies washed up by the waves and given to her from unknown deeps and times that still lay hidden out there. Because when does a story really begin? And when does it end? And when does a life begin and end?

The dead had arrived during the night. They were still missing two. But five forms filled the little room with a great, silent presence. Two were stretched across the kitchen table, still in their sea clothing, one already lay on the bench with his clothes off, and in the front parlor lay the last two. Outside the windows a cold wind turned the morning air grayish white, and the grasses in the sand trembled uneasily. But here inside it was warm, warmer than usual; she wondered if the corpses made it warm. They were so silent. Their hair had already been combed and hymnbooks laid under their chins. They did not yet have shirts on, but they were covered with the finest linen in the house to hide their nakedness. In the corner by the roaring stove lay piles of shapeless black sea clothing. She glimpsed some boots. A faint odor of saltwater vapors reached her from the dark clothes taken off the dead. The dead themselves were white and solemn. She walked around the rooms, from dead man to dead man, and looked at them. Josefa had never seen dead people like this before. And deep inside her something throbbed dully at the sight, cold and warm at the same time.

She had been awakened late at night by all the commotion, the men had come and gone. By the time she got dressed the worst was over down there on the beach. Things had gone badly, and the men had begun to return to the house already. She had to go out to the entry and open the door. Her father, the lighthouse master, towered before her in the doorway and she gave a start, he stood there in the darkness like the wet ghost of a drowned sailor; still, she was glad that it was he, safe and sound. Behind him she could dimly make out the other men, like more ghosts, in black oilskins, a whole procession. They were carrying something.

Her father looked at her in surprise, a bit disapprovingly.

"You're up."

"What's going on, Father?" she asked.

"A schooner has been aground the whole night. We didn't see her until it was too late."

"I see," she whispered.

"It broke apart before we got a rescue boat out to her. Stand aside now, Josefa, we need to get them into the house." She suddenly understood what the heavy burden was that the men were carrying, and she fled back into the house, into her own room, lit the lamp with numb hands. There had been shipwrecks out here before, but she had never seen anything, had been sleeping, had been small. The only thing she had noticed was that the next day her father and Aid and the other men slept or were scraped up and worn out, and that the scheduled watches were revised and did not follow their usual rhythm. Silent survivors were given lodging for a few days. Or graves were dug. But she had escaped seeing that. Now that she was bigger, they no longer hid such things from her, and she had gotten up by herself. The rest of the night she had sat in her room and heard the door opening and closing, heard them working and struggling out there, heard her mother's voice and Maja's, and in between, her father's calm statements and Aid's little grating grunts when they were in the house warming themselves. The whole time she thought: Soon they'll come and look in on me, say hello, stick their heads in the door and smile; at least Father, and if not Father, then Aid anyway, he never forgets me, because he's promised to rescue me from perils at sea and from every kind of danger. But no one came. The voices, grunting fragments:

"—we think seven in all—seven aboard—with coal to Visby—two are still out there—wait until it gets light—impossible to—" Aid agreed in between, oh, he so totally agreed; the cracked voice sounded submissive tonight, groveling, apologetic. It was strange. And none of them came in to her. But out there in the living room Aid said something. Her father's voice rose.

"—wait until it gets light, I said!" He was displeased with Aid. Josefa had never heard her father sound displeased with him before.

"Enberg," her father usually said when he talked about Aid, "Enberg is my best man. Lord knows what I'd have done without him out here." And then Aid would usually shrug and look down, a little embarrassed when the boss praised him. But tonight something was different.

And now it was light, and she stood alone in the living room looking at the silent guests.

No one seemed to notice her today—neither the living nor the dead. Her mother and the servant girl Maja appeared not to see her, she was alone even if those two bustled in and out. They were busy putting things in order, there were still two bodies to wash, and then of course they were still missing two. Perhaps the last two would drift in during the morning, so her father and his men walked around the island to search the beaches, despite how worn out they were from their hard work.

She put on a sweater and boots and slipped out the door unseen, out into the cold wind. The sea no longer roared as loudly as during the night, but it sounded as though it would still be a good while before it calmed down. After walking for ten minutes she could see the steel-gray ocean and the white breakers in its open jaws. Far to the south, at least a kilometer away, lay the rescue boat, pulled well up onto the beach. There was wreckage to be seen, but not much. Some timbers, some coils of rope, a few boards. Perhaps more would come when the sea began to calm down. All that could be seen of the shipwreck out on the reef was a dark, crumpled shadow amid all the gray. Light still shone from both of the lighthouses here on the island; no one had yet had time to extinguish them.

She stood for a while looking out to sea, then walked aimlessly across the island, into the woods and silence. She usually walked here every morning thinking her own thoughts, in almost all kinds of weather. It was her island, and her woods. But this morning the island seemed different, the island that had taught her *everything*. Today she barely recognized the pine trees, which otherwise were her best friends, erect and calm, and always had something to tell her. Today they seemed mute and dead, almost like the centuries-old petrified pines that stood here and there, dry and dead, whitening in the wind. Once again she felt a dull throbbing somewhere in her body, not really pain, but soreness, like fire and ice at the same time. Her mouth tasted like pewter. And she couldn't sing today. It was impossible to sing now, although she usually sang in here among the trees, and she couldn't go to the chapel, as she always did in the morning. She was suddenly afraid to go there and see the crucifix and the altar painting, which she usually liked to look at. She couldn't go to the chapel at all, not today, not as long as they were lying down there and two were still missing. Just imagine if they were in the chapel, those two. Just imagine if somehow or other they had found their way up from the sea and into the chapel and stood waiting for her with wet gazes. Such things had happened before, survivors had dragged themselves ashore and gotten lost on the island, and found their way into a building—both Father and Madam Westerberg had talked about that. To say nothing of the dead, they could *also* do such things, at least she had heard both Madam Westerberg and Aid say so with certainty.

But more than anything it was one of the dead men down there in the house that suddenly made it impossible to go to the chapel; she saw him quite clearly in her mind now, even though she had let her eyes rest on his face for only a brief second: a young man with a beard. She hadn't wanted to look at any of their faces, but nevertheless her glance had happened to strike his, and now she saw him clearly in her mind. His face was in profile, his mouth was open so his teeth and some of the inside of his mouth were visible, as if his lips had stiffened around an eternal, silent death rattle. And his eyes were not completely closed, but revealed white stripes under the eyelashes.

Once again she felt a dull throbbing inside her, and she looked around for something to focus her eyes on. But everything was far away. Besides, she could not go to the chapel because there was already a dead man hanging there, above the altar, and he was just as dead as the drowned men down there who had slowly swallowed seawater as they were washed back and forth in the surf, cold and bruised. For a brief moment things went black for her, and the throbbing was still in her body. A dead man in the church, she thought, what good does that do? The chapel, which usually was filled with sound and life, where she always put fresh flowers or leaves and heather, or pussy willow branches—and then a dead man? She hadn't thought about this before, and suddenly it seemed unnatural and strange, like the rest of the island that morning. She shrugged, walked farther, forced herself to keep going, even though she was really in pain now. Had she been standing like this a long time?

Through the mist she saw a hunched figure coming toward her on the path with a rolling gait; she could dimly make out a skipper's cap. At first she grew cold with terror because maybe it was one of the dead men, but then she saw it was only old Madam Westerberg limping along in a harbor pilot's jacket and cap, one of her many inherited uniforms. Madam—for that was all she was called on the island—Madam had a number of strange outfits like that, which either had been given to her by good-hearted people or belonged to the treasure chest of clothes she had gotten after a charity collection in Fårösund many, many years ago, a decade after she became a widow. Josefa was relieved when she saw who it was. The pain in her body lessened a little too.

The old woman limped over to her, stopped, straightened her back as well as she could, squinted up at her, and smiled. She smiled contentedly.

"Well, child, ship aground last night?" Still contented.

When Josefa was very small she had thought Madam a little crazy, and had always hidden in the coattails of her father's overcoat when Madam came to the lighthouse station or when they met her on one of her father's wanderings across the island. The toothless mouth, the shriveled face, the shining soot-colored hair pulled tight around her head, the strange clothes; Josefa had been afraid of her, afraid of her rancid cloying smell, afraid of her piercing blue eyes. She remembered this now. When she got a little older, old enough to have some understanding, she thought it was exciting to visit Madam in her low-ceilinged house and listen to her tell stories, sit on a bench in the drafty living room and look at all her strange things, her beach property, as she called it; when Josefa was *that* age they had traded coins and porcelain dishes, sinkers and glass balls, stones and unusual pieces of wood, for Josefa was the only child on the island and had no friends with whom to share her treasures. But now some of the anxiety seemed to return.

"Well, child, a ship aground last night?"

"Yes, Madam Westerberg," Josefa said politely. "A schooner carrying coal to Visby."

"Then it will be a cold winter in Visby," she chuckled. "Poor people. Maybe it will be as cold for them as for me."

"I've told Father many times that he should caulk your walls and fix the cracked windowpane."

"Ah yes," sighed the old woman, her blue eyes squinting at Josefa. "Ships go aground and men are washed ashore, that's how things should be; and old people shiver, yes, yes."

Josefa nodded, but did not reply. The old woman bowed her head, then glanced up at Josefa again.

"You've grown so tall, child."

"I'm going to be confirmed this spring."

"Imagine that. Your mother sent one of the men to ask me to come and help dress the corpses."

Josefa nodded again.

"How pale you are, child!" Madam Westerberg gave her a thoughtful, knowing look. "It's probably growing sickness," she lisped. "Well, if I just had a skilling for every dead sailor I've dressed in my life, I wouldn't be sitting here; no, I'd be living in a castle in Tallinn." Madam always said things like that. There was a legend along the Baltic coast that a troll lady lived out here, daughter of the Sandö troll who inhabited the hill in the middle of the island; an old woman who walked along the beaches collecting things and drew in shipwrecked sailors, living and dead, hundreds of years old. They must have heard about Madam Westerberg, her father thought. How old could she be? Josefa didn't know, nor did her father, and maybe Madam Westerberg didn't even know herself, although she had a son who had just died of old age in Fårösund. Old as the island.

"You mustn't take this so hard," Josefa heard the old woman say, as if from far away. "In the days of beach robbers, in old Gothberg's day, then things were different. Gothberg rode along the beach on stormy nights with a lantern in his hand, and made those at sea think he was the top lantern on another vessel. So they went aground on the reef then, and Gothberg and his people killed them as soon as they came ashore, and buried the corpses under Gothberg's farm, or under the Stone House."

"But that was long ago, Madam Westerberg," Josefa said dully.

"Not longer ago than that my mother could remember," said Madam Westerberg contentedly. "There was no talk then of preparing the corpses and burying them in Christian soil by the chapel, oh no, he buried them under the house, and that was it." Usually Josefa liked to talk with Madam Westerberg, but now she began feeling uncomfortable. She had heard all the stories before, about Gothberg and the beach robbers, about Gothberg's farm and the Stone House, about every shipwreck and each nameless grave on the island, and about still much more, but *then* it was a fairy tale. Today it was different. But Madam Westerberg was in full swing now, she sat alone in her house much of the time and you couldn't stop her once she had company.

"Oh, he was a bad man, that Gothberg," she went on, "and he ruled over the island like a King Balthasar, he did indeed. If one of the servants went against his will, he chopped him down and buried him along with the others under the Stone House, or sank him in the swamp. But my dear, how pale you are."

"It's nothing, Madam," said Josefa. "I need to get going."

"No," Madam Westerberg said firmly. "Your mother sent a message with the lighthouse boy that if you were visiting me you should go back to the lighthouse station with me and help them there at home with all they need to do today."

Josefa nodded, without understanding. She had just been at home, hadn't she? She just came from there. Or how long had she been walking around on the island? The sky was overcast, and it was hard to determine the time according to the light. Maybe she had been here for hours, spirited away by trolls, without remembering it. Or maybe she really *had* been invisible this morning.

Again she felt the pain deep inside her, and now a dark trembling seemed to rise in her, all the way up to her eyes. She heard her name, from far away. A moment later Madam Westerberg tugged on her, she opened her eyes and saw the old woman standing beside her.

"What's the matter with you, girl?" Madam said worriedly nearby, and her voice was suddenly soft and gentle, like a young mother's, and Josefa felt better. "I think I lost you," said Madam, and Josefa nodded. "I had to call you. You just stood there and wouldn't come back again." The old woman scrutinized her. "Come, we'll go to the station together, so neither of us will get lost on the way." She said it jokingly, but her voice sounded worried. Josefa looked at her, but only half understood what Madam said. She was frightened herself. She had never felt like this, it was as if the dark trembling lay beneath everything else the whole time, under the island and under Madam Westerberg, under the mist and the trees and the ground they walked on, under the sea and the sky and the shipwreck out there; yes, actually it was as if it lay under and behind her very self, and threatened to rise up in her again at any moment. Had she been away a long time? Josefa kept her eyes firmly focused on the path. Walking helped a little anyway; Madam Westerberg limped behind her and that made Josefa feel safer.

"To the left here," said Madam Westerberg, and Josefa had to stop. She really didn't recognize where she was. "My dear child," said Madam Westerberg behind her. "Surely you see we need to go to the left. We're right by your house, after all. There's your house."

144

Josefa looked around. Then the landscape fell into place for her. But for a brief moment it was as if she really were on another island, a place she had never been before, distant and unfamiliar. And this moment made her afraid, but not afraid as in dreams or anxiety, this was a distant and unfamiliar fear. As if it wasn't *she* who was afraid. She was as unfamiliar as everything else.

So they went down toward the cluster of houses between the tall towers. The lighthouse lamps had been extinguished.

THREE

THE WELL

The dead shine in the lamplight, white and yellow.

"There you are at last," says her mother impatiently. "Where have you been, and in this weather?"

Josefa does not answer. She stands in the living room, and just then her father and Aid arrive carrying a new dead man they found at Stora Beckrevet; he hangs between them, dripping, heavy, and limp as a bunch of seaweed. They maneuver him onto the table with a one and two and heave. "We found the other one too," says her father. "He's lying way down by Säludden." Madam has taken off her cap and jacket and stands in her tattered black muslin dress with a dirty gray sweater over it, carefully inspecting the dead man. Maja comes with yet another large wooden bowl of warm water from the washhouse; she gives Josefa a brief, dark look. Josefa's mother is impatient today. There is something that comes over her once in a while, a restlessness, a dissatisfaction with everything, especially on stormy days like this, or when the winter has worn on; she moves restlessly from one thing to another, from task to task, only half notices what happens around her or what is said, her face tense and expressionless under her knot of hair. She doesn't look at them then—at either Josefa or Father—

Mother, who usually is pretty and fun, and who reads and mends clothes and bakes and cooks and makes up party games and plays. If I had a castle in Tallinn. If I rode in a carriage at Haga. On those restless days she often goes to her potted plants, which stand on the windowsills in the living room next to clean white lace curtains; she pinches shoots and waters them carefully, moves them farther into the room if it is very cold outside. On such days, Mother *is not* there, she is in the silent, windless little world of the potted plants—she hides there, as in a secret garden, and the sound of wind and rain cannot reach her, not the deep dark forest, and not the sight of the endless Baltic Sea ice that surrounds the island, from horizon to horizon. The plants stand there growing so peacefully, and she pinches off every brown leaf in the white light. "Hush," says Father, "let Mother be, she's *weather sick*." Mother stands there with the small green flames of life and pinches and pinches. That's how she is today too, but it's the dead who have her impatient attention now. She is impatient with them, no matter how dead they are. Without a word she hands Josefa a sponge. She does not even look at her. Josefa swallows. The men pull the clothes off the dead, cover their nakedness. Josefa does not look at them, does not want to see, looks in another direction, looks toward the windows, looks toward the plants. And suddenly she understands something about her mother that she has not understood before. An odor rises from the sponge, it reminds one of vinegar and tickles the nose; and she does not protest when her mother carefully but firmly grasps her and turns her face toward the dead man.

"See here, Josefa, you're old enough now to help us. You must help to wash him."

Her father hears this, stops on his way out, looks at her mother in surprise.

"Have you really considered this carefully?" Her mother does not look at him, does not reply.

"You need to wash all the salt water off him, you see," her mother says firmly, but kindly. Although Josefa does not think it's so kind. Maybe it only *sounds* kind. She wishes her mother was *Mother* today, and not like this. Again she feels a small prick, like a needle, deep inside her.

"I'm talking to you, Rakel," says her father. He usually never uses

Mother's first name. He stands over by the door with Aid, his face gray with weariness. Aid stands there shuffling, looks down at his feet. Doesn't dare say anything. What's wrong? He seems out of everything today.

"Mmm?" says her mother.

"Don't you think this is too much for Josefa?" Tired, her father is so tired. But he's angry too. Usually he's never angry. Is he angry at Mother? At Aid? Or at the whole shipwreck? They hadn't seen a shipwreck for some time.

"I think she's old enough now to see what it's all about."

"She's a child," her father says calmly.

"I wasn't much older when you proposed and brought me out here."

"Yes, but—" Tired, he's so tired.

"It won't hurt her, Kalle."

"Yes, but *Rakel*! Josefa isn't like—"

"She may end up as a wife on a reef too," says her mother and smiles, but it sounds cutting nonetheless.

"Wife on a reef—" He has struggled with the breakers and rescue boat all night, and now this; Josefa feels sorry for him, and says valiantly: "I'm big enough now." She gives him just a quick look. He half raises his arms and lets them fall in a gesture of resignation, growls something to Aid, and they leave.

Josefa stands looking at the dead man. She lets out her breath in relief. He really doesn't look so bad, and his eyes are closed. Completely closed. Actually, it looks as though he is sleeping. His hair is wet. He is a middle-aged man, and he almost looks as if he has just taken a bath and gone to sleep on the beach. But something is different nonetheless. Josefa looks at him more closely. It's not that his face and hands are a little scraped up, not that he is so pale, not that he is completely motionless. But he has no breath. Something is missing. And then she sees that there *is* no one there. *Everything* is missing. No one is present. She holds the sponge more easily now, and begins to wash his right arm according to her mother's directions. Maja washes the left one. Her mother takes his legs, which are muscular and hairy. Madam Westerberg prepares the grave clothes. Josefa dips the sponge often, washes quickly and impersonally, as though she were washing an object. Her hands and face grow warm from the work, and her knees are still a bit weak in fact, but she feels better, and it no longer hurts so much either, inside her.

"You're doing a good job, Josefa," says her mother, and this time she sounds genuinely kind, sounds like *Mother*, and Josefa feels proud. This really wasn't so difficult. It wasn't so bad. It was just a thing after all, an arm without anyone present in it. And so she doesn't avoid looking at him naked when they dress him in a grave shirt, a task which isn't so easy for that matter, because he is heavy, twice as heavy now that he is dead, it seems. She had no idea that a man was so heavy. Josefa had thought he would be cold, but he is as warm as the air in the room. They lay him on the bench. Josefa feels almost happy as she stands there with the others looking at her work, her first corpse ready for the coffin. He lies white and peaceful and hasn't even noticed all the hard work they have done. He looks a little bored, to tell the truth. Josefa almost has to smile. What an ungrateful fellow he is. But he looks better than before, his hair is combed and his chin tied up with gauze strips; it looks almost as if he has a toothache.

"Well, that wasn't so bad," says her mother.

"No," Josefa agrees.

"You did a good job," her mother says again.

"Yes," says Josefa. She is still a little dizzy, a little distant, but strangely warm and calm, almost as if she'd had a swig of rum, such as her father has given her a few times when they have been out in an open boat in the winter; warm and golden.

But then her father and Aid arrive, and she feels the prick the moment she hears them rumbling out in the entry; they come carrying one more now, still another, and even before they are inside the door, she knows this will be different. She feels a very sharp prick, and for a moment she thinks she is going to faint. One more. The door opens. The first thing she notices is that her father and Aid move so easily. When they arrived with the earlier one, they shuffled across the floor with the strain of carrying him, but this time it's as if they have hardly any burden. It's just a boy, and they lay him on the table, light as a feather. The abrupt movement leaves his lower arm dangling in the air, a faint ring of water drops from his sleeve, and the palm of his hand hits the table with a plop, almost as if he wanted to emphasize something, even if he is so young and ought not to have anything to say. Her father glances quickly at her mother, but her mother just says that it went very well, Josefa did a good job, and with that her father can bear no more; he is worn out, he staggers into the bedroom and she hears him pull off the worst of the wet clothes and throw himself onto the bed. Aid keeps fumbling with the door, he tries to say something, oh, why doesn't he ever manage to say what he wants to say? He is *not* mute, he *can* talk. She sees the look he sends her, yes, he understands, he is trying to be considerate, but then he leaves quietly, clicks the door behind him, goes to his own room, and they are alone with the dead boy. Josefa is alone. They take off his clothes, she no longer hears what her mother says, or Madam Westerberg's cackling, she supports him under the back of his head while they pull off his oilskins and sweater, she feels his hair against her fingertips. He is about the same age as she, or a little older. He looks serious, a little stern, but at the same time has a gentle expression, especially when his head falls forward so his chin touches his chest. He is much more present than the previous one, he is much nearer, and she notices how heavy his head is. When the sweater, soaked with seawater, slips over his head, she loses her grasp, and he falls backward, hits the back of his head with a loud thud. She gives a start, and her heart skips a beat. "I'm sorry," she says softly, and she doesn't know if she is saying it to her mother and the others, or to the dead boy. She looks at him as if she half expects he will raise himself on his arm in annoyance and scold her for the way she handled him, but he lies as still as ever. A boy.

"Now, now, Josefa," says her mother. "It's not so bad."

"I'm sorry," Josefa says again. "I lost my grip."

"That's all right, Josefa. He doesn't notice it at all, you know."

"Don't say that," begins Madam Westerberg. "Nobody knows such things. Maybe the dear departed can—"

"Hush, Madam," says her mother sternly, and smiles a little. "You don't know anything about this."

Madam keeps silent, but continues to talk within herself. They take off the rest of his clothes. He is smooth and soft to touch, like velvet, with frail thin shoulders. And a slender neck. His hair is thick and tousled.

"This time you can wash his face and fix his hair, Josefa," says her mother, handing her a basin and sponge and comb. She stands with the dead boy's face between her hands and washes him carefully, trembling slightly. His eyelashes are very black against his white skin, his lips red and full. And now it happens to Josefa again, she can feel it, a dull throbbing deep within her, a feeling of heat and cold that trembles, trembles; she seems to go far outside herself, watches herself wash the stranger's face and hair. Then she takes the comb and lets it glide through his hair. He is naked and she can see all of him. She combs his hair, pulls out one tangle after another; he has sand and sea wrack and small pieces of starfish in his hair, his ears are small and pale, almost like her own, it feels almost as if she is touching her own ears, her own hair. He certainly hadn't combed his hair for a while before he fell into the sea. And his hair is so soft. Josefa notices how the room begins to burst around her, the kitchen, which she has known her whole life, fails her now, she has to keep busy, grasps his curls firmly, feels the dark trembling rise all the way up to her face, and she can't see the boy any longer, and she is sad about that, because she doesn't want to lose sight of his face, she thinks his face is one of the most beautiful things she has ever seen, she feels so sorry for him, even more sorry than for her father and mother and Aid and herself, because he is lying there and has hit his head with starfish and everything, and the last she sees is his face before she collapses in a blood darkness, which isn't even a darkness but a huge absence from everything, it's as if she falls into a well, a nothingness where she doesn't exist.

That was how Josefa got sick, at the same time as the first bleeding came.

Later they told her how everything had happened, gently, so as not to frighten her. But this first afternoon she only noticed that her whole body was heavy and sore when she finally awakened to life again in her bed, and her mother and father sat beside her. It was late in the day, and their faces were tired and a little blurred in the gray winter light. They sat talking together, quiet and worried, and for a while did not realize she was awake. She lay looking at their faces, heard them speaking, but without noticing what they said. Just heard the tone of their voices. That they were talking together in a way they almost never did otherwise. And in this light it seemed she could see their faces in another way, as young faces, and now she realized for the first time that her parents had also had faces before she was born, yes, before they met each other—their own faces, totally alone and individual. But the surprising thing was that at the same time Josefa could see that her father had begun to be an old man. His hair was nearly completely white after all. Whereas her mother still looked almost like a young girl. There was a great distance between them. Even more than the twenty years. They seemed both alone and together now. At the same time. Then they realized Josefa was awake. Her mother called for Maja, and Maja came with bouillon, proper meat soup it was, and her father held Josefa's hand carefully and just smiled for a long time, and he was Father again, had his face, the face that was hers alone.

"You frightened us," he said. Then he didn't say anything for a long time, but she could tell that he had been crying.

She drank the bouillon.

"I'm sorry, my child," said her mother, holding her hand. Mother. "I'm sorry. I shouldn't have asked you to do that."

"It doesn't matter, Mother," said Josefa.

"Yes it does," said her mother with lowered eyes.

"Where's Aid?" asked Josefa.

"Enberg sailed to Fårösund for the doctor." Josefa gave her father a frightened look, half sat up in bed.

"In this weather?"

"That's what I said too," said her mother. "But he absolutely insisted on going."

Her father shook his head gently.

"Like he did when you were born, you know, Josefa."

"Yes," said Josefa. The story of Enberg's two-day rowing trip before she came into the world was among those told every year, on her birthday and on other special days, or when her father would tell a guest what unusually good workers he had out here. "Nobody would go," her father would say. "There were large vessels lying weather-bound at Krykudden that didn't dare to go to Fårösund, but Enberg rowed two days in an open boat to fetch the doctor, like the first-rate fellow he is. Yes, as I always say: Enberg is my best man out here. Lord knows what I'd have—" The birth was long and difficult, and old doctor Johansson arrived just in time. As her father always said later: Enberg seemed to have had a feeling about it in the last weeks before the delivery, again and again he had talked about getting the doctor. No one had taken him seriously, not even Josefa's mother, despite the fact that she hadn't been well and had pain. But she said old Madam had helped more children come into the world out here than there lay seals on Säludden on a sunny day, and it always went well because this was a lucky island. It was a lucky island. But Enberg would not give up, he rowed away as soon as the birth pains started and it was obvious that something was wrong. The doctor arrived just in time.

Today he had sailed to Fårösund again.

Josefa thought about him as she lay in bed, thought about his being all alone out in the rain and heavy sea spray, and he was already worn out from before. She hoped he would have a favorable wind and didn't have to tack or row. She hoped he didn't feel too lonely out there, without her. She hoped that it wasn't too cold on the thwart, and that there would be no fog. She hoped he arrived safely in the harbor. Because Aid was her friend.

For a while she let the soup work in her body, then she felt herself growing tired in another way, tired as if she had run the length of the island, from Tärnudden to Bredsands Udde. Her brain was tired too, she felt light-headed, as if she had been out in the icy wind for many hours. She lay on her side and fell asleep just when her mother lit the lamp. She did not know what had happened. She did not know that she'd had a convulsive attack that had knocked her to the floor, that she had lain there, trembling and shaking, for a long time, while the whites in her eyes came and went, and her heart and breathing worked so hard they thought she would burst. She did not know that she had made strange sounds, or that she had soiled herself. But she understood that something was different, that she was different now. She had bled, this she knew without asking, because she could feel it, and in the moment before she fell asleep she thought about the dead boy and about his face.

FOUR

REPORT ABOUT A BUTTERFLY

The island is a long stretch of forest in the middle of the sea, eight kilometers long and six kilometers at the widest point. Within the forest, the air is always calm and silent. When you come to the edge of the forest and out onto the heath leading down to the beach, you are met by a gulp of wind and surf.

Josefa's childhood was a long silence in the forest. There were her father and her mother and then her. And Aid. Her father was enthroned above everyone, higher than the others, yes even higher than God. Big, with white sideburns and a uniform, king of the island. One of the guests from some summers back, she did not remember whether it was a painter or a botanist, had called her father Hottentottenpotentate, and her father had thought that was splendid. He ruled mildly and absolutely from his office in the annex. As *his* father had done before him. There he had all his books and memoranda, his tobacco pipes and trophies. Her father was not an educated man, but he had read a good deal on his own. Above all, he knew everything about his island and about the surrounding islands and coastlines, and about everyone who had lived there. He knew the truth and he knew all the tall tales, and he could pass the one thing off as the other, if he was in the mood. He was in his element telling stories over the punch bowl or with a long-stemmed pipe, especially on the rare occasions when guests came from Gotland, or even better, from the mainland. Then fun and jokes blazed around her father, and Josefa had often thought that he could have been a ship's captain. But in everyday life he was a serious man with orderly habits; he made observations and kept the lighthouse logbook very systematically. He had learned from his father that it is dangerous to sit with your hands in your lap at such a place, for then you finally end up just sitting. So he was busy from early morning until late evening, also when he had off-duty watch, even though he was certainly no longer a young man. He repaired buildings, went seal hunting, set nets, made inspection tours, fed the horse, tarred the boat, worked with his collections, wrote letters, sent for packages of books, read to Josefa and taught her, because as the highest public official on the island he was responsible for seeing that the island's children—namely, she—received the necessary schooling. And he demanded equally strict order and discipline from the lighthouse keepers and the other workers, to keep them from squabbling too much among themselves. This especially applied when the men brought their families along. When Josefa was smaller, two lighthouse keepers with wives and children had lived next to each other in a lighthouse station building for a couple of years, and there had been nothing but wrangling from New Year's to midsummer and absolute Indian war from midsummer to Christmas. Josefa missed the children when the term of service was over for the two families, but her father did not miss them, and certainly not their mothers.

It was different with Mother. Like her husband and Josefa, she felt at home on the island, it belonged to her. She took care of the new lighthouse folk who came, helped them get settled, maintained discipline with them and made sure they scrubbed their rooms regularly and wore somewhat decent clothes. She served Sunday dinners and coffee and sweets, so people would feel like fine folk; she kept the maid busy all day and as far away from the lighthouse fellows as possible. But those girls never stayed more than a year or two; by then they needed, and wanted, to go ashore. She held devotions and ordered supplies, she wrote letters, long letters, to everyone she knew and did not know in other places, and she constantly sewed the finery they would wear during the fourteen days in the year when they had vacation and went to the mainland. She also came up with games and playacting, and when they expected a visit to the island, whether it was inspectors or artists or scientists, she looked forward to it. These visits were her mother's moments even more than her father's; she worked for weeks, and put Josefa and the maid to work with the preparations. The lighthouse master's house shone from top to bottom then, the fish soup simmered, the damask tablecloths glistened, the silverware gleamed, so the mainland people would see they did things properly out here. And when she wasn't weather sick, she was Father's best friend and helper; it was enough just to see them walking together, hand in hand, to the chapel each Sunday. She supported him in everything, made clean copies of his letters (his spelling was a little uncertain), and packed him a good lunch when he was going out on a hike. She worried when he was at sea, and she was proud of him when he came home with fish or seal. There was rarely a harsh word spoken between them.

Her father took hikes with Josefa from the time she was small and showed her the special places he'd had in the forest when he was a boy, and they went to say hello to Madam and to the woodcutters who stayed in huts on the island during the summer. He showed her birds and seals, explained to her that she shouldn't disturb the gray sea eagle when it had young, told her where dead people were buried, and took her along to set nets. And he knew better than anyone where the sandbanks and underwater reefs were, and how they moved when the wind was from the east or north for a long time; he knew where the currents flowed and where it was dangerous to swim in an east wind. Or they rowed out and fished. But when he went seal hunting, she was not allowed to go along.

The other man in Josefa's life was Aid. He wasn't one of those who came for a couple of years and later disappeared; Josefa couldn't imagine but that he had always been there. Although actually she knew that he had come as a lighthouse assistant the year before she was born and never went back to the mainland again, never asked to be transferred. Something had driven him out to them, and something kept him there. He was silent, some thought mute, but that was because of his voice, which was cracked as the result of an accident. He was embarrassed to use it. He never talked about the accident nor about the time before he came out here; maybe that was why it seemed as though he had always been here. On the whole, he did not speak unnecessarily, and if he spoke it was softly in monosyllables, so the crack in his voice would not be so noticeable. But he talked with Josefa when they were alone. The cracked voice had settled in all parts of him, in his eyes and in his movements. That's how he was when he came. His position had quietly improved; now he was her father's next in command and his right-hand man. She knew that her father, like most others who only experienced the *half-mute* Enberg, didn't have very high regard for his intellect. Her father *knew* there was nothing wrong with Enberg's mental capabilities and that he was certainly not mute. Aid could both play music and read well, and moreover, he collected insects and natural preparations from the island; his collections were even better than her father's. But perhaps something still remained from when Aid first arrived out here: her father repeated everything he said to Enberg twice, the way one does to children and dull-witted people. Aid paid no attention to it. Just now and then sent Josefa a strange smile if the boss was especially thorough in explaining something. Listen to him, said the smile, he still thinks I have trouble understanding.

But at the same time she could see that her father depended on Aid in everything; like a loyal dog, Enberg accompanied her father when he went hunting or out in the boat. Sometimes they walked arm in arm along the beach, her father talking and gesturing, Aid listening patiently, and a stab of happiness would go through Josefa at the sight of them. Her father and her best friend. Because she loved Aid, loved his hands, which mounted insects or nailed together boats and could play so beautifully on the reed organ in the chapel, loved him because he had rowed to get the doctor when she came into the world, loved him because he had promised to save her from all dangers, loved him almost like a father. And she loved to hear him tell her things in his grating voice, no matter how bad it sounded. When he spoke it was as if fine gravel were washing back and forth in his voice, and for Josefa that was a reassuring sound. Only with her was he unashamed. He helped her to study her lessons. And he went to the chapel with her, just the two of them, and there they had their lessons together. Almost every day, miracles occurred—miracles that no one knew about, and that made her giddy and happy—when Aid paged through some new music he had ordered, seated himself at the keyboard, pumped the bellows, and she stood beside him and took a deep breath.

But otherwise he was silent.

Silence reigned in the forest, and this was Josefa's world. Here she grew up with the morning light and falling dusk, with the mist and the snow; here she was created in the fragrance of heather and moss. She knew every tree and every clearing and every root, and at the same time they were new every day. Every place was new each morning, and she inhabited the island with invisible figures and animals, friends she made up herself or knew from her books. She talked with them and surrounded herself with them; they had their own places and their own lives, and she spun long, endless tales in which both they and she took part. Some stories were sad, others were exciting and fun. In reality, there were no creatures in here other than the birds and insects, along with some sheep and cattle. Here she was away from the sea and the wind. The only sounds were those of the woodpeckers and the crows, the cuckoo and the green siskin. A quiet rustling in the treetops. The droning of dung beetles and wasps. Almost never a butterfly, so far from the mainland.

The first time Josefa saw a butterfly she thought it was a flying flower. She had been picking flowers on Höga Åsen when one of the flowers flew up in front of her nose and headed into the forest, fluttering like a petal in the wind. She described this strange phenomenon to Aid, who grew very excited.

"What are you saying, child! Have you seen a *butterfly*?" The cracked voice cracked even more on the rare occasions he raised it; the sound seemed to divide in two and vanish into thin air. "*Here?*"

"It was a flower that flew away." She was nine years old that summer. Aid got the insect net and portfolio, pad and pencil, and together they went out into the light and the grassy turf to discover where the little sun-yellow guest had hidden itself on their island.

"It can't have gone far," said Aid. "It doesn't have many places to go, you know."

"That's true," said Josefa.

"We'll find it, I'm sure," said Aid. "Well, well, so you've seen a *butterfly* here on the island—that's not bad. That's big news." This was a long sentence to come from Aid, even when speaking to her.

Aid was tall and lean, with thin brown hair. He had brown eyes and a gaze light as a breeze. He didn't look very strong, but was strong. He didn't look particularly intelligent either. Quite ugly. His nose was long and crooked. Josefa liked to look at him. He was her best friend after all. Next to her father, of course, but it was different with someone who stood above God.

"The association in Stockholm will congratulate me when I report this."

"Why, Uncle Enberg?"

"Until now, only moths have been registered out here—you know what they are, don't you? They're the ones that fly against the window on summer evenings."

"Yes." She shuddered a little at the thought. They were those dark, winged creatures that could fly into the room in the evening if she lay reading with the window open, that swarmed around the lamp with a humming sound, round and round the glass chimney, wilder and wilder, until they were unlucky enough to fly right over the opening and get burned. Then they fell down, sometimes into the blue flame where they burned up with a disgusting smell, and Josefa swore that she could hear them scream when they got burned and fell. For them, the lamp chimney must be like a dreadful shaft, a well right down into the lake of fire and brimstone itself.

"Butterflies are creatures similar to moths, but they belong to the day," said Enberg. On summer nights insects collected on the glass panes at the top of the lighthouse, and there Enberg harvested his largest catches of the island's tiny creatures. It was simply a matter of pouring handfuls of potassium cyanide onto them right on the windows. "They think the lighthouse is the moon," Enberg would say, "and that I'm the man in the moon."

Traveling entomologists, who stayed on the island for a few weeks at a time to register insects, did not understand how Enberg could have gotten such a complete collection, because they rushed around with scoop nets and did not think about the two large alluring lights that hovered above their heads at night. Or perhaps they were too dizzy to go up there. And Enberg did not tell them.

"We have five regular moth species here," he said, "but not butterflies. We lie too far out to sea. Yes, yes. Much too far out to sea."

The whole morning they walked around hunting for the little yellow butterfly. It was Josefa who finally caught sight of it, and they captured it, she remembered that well. She was nine years old. She sat with the little butterfly in her cupped hands and she was nine years old and the sun never set, and Aid was there and the island was there and she was alive. And the butterfly was the most beautiful thing she had ever seen. Its legs clung to the palm of her hand and it was almost like a tiny boat with a sail and crossbeam when it gently moved its feelers and its tall wings, which looked like very thin bits of paper. Even more beautiful than any boat Aid could whittle for her.

"Come now, princess," whispered Aid, and when he whispered his voice was completely different, completely normal, because you didn't hear the crackle. "We have to put this under glass so I have something to show the fine gentlemen in Stockholm."

"Oh no," she said, and the thought made things turn black inside her. "Do we have to?"

"Of course we do," said Aid, and he was no longer whispering. "Otherwise they'll just think I'm not telling the truth, and you certainly don't want them to think that about your poor Uncle Enberg, do you?"

She gave him a dubious look. Was he really going to put this sunny little friend on a needle in a box? Aid already had a glass jar in his hand, the cotton at the bottom was as innocently white and soft as a pillow, but under it was a layer of gypsum that contained potassium cyanide. The thought revolted her, and she said: "But the butterfly is so alone out here."

The jar was already open, and she could smell the vapors. Aid looked at her, then he screwed the cover back on.

"Let them think I'm lying," he said firmly. He was whispering again. "Let it fly away," he said, and nodded to her. So she let it fly away and did not see it again that summer; but the next summer there were two, and they flew across the heather together. And that's how the little *Sideris pallens* came to be registered as the island's single butterfly species (*observed only*).

FIVE

A FINE CARD GAME

That was how Josefa entered young womanhood, and on the third day Aid returned from Fårösund with a very reluctant doctor. It was not the same man who had delivered Josefa. This was one of the new breed, one who was miserable sitting in an open boat for a whole day. He was wet and irritable when he arrived at the house, and it took a long time by the stove and plenty of meat soup before he thawed out. He talked with her parents for a long while. Then, wearing her father's best Icelandic sweater and with her mother right behind him carrying a cup of coffee and his medical bag, he went in to see Josefa, who was sitting in bed reading.

"Well," he said a bit crossly, "you don't look so bad." He sat down. Josefa put aside her book. He motioned to her mother to leave them, groped in his bag for a stethoscope and tongue depressor; Josefa had to lift her slip and undershirt, and he listened. Then he looked down her throat, and tapped her knees with a hammer, and he stuck her with a pin while she had to keep her eyes closed and say where he stuck her.

"Are you dizzy?" he asked.

"No," said Josefa.

"Has anything like this happened to you before?"

"I beg your pardon?" said Josefa.

"Have you ever . . . lost consciousness like this before? Fallen down, I mean."

"No," said Josefa.

"Hmm, yes. What's your name?"

"Josefa," said Josefa. "Josefa Jacobsson."

"I see. My name is Doctor Brunsell. And how old are you?"

"I'm going to be confirmed in the spring," said Josefa.

"I see. Turn toward the light," said the doctor, "and look at my finger." She looked at his finger, which he held up in the light. It was long and pale and slender. He had nice hands. With his other hand he pulled out her eyelids and peered into her eyes through a tiny telescope.

"Do you see anything, Doctor?" Josefa asked.

"No," he said. "How are you otherwise, miss? Do you have a good appetite?"

"Yes," said Josefa. "I'm fine."

"Have you had monthly bleeding before?"

"This was the first time," Josefa whispered.

"Can you read without getting tired?"

"Yes," said Josefa.

"You don't get a headache or anything?"

"No," said Josefa.

"What are you reading?"

"*The Jungle Book*," said Josefa.

"That's exciting," said the doctor. "How much is eleven plus thirteen?"

"Twenty-four."

"What letter in the alphabet comes before L?"

"K."

"Good. And you haven't had any further attacks since that morning?"

"No," said Josefa. "I feel fine."

"Then you *are* fine," said the doctor. "You can get up and go out in the fresh air."

"Thank you," said Josefa.

"How did it feel, when you got sick?"

Josefa looked at him, thought about the question.

"I don't know," she began, "I was just gone."

"How did you feel immediately before it happened?"

"Far away."

"Did you have pain?"

"I felt sore. And I was warm and cold."

"Do you remember anything from when you were gone?"

Josefa had to think again.

"It was yellow," she said. "Everything was yellow. But that was at the very end, just before I woke up. At first everything was dark."

"Aha," said the doctor. He had red sideburns and seemed more pleasant now after they had talked a little. "And you're quite sure that you've never been—ah—gone like that before?"

"No," said Josefa, "I'm not sure, because how could I know, if I was gone?"

The doctor smiled.

"Well, well," he said. "Which of the animals in *The Jungle Book* do you like best?"

"Bagheera," said Josefa without hesitation. Then she added: "But Baloo is kinder. He reminds me of Aid."

"I beg your pardon?" said the doctor.

"Uncle Enberg, I mean," said Josefa. "The man who went to get you in Fårösund, Doctor."

"I see," said the doctor, and smiled again. "Yes, that was certainly . . . kind of him."

Her mother had been standing outside the door the whole time. Now she knocked and came in. Her father followed right behind her. The doctor looked at them.

"She's fine," he said, "for the moment. But it sounds as if perhaps she's had an epileptic seizure."

They gave him a long look.

"Epilepsy," said the doctor. "It means one gets attacks like that now and then. It's usually not dangerous, except that one can get hurt when one falls."

"Is there . . . any medicine," her mother began.

"Unfortunately, no," said the doctor. "One has to live quietly and calmly, and avoid excitement. And somebody has to take care of the sick person, while she's sick. A classic illness, as far as that goes," he said, this time turning more to her father. "It's described in the early literature.

Many great historical figures have had it. Saints. In olden days they called it the holy sickness. A person could have visions. Caesar had it, and perhaps Alexander as well. And Paul, on the way to Damascus."

"What causes it?" asked her father. "Has she been infected, or—"

"We don't know anything about the cause, unfortunately, Mr. Jacobsson. But it's not infectious, that's certain."

"Isn't there something we can do?" asked her father.

"No," said the doctor. "If the attacks should become more frequent, you can give her bromine drops twice a day. I'll leave you a bottle. She can take it in bread or tea. It makes one very tired. But you can adjust it according to the frequency of the attacks. With women, the attacks usually come once a month."

Her father gave the doctor a bleak look. He bit his lip. For a moment Josefa thought he was going to cry.

"She's only had one attack, after all," the doctor said comfortingly. "And it's not certain she will have any more, or that they will be so strong, for that matter. She doesn't seem like a typical epileptic in other respects; she's lively and intelligent. We'll have to wait and see. But if she gets many violent attacks, send me a message again. And if it happens, the most important thing is that she be lying on something soft and be kept warm. Rubbing the long muscles can help. It's easy to be frightened when you see the attack, but the patient isn't in pain. You must keep her from biting herself. A wad of cloth between her teeth will work fine."

Then he turned to Josefa. "Most people can sense when an attack is coming," he said. "They feel strange and dizzy. Might feel some jerking, in a hand or other parts of the body. If you notice that, you must sit down, or lie down completely, and call for someone."

"Call for someone," said Josefa.

The doctor was not particularly good at playing Knock and lost the first three rounds after dinner. He did not really know when he should knock and when it was best to trick. But Lighthouse Master Jacobsson and his wife were not especially in the mood for playing either, at least not at first, so Josefa won every time. She had been allowed to get up, had been outside and taken a long walk before dinner, and her cheeks were rosy from the fresh air and the toddy. She had been allowed to put on her best dress, a red velvet one, and had tied a matching ribbon around her neck. Pretty girl, thought the doctor. Or will be. Way out here. Well, well. It had become clear that Doctor Brunsell was not one who really appreciated a doctor's life at the mouth of a fjord. To tell the truth, he thought Fårösund was the outermost limits of civilization, a kind of Qaanaaq, and he was homesick for Göteborg. To him, Göteborg seemed almost like Paris; in his mind his hometown sparkled with towers and spires and lights and amusing people and parties and a festive spirit all day long, no matter how utterly boring Göteborg was in reality. To leave Fårösund—which he had to do from time to time, of course, in an official capacity—was something he did only when absolutely necessary. Each time was equally bad. Like the trip out here, with the thin silent fellow in an open boat through fog and wind. "You must come, Doctor," the thin man had croaked, standing there in his office two days earlier, dripping with rain and seawater. "You *must* come, Doctor. But bundle up well. We've got a long trip." It had been like a message from hell. The thin man would not be dissuaded, no matter how shy he seemed. So the doctor had gone, even though he knew it involved a long sea voyage and staying overnight out here, perhaps under wretched conditions. The weather was bad and the trip dangerous. He had been frightened and seasick. But he had to admit that right now it was cozy in the lighthouse master's home. Subdued, colored lamplight glowed on polished candlesticks and fine porcelain, the tablecloths were clean and white and perfect. And the napkins had been starched. He almost forgot how far away from people he was. He'd had a good, long nap that afternoon in a soft warm bed. And now there was a blazing fire in the stove; the food had been excellent: a chicken in wine sauce, Russian peas, and rice cream for dessert. The parents were a little downcast at first, poor people; of course they must be worried. That wasn't surprising. A hard diagnosis to get. But they had entertained him well, no one could say otherwise, and the lighthouse master had at least loosened up enough during the meal to tell fascinating and rather crude stories about his island, as he called it. The doctor did not believe any of them for a moment, but they were interesting and very entertaining and presented quite intelligently, and each story was eagerly encouraged by the daughter, who obviously knew them by heart. Now as they sat playing Knock, the lighthouse master poured more toddies and offered cigars. The mood improved, the wife grew livelier too, and Lighthouse Master Jacobsson began giving his messages with a chuckle. He knocked under the table. Doctor Brunsell, who was the next player, did not really know what to do. Knock or trick? Trick or knock? He still held his original ten points, and had no chance.

"No, no, no. You've got to decide now, seriously," said Josefa. "Do you need a little help maybe?" Doctor Brunsell took a sip of his toddy and noticed that he was beginning to enjoy himself, even though they were beating him soundly.

"Yes, thank you, miss," he said. "I think I do need a little help, in fact." She gave him a sly look.

"We're not allowed to look at anyone else's cards," she announced solemnly. Her parents nodded to her with satisfaction, glanced sidelong at each other and the doctor.

"That's right, Josefa, it's not allowed," her father grunted. "Not even for guests. You should be ashamed, Doctor Brunsell, asking a child to cheat; hellfire and fistulas! Pardon my French." Josefa snickered. Turning to his wife, the lighthouse master continued: "What do you say, Mother, shall we go to the kitchen and put on the coffee before playing this round?"

"Yes, darling," said the lighthouse keeper's wife, and at this moment she looked exactly like her daughter. She was radiant. "Let's do that. Before we play this round." They put down their cards and disappeared into the kitchen amazingly fast, the wife first, with the lighthouse master right behind her. The maid *was* already making the coffee out there; Doctor Brunsell could smell it.

"With such high clubs," whispered Josefa over his shoulder, "I'd knock. If the ace is played, go as low as you can. If not, you can clean up pretty well with what you've got there."

"You don't say so."

"Yes," said Josefa. "I do say so. Besides, I'm out this next round." The doctor almost didn't dare to turn his face toward her, but he did so anyway. He looked into blue eyes and a lively smile. Absolutely no epileptic characteristics. Josefa slipped back onto the sofa just as her parents returned from the kitchen. The lighthouse master's wife laughed, the lighthouse master chuckled loudly, and for a moment the doctor had the impression that they had been fondling out there. And maybe they had. By now he had almost forgotten that he needed to make the same cold, wet return trip tomorrow morning.

"Well," said the lighthouse master, "the coffee is perking excellently. Perking excellently. If I do say so myself. And have you had time to think things over, Doctor?"

"Yes, thank you," said Doctor Brunsell. "I've thought over my position carefully."

"And you, Josefa, my sly little one, you haven't helped him to cheat, have you?" the lighthouse master said sternly. Josefa shook her head innocently; so did the doctor. Then he took another sip of toddy; it was strong and sweet and went right to his head. Civilization at the mouth of the fjord, he thought—

The doctor was about to knock under the table when someone outside knocked first, and the group burst into laughter. "Come in!" shouted the lighthouse master. The door opened, and the thin ugly man from the boat trip appeared, a little hesitant, with his cap in his hand. He appeared to have been sleeping a long time.

"Aid!" shouted Josefa. "Uncle Enberg!" She got up from the sofa and ran to him, took his hand, drew him over to the coffee table. She hugged him. "Thank you," she whispered, "thank you so much." The thin man simply patted her head and smiled gently, as if he wanted to say: Are you all right again now?

"Did you sleep well, Enberg?"

"Yes, thank you, Mrs. Jacobsson, thank you," came the cracked reply. "Thank you."

"There's some delicious food in the kitchen. Maja has kept it warm for you. We thought you'd want to get slept out after that long trip."

"Thank you very much."

"Wouldn't you like to play Knock with us?" said Josefa eagerly. "Oh, can Uncle Enberg play Knock with us, Father; he's already knocked after all." The doctor laughed. But the lighthouse master had suddenly become serious. He looked at Enberg sternly.

"No, Josefa," he began, "I don't think so. Not this evening. I don't know if that would be right. The doctor is visiting us after all."

Josefa looked at her father wide-eyed, as if this was something she did not understand.

"But he plays with us every evening, and when we have other guests too; *Father*, he does." The doctor was about to say that it certainly didn't matter to him, although the sight of the thin man had been an unpleasant reminder of the imminent return trip, but Josefa's mother forestalled him.

"Kalle—" she began in a warning tone, turning to her husband. "*Of course* Enberg will play with us, if he wants to. He made that long trip. Josefa is right. He always plays with us otherwise." The doctor was about to say that the patient should decide, but did not want to put his host in an awkward situation.

"Of course," said the lighthouse master, and his expression softened. He looked embarrassed. "Of course, Enberg. Please forgive me. That was unreasonable of me." But he was not completely happy and seemed to be mulling something over in his mind.

"I really just came to get a little food," said Enberg, and walked quietly into the kitchen. He shut the door softly behind him.

After that the card party did not have the same gaiety, although the group did its best. Doctor Brunsell won the next round in fact, but it was not exactly the triumph he had hoped for. The lighthouse master seemed lost in his own thoughts, and the girl mostly sat looking at her father with wondering eyes.

Later, Doctor Brunsell went outside with the lighthouse master to get some fresh air. He got a little tour as well, even though it was dark and cold. Jacobsson had loaned him a loden jacket, which was so big he almost disappeared in it. The starlit sky was clear and the wind had died down. The doctor sent a small prayer of thanksgiving to the weather gods, and hoped the weather would hold until the trip home.

"Yes, here we have all the splendors of a lighthouse community," said his host with slightly forced ebullience and a wide sweep his hand. "It's no town, of course," he added apologetically.

No, God knows it's not, thought the doctor.

"But still, we call the station a community. In earlier times sheep-herders and fishermen lived out here; it was a whole little society, but when they built the lighthouses the island became government property, and now only one of the original inhabitants is left, an old woman. In those two buildings live the crew and the other two lighthouse keepers, and the room over there is where Aid—where Enberg lives. Besides me, there are seven men. Enberg, Quist, Frykman, Olsson, Wetterdahl, Simonsson, Skeppstedt. Then we have the washhouse and the office annex. And the equipment building. That's where the men who drowned in the shipwreck are lying. For the time being. In a few days people from Visby are coming to take our deposition."

"Do shipwrecks occur often out here?"

"Oh yes, they occur. Although rarely so dramatic as this time," he said seriously. "You must excuse me if I've seemed distracted, but something like this affects one, of course. We didn't see the wreck in time, and it troubles me to think about that."

"It was an excellent meal, and a very pleasant evening. Thank you so much, Mr. Jacobsson."

"And then of course my daughter was sick. We have our thoughts, don't we?"

The doctor did not respond.

"There are no reefs beyond here," the lighthouse master continued, "just banks where vessels run aground, so if we discover a shipwreck in time, things usually go well; we shoot out a line to them or row out. Unless there's a big storm like the other night, the vessels generally float after a few days, as long as we pump them out and dump the ballast. At most, we have a couple of shipwrecks per year. But we need to discover them in time." He fell silent, said no more.

The doctor pointed up to the two lights that hovered above them in the darkness. A faint whirring sound came from the mechanism up there.

"Don't the ships see the beams from the lighthouses?"

"Yes, of course, most of the time. We have double lights here, as you see, with half a kilometer between the two towers; each tower has a different kind of light, and there's one down at Bredsands Udde too, but in bad weather this isn't a satisfactory solution. They're thinking of removing one of the towers up here by the station and keeping the other, but at the same time they'll try to increase the light's intensity. Next summer a technical engineer is coming out here with a new apparatus from Stockholm; it has never been tested before. He's going to do experiments. We'll see what that leads to. Well, Doctor, what do you say, shall we go into my office and have a nightcap before saying good night? It's cold out here."

"Yes," said the doctor, "let's do that."

The office was furnished simply but cozily; an open rolltop desk had papers piled neatly on it, in the corner by the small woodburning stove stood a wing chair and an old beach chair; on the walls hung sealskins and rifles and fishing equipment, along with several navigational charts of the surrounding waters. Next to some meteorological instruments on the wall by the window, a few yellowed tables had been tacked up. Rust had run from the thumbtacks. Here and there lay fishing bags and all sorts of other things; two fish traps and a guide net that needed repair were slung on a bench along with a needle horn containing sail and boltrope needles. From hooks in the ceiling beams hung sinkers and glass balls, ropes and lines, cork floats, torchlights, caulking irons, blocks and marline bodkins. The bookshelves held an abundance of reading material as well as a couple of homemade ships in bottles, and the doctor also caught sight of some books about herbs. The air smelled of tobacco smoke and sea wrack.

"Welcome to my poor pigsty," said the lighthouse master. "You must excuse the mess, but I don't have permission to have all these things any-where else but here. Just a moment and I'll light a fire in the stove." It was done with one match. He lit lamps, took out two glasses and a bottle from somewhere in the bowels of the desk.

"Please sit down—no, not there, sit in the easy chair. That's for guests. I'll sit in—" He took a quick look at the beach chair, as if judging how much weight it would stand, then he sighed deeply and chose the old office chair. It sighed too, even more deeply, when he sat down in it.

"Aah," he said comfortably, and poured two glasses. "It's not often guests come during the winter," he said. "That is, unless we have a ship go aground, as I mentioned. But they're not invited guests exactly. If we res-cue a crew and get them to shore, they're not much company; they're mostly busy saving the ship, the few days they're here, and maybe the cap-tain can't speak Swedish or any other Christian language. No, that's not much fun; and food needs to be brought to them all day long, and if some are hurt, they have to be taken care of, and there's a lot of paperwork in-volved." He sighed again. "You should come in the summertime and go seal hunting, Doctor; we have a good time here then."

"Thank you," said the doctor, who had never killed a wild creature larger than a whiting. "That sounds very nice."

"Yes, I want you to know we get scientists and other fine folks out here in the summer," said the lighthouse master. "They're so fascinated by the flora and fauna here, which is evidently quite unique. Painters come too. There's a lot of social life in the evenings then. Yes, this is a beautiful island in the summer, believe me. Like a garden in the sea, I usually say. I've lived here my whole life. My father was the lighthouse master before me. I wouldn't live anywhere else either. One is free here, and one's thoughts are clear, like the air. I've been to Stockholm several times. An awful place. And the smell. Do you like Stockholm, Doctor Brunsell?"

"Well," the doctor began, "it depends on what one is used to. I'm from Göteborg myself, and—"

"No, cities aren't for me," said the lighthouse master with calm conviction. "And the way people rush around!"

"Yes," said the doctor indifferently, "and all the restaurants."

"Yes, cities are awful."

"But don't you miss—well—being around other people, Jacobsson? And the flow, the flow of ideas from outside?"

"Did you know that scientists in Germany have discovered rays that can penetrate matter?" said the lighthouse master.

"What—what do you mean?"

"Well, I don't know if this is correct, and I have no education in this field, so forgive me for expressing myself as a layman, but as far as I can tell, this German doctor or professor has discovered some rays, some sort of invisible light, whatever that may be, which can penetrate almost anything."

"Surely they must give out a faint light . . ."

"If one directs these rays toward the human body, for example, and puts a photographic plate behind it, one can see right through the body when the plate is developed. The bones become visible; for example, one can see where there's a break or where there are other internal injuries. Oh, haven't you read about this? I think they're called X rays. This must be an enormous step forward for medical science!"

"You're right," admitted the doctor. "Where did you learn this?"

"Oh," grunted the lighthouse master with satisfaction, "the flow of modern ideas."

"Hmm. You must really forgive me."

"I got you there," the lighthouse master said with a smile. "But of course it's because one reads as much as possible out here during the winter, to make the time pass. Nothing major. But we get a case of books from the reading society in Visby each fall, and I subscribe to some magazines along with Aid. With Enberg, I mean."

"Röntgen, that's the name of the German professor you're referring to. Now I remember. Wilhelm Röntgen."

"Right," said the lighthouse master. "That was it. Wilhelm Rönken. But of course—I often think about Josefa. If I'd had a son, he would have walked in my footsteps. But we had her. And perhaps there is no future for her out here. In the long run. But she doesn't know anything except the island. I don't know how she would manage on the mainland." He looked worried again. "And now this. Why should she get sick, when she has always been healthy as a herring? Listen, Doctor Brunsell, do you think these X rays can help my little Josefa?" The last words were said urgently.

"Well," said Doctor Brunsell evasively, "these rays haven't really been put to use yet, and besides, one still doesn't know all their possible applications. Or their limitations."

"Yes, but rays that can penetrate everything," said the lighthouse master eagerly, "that's marvelous. It's fantastic. What times we live in! One could see—see into the brain and see—see—well, maybe see where this sickness is located."

"Listen," said the doctor, "I'll be completely honest with you, Mr. Jacobsson. You mustn't hold out too much hope for any cure."

"What do you mean?"

"Epilepsy is a sickness that often leads to severe injuries in the brain and nervous system. One sees many epileptics in institutions for the mentally retarded. It's a sad sight." The lighthouse master looked at him open-mouthed. It took a few moments for the doctor's words to sink in.

"Good Lord, what are you saying, man?"

"In certain cases the epilepsy gets worse with the years. And if that's what happens to her, she must go to the mainland."

"To the mainland," groaned the lighthouse master hopelessly.

"On the other hand, I emphasize again: Josefa seems healthy and happy, and does not show typical epileptic traits. She completely lacks the stodgy, melancholy nature and appearance that the literature describes as characteristic. Maybe she will only have sporadic attacks. That's the most you can hope for, I believe."

"I see," said the lighthouse master dully. "What shall I tell my wife?"

"Nothing, perhaps. Wait and see how things develop, as I said."

The lighthouse master suddenly seemed old and sagging. He finished his drink, and drank one more. Only then did he pour another for the doctor.

"Now, now," said the doctor. "You mustn't take it so hard. You'll see, everything will be fine."

"First the shipwreck," said the lighthouse master, "and now this. Poor little Josefa, what have we done to her."

"You mustn't blame yourself for either of those things."

"I feel as if there's some sort of connection."

"You should not feel that way. You're not to blame for either of them. Shipwrecks occur—"

"We didn't see the wreck in time. I should have taken that watch myself. It's my fault."

"—and you're not to blame for Josefa's illness. This illness often lies latent for many years. It may be due to a head injury when she was little, or a difficult birth, or it may have completely unknown causes. One doesn't know for certain. There's no reason to blame yourself."

"I didn't notice it in time. An idiot. An idiot in an insane asylum."

"Not at all," said the doctor. "Listen to me: that certainly doesn't need to happen. Pull yourself together. She's not going to an asylum. All I said was—"

"To an asylum. With screaming people. A madhouse. Where they drool and— Isn't there anything at all one can do?"

"I promise you," said Doctor Brunsell with great self-control, "that I'll make another trip out here this summer and look at Josefa again."

"Yes, and won't you please investigate whether these X rays of Doctor Rönken can help her? Or if there's any other medicine or treatment or . . . something. Something electric maybe."

"I promise I'll do that. I'll write and inquire before this summer. And then we can go seal hunting together as you suggested."

But despite the doctor's optimistic promise it took a long time and a few more drinks before the lighthouse master became more cheerful again.

Though the doctor did his best, he seemed unable to rid Jacobsson of his notions. But the lighthouse master gradually pulled himself together, as a good man of the sea should do, and related many things about the island to entertain his guest, yet without either him or the doctor really being involved in the story. And when the doctor left to go to bed, Jacobsson kept sitting there, looking dejected.

SIX

MUST AID BE REPORTED?

I'm an old man, he told himself. An old man, and very simple besides. It was still dark outside. It was late. Or early. He never had to look at the clock, he had it inside him, he'd had it in his body for nearly sixty years. It was past five now. Had he been asleep? The fire had gone out in the stove, and he needed to lay a completely new one. I'm a simple man, he thought. I have things to think about that would have driven far less simple men into a corner. He struck a match. It was quiet outside, and in the silence he could hear that it had turned even colder. When he saw that the fire was burning well, he rose heavily, carried the office chair over to the desk, lit the work lamp. On one of the shelves in the desk he saw the book spines lined up, the most important ones; first-aid handbook, Russian and German phrase books, lighthouse technical manuals, the regulations, and, most important of all, the logbook. He hadn't opened the logbook since Josefa became ill. This was the first time it had happened, that he hadn't kept the logbook for three days. It was the station's logbook and had to be kept every day. It was a legal document. They'd had a serious shipwreck out here. In a day or two, officials from Visby would come to take a deposition and decide what should be done with the drowned men lying in the cold shed. Whether they should be taken to Gotland or be buried in the little cemetery out here. The log had to be up-to-date then. He had to do it now. The question was whether Aid needed to be reported in the logbook. If he put him in the logbook, he would probably have to report him too. The responsibility was entirely his own. He was the lighthouse station master after all. People had confidence in him. He was known far and wide for his sense of duty. He had been in charge of the island for more than thirty years, without incident, had kept everything in order. He had reported people before—it wasn't his problem if they chose not to heed his warnings. Hansson in '82, for example, on the lighthouse crew; he was one of those who came back late from his furloughs. Had a girl or something in Visby. Can't you marry her, then you can have her with you as much as you wish? he had suggested to Hansson. But no. It wasn't *so* important for Hansson, because he was too poor to get married. Yes, but you mustn't come back a day or two late, Hansson. There are others who need days off, and we need to have a full crew out here. But Hansson wouldn't understand. Can't you just deduct it from my pay? he said, putting his hands in his pockets. I'm warning you, Hansson. If this happens several times, then— And it happened several times, of course, and each time it was noted in the log, and when it was noted for the fifth time that he had come back too late, the lighthouse master sat down with pen and ink and reported Hansson. The fellow was then dismissed, and that was the last they saw of him. And he didn't marry the girl in Visby either. But this was different. This was very serious. And Jacobsson felt like a simple man.

He sat looking at the logbook there on the shelf. It was a leather-bound book, heavy and solid. Still, he'd had to glue a piece of canvas to the upper part of the spine to strengthen it; the headband had been worn out by his finger pulling at it, taking the book out every single day for many years. Most days it was only necessary to write two or three lines, so the logbook lasted for a long time.

He pulled himself together, took out the logbook.

He opened it. On one page was a record of who had the day's watches in which tower. On the facing page were the entries. And when he read his own slightly stiff, delicate handwriting, he could see the way everything began.

12/10/98. Fresh breeze NNE all night. Good visibility. Morning sun, fresh breeze NNE increasing to moderate gale force 7 after noon. Good visibility. 1400: Two cutters traveling north to the SW. Moderate gale shifting to NE, diminishing somewhat by evening. Quist has a sore throat and fever and must stay in bed. Frykman takes his watch.

12/11/98. Moderate gale NE, increasing slightly toward morning. Good to moderate visibility. 1100: Naval vessel traveling north to the NW. Visibility unchanged, moderate to good in the afternoon. High seas. Overcast. Light snow showers in the evening. 1500: Three-master traveling south to the NW. 1500: My daughter sees from Bredsands Udde a steamer traveling south. Quist still has a sore throat and fever but says he is ready for watch tomorrow. Put him on tomorrow evening.

12/12/98. Overcast, low clouds. Heavy snow showers in the squalls, minus 8 degrees Celsius. Moderate to poor visibility. 0900: Wind increasing to strong gale 8 from NE in the afternoon. Filled kerosene, inspected equipment at both lighthouses and at Bredsands Udde. 1500: Barometer fell 8 millibar since noon. Very rough sea. Wind increasing to light storm in the evening. Snow showers. Poor visibility. Quist on watch in the south tower, Enberg north.

He picked up the pen. Looked at the blank page. Then he dipped the point in the inkwell.

He wrote "12/13/98."

Then he sat a long time without writing a word.

It had been well past two in the morning when Rakel awakened him.

"Kalle," she said, softly and urgently. "Wake up. Aid is here. A ship has gone aground at Stora Beckrevet."

He had been dreaming, dreaming something about when he was a boy, something about his father here on the island and about the time they built one of the two new lighthouses here at the station; he could hardly remember that time when he was awake, but in his dreams he constantly replayed it, all the men who came and went and the tall tower that rose in the sunlight. He was wide awake immediately, and even before his feet touched the floor he knew from listening to the weather outside that it had not improved; rather, the wind had grown worse. He had been relieved at four that afternoon, after having stood the tower watch since morning, and Aid had taken a double watch until two the next morning. The weather had deteriorated all evening with a strong gale from the northeast; visibility was very poor when he went off watch. They expected a strong to full gale during the night and he had felt it was very important to have a steady and reliable man in the tower on such an evening, so Aid had taken an extra watch. Lighthouse keeper Quist, also a dependable man, was on duty in the tower to the south.

Kalle Jacobsson put on an extra layer of wool underwear, bundled himself up well. At three o'clock that afternoon the thermometer had shown minus 9 degrees Celsius, the wind had been gusting to force nine or ten, snow was falling in small sharp grains, and the gusts of wind on the balcony had burned his cheeks like a rain of sparks. It had probably gotten considerably colder during the night. He quickly put on his outer wraps and oilskins; finally his boots. Rakel helped him.

"Thank you," he said. "What time is it?"

"It's ten after two. Be careful now."

Aid was waiting in the entry, wet and pale.

"Quist has gone to rouse the others," he said. "It's an unknown vessel, it's quite far out."

"Is she sending signals?"

"No rockets," said Aid, "but I saw a swinging lantern."

"And Quist, has he seen anything?"

"Hmm," mumbled Aid. "Quist . . . was probably keeping watch toward the south."

"Oh yes," said the lighthouse master. And suddenly, for the first time that night, it struck him that something was wrong.

"Has she been aground long?" he asked. Aid looked down.

"I don't know," he said. "I saw her in a clearing between two squalls."

They went out into the wind together. The other men already stood in the yard, all six of them, serious, somber, each wearing a life vest and carrying his lantern. The wind beat against their cheeks, but it would be worse when they got down to the beach and out of the lee. It was snowing less now.

"Well," Quist began, "I've been down to the beach with Simonsson and fired off a couple of flares. There was no reaction from out there. Enberg thought he had seen a swinging lantern, but in any case it's out now. But there's light in the aft lantern still."

"Has she been aground long, do you think?"

"I think so."

"And you didn't see anything from your post, Quist?"

"No, I was watching to the south. Aid came and got me."

Nothing more was said. They walked quickly to the ridge where the rescue boat, line-throwing rocket, and rescue lines lay ready in the boathouse. From the boathouse, paths went toward the beaches in different directions, so that the boat could easily be carried to wherever it was needed. The weather was colder up here, but that was nothing compared to the open jaws of winter that met them when they got down to the beach. The storm had increased to almost a full gale now. Despite the oilskins, it felt as if the wind were striking naked skin, and the gusts were laden with sea spray. The whirling snow froze to ice the moment it struck the oilskins, and the other men's hair and beards were already white. Ice crunched under their feet.

"Fy! It's like—" began one of the men, but the wind blew the rest of his words back at him. They put the boat and the line-throwing rocket behind a sand dune, and then the lighthouse master took Enberg and Quist and went farther down toward the breakers. Yes, between the squalls he glimpsed a faint blue light out there. It was no longer snowing so hard, and visibility was not too bad, much better than in the afternoon. Not too bad at all. While Aid peered out to sea, the lighthouse master drew Quist a little aside. The sound of the surf was no longer a sound, but a force in the air around them.

"Quist," he roared into the other man's ear. "Has visibility improved?"

"No!" Quist roared back. He was coughing badly. The poor fellow was still not over his sore throat. "It's been—" he had to catch his breath, "this good all night! Ever since the storm abated at about nine-thirty."

"Strange Enberg didn't see her earlier!"

"Yes!" shouted Quist. But then they were given other things to think about. Aid fired two flares, and in the bursts of light they could see her. It was a three-masted staysail schooner. Nice vessel, but she had been lying there a long time and was in bad condition. There was no life to be seen on board. In the garish phosphorescent light the hull looked yellowish, like a corpse; it lay deep in the water. Jacobsson put the binoculars to his eyes. The mainmast was broken, and the deckhouse appeared to be crushed, but it was difficult to see because of the tangles of rope and pieces of wreckage. And between the vessel and the beach, a frothing belt of surf and foam and raging movement. Slightly more than a cable length. Two hundred meters, at the most. It could just as well have been two hundred miles. Then the flares went out, and the sad picture disappeared into blackness. Aid started toward him. He was pale, staggered a little. The lighthouse master looked at him in surprise. Was he sick? He waved both men nearer.

"Could either of you see if the lifeboat was gone?" he shouted.

The men shook their heads. They trotted up toward the sand dunes again, where the others were waiting. Compared with the noise and the wind at the water's edge, it seemed calm and sheltered up here.

"There's no sign of life!" shouted Jacobsson. "They don't reply to signals."

"They're gone, every man," said Frykman. The others nodded in agreement.

"That may be!" shouted the lighthouse master. "But we have to go out to her anyway! We have to try with the line-throwing rocket, maybe there's someone alive out there who can receive it."

They hauled the heavy device farther down on the beach, and Aid adjusted it. Quist fired two more flares, and the ship appeared out there again, unchanged.

"Not good!" shouted Frykman. "Not good!" He shook his head. Enberg aimed long and carefully in the light from the flares, then shot the rocket. It flew away with a whine, pulling the line after it; in the intense glow of the flares they saw the projectile's path like a long white streak through the snowy air.

"Too short!" groaned the men, even before the rocket had missed the mark, and Enberg swore inaudibly in the storm. The projectile went into the water. Much too short. The flares went out. So there was nothing to do but haul in the line. That took time, and the men's wool mittens became wet and full of seaweed and filth; the moisture and cold went through the mittens immediately. Aid laboriously rewound the line on the device, slowly fastened it to a new rocket. The lighthouse master watched impatiently, thought it was taking an eternity, but restrained himself. It was important that the line be wound properly in the device. Better that Aid took a little time, than that they ended up with two hundred meters of granny knots.

"Set it at 230, Enberg," roared Jacobsson kindly. "You weren't far off, by God."

Encouraged, Aid took new aim, new flares were fired, almost soundless in the roar of the surf, and once again the rocket flew out of the device. Jacobsson thought: He's got to hit it now. He's got to hit it. If there are any men clinging to the ship out there, he's got to hit it now. They don't have much time left if he doesn't hit it.

New roar. New disappointment. New darkness.

"Too short!"

"Is there a head wind?" shouted Jacobsson.

Enberg shrugged his shoulders.

"Did you set it at 230, like I told you?"

Enberg moved aside. The lighthouse master held a lantern toward the lever. It was adjusted completely wrong.

"It's at 160!" he screamed furiously. "Did you forget your glasses at home with your mother?!" He gave him a shove in the chest. Aid looked down. Mumbled something that cracked and disappeared in the storm.

"What!" The lighthouse master put his ear right up against Aid's mouth.

"I heard wrong, sir. I thought you said—"

"Nonsense!" snarled Jacobsson. "You must know that 160 was far too little. You've been here fifteen years! You're the best shot out here! Next time I'll shoot it myself!"

So then it was a matter of waiting long minutes while the line was hauled in and rewound.

Jacobsson reset the device, waited for the wind to lessen, gave the sign. More flares were fired, the vessel came into view. The wind quieted a little.

He aimed carefully, shot. The line ran. It will hit, he said to himself. It will hit.

He hit the vessel on the first try, amidships.

"Hurrah!" shouted the men.

"New flares, hurry, goddamn it, new flares!" Jacobsson ordered. "We've got to see if anyone fastens it!"

More flares flew into the air, the men stood shivering and hopping from one foot to the other, but now were more concerned about the line than about the cold and stared toward the shipwreck; everything depended upon someone securing it out there. They waited for a few minutes. Nothing moved on the wreck. Two more flares were fired.

"Poor devils," said Frykman. "They're gone, every man."

"Has the projectile caught itself out there?" Quist wondered. Skeppstedt went and tugged at the line.

"Slack as seaweed!"

"We'll leave it there!" shouted the lighthouse master. "We have to go out to her!" And quick as the devil, he added to himself. He gestured with his head for them to come with him. They followed him up to the sand dunes and got the rescue boat.

They launched from a hundred meters farther down the beach, because the current would be strong. It was hardest to get the boat through the breakers near the shore, but the men rowed as if possessed. The lighthouse master sat at the helm, Aid forward with a line and boarding hook. The boat was self-bailing, but they sat in water to their knees most of the time anyway. It was a matter of avoiding the worst breakers, which could sweep them overboard or overturn the boat. The sea was white with seething, swirling foam. The men rowed furiously on the way up the troughs of the waves and backed the oars on the way down, while the sea towered above the boat. It was hard to know in just what direction the breakers would come, but Lighthouse Master Jacobsson was very good at guessing. He had been out in rescue boats before, at the same beaches, and he guessed well. He sensed it more than he saw it. Now, now, now, something said within him, that one from starboard, that crest is going to break, it's going to break now, I know it. Then he roared at the top of his lungs and pointed, and the men rowed as one, so the boat would pierce the breaker with the bow first. Several times some smaller waves washed into the boat, then they leaned over and clung to the thwarts while the water hammered their backs like fists. Once they took in a larger wave, it was like having a load of stones poured over them. Just after that, they hung on the top of a crest, and the oars bristled uselessly in the air; the lighthouse master thought they would lose their balance and capsize then. But each time they stayed afloat.

At first it was impossible to see where they should go, and the lighthouse master had to choose the direction by intuition. Only when they had gone out some fifty meters could he see the top lantern on the shipwreck appear behind the crest of a wave, like a faint misty star, straight ahead. He hadn't aimed too badly. With the current and all. Not bad at all. They just had to set course slightly to port, then they would come right to her.

It was a little easier to maneuver when they came into the lee of the vessel, but the countercurrent was as strong as in a river rapids, and the men rowed madly, precisely, deeply. They let out a shout each time the oars cut the surface of the water, and each thrust gave the boat a tremendous spurt. From his place at the helm Jacobsson saw their faces rock up and down in rhythm with the thrusts of the oars; now and then a gaze met his, calm, serious, controlled. As if asleep. He held fast to the tiller.

"Steady now. Starboard! Starboard! Port!" They had reached the side of the ship, and now what they needed to do was lie to, if that was possible. There was considerable wreckage and jetsam in the water, and the vessel rocked violently with each large swell. At regular intervals a giant wave crashed over her, and the hull and woodwork creaked ominously. In the bow Aid struggled for elbowroom to throw a grapnel. Finally he succeeded, and they pulled themselves in. The ship lay with her starboard side toward land and was really in bad condition. A rope ladder dangled loosely along her side, and they backed the oars toward it. The moment they reached it, they all saw the same thing simultaneously. Above them, the lifeboat davit was empty.

"They've left in the boat," Olsson shouted.

"Then they're gone!" shouted Frykman, shaking his head.

Without a word, Jacobsson gave the tiller to Quist and crept forward. He nodded to Aid, who gave him a steady look. Did he smile? It was hard to see in the dark. Was it because of the reprimand for the bad rocket shot? And now the lighthouse master knelt here in the boat and silently asked

Aid for something. No, demanded it of him. He was in charge, had to go aboard himself. But he could not go aboard alone; it was dangerous and he needed to have someone with him. Such a task was of course voluntary for those under him, they might be their family's sole provider or have some other reason. Although several would surely have offered, had he asked. Many of the men were younger and more limber. Nonetheless, the lighthouse master could not imagine going aboard without Aid. Who else would he go aboard with?

"It's best that we go aboard," said Jacobsson, "we have the highest pensions." He lit two lanterns, put one in Aid's hand.

"In God's name," said Aid. He smiled a little again, with closed lips, almost secretively. He grabbed the rope ladder. Lithe as a cat, he suddenly dangled above them, kicked against the huge rocking side of the ship, and then he was up. Once aboard he leaned over the railing, and the lighthouse master glimpsed his face. Do what I did, said the face. The lighthouse master took a deep breath, grabbed the ladder, kicked out. And he felt in his arms and legs how heavy he was. For a moment he hung there absolutely still, but then his will took over, completely filled his limbs, his legs and feet and arms *became* his will, pure will, and his body began to move, and then he was up, everything went fine.

"Careful now," croaked Aid as Jacobsson swung himself over the railing. "It's slippery as hell."

The wreck was a sad sight. Amidships everything was a swaying chaos of rope and splintered wood, and waves crashed over her. With each wave she took in, the hull shook threateningly, and water washed ankle-deep over the entire ship, which was slowly freezing over. She lay there like an ice bird, a sad disabled storm swallow or seagull, frozen to death. Icicles hung from the rigging like long fingers of a corpse, and the ropes and backstays were white and ankle thick. She must have lain here for several hours. The deck was just one long, dangerous, slippery surface and it was very hard to keep one's footing because the sea struck the vessel's port side, she rocked violently with every swell, and waves washed over her deck at regular intervals. Almost as soon as the two men began to move, they fell down. The lighthouse master hit his knee, swore, got to his feet. They pulled themselves along the railing, more creeping than walking. Something crunched strangely under their boots; at first Jacobsson thought it was the ice, but then Aid picked up a shard and held it in the lantern light, and they discovered they were treading on pieces of coal that were being washed back and forth. So this was a coal boat, and there must be some serious damage to the hatches or hull if water had gotten into the hold and reached the cargo. They looked at each other. They had to be quick now.

"Ahoy! Is anyone aboard!"

Nothing but wind and waves.

They carefully moved aft, toward the deckhouse, which was partially crushed by the mast. There they found the first dead man. He crouched quite still behind the port railing aft, in the lee of a huge jumble of rope and woodwork, and looked as if he were trying to keep warm. At his feet was a lantern that had gone out. Jacobsson knelt in front of the sailor, shone a light on him, looked at his face; it was stiff and blue like paraffin. He shook the man, who was hard as rock. Jacobsson shook his head. As he stood up, he slipped and was about to tumble backward and slide down the slanting deck; it could have been terribly bad. For a moment he lost his balance, stood waving his arms, but Aid grabbed his arm and held him up until he regained his balance.

"We're getting old, sir!"

Slowly they made their way farther. They crawled, skidded, bumped themselves. A slippery film of ice formed on their mittens and the soles of their boots. Behind the remains of the deckhouse they found what had been the skipper. An older, gray-bearded man wearing a cap. He lay stretched out on his stomach with his right hand clutching a backstay. They had to tug him loose, finger by finger, in order to turn him over. His face was swollen and frozen, his hair and beard had turned to cakes of ice. His eyes were closed. His left arm was tucked inside his jacket and held a worn, bound notebook pressed tight to his body with a protective gesture; the logbook, no doubt. It had gotten wet, and now it was frozen fast to the captain's ulster.

While Aid held the lantern, the lighthouse master loosened the frozen logbook carefully, so as not to damage the pages too much, and put it beneath his own oilskin, under his sweater.

Other than that, the ship was deserted as far as they could see. They did not venture below deck or into the forecastle; the cargo holds were probably all under water. The remaining crew members must have tried their luck in the lifeboat. Jacobsson and Aid looked at each other. Jacobsson shook his head. Aid somberly lowered his eyes.

They maneuvered the two dead men toward the starboard railing and found the rope ladder near the davit.

"Ahoy!"

Below them, six faces blue with cold looked up eagerly. The men lay on the oars and back paddled to hold their position. The vessel seemed to lie deeper now and offered less lee.

"Just the skipper and one other!" shouted Jacobsson. "Both dead."

The faces below fell in resignation.

"We'll tie the ropes and send them down!"

They put a noose around the crouching sailor's feet and dropped him over the railing like a ball, held the rope firmly so he would not sink while the men in the boat struggled to get hold of him in the icy sea. Olsson and Frykman hauled him aboard the rescue boat, laid him forward. Aid and the lighthouse master let the skipper go the same way. Frykman took him with the boat hook; Wetterdahl and Simonsson laid him on top of the other man. Then Aid went down the rope ladder, and finally the lighthouse master started down. Carefully, because the ladder was slippery, and he knew if he landed in the water he would be dead in a minute. It seemed to him he was even heavier now than when he went aboard. His feet felt like unwieldy lead weights that wanted to pull him off the ladder, pull him down and away. The boat kept slipping away from him, and he hung there flailing for some time. Then he felt the sheer strake under his right foot, and a moment later was sitting in the boat.

No sooner did he have the tiller in his hand than the men started in toward the beach. It was easier now that they had the wind at their backs, but they knew the return trip would be the most dangerous when they got in toward land and had the breakers behind them. But now at least the rowers could *see* the breakers that rose threateningly behind them, and the sight gave them new strength; they rowed like wild men, in even faster rhythm than on the way out, and without saying a word, rowed in silent terror, until sand scraped under the boat and a little farther still; then they were over the side like one man and began shoving the boat up on dry land, they pulled and shoved with all their might, away from the current that grasped for them, away from the breakers that thundered in over the boat and the beach. They shoved and pulled, pulled and shoved, one more meter, two more meters, heave-ho! Still farther. And farther still.

For the final distance Jacobsson sat quietly at the tiller; he wasn't able to jump into the sea to help them, he was cold and worn out and sad. It was a couple of years now since he had been out in a rescue boat in a heavy storm, and he could feel that. I'll soon be sixty years old, he thought. I've done this year after year for over forty years. Usually, things have gone well. You've even saved some lives. There's even a medal hanging at home. Things have gone well most of the time. Things went well this time too.

Not until the boat had been dragged far up on the beach and turned onto its side did he stand up with difficulty and stagger onto the sand. Suddenly he could feel his heart pounding way up in his throat, and he had never felt that before. Tiny, annoying bluish pricks came and went before his eyes, and there was a salty cloying taste in his mouth. The dead captain's logbook was like a clump of ice against his chest under his sweater. He took a few unsteady steps, then straightened his back.

"We need to start looking for the others," he said. "Maybe the lifeboat managed to get to shore."

The men looked at him gloomily.

"Not a chance," said Frykman.

"We have to look for them anyway."

They divided into two groups and each began minutely examining the beach in a different direction. Here and there they found planks and ropes that had washed ashore from the shipwreck. And after just half an hour they found two drowned men about three hundred meters farther south. There was no sign of the lifeboat.

12 December 1898. 1800: Unable to get a fix to determine correct position since early yesterday and navigating by dead reckoning. Small storm 41 knots and strong current NNE to NE. Much icing. Reef spanker and foresail. Probably badly off course but believe we are 18 nm NNW off Gotland coast.

1940: Mate thinks he sees light in SW.

1950: Reef all sails. Damage to the rigging, the wheel moves slug-

gishly. Strong icing despite hard work with the axes. Maneuvering soon impossible.

2010: Light aground near?? On sandbank. Collision quite mild. Checked vessel to examine damages more closely. Every man ready at the pumps. Can perhaps refloat if weather improves a bit. Vessel seems tight at the moment.

2040: Believe we're aground near Sandön. Can glimpse the lighthouses, but heavy weather. No leakage. Await weather.

2100: Visibility improved, steady wind. Fire distress flares every fifteen minutes.

2120: Hellström overboard with sudden wave and no one could save him. Dangerous on deck, much lurching. No reply from lighthouses.

2130 ca.: Continue shooting flares. No reply. But visibility significantly better and we're of good cheer. They will surely see us soon. Wind increasing. Janson believes we have leakage in the forward hold.

2230: No reaction from shore. Eight flares remain. Waiting.

2320: Five flares remain. Deck crew in poor condition. Frostbite. Leakage increasing, pumping useless, hull shifting on sandbank.

Midnight. 12/13: Mainmast toppled at 2340, prob. as result of constant shaking, for it cracked at the mast collar, splintered deck amidships. Much damage, prob. also to hull. All safe and sound, but deckhouse damaged and cold is intense. Janson broke his arm. Talk with mate about sending four men ashore in lifeboat for help. Terrible sea. All rockets expended. God.

"Quist," said the lighthouse master as he lit the lamp on Quist's night table, "I want to know about a certain matter, and it must be kept just between the two of us."

Quist sat up in bed.

"What—?" he began, coughing at the same time. "What time is it?"

"It's six-thirty," said the lighthouse master.

"That's the middle of the night," said Quist.

"When the shipwreck occurred, you told me that visibility had been moderate to good ever since about nine-thirty, didn't you?"

"Did I say that? That's possible." He shivered and yawned—the yawn turned into a new coughing spell, deep and nasty. "I've got a fever," he explained.

"I can see that," said the lighthouse master, and handed him the mug of cold tea that was on his night table. "I shouldn't have dragged you out the other night, as sick as you were."

"Nonsense," said Quist. "That was fine. I'd reported for watch, after all. Let me think. Yes, visibility was quite good, yes. Better than the thick snow porridge we had earlier in the evening. I'd say visibility was a couple of miles, at least. Yes, a couple of miles, toward the south."

"You held watch toward the south."

"Yes."

"And didn't watch toward the north, where the shipwreck occurred?"

"No. I figured Aid had a complete view to the north."

"You didn't see any distress flares or anything like that?"

"No."

"Not at all?"

"No."

"And you were in the lighthouse the whole time."

"Yes, except for the time it took to inspect the equipment and make a cup of tea." Quist examined the lighthouse master with interest. "Why do you ask?" He coughed again.

"Oh—nothing, perhaps. When Aid came up to the tower to warn you, what time was it then?"

"About one, one-thirty."

"You can't be more exact?"

"One-thirty."

"What did he say?"

"He said he'd just sighted a vessel gone aground on Stora Beckrevet, and that was that."

"*When* had he seen her?"

Quist coughed again, a deep harsh cough. He shivered a little.

"What a wind," he said.

"It gets in your bones."

"It does. Well, he didn't say anything about that, exactly. He'd probably seen her just before. Pretty strange, actually."

"Yes, because she had been aground a long time."

"She had, yes."

"What was your impression of—Enberg, when he came up and warned you."

"Oh."

"Nothing you noticed particularly?"

"Oh." Quist coughed deeply again and leaned forward. In the lamplight the lighthouse master could see how sick he was. Drops of sweat glistened on his forehead.

"I think you've got a very high fever, Quist."

"I probably do."

"Maybe I should get you something warm to drink, and stop bothering you?"

"It's no bother. Listen," his teeth chattered a bit and he was shivering, "maybe I shouldn't say this, but you know very well that—"

"What is it, Quist?"

"No, it's the fever. I'm not talking sense. I shouldn't talk about others that way. It's just something I believe."

"What do you believe?"

"Well, maybe there are a couple of us men who believe it for all I know, because we notice things in everyday life, things that maybe you don't notice . . . But who's going to tell lies about a first-rate fellow's name and reputation? Not me, at least. So it's only something I maybe *believe*. I don't *know* it."

"What do you believe, then, Quist?"

"Well, you must surely know that Aid drinks?"

The lighthouse master sat for a long time, looking straight ahead, without saying a word.

"Drinks while on duty, I mean," coughed Quist.

The lighthouse master still said nothing.

"Well, this is just something I believe," Quist continued, as if to himself.

"Why do you believe that?"

"Oh . . . little things. But good God, I don't like to talk about it. Maybe I'm wrong. Just think if I'm wrong—good God, that would be terrible." Quist got a new coughing spell.

"What things?"

The coughing spell continued.

"What little things?"

But Quist's coughing spell would not stop, and when he finally looked up, Jacobsson could see that he was no longer completely lucid.

"Go to sleep now," he said.

SEVEN

MEMORIES OF A MARRIAGE
(AND OF LOVE)

The morning was cold and clear. He walked for a long time. Black bundles of bladder wrack had washed far up on the beach. Ash-white driftwood lay here and there, like hollow bones. Color began to tint the eastern sky, above the horizon a glimmer of green and gold could be seen. Soon the stars would be gone. Ice crunched beneath his feet. He breathed deeply, looked out to sea.

You breathe your entire life, he thought. You breathe your entire life, and it's love. You see the stars and the sea a whole life, and it's love. You row out on quiet mornings and it's love, and the fish in the net are love. Every glance and every breath are a prayer, without your knowing it. And each stroke of an oar and each silvery wriggling life is a hymn.

In those days, long ago, he had been afraid he would have a hard time finding a wife, but it happened easily. He had known, in a way, that he would find her if he was just in the right place at the right time. It was a matter of waiting for the time. He had grown up on the island, and could wait. He had always been here, if he didn't count the five years at sea as a young man in order to get his certification. Then he had come back to his parents and to the lighthouse, which was waiting for him, and it had not been difficult to say good-bye to the larger world, because if one has grown up on Sandön, no other worlds, large or small, would ever be as beautiful. At least that's what Kalle Jacobsson thought. While his father, the old lighthouse master, slowly became an old man, became part of all the legends and stories he remembered and glided into his own memories, he, Kalle Jacobsson, became the lighthouse master, became strong, became an adult. In the end, his father no longer went out but just sat in his rocking chair and thought. Listened into the air a little, looked out the windows. Then one cold day like this the old man said: "You should go to Fårösund now, and find a wife."

And Kalle Jacobsson listened to his father, even though he had plenty to do, even though he was approaching forty and in charge of seven men and absolutely did not have time to take pleasure trips when he wished. But Kalle Jacobsson had read the Bible and there it said that if I speak in the tongues of men and of angels, but have not love, then I am sounding brass or a clanging cymbal. And if I understand all mysteries and all knowledge, and if I have all faith, so as to move mountains, but have not love, I am nothing.

So he lay aside his tasks, put on his best uniform overcoat, went to Fårösund, and found a girl almost the moment he set foot on the wharf. He had to walk only nineteen meters, to be completely precise, or just sixteen steps (he had counted them many times later), and he came to the general store, where Rakel worked as a clerk in her father's business. And she was so fine. There was something strong and lively about her, she could move and didn't just stand there loafing. Was like a helmsman behind the counter. She had a nice smile and her hands moved quickly when she filled his cone-shaped paper container with lemon drops. He hadn't tasted lemon drops in months. He was in Fårösund for three days, and he ate lemon drops several times each day. He groomed his mustache and polished the buttons on his uniform, and he no longer understood and spoke haltingly, but straight out; at any rate he felt that he was very well spoken. Maybe Rakel thought so too, because the last evening she let herself be convinced and they went for a walk together along the wharves.

Afterward he set his homeward course, waited fourteen days, cared for his father and played chess with him, tended his mother's grave, and then sailed to Fårösund again.

Three times fourteen days he did this, and the men laughed at him a bit because they certainly knew what was going on. His father said nothing, sat in his chair and rocked, peered at him now and then, a little slyly. And what might the old man have been thinking? Did he think that in his day he had planted his small son in a narrow strip of sandy soil far out to sea, without asking whether the son wanted that? Did he sometimes think that the child did not get proper schooling or an education, even though he was a bright boy? And maybe not even a good wife, being so far from people? Did he think such things? He said nothing. He never said a word about such things. Once, as a very young man, in an earlier life, he had been an artillery officer, but that was some time ago and almost no longer true; now he was a sea legend, a ghost, a man who with his own two hands had saved scores of lives, who had fulfilled his duty for more than forty years, who had built houses and boats and set out to sea and found harbors in all kinds of weather; he no longer needed to talk, he had found God. He just looked at his son with a sly, ancient gaze. Every evening they played chess. They beat each other about every other time.

Three times fourteen days passed like that. And the third time he brought Rakel's word back with him, despite how young she was, and despite the fact that her father almost wept a merchant's blood over the life she would now have to endure out there at the mouth of the fjord; but he had so many daughters he needed to marry off.

"That was a good move with her," said his father over the chessboard, when he had seen his future daughter-in-law. But Kalle Jacobsson did not know for certain which lady his father referred to, whether it was the queen on the board or the lovely blond girl who began to fill the rooms in the lighthouse master's house with herself, with soft breathing and a bright voice, with new colors and light curtains.

"Love suffereth long and is kind; love envieth not; love vaunteth not itself, is not puffed up, doth not behave itself unseemly, seeketh not its own, is not provoked, taketh not account of evil; rejoiceth not in unrighteousness, but rejoiceth with the truth; beareth all things, believeth all things, hopeth all things, endureth all things. And I ask you therefore: Karl Jacobsson. Will you have Rakel Warmann as—"

Yes, yes.

Rakel. Life itself became different, and the island became different. He was well on in years, and looked forward to the sons who would come; he wanted many. He painted living room walls and brought furniture from Gotland, yes even *wallpaper*; he repaired the kitchen worktable and plowed up a long-neglected kitchen garden; he knocked down walls and moved the stove, and they loved each other deeply, morning and evening; she was still somewhat ladylike in everything (or almost everything); she introduced the use of a parasol on the island, and they took promenades together under it each Sunday, arm in arm, as elegantly as a merchant couple strolling an esplanade; at first the men laughed, later she graciously gave them permission to walk with them, at a proper distance and only in their Sunday best. And Kalle Jacobsson didn't give a damn if they looked ridiculous, because who could see them as they walked out here, her hand on his arm? He hadn't been mistaken about her hands, they were everywhere, changed the island and his home, changed him, took hold of everything and changed it. He showed her his island, and she loved it as he did. And she laughed at him and with him, and all his stories were still new. He was a lion, and he continued to see and understand and speak well, and not in fragments.

Then came the winter his father died, and he made a coffin and placed him in the ground. After that it was just the two of them.

But no sons arrive. No daughters either. And several years go by. She is always the same, depends on him, still loves him; he can see it in the way she sets the food in front of him, senses it in the movements of her hands when she helps him into his sea clothing. There is tenderness in everything. But during the winters he can tell what she misses; she walks slowly along the windows pinching shoots on the plants, cares for them, feels the soil and roots with her fingers; her mouth develops a sad expression, and her eyes become distant and empty. Or she takes out her longing on the men; never has a rough lighthouse crew received better attention. She is like a mother to them, takes care of them, tends to their clothes, asks them to shave on Sundays, maintains a strict watch over their use of language and their heathenism, keeps them working; yes, she is Kalle Jacobsson's wife in everything. During the summers her need for activity is showered on the guests who come, not just relatives, but all the odd scientist fellows and land crabs who now start coming to look at the animal and plant life, or to paint and draw motifs from the island; soon articles about their island appear in magazines and newspapers, and lectures about it are given in learned associations and societies in the capital city itself. More and more fine visitors come, so they have to fix up guesthouses. And each guest brings gifts or leaves generous sums of money for their summer lodging, and slowly they can fill the cupboards with genuine porcelain and small crystal objects. Rakel blooms in the summer; the island is no longer so desolate and distant, but a place that has been featured in the newspapers, it has become an exotic and sought-after place, even if it is still only Sandön, that's the strange thing. Even Rakel's father slowly comes to terms with his eighth daughter's fate; he no longer thinks loneliness was Rakel's dowry, but comes to visit himself and hunts seals and goes fishing and smokes cigars on the balcony on light summer nights, and calls his son-in-law Kalle. They're almost the same age, after all, so why not.

"Yes, Kalle, I'm a grandfather many times over already, and you aren't even a father; how can that be?" This comment generally occurs over the fourth or fifth drink. With a slightly reproachful look, obliquely wondering. "Maybe you get too much fresh air out here?"

"Well," says Kalle Jacobsson evasively, "children will come I'm sure."

"Yes," says Warmann, "one shouldn't try too hard either. Look at Lina and me. Nine daughters and no sons, good God. Ah yes. We finally had to give up."

"Yes, the wish for a son is the father of many daughters," Kalle Jacobsson says lightly.

"Yes, but whether it be sons or daughters, one must have children. They're the joy of our old age and our final comfort. God intends people to have many children, so we don't fall into doubt and disbelief. Children don't give you time to think too much, and those who don't think so much aren't troubled by doubt, but are content with life as it *is*. Skol. Besides, children are a good investment, for those who *have to* earn money quickly learn to get moving early in the morning." This is what Warmann says to his son-in-law with the seventh drink. But Kalle Jacobsson does not answer, he is no longer whole and complete, but fragmented. And his steps are held back by doubt. Rakel says nothing, just looks far out across the sea, and in the winters she puts lighted candles on the windowsill.

Several years pass like this. Then Aid comes.

It was actually by accident, although what is accidental? One of the lighthouse assistants has requested a transfer to a lighthouse in the south. Kalle Jacobsson is sorry to lose him, but all the man's siblings are in America, and as the only remaining son he wants to be nearer his elderly parents, so the lighthouse master has no choice but to approve the request and ask the administration in Stockholm for a new man. The replacement they assign is a reliable and experienced fellow from Båhuslen, but scarcely a month before the man is to take over the position, he falls into the sea and breaks his skull, a sad story. But such things happen. So the administration in Stockholm finds a new replacement, also an experienced man, from Kristianstad this time, but he gets appendicitis the same day he is appointed, his appendix bursts, and he is out of the dance. The final alternative is a man from Visby, but Kalle Jacobsson knows him from before and knows that he is a lazy fellow, and earnestly requests not to have him. In the end, the administration in Stockholm has nothing else to offer than Bernhard Enberg, a former naval cadet, partially crippled after a shipwreck a few years ago on the southern coast of Norway; he distinguished himself by his bravery at that time, but the injuries have made him unfit for sea duty. He has also become a bit strange in the head. But one doesn't want to leave such a fine fellow with no means of earning his living, so one seeks a suitable position for him; maybe Sandön is just the thing? At least for now? "A fine and capable man with good references and our high recommendation, strong and sober as well; after his hospital stay and convalescence one could almost say he is fully recovered in every way, but unfortunately no longer fit to serve as a naval officer. His defects are not at all noticeable in everyday company." There is a pleading tone behind the administration's formal communication to Kalle Jacobsson, and he understands that they are looking for someplace to get rid of the man, so he has his doubts, but he has no choice. It has to be Bernhard Enberg, lieutenant junior grade.

Eighteen days later, a calm, warm sunny afternoon in April 1883, he wades ashore onto the beach, wearing a black suit and bow tie and carrying an umbrella at his side, like some traveling lay preacher. The funeral mood is lightened only by his sea boots, which he has pulled up well over his trouser legs, and the heavy well-worn sea bag he carries easily over his shoulder. He looks very odd, like a tall black raven wading ashore, and the men glance sideways at one another as he comes sloshing toward them, then look quickly at the lighthouse master. What in the world have they sent us, the looks ask. Kalle Jacobsson does not know what to think. The skipper on the cutter that brought Enberg here sits in the boat half a cable length out and shakes his head at the tall apparition striding toward the shore. He spits into the sea, looks at the men who stand dubiously watching the arrival of the island's new inhabitant, then the skipper laughs, he laughs, indeed laughs heartily, shakes his head once more, and heads out again.

Bernhard Enberg slogs slowly and carefully onto the beach, looking down the whole time, as if he is afraid of stumbling. Not until he has both feet firmly on dry land does he raise his eyes. They are brown and their gaze seems steady, but Kalle Jacobsson realizes that the new man has practiced that for a long time. Perhaps this Enberg actually had a strong steady gaze at one time, one with no weakness or uncertainty, but then he lost it. And now he has to be content with practicing an imitation of his old gaze, so the gaze *itself* is deceptive. Enberg looks up, sees the group, then walks over to Kalle Jacobsson, sticks the umbrella into the sand, and holds out his long thin hand. There is something deceptive about his hand too. It is firm but flabby. Like the straight bow tie at his neck; up close one can see it is hanging loosely and has seen better times.

He says nothing. Simply shakes hands.

"Well," says Kalle Jacobsson. "You must be Enberg."

The tall man nods, shakes his hand again. Meets his gaze for a moment, looks down.

"Well," says Kalle Jacobsson again. "Welcome. I am Lighthouse Master Jacobsson. Don't you have any other baggage?"

The thin man shakes his head, puts down his bag. Now he says something, but it's so weak they can't hear it.

"Speak up!" says Kalle Jacobsson.

The thin man clears his throat, hawks, looks at them pleadingly at first, then apologetically. Then he speaks. And it's as though the sound comes from inside a drainpipe; it's almost as if they hear two voices, the one high like the overtone in a cracked woodwind instrument, the other grating and guttural like the low trembling notes of a tuba. In between these tones there is nothing, except a faint huffing murmur. He looks at them regretfully. Some of the men can't help smiling, must look down.

"I have," he hawks, "no other baggage. This is what I've got."

Kalle Jacobsson looks at the thin man uncertainly, then pulls himself together.

"Have you injured your larynx?"

"Yes," whispers Enberg. "It was the accident." He looks down, mumbles something, but it is impossible to hear what he says. They stand looking at him for a while to see if he tells them anything further about the accident, but he says nothing more.

"I see," Kalle Jacobsson finally says. "Well, welcome. These are the men."

Enberg takes his umbrella and sticks it under his arm. He shakes every man's hand, rather solemnly, and each time he shakes a hand, he hawks: "Enberg. I'm here to help with aid."

He grates his way around to everyone.

"Enberg. I'm here to help with aid."

"Enberg. I'm here to help with aid."

"Enberg. I'm here to help with aid."

The men are overwhelmed, this is too much of a good thing; nevertheless, they manage to contain themselves until almost the very end, but the last man can't restrain himself and beats Enberg to it.

"You must be Aid, who's here to help with Enberg."

Enberg looks down while the roars of laughter stream over him. He waits until they have stopped laughing, then he raises his head cautiously.

"No. Quite the contrary. You misunderstand. *I'm* not . . ."

New roar of laughter.

"All right," says the lighthouse master, "that's enough."

The black-clad figure is among the long line of men that makes its way up from the beach.

But already that evening he appears in working clothes and an Icelandic sweater and looks almost normal. He limps a little, and something is crooked in his face and neck, but his movements are strong. It's clear that he doesn't know the least thing about the Coast Guard lighthouse service, but he enters the steep, narrow, winding stairway just as quickly as any of them. If someone explains anything to him, it's hard to know if he has understood. He looks down, looks away, looks everywhere else, says nothing. Nods, somewhat absentmindedly. He quietly goes his own way around the island, avoids conversations and companionship. Not so strange, thinks Kalle Jacobsson. The men laugh at him, and shake their heads about him behind his back. From then on, he is called Aid, that's unavoidable. And he gives aid. Not many weeks go by before they begin to think Aid can be several places at the same time. The lighthouse master's worries are thoroughly put to shame. If Kalle Jacobsson stands in the narrow engine room swearing as he bends over the engine with pipe wrench and screwdriver and pliers and his face covered with oil, a long thin hand is immediately there to hand him the tool. Or unloading supplies and stores: there is a long shallows by the island, so everything must be carried ashore laboriously—what previously took three men two hours is suddenly done by itself, as if by invisible hands, carried into the buildings, stowed carefully and properly in place. Rakel especially likes the new man's eagerness to help; in the morning she and the maid find the potatoes scrubbed and put nicely in water, or the salted fish soaked—has he done it in his sleep? Maybe, thinks Kalle Jacobsson, maybe it's the naval cadet in him—they need to have absolute discipline aboard navy vessels, that's certain. As the summer goes on, the men laugh at him less, or at least they laugh more kindly, because it's good to have a helping hand.

"He doesn't say much, that new fellow, poor man," says Kalle Jacobsson one evening as he sits alone with his wife. She looks up from her knitting.

"He speaks with his hands," says Rakel.

At meals Aid sits by himself. In the evenings, lying in his bunk in the crew's three-man room, he reads a lot, often from the Bible but also from various other books.

On Sundays he dresses in his funeral suit, but now with more proper footwear; and as soon as he puts on his patent-leather shoes they can see it was once a good-looking suit, one can see that by the cut. It fits as though painted on him, despite how tall and odd his body is. The sleeves are not a hairsbreadth too short or too long, the shoulders not too loose or too tight, the buttons shine with the finest pure resin, lapel and pockets are discreetly elegant, lined with velvet, everything bespeaks nobler times in Aid's life. And Kalle Jacobsson suddenly imagines him in uniform—he must have been a handsome man. But the sleeves and trouser cuffs have become frayed now, and his trousers have been brushed with coffee grounds a few times. He sits quietly in the pew in the chapel with his hands folded while the men drone out a few hymns. *A. Mighty. For-tress. Is. Our. God.* It's not exactly a cathedral choir, most of the men sing all the words of all the hymns to the same melody. *Make. High. The. Door-way. Make. Wide. The. Por-tal.* A couple of them have better singing voices; powerful sea voices blend with the monotone mumbling from the others. Aid sits with his lips tightly closed, his eyes too, his head bowed.

The fourth Sunday he goes to the altar after the devotions.

The island's house of God is a tiny little chapel, scarcely room for more than a dozen or so, but there are rarely more churchgoers on the island. Once during the year, generally in the spring, the pastor from Fårösund comes to give communion or conduct delayed ceremonies—and then there is a constant round of gatherings. Kalle Jacobsson can remember an especially memorable spring Sunday during his childhood when the pastor officiated at communion, two baptisms, a wedding, and two funerals within the course of one church service. But normally the Sunday devotions are something the lighthouse master takes care of himself, with the good help of Rakel, who chooses the text and hymns and brings in flowers. The chapel is beautiful, even if it is small, with lovely green wooden pews and rafters. It has quite a fine crucifix, carved by Madam Westerberg's long-dead husband in the days when there were permanent inhabitants out here. Madam Westerberg often touches the crucifix before the devotions, entranced, as if she were touching a hand. The altar painting is quite a lovely Madonna and child, painted by a carpenter in Visby who often created such things—at any rate Kalle Jacobsson thinks it's lovely; it is the only painting he has actually looked at carefully in his life, and he has seen it his entire life. Our Lady reminds him quite a bit of Rakel, he has discovered that now, after they got married; he has always thought she was beautiful. The baby Jesus is round and plump and slightly cross-eyed. Our Lady is holding an orange fruit in her right hand; it must be an orange. The side panels depict the Savior's torments; the flogging by Herod and the crucifixion. The flogging scene is the least successful, because the Roman centurion in Jerusalem has such puffy cheeks it looks as though he has mumps. He is more humorous than biblical, that's what Kalle Jacobsson thought even as a child, so he can't really follow the painter's intentions as far as Herod is concerned. But the Roman soldier lashing with a whip is terribly ugly and his face is the color of red lead. The painter has provided the crucifixion with a wonderful solar eclipse—wherever he may have gotten that; he has painted a total eclipse, with a corona and everything, and Kalle Jacobsson especially appreciates this detail, surrounded as he is by the sun and stars in their courses, year after year, every night and day.

The crew have already shuffled out with Madam Westerberg at their heels, along with a few of the summer's woodcutters; Kalle Jacobsson stands in the tiny vestibule waiting for his wife to tidy up and move the vases of flowers out of the sunlight from the window. He likes to stand there and watch her through the crack in the doorway after the devotions, see her movements, which are so busy and at the same time so gentle. Now he sees Aid steal up toward the altar, to the organ, the little organ with foot-pump bellows, which stands beside the altar and suffers from lack of attention.

Aid seats himself at the instrument, opens the keyboard cover, blows dust off the keys. His feet begin pumping the bellows. From within the instrument comes a wheezing noise, like a large animal, and Rakel gives a start, half turns, sees Aid sitting there.

Aid presses his long fingers on the keyboard.

The keys make no sound, but the wheezing becomes a bit different. Sometimes the instrument whines a little, then it growls. He pulls out stops, tries different combinations. He gets a few hoarse squeaks out of it, nothing more.

Rakel goes over to him.

"You poor fellow," she says. "It's impossible to get a note out of our organ. Kalle has told me that there's been no sound in it for many years, not since he was young."

Aid nods. He says something, very softly, which Kalle Jacobsson can't hear out in the vestibule.

"No, alas," laughs Rakel heartily. "Not since he was young."

Aid says something again. And again Rakel laughs.

"Not *that* long," she trills. Then she gets her shawl, smiles at him, and wishes him a good weekend.

"What was so amusing?" Kalle Jacobsson asks as they are walking home.

"Oh—nothing. He said mice had probably gotten into the bellows."

"Mice?"

"In the bellows."

"In the bellows?"

"Mice in the bellows. Yes."

"In the organ, in other words." She laughs.

"I see."

In the days that follow, Aid sometimes goes to the chapel on his off-duty watches and when he thinks nobody sees him. But Kalle Jacobsson sees him, because Kalle Jacobsson sees everything that happens on his island, or almost everything anyway; he sees him from up in the tower, sees that he disappears up the path and between the trees in the direction of the chapel, or he sees him from the window in the office as he comes back down the same path.

One calm summer afternoon Kalle Jacobsson looks out the office window and sees Aid ambling off again. And now Kalle Jacobsson gets curious and decides to amble up to the chapel himself, to see what Aid is doing up there.

The door is shut but never locked. No doors on the island are locked, except to the lighthouses and the office annex, because it sometimes happens that someone comes ashore unexpectedly and needs shelter for a night. So Kalle Jacobsson silently opens the chapel door and walks into the vestibule; there is no sound from within the chapel; he opens the inner door a crack. Aid is seated at the organ. He rocks back and forth. Beneath his hands is a rhythmic ticking, small muffled thrusts on the keyboard; his fingers move softly, undulate, like the cilia on a shrimp. Then a wheezing sound is heard. For a moment Kalle Jacobsson thinks the wheezing is coming from the bellows, the mouse-eaten bellows, but Aid does not have his feet on the pedals; it is Aid himself who is wheezing. He lets his hands move across the keyboard, his eyes closed, and his body moves back and forth as in heavy seas, and he wheezes, growls, and breathes, rhythmic thrusts, long and short. The silent keys tick. He plays, without a sound.

The lighthouse master stands looking at him for a while. He has never seen such a thing before, and he doesn't know what to think or believe. It's almost a little eerie. Finally he steals out again, as quietly as he came. In the days that follow he often thinks about the thin swaying figure at the organ, and it gradually becomes clear to him that this isn't madness but a secret. And Kalle Jacobsson knows that on such an island there are not many secrets in the long run, so the few that exist must be well protected.

So one morning when he and Aid are alone in the tower, he just barely mentions it while they are out on the balcony polishing the glass. The sun is still red and a brisk wind is blowing. There is always a brisk wind up here. It makes the windowpanes clatter. Inside the lighthouse a lantern glitters in the sun like warm ice. Around the balcony is a low, simple iron railing, nothing more. They lean against it to reach the highest windowpanes.

"Please hand me the sponge, Enberg."

Sponge.

"Thank you."

Ammonium chloride water, knuckles, polishing.

"Are you happy here on the island, Enberg?"

Rinse water, new sponge.

"I said: Are you happy here on my island, Enberg?"

"Yes, thank you," he says, whispering.

"That's good. You do good work, Enberg; everyone is satisfied with you."

"Thank you."

"I'm going to write to the administration in Stockholm and inform them that you perform your work to everyone's satisfaction, and that we would like to have you stay here after the trial period. If you want to do that."

Enberg lets the sponge fall into the bucket. He looks at Kalle Jacobsson. Something golden comes into his brown eyes.

"Thank you," he says. "I'd like to stay here."

"You mustn't let it bother you that the men make fun of your voice a little. It's not meant unkindly. Everyone knows you've been injured."

"I don't let it bother me." Still something golden in his eyes.

"But if you go to the chapel, you must lock the door behind you."

Enberg looks at him. His eyes narrow. For a moment he is serious. Then he smiles. It is a strange smile.

"I'll remember that," he says.

"Well, what I wanted to say: if you keep on doing such good work in the future, Enberg," the lighthouse master continues quickly, "then it's very possible you can have a future out here on the island."

"Yes, that's possible," says Enberg, and wets the sponge.

Then autumn comes, and in the autumn the island has a different color. From up in the tower the treetops look like small sponges in many tones of red and gold, and it's chilly to be on watch. The hours pass quietly up there between sky and sea: every twenty minutes a round on the balcony to keep a lookout, an inspection of the flame and oil level, otherwise silence and the monotonous drone of the engine. There is such a difference in what lighthouse keepers do to stay awake. Kalle Jacobsson usually reads when the watches grow long, others carve wood or tie nets. Some hundred meters away the other tower is visible, a man can see his neighboring lighthouse keeper like a tiny silhouette against the light when he is out on the balcony making observations. Now and then the mist lies so low that the towers rise like two lonely spar buoys in the sky. The island and everything else is gone, and there is only the sky and the clouds and two people, high up, each in his glass house. If the autumn sun is shining, the towers cast disproportionately long shadows across the mist, and huge shining haloes surround the silhouettes with all the colors of the rainbow. And the men sit there, each in his own tower keeping busy with his tasks.

Aid begins to take watches alone that fall, and he too takes along a bundle with something to do up there in the light of the shielded reading lamp; once Kalle Jacobsson sees that he is doing some leather work, but the lighthouse master doesn't ask, thinks it's perhaps a fishing pouch or a pair of sturdy work pants. In reality, Aid has begun to restore the voice of the mute organ. He has opened the instrument and has found a nest in the bellows with room for a whole Bedouin camp of mice, grandparents and great-grandparents and a couple of huge males along with a harem of females and young. So he has gotten leather and cobbler's thread and, using simple materials but without the proper tools, he is slowly repairing the organ. However, no one knows this, because he keeps it hidden; he makes sure that all the outer parts are in place, so no one will discover it on Sundays.

But one person knows about it anyway; he needs an ally, and that is Kalle Jacobsson's wife. It's to be a surprise when the pastor comes for his spring visit, a surprise for everyone. Rakel helps Aid find materials or orders things from Gotland, so he has everything he needs for his work during the winter; the last vessel departs from the island at the end of January and the next one doesn't come until the ice clears from the sea in March, so if he is to have the instrument ready for spring, he needs to think things through carefully before deciding what materials to order. And Rakel Jacobsson writes the order for him, she accompanies him to the chapel very early in the morning or late at night and helps him, she uses every possible excuse and subterfuge so that neither her husband nor the others will know anything, and the remarkable thing is that she is successful. No one discovers it, not the maid and not the men; they think she really is gathering mushrooms or berries, or that she is going to beat rugs in the snow; in reality, she steals away with her roll of rugs filled with leather and steel thread, disappears among the trees, turns in a different direction, goes up to the chapel, where she meets Aid and the secret they share. The secret makes her bloom, she becomes happier, she looks forward to spring and to the music. She helps him pull out the wind-chest, bellows, and pipes, clean them with steel wool and scouring powder, wash them thoroughly, remove spiderwebs and dust, along with a whole Augean stable of mouse droppings, thirty generations' collected output. Aid works calmly and silently, says little, but his hands speak, and she wonders *what* they say, how he knows how to do this, where he learned it. Because he knows. He has the scales and the intervals written somewhere inside him, somewhere within his hearing, and he listens to the notes, is aware of the least vibration, the slightest impurity. He has it in his hands too; they are long, thin sailor's hands, the skin is chapped and callused, but on the instrument they are at home and become completely different; it's as if they are swimming in deep, clear water. He tunes the pipes and solders damaged pewter; gets the keys and registers to slide smoothly and easily. Finally, there is sound in the instrument, a clear tone, pure and gentle, almost tender, and he can begin to tune it; one Sunday morning when they are in the chapel together he plays for her for the first time. Until now she has only heard him play single notes, chords, intervals, and scales as he was working and tuning, but now he plays for her, a very simple chorale; his fingers bring out the voices of the upper registers and the lower registers; the organ does not have a powerful sound, but a fine subdued resonance. His playing moves her and delights her at the same time. No one knows anything about this—not the men, and not Kalle Jacobsson; it's a secret and is to be a surprise. The island is small and secrets must be protected, including this one.

But one of the island's inhabitants must have found out anyway; when Kalle Jacobsson happens to meet Madam Westerberg in the woods during this time he gets the impression she is mocking him a little, and he doesn't understand why. He can remember a conversation when he met her in the woods near the chapel as she came hurrying between two spruce trees on her way to her little tumbledown house and he stopped her and said hello.

"How are you, Madam?" The years did not seem to affect Madam Westerberg, it was as if she were outside time; as far back as he could remember she had looked the same, hunched over and gray as ash.

"Just fine, thank you, and what about yourself? Is everything as fine as you think?"

"What do you mean, Madam?"

"Mean or *mean*." She looks at him slyly. "I don't mean anything. It's best to have no opinion about anything."

"I don't really understand," he says kindly.

"No, and that's probably best," is the toothless reply. "It's best that we don't understand too much of everything that happens in this world, ah yes, ah yes."

"That may well be."

"I'm an old woman, and still I understand more than you about many things."

"That may well be, Madam."

"It may be, and it may not be. Sometimes one understands everything one doesn't see, but doesn't understand what one sees happening right in front of one's nose."

"I guess so," he says, a little stiffly.

"And everyone knows how people look when they have their eyes open, but who knows what it looks like behind their eyelids when they're closed? That's two different things indeed. They can be two different people, depending on whether their eyes are open or closed."

"Now you're talking nonsense, Madam," he says. "Your words have no meaning."

"Maybe, maybe not, I don't have any opinion about that; but I wouldn't be too sure, and you shouldn't be either. Remember, I've seen you as a tiny baby, when your father and mother came to the island right after the lighthouses were built and everyone who had lived here was sent away, except for my husband, dear departed Westerberg, who got work in the lighthouses. I saw you as a baby then."

"That's true, Madam."

"It's so true that if I close my eyes I still see you as a tiny baby, and I see the farm we had before the lighthouses were built, and I see everyone who lived here before it became the government's land, and I see the Sandön troll and the gray lady when she walks around here in foggy weather, and old Gothberg—I've seen him many times, ah yes, and still see him from time to time as he rides along the beach with his lantern, but I saw him even more often before the lighthouses came with their engines and bright lights."

"That's really too bad, Madam. You shouldn't imagine seeing such uncanny things with your eyes open."

"And which eyes do you think I should I see with? I've seen ghosts and phantoms with my two eyes open, just as I saw you as a little boy and now see you as a grown man; I see neither of those two now, but when I close my eyes I can see both." She closed her eyes a moment, opened them, looked at him, and smiled, as radiantly as a young girl.

"That's ungodly talk."

"Yes, it is. But godly or ungodly, what one sees isn't always what *is*, you ought to know that. Not out here in the woods, where ghosts live, or inside God's little chapel down there, where God lives, but the chapel is in the woods, ah yes. Just pay attention. Close your eyes and pay attention. It often helps to listen too. As we know, we can't close our ears. Ah yes. Ah yes. I've said enough. I'll say no more."

But he hadn't understood.

And at the end of April, after a quiet winter with a great deal of ice, one year after Aid came to the island, the day arrives. Pastor Selander comes ashore to conduct the spring worship service.

Kalle Jacobsson hadn't understood. He hadn't realized anything. Even when Rakel made an excuse for not going along to meet the pastor, he didn't realize anything was afoot. She hadn't finished getting things ready in the chapel, she said regretfully. Kalle Jacobsson looked at his wife in surprise, because it was the first time in his experience that she hadn't been finished with something in time, but for precisely that reason he didn't object and went alone to the beach to meet the pastor; he was expected about noon.

With a stiff salute he greeted the clergyman wading ashore with his coattails and clerical robes pulled well up over his short legs. Once ashore the pastor put on his clerical collar, greeted Lighthouse Master Jacobsson, and they began walking up to the chapel, slowly and sedately, chatting.

"And your wife?"

"My wife didn't come to greet you," said Kalle Jacobsson apologetically. "There is so much to do when we have a fine visitor."

"And how has the winter been?"

"It's been a good season, no shipwrecks. No one has gone aground."

"I hope all is well with the people living out here?"

"Yes, thank you, everyone is in good health; no deaths and no accidents of any kind."

"And old Madam Westerberg?"

"Yes, she's alive. Sits down there in her house. But she's beginning to be a little odd."

"Beginning or beginning."

"Well, yes, she's always been odd of course. So we're all fine, all of us. Thanks to Divine Providence," he added.

"Well, then there will be a festive worship service," said the pastor as they reached the chapel. He clapped Kalle Jacobsson on the shoulder, opened the door, they went into the small vestibule, and the music met them.

Later Kalle Jacobsson would remember that moment as one of great joy. At first he hadn't realized what it was. It had been like flowers in the air. He hadn't heard organ music since he was a small boy, when his heart was still as soft and unprotected as a bud. And now the music was there, all around him, and it spoke to his innermost heart. Suddenly the chapel was a completely different building, constructed of other materials; Pastor Selander gave him a radiant look of joy as they walked toward the altar. He didn't understand anything, simply saw Rakel's flaming face, saw the laughing face of Madam Westerberg—oh how she was enjoying this, she had fooled him now! He saw Aïd's swaying back as he played the processional, the pastor congratulated him, the pastor was moved, moved almost to tears, after ten years of worship services out here without an organ. Again and again that day the pastor congratulated him, as if this was all due to Kalle Jacobsson, all of it.

"Just think," said the pastor, "what a happy moment. What a happy moment. What a marvelous idea. It's as if the island has regained its voice. Congratulations, Jacobsson. Congratulations. Just think."

"It is—is, is—one of the men who—and my wife, who—have—have—"

"Yes, you're a fortunate man, Kalle Jacobsson. What a sound, so pure and delicate."

"Yes, it's, as I said, one of the men who is—who has—who can—"

"A fine fellow. You're fortunate. Congratulations. Just think. A happy moment."

It was a happy moment and a happy day. As he sat there in the chapel and the notes flowed clear as water from the little organ, it was as if Kalle Jacobsson felt something, a presentiment, a vision of something great and beautiful that would come. It was as if he knew. He knew, as Aid played a new, unusually light and gracious "A Mighty Fortress Is Our God" (who would have thought it could be so beautiful?), he knew, as the men sitting around him sang, restrained, so as not to disturb the bliss in the air. Knew, without knowing, knew that he knew. Something great and beautiful would come.

He knows this every Sunday when they hold devotions and Aid, wearing his black suit, plays, first the familiar hymns, then he lets go and plays other hymns and new hymns, and later melodies and music Kalle Jacobsson didn't even know existed, music that no longer can be sung but is simply played, music that can't be created for ordinary people, but for angels and such beings.

And he still knows it when Rakel tells him later that summer. He is hardly even surprised; it's like when he went ashore and found Rakel in the general store in Fårösund, he had *known* it then, and he *knows* it now; he has regained his certainty, once again he understands completely, he no longer doubts. Everything has meaning again. And as Rakel grows bigger and happier day by day, week by week, and the birth approaches, he fusses and fixes along with Aid, paints walls with linseed oil colors and builds a cradle. Kalle Jacobsson is strong and rich now, and is not nagged by doubt; he is going to be a father. All this, all this tremendous happiness, he thinks, is because Aid repaired the organ. Selander was right: the island has regained its voice. But he doesn't manage to thank Aid properly, Aid isn't one who lets you thank him; he slips away, wary, his glance both uncertain and deceptive. Smiles a little. And so forth. Is, of course, somewhat proud of the instrument he has repaired so well; as he sits at the organ playing he grows larger and becomes another person, an Aid they don't know, a Bernhard Enberg from an earlier existence. But the moment he puts his hands in his lap and the music stops, he is the same, looks at them a little embarrassed, withdraws. He seems slightly afraid. Afraid of what? Maybe he is afraid they will think he shows off too much with his playing. Or maybe he fears something else. He speaks in monosyllables, soft and squeaking. Slips away.

Kalle Jacobsson may not be the best person at saying thank you, but he thanks Aid in a way nonetheless. They build a cradle together, as mentioned, and more and more often Kalle Jacobsson takes Aid along on seal hunts or fishing trips. Does he think he needs to? Yes, perhaps, but not only for that reason; Kalle Jacobsson has experienced a miracle, and he thinks Aid is somehow part of it. Aid does not say much of course, but Kalle Jacobsson talks for both of them while they fish or do carpentry, talks about the island and about his sea, about his father and mother, about his life growing up out here, tells yarns and legends, draws Aid into his life. He rewards him, invites him to Sunday dinner and card playing and reading aloud, just the three of them, Aid and he and Rakel, who reigns, no, who radiates at the table. She grows round and beautiful. Kalle Jacobsson talks. Aid says little, gives him brief embarrassed looks, smiles. Laughs when Rakel says something amusing, laughter that is just hoarse breathing behind lips he tries to hold closed. If he opens his mouth too much, the laughter sounds like the death rattle of a man just hanged; it's an awful sound, and they were frightened the first time he laughed out loud; they stopped laughing themselves, put down their cards, gave him a worried look, afraid. He immediately stopped laughing, looked at them apologetically, and then away. It took awhile for him to get over that incident; he hardly ever laughed like that again.

But every Sunday he plays in the chapel.

And then came the terrible trip to Visby in October that year, when he and Aid got lost rowing home in foggy weather; they strayed off course and ended up far out to sea. Six days and nights they drifted there, with no sign of clearing. The last two days were the worst because they had no more water and no more provisions. A milky gray silence enveloped them. They rowed just a little to keep warm, because they had no idea where they were and did not want to go even farther astray. They said very little. The days out there in the fog were like a rocking dream. Everything went fine the first couple of days, and they were of good cheer. But if Aid had not been along, Kalle Jacobsson would not have returned from that trip, because near the end he grew very weak and had to lie in the bottom of the boat. He was not cold. Rather, he felt calm and pleasantly lethargic. If he thought about Rakel waiting at home, and about the child, his thoughts were distant and tired and strangely contented. He glided in and out of a strange sleep that was as soft and safely formless as the fog. Now and then Aid knelt over him and wet his lips with a piece of sailcloth he had moistened with water that had condensed on the thwarts. Actually, the only thing that bothered the lighthouse master were Aid's attempts to shout across the water at regular intervals in case another vessel might be lying nearby. It sounded like terrible bird noises, and it irritated him. He should ask Aid to turn on the bailer or to do something else instead, but he couldn't manage to do that. He lay like that for more than a day and a night, until something changed around him, and with great difficulty he was able to slowly raise himself a little and look over the rail. Where there had been a white wall, he now saw waves and movement. The wind had risen. They could not see land, but Aid began to row south until they sighted Gotland. Then, without a word, he turned sharply and rowed home, while the wind rose even more, while it began to rain, rowed without stopping, with no sound other than the small grating gasp with each stroke of the oars, hour after hour. The last part of the trip Kalle Jacobsson later remembered as just one long cold feeling. He was wide awake now that they were headed homeward and could keep watch. And along with the cold, with the wakefulness and the thoughts, the anxiety returned. He thought about Rakel sitting at home, and he thought about the baby. He thought about what would happen if the storm grew even worse.

But Aid rowed them safely all the way home. Kalle Jacobsson would never forget it. And he would never forget Rakel, how she began to cry when they finally entered the house, and how tightly she held him, and how she thanked Aid over and over again, and then suddenly her face grew very serious, in fact almost terrified, as white as the fog they came in from. She stopped crying, went in and lay down. For many days she did not speak, did not say a word to him or Aid or anyone else; she simply collapsed, lay in bed in her own silence and said nothing. She was different after this, more serious, more silent. Walked from window to window.

But then Josefa arrived. And again it was Aid who rowed in bad weather, this time to get the doctor, and saved the daughter and perhaps the mother too.

Josefa, his only, beautiful, white child. This marvelous Josefa, who was his daughter, regardless of how dissimilar they were. Who could look at him so seriously, and sing so beautifully.

And now she was sick.

Kalle Jacobsson stopped walking. He had gone far this morning, almost around the island. He had often thought about how everything would have been out here if he hadn't had Rakel and Josefa. If things had gone badly with the birth. Would he even have been here? Would he have sat drunkenly in his living room while an unused cradle stood gathering dust in the attic? Everything that *does not* happen, he thought. Everything that *could have* happened. Why doesn't it happen? You are still here. Everything is here. You breathe your entire life.

But the seven dead men lying in the shelter, what about them? And all those they left behind? This happens. It has happened. It's terrible, but it has happened. And in a little while you must write in the logbook, and you must write what has happened.

What should he write?

Kalle Jacobsson had walked for a long time this morning, and thought through half a lifetime and many things he did not think about usually. I'm a simple man, he thought. And he had made his decision now. So he went back to the house, ate breakfast, asked Rakel to pack a lunch for the doctor's return trip, went to see Quist again. Quist was still very ill and talking irrationally.

Later he woke Doctor Brunsell and got Frykman to sail him to Fårösund as soon as he had eaten breakfast. Only after the doctor had left did he sit down to write in the log.

EIGHT

A PRACTICAL DEVICE

They all ended up here. Quist too. But first Aid had built a channel. He took four long boards and nailed them together to form sort of a squared tube, ten centimeters in diameter and two meters long. At one end he made a lid that was screwed tight over a layer of tar paper, almost like a roof, so no moisture could get in. Then he tarred that end. Josefa had sat in the corner of the workshop watching him, the work took only about an hour and yet it was a big job; Aid pounded the nails painstakingly, took them from his lips one by one, somber, silent, and without looking at her. He was serious, despite his smile of nails.

Then he was finished.

"You can help me carry it where it's supposed to go. No, take the other end, otherwise you'll get tar on your dress."

"Mother wouldn't be happy about that," said Josefa.

"No," he agreed.

"Are we going to the chapel afterward?" she asked.

"No," said Aid. "Not today."

They carried the channel from the workshop, up through the woods. Up there. The lighthouse crew was still digging. They stopped when Aid and Josefa came with their burden, stood looking at the two, leaned on their shovels and spades. On the white snow lay dark shadows of sandy soil. They had dug almost deep enough now, and it was hard work, because there was a thick layer of frost in the ground. But fortunately they did not have to dig seven more graves, because it had been decided that tomorrow the shipwrecked men would be picked up by boat and brought to Gotland. Only Quist would remain.

The crosses stuck out of the snow, and in front of the crosses were objects like small square houses. They looked like birdhouses on the ground. That was how Josefa imagined it, that these were the small houses where the dead lived and kept watch. Now and then perhaps they invited a little nisse inside, or a small animal that was outside and needed warmth. That's what she had pretended. But it was actually only a practical device. These were the uppermost ends of channels, exactly the same as the channel she had seen Aid nail together today; one end rested on the coffin lid, far down there in the dark earth, and the other end stuck out of the ground, so that when Pastor Selander came in the spring he could perform the ritual of casting earth on the coffin and mumble his delayed blessings down through the channel to the person buried there. They filled the channel with earth afterward, but let it remain.

"I made it two meters long after all," said Aid. "I thought that was best."

"Hmm, so that's what you thought, was it?" said Frykman. He spit, looked away. "Then we have to dig out one more meter, fellows. So the dumb thing fits. Because we can't ask him to saw it off, can we?"

Josefa didn't understand.

"Two meters," said Aid softly but firmly. "That's the regulation."

"The regulation—you." Frykman did not look at him, turned his head away, mumbled something. His face was dark. Josefa became frightened. Frykman thrust the point of the spade into the ground with a sharp sound. Josefa felt her scalp prickle, she didn't understand anything, just that they were angry. Were they sad because Quist was dead?

Dead. Kind Quist, who had died of pneumonia. And no one had realized how sick he was before it was too late; he had lain there so quietly and nicely—until he began to talk irrationally on the third day. And by then it was long after the doctor had sailed back to Fårösund—Doctor Brunsell hadn't even seen the unfortunate fellow, and everything was too late for poor Quist.

"It's supposed to be two meters," said Aid quietly. He looked at the men, they stopped digging, but no one met his gaze.

"Does anyone want to come and play circle tag with me afterward?" Josefa asked loudly, making her voice as normal as possible, but no one replied. Instead they thrust the spades into the ground again. She went over to the open grave, looked down at them. Their faces were far away. But their contempt was close by; it rose from the earth like a breath, right into her face.

"We can play circle tag," she said, softly this time.

"Come," whispered Aid, and put his hand on her shoulder, drew her away from the grave.

"It's extra-good snow for tracking," she said, almost desperately. What was wrong with the men today? Frykman mumbled something in reply.

"Stop it. She's just a child," Skeppstedt objected crossly.

"I don't give a damn," said Frykman.

"Stop it," Skeppstedt warned again. "Remember, she's the boss's daughter."

"Is that so," said Frykman with terrible calm. He looked up, fixed his eyes on Josefa. "Then she can go home to that so-called boss with this monster. I don't give a damn about that either. He's not my boss any longer, if things are going to be handled like this."

"Enough!" Olsson warned him. Then turning to Enberg he said calmly: "Go away, Enberg. We don't want to talk with you today."

Josefa began to tremble.

"Come now," Aid said reassuringly to Josefa. "Come. We'll go home."

"But—" began Josefa. Her scalp prickled terribly.

"Come," whispered Aid. "Come."

Josefa's eyes searched for a friendly gaze among the crew. They were the lighthouse crew after all—the men who had been around her always, her whole life, whom she saw every day and who only wished her well, with whom she played hide-and-seek and card games, or for whom she sang, the men who were her audience when she did playacting and who made up games for her on their off-duty watches. What was wrong with them today?

"Wh-why," she began, and she could hear there was something wrong with her voice, it stuck so strangely to her mouth, to her teeth, her tongue, her teeth, her-her teeth.

"Why are yo-o-ou s-so nasty?"

"Come," said Aid.

"You don't want to know anything about this, Josefa," said Olsson. "Go home now."

"D-d-don't want to know," Josefa began, but then Aid pulled her away, he pulled her by the arm even though she struggled against it, away from the graves and the black sand shadows on the snow. She kept looking back at the dark staring faces by Quist's grave, until at last they disappeared among the trees. The inside of her mouth became thicker. And they hadn't walked for many minutes before she suddenly showed the whites of her eyes and fell down.

She lay in the snow kicking and flailing, and for a moment she could see herself from above, she looked as if she were making a snow angel, that's how she looked; Aid's dark figure crouched beside her. Then she saw how the dark lines of the pine trees rose above her for an eternity, pointed up and up toward a zenith far overhead, far up in the whiteness that only grew whiter. Red foam colored the snow and her cheeks.

Aid had made his practical device, and Quist was laid in a coffin and buried two meters underground the next morning, as soon as the lighthouse lamps were extinguished. But before they carried him to the grave, they held devotions in the chapel. Lighthouse Master Jacobsson read the text. It was an uncomfortable situation, and Kalle Jacobsson had a hard time keeping his thoughts focused while he read. The men mostly sat looking down at the floor, scraped their feet a little. And when they came to the hymn, it was clear that something was missing, because Aid was not there, nor Josefa either; the organ bench was empty and the air was empty, the island had no voice today.

Kalle Jacobsson looked at the men as they sang, but none of them met his gaze. And in reality he was glad for that. He felt very weary when they carried Quist's coffin out of the chapel. It was just before the winter equinox and already dark outside. He should really have led the procession but could not bring himself to do that, so held back. If only Rakel had been here and held his arm. But Rakel was at home caring for Josefa and getting ready for Christmas. Kalle Jacobsson walked farther and farther behind the coffin as the men carried it between them with no visible effort. The snow crunched heavily beneath his steps, and he noticed that his breath did not come as calmly and deeply as usual.

But once at the grave he pulled himself together. The men already stood beside the coffin with bared heads waiting for what he would say. What should he say? They were expecting something from him.

He straightened his back, went to the foot of the coffin, looked each of his men directly in the face, one after the other, and said what should be said; what he *had* to say now, there in the winter darkness.

The men mumbled among themselves somewhat embarrassed, but Kalle Jacobsson gave them no time for second thoughts right then, and immediately began to say the Lord's Prayer.

Then the coffin was lowered, the device put in place, and the grave covered with earth. Afterward, Kalle Jacobsson walked home alone. He did not weep but thought about his daughter.

Josefa lay in bed for several days after the seizure in the snow under the pine trees because she was very weak, and during the first day and night she also had some small attacks that caused spasms and incontinence. Her mother and father stayed with her and cared for her together with Maja; she didn't see anything of Aid. Most of the time she just lay dozing. She was given bromine, and that made her tired.

Her father and mother were worried, and her father hardly dared to read aloud to her in the evenings, fearing it would be too much for her. She was so exhausted that it didn't matter much anyway whether he read or not, her whole body felt tired and heavy. She understood that the illness had come back again and that it was more serious this time, but Aid had not gone for the doctor, because ice was forming in the bays and inlets. She remembered little of what had happened that morning by the grave, just before the seizure, but she could remember that she had been with Aid when it happened, and she asked her parents about him, but only got evasive answers; he was busy, they said and didn't look at her.

She was too tired to wonder about it, and besides something strange had happened to her voice which made it hard to talk; the words stuck to her teeth and lips and wouldn't come out, but broke into pieces.

Then late one evening as she lay dozing, Aid suddenly sat beside her bed, wearing all his outer clothes, and just looked at her. She sat up in bed and was about to say his name, but he gently motioned her to keep silent. Maybe it was late at night. He smiled somewhat sadly as he stroked her hair.

"I miss you in the chapel," he whispered.

She just nodded.

"The ice is forming," he whispered.

"Mmm," she murmured. "Th-there's frost patterns on th-the windows. I can see that."

After she had gotten out the words, he looked at her for a long time, stroked her hair. His eyes were sad. But still, he smiled. She closed her eyes. He sat there like that for a long time, until she fell asleep again. And she dreamed that he talked with her, and in the dream his voice was completely normal, it was a beautiful voice, deep and musical, and he told her strange fairy tales, so she knew things she had never heard about before, about his life as a naval cadet and about all kinds of dangerous experiences, and about a king whose queen died and a princess white as snow and red as blood, and everything that happened to her, but then suddenly his voice was broken and cracked in the dream, like it normally was, and he said: "Why do you think I stayed on the island all these years?"

It is a very cold Christmas and an even colder January; there is little snow, the temperature is low and stable. Now and then some fine specks sift down from the air masses high in the cloudless sky; just pure crystals, frozen air. Ice begins to form around the island, soon it is like a blind eye in all the whiteness.

In the rooms at the lighthouse station, life returns to its usual pattern; the men take their watches and write down their observations, do the necessary tasks. Celebration of Christmas is very quiet, for Josefa is still weak and it seems to Lighthouse Master Jacobsson and his wife that there is actually very little to celebrate this year. And Josefa does not get the new sled she had wanted; she has gotten too big for such things, her father explains—but in reality her parents have decided, after much deliberation, that they don't dare to give her a sled, because just think if all the exertions on the hill caused another seizure? Josefa has already seen the fine new red-and-blue sled that is wrapped in gray paper in the shed, but she doesn't let them see that she knows, doesn't let them see that she is disappointed; she is happy for the books and sheet music she receives, says thank you nicely anyway.

Everything is the same as before. Well. Almost the same. And the men talk with Aid again. They talk with him, when they have to. It's the same as before, and if it's not exactly the same, it's almost the same. Anyway, things are almost the way they were before, or try to be the way they were before. Aid is never inside with the men in the evenings anymore, but mostly sits alone in his own room, reading perhaps, or doing something else, the thing nobody talks about. He is at the lighthouse master's less often, rarely comes to play cards, but on Christmas Eve he is allowed to come because Josefa misses him so much and her parents realize that; they let him come because there is no Christmas for Josefa without him, and Aid does not need to spend Christmas with the rest of the men, that way they don't need to have him there. He does not touch the glass of liqueur, it stands on the white tablecloth in front of him all Christmas Eve. On Christmas Day he plays in the chapel, but Josefa does not sing. So everything is almost the same as before. Aid plays rather poorly that Christmas Day. Josefa doesn't understand why everything is *almost* the same as before and not *as* before, and it occurs to her that no one knows, no one knows what has happened, and no one knows why she no longer is allowed to go over to the men's lodgings and talk with them on their off-duty watch, as she always used to do. That simply isn't permitted. No one has said anything, but she can tell that her mother wants her to stop going there, and she doesn't ask why. No one knows. Just as no one knows what makes her sick, and it's best not to think too much about it and not to ask. Things are getting worse with Aid this winter, and that's something *everyone* knows, but nobody talks about it because this is something they don't *want* to know; they talk with him when necessary, and otherwise he is by himself. Now and then he has a strange, distant look and a slightly ruddy face; everyone thinks they know why, no one wants to know.

And no one knows that during the days an old man is walking along the beaches, where sand meets ice, while snow sprinkles from the sky, an old man who has no purpose in being on this island. Who is he? Josefa sees him now and then when she is out walking; he doesn't frighten her, even though she thinks he must be a ghost. But he just gives her a kindly, slightly squinting look, a look that comes from far away, that doesn't belong to the island here or to its time; someone from very far away. She isn't afraid of him, because this tall old man is just as light and distant as the delicate snowflakes that fall from the sky. He has white hair and a fine, noble face. So it can't be Gothberg or another of the local ghosts, whom Josefa has never actually seen herself but only heard described in vivid detail by Madam, who *has* seen them, many times, ah yes, yes, many times. But Josefa can see the old man, and he likes to walk along the beaches while snow crystals are falling. He is dressed all in black, and he stops and looks at the crystals that have landed on his jacket sleeve, peers at them intently, smiles. Sees Josefa, smiles. Or he looks at the ice growing along the beaches. Then he is gone in the blink of an eye. And Josefa doesn't find it the least odd to have this guest from far away; instead she finishes her walk, goes home. She doesn't go to the chapel, where Aid is sitting. Nowadays he more often spends his off-duty watches in the chapel than down at the lighthouse station. But he doesn't play, just sits there, motionless, at the organ. She has seen him through the window. Everything is almost the same as before.

Nevertheless, Aid is the one who gives her confirmation lessons because he knows just a little about theological questions—if indeed there will be any confirmation, because it has become somewhat difficult for Josefa to remember things. He reads with her and hears her lessons in the evenings. But they are never in the chapel together, because Josefa isn't allowed to do that; her parents are afraid she will overexert herself, use too much air, increase her pulse rate, and besides Aid doesn't play anymore. At least not for the time being.

"Fifth commandment. Well, Josefa?" Aid gives her a dissatisfied look, but smiles a little nonetheless.

"Thou shalt not commit adul—"

"No, that's the sixth. The fifth. The most important."

"Thou shalt not kill."

"What does this mean?"

"We shall fear and love God so that we—"

"So that we—do not—"

"S-so that we do not—not—"

"—so that we do not ha . . ."

"—so that we do not h-harm our neighbor's body nor do him any wrong, but h-help him when he is in n-need."

Aid clears his throat, tries to clear his voice, which will never be clear.

"That's right," he whispers. "One more time. Fifth commandment."

"Fifth commandment. Thou-shalt-not-kill. This means: We-shall-fear-and-love-G-God—so-that-we-do-not-harm-our-neighbor's-body-nor-do-him-any-wrong—but help him so he is in need."

"*When* he is in need."

"*When* he is in need."

"It goes along with the Love-your-neighbor commandment, which is just as important. How does that go?"

She looks at him, slightly annoyed.

"You'll see, your catechization will go just fine this spring," Aid says encouragingly.

"Do you think so?"

"Yes, I think so. Now, the Love-your-neighbor commandment?"

"Can't you tell me more stories?"

"No, not now. You don't take this seriously enough. Your catechization won't go well if you don't take this seriously. Just think if you were to stand there looking stupid in front of the pastor and everyone else." He is obviously trying to startle her. "This is *important*."

"You shall love your neighbor as your-s-self," she says quickly.

"Good. And why do these two go together?"

But she doesn't know.

"It's written in the Gospel of Matthew," Aid explains. "Seventh chapter, twelfth verse: 'Whatsoever ye would that men should do to you, do ye even so to them.' And in the Gospel of John: 'Whosoever hateth his brother, is a murderer.' "

"What does that mean?"

"It means," Aid says slowly in his grating voice, "that we're all brothers."

"Can't you tell me a story instead?"

"Of course I can," Aid rasps, "but I don't want to. Not when you don't pay attention."

"I d-do pay attention."

"Josefa," he whispers suddenly, "it's too bad you've developed this trouble with your voice." He gives her a serious look. Does he have tears in his eyes?

"Yes."

"Is it . . . because of the sickness, do you think?"

"Yes," she whispers back. She has tears in her eyes herself. "I'm sure it's the s-sickness."

He clears his throat, clears it again, but does not say anything.

"So b-both of us have ruined v-voices," she says quietly.

He looks at her for a long time.

"Nonsense," he says. "Voices aren't ruined so easily."

"Maybe I can't sing anymore."

"Oh yes," he says with a solemn look. "You can sing. I'm absolutely sure of that. Soon we'll go to the chapel again, whether or not you get permission from your father and mother."

"Yes," she begs. "Can't we do that?"

"Or at least in the spring, after the doctor has seen you. He'll certainly give you permission to come and sing again."

"D-do you think so?"

"Yes," he says. "You'll sing again. I'm absolutely sure you will. Voices don't get ruined so easily. I'm absolutely sure about that."

NINE

THE SILENCE

He lay for many days without knowing anything but his own name. Besides, something heavy and hard was on his face; he didn't know what it was. It felt as if someone had made a cast of a death mask and forgotten to remove it. Maybe it was the smell of plaster and bandages that made him think of death masks—in any case, he was lying inside the mask now, and he remembered his own name, his own name above all. Bernhard, he thought, I am Bernhardbernhard. He clung to this name. He couldn't see because of whatever was on his face, and he couldn't move. But he thought he was lying in a bed. It was quiet around him for the most part. But now and then he could hear a loud, resounding clang; it reminded him of something dear to him, and he realized that this clang wanted to awaken him. That's what it wanted to do. It called his name. Bernhardbernhardbernhard, he thought. It's steeple bells, it's huge bronze bells. Yes. Sometimes he could also hear a window rattling, rattling, right by his head, and that annoyed him greatly, it hurt his ears, but he couldn't move and couldn't talk, and his eyes saw only darkness, and this actually didn't seem the least bit strange to him, any of it; he smelled plaster and someone had covered his face with a death mask again. Now and then there was another sound too, one that affected him strangely and tried to frighten him—it sounded almost like a sick animal or a headless rooster, whimpering and whining for long periods at a time. That was even worse to listen to than the clattering window. But when the bells rang, the headless whimpering stopped and he felt calm inside. Bernhard, he thought, Bernhardbernhard. Someone came and changed him if he was wet, and two strong hands lifted him if he needed to be rubbed with lotion; he felt pain in his whole body, and in the back of his neck. In moments of clarity he assumed he was sick, and wondered if it was his mother caring for him, or his good friend and benefactor, Cantor Bach. But no one said anything, so that could hardly be the case, so to speak. Speak. Then sleep and unconsciousness overcame him and he forgot everything again. Once he thought he heard the sound of something wonderful, music playing and a group singing, and the sound almost made him weep, and he heard the headless rooster again, and suddenly realized that maybe it was himself he heard. But then the music disappeared like a puff of wind and the whimpering with it.

Far away he saw his father, bearded, stern, and spectacled; he looked grimly at his son, but never said anything. It was a picture of Morality with a beard, and Bernhard had been very afraid of this picture when he was small, yes, more afraid than when he was sent aloft in the rigging for the first time as a seventeen-year-old sailor, and even more afraid than the first time he received a rope flogging. As a matter of fact, it wasn't the first time, because Morality had always had—if not a rope then at least a rattan cane at his disposal, and he had used it regularly when his son had not lived up to Morality's expectations. It was all very strange, because when Bernhard was only nine years old, Morality with a beard was taken away to a place where only the most immoral people are sent. Morality was put in prison and never got out, but died there rightfully, like the charlatan and swindler he was. Social climber and swindler. And that was perhaps best, for then his wife did not have to live with the shame, but could get rid of the swindler's name, put the headlines and rumors behind her, restore her maiden name, take her small son and move to a place where no one had heard of the scandal or knew who they were.

"Enberg," his mother said to him. "Remember that, when anyone asks you, Bernhard. Bernhard Enberg."

Bernhard was quick to learn and never said the old name, because his mother had wept when she told him this, and she never cried otherwise.

She hadn't cried in the difficult days after Morality was suddenly gone and had left his affairs in the lurch, and all the men came and demanded to talk with the director, demanded to know when the director planned to show his face in Stockholm again, or damn well wanted to know where in the world the scoundrel was. She hadn't cried *then*, but answered them with quiet dignity, even when they shouted. She hadn't cried either when the director in fact turned up again, in Ystad of all remarkable places (he who loved Paris), and she hadn't cried when he was arrested or during the trial. The only time she cried was when one day many men came again—not shouting now, just silent and obedient and never looking at her—and took away nearly all the furniture. The furniture, all the jewelry, even Bernhard's steam engine and his wonderful sailboat, the one that stood on the windowsill. But it wasn't any of those things his mother cried about, it was the grand piano. She begged them to let it stay, in fact she fell to her knees in front of the mover's foreman and asked him to take everything, just not the piano, it was hers. But he showed no understanding, just pointed to the piano with his face, and his silent men came with harnesses and took it away. Then his mother cried. Then, and when she explained to him about the name.

However, Bernhard was only too pleased about the name. He understood. Because it really hadn't been any fun to be Morality's son, never, and especially not during the last months; he didn't have a single friend left at school, and longed to get away from the whole situation. Anyway, he had only seen Morality on Sundays, and at nice dinner parties. That meant a sailor suit and starched collar and "Yes, Father," "No, Father," accompanied by Morality's displeased growl if things went *well* at school, and his even more displeased growl if they went poorly. Or the rattan cane. The son didn't meet Morality's expectations of manliness and showed signs of avoiding work in the simplest things. So Bernhard didn't particularly miss his father when he had to go to prison, at least no more than he had missed him before. On the other hand, it was sad about the piano, because that had been their dearest possession, his mother's and his. The two of them had spent many of the lonesome evenings, when his father was at the club or out of the country on business or merely away, in the light of the single lamp on the piano. After the maid had cleared the table, after his schoolwork had been avoided, and the apartment—room after room, large and dark and elegantly unused—surrounded them like a black lampless sea, they sat there, his mother and he, and she played in a safe circle of light.

And then his mother's fingers on the keys told of another time, another coast, long ago when she wasn't married to Morality; a time when everything was light and happy and beautiful, when she was a promising young pianist. That's how Bernhard imagined her: young and beautiful and promising, with joyful curls in her hair and Chopin flowing in her long slim arms, surrounded by admirers and friends. Until one evening after a private concert, when suddenly an evil, bearded troll-man stood behind red portiers and watched her, waited for her, and bewitched her. And she married Morality. This was how Bernhard imagined it, and it probably had little to do with reality; he actually had very little idea how everything had happened, how these two people who didn't fit with one another had met. He never asked but was satisfied with his own conception of the matter. The idea that Morality had any deeper involvement with his mother, or with himself, seemed strange and incomprehensible, in fact irrelevant. And his father disliked that Bernhard played the piano; perhaps because it wasn't masculine enough, or because that was his mother's domain, her frivolous memory, and Bernhard ought not to have any part in it.

No, it was worse that the grand piano was gone than that his father had to go to prison. For many weeks afterward he felt as if he had lost a limb, lost his hands, lost his voice; if he came home from school and wanted to sit down to practice, it wasn't there, no keyboard was there to meet the longing of his hands; it was incomprehensible, he almost didn't believe it could be true. Later, when they had moved to the new place, to the small town farther south, Bernhard took a long piece of white wrapping paper, a ruler, and a pencil, and drew keys, a whole keyboard, on the paper and pinned it on the kitchen table. There he practiced, silently, when he came home from school. It wasn't the same, but it kept his fingers firm. But his mother could never be persuaded to play on the paper. Never. Besides, she had more than enough to do creating some order and security in their new environment; she nearly wore herself out, day and night, finding a solution.

Bernhard now understood, better than before, that he had an exceptionally good and self-sacrificing mother. Perhaps she had been a promising pianist, perhaps that was just a fairy tale, but she was certainly stubborn and capable. She could hardly cook, they no longer had maids, ergo she taught herself to cook. And that's how she got the idea. She bought a secondhand copy of Hortense v. Pfauendorff's *Big Cookbook for Better Households*; it was stained, page 342 was missing (chicken liver pâté I & II, with and without truffles), so she got it cheaply. After scarcely a year, with much hard work, she had gone from burned béchamel sauce to perfect poached eggs in tarragon-flavored veal broth aspic; but during this period his mother had little time left for Bernhard. She had received a little help from family and friends, to *get going*, to *start* with, they said; now she bought all the required appliances, containers, and kitchen utensils. For his mother, who had been married to Morality, who had held dinner parties for twenty-two guests when she was still the director's wife and Morality was still a popular and boldly creative industrialist, and who had also been out in the world as a young woman—his mother instinctively understood what was needed in the sleepy little coastal town, namely, stuffed partridge, capons filled with mincemeat, fried chicken livers on a bed of lettuce bits, champagne sorbets, and asparagus soup with quail eggs. Precisely the kind of fare they had served in those days when they still had three maids in the house. For none of this was to be found in this little town, but one did find an ecclesiastical dean and a mayor, a stationmaster and a chief of police, a consul and still another consul, as well as a couple of directors and other citizenry of various proportions. And above all, the town included the aforementioned persons' wives, who dreamed of the world beyond.

So the three rooms in which Bernhard and his mother now lived were regularly transformed into a workshop, a large kitchen where a pot of chilled consommé was clearing on the coffee table, where trays of roasted hazelnuts were cooling on the bed, and where the kitchen table was the scene of stuffed crayfish tails with peas baked in mille-feuille; at such times, the paper piano had to relinquish its place. The town had a new professional cook, and soon she was greatly sought after; social life blossomed as never before, the times were good, the times were peaceful, and it was a time for dreams among the wives of captains, consuls, and engineers. This Mrs. Enberg, her cooking tasted of names, of words one had heard about, places one had been in one's youth or pretended that one had been. Maxim's. Procope. La Coupole. She became very popular among the town's upper class, her culinary arts attracted attention beyond the town, and soon she was traveling by train back and forth to neighboring towns—towns that were equally sleepy, whose petty bourgeoisie did not want to be outshone—with Hortense v. Pfauendorff in the large midwife bag she had procured. Gradually more cookbooks were added, always more advanced. Furthermore, his mother, who in her day had entertained generals and ambassadors at her table, even people of royal blood, was very reserved in her manner, but at the same time very decided. She made it quite clear if she disagreed with the hostesses' proposed menus for various occasions, if she found them too lavish, too dull, too unimaginative, too impossible, too expensive, too cheap. She knew what kind of wine one drank and what one did not drink, knew the vintages and the mysteries of tempering, knew that one removed one's galoshes in the entry, knew the order in which to make toasts, knew the correct moment for applause after someone made a toast—on all these important points of dispute, which under certain circumstances can occupy much of a person's mind if they remain unanswered, his mother was a walking reference work. She knew *more* than they about all such things, but never boasted about it, simply let her knowledge discreetly sift through to the hostess who needed it, always made her insights available. She possessed a sort of musicality for such things, and the fact that nobody really knew where it came from or who she was made her doubly interesting. Moreover, she had dark hair with long beautiful curls that kept escaping from her topknot, and she always dressed in black (always, always). But she never mingled, she knew her place. And of course she had her secret to guard. Still, they noticed it, there *was* something, something about her manners, her speech—she was a mysterious, foreign bird among them and won their minds with her dignified modesty, and their stomachs with her blue-shell clams sautéed in white wine and served with ginger and strips of leek, her Caneton Montmercy, and her orange fromage with a liqueur sauce. When she began she knew nothing about the art of cooking, other than *how* food should taste. That was the musicality. She always wore black after Morality died, but had traveled alone to the funeral when he passed away during the first year of his imprisonment (from a broken heart, the letter said); she traveled alone, so as not to expose Bernhard to shame and whispers, and so as not to make her absence from the little town more noticeable than necessary. That way she succeeded in keeping her secret and maintaining her renown. During all these months of toil she had little time left for Bernhard, so he was often alone; she worked hard, grew thin and pale. But after a year as a gourmet cook his mother reached her first goal; one afternoon when Bernhard came home from school the piano stood there.

No Bechstein, of course, but a perfectly fine piano from Gebr. Zernikov, used, very nicely used. It was a strange moment, for Bernhard had scarcely touched a piano in almost two years, and his mother was moved when he sat down and awkwardly began to play a few notes. It was strange and unfamiliar, as if his hands had gotten too big for the keys—and maybe that was true, he was now almost twelve years old and had grown a great deal.

But the two years without an instrument had created a new voice in Bernhard, it seemed to have forced itself out on its own when he no longer had a keyboard as an outlet. Besides, he had often been alone and had found it hard to mix with the boys at school; he wasn't from the town, was different, spoke differently. And in this blend of loneliness and a need to perform music, a voice rose in him. Fortunately, there was a boys choir in town, at the cathedral, led by the organist, Cantor Bach. (That was actually his last name, to the great amusement of the small town's witty snouts, but his first name was quite ordinary, Björn.) And this Cantor Bach directed a small boys choir, just sixteen or seventeen boys, and no men's voices, but nonetheless a proper choir. Bernhard's mother had signed him up as soon as she learned about the choir; besides, it was free. And there Cantor Bach discovered that Bernhard had a voice. A beautiful soprano voice, clear and pure, with remarkable fullness. As long as Bernhard and his mother had had the piano in Stockholm, while Morality still ruled, his voice had remained unnecessary and undiscovered. But now, when Bernhard no longer had an instrument to play, his voice emerged. It happened at the first choir practice when Bernhard auditioned; he stood there, an outsider, a newcomer, well dressed but with the slightly evasive gaze of the déclassé. Sitting in front at the piano, Bach asked him to sing a scale. Bernhard stood erect and began with a scale so pure and true that it startled the other boys, cantor Bach, and, not least of all, Bernhard himself. He knew he was musical, but had never sung like that before. The cantor was exhilarated. Because as soon as Bernhard had sung the scale, Bach knew that a prince had landed among them, here, far out in the provinces. He gave Bernhard an arpeggio to sing, and still another, and finally "Bist du bei mir," and Bach listened blissfully; this was a prince, a music prince, a rare talent; he had never heard such a beautiful voice. The very next Sunday, Bernhard sang a solo in the worship service.

He could thank his voice for many things; his voice protected him. It protected him from teasing at school, where he was a stranger with a different accent and a different temperament, where things could easily have gone badly. But since Bernhard sang in church every Sunday—sang so it sent chills down one's spine and the women got tears in their eyes and the men opened their eyes after the sermon—he was protected. For the parents of Bernhard's classmates were among these good citizens, of course; his teachers also sat there, as well as all the other authorities. So Bernhard was spared any trouble because he was something special. His voice preceded him and protected him. Even if he did not have friends among the boys, he had respect, almost awe. They moved aside for him, did not touch him, never ridiculed him. But they never talked with him in an ordinary way, because what in the world would you talk about with somebody like that? He belonged to the grown-ups somehow, his *voice* belonged to the grown-ups; it was bigger than them and more serious than the schoolboys' world—so it was best to stay away. No one thought about whether Bernhard's extraordinary voice also was too big and too serious for the boy himself. "Bist du bei mir." So Bernhard was lonely. But he wasn't unhappy.

When the piano arrived, it was a different Bernhard who touched it; he no longer missed a piano in the same way, because something greater had appeared, his voice, which had become the most important thing for him. Still, he was happy when the instrument stood there, because he knew it had cost his mother two years of hard work, two years of systematic saving; it was the most wonderful surprise he had ever received. And he practiced it diligently. But his mother rarely touched it anymore, they never sat together in the lamplight fantasizing on the keys as before. She couldn't bring herself to do that. It's possible she missed the grand piano, or perhaps it was something else she missed. There was just silence inside her, as if something had broken. And she expended so much of herself in cooking; it demanded all her creative energy and anything else that remained. Only now and then would she play the piano, but not as before; mostly a few small pieces, played somewhat listlessly and uncertainly. You could hear that she *had* been able to play, in an earlier life, her touch revealed that, but her vitality was gone. You could say her voice had shifted from one medium to another, to pots and menus. Now that she had a piano she could have expanded her activities of course, become a piano teacher, but she restricted herself to the pots. Besides, cooking required all her time, and it was not particularly well paid. It was also affected by the seasons, so she had to work hard; to make ends meet she burned her candle at both ends. She grew very thin and got dark shadows under her eyes.

She put aside money for Bernhard's education.

Now and then she spit blood. That became yet another secret she had to hide, because she was a cook after all. She didn't tell anyone, not even Bernhard. And Bernhard was good at not seeing what he had seen. What else should he do? She put aside money for his education, for fame, for everything that *must* come. Would he be a bass, would he be a tenor, a baritone?

Bernhard grew, along with his voice; he did his voice exercises faithfully, practiced the piano, and one evening Cantor Bach came to talk with his mother at their home and they laid great plans for Bernhard's future, for the future of his voice, as soon as his voice changed. Every Sunday he sang in church.

When he was fourteen years old, he got measles; they came late, it was a severe case, and he was in bed for three weeks. Much of the time he lay in the dark because the light hurt his eyes. His mother cared for him anxiously.

A strong, kind male voice.

"Can you hear me, Lieutenant Enberg?"

There was something strange about the voice, something foreign and singsong, and the words were different. Lying there in his bandages, he couldn't really grasp what the difference was—he understood what was said, but it sounded strange nonetheless.

"Do you understand what I'm saying, Lieutenant Enberg?"

Good question. But he understood.

"Don't try to talk, just move your hand if you understand me."

Bernhard moved his hand, it was strangely light and numb.

"You've had a serious accident, Lieutenant Enberg."

Lieutenant Enberg.

"We're going to remove some of the bandages around your head now, but you must try not to move, even if it hurts. Do you understand? Move your hand, please."

His hand.

All that light—it was awful. He glimpsed a face, two faces, then everything grew dark because he had to close his eyes.

"That went fine, Lieutenant Enberg."

. . .

"Don't try to talk. You got quite a blow. Use your hand. Do you know where you are?"

No. Yes. He opened his eyes just barely, squinted toward the face and the friendly voice. Then he understood why it had sounded so strange, the man had spoken Norwegian.

And Bernhard knew where he was.

I know what happened. The cruiser *Queen Josephine* of Karlskrona was a large three-masted ironclad vessel with full armament. During my six years in the navy I had served aboard the *Josephine* for three years, and had been promoted to the rank of a junior officer, to lieutenant junior grade. The *Josephine* had patrolled the Skagerrak in heavy weather for three days and nights when it happened. On the first of October, as a part of a squadron of five ships, the *Josephine* headed north from Hälsingborg, where we had stopped enroute from Karlskrona to embark the commodore, Captain Windtler, and was en route to Bergen for a port visit. On the third of October in the morning the squadron passed Skagen's lightship one mile to starboard, in good visibility.

There was a fresh northwesterly breeze and we sailed northward close-hauled under full canvas. But that evening a small storm arose and the wind shifted to the west. Visibility was poor, and the squadron dispersed. The following day Captain Windtler tacked to about twelve or fifteen miles off the Norwegian coast. Then the weather deteriorated into a small storm, so he had to veer and tack against the west wind, which was gusting to a small gale. The temperature fell. The crew worked very hard. On the third night the forward mizzen ripped, and just before dawn, both jibs. The crew hoisted the reserves as quickly as was possible under those conditions. Several men suffered blows and falls, but I escaped without injury. We were worn out, but of good cheer. The *Josephine* was a fine ship, and she had a full, young crew with first-rate military discipline. However, the weather did not seem to be improving. Judging that the voyage could not continue much longer, Captain Windtler wanted to seek harbor as soon as possible and had set a double watch. Just before daybreak a lighthouse was sighted on the Norwegian coast to the northwest. Everyone on deck saw the light at the same time and let out a cheer. "It must be Egenes lighthouse," the lookout said. But the sight lasted only a few minutes, and then disappeared in the fog.

Then followed three days of heavy weather, during which the *Josephine* navigated as well as possible by dead reckoning. The leeway was strong—stronger than anyone realized, we would discover. We used only the essential sails, and there was lesser damage to the mainmast and foremast.

The seventh day at five o'clock in the afternoon, just before the shipwreck, the fourth officer, Lieutenant Borg, reported that he had seen a light to leeward. I wrote the night orders for the commodore that evening and was in the chart house when Lieutenant Borg came in with his report. Borg and the commodore stood for a while discussing which lighthouse it could have been; the second in command, Captain Knutsson, arrived and they all stood for a long time studying the charts. The commodore thought we must be twenty nautical miles west of Lysekil on the Båhuslen coast, and assumed the leeward light had been a steamer. We had lain like this for five days; the weather showed no sign of abating. Now Windtler wanted to set course south into the Kattegat to seek calmer waters.

At that moment we went aground. We felt a mild jolt, every man rushed on deck, we in the chart house rushed to the bridge. A more powerful jolt now followed, and yet another. The order was given to turn out.

"We must have been closer to the Swedish coast than we thought," shouted the commodore, who probably thought we had run into one of the reefs near Smögen. For a while it seemed as if the vessel was clear, then she suddenly began rocking violently. The helmsman reported the ship had lost steering. So she was hard aground. At that moment the weather cleared, and we again saw the light to leeward. It was clearly a lighthouse, not a steamer, and not many miles away.

"So it's the Norwegian coast," said the captain; the words came with gloomy resignation. The ship had been pressed westward the entire time, and had not crossed Skagerrak at all. In fact, it was the Egenes lighthouse we saw again.

Almost at once breakers began crashing onto the deck and the crew sought shelter in the cabins or rigging. We immediately began to launch distress signals and fire the signal canon at short intervals. Spirits were reasonably good; the weather had also improved somewhat, and the ship's iron hull gave no sign of breaking apart, despite considerable leakage in the forward holds. The pumps were working at full power. The mainmast had been partially damaged where it still carried sail and some splintered wood dangled in the ropes, but it stood firmly. We probably had a respite of several hours, indeed in all likelihood the damage to the *Josephine* was not severe enough to prevent getting her afloat when the weather improved, but in any case we needed to get the crew ashore as quickly as possible, just to be on the safe side. No one knew these waters, and to launch a small boat to try to go ashore on our own could only be the last resort; we had to wait until someone on shore saw us.

And after scarcely half an hour the lighthouse responded with two flares; they had seen us. The commodore asked me to try to signal with the Morse lantern to request instructions from people ashore who knew the waters, but visibility was too poor. We could see the people ashore had a signal lantern too and were trying to answer, but after half an hour of confusing dots and dashes partially drowned in sea spray and mist, we had to abandon trying to communicate by the sculptor method—old Sam Morse, who invented the Morse code, was a sculptor and painter, so we like to call it the sculptor method; also, perhaps the signaling reminds one a little of short and long chisel strokes.

But now we could glimpse at least two rescue boats heading out to us. As mentioned, the weather had cleared, or at least gotten no worse, and the vessel still lay firmly aground on the reef, so there was no cause for hasty anxiety.

The commodore asked me to take three men and go amidships on the starboard side to receive the rescue boats when they came alongside. Some sailors had sought shelter in the ladder to the bridge, one of them young cadet Karlsson, whose naval service had just begun; he was seventeen years old, thin and apprehensive, and had quite a hard time on board. I thought he might need to bolster his self-confidence a little, so I asked him to come along. The deck was slippery, but the only real difficulty as we moved along the railing was having masses of seawater wash over us. We had boarding hooks and coils of rope with us, and I thought it would be a rather easy matter. We leaned over the railing as the boats neared, ready to throw the lines over.

However, we hadn't taken the wind into account, which at that moment began blowing strongly. The *Josephine* suddenly rocked violently, a breaker crashed over the deck, and young Karlsson was swept overboard, light as a feather. At the same time, some of the rigging in the mainmast loosened and fell into the sea along with other woodwork and deck rigging. I'm not really sure if I lost my balance as I hung over the railing, or if I reached out for Karlsson as he flew past to try to haul him in, but I saw the sea come toward me and realized I was falling.

All I remember about the time I was in the water is this: everything grew dark and confined. I hadn't taken a breath before going under, and I was quite convinced that I was about to drown. It was cold. I've never experienced such darkness. It wasn't just the black water. I noticed that there was movement around me the whole time, and that the darkness *moved*, that it *wanted to do something with me*. That's what frightened me most. I don't know if I had my eyes open under the water. Nor do I know if I opened them when, to my surprise, I reached the surface. I suppose I did. Because I remember that I turned my head to orient myself the moment I came up, at least I *think* I turned, and at that moment I think I saw the timber, part of the topgallant yard it must have been, which came rushing with a wave straight toward me, huge and shiny, along with a tangled mass of rope and tackle, and it wasn't possible to duck. I think I saw this. And I think I was thrown against the side of the ship. I think I was bleeding badly.

But I saw something else. When the crash came and things went black for me, I saw the ship. I saw myself dancing. Yes, that's right. Suddenly I was high above the seething water. I saw the ship, the *Josephine*, lying there, and I saw the rescue boats. Then suddenly I stood on the ship's rail, with both feet on the curved slippery railing, as easily as could be. I had no trouble keeping my balance and I moved as light as a feather, walked back and forth, while I saw that they were busy with their boat hooks down there in the water, as they tried to pull something dark out of the even darker water. It had nothing to do with me. I was standing on the railing, I actually danced across the slippery curved railing, and I was very light. They shouted and noisily thrashed around me, more people arrived. It hadn't mattered, but then I saw that another person also lay in the water; I saw young Karlsson who had been washed overboard with me, even though I don't know how I saw him, because he wasn't visible, he was under the water, surely half a meter under; I scarcely knew him, he was just a young deckhand who didn't concern me, but I thought that *still . . . somebody for God's sake must grab his sweater so he doesn't go under forever*. And the moment I thought this, everything grew dark again, and I was under the water again, and I only know that I held fast to Karlsson's sweater, and the reason it was so difficult, so terribly heavy to pull me up, was that it wasn't one, but two; I held fast to the boy and they pulled us up together.

"I must say you did a good job, Enberg."

. . .

"You're a real craftsman. Just think, it had hung there all those years gathering dust, and become really worm-eaten, and now you've helped us to get it repaired."

. . .

"No, don't say anything. I understand. Don't say anything."

. . .

"Do you want your slate to write on? Just a minute, I'll . . . Here. Here it is."

. . .

"My wife and I have come to consider you a guest here at the parsonage. Yes, you know that my wife cared for you when you were on the verge of dying? The doctor had pretty much given you up, didn't even want to move you, so you stayed here at our home."

Yes.

"You were so battered we didn't think you would survive. You were in terrible condition. I don't know how many broken bones you had—aside from the—oh, well. And now here you sit making repairs. After only three months. It's a miracle."

It's the least I could do.

"It's an old ship model, you know. It has hung from the ceiling here for more than a hundred and fifty years."

Why?

"Oh—as far as I know, in gratitude for a shipwreck where everyone was saved. One of the Danish king's silver vessels, filled with expensive cargo and noblemen. We're exposed to harsh weather out here at Egenes, and there are sinister shallows; a veritable ships' graveyard. So for that matter—yes?"

It's appropriate that I repair it.

"Just what I was about to say."

. . .

"Yes, we've come to consider you a guest here in our home, Lieutenant Enberg. A guest. My wife is very happy that you came to your senses again."

. . .

"Have you thought about your future?"

No.

"No. I understand."

I don't want to be a burden.

"Oh, no, no! You misunderstand. You can stay here at Egenes as long as you wish. As long as you wish. Until you've regained your strength. Furthermore—the proprietor at Ekelund has been kind to you; when he heard about your fate he sent some money toward your support beyond what you get from the navy, which will give you time to recuperate. Besides—"

. . .

"And . . . Besides, a letter has arrived saying that you're going to receive a medal for your bravery."

A medal?

"Yes. You saved that boy, after all."

Don't need a medal.

"Yes. You need that medal, Lieutenant Enberg."

Maybe.

"People have told me that you're a musician. That you play the organ."

. . .

"Won't you play a little for us? It's not a good instrument, but it would please us very much if—"

. . .

"I see. You don't want to."

There is an organ in the church. But he cannot touch it. He leaves the church quickly if anyone is playing it. He leaves if the congregation is singing. He goes down to the sea.

Voice change. His voice changed over several years. Both his mother and the Cantor Bach admonished him: Don't push, don't try to sing, just do small humming exercises. Mmmmm-mmmmm, up and down in your register. It was terrible to lose his voice for the second time, when he recovered from the measles and his voice change was suddenly there, inflicted on him—it was worse than the first time, when the grand piano disappeared. But he was brave. He drank egg yolks in whiskey, and got a little intoxicated, every afternoon. Almost three years without a voice. Of course he could take refuge in the piano, but that was no longer enough. He missed his own voice, he missed the dizzying freedom in the high notes, missed listening to himself, hearing his falsetto, perfect, high up in his head and even higher; his current voice, the one measles had given him, seemed false and impure, not his. It was like losing himself.

But within him, within the unfinished, rough adolescent voice, another voice was emerging, like a hawk moth in a chrysalis; his throat was a cocoon where the miracle occurred; he could sense it, he knew it, an emperor moth, a golden baritone, a perfect instrument, bottle-fed with care and egg yolks in whiskey, a golden expectation, a voice with no other purpose than to be *heard*.

That had been the purpose. His voice was the purpose, it was what would finally rescue him. Yes, even finally rescue him from the navy, it *was* already his salvation. He continued to drink the little egg toddies as a cadet and later as a lieutenant, he warmed himself with them. Not a free weekend, not a furlough passed, without Lieutenant Enberg rushing away to practice. He practiced in his small attic room, he sang in the navy chorus; he gave small concerts at Free Church gatherings and for temperance societies, even in pubs and marketplaces, to supplement his income. Because he needed money; he had a voice teacher of course, a very good voice teacher, the best he could get. That had happened with Cantor Bach's intervention; the two musicians had known each other, a little, when they were young. And Bernhard could pay for the lessons. That was the most important thing. That was the only important thing, the very reason for everything else. For five years his navy pay was just sufficient for lessons from Royal Court Singer Topelius; the old lion was annoyed that the instruction was so irregular because of Bernhard's frequent sea duty, and he complained and scolded each time his pupil finally came back after many weeks at sea, tanned and thin.

"You don't build a voice this way, Enberg. You build it with consistency. *Consistency, practice, and correction.*"

"But I practice on board."

"Ha. On board. You ought to sing *here*, with *me*. Twice a week. Ah well. Please begin."

And Bernhard's great triumph was always that when he had sung for three minutes, Royal Court Singer Topelius had forgotten his annoyance, forgotten everything called consistency, but enthusiastically corrected him.

"I believe you actually get something out of singing there under the mast," he would say. "You get better and better, each time you've been out." And Bernhard laughed.

"One has a rich musical life in the navy," he said.

"That's nonsense," said Topelius, stroking his mustache. "Rich musical life indeed."

"It was the only way," said Bernhard quietly.

"Yes," said Topelius apologetically, "I realize that."

"I know it's not an ideal situation, Maestro. I'm very grateful that you nonetheless—"

"Now, now. That was stupid of me. We've tried to help you as best we could. The navy was the simplest solution. How old are you now?"

"Twenty-five."

"Hmm. And how many more years of service do you have?"

"Five."

"That's too long. You should get into a school as soon as possible. A conservatory."

"I realize that. But there are certain requirements."

"I was unsure to begin with," said the royal court singer, "when Bach wrote to me about you. I'll be honest: I didn't have much faith in either him or you. But you are gifted."

"Thank you, Maestro."

"It was evident from the first time you sang for me. Now things have progressed to the point that you should go further. You can't stand at the helm and sing any longer. You should stand on a stage, or in a cathedral. You should sing in Stockholm, in Berlin. But then we must get you out of the navy. Five more years is too long."

"My mother had plans to make that happen. And Cantor Bach. But then Mother became ill."

"I realize that."

"There was no money. The treatment took everything, and the sanatorium." Bernhard lowered his voice, looked down. "And there was the scandal too—my mother cooked in upper-class homes and continued doing that for several years even though she was ill, against her better judgment. When this became known, naturally there was no help to be had from those upper-class people, either for her or for me. So my only recourse was the sea."

"I realize that. I know what happened, Lieutenant Enberg. I've made inquiries."

Bernhard fell silent, looked down into the grand piano, saw the strings moving. Topelius struck a chord. He looked up.

"You are quite a—what shall I say—scandal-prone young man, Enberg," said Topelius. "I know who you are. Now, now, don't look so dismayed. I've made inquiries. I know who your father was. Do you know that I was quite well acquainted with Director Sachs when he was young?"

Bernhard did not say anything.

"Yes, I'm speaking about your father. Now, now. Don't look so gloomy. Sachs was basically a good man. He was very musical, did you know that?"

"No," said Bernhard, "I had no idea."

"Really? Played very well, both violin and piano. And he had a wonderful voice. In his youth. Came from an old organ-building family in Saxony, I believe. An excellent fellow. Cheerful and happy, a real life of the party. Capable with people and clever with money. Too bad that he tried to bite off so much more than he could—oh well. You must excuse me."

"That's all right."

"You must have inherited your musical gifts from him. And your voice. Yes, because a voice like yours can be inherited, passed on from one generation to the next, Enberg. That's your mother's name, isn't it?"

"Yes. She—"

"Well, I didn't know her. She must have had great hopes for you."

"Yes."

"You should have been at the conservatory long ago. The way things are now—well. Five more years without systematic training will not do. You must come ashore."

"And how can I manage that, Maestro?"

"We'll see. I still have various connections, old as I am. We'll see. If I don't know the rear admiral personally, at any rate I know his wife very well. You can add luster to the navy, Enberg, if only you can leave it. There isn't a rear admiral alive who is able to resist casting a little luster on his epaulettes and his squadron. I'll do my best. You're throwing away your life by sailing back and forth and playing war, and you're ruining your voice by giving concerts in those drafty halls early and late."

"I need the money."

"Money, young Enberg, is a problem that merit will solve. I believe it can be solved for you. But we mustn't spend our time talking. We must practice. So. *Wer nie sein Brot mit Tränen* . . . Please begin."

Bernhard sang. And the old man smiled, entranced, closed his eyes.

At the Free Church meetings the women wept when he sang about the great white hosts, and in the public squares the young people cheered and the women in the market stalls stopped their cackling when he sang about the penniless fate that can strike us all in the middle of life's morning. The pubs grew utterly quiet when he sang seductively about love and the sea, men and women pressed closer to each other; he made friends, best friends for a single night, and sometimes girlfriends too; people bought him food and drink. People bought him many drinks, and that was better than egg toddy, because it was without the egg. It warmed you better. And the warmer he became, the better he sang. He sang so they could hear the sound of the water rushing along the side of the ship, hear the gulls shrieking in the sunrise, hear the creaking of the helm on the midwatch, hear the stars. Bernhard Enberg needed nothing except his voice; he needed no money, no books, no weapons, just his voice. It was like reliving his childhood years. His voice preceded him and protected him, he was a prince. Even aboard the ship he escaped most of the harassing and fights, because with his voice he could make the whole ship sing, because the men got chills down their spines when he stood alone astern and sang in the evening, bowed his head, directed his voice down into the ship's wake and lit the phosphorescence with the notes. Or when he stood on the forecastle and trained his breathing by singing against the wind.

He needed nothing. He had his sorrow and his loneliness, but neither of those things could hurt him. He had worried and felt sad when he had to choose the sea, but his voice had smoothed the way for him, and he had become powerful and strong. It had been good for him, and his voice had grown, from the air and his efforts. And soon—hadn't Topelius almost promised it?—soon his voice would lift him up there where it belonged, to distant constellations of stars, Orion, Lyra, Stockholm, Berlin, Pegasus.

During the time in the parsonage, as well as all the years that will follow, he will often think about this, about what he has lost and what he has been separated from. This really seems to be the motif in his life. He eventually calls it the Separation Problem. He is no great metaphysician, and is an unpracticed thinker (because he'd had his voice, after all, so what would he do with such theoretical things), but now, when he no longer can open his mouth and say the simplest thing—to say nothing of singing—without people looking at each other uncomfortably or looking away, now, in this silence, he begins to reclaim what he has neglected. He thinks, he reads a little too. But the question was, what is the *meaning* in the fact that one can so easily *lose* something? People, home, instruments? The problem of separation seems especially hard to fathom when one is right *in the middle* of separation, and can't communicate about it. And already one year after his "good health report" with a crushed larynx he begins to long to go *away*,

away from people, away from cities and streets and voices; he begins to long for a place, a quiet place, a silent place, an outer isolation that matches his inner isolation, a place where perhaps he can—

No, he couldn't touch the organ that winter and spring when he lived in the parsonage at Egenes church, recovering. How could he *recover*? He drank a little, but no longer to warm himself. Not much, just every time he had a chance. He surreptitiously drank the pastor's sherry and stole bottles of beer from the icehouse, or drank a little of the wife's bitter table wine. He left the white wooden church if the congregation sang, walked across the fields. High above him the swallows shrieked, very busy with their concerns, the insects hummed; he practically ran through all of this, all the golden life that awakened around the parsonage, ran down the gravel path toward the bare, rough, sloping rocks, just as rough as his own larynx; he had to see stones and water. It had become almost unbearable for him to hear even the gruffest speaking voice, he had to press his nails hard into his palms in order not to rush out in despair when the pastor or the pastor's wife talked with him, he felt pressure in his chest, a deathly anxiety, and it was the worst if anyone sang or merely hummed. The sea, he thought, the sea. He put the land and the people behind him, all sounds of voices.

Then only the sea remained, the sea and the muteness.

And there on the sloping rocks, all that was in his mind as he looked down into the gray water, wondering and somewhat tentative—all that was in his mind were two things.

First: What was it like to sit on the bottom of the sea? Sit there, naked, on a stone and feel rough shells on your behind, peer up through the seaweed and into the bright undulating surface, chatter with the small fish. He took off his clothes several times and began to walk out, but always turned around, because something else was clear to him and would not let go of him.

Second: Such a voice can be passed on.

TEN

JOSEFA ADJUSTS

In early January the ice begins to form for good, but there are still open channels far out. The sea becomes silent, the pounding of waves is gone, it's as if something stops breathing. Here and there one sees animal tracks on the ice; close to the beaches the frozen water builds strange gray-and-white forms around stones and tree trunks. The days are brief flickers in the darkness. Josefa's mother is weather sick for days at a time. Kalle Jacobsson has become silent and introspective, and the men begin to talk about how suddenly he has grown old. Things get worse with Aid. He putters around all alone. The men are civil to him (what did the lighthouse master say to them at Quist's grave?) but keep their distance. Josefa is not allowed to go to the chapel with him, because her parents fear what the exertion could lead to—another seizure, or even worse, a new injury (that's what they say). She has begun to stutter. A little. Mostly when she is excited or happy or concentrating. The lighthouse master and his wife agree that it's best she take things very easy until Doctor Brunsell can come and examine her again. It's hard to say what Josefa's parents imagine Doctor Brunsell can actually do, what kind of miracle he can bring about by such an examination, but for now Josefa will take it easy. She is given bromide.

But they can't keep her from walking around on the island, or from populating the woods and beaches with imaginary beings as she has always done. The strange thing is that now, when she has begun to stammer, after the last seizure, now she sees everything far more clearly. Not just the old man who sometimes wanders on the beach, but all sorts of other things too. She sees the colored clouds in the air around the trees and she sees the light that rises from the old sailors' graves; if she goes to the Stone House, Gothberg's bandit hideout, she sees the blue outlines around the windows and at the threshold, and can see that someone is moving inside, even though the building is empty (it's otherwise used only as a guesthouse during the summer). Everything she reads is also much more vivid to her now, and when her father or Aid tell her fairy tales, there is scarcely any difference between pictures and reality. It takes a few months to adjust to this new situation; her parents are worried, perhaps they think she has grown lethargic, but in reality she just needs time to learn to know herself in a new way, the way she is now. So she doesn't sing either, not even when she is alone, not because she obeys her parents, but because she must first learn to *stand* in all this newness, to recognize herself in everything that goes on around and in her. Somewhere within her she knows that she can't endure even a single note until she understands more about how everything is now, and who she has become. Everything has become a *little* different. She sees so much, and it gives her so much to think about. She never tells anyone. It's hard to concentrate on lessons and Bible verses, to say nothing of the catechism. Besides, she thinks about the dead boy that morning she got sick for the first time, the boy who is dead and buried now. She thinks about his hair with sand in it. And she feels both cold and hot when she thinks about that hair between her fingers. The whole time she has a strange feeling that someone is going to come. One morning she hears a lone gull shriek loudly above the expanse of frozen whiteness, a gull shrieks, and it's as if a boy shrieked, an uncouth boy with a cracked, immature voice, a boy flying with white wings and hungry for food. She has to smile, but she's frightened too.

ELEVEN

A MESSAGE

The night of January 29, Lighthouse Master Jacobsson and Enberg assume the watch each in his own tower. The lighthouse master has begun to put Aid on night watches again, and there is no particular risk in that either, considering how much ice has formed in the channel; not a ship in sight as far as the eye can see, but of course the lighthouses still must be manned and lit.

They stand in the annex for a while and exchange a few words, but contacts between them are brief now, short and long at the same time. Kalle Jacobsson is sorry about the change, it hurts him, but he can't bring himself to treat Aid as before. He has protected him, he has borne the brunt of the responsibility, taken it on his own shoulders by not reporting what happened. But as a result, something seems to have gone to pieces between them. They have never talked about it, but Aid seems to understand, places on himself a quiet punishment, like a cape. Now and then Kalle Jacobsson thinks it would almost have been better if he *had* reported his old friend, then neither of them would have had to endure this *nothing*, this halfway condition. Oh yes, Enberg probably understands why people reproach him. But he doesn't protest either, just putters around by himself.

And Kalle Jacobsson can only interpret Aid's silence as some sort of admission.

Yet when the inspector came to take a deposition regarding the accident at sea, he had said that visibility was poor, much too poor. Look in the log, Kalle Jacobsson had said, it's all written there.

> . . . *the regrettable fact that lighthouse keeper Enberg did not see the shipwreck in time cannot be held against him. Quist did not see the distress signals from his lighthouse either. Unfortunately, Quist died unexpectedly and cannot testify, but it has been established that visibility was so poor during the hours in question that neither of the watch-standers could be held responsible. Quist and Enberg are regarded to be the most experienced out here.*

He had struggled a good deal with these sentences, written several rough drafts before he found one watertight enough to be written into the log. But—the men don't agree, and they have let him know that. None of them said anything, none were disloyal to the lighthouse master, because the lighthouse master is the island's king, it's *his* island. But they don't talk with him as before. He doesn't know what they say among themselves either, but several of them were with Quist during his final days; they surely must have talked with the sick man about what had happened, and probably have their own ideas. He *knows* they have their own ideas.

To think that he let the doctor leave so soon, without looking at Quist. But good Lord, it was just a bad cold. Wasn't it? He had been sure that Quist would be fine. The man was strong. Kalle Jacobsson had had so many other things to think about. He hadn't thought about all eventualities. There had been so many other things. Wasn't that why? Kalle Jacobsson is convinced that was why. But things are not as before; nor can he *say* anything, can't defend himself. The men keep a respectful but chilly distance from both him and Aid, and he is no longer able to look his old friend in the eye. It makes him feel lonely, and old. He knows it bothers Josefa that things are like this, but can't help it. He has taken the brunt for Aid, it cost him the friendship. Can one go so far to protect somebody to whom one is greatly indebted that one sacrifices the friendship? Rakel feels sad about it too, but says nothing. She is weather sick. Worries about

Josefa. If only they had been able to *talk* about this. But the silence grows, rises between them.

The words at the grave are all that has prevented things from falling completely apart with the men. Words about how in the final analysis it was the lighthouse master's responsibility to judge the situation and keep the log, and that he blamed himself too, that no one could know anything for certain, so to doubt would be the best for everyone, both the dead and the living, and also that Quist was looking down from heaven at his comrades and expected them to show friendship to each other, and forgiveness. Quist had died without a harsh word crossing his lips, and Kalle Jacobsson would never forgive himself for not getting treatment for Quist when it was possible. That was a serious and irreparable mistake, for which I am solely responsible. Our Father, Who art in heaven—

Besides: Was Quist correct? Was Enberg addicted to alcohol? Aid has always been odd, and if he slurs his words it's impossible to tell by his voice. If he drinks, nobody knows where his stock is hidden, where he gets the liquor, or when he finds time to drink. No one has ever seen him drink.

What do the men think? Does his breath smell of alcohol? Some think yes, others no. One sees what one sees. Sometimes when Enberg walks in the woods his gait seems a little strange. People have seen that. Kalle Jacobsson has seen that too. Or that he is flushed and his face and eyes look a little bleary. Now Aid can sail in his own sea; no one wants to walk with him anywhere, if they can avoid it. The men let Kalle Jacobsson know in various ways what they think about Enberg's possible addiction and about what he did or did not do that unfortunate night; a glance now and then, a passing comment, a word or two, that's enough. Kalle Jacobsson knows how to interpret his men. Things can't go on like this out here, Kalle Jacobsson thinks. Not much of his authority and power remain; he can't be the master, not as long as this is unresolved, not with the *entire* lighthouse crew against him. He hasn't reported his old friend. Hopefully the men have understood why and tacitly accepted it. But they *expect* something of him, expect an action, a reaction that can resurrect respect for him.

The worst part is that Aid is silent about the whole thing, never responds in either word or deed. He surely knows what they think about him, but doesn't defend himself. That disappoints Kalle Jacobsson more than anything else.

Next summer an engineer is coming to the island to experiment with new and brighter lamps that use acetylene gas. The idea is to no longer have twin lighthouses out here and to tear down one tower within a year. Then three of the men will have to leave. Bernhard Enberg earned himself a good pension long ago. But the moment Lighthouse Master Jacobsson thinks such thoughts, he rejects them again. How can he think like that, about Enberg, about his friend, about Josefa's friend? About the man who gave the island its voice? At the same time, he knows this is perhaps the only chance he will ever have to repair the damage that has been done.

His thoughts have gone back and forth like this for over a month. And he knows he will keep right on thinking about it until summer, if no changes occur.

The thoughts continue to raid Kalle Jacobsson's mind as he stands in the annex with Enberg preparing for the watch. It's eleven o'clock.

"It's going to be quiet tonight, Enberg."

"Yes," whispers Aid. "Probably so."

"There's a channel open in the northwest. Keep your eyes open."

"Yes," nods Enberg. Looks down.

"If anything should happen far out, beyond the horizon, someone might try to walk across the ice toward the island." Why does he say that? Enberg knows all this, of course.

"Mmm," nods Enberg. "I'll keep an eye on the ice."

"Visibility is good, a fine starry night," says the lighthouse master, and looks at Aid. "Come and tell me right away if there's anything to report." Why does he say all this?

"Mmm," nods Enberg. Does he smile a little? Is he mocking him?

"I'm sorry Josefa isn't allowed to go to the chapel during the day. I know she misses it. She keeps begging to go."

"She's ill," says Enberg. "I understand."

"I counted on that."

"Mmm." Again that little smile, if it *is* a smile.

"Well," says Kalle Jacobsson. "Have a good watch."

"Have a good watch, sir."

It's a long, quiet watch for them both. Each man sits in his tower. Every hour they walk around the balcony, look through the binoculars, search the horizon and the ice for any sign of a vessel, but all is calm. Kalle Jacobsson reads a novel, an amazing yarn by this fellow named Verne. But it's exciting, keeps him awake. Besides, he is interested in astronomy. Even so, the idea that it would be possible to travel with a comet, a tiny frozen globe, through the entire solar system is a bit too exaggerated for Kalle Jacobsson. But he reads. The heavy engine runs smoothly in the background, he doesn't hear it. Now and then he puts the book aside, walks out onto the balcony, takes deep breaths of cold air, keeps himself awake. Far away, on the balcony of the twin lighthouse, he glimpses Aid like a small dot; he assumes Enberg sees him too, but he doesn't wave.

He goes inside, continues reading.

A few minutes past two he hears someone on the stairs, heavy, shuffling footsteps. He looks up from his book, is taken aback. It must be Enberg. Surely it must be Enberg? Has something happened? Thick ice surrounds them for many kilometers, they haven't seen a ship for several days, what could have happened? He hears the footsteps on the wrought-iron stairs, but doesn't recognize them. Somehow they seem weary, seem weak—which doesn't sound familiar.

He hears a knock at the door, firm and loud.

Lighthouse Master Jacobsson puts his book away, rises from his chair, goes over to the door and opens it.

There is no one on the landing outside. He is startled.

"Hello?" he calls into the dark stairwell. He peers down the stairs, there is no one there either. Then he goes back to the room, gets the lantern, walks down several steps shining the light, but the stairway is empty.

"Is anyone here?" he shouts, and the sound reverberates against the walls. "Enberg?"

Silence.

He quickly climbs the steps again, puts on his jacket and scarf, grabs the lantern and goes down the stairway, shining the lantern in every corner.

When he reaches the bottom he opens the door carefully. But no one is standing outside. In the fine powder snow by the front steps he sees his own boot tracks and some other, older footprints.

"That's strange," he says half aloud. Then he strides firmly into the night toward the south tower. It's a five-minute walk, but he feels strangely ill at ease. Snow sprinkles from the trees around him as he walks.

He arrives at the south tower, opens the door, begins to climb the stairs.

Aid is standing in the doorway above.

"Is that you, sir?" he whispers down to him.

"Yes," says Kalle Jacobsson.

"Hmm," says Aid. "That's strange."

The lighthouse master takes the last stairs. Aid lets him in. Kalle Jacobsson gives him a quick inspection. He is in his shirtsleeves, his boots are dry. They stand looking at each other for a moment.

"I thought I heard you a little while ago," says Aid.

"Oh?"

"I heard footsteps on the stairs," he continues, "and somebody knocked. But no one was there."

"Oh," says Kalle Jacobsson again. "That's strange, Enberg, because the same thing just happened over in my tower."

"Oh?"

"About fifteen minutes ago."

They look at each other for a long time.

"You haven't been outside?" asks Kalle Jacobsson.

"No," says Aid, "but the more I thought about it, the stranger it seemed. I was just about to go over to see you, but you beat me to it, sir."

They look at each other again.

"Someone knocked," Aid says softly.

"Yes," says Kalle Jacobsson. "Someone knocked."

"I wonder who he was."

"We'll look into it tomorrow," says Kalle Jacobsson thoughtfully. "I'm sure we'll find out."

"Yes," Aid nods slowly. "We probably will."

"There's something strange going on."

"Yes," says Aid. "There's something strange here."

"We'll see tomorrow. Have a good watch—Enberg."

"Have a good watch."

The rest of the night is uneventful, nothing else happens, and they go off watch at six o'clock.

But just after midday Aid stands in Kalle Jacobsson's living room, warmly dressed.

"Father. *Father!* Aid is here!"

"Hmm?"

"He's waiting for you. *Father!*"

"What—who?"

"He says you're going for a walk together!"

"What time is—is it after twelve?"

"Ten after. Are you going for a *walk*? Can I come along?"

"Hmm," says Kalle Jacobsson. Then he remembers last night's events.

"Oh please, *Papa.*"

"Now, now, Josefa." Rakel's voice. But she too sounds happy. "If Father and Enberg are going for a walk, I'm not sure they want—"

"Hmm," says Kalle Jacobsson. "No, Josefa. Not today. I don't think so. Aid and I are going alone this time."

"But it's so long since we've taken a walk together—any of us."

"No," says Kalle Jacobsson, a little more sternly. "Another time."

"But—"

"We have work to do."

"Do you want to take some sandwiches along?" asks Rakel.

"Oh," says Kalle Jacobsson. "No. No, I don't think that's necessary. We're only going to inspect the beaches a little."

"I've already made some sandwiches," says Rakel.

"I see. Well. All right. I just need to get dressed first and wash up a bit." Josefa gives him a pleading look, but he only smiles at her and shakes his head. "Another time, Josefa, do you hear?"

"Awww." She makes a face as long as the word.

Aid stands waiting for him, well bundled up in a scarf and heavy sweater. It's very cold today; the thermometer showed minus 21 Celsius when they got off watch. For a moment Kalle Jacobsson is happy, the day is clear and cold, and he is going to walk in it for a while with Enberg.

They walk quickly down toward the beach together, in step with each other as usual. Neither man says anything. Without asking one another they walk southwest, toward the island's southern point. They walk at the edge of the beach, ice crunches under their feet, and they look carefully at every stone, every inlet, every barrier of packed ice piled up near the shore, looking for anything unusual.

After an hour in silence, they meet Madam Westerberg, who is also out walking on the beach.

"But Madam," the lighthouse master greets her, "isn't it too cold to wander along the beach today?"

Madam Westerberg gives them a dark, vacant, uncomprehending look. Her eyes are like pieces of coal.

"All right," says Kalle Jacobsson kindly. "But you should tie your shawl a little tighter around—"

"You should be careful yourself, Kalle Jacobsson," she says suddenly. "Just be careful. And you too, as a matter of fact!" she snarls at Enberg. They look at her in astonishment, but she has already walked past them, her body rocks quickly back and forth as she hurries north. A cloud of frozen breath appears in the air around her.

They look at each other, smile slightly. Then they become serious again, continue their walk.

Half an hour later they find what they are looking for; it's not so difficult to discover either. Some distance out on the ice, among some rocks, he lies firmly frozen into the ice, facedown. A little of his oilskin sticks up, his posterior and part of one arm, but otherwise he is covered with ice and snow.

"Uff," says Kalle Jacobsson. "That's him."

Enberg nods.

Without a word they go out to him, he is lying a good fifteen meters out on the blue ice. They kneel down beside him.

"Yes," says Enberg. "He's probably a traveler from far away."

"A Russian?"

"Maybe. I can't see his boots."

"Hmm," says Kalle Jacobsson. They walk stiffly back to land again, sit down on a tree limb protruding from the snow. Kalle Jacobsson takes out the sandwiches and a hip flask and they eat hurriedly.

"Rakel makes good sandwiches," says Enberg.

"Yes," says Kalle Jacobsson. "She does. Here, have a sip to keep warm."

"Thanks," says Aid.

"You're welcome. Skol."

"Skol."

"So we know who visited us last night."

"I think so, yes."

Kalle Jacobsson considers the situation.

"Terribly hard work to chop him loose now, and in this cold too."

"Yes," Aid agrees.

"Don't you think—don't you think if he managed to tell us he's lying here, then he'll manage to tell us when he's come loose and wants to go into the ground?"

"Yes," says Aid. He smiles a little. "I'd say so."

"Then we'll leave it at that," says the lighthouse master.

They walk home together. On February 3 there is a big snowstorm, which covers everything.

TWELVE

NEW MESSAGE

The weeks go by, and the days' flickers of light become longer and longer, become real days. Josefa has started to go to the chapel again, at first in complete secrecy; later, she does not care if her father and mother discover what she is doing.

It is quiet on the island, everything and everyone are quiet. Josefa slowly begins to find herself again; she has not been ill since that time before Christmas. She goes to the chapel, meets Aid there. And they have much to catch up on. With his cracked voice, without ever being able to demonstrate with his own voice what she should do, he painstakingly explains to her in words. And she sings. The first few times she is somewhat uncertain, almost a little afraid to let her voice fully ring out, but then she lets herself go. Her voice has changed, she can hear it herself. Aid explains about how the larynx develops and what happens when she sings, but above all he describes what she must do, and he explains hurriedly, as if he has little time; there is so much he needs to say to her. Her voice has become more open and at the same time larger. She must aim her voice now, he explains to her, aim toward the ceiling and the walls, she must notice how it emerges from her and reaches the wall and returns, she must stay with it the entire time, fill it completely. That way she grows beyond herself when she sings, and that's the essential thing. He is proud of her when she does it. Now and then it seems as if his eyes are wet.

"Are you sad about something, Uncle Enberg?"

"No, Josefa. I'm happy. Happy because you come and sing again."

"Are you sad because the others won't talk to you like before?"

"No," he says. "That's not so awful."

"Yes," she says, "it is awful. I can see that. They think something bad about you."

He does not reply.

"Father too," she says softly. "And mother."

He looks down at the keyboard.

"Shall we sing 'Heidenröslein' one more time," he suggests.

"But not me," she says. "Never."

He just looks down at his fingers. Now it's absolutely certain his eyes are wet.

"It's not fair," she says. "You haven't done anything wrong."

He looks at her, looks and looks.

"Oh, Josefa," is all he says.

Then he starts pumping the pedals, and she has to sing again.

When she has sung "Heidenröslein," he tells her.

The spring equinox approaches. The sun shines above the ice, and the white surfaces turn golden during the day. Soon there are small black zigzag lines from horizon to horizon. Early one morning Josefa is standing in the washhouse alone, helping her mother do the laundry. Her mother has just gone inside to get a new basket of clothes, and Josefa has lifted a heavy load into the rinse tub; she has permission to begin exerting herself again now, since she has been well for so long. Outside, the March sun is shining. Deep snowdrifts line the wall, all the way up to the window. She hums. She thinks about many things and places, places she hasn't been; she thinks about fresh bread and butter, she thinks about the fact that it will soon be spring and will be green in the woods. She avoids thinking about her father and mother and, above all, avoids thinking about what Aid told her. Instead she thinks about summer guests who will come. She thinks intensely about such things. She constantly asks her mother who she thinks will come in the summer.

"I don't know," her mother laughs. "Are you wondering about that so much?"

"Yes," says Josefa softly.

"You're a strange one," says her mother. "I guess those scientists will probably come as usual, and maybe a painter. Oh yes, that's true—there's an engineer coming too, to test a new lighthouse lamp."

"But just imagine if *exciting* people come," says Josefa. "That would be thrilling."

"It certainly would," says her mother. She gives Josefa a puzzled look. "Do you think life is boring out here?" she asks.

"Uff," says Josefa, flushing, "what a stupid question."

Her mother laughs a little, but without really understanding.

"You're at a strange age now, Josefa," is all she says. Josefa does not reply.

The air smells of soap and clean clothes, and Josefa rinses large white tablecloths and sheets. All at once everything becomes so strange; it's as if she's very cold, and her humming suddenly sounds confined, as if it doesn't go farther than her lips.

She hears a sudden loud knock on the windowpane. Startled, she drops the clothes from her hands and looks out. Against the pane she sees a man's fist; now it knocks again, and the glass rattles violently. She knows she has never seen quite such a fist before. She is taken aback, screams loudly. Then everything goes black around her.

When she regains consciousness, her mother and father are leaning over her, she is lying on the couch in the living room. Aid is there too, standing at a distance over by the door, wearing his winter jacket.

"Thank God," says her father. "We thought you were sick again, Josefa."

"No," she says, a little surprised. "No. I'm not sick. I don't think so."

"Aid was walking past the washhouse. He heard you scream and found you on the floor inside."

"It was so strange," says Josefa thoughtfully.

"What was strange?" asks her mother.

"Someone knocked on the window," says Josefa. "I got so scared." Yes, now when she thinks about it, she knows she isn't sick, she only got frightened. Maybe, she thinks, when I got so scared I was just a *little* sick.

"Knocked?" asks her father.

"Yes," says Josefa. "A man. I saw his hand."

Her father stands up, puts on his jacket, and disappears with Aid. They return a short time later.

"Josefa, my child," says her father, "there's a huge snowdrift outside the washhouse window, and we didn't see any tracks going over to the wall. Nobody has been there and knocked."

Rakel gives her husband an anxious look.

"Yes, someone *did* knock," says Josefa firmly. "I saw the hand and I heard it. Loud. Several times. It was horrible."

"I think you're starting to imagine—" her mother begins.

"No," says Josefa firmly. "I *saw* it."

Her father looks at Aid.

"It doesn't matter," Aid says to her mother. "I think she did see it."

"You too?" says her mother, without looking at him.

"Hmm," says her father, half embarrassed. "Aid may well be right. It's a message."

It's a young sailor, and the winter has treated him badly. All they can see is that he once had a beard. They pry him loose without difficulty now, carry him ashore. He has no papers in his pockets. They wrap him in sailcloth and put him on the fish sled, tie him firmly to it, pull him home. It's true as can be: a dead man speaks.

"Let's hope," says Kalle Jacobsson breathing heavily, "let's hope he stays there, when we finally get him into the ground."

"I think he's a Russian," says Aid.

"Does it matter?" asks the lighthouse master. Aid makes no reply, just pulls the sled. The snow has begun to melt here and there, and the sled does not glide easily.

"Tell me, Enberg," begins Kalle Jacobsson. "It's about time you tell me what's wrong with you."

Aid stops pulling, turns, drops his harness.

"You don't want to know," says Aid.

"Things can't go on like this." Kalle Jacobsson drops his harness too. They stand there looking at each other, breathing hard.

"You don't want to know," says Aid.

"Listen, after what Quist told me about that night. What actually—"

"You don't want to know." There is something strange about his monotone grating now, almost as though his voice has taken on color. Kalle Jacobsson looks at him grimly.

"All right," he says. "We'll leave it at that."

"It's best that way," says Aid firmly.

"Best that way." But Kalle Jacobsson can't interpret the strange look Enberg sends him now; it is firm and sharp, not like his usual gaze. He has to look away.

Aid leans over, picks up both harnesses, pulls the sled home alone, quickly and easily, as the lighthouse master stands there watching him for a while. Then he follows Aid's tracks home—home to the lighthouse station, to Rakel and Josefa and to the men; funeral preparations had to be made for the unknown man.

⸎

"The world is a strange place after all, isn't it? There is no space anywhere, except in itself. Like an island."

"This is amazing," we say, because we see who it is. "*You* here? On the beach?" We see who it is, and it seems natural to speak to him like an old friend.

"Where else?" He looks at us, white-haired and black-clad. He is very old, but moves easily and lightly across ice and snow, just the way Josefa thinks she has sometimes seen him.

"In this story?"

"Yes. Right here. Don't you understand? This is simply one of my memories. Simply a journey. I have to follow my tracks. My very specific tracks. You could say that remembering is my assignment."

"But this is the tale about Josefa."

"That's true. One of my most necessary memories. Although I should perhaps add that my recollections are not conventional *memories*. One could speak of an expanded concept of memory. Yes, one could. I must say that I remember much *more* than before."

"Those are puzzling words."

"Not at all. But we must leave this story now. The first act is already over."

"Leave it—what do you mean?"

"Many other things will happen here on the island," he says. "Many other things, all of which were necessary for what will happen later, but we can't really understand it yet. Next summer the stranger will come, and much will occur. For instance, Aid, lighthouse keeper Enberg, will die, quite unexpectedly, and thus will experience the Separation Problem in the truest sense of its meaning."

He looks at us.

"But what will happen to Josefa?"

"Just wait," he says. "Great things will happen to her soon, wonderful things, which will take her away from the island and lead her tracks far away, into the heart of today. Right now someone far from here is wondering about those tracks. They are invisible, the person wondering can't see them, but nonetheless they are felt in the wondering itself. Wait and see. We must understand something else first. We must go to another place now."

❧

There was once an island, more specifically 58°23'30" north longitude, 19°11'45" east latitude; there was an island and a winter that came and ended. A slightly unbalanced lighthouse keeper told a girl his secret; his and hers. The earth turned in its orbit and the spring equinox came, the wind began blowing from the southwest, a warm, temperate wind that broke up the ice completely in two days. Slowly the winter night withdrew northward, sea and sky lightened. The snow melted. People on the island could sense the air slowly begin to smell hopefully of earth and summer; Josefa could sense it. Especially at night, now when she could have her window open so the smell of mold and moisture came all the way into her room, all the way to her pillow and her face. She slept easily these spring nights, the fragrances entered her dreams and became longing, a longing that lasted all through the night and until the birds began to sing, and above the island the sky slowly

PART

THREE

ONE

Nondimanco, perché il nostro libero arbitrio non sia spento, iudico potere essere vero che la fortuna sia arbitra della metà delle azioni nostre, ma che etiam lei ne lasci governare l'altra metà, o presso, a noi.*

MACHIAVELLI, *Il Principe*, XXV

turned to dawn. Like a secret message from the clouds, the insect tapped carefully and clumsily on the shutters, which were closed almost completely. The dung beetle was traveling westward, it was tired, for it had flown a long distance, and it wanted to get inside. It struggled quite a while to find a suitable crack, aimed, took flight, missed, tried again. Despite the difficulties, its wings whirred evenly, with a deep, patient tone. But if you are a dung beetle you must accept that the simplest things take time. Now the sun rose and the beetle's greenish gold carapace glistened as it tried to enter the room. It came from far away, had flown through the wind and night rain and was very weary.

Inside the room's cool darkness, in the bed beneath the magnificent, luminous ceiling paintings, Lorenzo del Vetro awoke, sat up in bed, and was about to call Fiorello. He took a deep breath, because he had slept extraordinarily well; he could not remember having had such a deep, refreshing, wonderful sleep for many years. Usually as soon as he awoke he shouted furiously for the boy, his page and factotum, but this morning was

---

*But to not preclude our own free will, I think it probable that Fortuna indeed reigns over half our deeds, but she leaves it to us to determine the other half, or at least almost.

different. It must still be very early, pure white light fell at a sharp angle through the slats of the shutters. Outside in the trees of the Palazzo Fili garden, the birds still noisily chirped their morning song. The water in the fountain splashed cheerfully.

If Lorenzo del Vetro had dreamed, all he could remember of it was a soft, tender, happy mood, as if he were still a young boy, a child sleeping in his mother's arms.

"Fiorello!" he shouted good-naturedly. Beyond the birds and the water fountain, the city's sounds could be faintly heard. A wagon clattering past the garden walls, clanging hammer strokes from a royal smithy, handcarts rattling on the way to the market, crowing roosters. Fiorello was probably still asleep; usually his master did not want to rise at such an early hour.

"Fiorellino!" shouted Lorenzo del Vetro, as loudly and happily as before. He stretched his arms, feeling no unpleasantness of any sort, rose from his bed, walked barefoot to the window, and threw open the shutters. Fresh morning air rushed to meet him. It had rained during the night, and the day was clear as crystal. Maybe he had slept so well because of the rain.

"Fiorello!"

Someone called his name, but the boy Fiorello did not hear it. He lay in his bed in the alcove just outside Lord Lorenzo's bedchamber, having a wonderful dream. He dreamed he was at home, in the country outside Florence, and the men had just returned from hunting. He dreamed that the hunting party slowly entered the courtyard, the horses wet from rain, with lowered heads and mud-splattered flanks, and that the men dismounted, equally mud-soaked and melancholy. He was standing somewhere that was sheltered from the pouring rain, two hands held him back so he would not get wet, but he tore himself loose and ran toward the men, shouting happily. The biggest man saw him, brightened, opened his arms, kissed him, lifted him high in the air with a laugh. Fiorello got soaked to the skin, but laughed and laughed. His father said his name, softly and tenderly. But somewhere behind him in the rain he heard a woman's voice shout, ominously reproachful: "Fiorello!"

There was something wrong, with both the voice and the name.

He awoke and looked around, not quite sure where he was. Then cold terror gripped him. He had overslept. He who never overslept. His master shouted again from in there; the boy leaped to the floor, but his sleepy legs would not support him properly; he waited a moment until his limbs gathered strength, then he hurriedly put on his trousers and shirt. As he dressed, he heard his master's voice call his name again. Suddenly—he did not know why, perhaps it was the dream—suddenly he felt tears in his eyes. His master cannot bear to call more than once. Never let him call more than once. It must never happen. And how many times had he called already? Fiorello rubbed his face, swallowed, bit his tongue hard, smiled. Always smile. It's your task to smile every morning; not too much, not too little, a pleasant expression, something to rest one's eyes on, a friendly face, a friend, he calls you his friend, you're the only one who manages him. Poor you, because you're the only one who manages him.

He heard his master's voice yet another time, but not wailing as if in deep sorrow, not piercing like an old woman's, not furious like a whipping; somehow it sounded different than usual. God help me, thought Fiorello, and bit his tongue again (his well-tested way to combat tears), maybe I'll be lucky today.

Something small and friendly flashed past Lorenzo del Vetro and flew into the room with a whirring sound. He was immediately reminded of something, he could not really remember what, something from the day or the evening before, or a memory from a dream. He tried to think back to yesterday, then he heard Fiorello's steps outside the door. The boy rushed in, his hair uncombed, his feet bare, and his shirt not properly buttoned.

"Good morning, Lord Lorenzo," said Fiorello looking distressed, his eyes still filled with sleep. "I deeply apologize for having overslept. Has Your Lordship called many times?"

Lorenzo del Vetro looked at him kindly.

"You're not late, Fiorello. I'm early. Even though we had guests last night."

"I see, Your Lordship." Fiorello bowed, opened the other shutters. Then, suddenly wide awake, he fixed his large gray eyes on his master and mischievously inquired: "Perhaps we're going on a morning hunt?"

"With you at my side, I don't need a jester," said Lord Lorenzo. That was what he always said when he was pleased with him.

"My mother laughed when she brought me into the world," Fiorello said seriously. Then he smiled a little. But Lorenzo del Vetro did not make his usual, gloomy reply to this statement. Instead he said: "And what prey should we hunt in this foul town?"

Still no screams, thought Fiorello.

"Your Lordship has only to recommend the prey," he said eagerly, "and I'll flush it out for you. What about ambassadors? Emissaries, envoys, fat and fine from faraway cities but fleet as foxes, are best hunted with bow and arrow—"

Lorenzo del Vetro shook his head seriously.

"—or how about trapping some rutting Dominicans, well-foddered cardinals, furred bishops—"

"No, no, no! Fiorello."

"—downy dreamers, purring painters, fresh philosophers, hairy humanists—"

"Absolutely not."

"—or we can fish for curly-haired courtesans, libertine ladies, appetitive abbesses—"

"No." He laughed.

"—poisonous Jesuits—"

"Worse and worse."

"—hawk hunting for hypocritical helots—"

Lorenzo del Vetro laughed so heartily into the morning that a flock of birds flew out of the cherry tree. He's laughing, thought Fiorello.

"Your choice of prey is getting lower and lower."

"Even lower!" Fiorello continued in a dramatic tone. His eyes narrowed, and he held his hands to his temples, his fingers bristling sinisterly. "At the very deepest, in the deepest darkest mud pool in the Tiber, in a secret hollow, is His Holiness Great Pike himself—but difficult to catch. There's only one of him. His prick is shaped like a poisonous snail and his balls are like mussels that have lain too long in the sun. He lives with his daughter, who is a very small poisonous pike. And he is *very* holy." The final words were pronounced in a hissing whisper.

"No," said Lorenzo del Vetro, and looked down at the boy who stood smiling in front of him. He rumpled his hair gently. "It's too nice a day, Fiorello. We had enough of such people yesterday, and all the days before. I want you to sing for me, and later we'll read and converse. No visitors.

No visits, no official matters. You won't have to run around the city for me today."

"Very well, Lord Lorenzo," said Fiorello happily.

"But first you can awaken the whole chicken coop downstairs and draw my morning bath." Suddenly he looked at the boy seriously, and a strange expression crossed his face, which Fiorello could not remember having seen before. "Just think," said Lorenzo del Vetro, "last night I had such good dreams. I dreamed calmly and deeply, as if I were floating in water. But I can't remember what I dreamed, Fiorello." Fiorello looked at him, his eyes narrowed again, but now they shone, almost as if with tears. He swallowed, smiled with closed lips.

"Then it is truly a fine morning, Your Lordship."

"Yes, my friend. Did you dream?"

"No," said Fiorello. "I never dream. I have such a terribly strict and demanding master, who gives me too many unbelievably foolish tasks and crazy errands to accomplish during the day, so I can't spend the night running around as well."

"Out with you," said Lorenzo del Vetro, very kindly.

Fiorello obediently turned on his heel, hurried toward the door, then stopped abruptly.

"I'm getting old," he said sadly, clapped himself forgetfully on the forehead. "I'm very sorry about that, Lord Lorenzo," he said. They looked at each other somewhat in surprise. Fiorello brought his master's clean white dressing gown and laid it on a stool by the bed. Like Lorenzo del Vetro's nightclothes, it was of the finest silk, the smoothest and purest to be found in all of Italy, purchased by special agreement with Florence's leading silk merchant. Fiorello very carefully helped his master take off his nightshirt, just as gently and carefully as he always did, so that the scabs would not crack. Most other people would have turned their eyes away, but Fiorello thoroughly examined the scaly reddish brown scabs on Lorenzo del Vetro's back. With tiny movements he brushed away a few dry flecks that had loosened while his master slept.

"See!" he exclaimed in admiration. "Not a single new one during the night."

To Fiorello, Lorenzo del Vetro's skin was a constantly shifting landscape, where each night could bring a sudden unpleasant change. Fiorello knew each feature of this landscape, each pockmark, followed each sore from when it began as inflamed, stinging blisters filled with yellow pus that had to be pressed out, until they dried up and became itching scabs, fell off and left shiny new red skin underneath, where other blisters would soon burn through again. The sores were like continents floating in a sea of skin, and Fiorello followed their development with great attentiveness. He was like the hunter who tracks an animal for days, or like the gardener who painstakingly follows the rose from bud to bloom. For these sores were his domain, he read his daily horoscope in them, everything depended on them.

"Not a single new one," he said again, and swallowed.

"Are you sure, boy?"

"Yes," said Fiorello quietly and solemnly, because he could count on one hand the mornings during the year when he could report such good news to his master. He lightly brushed across the loosening scabs on Lorenzo del Vetro's back; completely dry. He blew on them carefully and coolly, sniffed their odor, not a trace of sour decay. Completely dry. Then he examined his master's arms and chest. The ugly inflamed blisters that had appeared in his armpits the previous morning were still filled with mushy puss, but were no longer such an intense yellow. Then he carefully slipped the dressing gown on Lorenzo del Vetro, who stood with his arms outstretched and his eyes closed as usual. But it did not hurt this morning, and he made no sound. The reddish brown scabs shone dully in the sunshine, as if he were a statue covered with a myriad of unpolished garnets.

Lorenzo del Vetro stood quietly by the window for a long time after his servant had left him. He took deep breaths, several times, stretched, without the sores hurting or the scabs pulling. Then he padded into his workroom, which was next to his bedroom, went to his writing desk, and looked through the papers lying there. A coded letter about the situation in that treacherous Florence; he had not yet decoded it, but could imagine the contents. Then eight or ten unanswered business letters. He cast a quick embarrassed glance at his father's portrait on the wall; the old man looked at him sternly and spartanly. That picture must go, he thought. Besides, it's not a good painting. Let me see. The oldest letter, from the office in Paris, marked "Urgent," had lain unanswered for a week. Had he read it? He did not remember. He would have to ask Rizzoli, the secretary. He had probably read it. Or had he? Had he read it? He stole another glance at the old man on the wall. Had he? What was it his father had always said? Keep a record of your letters: when they arrive, what they contain, what you reply, when you reply. Write every least thing in your journal, write everything that is said, all the gossip you hear, every number you pick up. The world is won with numbers and letters and memoranda, not with swords. Indeed. And here he sat, in this vile disgusting city, forced to flee with saber and sword. He sat here waiting. He looked with shame at the journal, which lay open under a pile of closely written papers. He could not remember when he last touched it. All at once he sternly pulled himself together, picked up the papers covering the journal, threw them on the floor, looked at the journal. Good God. The last entry was more than two weeks ago. With a spurt of activity he gathered quill and inkwell, quickly sorted the letters into private and business letters; the letter from Florence, the letter from Paris, business pile. A ridiculous letter from a madam and her daughter at Piazza Navona, private pile. A letter from one of his spies at the French king's field camp about the war in Toscana, business pile. A letter containing venomous gossip about the pope from Cardinal Cozzegrande—he hesitated a moment—business pile. A half-finished epistle about Virgil written by himself, addressed to the poet d'Argento, "Concerning the Orpheus Myth in the *Georgics*." He let his eyes follow the first sentences: "Quid faceret? Quo se rapta bis coniuge ferret? What should he do? Where should he go, now that his wife had twice been torn away from him? This is what Virgil writes, and I believe one can agree, it is as painful as—" He tore himself away from his own sentences. Private pile, no question about that. Or even better, the charcoal basin. He quickly entered the dates of incoming letters in the journal, put them in a neat pile to look at later in the day.

What kind of night had it been, last night? A May night like all the others, apparently, in this year of Our Lord 1497, with clusters of stars above Rome, which lay in the darkness like a warm sleeping beehive. Now and then a voice, now and then noise from a boisterous drinking party, a cry of pain or joy, a muffled horse's whinny, a bleating goat, frogs at the river's edge. The river as dark and deep as the heavens. A night in Lorenzo del Vetro's house, the remains from a banquet; some Florentines in exile, some prelates and prostitutes, nothing unusual: they had wandered out into the night, then they stopped wandering, and then morning came. But in the months and years to follow Lorenzo del Vetro will think back on this night, he will try to fathom what really happened, he will research, as carefully as a scientist, this brief quiet darkness that marked a dividing line in his life. For this was the night when everything changed, it did its deed quietly and imperceptibly, like a Good Samaritan, like a mother comforting her child who is crying in its sleep. Such a short night; it brought a miracle.

But Lorenzo del Vetro does not yet know about this transformation as he stands in his room looking out into the garden and feels in such a strangely good mood; last night is still just another night that has passed. And Fiorello does not know anything about the change either, although perhaps he has a brief inkling of it as he runs barefoot through rows of rooms, from double door to double door, past paintings, tapestries, and sculptures. All the magnificent splendor that fills Palazzo Fili becomes figures that flicker past in the pale morning light, gods and goddesses, graces, water nymphs, Pallas, Juno and Venus, Jupiter and Ganymead; it is as if he runs through a crowd of people who have been turned to stone, a group of party guests; mute and motionless they watch him run past. The soles of his feet slap against the cold marble as he rushes down the great staircases in high spirits; maybe it's a good day, he thinks, he forgets to watch when he rounds the landing, hits his foot against a sharp edge, screams in white pain, is falling, must do something, grasps the ankle of a Jupiter standing there sending lightning down the hall; he sees in a flash that a toenail is gushing blood but doggedly continues. Let's get the riders inside the walls first, he thinks, we can shoe the horse afterward. He leaves spots of blood on the marble as he runs. He seems to hear the voice reverberating from the evening before, raging with pain and anger: "I'll have you beaten bloody. No, beaten to death! I'll *kill* you! *Kill* you!" Fiorello bites his tongue.

TWO

The servants had just sat down at the table in the kitchen when Fiorello burst through the door. Hands sank on their way to mouths, the servant girls looked at him in fright, the butler Pippo Golaccio stopped chewing, the cook Rosario halted in the middle of a word. For a moment they sat as unmoving and purposeless as the gods upstairs where the aristocrats lived. The kitchen still overflowed with dirty platters and wooden vessels from the evening before, and the servants looked drowsy. Fiorello stood looking at them, planted his hands on his hips.

"Well!" he said. "Lord Lorenzo is up."

"What the devil! Already?" the butler grumbled irritably, threw down his bread and cheese, got to his feet. Suddenly there was great activity beneath the vaulted ceiling, the master's breakfast was hastily prepared, the maids scurried back and forth, fixed each other's hair in passing. The water for Lorenzo del Vetro's bath was already being warmed, Fiorello tested the temperature disapprovingly, stoked up the fire. Pippo returned, dressed in his livery. He gave Fiorello an ingratiating smile. Fiorello did not like that.

"He's awake terribly early today, isn't he?" said Pippo, a little uneasily. "Shouldn't he have slept like a bat during morning mass, after yesterday's debaucheries?"

"He slept well all night. No new sores."

"God help us all," said the butler. "I say again, boy, what would we do without you?" He sent Fiorello an inquisitive glance, malicious and worried at the same time: "Although now perhaps we must prepare ourselves for a life without you, Fiorello, after your little accident last night. Yes, yes, it had to happen, sooner or later." Fiorello ignored the comment, gave Pippo a cold look, as if nothing in the world had happened. It worked. The other man grew uncertain.

"Tell me," he said, just a bit lasciviously, "did it go on for a long time last night? I mean, after you did yourself in?"

"No," said Fiorello curtly. "He had a great deal of pain and sent them away." Fiorello, who had a highly developed sense of whom one could trust in this world, saw no reason to tell Pippo the details of what else had happened the previous evening.

Pippo clapped his hands for the servants to line up, inspected the maids' attire and hairdos before they were allowed to take the master's breakfast upstairs to him. This was Pippo's daily privilege, and despite being busy, he did it in his usual way, slowly and pleasurably, especially with regard to the youngest maids; he stood close to them, pushed a curl into place behind their ears, told them to open their mouths, smelled their breath, stuck a searching finger between their lips, let a hand lift their breasts as if by accident while tying their bodices tighter, pretended to brush dust from the small of their backs and their thighs with a stroking hand. The girls giggled or looked down furiously, blushing with shame. Fiorello, who sat on a stool by the fire, looked wearily at the boring scene, then looked away. He turned around on the stool toward the little table lined with jars and baskets from which the medicinal herbs were dispensed—his table, where only he was allowed to sit. He took out the silver knife, measuring spoon, and mortar, set up the balance scales, and with a precise, sure hand began weighing out the herbs that were to go into Lorenzo del Vetro's bath.

Three measures of rose petal oil from the alabaster jar; he had personally cut the most luxurious full-blown flowers in the garden and they had lain for exactly fifteen days, the oil was ready for use precisely this morning, and never again. Fifteen such jars stood before him, with rose oil in different stages.

"You're bleeding," said a voice nearby.

"Leave me alone," said Fiorello. "Don't you see I'm working?" Where was he? *Ten dried achillea leaves; pound eight of them with a mortar.*

"Yes, but your foot—you've hurt your foot." He gave her a quick glance, one of the maids had knelt down by the stool and reached out a slender hand for his foot. *Steep one hundred borage petals for four days in one measure of cold morning dew that has been collected on a silver platter; strain the dew and add to the medicinal mixture.* For a moment his foot rested in her hand; her hand was soft, he felt her warm breath when she leaned her head to examine his toes. She was pale and slender, with smooth brown hair. One of the new ones. They never stayed long. *Eight measures of hyssop leaves harvested at the new moon; press to a fine oil.*

"Let me look at it." She smiled at him gravely, half opened her mouth, moistened her lips with her tongue. "I want to see it," she said softly.

"Don't bother me," said Fiorello. He pulled back his foot, put the leaves in the press, set the beaker under it, screwed tightly.

"Yes, but you've hurt yourself." *Pound fresh calendula flowers to a mash.*

"Thank you," said Fiorello, "I know that." He did not look at her.

"I was there last night," she said, "when the accident happened. I mean your accident. I saw you. I danced with the crystal glasses."

"I see," he said curtly.

"I felt so sorry for you."

"Thank you," he said without warmth.

"I wish I could have given you one of my glasses instead."

"But you couldn't do that," said Fiorello icily.

"It looked as if you were bleeding, with all that wine on your clothes."

"I didn't cut myself," he said.

"But you're bleeding now."

"Oh really?"

She rose without a word, turned her eyes away, and left. They never stayed long. *Blend the liquid from the rose water, dew, and hyssop and add enough engle-herb oil to make ten measures; then add the crushed achillea leaves and calendula flowers. The final two achillea leaves are added whole to the bathwater, which should be pure springwater and pleasantly warm.* One cannot be too precise. Fiorello sighed as he conscientiously followed Doctor Bevila-qua's most recent, promising directions. Was this the twentieth cure, or the thirtieth? From the fifteenth physician, or the eighteenth? Be happy, Fiorello, for every least hope, for hope springs eternal. There had been so many doctors and cures, and each cure had fervently sustained the flame of hope. That was also the only thing that got sustained, aside from the doctors' money bags. Oh, faithful servant, imagine a *warm porridge compress of pulverized rose of Sharon*. Restore your soul with the memory of *tormentil roots, leaf nettles, and alum blended to a salve with retsina oil and wild-swine fat*. Illuminate your dark day, young page, by remembering again *fresh angelica leaves mixed with the ashes of charred southernwood, added to an ice bath along with powdered pyrites, one measure of cooked calf urine, and four knife tips of gold dust*. That too was ineffective, despite the heart-strengthening gold dust. On the contrary, the gold appeared to make the yellow blisters more inflamed and more combative, like an army of lansquenets; Lorenzo del Vetro's skin never looked more ravaged than in the gold-dust days. Or maybe it was due to the calf urine. Fiorello (who had personally cooked the brew) shuddered at the thought. *That* doctor did not last long.

He took the jar, mortar, and knife out into the garden and sun and harvested the final herbs. The insects hummed contentedly among the flowers and numerous medicinal plants that Fiorello tended each day and watered so attentively. How many such prescriptions had he followed? How many doctors had there been? Tall and short, all shapes, colors, and sizes, with and without beards, from the universities in Bologna, Padova, and Salerno, Heidelberg and Prague, yes, even the great Chrysoloras himself had tried, and that was a whole story in itself. Chrysoloras was a venerable old man from Greece who was an entire university of knowledge in himself; as a youth he had served the court in Constantinople and with his own hand had helped the court physician to blend the empress's perfumes and medicines. Later, after the fall of Byzantium, he had practiced medicine as a slave of the Turks for half a year, and now he served as court physician to the doge of Venice. He had such an excellent position that he accepted no fees unless the patient was completely healed—and even so, had become a very rich man; he seemed promising indeed. It took much persuasion and many rich gifts from Lorenzo del Vetro to induce the old man to undertake the long trip to Rome (to say nothing of the bribes to Venice's signor, who did not let his best doctor simply leave). But finally Chrysoloras arrived in the pope's city, where Lorenzo del Vetro lived a dreary existence of luxurious exile from his native city; he was given Palazzo Fili's most sumptuous guest room and treated like a prince.

Chrysoloras's examinations were long and laborious; he inspected Lorenzo del Vetro's sick skin for two whole weeks, day after day, while mumbling Greek and heathen words under his silk turban; before he began his treatment he analyzed how skin scrapings reacted on different substances, and took similar tests of Lorenzo del Vetro's spit, stools, and sperm. He burned scrapings of Lorenzo del Vetro's scabs to ashes, which he then mixed with quicksilver, heather honey, and nard balsam to make a salve that was applied three times a day. When this did not help, he ordered other ingredients, oriental herbs and essences, myrrh, the bark of cedar trees and Indian cypresses, rose of Sharon from Cos, said to be from the very same althea root that Hippocrates had used—but without success. Finally, he was so perplexed that he even tried water from the Jordan River (which stank terribly, although it cost eight florins a jar). In vain, of course in vain. Then the wise old man from Byzantium had looked at Lorenzo del Vetro with tear-filled eyes (Fiorello had witnessed it), with eyes that seemed to have faded away like the magnificent lost kingdom to which he had originally belonged, a kingdom no longer found on this earth, except as a memory. His eyes were like two deep slits reaching back through time when he had to declare that all his art could not accomplish this task; he stiffly fell to his knees, old as he was, and humbly asked Lorenzo del Vetro's forgiveness, kissed his scab-infested hand, rose just as stiffly and sadly, made the sign of the Greek Orthodox cross, and left them—left Lorenzo del Vetro, who wept from bewilderment and fright. Even Fiorello wept, who never cried otherwise. As promised, the old Greek took no payment for his consultations—but he took generous payment for mixing his medicines, the old scoundrel, so Chrysoloras had considerably enriched both his reputation and his bank account when he set out for his home in Venice.

Later there were still more doctors, and more cures and miracle medicines than Fiorello could bear to think about. For the past half year, out of pure resignation, they had restricted themselves to the local physician, Doctor Bevilaqua who, it is true, promised neither healing nor freedom from pain, but who ordered daily baths and liniments that had a somewhat cooling and alleviating effect. That was at least something, after all.

Fiorello cut the last herbs, went back to the kitchen, felt the bathwater, it was almost boiling hot now. He clapped his hands as a sign to the four waiting servants that the tub should be carried up to the terrace. He followed with the tray of medicinal preparations, and behind him came four maids with eight buckets of cold water. On the stairway the servants chattered and bickered among themselves, but as soon as they reached the second floor they fell silent, for in Lorenzo del Vetro's quarters no noise was tolerated, no unnecessary words, under real threat of dismissal. In the master's rooms silence prevailed each day, it lay like a white mist on all the books and works of art. Fiorello was the only servant who could begin speaking on his own up here, and he used this privilege only with the utmost care and consideration. The servants huffed and puffed under the weight of the water, the yokes creaked, the buckets splashed. Their steps were slow and heavy, like a funeral procession; the steaming vat was black with soot.

The large bathtub stood gleaming in the sunlight; when the men poured the water into it a cloud of steam rose into the air. Fiorello tested the temperature. He poured in the medicinal mixture, then the additional herbs, and finally some fresh rose petals and mint leaves for the sake of the smell. He stirred them with a long thin silver staff twisted like a unicorn's horn; first four times counterclockwise, from west to east, then eight times from east to west, being careful to turn the staff when he shifted direction, so the twists in the silver always followed the direction he stirred. Then he felt the water again, stuck his elbow into it.

"A little cooler," he said. One of the maids came forward, poured in half a bucket of the cold springwater. She glanced at his bare foot. It was she again. He followed her glance. The toe was black and blue and bloody. It suddenly hurt.

"What's your name?" Fiorello asked.

"Simonetta," she said in a low voice. "I started here a week ago."

"I know," he said sarcastically. "I helped to choose you." He looked at her. Quite presentable, now that she wasn't on her knees. She had been among those who danced and clowned for the guests at Lorenzo del Vetro's party the previous evening, for in this house there was a constant need for new entertainment, and she had been added to the servant staff because she had several talents; Fiorello had no desire to know exactly what that meant, but left this aspect of the work to the butler Pippo Golaccio.

"Well, Simonetta," Fiorello said quite kindly, "you can go and see how far the master has gotten with his breakfast. Take a careful look through the keyhole. Walk quietly, because the floorboards creak outside the door. And if he's still eating, maybe I'll have time to wash myself and get something on my feet."

She disappeared, came back.

"He's still eating, young master."

"And his appetite?"

"I—I don't know. I didn't notice. This morning is the first time I've come up here."

"You're a fool," said Fiorello. "You must learn to notice all such things, or you won't grow old in this house. Here there's a different law during the day than at night, because at night happiness and beauty rule, comedies are performed under torch lights, but in the morning it's a dance of pain. You must be able to tell me if he eats slowly or hurriedly, if he just picks at his food, if he has ordered other dishes, once or several times, if he looks furious or seems nauseated, if he speaks to the butler or if he simply gestures with his hands, and *if* he speaks to him whether he talks the way one talks to a parrot or if it seems as if he's in fact speaking to a grown-up, despite that it's Pippo; and if he makes gestures, whether his hands seem tired and heavy or lively as butterflies, or if when he lifts his knife to his mouth—"

"He was eating like any normal person does in the morning," Simonetta interrupted. She raised her head and looked straight at him. "Bread and cheese and porridge. He seemed completely normal. He was about halfway through his meal."

"I see," said Fiorello quietly. "Completely normal, yes, of course." He shook his head slightly in resignation. "All right, then you can go and station yourself outside the door again—and run to get me as soon as he gives a sign of rising from the table. But don't let him notice that you're standing outside, he doesn't like that."

"No, young master."

Feeling somewhat annoyed, Fiorello limped into his room, poured water into the washbasin, washed his face, hurriedly brushed his hair. You have dark rings under your eyes, he thought, blue as velvet. Using two fingers, he rubbed a little saffron onto his face while it was still wet. That helped; he looked tanned and healthy. He took off his shirt and trousers and dressed properly, then looked at his toe. It was ugly. He splashed a little cold water on it. The nail was crushed, it stung terribly and started bleeding again as soon as water touched it. He swore, clenched his teeth, drew on his stockings. Blood seeped through the stocking foot, but he had no time to bother about that, put on his boots. He dressed in the black-and-yellow uniform with a silver dagger hanging from his belt, even though it was not Sunday, but Monday, and put on his beret with the big peacock feather. Then he heard quick steps in the corridor, hurried out, trotted back to the terrace with the girl. When the door opened and Lorenzo del Vetro strode out into the fresh air, Fiorello stood by the bathtub. At that moment he remembered he had forgotten his instrument, and whispered to the girl, scarcely audibly: "My lute. Go and get my lute." He gestured with his head in the direction of his room.

For a moment she looked at him without comprehending, then she understood. She disappeared inconspicuously, almost invisibly. Not bad, he thought, perhaps he had been mistaken about her. Then he took a few steps toward his master, bowed elegantly, took off his beret with a sweeping gesture.

"Your bath is prepared, Your Lordship."

"Thank you," said Lorenzo del Vetro.

"If Lord Lorenzo wishes to test the temperature—"

"I'm sure it's fine, Fiorello."

Fiorello was taken aback, quickly felt the water one last time with the back of his hand, then he helped Lorenzo del Vetro remove his dressing gown. Simonetta came out to the terrace at that moment, with the lute hidden behind her back; she gasped and stopped short when his dressing gown fell, revealing his back with its carapace of scabs. The others looked down too. Lorenzo del Vetro stepped into the bathtub stiffly, like an arthritic.

"A little cool, perhaps," he said, and Fiorello gave a sign to one of the maids, but Lorenzo del Vetro added: "No, actually. It's fine as it is. Just like this. Aaah." Slowly he slid down into the water. He sighed contentedly when the water covered his body. Fiorello was taken aback again. Still no screams.

"Is everything all right, Your Lordship?" he asked.

"Yes, yes, Fiorello. It's fine." Fiorello gave a sign that the others could leave; they set down the buckets and vat and slipped out quietly. The lute lay on the couch by the wall. Fiorello sat on a low stool near the tub so he could help his master by handing him linen cloths, sponges, and scrapers. For a while they sat in silence, while Lorenzo del Vetro enjoyed the warm bath. Fiorello put his head in his hands, listened to the birds and the fountain. He was very tired. Then he pulled himself together, struck a few chords on the lute, and began to hum.

"We should have been at home in Florence now," said Lorenzo del Vetro quietly, as Fiorello hummed the melody. It was an old melody, a very simple craftsmen's song; he had learned it as a child.

We should have been in Florence now. We should have ridden out of the city, out into the hills and mountains, among swaying treetops, we should have rested our horses in the shade. We should have drunk water from a brook. Everything should have been blue and green in the midday sun. We should have gone hunting. The whir of the bowstring when released, the cry of the bird when it falls in flight, amazed, suddenly heavy and transformed. Was that how it was, thought Lorenzo del Vetro, was that how the days were before?

Lorenzo del Vetro sat up in the bathtub, signaled to the boy that he was ready.

Fiorello took one of the pure silver scrapers and one of the fine soft sponges, the softest that one could buy, grown beyond the coast of Patmos. Humming the whole time, he began to wash Lorenzo del Vetro's back, carefully, gently, as he always did.

There was, for example, the large eruption shaped like a grape leaf on the left shoulder blade; it had lasted a long time, more than a month, but today it seemed dry, and it looked as if the scab could be removed. He had to be careful, because if he removed too much of the scab it would start to bleed, which not only hurt terribly but could also cause scars. After having cautiously washed the shoulder blade and pressed a sponge against the crusted skin to let the moisture seep in well, he placed the silver scraper gently on the skin, at the edge of the sore, pushed it under the scab, humming soothingly the whole time, and carefully lifted the scab; over the years he had developed his own knack with this, he rarely made a mistake. He peered under the scab. As he had thought, fortunately. Just red skin underneath. He decided to remove about one-third to begin with. Usually this was a tiring, meticulous job, because parts of the scab often clung to the skin beneath with white threads, like roots, and he had to work around them. But today it went easily. It went amazingly easily. Fiorello hummed, the same song. Lorenzo del Vetro made no sound, none of the usual small painful cries when the boy pulled off the dry flakes or happened to tug a scab root. He was completely silent. Fiorello worked. Soon he had removed the first third, he shifted to another scraper, tested the edge, sprinkled the area with more water from the sponge.

"How does it look, Fiorello?"

"Good, Your Lordship."

He continued working. No scab roots, no blood. The skin underneath did not look as fiery red and wrinkled as usual, but seemed pink and fresh. This third also came off easily. Fiorello did not change scrapers, but went right to work on the final third. This time the scabs seemed to fall off by themselves. Finally, he washed the area one more time with a linen cloth, brushed the skin with his hand, removed some small flaking shreds of skin. It did not look bad. It looked a little sunburned.

Fiorello enthusiastically worked his way down Lorenzo del Vetro's back. Everywhere the scabs fell off, like the shell of a hard-boiled egg, like the cocoon around a fully formed butterfly. He worked more and more eagerly, stopped humming, forgot to use the sponge, forgot to scrape; in the end he just used his fingers. It was as if the scabs melted off Lorenzo del Vetro. His master must have noticed that something was different, because he turned his head and asked over his shoulder: "Are they coming loose?"

Fiorello nodded elatedly.

"There are only a few that won't loosen, down near your tailbone."

"Is that possible?"

"Turn around," Fiorello said without thinking, simply out of eagerness, in an objective and commanding voice, the same tone a painter uses to his model or a mustache trimmer in a marketplace uses to a bearded carriage driver. "I want to see the sores in your armpit." Lorenzo del Vetro turned good-naturedly, sat on his haunches in the tub.

"As you command, master," he said mockingly.

"Forgive me," said Fiorello looking genuinely regretful. "I didn't mean it that way, Your Lordship." Lorenzo del Vetro, who now was as elated as Fiorello, just nodded indulgently. And the regretful expression on Fiorello's face quickly disappeared when he saw the eruptions under his master's armpits. He reached for the small spatula and the little triangle he used to press out pus. Was it possible these were the sores that had been full of yellow pus this morning? It couldn't be possible! Just an hour ago they were pus-filled blisters, and now? Dry red scabs. He sprinkled them thoroughly with water, took the linen cloth in one hand, the spatula in the other, folded the linen cloth around an index finger, held it against the skin, pressed with the spatula, gently and firmly at the same time, the way he usually did. But no yellow mass spurted from the scabs, no colorless substance trickled out under the weak pressure of his fingers. Instead Lorenzo del Vetro said: "Ow! That hurts."

"Forgive me, Your Lordship, but I'm trying to press out the pus."

"Don't you have eyes? They're dry, Fiorello."

"Excuse me, Your Lordship, but that can't be true."

"Are you disagreeing with me?"

"I beg Your Lordship's forgiveness a hundred times, but just an hour ago they were infected; I swear it. I saw them myself, and I always note very carefully where I need to work. Excuse me for saying so, but you know that very well, Your Lordship."

"Well, they aren't infected anymore *now*."

They looked at each other.

"This is confusing," Fiorello said finally. "They were yellow an hour ago." He pressed the scabs carefully one more time, but without result.

"Oww!"

They looked at each other again.

"They *are* dry, Fiorello," said Lorenzo del Vetro. "*I* ought to know that better than you, after all. In spite of everything, I'm the one living in this skin."

"God help me, I believe it's true, Lord Lorenzo. They *are* dry. If things go as usual, the scabs can be removed tomorrow or the next day."

Lorenzo del Vetro stood up in the bathtub, looked down at himself. More than half of the scabs were gone, and where the disfiguring sores had been, there was now only pink skin.

"And my back?"

"More than half are gone, Your Lordship." Fiorello brought the large linen towel and began to dry Lorenzo del Vetro, who smiled the whole time. Fiorello had almost forgotten how that looked, and he had never seen his master smile like this.

"Well," said Lorenzo del Vetro. "Let's not rejoice too soon, Fiorello. It may be just a random remission."

"Yes, Your Lordship. It may be just a random remission." But Fiorello could see that his master really could not stop smiling, and the smile remained long after Fiorello had helped him dress.

Lorenzo del Vetro kept his promise from that morning: Fiorello did not have to run errands in the city, his master deferred his work and his correspondence and did not call either his private secretary or the librarian. Instead, he and Fiorello walked together in the garden, where Pippo had set out platters of fruit and grapes and dishes of currants and sweets, as well as a carafe of sweet wine. There Fiorello read to Lorenzo del Vetro from Ovid's *Metamorphoses*, more specifically from Book Ten, and together they accompanied the Singer down into the Underworld to search for his dead beloved, saw her glide back and forth among the shadows, followed the unhappy Orpheus back up into the light. Fiorello read attentively, but noticed that Lorenzo del Vetro was unusually moved, he sat with his eyes closed, but came to himself somewhat when they left the Underworld, enjoyed the poet's marvelous listing of all the trees and plants that came to cast shadows around the Singer when he needed it; laughed about the story of how Myrrh was transformed into a tree as punishment for having lain with her father.

"In our day, certain noble ladies of Rome would begin sprouting buds immediately," he said, "but I'll mention no names!" He gave Fiorello a sly look. "Their roots are rotting anyway," he added. But then followed the story of Pygmalion, and afterward Fiorello read about Cyparissus, and once again Lorenzo del Vetro was moved by the verses.

Fiorello read slowly and attentively, without stumbling on the words, in a soft, almost whispering voice, an overtone to the sound of the fountain. He knew it was not least his clear, pleasant voice that made him suited for such a prominent position in Lorenzo del Vetro's palace, because after his illness developed Lorenzo del Vetro could no longer tolerate any sound or voice that was grating or cutting; on the worst days merely having to walk across a field in the morning was more than he could endure. Nor could he tolerate that a glass was chipped or a sword clanked in its sheath, and a false note in a piece of music irritated him no end. It was as if Lorenzo del Vetro's other senses took on the same unbearable sensitivity as the painful new flaming red skin that appeared where the blisters hardened and the scabs fell off; he could not bear that any object or person around him had flaws or defects. The maids needed to be lovely young girls, their teeth had to be clean, even, and not decayed, their bosoms beautiful and perfect; the dancers had to be graceful, the musicians musical, the entertainers guaranteed to be amusing. His food and drink needed to be perfectly prepared, with no aftertaste, not too salty, not too sour, the wine excellent, the vegetables fresh, an apple had to be clean, shiny, without spots, and certainly not worm-eaten. And God have mercy on the cook who served a tough piece of meat—expensive crystal and silverware could fly at the wall, or he swept the table clean with a long, sad movement, his eyes bloodshot, his pupils constricted from too little sleep and constant pain. Even when he gave banquets one did not feel safe. No servant stayed long, with the exception of the butler Pippo and Fiorello. It seemed as if the sickness itself was so painful that Lorenzo del Vetro did not tolerate the least additional pain, not the least resistance or irritation in his surroundings.

With the same irritated impatience he collected all his valuable art, both modern and from antiquity, paintings, tapestries, statues; he collected books and ancient manuscripts, along with coins and rare preparations and treasures from around the world, but nothing seemed to satisfy him. As soon as a work of art, a manuscript, or an object had come into the palace, and he had looked at his new acquisition a moment or two (Lorenzo del Vetro was a great patron, who supported many painters, poets, and scholars), he impatiently hurried on, without resting, to more and more new things, new experiences, new knowledge, or new sensations. It was as if his soul itched, as if the inflamed eruptions had settled in his very heart, or clung to him like scar tissue on the optical membrane; nothing satisfied him, nothing gave him peace or equilibrium. Take yesterday, for example. Yes, thought Fiorello, as he continued reading, take yesterday, for example. It was a strange day; a strange and terrible day. And while his mouth formed the words he read, and without losing the thread of the story about Cyparissus, his thoughts went back to the previous day, and the remarkable events at the end of it.

By thee, to pastures fresh, he oft was led,
By thee oft water'd at the fountain's head:
His horns with garlands, now, by thee were ty'd,
And, now, thou on his back wou'dst wanton ride;
Now here, now there wou'dst bound along the plains,
Ruling his tender mouth with purple reins.

THREE

". . . But the most important thing about today's painting, my distinguished friends, is not simply the ties to antiquity—its empires, its world of ideas, and the noble godlike figures who, as I've shown, represent the forces of Nature. Above all, it is modern painting's new ability to *imitate*, to reproduce the world around us in its true colors; so the painter's motifs, whether Christian or mythological, can be mistaken for scenes we see in our city streets and marketplaces, and the new techniques enable the painter to reproduce each face so freely and plastically that you believe the actual person—bishop, baron, or bondsman—is standing before you."

"Hear, hear," mumbled the painter Enzio da Castelnuovo, "those are wise words."

Da Castelnuovo, a tall, handsome man with a blond well-trimmed beard and elegant dark blue velvet cape and hat, followed Lorenzo del Vetro's lecture with an open, clear-eyed gaze, leaning forward eagerly in his chair with his chin resting on the back of his hand. The other listeners' attentiveness varied according to their degree of intoxication, satedness, and interest in the subject, but most of them seemed to appreciate Lorenzo del Vetro's painstakingly prepared interpretations of modern painting, even if he had already talked more than long enough.

"Not bad at all, coming from a nobleman," one of the learned doctors—Verduccio—mumbled to his neighbor, the poet d'Argento, as one of the courtesans, beautiful red-haired Luciana, yawned.

"I think it's boring," she whispered, but was quickly hushed by Lorenzo del Vetro's physician, Doctor Bevilaqua.

"You must understand, Luciana, a symposium is *supposed* to be like that. But he'll soon be finished, lovely lady, and then we can turn to sweeter pleasures more in your domain."

"Oh yes, I know what kind of sweet pleasures you prefer, Doctor."

"It wouldn't be tarts, of course," said the husky voice of Cardinal Rizzi.

With Socratic high-mindedness, Lorenzo del Vetro ignored the snicker caused by the clerical comment, drew a breath, leafed forward to the last page of his manuscript, and began the summation, on which he had worked very hard.

"Indeed, the new paintings are so strikingly lifelike that people exclaim at the sight of them, half in fear, half in delight, as if it were reality and the sunlit day before their eyes, and not an illusion in oil and colors. With the aid of a charming perspective, the painted figures meet the observer's eye quite as if they came strolling toward him, and he has the impression he could walk into the painting himself, wander toward the horizon, or disappear behind the corner of a house. But above all, this new resemblance is due to the new oil paints, which are a far better and more compliant medium than the old egg tempera. Just consider what paintings looked like only a few decades ago—so old-fashioned, so stiff and awkward, as stiff as the hardened egg yolks from which they were made, and where each face necessarily was aloof and bore little likeness to the model, because it had to be sketched and painted one part at a time, color by color, whereas today's painting allows the artist to mix the face and hair colors in the finest nuances, to paint over and change the contours, again and again, just as he wishes, with complete freedom, until he has reached the outer likeness and lifelike expression he desires. And thus today's painters, using the new techniques, have created a new perception of both Nature and divinity, for in Nature's physical, visible, and material forms we find secret images of divinity reproduced; God himself has put his stamp on each lily and on every woman's breast, on each child's face and every old person's hand.

This is the world as we see it. And now, with the new techniques and artistry, with oil and canvas instead of wood panels and egg tempera, with perspective and anatomical studies, the artist is able to put his own stamp, his own mark, on the world, not merely by reproducing it, but by re-creating it, ordering it, elevating one moment, creating *in addition*, just as the poet tightens an experience to a poem which expresses more than the experience." Lorenzo nodded slightly toward the verse artist who was present, the poet d'Argento.

"Brilliant!" exclaimed the poet, who was already glowing with happiness over the beautiful evening in Lorenzo del Vetro's halls—the food, the women, the wine, all this obvious wealth and beauty—and now blushed deeply at hearing his art praised in the host's speech and seemed completely without words, he felt so honored.

"And this," continued Lorenzo del Vetro quietly, "makes people of today both happier and more unhappy than people of all earlier times. For in our day, he who misses his native city—like many of us Florentines here this evening in our forced exile, in this wretched time of strife and fervor and fratricide—misses not only his native soil and the taste of his native city's water, not only his own dialect and his brothers and friends, he also misses the revelations of beauty that art has showered on his city, the magnificent paintings that shine in the churches' chapels and the citizens' halls, that are more beautiful than reality itself, because they reproduce it and elevate it to timelessness and truth, and therefore they glow in the memory of the homeless one as the very essence of all he misses. And because he experiences this double beauty, he is doubly unhappy in his bereavement, but three times as happy the day he is able to return. And here I conclude my speech."

"Bravo!" exclaimed the painter da Castelnuovo, and immediately began clapping with strong, steady hands. The other symposium guests gradually joined the applause, especially the Florentines. Only a couple of the highest prelates continued to sit with their hands buried in the women's low-cut necklines.

Lorenzo del Vetro sat down in a daze. He was in a great deal of pain now, and Fiorello, who had stood leaning against a pillar half asleep, woke up and rushed over to help his master sit down.

"Thank you, thank you," Lorenzo del Vetro mumbled to the listeners. "Wine," he whispered to Fiorello, but Fiorello had already filled the wine cup to the brim and handed it to him.

"A brilliant lecture, Your Lordship." Doctor Bevilaqua leaned forward toward Lorenzo del Vetro to congratulate him. "Truly sublime."

"Oh yes," agreed the courtesan Luciana. "And when you speak, the sight of you is—is—it's like the moon," she exclaimed. She looked at him a little uncertainly.

"That was nicely put, my beauty," mumbled Lorenzo del Vetro. "Very nicely."

"The city of the Florentines," began the learned Verduccio, "misfortune befalls it, when it can thrust away such noble blooms, if not *the* noblest, well, I'm speaking freely, you understand, *the* noblest, not merely in the area of commerce, but also in art and science, a man who unites the prince's power with all the demands of the practical life, and thereby realizes antiquity's ideal of versatility and education; in short, a prince in the world of the spirit as well. What a generous mentor and support you are for us all! How sad for your native city that you must languish here among us. But your presence is a double joy for us Romans, of course."

Lorenzo del Vetro looked at him with a smile during the whole tirade, and only close to the end did his eyes narrow a little.

"Thank you, thank you. You're much too kind, esteemed doctor," he said, and turned away.

"I liked what you said about the divinity in pleasures of the senses," Cardinal Rizzi said fervently. "There is a deep hidden truth in that. You should absolutely develop the subject further."

"Thank you, Your Eminence."

"I am moved," murmured the poet d'Argento. "Your talk treated the subject extremely well. It could not be said better—no. It was brilliant! I find no response. I find no words. I must write a poem." He hastily withdrew into the next room, where he sat swishing a goose quill for a long time as he wrote a sonnet in honor of his host.

The other guests praised the speech similarly, one after another. Only the painter da Castelnuovo remained silent, saying no more than his single, deeply felt "Bravo!"—even though he was in the process of creating an expensive pietà commissioned by Lorenzo del Vetro. He gazed straight ahead, his clear eyes shone, his look went beyond and above the other people present, resting instead on the paintings and statues in the hall, a quiet smile on his lips.

Fiorello looked at his master; he appeared expectant, still elated by his own words, his cheeks flushed from his long and well-formulated speech. But when the right conversational atmosphere did not arise among the symposium guests who, after expressing the obligatory praises, quickly returned to their ordinary festivities, Lorenzo del Vetro sighed with a grimace, and Fiorello hastened to bring in the dancers, musicians, and clowns, who had been sent out to eat when the speech was about to begin. The performers were both beautiful and talented, but Lorenzo del Vetro looked at them without pleasure or interest. Instead he drank deeply from his wine cup and began impatiently shifting back and forth, rubbing himself against the back of the chair. He's in a ferment now, thought Fiorello. Now he's noticing how much pain he has, and then something terrible will happen. Lorenzo del Vetro looked with evident disgust at the cardinal, who was as drunk as a—yes, as drunk as a cardinal, quite simply. This is certainly not what his master had imagined, thought Fiorello; this isn't exactly Florence. God have mercy on us if something happens this evening; we're not in Florence, we're strangers in this city, and he'll forget that soon. If only I hadn't been so tired. I must find something to distract his thoughts.

But Fiorello was tired, so tired he almost fell asleep standing there, because he had been on his feet since early that morning, completely occupied with preparations for the banquet, and it had been like this for nearly two weeks. The morning's many errands were no sooner done than the master awoke toward noon and needed to have his care. Then Lorenzo del Vetro busied himself with the speech he was working on (the speech he had just presented to the group of banquet guests), worked without stopping, hour after hour, interrupted only by more baths and more liniments as the afternoon grew warmer and the pain increasingly unbearable; often he had no appetite for food (and Fiorello did not get to eat much either). Fiorello had to take dictation, or make clean copies, or read to Lorenzo paragraphs that the master had just written, often the same paragraph several times. All this continued until late at night, until Lorenzo del Vetro finally fell asleep from sheer exhaustion, and Fiorello could stagger to bed, bone weary after serving his master since cockcrow. His master had worked as if intoxicated for more than a week; Fiorello had never seen him like that: he never paused, he never rested. He had worked like a madman.

At first Fiorello had been pleased with his master's idea. Lorenzo del Vetro had come up with the thought one morning in the bathtub, had said he was tired of his barren existence in this horrible, hot, vulgar city, was tired of the whole band of parasites, prelates, ambassadors, and envoys.

"Let's give a banquet, Fiorello," he had said, "a banquet such as we used to give at home, a true symposium." And Fiorello had definitely approved of the idea, because he really felt sorry for his master, who had been forced to spend three dreary years far away from his native city, away from his magnificent home with all its treasures, its luxury, and its art (for Palazzo Fili, the del Vetro family residence in Rome where Lorenzo del Vetro had sought refuge, was like a shepherd's hut in comparison to the Palazzo Vetro in Florence), and unable to use his country villas. For the third year now, Lorenzo del Vetro could not tend to his business and other interests properly, and had to bear the yoke of his illness as well.

Fiorello had been happy at the thought of a banquet in the fine old style, because he saw what the late nights of drinking did to Lorenzo del Vetro, he saw his master slowly degenerating, saw how he lost fortunes playing dice and squandered money on courtesans and parasites, all the while becoming more and more surly and sullen, getting wrought up and irritated at the least little thing. Furthermore, Fiorello could tell his master's state of mind by the eruptions, how they came and went, how they constantly became more inflamed, constantly more pus-filled and painful, as Lorenzo del Vetro's dissatisfaction with his environment increased. And it was Fiorello who suffered, he was the one who got the washbasin thrown at his head and his shins kicked if something hurt or if things were too slow. It was Fiorello who had to bring Lorenzo del Vetro's bad news to the other servants, that this or that one was to be beaten for inattention, this or that one fired because of his appearance, this or that one degraded to stableboy because he had bad breath. So Fiorello had wholeheartedly supported the banquet idea and encouraged it in every way, because he still remembered Lorenzo's banquets in Florence in earlier days, what they had been like, grand and beautiful and temperate (that's how he remembered them now at any rate), with music and song, with noble speeches and conversation; banquets that had gathered the best Florentines, merchants, scholars, theologians, and artists in free and cheerful company in Palazzo Vetro's halls or out in the country villa on mild, velvet-soft evenings (that's how he remembered it). It had been *graceful*, all of it, and wonderful. And so Fiorello immediately clapped his hands and lavishly praised his master's resourcefulness, and began thinking at once about plans for the banquet; they must have dancers, he thought, and musicians, the best to be found, better than those they had in the house now, much better, and the food must be easily digested, and summery, honey cakes, songbirds stuffed with mincemeat, liver pâtés, a whole peacock with its feathers replaced after it had been roasted and with grapes in its beak, along with trout, Tiber crayfish, figs, fancy dates, peaches, pears, pigeon eggs—

"And I'll speak about art," said Lorenzo del Vetro, "about modern painting."

"Yes," said Fiorello absentmindedly, "that's an excellent idea, Your Lordship."

But then Lorenzo del Vetro began to write his speech about modern art, nicely and neatly at first, almost as he would have written such an evening speech at home in Florence; some observations about the role of perspective, nothing complicated; as an art connoisseur and collector he believed he should be able to express himself on this subject with considerable confidence. But as soon as he started to put the words on paper, words began flowing from him. Fiorello could see how the subject seemed to grow in his master's hands as he wrote, he wrote so quickly he scarcely could dip his quill; he began logically, explaining perspective and the technique of oil painting, but he had no sooner described their practical execution and given examples of particularly successful results than he was into the works themselves, giving elaborate, detailed descriptions of individual paintings, at home and here in Rome and elsewhere, and their effect on him. He described their geometry and their secret mathematics, their symbols and their numeral magic. He wrote from his memory, as if he saw the paintings in detail before him. And he wrote with increasing amazement, because he had no idea all of this was inside him. The more he wrote, the more enthusiastic he grew and the better he wrote—the words became a medium he floated in, he did not have to fumble for concepts, they came to him the moment he needed them; his style became easy and yet concrete, his observations free and original. Fiorello scarcely recognized his master and did not understand what was happening to him. Lorenzo del Vetro did not completely understand it either. It was as if an abscess had been punctured; three years of idleness and silence had collected in him. But also a whole life's bondage in the business firm, his proud patrimony, which burdened him with all the bookkeeping, business records, transactions, secret agreements, correspondence, and intrigues, along with his illness and its afflictions, which no medication could overcome—all this now gathered to a force within him that went far beyond the limits of an evening's contemplations on artistic perspective. But he could not stop, the speech would be as long as it had to be, and the guests could say what they wished. "They're going to eat my food, aren't they?" he said to Fiorello, who had his own concerns. Because whom would they invite to the symposium? The foremost artists in the papal city at the time, of course, and Rome's finest scholars, along with outstanding representatives of the Florentine merchant nobility in exile; Fiorello had prepared a list of glittering names. But things did not turn out as they should. First, it was short notice and many sent word they could not come for that reason, and most of the foremost artists were busy working on commissions in other cities that were more lucrative and less infested with intrigue. Of the great names, only da Castelnuovo was in Rome, and only because he was creating a work for Lord Lorenzo himself. Secondly, a number of those invited were already on their way north again to see the lay of the land and to position themselves in time, in case changes began to occur in their native city; certain things would seem to indicate this might happen. A third reason was that there were a number of guests one could not avoid inviting simply out of politeness; they would have been mortally offended if they were not invited—and an offended cardinal is as dangerous as an angry wasp, no, even more dangerous, because he stings secretly and the sting more often results in a hasty burial. So the guest list was far from being what it should have been. It was impossible to overlook Cardinal Rizzi, of course, with his whole retinue, and a number of papal officials, and in addition there were a great number of the usual bootlickers, noblemen, and diplomats of varying carats whom one could not overlook either in a city like this, and in such people's company there were inevitably a number of independent trade women. All in all, the guest list increasingly resembled one of Lorenzo's usual bacchanalian parties than the magnificent, philosophical occasion it was intended to be, and which would have been worthy of Lorenzo's speech. But if Fiorello did so much as cough a slight concern about the list or suggest that perhaps his master should think about delaying the banquet until a later time, Lorenzo del Vetro would glare furiously at his servant with bloodshot eyes over the manuscript he was writing and refuse to be distracted; he was working. Fiorello thought he knew his master well, knew all his difficult and unpleasant sides, but this was new, yes indeed. Lord Lorenzo usually was very concerned about whom he invited to his house, and how they should be entertained, for careful attention to such matters could pay off. But now the only thing on his mind was working on the speech; the speech cleared a path for itself, past all other considerations; it should and it would be presented *now*, as soon as possible, while the material was still new. Lorenzo del Vetro did not worry about the guests, but entrusted all such worries to Fiorello. And perhaps he thought because he had *imagined* a banquet that would be as beautiful and temperate as those in Florence, which he so longed for, and *believed* this, therefore it would *be* that way of itself. Perhaps Fiorello had also *imagined* this, and had not foreseen the difficulties, but been seized by a dream. So the evening turned out as it did.

Now Lorenzo del Vetro sat glowering with dissatisfaction at the festivities, which more and more resembled one of his usual banquets—the guests had sat without food and drink for a long time, and were making up for it; a couple of them had already taken out the dice. Now and then Lorenzo sent Fiorello a furious look. It's my fault, thought the boy, it's my fault that the evening didn't turn out the way Lord Lorenzo had imagined. He desperately tried to think of something that could lighten the mood and distract his master. Right then two of the new servant girls were performing a dance where they juggled crystal glasses on which they had just played a melody; the act met with hearty approval from the guests, whereas Lorenzo del Vetro watched with great disgust. But the crystal glasses gave Fiorello an idea, and he sent a lackey to get the large crystal chalice, Il Vetrone dei Vetri, one of the house's magnificent decorative objects, given as a gift to Lorenzo's father by old Cosimo de' Medici himself as a sign of eternal peace between the two families—ah yes; it had been transported with great care and effort the whole long way to Rome to console Lorenzo del Vetro in his misery, but it was never used. Now, thought Fiorello, now perhaps the moment had come; Lorenzo had given a great speech, at least as far as Fiorello could tell, and he wanted to honor and surprise his master, to show that at least he, Fiorello, his loyal servant, valued and admired the effort Lorenzo had mustered during the past days and nights. And even if Fiorello perhaps didn't understand everything that had been said, at least the effort itself hadn't fallen on stony ground with him, as it apparently did among the other people present. (And perhaps this thought was a tiny bit selfish on Fiorello's part, but who can blame him for that?) True enough, it was a daring deed, to get the chalice, for Lorenzo del Vetro had not asked for it, and it was a family treasure, but his deed would have to stand the test. Sometimes precisely such unexpected surprises could put Lorenzo del Vetro in a better humor, and perhaps the chalice would remind him of the finer times and nobler company he had tried to recall now this evening.

So when the lackey signaled from the doorway that the chalice had been brought up from the silver room in the cellar, Fiorello asked his master to excuse him and slipped out quickly. There it was, even more magnificent than he remembered it. Large and gleaming, with the reliefs and ornamentation so true to nature, and then the marvelous inscription: FIDE, SPES ET CARITAS. The chalice was a little dusty, especially the grapevine forms on the glass; Fiorello took the lackey's towel peremptorily and wiped the glass. Beneath his fingers the crystal was unexpectedly slippery, clear and exquisite, every touch told him what a precious thing he held in his hands. The crystal was so flawless that the chalice seemed to be a grapevine of flowing light. From the base of the chalice rose an intricate ornamentation of stalks and roots, which branched into two powerful, entwined stalks—they were the handles on either side—and then leaves, grapes, and flowers spread across the whole magnificent pointed cover. Around the chalice, in the spaces between the handles, masterful reliefs were engraved. On one side the reliefs showed a splendid procession of del Vetro family images; Lorenzo himself was portrayed, as a young boy with curls and a gentle, angelic expression on his face, but the engraver had reproduced his profile so realistically that anyone who knew the man had no doubt as to who the boy on the glass had become. On the opposite side one saw the Medici in a similar parade; the chalice was invaluable, extraordinary, and for a moment Fiorello was seized with doubt and awe. He suddenly heard some words within himself, some words from long ago, but he heard them as if they were said close to his ear, and it was as if his ear still hurt from the cuffing it had received that time: "You'll be among noble and expensive things, Fiorello." It sounded like a warning. But perhaps because he was tired and lacked judgment, or perhaps because he thought it would be too bad to simply have the chalice carried down into hiding again, Fiorello called for the finest sparkling red wine the house could produce, and he lifted off the cover with careful hands, filled the chalice to the brim, replaced the cover, gave a sign to the lackey, who threw open the double doors.

The moment he re-entered the hall, with the chalice carefully balanced between his hands, he saw by Lorenzo del Vetro's alarmed expression that he should not have done this. But an expectant sigh rose from the guests at the sight of the large magnificent Vetrone dei Vetri, which shone like a deep red ruby of wine in the torch light. Slowly, solemnly, Fiorello walked toward his master, who still looked at him in alarm, but whose expression had perhaps softened somewhat; indeed, as Fiorello gradually came closer it seemed to him that Lorenzo actually smiled for a moment, one of his rare, slightly unrestrained, admiring smiles, and a feeling of triumph, as bubbling as the wine, flowed through him as he strode forward; the music had changed tempo, the guests applauded, Lorenzo del Vetro rose, Fiorello bowed deferentially, and something happened, something or other happened, he felt it more than he saw it, something slid, the chalice cover slid, and with a terrible sound it fell to the floor where it shattered like ice. Fiorello watched in horror as the cover instantly became a myriad of white meaningless crystals that burst across the floor like a swarm of shooting stars; he gave a frightened start, and something in him made him want to grasp for the shooting stars down there between his feet, stop them in their flight, stop time, bring them back to their crystal sphere, to the heavenly home they came from; the Devil himself must have been visiting in Lorenzo's home this evening, indeed the Devil who said to Fiorello, now Fiorello, you must reach for the shattered lid and let go of the whole chalice, that's the wisest thing to do. So Fiorello did this, he no longer seemed to know the difference between up and down, he dropped the chalice, and shooting stars again streamed across the heavenly floor, but now they were red as blood.

For a moment there was absolute silence.

"Fiorello!"

Red.

"*Fiorello!*"

Silence.

"I'll have you beaten bloody. No, beaten to death! I'll *kill* you! *Kill* you!"

Fiorello drew back a few steps, as if standing in front of a wild animal, without knowing what had happened. The walls in the hall still echoed from Lorenzo del Vetro's shout, several guests had risen in alarm, the musicians had lowered their instruments, Lorenzo del Vetro's mouth looked like a gash in his face, and Fiorello heard again the voice from that time long ago: "You'll be among noble and expensive things, Fiorello." But now he also heard the words that had followed, so clearly that it completely drowned out Lorenzo del Vetro's repeated shout, but this time with an outstretched, commanding hand; close to his ear, which still hurt from the cuffing it had received, which would always hurt, Fiorello heard the voice, heard the whole long, admonishing tirade, ending with the words: "You're a work of art yourself, never forget that, and one day someone can decide to get rid of you." Lorenzo del Vetro's mouth moved, trembled like a wound just after the arrow has been pulled out, he had bellowed again; some of the worst guests were already shouting encouragingly to Lorenzo, asking to see the punishment here and now; and, without really wanting to, Fiorello fell to his knees among the shards.

If at this moment he had begun to brush together the shards in despair as was his impulse, indeed as his hands wished and had already numbly reached out to do, then the Devil's purpose in playing this trick on him would surely have been fulfilled, *then* he would have been finished, as so many other servants had been finished in Lorenzo del Vetro's eyes the moment they lost their worth and beauty; then he would have found himself on the street faster than the chalice had been broken, or worse: in the cellar. He saw Lorenzo's face, it seemed like a complete stranger's; he could already feel the cold, damp stone against his bare skin and waited for the whiplashes; he saw Lorenzo's face, and the entire previous week, the work on the speech, the preparations for the symposium, his joy at his master's diligence, his happiness at his master's happiness—it all seemed to be erased from his life. All the years as a servant in the del Vetro palace, suddenly they were nothing, gone like the fragile chalice, had never existed, and he no longer knew Lorenzo del Vetro, had never known him, never been his servant, was no longer Fiorello, had never been Fiorello, was someone else, was the person he had once been, was—

But someone helped him to his feet.

"Oh, honorable Lord Lorenzo," said the deep, kind voice. "Have I told you how my mother once crushed my father's testicles?"

"What!" snarled Lorenzo, nonplused.

"Fortunately," the voice continued, "fortunately it happened after Your Lordship's humble servant, yours truly, had been conceived, otherwise I would neither have stood here nor been able to paint my pictures. Or," continued the painter da Castelnuovo, for it was he, "*if* I had stood here anyway, then I would not have been the son of my father, that's certain, but perhaps of a neighbor."

Some people laughed, a little uncertainly.

"We had a neighbor, you see," da Castelnuovo doggedly continued, "a truly elegant fellow he was, and ingratiating besides, and my mother, who had a weakness for such things, like most women, was surely often tempted to seek comfort with this neighbor for my father's embarrassing, to say nothing of physical, misfortune, but the cleric forestalled the neighbor, fortunately, so a proper annointment took place."

Now Cardinal Rizzi laughed.

"Alas, all flesh is fleeting, to say nothing of chalices, but smashed testicles are worse, at least for the person to whom they belong; it doesn't happen often, at least not in times of peace, and rarely by accident, but anyway it can happen," da Castelnuovo went on.

"But—but how—?" Lorenzo's voice demanded, half furious, half curious.

"Oh, it's a tragic story, so Your Lordship must promise not to laugh. Promise me! My mother only wanted to free my father from a harmless affliction! You see, my mother was a simple, trusting soul, demure and pious, raised in a small village, where she had gained all her knowledge of life. Unlike certain others, she hadn't had the good fortune of being trained in a convent or at a convent school, and therefore was quite unacquainted with life's realities. As a matter of fact, she went into marriage utterly innocent and ignorant, and her ignorance included important parts of the male anatomy, if I'm not extremely mistaken. My poor father, God bless his soul, had for many years suffered from carbuncles on the back of his neck, nasty boils, and he constantly poured out his troubles with these horribly painful carbuncles to my mother. She went to an old woman widely reputed to know cures for everything, and asked for advice: My husband's carbuncles trouble him day and night, they spread so terribly, he says, and I'm pregnant with our first child and need rest at night, and I can't sleep properly because of the way he twists and turns in his distress. The old woman said: Madam, you must simply squeeze them out, quickly and brutally, preferably while he's sleeping, and pay no attention if he screams and carries on; just squeeze hard. He'll be doubly grateful for your vigor afterward, you can be sure."

Snickers were heard in the hall.

"No sooner said than done. The next night my mother found what she thought were the spreading carbuncles . . ."

Laughter.

". . . but they were big, so she needed something that could squeeze them out really effectively. So she went to the kitchen and got the largest mangle . . ."

More laughter. Lorenzo del Vetro laughed now too.

"This isn't funny at all! . . . got the largest mangle and carefully, carefully, without awakening him, she placed my father's carbuncles between the mangle board and the roller. And then she pressed hard! And paid no attention when he screamed and carried on . . ."

"It can't be true," laughed Lorenzo del Vetro.

"True or not," said the painter, "this is what I've heard, and if it's not true, it's a good explanation, although of course other explanations are possible . . ."

"Come and sit with me," Lorenzo del Vetro said to the painter.

"It was a tragedy, of course, that my father lost his carbuncles in this sad way," the painter said with deadly seriousness as he walked forward to Lorenzo del Vetro's seat. "And yet there was nothing to do about it. For as I said earlier: all flesh is fleeting, be it carbuncles or chalices or life itself, they are lost in the end and go the way of everything else."

Fiorello collected himself, went into action, held out the chair for the painter, who settled himself comfortably next to Lorenzo del Vetro, handed him a glass, bowed deeply, and then twice as deeply to them both. Lorenzo gave him a furious look, but the painter said: "Things can happen as they did with my mother and father, when faith is strong enough. For my mother truly believed that she was healing her husband's painful carbuncles in this unpleasant way, she believed the wise old woman's words more than her own healthy good sense; had she stopped to think, she surely wouldn't have done it."

"But she didn't stop to think," said Lorenzo del Vetro, and raised his glass to the painter. He was feeling better now, Fiorello could see that.

"No, she didn't stop to think, just like your poor servant here."

"Indeed," said Lorenzo del Vetro, with another dark look at Fiorello.

"There could certainly be worse things to feel sad about than a little chalice," said the painter quietly. After a brief pause he added: "My mother didn't stop to think, as you said. And in a strange way, it's exactly this aspect I sat here thinking about for a long time after hearing your excellent speech, Lord Lorenzo."

"Oh?"

The other guests had sat down again, closer to Lorenzo and the painter, in order not to miss out on the conversation. The entertainers had quietly withdrawn, the painter held everyone's attention in the palm of his hand. Fiorello, who had now half regained his presence of mind, signaled to have the wineglasses refilled and, just to be safe, discreetly withdrew from Lorenzo del Vetro's line of vision, but stood just behind him, so that for the rest of the evening he could assist him immediately without fail. The circle around the painter and Lorenzo started to look exactly like a symposium.

"You began," said the painter, "by describing the effects created by modern painting purely from a technical side, Lord Lorenzo. You mentioned perspective and anatomy, and then you went on to describe the new mediums for painting, namely oil and canvas. With these new techniques, as you indicated, painters have come increasingly closer to a lifelike representation of the reality we see around us, and gradually have distanced themselves from the more stylized abstract method of painting that prevailed until very recently. Painting has made this leap in less than a hundred years. And as a result, you said, painting has come closer to its ultimate goal, to what it has always sought, namely to resemble its motif."

"And to elevate it, concentrate it," said Lorenzo del Vetro.

"That's right, Lord Lorenzo, and I agree with you. One can't imagine any higher goal for all human art than to skillfully reproduce what it presents and at the same time elevate the motif to a more meaningful sphere."

"Precisely," said Lorenzo del Vetro. He seemed to have completely forgotten the chalice for the moment. Several of the guests nodded.

"People painted as they did for hundreds of years out of pure ignorance; they had no knowledge about perspective, about anatomy, and lacked an elastic technique. All the altar paintings from olden times that we know from our churches and chapels are painted in this way. When we see these pictures today, the style often seems clumsy and awkward."

"Almost childish," said Lorenzo del Vetro.

"Quite right."

"In my own case," said Lorenzo del Vetro, "I exchanged the old altar painting in the family chapel at home in Florence for a new one, painted in today's spirit. The old one was terrible. Completely . . . *flat*. The figures' faces scarcely looked like real faces, but had only the outline of faces, with simplified geometric strokes to mark eyes, nose, and mouth, and were shaded in the most elementary way, as if they were cone-shaped, and the clothing was merely colored surfaces. I exchanged it, as I said."

"You were right in doing so, Lord Lorenzo," the painter replied emphatically. "But nonetheless let me add that one element, or more correctly, one point of view was lacking in your otherwise perfect speech, and since this is to be a symposium, I could well imagine developing some thoughts about that."

"Let us hear!"

"I'll be brief, because it's a short and simple question," said the painter. "Today when one sees a painting of, let's say, for example, the Magi's adoration of the Virgin and child—commissioned by one of our day's great princes and art patrons, like yourself, Lord Lorenzo—nothing is lacking in this portrayal of the world. If we look through the windows and doors of the stable, we see the forests and mountains in the distance, and they are painted so realistically that one wants to saddle a horse and ride up there for a hunt. Between the mountains and the stable stretch the fields, where shepherds watch their grazing flocks, and outside the stable perhaps stand the Magi's horses, magnificent steeds, all three."

"Or a camel," interjected the cardinal.

"Quite true, or some such animal. And in the stable sits the radiant Madonna, and she is beautiful and young, clad in her blue cape, and the cape is woven in a pattern everyone recognizes; it comes from Pentitti's textile shop near Rubaconte da Mandela above the Arno and is the latest fashion; her shoes, for example, are made by Master Giacomo at the cathedral square, with a gold thread design embroidered into the suede upper part of the shoe, her ermine collar is imported from Novgorod, the book she holds in her hand comes from the new print shops in Mainz, and her simple necklace is expensive—as everyone can see—and made by Florence's foremost jeweler or perhaps it's a Moorish piece imported from Spain; indeed, isn't it—thinks the churchgoer—yes, confound it, it's the same piece of jewelry that can be admired during Sunday mass adorning the wife of the man who gave the commission, or his fiancée, or his mistress . . ."

"Or sister," the cardinal pointed out.

"Or the like," the painter granted. "And if we more closely examine the Virgin in the painting, she often also has the features of the wife or the fiancée or the mistress . . ."

"But no one knows what the Holy Virgin looked like," one of the theologians objected.

"That's right," said the painter, "no one knows that, and yet everyone knows in his heart, everyone who has prayed to her." The last words were said with quiet emphasis.

There was a painful silence; no one dared to look at anyone else, neither theologians nor noblemen, until the painter continued.

"But this image one carries in one's heart, gentlemen and ladies, is of course one's own and very personal, and perhaps this image has long been only a memory from childhood's innocent prayers, but still: as a painter who must paint the world around us, one seeks an external model who corresponds to the inner beauty one has imagined when praying to the Virgin Mother."

"And of course the patron must get something for his money too," said Lorenzo del Vetro.

"Quite right. Why shouldn't he see his wife or mistress or mother or whomever in the Virgin's role, or even his own features in one of the

Magi's faces, or as Joseph, or at least as one of the humble shepherds in the field. But then the question is: When the whole motif is reproduced in this way, when every detail is true to Nature and painted with devotion, and every churchgoer can recognize everything as real, then is it really God's mother and the adoration scene we have before us, or in fact a picture of the same men, women, and objects, the same streets, the same mountains, and the same Nature we see around us every day, now merely elevated to new and unaccustomed esteem?"

"That's precisely what I considered as the primary characteristic and goal of painting," Lorenzo del Vetro objected enthusiastically: "To elevate the reality we see around us."

"But then isn't it irrelevant what the painting depicts? Couldn't it just as well be a profane scene from our own city? Something that has actually happened? Why even paint the adoration of the Madonna and child? Indeed why, when the Virgin's most important purpose in the painting is to resemble the features of the living woman who was the model and to display the clothes and jewels she was wearing?"

"This is blasphemy," said the cardinal, with no outward sign of shock.

"It's like listening to Savonarola, isn't it?" said one of the exiles with disgust.

"Not at all," smiled the painter disarmingly. "I simply allow myself to raise the question. And it's interesting that you mention our great enemy, the zealous priest and agitator in Florence who has caused so many of us such unhappiness. Because perhaps in precisely this question," he continued, "lies part of the reason for this iconoclast's great appeal among the common people. Savonarola seeks the inner, the heartfelt belief, not the outer portrayal of what is transitory, and unfortunately many people have joined him in this madness—not just laymen, in fact, but also learned men, yes even several of my esteemed colleagues have been affected by his sermons and have completely stopped painting profane or hedonistic motifs, not even so much as a little Bacchus, and for the time being they paint only simple, chaste Madonnas and crucifixions stripped of all external beauty. This brings me back to my innocent mother and her blind faith in the advice she received from the wise woman. For my mother believed in all higher things the same way—blindly. In religion as well, she was the same:

faith-full, trust-full, and trust-worthy. She was that way in anything and everything. She was faithful in little and faithful in much, as the Gospel of Luke says. She *had faith*. She didn't desert her belief, and it never deserted her but was always in her heart. If her prayers were answered, well, then she thanked all the saints and God's mother, and if her prayers were *not* answered, she told herself that the saints and God's mother knew what was best for her, were on her side and wanted what was good for her, and therefore were her greatest comfort in sorrow and misfortune, and for this she was doubly grateful to them. She was no saint, but an ordinary person who to the best of her poor abilities tried to practice goodness and do what was right, and her faith gave her strength to do this, while at the same time she had to endure an everyday life that consisted of drudgery, toil, and sorrow. For her, the Virgin and child were identical to the images she saw when she prayed in church and elsewhere, and these internal images corresponded to the altar paintings she saw in her village church. There was no difference between the eye's outer and the heart's inner image."

"I don't understand this," said Doctor Bevilaqua. "This is an emotional and old-fashioned faith, a sort of faith in miracles, and as far as I can see, has nothing to do with faith in the higher sense, that is, as an intellectual occupation, where one seeks signs of God's will through understanding the world and through thinking itself, much like the Greek philosophers. Only *thereby* does faith become an act of the will, a tool for our insight, and the cardinal virtue it is meant to be. Otherwise we might as well believe in magicians, wise women, and—ugh—miracle doctors, just like your esteemed mother."

"Now, now, Doctor," Lorenzo del Vetro warned, and cleared his throat, "even the most learned doctor doesn't always achieve the desired results, and is often just as helpless as the quack doctor."

"Mendaci homini, ne verum quidem dicenti, credere solemus," objected the doctor indignantly, and continued: "Blind faith is and will be blind—" but the painter interrupted him.

"Yes, Doctor, I agree with you. But as it is written: Blessed are they who do not see but still believe. Or let me describe it another way, by telling a little story about something I witnessed recently.

"As you ladies and gentlemen may know, my simple home and studio are located not far from here, down by the river. The air isn't always so healthy, it's true, but I have my small boat down at the shore and can row out to see the city at a little distance and fill my eyes with light. Well then. Near my studio, indeed just a few blocks from the palace where we now sit, at the end of a narrow passageway, stands a little church, San Luca al Mare it's called, even though it doesn't stand by the sea at all, but at the edge of the Tiber River, not far from Ponte Sisto. Perhaps some of the ladies and gentlemen from this neighborhood know that little church?"

"I vaguely remember it," said Doctor Bevilaqua. "Doesn't your family have an altar there, Lord Lorenzo?"

"That's possible," admitted Lorenzo del Vetro, scratching himself on his crusted neck. "To tell the truth, I don't know."

"Yes," said the painter, "you have an altar there, and that particular chapel, which your father established in his youth when he bought the palace here, plays a certain role in my story."

"He did?" said Lorenzo del Vetro. "Unfortunately, I've neglected it, without realizing so. But I've given paintings to other churches here in the neighborhood," he added.

"You're not the only one who has neglected it, Lord Lorenzo, if that's any comfort, for the entire little church of San Luca al Mare is neglected. Its golden days are over now, there are no longer many lamps burning before the holy paintings; the chapels and altars are turning to dust due to lack of attention from the families who previously kept the church in good repair. Only a few decades ago candles burned before each altar painting; now only a few flames remain, and the guardian patrons no longer donate new paintings, altars, and candelabra to San Luca al Mare. There are no more processions and parades, and nearly all the priests have left. It has become a poor church, for the poorest people in the area, beggars and street wenches and old women. Its time is nearly ended; there one finds only old altarpieces, painted in the traditional way, with egg tempera on plaster. There one finds nothing of the beauty which characterizes the neighboring churches: new oil paintings, lifelike, filled with light, air, and depth perspective. San Luca al Mare's paintings are stiff and old-fashioned. For new times prevail now, the people have found new gods—knowledge and beauty they're called—the priests desert their duties or stop taking them seriously, indeed, at the pope's palace one speaks more about Cicero and Ovid than about Peter and Paul, one thinks more about astronomy than about transubstantiation and praises today's poets and painters more than saints and hermits."

The cardinal cleared his throat.

"Oh well," said da Castelnuovo, "let's speak no more about that. What I wanted to tell you is this: when I first moved to this neighborhood, I peeked into the little church a few times, but found it dark and sad and poverty-stricken. None of the paintings there gave me pleasure, and it was managed by one lonely priest of the worst sort, a man without humor or learning; when he spoke with me he positively poured out his rage about the decadence of the times, and he chanted the mass in a false, piercing voice. The fellow was an old billy goat, rarely sober I think, who had both choirboys and local street wenches. So after a couple of introductory visits, my path never again led past San Luca al Mare—until recently. I had taken a break from my work and rowed quite a distance up the Tiber. The river was very high, as it usually is at this time of year, and my own quay was flooded, so when I returned I docked by the church, where the quay is higher. Carrying my oars, I walked quickly past the church door as I headed home to continue working on the pietà I'm creating for our esteemed host; the rowing had done me good, and I was eager to get back to my work."

Enzio da Castelnuovo paused for a moment, drained his glass, held it out. Fiorello filled it, and took care to fill Lord Lorenzo's glass at the same time, but his master did not look at him, his entire attention was directed toward the painter.

"Well," said the painter, "outside the church, which had always stood there wretched and unvisited when I'd gone by, I saw a large group of people cackling to each other. I became curious and went inside. Nothing was changed in there, the same dark mournfulness met me from all corners—with one nearby exception. In one of the side chapels a mass of candles had been lit before the altar, incense burned freshly in all the corners, and many people either knelt or were on their hands and knees on the floor. Some lay fully stretched out. Mostly old women, but also some younger ones, a couple of whores, and even a few men from the neighborhood—

simple craftsmen by and large, a smithy, a baker, a mustache clipper, and so forth, judging from their dress, but I also saw a money changer and a scribe on the dirty floor before the altar.

"Good heavens, I thought, what's happened? I went closer; near the altar it was very crowded. Some of the poor old women were singing, and it sounded awful. Do you know what, Lord Lorenzo? *Your* chapel was the cause of all the uproar."

Lorenzo del Vetro looked at the painter with curiosity.

"Well," continued da Castelnuovo, "I took a closer look at the chapel, and at the altar, and there was nothing to see other than a very simple Madonna and child, painted in the old manner, not especially beautiful or wonderful; I hadn't even noticed her on my earlier visits to the church, she was so modest and pitiful—yes, Lord Lorenzo, I hope I don't offend your honored father's memory by saying this, but that painting is surely not the most beautiful altar he donated during his life, nor the most important commission he gave, God bless his soul."

"It can't have meant much to him," said Lorenzo del Vetro. "But after all, the family has never regarded this city as its home."

"Precisely what I thought myself," said the painter. "Perhaps he donated it with regard to his reputation as a visitor in the quarter at the time he bought the palace here, and later forgot the entire matter. However that may be, this Madonna is not especially wonderful, but she has a certain charm simply because she has an orange in her hand and the baby Jesus is reaching for it; rather sweet. But the work is stiff and rather awkward in its expression. A poor painting, all of us here would agree. And old-fashioned besides. Fifty years old, or more. I tried to think who might have painted it, but no name came to mind, so undistinctive did the work seem. On the other hand, I saw the priest, the terrible old billy goat I'd met before, and he was still just as terrible, yes, please excuse the expression, Your Eminence, but the church has its black sheep too—anyway, he was the same as before, except worse, because now he was happy. 'Master Enzio,' he shouted, and came over and caught hold of me. 'Master Enzio, Master Enzio, what a pleasure and honor to see you!' I greeted him and asked what had happened, since so many people were flocking to his church. 'What's happened indeed!' he shouted. 'What's happened indeed within these humble walls! A miracle has happened, esteemed Master Enzio. God be praised!' He continued to babble like this for a long time, because he was already drunk, even though it was early in the afternoon, so I drew him aside and out into the fresh air. And little by little it became clearer what had occurred. One evening just a few months ago, the priest told me, an arthritic old woman had entered the church, a woman he had never seen in the neighborhood before. The priest, who feared she came to sleep in there, asked what she wanted. 'Oh,' said the old woman, 'I've come to pray to the Madonna over there for my arthritis.' The priest thought that was a strange reply, because he had never heard that the Madonna was supposed to have any effect on arthritis, but he asked her to hurry, because he wanted to extinguish the lamps. She walked stiffly over to the altar and kneeled down with great difficulty. The priest busied himself with his own concerns, but after some minutes he went over and told her to leave. She rose obediently, thanked him, and went her way. Only afterward did he realize something had been strange. Hadn't she left much more quickly than she arrived? The next day another old lady stood in the doorway, this time with urinary canal troubles. She had so much pain she could hardly walk and her daughter had to help her to the altar. But—this is important—she needed no help when she left."

"I've heard rumors about this miracle-making in San Luca from some patients," said Doctor Bevilaqua. "But there is no reason to trust these so-called cures. None of the patients I spoke with had obtained any result."

"No, of course not," said the painter, "I'm simply telling you what the priest said. The next morning there were four old women in front of the altar, each with her own pain, and all went home satisfied, though the priest could not determine whether they were actually healed or not. But some days later a young mother came with her sick boy, he had mumps and was near death. 'And,' said the priest, 'the miracle occurred before my eyes, when the boy saw the miraculous Madonna's face, the swelling went down, the feverish spots disappeared from his cheeks, and his natural healthy color returned.' I wondered how the priest could determine this with such certainty in the dark church, he undoubtedly has poor eyesight as well, but these were his words. Later, he said, more and more people came to pray to the Madonna delle Arancie—people with large and small physical problems, mostly poor folk from the area but also a few good citizens. The Madonna treated everyone the same, said the priest, she gave help for a florin or nothing, but still there was a nice sum of money in the collection box, so he could light proper candles that didn't smoke and still get his wine; and plenty of people came to mass, just as in earlier days, and he was able to express so many of the terrible things that concerned him. So the priest was very happy. She healed everything, from head lice to kidney stones, and right now she was a poor person's best remedy for every physical affliction, whether large or small, because—as you'll admit, esteemed doctor—not everyone has the means to consult a real physician, so some must content themselves with miracles and the advice of old women."

"That's how it's always been," admitted the doctor. "One day it's a miraculous painting of a Madonna, the next day a marvelous tincture sold by an articulate gentleman at the flower market."

"Quite right," said the painter, "and when I questioned the priest he didn't have particularly high hopes that people would keep flocking to the church forever. But the great and small miracles of faith he had witnessed had done him good, he was overwhelmed, and his faith had regained some of its original, youthful fervor. 'The most beautiful healing,' he said, 'the most marvelous one, was the young woman with leprosy, once a lovely courtesan, whose face and body had been ravaged by this terrible sickness, but with the Madonna's help the young woman lost her sores completely, they dried up and disappeared within a very short time after she prayed in front of the miraculous painting, and she became beautiful again, and now she's going to get married, and she richly deserves that,' the priest said."

"I'm sure he thinks so," said one of the listeners, and others laughed.

"Well, I don't know," said the painter. "And I didn't know what I should believe as I stood there with the poor priest either, so I left him and went into the church again, and stood before the altar where all the poor people were kneeling or lying with their faces turned toward the altarpiece. I looked at the painting. It was just as old-fashioned and inferior as ever. But—if one was to believe the priest—it also worked miracles. At any rate, it was miraculous in the eyes of all of those who lay and knelt around me, poor simple souls from all parts of Rome. And I thought: Why *this* painting, this inferior old-fashioned painting, and not one of the marvelous new ones? What is it about precisely this pitiful, simple Madonna that makes people from far and near come to *her* for help with their inflammations and infected fingers, broken hearts and barrenness? And when you gave your excellent speech just now, Lord Lorenzo, I thought again about this Madonna, whom your own father donated without knowing what it would lead to, and I happened to think about the many magnificent new perspective paintings of the Madonna with necklaces and ermine collars, Madonnas who look exactly like fiancées and lovers and sisters and other beautiful women whom everyone recognizes, and who don't cure so much as a wart, while this poor plaster of paris Madonna in San Luca al Mare who had an unknown model, *she* performs miracles. And I thought about my mother's blind faith, and about the many Madonnas I've painted myself, which are admired and praised by people with good taste and insight; the most beautiful women were models for all of them, but they will never approach the Madonna I saw in my prayers as a boy and have now almost forgotten, and as far as I know they haven't performed any miracles other than for my own money purse. And I don't know if my mother would have recognized *her* God's mother in my paintings either, but would have preferred the old one she was used to from the village church. And I began to wonder about which painting really came closest to the *actual* Madonna, and if it isn't also the task of art to touch *her*, whose appearance no one knows, but who simply works in us, like a secret spoor in our soul, faceless and unknown—just as the miraculous Madonna delle Arancie in San Luca al Mare obviously touches the souls of the poor believers so powerfully that they are cured, indeed, in their eyes she is *identical* to the true Madonna they pray to, indeed *is* the miraculous God's mother.

"What is the task of art, actually? What should it mean? Should it mean anything at all? And what should painting actually strive for and portray? The visible and temporal, or the eternal and amorphous, the abstract divine principle, whose true face no one knows?"

Lorenzo del Vetro was about to take the floor with objections, as were the cardinal and the doctor and several others, but unfortunately the symposiasts were interrupted at this important point in the conversation by the poet d'Argento, who now rushed in from the next room with the sonnet he had finished composing in honor of his host, which he immediately began to read aloud, but which we will bypass in respectful silence.

Meanwhile, the Devil, who had not succeeded in his evil purpose when Fiorello dropped Il Vetrone dei Vetri because the painter da Castelnuovo had prevented it—the Devil still stood in a corner of the room pouting like a schoolboy. He bit his nails nervously. Now, when the poet was reading his work, the Stranger saw his chance to get even. In a wily, devilish way (God knows how the Devil manages such things) he allowed a wave of laughter to go through the whole group, from the highest to the lowliest, right in the middle of the poet's emotionally charged declamation, and when they saw the poet's offended expression the guests needed no further encouragement to guffaw loudly; so the Devil could withdraw, satisfied with his vindictive little trick. The poet's sonnet on top of the painter's grandiloquence was too much for the guests; da Castelnuovo laughed the loudest of all, although perhaps not as heartily as Lorenzo del Vetro himself, who, despite the fact that the interesting conversation had now been cut off, still had experienced some of the atmosphere of the earlier banquets that he had wanted to re-create, and no longer thought about the loss of his family treasure but was happier than he had been in a long time. In the end, the poet had to give up and laugh too, perhaps not as wholeheartedly as the rest of the group, but noble self-conquest benefits everyone, even poets, on the Day of Judgment.

When the laughter had subsided, it would still have been possible to collect the threads of conversation and continue, for Lorenzo del Vetro and several of the guests still had questions and objections on their tongues. But the laughter on top of the wine and the poetic laurels had their effect on Lorenzo del Vetro, just as happened with Aristophanes during the classical Symposium in Athens; the moment Lorenzo had settled his face into a serious expression again and opened his mouth to resume the discussion, he let out a hiccup. He drew a breath, was about to begin again, then he hiccuped again, and again. Soon the guests began laughing anew, and Lorenzo with them, which of course just made the hiccuping worse. Now the thread of conversation was irrevocably cut, and the party's collective interest began to concentrate on the host's hiccups and on finding a remedy for his suffering. But we will not say whether this was the Devil's intention, or simply by chance.

"Huge amounts of water," Luciana the courtesan suggested objectively, "but it has to be ice cold." Fiorello ran for fresh water.

"Shouldn't he hold his breath for a minute afterward?" asked the cardinal.

"Yes," said Luciana, "and I'll help him. Drink, Lord Lorenzo, all in one gulp." When Lorenzo del Vetro had drunk the water, and Luciana began kissing him, the group started counting aloud, but before they had reached thirty, the kiss was over.

"That wasn't even half a minute," shouted the painter.

"He's cheating," said the cardinal. "He wants to do it again."

"Not at all," said Luciana. "But it's impossible to kiss him, the way he's hiccuping. I get air in my stomach."

New roar of laughter and a series of wheezing hiccups from the patient.

"Perhaps we should frighten him?" the cardinal wondered.

"Doctor," said Verduccio, "I've heard that salt is supposed to be good for hiccups. What does science say?"

"I think we ought to frighten him," the cardinal insisted, but the doctor said: "Such household remedies are for those blinded by ignorance. Salt can be excellent for one patient, ineffective for another, and exacerbate the situation for a third. Science is the light, but I would no more tell you why this is so than I would ask you to stare straight at the sun without protection (it would blind you irrevocably); I would illuminate your layman's soul with only as much light as it is capable of receiving, since it doesn't know the true background of the art of medicine."

"Get to the point!"

"In order to prescribe the correct medical remedy every time, one must not only know the herbs' effects but also have deep insight into astrology and human temperaments, for physiology without astrology is like a lamp without oil. If the patient is choleric, the medical remedy must be antipathetic toward this; if the patient is phlegmatic the medical remedy must repel the weight of impassiveness, et cetera; and if the patient's horoscope shows the seventh house is dominated by, for example, the moon or Saturn, I would choose medical remedies that respectively support or counteract these celestial influences, depending upon which aspects they are in, positive or negative, in balance or out of balance, all according to the patient's horoscope and constitutional temperament."

"Boo!" shouted the cardinal.

"Salt or no salt?" the poet persisted, and reached for the saltcellar.

"Lord Lorenzo just happens to be my patient, and judging from my knowledge of his temperament and horoscope, in this instance I would not prescribe salt for hiccups, although it can hardly hurt, but rather *Anethum graveolens*—just ordinary dill—either cooked in wine or simply crushed and the aroma inhaled, because dill is protected by Mercury and strengthens the brain and quiets a restless mind. Or I would prescribe *Foeniculum vulgare* or *Peucedanum officinale*—fennel and sulphurweed, pure and simple, as tea or decoction, for Mercury also controls fennel. On the other hand, I would advise against *Mentha viridis*, spearmint, which is otherwise regarded as being a good remedy for hiccups, because this plant is influenced by Venus and Lord Lorenzo's relation to this star is of a very questionable na—"

New wave of laughter. This time it was Doctor Bevilaqua's turn to be annoyed; he did not take it as well as the poet, and sat looking out at the gathering with a sardonic smile.

"Fi-ik-kiorello, do we have any dill in the house?" asked Lorenzo del Vetro.

"Dill is coming, Lord Lorenzo."

"Boo!"

"Of course," giggled Luciana, "Your Lordship could do what the common people do and go to Your Lordship's family altar in San Luca al Mare and pray to the miraculous Madonna delle Arancie."

The roar of laughter rose to the ceiling so loudly the plaster moldings trembled.

"Uaaaaaah!" cried the other courtesans and the papal officials.

"Hear! Hear!" shouted Cardinal Rizzi, and was about to say something more, but an inner gust of wind got in the way, and he belched while protesting his innocence.

"That's the best," laughed Enzio da Castelnuovo, "that's the best suggestion yet this evening!"

"I think . . . ! I think . . . !" continued the cardinal, but was overtaken by the wind again, and shut his mouth suddenly against his inner life. Everyone laughed. Even Doctor Bevilaqua.

"It would be a brilliant triumph of spirit over flesh," he said. "Science would be distressed."

"I think . . . ! I think . . . !" the cardinal tried once again, was almost overwhelmed by a new belch, which caused a new gale of laughter among the guests, but he fought his way through it, as a sailor maneuvers a ship through the sea in a storm, got everyone's attention, surveyed the gathering with his beady eyes, and struck: "Just imagine if the pope heard about it!"

"Uaaaaah!" New roar of laughter.

"He would die of shock."

"Or at least be cured of hiccups forever."

"Poor pope."

"They would have to elect a new one."

"Oh God! Oh God!"

"Eighteen nights' conclave!" cried the cardinal. "No, for God's sake. And just because of a hiccup."

"And think of the poor pope's family."

"Well, his daughter's life is lively enough—whether with the father or with the brother—"

"Good people!" shouted the poet d'Argento. "We'll do it! We'll do it tonight!"

"Do what, my friend?" asked Luciana charmingly. "Are we all going to do it, all of us together?"

New roar of laughter.

"No! No!" The poet tried to put a damper on the mood. "We'll put on our wraps and go to the church, all of us."

"Wonderful! Wonderful!"

"I—have more faith in the di-hill," Lorenzo del Vetro began, and Fiorello gave him a questioning look.

"Should I go down to the garden and cut some dill, Your Lordship, or shouldn't I?"

"Forget all this dill-y-dallying, and come with us, Lord Lorenzo!"

"Yes, come with us, Lord Lorenzo!"

"Then we can see this miracle-maker the painter has been talking about for half the evening."

"Well!" said Lorenzo del Vetro, rising in resignation, "I th-hank my guests for their concern about my hiccuping, and so let's—just h-hope and pray-he it doesn't stop on the way down to the ri-iver, but lasts long enough to be cured. Master Enzio, you sho-ow the way."

It took a while to gather the guests' retinue of servants and guards, who lay drunk or sleeping in the kitchen, and to get the lamps and torches lit, but finally the procession set out into the dark streets. They laughed and sang and hiccuped going down the stairs and into the illuminated entrance to the courtyard. But as soon as they came out into the dark, chilly silence, some of the mood was lost. For everyone could tell that the city was not a city but an enormous rat breathing in the darkness, and that they found themselves in the rat's belly, and that this labyrinth of streets was nothing more than the bowels. The women in particular took this realization to heart. The men held their hands on the shafts of their swords, for one could meet both murderers and bandits at so late an hour. Therefore a number of the guests lost their desire to visit the church, and chose instead to discreetly take their entourage and go home or to other parties and other pleasures. But there were still a dozen or so when they arrived at the entrance to San Luca al Mare. The stench of sewage and slime rose toward them from the Tiber, and they could hear the rhythmic sound of oars from a solitary flat-bottomed rowboat on its way to the other side of the river. Otherwise it was quiet, except for some half-choked hiccups from Lorenzo del Vetro.

It was indeed an unpretentious little church, very old, with Romanesque portals and window arches and a simple nave with a small adjoining campanile. Above the loggia could be seen the remains of a mosaic, but it was so damaged that it was impossible to tell what it had depicted. The rest of the church had no outer ornamentation. For a moment the group of revelers stood looking at the closed door without finding courage to knock in the quiet night.

Then Enzio da Castelnuovo strode forward, walked fearlessly into the pillared entry where the darkness seemed even thicker, and began to pound loudly on the door's oak timbers. The other guests were startled by the sudden, thundering sound, which echoed doubly loud beneath the arched ceiling of the loggia; at the same moment, all the dogs in the neighborhood began to howl, and the houses in this quarter were so close that the whole pack seemed to be barking in their ears. Here and there small lights appeared in dark windows, voices could be dimly heard, but nobody shouted at them, for people could see this was a retinue with swords. But the group felt the eyes on them. And the beggars, who slept between the loggia's pillars, moved and mumbled in the dark. The painter kept pounding on the door for quite some time, until a shapeless figure crept out from behind a pillar, darker than dark, darker than the darkness.

Enzio da Castelnuovo stopped knocking and went over to the creeping bundle, which stretched out a white arm that had no hand; a tin mug was chained around the stump of his arm.

"Where is the priest, beggar?"

Some unintelligible sounds came from the bundle.

"Where is the priest!"

"Internal dissension," said the bundle.

"What did you say?"

"Internal dissension and the church's disintegration. Yes. Three hundred years of misfortunes and violence and pestilence, fourteen popes and fifteen antipopes, conclaves without goals and the Holy Spirit on Sunday holidays in the country, while the pope whores with his daughter, yes, and Christ's brother battles Christ's brother in the middle of holy Tuscany. Sancte Michael Archangele, defende nos in proelio! While Turkish dogs tear at the rotting cadaver and destroy us with their cannonballs. Yes sir, yes indeed."

"Are you mad?"

"Yes sir, yes."

"You appear to have been an educated person at one time."

"Yes sir, at one time, but now I'm as stupid as an astronomer."

"Do you live here under—"

"Rent. They charge rent. And they chop off the hands of people who have done nothing wrong and who can't provide money in a war that doesn't even concern them. These are surely strange times, I must say. What do you believe God thinks about this matter of the rent, sir?"

"If you live here," the painter went on stubbornly, because he had little desire to start a discussion about the banking system's loan policies right now, "if you live here, as you say, you should know where the priest has his lodgings."

"It's the fault of the abacus."

"What?"

"This Turkish nuisance, this Saracen heresy, this godless nothing. Yes. Plip, plop, they move the beans on the abacus up and down so nicely on the rod, plip-plop-plop. Presto here and there. Soon the one column is empty, and they move another down, because where it's empty, they say, there it's nothing and null, they call it, but still this is nothing more than everything else combined, whoever can understand that, how nothing can mean something; in truth, that's heresy and black magic, and still they're allowed to continue on their reckless course with their abacuses, and neither the church nor the prince takes action against this heathenism."

"Listen—"

"No, it was better with the old numbers, then one was one and five was five and equal inside and outside, and ten was always ten and was just as many fingers as I once had on my two hands, akk, ten was ten and neither more nor less, and one less than ten was nine, while one more than ten was eleven, and ten less than ten was nothing and irrevocably nothing, of which I myself am a wandering proof. While now, a person moves his beads here and there and says: One bead plus no beads, that equals ten! And if one adds still another nothing to this miserable number ten, then suddenly it's one hundred; this is an abominable and strangely ingenious number ten, I must say. And with this new godless number ten, which people have discovered without asking anyone about laws, people demand rents and chop off the hands of people who have done nothing but simply perform their trade in peace and quiet; there's no sense in this, sir. May I go to sleep now, sir, or at least have a few coins for the conversation?"

"You're mad," said the painter, "wretched and mad."

"Yes, sir, a few coins. Many people pay me to listen to my opinions about the number ten."

"Have you tried praying to the miraculous Madonna in there instead, asked her to give you some wits in your head?"

"Unfortunately, young man, my wits were in my hands, because I was a carpenter, made the finest furniture, that's what I was, and I was an artist, yes that I was indeed, and my work was found in the most aristocratic houses. But the war came and with it came plundering and all sorts of extortion and swindles, with rents and interest on rent, and treachery and deception and rents and nothing numbers and extortion and rents and I lost my hands, both of them, ten fingers, five on each, just as God had created them. The Madonna can't give me back my hands, or give humanity back its ten—and I think there are limits to what even a Madonna can do with the wave of a hand, if you understand my little joke—so I'll keep my fingers out of it and stick with my number ten, here outside the church door."

By now the painter had completely changed his mind and put a generous sum into the cup chained to the beggar's arm.

"Thank you," said the beggar. "I can see you are a noble gentleman, despite seeing almost nothing in this deep darkness, for your figure shines and glitters, there's a glow around you wherever you go, your words and voice gleam, so you've surely always had good luck with women, and haven't had to exert much effort in that regard, whether you were poor or rich, child or grown-up, for this glittering attracts women more than any other characteristic; that's a secret not everyone knows."

"So you still have your eyesight?"

"As one sees it, sir, as one sees it. For that matter, they could just as well have blinded me too, because my hands contained the light, and through the work of my hands the light rose to my eyes and lit their fire, but now when my hands are gone my eyes are closed too and can no longer cast their light on the world, they find no joy or meaning in the little they glimpse, but prefer to remain here in the darkness. So in reality I'm blind too, blind in my soul, for my inner light has disappeared, and in its place is only darkness."

"The eye is the light of the body," said the painter, "if your eye is healthy, then your whole body is light, but if your eye is sick, your whole body becomes dark. So if the light in you is dark, how great then is the darkness!"

"That's exactly the situation, sir."

"We want to go in to see the Madonna now, tonight," said the painter kindly, "because we want to test her miraculous powers."

"That's certainly not wasted time," said the beggar, "certainly not, but the priest is drunk as a bandit and sleeping heavily. Still, he would probably have been awakened by all your pounding, if he had heard it, but he can't hear it, because you're knocking on the wrong door."

"What door should I knock on then, craftsman?"

"The sacristy door, honorable sir; you should have thought of that yourself, then all of us would have had peace right away. And now with your permission I'll withdraw to my beauty sleep; for it's true that vanity is a deadly sin, but ugliness is worse, and I think I have a right to be able to sleep and dream about the beauty of my hands."

The others had listened to this strange conversation with a mixture of interest and boredom, depending upon each guest's temperament, and several of the women began to complain about the darkness and say they wanted to go home. But the servants lit new torches, and the group started toward the sacristy in somewhat better spirits. The painter was in the lead; behind him came Lorenzo del Vetro and the others, laughing and talking enthusiastically about all the strange things the beggar had said. Farthest back, outside the circle of light, came Fiorello; nobody noticed how pale he had become. The painter began pounding on the sacristy door immediately. After a few minutes they heard someone begin to move around inside, a thick voice hawked and shouted: "Who's there? Go away! This is a church!"

"We've come to loot it!" Cardinal Rizzi called out with the voice of a prophet. Everyone laughed, but the voice inside grew high-pitched and abject.

"This is a poor church! There's nothing to steal here! Not so much as a candlestick. Just rats and lice. Go away!"

"Take it easy, priest," said the painter, "he's just joking. It's me, the painter Enzio da Castelnuovo, and a small company of distinguished friends who would like to see the Madonna now, tonight, if that's possible—"

A small window opened in one of the door panels, a round face stared out with watery, distrustful eyes.

"Why didn't you say so immediately!" he said beaming with pleasure. "Esteemed master!" The priest stuck his head out the small window and looked at the company with wide eyes. "Oh, oh my! What an honor! Welcome. Eh. Welcome. Welcome. Oh! Monsignor!" cried the head when he saw the cardinal, and gave a little bow over the edge, almost like a doll in a puppet theater. "Welcome! What an honor! I'm sorry that I'm not—I mean, I'm sorry that you gentlemen have had to wait. What an honor! And Lord Lorenzo!" he squeaked desperately as he pressed his head even farther through the opening, almost as if the church were giving birth to him. "Welcome to San Luca al Mare."

The cardinal looked at him with narrowed eyes.

"Aren't you going to let us in, Father?"

"Yes! Of course! Of course! Why am I standing here idle? Just a moment, and I'll—" The head disappeared and the small window shut with a bang. A few minutes passed without anything happening, but they could dimly hear shuffling steps and lowered voices; the priest hissed something. The cardinal laughed quietly in the dark. Then they heard new steps, and keys jangling, and the door swung open.

"I'm sorry," said the priest. "I had to get the key, and make myself a little more . . . presentable." Despite how dark it was, they could see that he blushed as he bowed them in. The servants remained outside with the torches.

"We want to see the Madonna," said Enzio da Castelnuovo with no further ado.

"The Madonna! Yes, of course! The Madonna. The miraculous Madonna delle Arancie, who adorns and honors the church. Yes, of course. What an honor too, that such noble gentlemen, indeed the noblest in the land, together with one of the foremost men of the church, have heard about her and want to see her. This way, ladies and gentlemen, I'll light candles. No, not in there, that's my cell . . . Not in there. It's so . . . untidy." But the cardinal had already peeked through a crack in the doorway to the priest's boudoir. He immediately turned toward the priest.

"Not bad," he said, and winked.

The poor priest became completely befuddled, and with a litany of regrets and thanks he led them into the dark church, stumbled on his robe, and awakened a whole swarm of rats that scurried away in fright between their feet. The women screamed, and Luciana clung to Lorenzo and said she wanted to go home, preferably to his home.

"How are your hiccups, Lord Lorenzo?" the cardinal asked maliciously. "Didn't you get frightened just now?"

"I still have them," mumbled Lorenzo del Vetro. He was not particularly enjoying himself either; from the floor of the church rose the stench of dead bodies. But the priest had lit candles now, and led them down to the del Vetro family's chapel. A few stumps of candles still flickered in front of the Madonna; they stood in a sea of burned-out wicks.

Lorenzo del Vetro called for Fiorello, who appeared immediately.

"Take a candle and hold it up under the painting, Fiorello, so we can get a better look at her." Fiorello obediently leaped over the altar railing, took one of the large white altar candles, lit it with one of the small candles that was almost burned out, and raised it toward the Madonna's face.

The group stood looking at the picture for a while.

"My father must have been out of his mind," Lorenzo del Vetro said firmly. "You didn't exaggerate, master," he said to the painter.

"No, I certainly didn't."

"One would think it was painted more than a hundred years ago."

"It's not that old, Lord Lorenzo."

Lorenzo del Vetro took a step closer, looked intently at the Madonna. This is what he saw: a woman in a simple blue cloak with a child in her arms. With a rather stiff hand she held out a fruit toward the child, but it was hard to tell what kind of fruit, because it was painted so imprecisely; it could well have been an apple. The child was reaching for the fruit, but its gaze was turned in a completely different direction, outward. So in this aspect as well it was not a very believable painting. Gold leaf was richly laid around the heads of the mother and child, and large parts of the background were also covered with gold; only in this lavish embellishment (which in fact was quite well done) could one see that the person who commissioned the painting had not been just anybody. The background was flat and consisted of stylized hills and round trees, where one could glimpse other fruits. The Madonna was looking at neither the child nor the fruit; her eyes squinted a little and had a vague, inscrutable gaze; the pupils did not seem properly round. The painting was neglected, the plaster had become cracked and ulcerated (perhaps due to moisture from the Tiber's annual flooding), and the colors were stale and conventional.

"Well," said the painter, "what do you think?"

"Rather bad," said the cardinal.

"Insignificant," said the doctor.

"Tell me, Father," asked the cardinal, "is it really true that the Madonna performs miracles? Or is this something you've concocted to get people to come?"

"Oh no, Your Eminence," said the priest, bowing almost to the floor, "all kinds of things really happen here, no question about that. Last week a woman came who was purblind but didn't have the means to undertake any treatment with a needle, and she regained her sight, that's certain."

"Remarkable," said the cardinal. "Truly remarkable. Doctor?"

"It sounds amazing," said the doctor, "but treatment with a needle isn't the only course of action, because a needle is both risky and difficult to use, and moreover it doesn't provide a lasting cure, but only delays eventual blindness. So one can also use *Chelidonium* or caustic plant juices. Or the woman's cure could have other causes. As we know, purblindness is due to an imbalance of body fluids, since nourishment from food is transformed to spirit through the organs; first through the liver, where the nourishment becomes natural virtue, then to the heart where it becomes spiritual virtue, and finally to the brain, where it is transformed to shining spiritual wind that ignites the light in the eye's lantern. Unbalance, for example in the liver, can develop into impurities that rise to the eye and darken the membrane in the form of crusts. The woman you mention may have changed her diet."

"But you do agree that it could also be a miracle?"

"Yes," the doctor granted. "With God all things are possible."

"Amen," the priest and the cardinal said in chorus.

"Do you really believe that, Doctor?" asked the painter. "I mean, what you said about the eye's light?"

"What do you mean?"

"That the eye sends out light like a lantern, or do you believe that all light comes to us from outside and is reflected into the eye, so that in some inexplicable way the whole world enters through that tiny little hole in a camera obscura and becomes visible on the opposite wall? In other words, that it's dark within the eye itself, until light comes into it?"

"What do you mean?" asked the poet d'Argento.

"When the great, divine master Brunelleschi, God bless his genius eternally, created perspective, the youngest and sweetest of the free artist's muses—and it's no more than seventy-five years ago that this miracle occurred—he stood on the cathedral steps in Florence with a board one sunlit morning and let people peer through a tiny little hole from the back of the board. Through the hole they saw the market square and the baptistery, and were willing to swear it was the reality they saw. What they did not know, was that the master held a mirror in front of the board they were looking through, so that what they actually saw was the motif he had painted on the front of the board which, with proper perspective but in mirror image, reproduced the entire square and the baptistery. To heighten the effect he had laid silver leaf on the sky in the painting, so that the actual sky and the moving clouds were reflected in it. The illusion was complete. With that, painting became a whole new art, and Brunelleschi became famous."

"What does this have to do with the eye?"

"If the old ideas are correct, a beam of light goes out from the eye to seek and blend with the forms of light in outer reality. The gaze is *out there*. But Brunelleschi knew this could not be the case when he created perspective, because the eye could be fooled by his trick. In other words, he knew it depends on only the outer light. The same is true in a camera obscura, where one lets a thin, thin beam of light seep into a darkened room through a black, impenetrable curtain, and a complete picture of the world is created on the surface the beam of light strikes. Perhaps the eye is a dim chamber such as that."

"I'm inclined toward the latter idea, even though it's indoctrinatory," admitted the doctor. "And there is also the problem that the light picture in a camera obscura always appears upside down, which doesn't happen when we see reality, fortunately. But if, for example, one slices the eye of an ox—"

"Yes, have you also done that splendid experiment!" the painter exclaimed enthusiastically, while several of the guests stole away, tired of the conversation and the gloomy church, and certainly very thirsty as well. The gathering was breaking up more and more.

During all of this, Lorenzo del Vetro stood looking at his family's Romanesque Madonna, which he had never seen before. Fiorello held the candle in his outstretched arm in front of the painting. Lorenzo del Vetro sighed, yawned, peered toward the painting. For a moment a mood came over him, as if he dozed off, like a stone that falls into a lake causing rings that spread out and gradually disappear. Then he shook off his weariness. He looked at the young woman in the painting, but it was impossible to determine whether the model had been pretty or quite ordinary in appearance.

"This is absurd," he mumbled. "Tell me, Master Enzio, who was the model for this Madonna?"

"I don't know," said Enzio da Castelnuovo, pulling himself away from the interesting conversation about the eye's characteristics.

"The painter must have had a model for this painting."

"Most certainly."

"Yes, because even if he painted his inner picture of the Madonna, the unknown master of wretchedness must surely also have had an actual woman and an actual child to look at while he painted. Yes, and even real oranges or peaches or whatever those round things are supposed to represent."

"Very likely, Lord Lorenzo. You have a point there."

"So in principle she is no different from today's more perfect Madonnas, who are also painted from a model, and hence all your fine rhetoric in our conversation falls to pieces."

"It seems your hiccups are gone, Lord Lorenzo."

"That's unimportant."

"It's probably because he got frightened," the cardinal said with satisfaction.

"Can we leave soon?" asked Luciana. "I'm tired of being here."

"She's right," said the cardinal discontentedly. "Well, Father, surely you wouldn't deny a poor servant of the church something to drink since we're here?"

"This painting," Lorenzo del Vetro insisted stubbornly, "doesn't resemble anything. It's possibly one of the worst paintings I've ever seen. My father must have bought the cat in the bag, I can't find any other explanation for his having chosen such an old-fashioned artist to create a Madonna for him. The painting must depict something inner, for it surely can't be anything outer. But what this 'inner' might be, other than vagueness and mystery, is incomprehensible. It reveals nothing. I see neither truth nor beauty in this, no visible divinity and no maternal joy, no real play with the child, but no pain or sorrow either, which one would have expected. On the whole, it's impossible to see what this Madonna feels, or who she is."

"I quite agree, Lord Lorenzo, she is utterly expressionless, and yet that shows what difficult and confused times we live in, when people are drawn to this dismal, old-fashioned wretchedness."

"Who painted it, by the way?" asked the poet.

"I don't know," replied the painter, "perhaps the priest knows." But the priest was no longer there, nor was the cardinal anywhere to be seen.

"Please," said Luciana. "Can we leave now? Being in here makes me ill. It's disgusting."

"Yes, let's go," said Lorenzo del Vetro.

On the way out they heard loud, intoxicated voices from the priest's room; the painter peeked through a crack in the doorway. "Everything is fine," he whispered to them, and they stole past quietly.

"Now that we're rid of the cardinal," the painter said softly when they were out in the street, "perhaps the remaining gentlemen and ladies would be interested in seeing a *real* work of art, if I may modestly say so, one that truly resembles something, along with what it resembles."

"Yes!" said Lorenzo del Vetro. "I want to see my pietà, now, tonight!"

"Yes, let's do that," the poet agreed, "because I long to see true, beautiful art, after that horrible miracle Madonna."

"All right, but let's hurry, because it's impossible to visit my atelier with His Eminence, for reasons you'll soon understand, and he might discover that we've slipped away, and follow us."

The group now consisted of only the painter, the poet d'Argento, Doctor Bevilaqua and Lorenzo del Vetro, and three women, including the beautiful Luciana, as well as the servants of course, who wearily staggered ahead of them.

"For that matter, he has a lovely apartment on Gianicolo," said Luciana. "The cardinal, that is."

"So, my beauty," asked Lorenzo del Vetro, "you *have* visited it?"

"Oh no, I've only heard the *rumors*," she said, not sounding particularly convincing. "It's next to the church and has a direct entrance from the confessional, so he can take the sinners into his room unseen, for further forgiveness of their sins in more pleasant surroundings."

"An excellent move," said the painter. "Is he rich?"

"He's very careful not to display his wealth too conspicuously, as everyone can well understand, otherwise he would meet the same fate as the others."

"Oh yes, Cardinal Furbizio, God have mercy on his sinful soul; old Furbo beat the drum too hard, as you recall. Everyone thought he was good for eighty thousand ducats or more, perhaps a hundred thousand, the way he threw money around, with bacchanalian feasts and marvelous satyr plays—yes, you all remember old Furbizio's feasts, of course; they were magnificent, and truly enjoyable, with no lack of worldly pleasures, and that became his misfortune. For as soon as the pope got news of his wealth, old Furbizio got sick and died of an unfortunate stomach ailment. As usual, His Holiness was just in time to receive the dying man's last confession and to sweep the apartment clean of silverware and textiles. The Venetian ambassador, a friend of mine, immediately sought an audience at the Vatican to sniff around, but of course wasn't given an audience for several days, while the pope counted. He was still counting, for that matter, at the time of the audience, and this was the first subject His Holiness brought up: 'Eighty thousand,' said the pope, in an offended tone, 'the whole city is saying that we've gotten more than eighty thousand, but there was no more than exactly 23,832 in the chest, the old swindler.' "

They laughed.

"However, my friend the ambassador claimed to know with certainty that in fact it was a matter of more than 150,000, but I don't believe that, not about old Furbo; he had spent it all. So he got something for his money while he was still among us."

"Yes," said Lorenzo del Vetro, "one needs to be careful not to throw money around too much."

"Yes, my honorable friend," said the painter, "and you should be careful yourself, because from what they say, Cardinal Rizzi enjoys His Holiness's favor, and he noted with wide-eyed attention everything that was served and what valuables were displayed this evening. I certainly noticed that. And it takes no more than that before your secure exile becomes a wasps' nest, and you have to flee hastily, with a ransom placed on your head; and then you're no longer a human being but a check, which others can pass from hand to hand like any financial document."

"Don't worry," said Lorenzo del Vetro with a thin smile. "We all have a grip on each other's balls, and I too have one thing and another on certain persons, whose names won't be mentioned here, which makes me feel quite safe at the moment anyway."

"I completely forgot that you were the son of your father," mumbled the painter. They walked through the narrow passages. At one point they had to stop for a moment because two men came around a corner toward them with their knives drawn; the servants gripped their swords, but the two just stared at them with bloodshot eyes and disappeared into the darkness without starting a fight.

"Fortunately, their business had nothing to do with us," the painter said in relief. "Those two appeared to be quite certain where they were coming from and where they were going." Soon afterward the group came upon the corpse the two had left behind; it was still warm: a younger, well-dressed man, lying facedown. The passage was so narrow that they had to step over him.

"Ugh," said Luciana. "You live in a bad neighborhood, painter. I'm getting completely out of the mood for this."

"Just wait until you get to my home, little friend," said the painter. "Then you will have a chance to read deeply in both God's book and Nature's book, that is to say, the book of experience. We'll see how your mood is then."

"Deep sounds good," mumbled a girl who until now had simply straggled along somewhat timidly. She barely whispered it, but something about her voice made everyone give her an eager look.

They found themselves in a large, dark, sparsely furnished room, almost a hall, where the walls seemed to lose themselves in arches high above them. The painter lit lamps and candles, drew out chairs and a couch, and asked his nocturnal guests to make themselves comfortable. While he went to get wine, they looked around the room. A pile of sketches and books lay on one table, on another were the artist's tools along with a row of jars from which came an unpleasant smell. In a corner one could glimpse a huge rough block of marble. In the middle of the floor stood another large object, covered with a cloth, and beside it, a low table on which there also lay a large covered object. The artist returned with a tray of expensive crystal glasses and a carafe of wine. He poured. It was a marvelous wine, sparkling and refreshing in the early-morning hours, and the group expressed its recognition with small sighs.

"It's been a long night," said da Castelnuovo, "and soon it will be over, so I'll come right to the point, while the ladies and gentlemen fortify themselves." He went over to the covered object, held up a candelabra, removed the cloth, and there, in the flickering light, was his pietà.

They stopped drinking. They went over to the work of art, stood there stunned, even the prostitutes. They stood before it. They wiped their eyes, deeply moved. The dead man lay outstretched with his mother, as if he had just been taken down from the cross and had given up the ghost. Every muscle showed how much he had suffered, his face still bore traces of life and pain. His mother, whom the master had chosen to make young, looked down at him with a quiet, inscrutable look, and her face was as innocent as a child's, and at the same time it held every innocent sorrow. The folds of her cloak, her hair, and the dead man's muscles, all were reproduced with precise accurateness, and yet the surface was endlessly rich and living in its play of light and shadow.

"Master Enzio," said Lorenzo del Vetro quietly, "it's sublime."

"It's marvelous," said the doctor. "How do you manage to re-create the body so true to nature? And in particular the *dead* body? It's incomprehensible. One *sees* that it's dead, and yet that it has just been alive. It's very well done."

"Well," said the artist, and went over to the low table, "one must have a model. See." He pulled the cloth to one side. "Ecce homo," he said.

On the stone table lay the naked corpse of a young man. His skin was extremely pale, with blood extravasations under his arms and around his neck and abdomen.

"The day's corpse," said da Castelnuovo.

The women crossed themselves and turned away, while the men stood looking at the body with interest.

"Who is it?" asked Lorenzo del Vetro. "And where does he come from?"

"I saw him die," said Enzio da Castelnuovo. "Last night, to be exact. Castel Sant'Angelo lies just a short rowing trip from here, over on the other side of the river, and I have become friends with all the guards and officers there, and have brought them generous amounts of good wine and bribes, so they let me in to see what's happening."

"He was a handsome man once," said the timid girl. She looked fearlessly at the dead man as she placed herself beside da Castelnuovo and took his hand. "What did he die from?"

"Oh," said the artist. "I don't know. Does it matter? They worked on him for several hours in the cellar before he gave up the ghost. They wanted him to say something or other, I don't know what, and it's of no interest to me either. But he didn't say anything, even though they tried things with him that make most people jabber like a Hebrew merchant from Alexandria before they're finished. But this one here was odd." He searched his memory a little. "Odd. Yes, he was. He lay there and they worked on him. At first he groaned and screamed terribly when they put him on the wheel, but then it was as if something happened with him; it was as if he suddenly wasn't *there* any longer, although everyone could see that he was still conscious. He found his way to a place within himself where none of the pain could reach him, a place where time no longer existed, but stood completely still, or simply didn't mean anything anymore, whereas otherwise it's usually *time* that means something to the person lying there, since time goes more slowly when one is being tortured. Everyone who has been tortured says the same thing: the pain makes time go so slowly that one is willing to do anything at all to make it pass at a normal rate again. But for this one here, time seemed to no longer mean anything; he turned his eyes inward and there he saw something or there *was* something that made him endure everything they did to him. Such things happen, the men told me, such things happen; every now and then they run into a fellow who just disappears from them, and it doesn't have to be one of the big strong ones. Quite the contrary, it's often a little whippersnapper, and it's equally tiresome each time it happens, because they know such a fellow can keep them busy for days, seeming oblivious to them, to water torture or fire torture or even worse things, though he is certainly feeling pain. It's just not *his* pain any longer, or rather let us say: It's outside him, and he's outside it. They could just as well kill him right away, and they did that with this poor fellow; he died like a Christ, and his manner of dying made such an impression on me that I asked to take him home with me, to study him more closely. He interested me."

"And have you found anything?" asked Lorenzo del Vetro.

"No," said the artist. "He's like all other dead bodies. I've cut into him a little, as you see, but it's not primarily the inner anatomy that I'm interested in this time, but more the play of muscles in his underarms. They cracked his bones, just as with the dead Christ, and then interesting things happen with the muscles."

"Do you often bring corpses here?" asked the doctor with distaste.

"It's not allowed, of course," said the painter apologetically, "but to read in Nature's book, that is to say the book of experience, one must break some rules now and then. I regularly bring corpses here and cut them up, so I have something to sketch from. Not only from Castel Sant'Angelo, for that matter, but also right from the street, or fresh corpses I pluck out of the river, if they haven't been there long; there's no lack of bodies, both old and young, women and children. In the river especially one finds a preponderance of pregnant women. It's unbelievable how much more one understands of the human body when one has cut into it a little. It's a machine where God has placed his fingerprint in each sinew, each limb, each bone. So ingenious. So incredibly ingenious, and at the same time so simple and vulnerable."

"What happened when he died?" asked d'Argento.

"This one here? Oh, he leaned over to the side and stopped breathing, that was all. Isn't that how everyone dies?"

"I mean, his soul?" said the poet. "He had a strong soul! Did he say anything?"

"No, he didn't say anything. He just let out his breath, and otherwise there was nothing to see or hear. He looked exactly as before, except that every movement stopped. He looked the way he looks now. And that's also how he looked when he was alive, except that he wasn't so calm. Isn't that how it is with all who die?"

"How can you say such a thing!" shouted Luciana suddenly. "That the only thing that happened was that he stopped moving! He died after all!"

"Yes, and what else do you think death is, my beauty?" asked the artist. "One day you too will stop wriggling, stop moving, lie as still as a fish on a counter, and then you'll be dead; even if you're as beautiful as a goldfish with a tail, you're just as dead."

"Ugh! You should be ashamed!" But the timid young girl stole even closer to the artist.

"Can you tell me how I'll look when I'm dead?"

"Completely motionless. You *aren't there*, miss, don't you understand? That's all. You aren't there."

"So strange," she said. "To not be there." She looked at her hands.

"Yes, your hand is there, and I can see it, but you can no longer see it."

"You have a very frank view of death," said Lorenzo del Vetro. "And of the soul."

"Lord Lorenzo," said the painter, "by now I've cut up surely fifty corpses in here, old and young, criminals and innocents. I cut them up and look inside them, see the veins, the heart, the nerves, the brain, the muscles. Slice through them and take them apart into their individual components. The muscles in particular interest me, for purely practical reasons, because it's the play of muscles that one must reproduce, after all. I preserve especially fine examples in alcohol, in the jars you see there on the table, for later study. I cut them up, and in the end all that's left of them is a large number of loose organs. I can no longer see which gallbladder belonged to which corpse. There's nothing left of them, and nobody objects to the treatment. If anyone is there, that person is invisible."

"Invisible?" said Lorenzo del Vetro.

"That's my experience. The person is invisible. Not present. If we did an experiment in which you killed your young servant right now, he would scream and flail about for a short while, but then he would be absolutely still. He would never be able to tell us what he experienced in the final minutes, nor can we imagine it. If before you killed him you had forgotten to ask him where he put your comb, you would ask the corpse in vain, and you would probably have to buy a new comb. He would become invisible to you, just as invisible as he actually was the whole time he was alive. Because what did you really know about him while he was alive? Nothing."

Fiorello cast a quick look at his master, but Lorenzo did not look at him, just stared at the painter and at the painter's mouth, which continued speaking.

"I think it's *dark* in the closed eye, dark as in a camera obscura, and dark in the soul that can no longer see the clear light out there in the world when the body is dead and begins to decay, and the eye with it. A person who goes blind in life can't see anything either, so why should one see more when one is dead? Once, when somebody hit me with a heavy hammer because of a disagreement in a matter of the heart, I lay unconscious for three days, and I don't remember one iota from those three days; when I awakened I believed it was still the same day and wanted to keep on fighting, but people managed to convince me to stay in bed and take it easy for a while. From those three days there's not so much as a gleam of light in my memory, and perhaps the same thing happens when one is dead. But I may be wrong. I hope so. I just don't know how I could be mistaken in such a serious matter, which I've researched for many years; and that's precisely why this young man interested me when I saw him die in Castel Sant'Angelo. Because he died differently."

"But he died, all the same."

"He died, just like the others."

"Tell me more about this, master," said the young girl, and began to touch the painter.

"I think it's time to say farewell," said Lorenzo del Vetro understandingly. "Thank you for the evening, Master Enzio; thank you for the conversation, and thank you for allowing us to see your marvelous work of art here in your studio."

"You're welcome, Lord Lorenzo, the pleasure was all mine. And the honor." He bowed deeply, as the girl beside him began loosening her bodice.

"It was a relief to see it, after that ridiculous Madonna," said the doctor.

"Never laugh at what you don't understand," said the painter. He turned toward the girl, who sat with her legs crossed on the table beside the dead man. He looked at her preening there, then turned to the doctor again. "Who can really say that he understands anything at all? I can't, because I understand nothing. Especially not now."

The doctor snorted and left. But Lorenzo gave the painter a friendly smile.

"Sublime," he said, casting a final look at the master's pietà on the way out of the painter's dark studio.

Outside, the servants waited with torches and lamps to escort the remaining revelers home, but the courtesan Luciana no longer wanted to return to Palazzo Fili with Lorenzo del Vetro. She was tired, she said, and furthermore was offended by the painter (whether that was because of his rash comments about death or because he had chosen the younger girl will remain unsaid), so Lorenzo del Vetro let her go, but sent a couple of men to guard her. The other guests also went off in their separate directions, and Lorenzo del Vetro walked the short distance back to the palace with an exhausted Fiorello, while the stars in the east slowly began to pale for the sun that would arrive. Fiorello hummed for his master, but neither of them said anything.

FOUR

There is a church in Rome, San Luca al Mare it is called. It is a pitiful little church way down by the shore of the Tiber. In the spring, when the river rises, the water often washes in across the floor of the church and fills the crypt, and the air smells of corpses in the summer heat. It is dark and deserted inside, and everything is filthy; the church is no longer kept clean and orderly because nearly all the priests have left, the altars are neglected and no one walks in procession with the holy pictures of Our Lady anymore. And why should they? There are so many other interesting ways to spend one's time during these years. Because people serve another lady, a much greater and more present sovereign, rich and all-powerful, and that is Lady Angst. She is harsh toward the earth in these times. And that gives one other interests than the question of eternal salvation. One might go to hell, it's true, but why shouldn't one go to hell? There are so many good people in hell. Just look at who is already there, or is on a sure path toward it. We hardly need to mention the little girl who was starved to death by her mother here in the neighborhood recently; a little girl from the nobility she was, quite lovely and charming with slender hands and milk-white skin, and now she is in hell. One cannot do such things as this little girl did without being punished; it's a long story, but one does not do such things, no matter what. She was cruel toward her pets too; she hung them by the neck if they were naughty, and that happened often, or she gave them different kinds of poison. When she got married at the age of twelve, her husband soon met the same fate. And as if that were not bad enough, later her father got the same treatment. And so she was locked in her room, while her mother, the widowed countess, sat outside the door the whole time listening to her daughter's terrible screams, day in and day out, until they grew weaker and finally stopped completely. She was from a very good family, and now she is in hell. Her father probably finds himself in the same place, and they are surely better off there. And the widowed countess, the daughterless mother? She will follow, most certainly, but not because she proudly set in motion what was essentially a just punishment of her daughter, but because she already had on her conscience that at her instigation her first husband had his throat cut one night, because he had crossed her interests in an unpleasant inheritance matter and had killed her uncle and brother at the same time. On the whole, it was a very fine family, extremely interested in art besides, and soon, in a very few decades, they will all be reunited in hell.

Nor do we need to talk about a certain beautiful, peaceful cloister nearby, but its name is whispered from man to man. There the well-known revered abbess (also from a very good family, but people have forgotten her original name and call her just Mother Misericordia) not only serves as procuress—among monks and nuns, monks and neophytes, neophytes and novices, novices and novices, neophytes and bishops, cardinals and novices, abbesses and abbesses, and so on—no, she does not content herself with these simple diversions in the routine cloister life, but allows large bacchanalian revels to take place in the cloister church itself, before the altar, where anyone with money in his purse can come and expand his religious horizon, and where the price of a novice's or neophyte's virtue is a generous and welcome offering to the collection plate. Mother Misericordia's cloister thrives in these days, and where will she spend eternity?

We will refrain almost entirely from mentioning Christ's deputy in the warty person of His Holiness Pope Alexander, from the aristocratic Borgia family, who most certainly will go straight to hell with his closest family and co-workers. Not only has he bribed and bought his way to his office, not only does he dance and revel all through the nights while indulging alternately in every enticement and delicacy of the table and the flesh, not only has his celibacy given him seven children and more mistresses than warts, not only does he have a veritable guild of Corsican assassins running around Rome for him at night, not only does he let his son Cesare ravage and plunder and steal like a warlord throughout Italy and also let loose with private knife killings late at night—nobody goes free, neither bishops nor chamber servants, when Cesare has a party and wants to relax a little with his knife—no: this prince of the church, this proud Spanish lion, Christ's vice-regent, also has a daughter, she is already divorced, despite her very young age, but this year she gives birth to a son, and he is the son of his mother's father and the daughter's son at the same time, so to speak; later she will marry Alfonso, prince of Naples, whom her brother and lover, the aforementioned great charmer Cesare, will murder in a fit of jealousy. Later Cesare kills his and his sister's little brother, for the same reason. He wants to have all the sisterly pleasures to himself, and will share them with no one except his holy father, whom he reveres and loves above everything on Earth. The pope has reason to be proud of his children, and he does not hide that, but treats them royally and allows scores and scores of rich people to be murdered in order to keep himself and his family from suffering hunger or thirst. Or he just throws the rich people in prison and lets them buy their way out, again and again. That way they last longer. This pious man does not fear hell, that's certain. And when God's vice-regent finally dies—not, as people say, of a poison he had intended for a cardinal, but of a fever he brings on himself late one night when, worn out and perspiring, surfeited with delicacies of all kinds and drunk with wine, he is making his way home from a dancing party at his son's, and his body begins to swell up in the August heat to almost twice its size. His figure becomes completely unrecognizable, a huge purple balloon of gas and decay, people vomit at the sight; it is much too large for the coffin and in the end people have to pummel and bend the shapeless lump, warts and all, in order to get him under the lid, and throw in the tiara afterward. No one can bear to conduct a funeral mass.

Nor shall we waste time talking about the war, this war which continues to rage back and forth across the peninsula, which sweeps misfortune from city to city, from family to family, with no purpose and with no goal, year in and year out. The truth is that this war no longer has any goal, it is no war, it comes and goes, it is just a way of living, for both the tortured and the torturers, for both the lancers and their victims, for both the besieged and those who besiege. Take for example Caterina Sforza, the great duchess of Imola and Forli in Romagna, a tempest of a woman, a cunning politician and a terrible adversary; more man than most men. Her calculating cleverness and cool shrewdness save her, protect her from all kinds of dangers, ensure that she survives in this terrible time and does not succumb like all the others. One day Cesare Borgia—the aforementioned condottiere and thief, the pope's son, the most powerful warlord on Italian soil—stands outside her gates, stands there holding prisoner her two innocent young sons, the apples of her eye, and threatens to kill them if she does not open the gates (and in such matters Cesare does not engage in idle talk, as one will have understood). But she gives him the finger, she stands there and gives him the finger, says that he can just kill them, cut them up, go ahead; she can produce new sons. Will she go to hell? Probably, and she will have a long-range view of it. In short: hell is not what it used to be.

No, let us not talk about all this. Let us talk about the powerful lady, whom all serve. There is a small church on the shore of the Tiber, and it is dark and sad, but not completely so any longer, because candles are burning by one of the altars, and this is the candle of angst. And this morning, when the weary, naïve priest comes into the church to open it and light lamps, he is happy about the candles burning there. He is content, because people are coming to his little church again. They come streaming in from the bright clear day glimpsed through the doorway and kneel on his dirty floor. He walks about in there and he does not know it is angst that comes into his church. He believes it is poor people who shuffle in each morning, he believes they come out of faith, and that makes him happy. He does not know who comes. He goes confidently to the door this morning too.

Truly, he thinks; he yawns wearily and lazily scratches himself under his arms, where he is bothered by a miserable fungus growth. Truly, truly. He does not think much more, bows before the Madonna, lights the lamps, looks around. Truly, it could have been worse. It could have been better too. He yawns. Before, when he was young, the church was always full, and there were more than twenty holy paintings, which were all kept in good condition. But then bad times came, and everyone left and found better things to do. Why was he the only one who remained? Earlier he had cursed his own inertia, thought it was due to his naïveté and lack of initiative; he has shuffled around here, as if in a swamp, as if in a voluntary prison, he has thought—whether that was due to the flask or early apathy or simply because he is too stupid to do anything else. But now he doesn't think that any longer. He has completely forgotten it. On the contrary, now he thinks it is due to his perseverance, his loyalty, and his steadfastness in faith that he has been rewarded for his patience with the marvelous things that have happened, and that his flock is returning to its shepherd through a great miracle. People have even begun to go to confession again, almost as much as before. Even a cardinal has visited recently, just a little over a week ago, late at night, and he certainly was a lively and enthusiastic man. To tell the truth, the priest thinks of himself as almost a saint in his perseverance. Even his sins of varied and carnal nature—and they are many—seem fewer and appear in a different light than before. He is no longer disgusted by them, but feels forgiven and redeemed. They could have been worse, those sins, now that he thinks about it. All things considered, compared to certain other people he is a pure ascetic, a stylite. Truly, he thinks, and opens the door to the light.

Already a whole flock of old women are standing there, and other needy people, who cross themselves and disappear in toward the altar even before he has opened the door properly. He stands for a while squinting toward the light, then he slips into the church to prepare his morning mass. The sexton is late today. Up at the altar he lays out the things for the mass, opens the Bible to the correct passage, half turns at a sound by the door. In the lighted doorway, a figure stands pointing. For a moment the priest thinks it may be the sexton, so he shuffles into the nave again, toward the newcomer; but then he sees that it's not the sexton who has entered his church. It's not anyone else he knows either. It's a rather young boy, and he is accompanied by four guards and three other men in workmen's clothing who are carrying toolboxes. The boy is very elegantly dressed, he stands and points in the direction of the altar with the Madonna and says something to the men in his company. And when he looks at them he throws his head backward, as if he were looking down at them, even though he is shorter than they. The guards and the workmen obey the order and begin to walk up the aisle; the boy keeps standing there look-

ing down, holds his forehead. He sways a little. In the light from the doorway the priest can see that his face is white as chalk. He hurries toward the
newcomer, is nearly knocked down by the large men marching purposefully up the middle aisle, he turns halfway in confusion, does not know
what this means, is about to set out after them, but the boy farther back
sways again, and the priest rushes over to him, asks uneasily: "Is everything
all right, young man?"

"Thank you, Father," says the stranger coolly. "I'm just tired." He
stands rubbing his eyes for a while, then he pulls himself together and fixes
his gaze on the priest. At that moment it seems to the priest that he recognizes the stranger.

"But—isn't it—haven't I seen you before, young man . . . recently?"

"Perhaps," says the boy.

"What can I do for you?" asks the priest, rather uneasily, because now
he hears pounding behind him, and old women cackling.

"Nothing, for that matter," says the boy, and begins to walk down the
aisle, limping slightly. "Do you have any lamps, Father? I mean any proper
oil lamps or torches?"

"Have you hurt yourself?" asks the priest.

"Lamps," says the boy stubbornly. "We need work lamps over here."

"Lamps. Yes, lamps. Yes, of course I have lamps."

The boy stops, leans his head back, looks at him again.

"Then get them." And this priest is no more a saint than that the boy's
tone fills him with angst, a deathly angst; *now* he knows that it is fear that
has entered his little church, with a sword at its side, and he falls at its feet
at once, asks no questions, neither for the sake of his altar nor his faith, although his head buzzes with them like a beehive, and fearfully rushes away
for lamps. When he returns with them, the workers are already very busy
with the miraculous Madonna's altar, he hears sawing and the unpleasant
sound of wood being splintered by crowbars; the old women are cackling
in wild protest, and now more people have come from outside, many more
stream in each minute, and they stand and watch, as they murmur among
themselves, frightened and upset, they point and gesticulate, but the
guards hold them back authoritatively, standing with lowered lances and
feet wide apart, at a safe distance from the altar. They will scarcely let the
priest go past them, but the boy waves him forward. He holds out the

lamps, the boy looks at him; the workmen light them, set them up. The boy looks away, looks down, looks at the altar with an expression of indescribable boredom, leans back heavily against a bench, rubs his eyes. Finally the priest says carefully: "On what grounds—ahem—has our little church the honor—of—"

The boy straightens up, fixes his eyes on him again, sighs.

"Well," he says, and begins to rattle off: "Since it has pleased His Lordship, my lord and master, Lorenzo del Vetro, to live in this hospitable quarter, it is His Lordship's duty and joy to serve God with gratitude for his new home; therefore it has pleased His Lordship to remember his family's old altar in this little church, which regretfully has long stood neglected, with a new and marvelous altar painting, to replace the old one, which is in sad condition."

He stops a moment, rubs his eyes again, continues: "His Lordship has accordingly obtained His Eminence's permission to take down the old worn-out painting above his family altar, so that in the fullness of time it can be replaced with a new painting, which is commissioned from one of the foremost artists at His Holiness's court, the painter Enzio da Castelnuovo. Here are the papers, if you wish to see, Father. Everything is in the most excellent order. Is there anything else you are wondering about?"

"But—but—"

"Yes?"

But the priest could not speak. Before his eyes the workmen took down the miraculous painting from the altar and wrapped it in a sheet, and all that was left was a shining square of freshly scrubbed wood. If he turned around, he looked into the eyes of the congregation. They too were completely speechless now. Those eyes, thought the priest. He swallowed.

"Oh yes," said the boy, fumbling with his belt, "Lord Lorenzo has of course the pleasure of donating to you—I mean to your . . . humble little church—a small offering, which His Lordship hopes you will not reject, as an apology for the inconvenience." He drew out a well-filled money pouch and put it in the other man's hand. It weighed heavily against the priest's palm.

"If you're wise," whispered the boy with a slight smile, "you will take it and not say a word."

"Yes," said the priest docilely.

"Careful!" hissed the boy to the workmen. "The idea isn't to destroy it. You clowns."

"But—" began the priest once more, for he had looked again into the faces of the people who had gathered in the nave and saw that the Madonna was taken down.

"Yes?" The boy looked at him. And some of the despair in the priest's eyes must have gotten through to him, because he continued: "It's all right if you scream and carry on a little. Go ahead, do it, Father. Your congregation—or whatever you call them—" he glanced toward the gray figures in the church, "surely expect that of you. Go ahead. The guards won't do anything to you, unless I tell them to."

But the little priest became filled with a strange and inexplicable, defiant happiness; he had never felt that way before, it was like a golden light in him for a moment, and he said: "No, young man. Go in peace."

The boy looked at him in amazement with dark eyes that were a little dulled. His face could have been handsome, thought the priest, but something had settled in it, an expression, around the mouth, around the eyes. "Just go," he said quietly. "It's not your fault."

The boy looked down.

And they went away, out through the church, and no one stopped them; as the sword-clanking guards made a path through the crowd, the people just sighed softly, like wind whispering in the treetops.

FIVE

The house was in turmoil when Fiorello returned with the altar painting that morning. The servants scurried here and there, and high spirits prevailed throughout the palace, from cellar to loft, as before an important visit or before a trip; the mood struck Fiorello like music in the air the moment he led his little procession into the entry hall. Everything was different in the house this morning. For several days there had been rumors among the servants that the master of the house had been cured of the sickness that had plagued them all like a curse, and no one really knew why or how it had happened. And now people knew: it was true; the master—and they—were rid of their scourge. But the rumors about the circumstances surrounding Lord Lorenzo's cure continued to circulate, and through cracks in doors and from behind pillars curious eyes stared at Fiorello as he led his secretive procession through the hall, up the stairs, from room to room. Lord Lorenzo sat once more in the banquet hall, surrounded by a select circle of friends, Doctor Bevilaqua, the learned Verduccio, and the painter da Castelnuovo; his private secretary and the arithmetician Rizzoli were there as well. They sat in animated conversation, but rose expectantly as soon as Fiorello entered the room.

"There she is, finally!" exclaimed Lord Lorenzo, and strode quickly to meet the procession. "There she is. Fiorello, I want to have the painting on the easel over here." Fiorello gave a sign, and the workmen carried the panel over to the easel and put it down carefully. Fiorello drew the cloth aside. For a long time Lord Lorenzo stood gazing at the Madonna with the fruit.

"It's strange," he said at last. "I don't think it's a bit better than ten days ago."

"No, Your Lordship," mumbled Fiorello.

"Nevertheless," said the learned Verduccio, "nevertheless, it has performed a miracle."

"A miracle?" said the doctor irritably. "I'm not sure . . . At any rate, I simply raise the question. You may have a relapse, Lord Lorenzo. Don't rejoice too soon."

"Don't pour wormwood into our friend's cup of joy," said Verduccio.

"You're just afraid of losing a good customer," the painter commented frankly. The doctor gave him a furious look and was about to speak, but Lord Lorenzo said, without looking at them: "That's correct. He is afraid of losing a customer. But Doctor, you *have* already lost me as a customer, at least in this unpleasant matter. And as long as I don't have a relapse, I'm well. Even if it's only for one more day. Look at me. Didn't you examine my skin yourself this morning?"

"Yes, I did," admitted the doctor.

"And was it without scars, without sores, and without blemish?"

"It was, Your Lordship."

"Wasn't it like a child's skin?"

"Yes," said the doctor. "Perhaps my cure—"

"Fiorello!" interrupted Lord Lorenzo. "Fiorello, has the esteemed Doctor Bevilaqua's cure helped until now?"

"No, Your Lordship," said Fiorello wearily.

"Has it removed even the least scab or boil?"

"Not until now. Although it's had a certain soothing effect."

"Didn't we experiment by stopping baths, herbs, and liniments several days ago, to see if the improvement lasted?"

"Yes, Your Lordship, that's correct."

"And what was the result?"

"The scabs and sores continued to disappear very rapidly, Your Lordship, independent of baths and remedies. Two days ago my master's skin didn't have so much as a flaking speck."

"Gentlemen," said Lorenzo del Vetro, "my faithful servant Fiorello has followed my illness through all the years, he knows that nothing has helped. Until now." The doctor looked down, but said nothing. "And you, Doctor, should not take this so hard, but rejoice over my newly regained health and vitality."

"I do, Lord Lorenzo, I sincerely rejoice," said the doctor, albeit a bit forced.

"You'll see, Doctor, you'll still be invited to my table in the future," said Lorenzo del Vetro reassuringly. "But I didn't call you here simply to confirm what I can find out on my own; I have other reasons for inviting you here today. One always has use for a doctor, and I do too, even if I'm now rid of my detestable illness."

"God be praised," said the private secretary.

"For Doctor Bevilaqua is right in a sense," Lorenzo del Vetro went on. "The question, my friends, is simply: How?"

"One of God's wonders," said the painter.

"An inexplicable miracle," said Verduccio.

"Your prayers have been heard," said the private secretary.

"That's true," said Lord Lorenzo. "It's a divine miracle. Or isn't it, after all? Because . . . my *prayers* haven't been answered, but on the other hand—tell me, are you feeling all right, Fiorello?"

Fiorello was swaying a little on his feet, and had to support himself against the easel.

"Thank you, Lord Lorenzo, I'm feeling fine."

"You're pale."

"Just a little tired."

"He didn't take it too badly—the priest?"

"No," said Fiorello. "He took it well."

"As I said," said Lorenzo del Vetro, "a miracle. But *what* in this painting created the miracle, if there *is* a miracle? Why *this* painting? A painting that cures old women, on the same level as plantain and horsetail? Look at it. Well, *look* at it."

The painter shook his head.

"I'm inclined to stick to my first impression of it, Lord Lorenzo," he said. "It's even worse in daylight."

"This modest painting," said Lorenzo del Vetro, "which was in my possession without my knowing it, has transformed everything. Without my even asking, it has suddenly healed me of my suffering, which I had feared I would have to endure for the rest of my life. I'm like a new person. I can return to my native city, when that day finally comes, strong and healthy and as eager to work as a young man, praise God."

He paused after this proclamation. "So I have called you here, my esteemed, learned friends. Why? We'll try to discover that."

"Shouldn't you have called the cardinal too?" asked the painter sarcastically. "Isn't this question really more in his field?"

"Aside from the fact that His Eminence is indisposed due to a suspicious stomach affair, and aside from the fact that I think his theological knowledge has . . . paled somewhat with the years, this is not a matter of faith," said Lorenzo del Vetro. "It's absolutely not a matter of faith."

"Well then?"

"I have neither more nor less faith than before. I'm an equally good or poor Christian as before. I sin neither more nor less, and I have the same opinion of the painting as before. I have no thought of falling on my knees and praying to it. I have *not* prayed to it at all. It's contrary to all reason that I should have been healed by it."

"Lord Lorenzo, to speak frankly," the learned Verduccio ventured to object: "Where reason ends, faith begins. Your healing is itself a sign that from now on—well—it's a sign that you no longer should—but that you—"

"What is this man trying to say?"

"He means that you should acknowledge this miracle by letting it become a turning point in your life, that from now on you ought to thank God by living more according to His laws."

"Thank you, Master Enzio, for your enlightening explanation. But should I do that? My friends, I've lain awake at night. I've searched my soul. Tell me, Fiorello, aren't you feeling well?"

"Thank you, Lord Lorenzo, I'm just fine."

"Well. I've promised myself: I will give large gifts of thanks to the church; that's clear. But I won't be content with that, because it seems superficial and scarcely enlightening. My *faith*, the faith I needed to have, will not be strengthened by such a gesture, nor will it be strengthened if I blindly and irrationally accept the miracle as a miracle, without a reason and without an explanation. My faith would then have no *direction*, Master Enzio—when we visited the church that night, I asked you whether the painter, whoever he may have been, must have had a model for this painting."

"I'm sure he did."

"This painting was created under given circumstances, like all other paintings," said Lorenzo del Vetro. "With pigments and brushes. In an atelier. Why then has *this* particular painting performed this miracle? Who was the model for it? Who was the painter? What were the circumstances? Since *I* have done nothing except go and look at it, in complete disbelief and with no appreciation of it, my healing can't have had anything to do with my person and my actions. There are also many altar paintings that people pray to—pray in ardent belief—which have *no* special healing effect or miraculous power. To say nothing of relics.

"During my years of illness, I too have fallen to my knees at times and prayed earnestly to God for healing, to no avail. Then late one night I go to get my hiccups cured, purely as a joke, and what happens? No, the truth of this matter must lie in *the painting itself*. And since this painting was done at the request of my blessed father, by a painter of flesh and blood, and didn't descend from heaven, I've called you together to figure this out: Who painted it? What were the circumstances around its creation? Did a miracle perhaps occur when it was created? Was the painter a holy man?"

No one said anything.

"Only *then*, when all this is known, only *then* will I be ready to make the penitential journey. Only then will I know where my journey should go. In any case, I am grateful to God."

After a few moments the painter da Castelnuovo said: "It will be almost impossible to find out these things, Lord Lorenzo. The painting is certainly forty years old."

"Nothing is impossible, my father always said. The impossible just costs extra. Gentlemen, I will not tie my money pouch before this is clarified. Somewhere, here in the palace's archives or in the church, there must be a record of who painted the picture, and somewhere in Italy there must still be someone who can inform me about the circumstances surrounding its creation. You will all be paid royally, and the one who finds the answer will be rewarded accordingly."

They looked at each other around the table, raised their eyebrows imperceptibly, but no one said anything. Fiorello, who stood in a cloud of pain and fever, had understood only bits of the conversation. The room around him seemed to have become very large, and the voices sounded as if they were whispering; he could scarcely hear what they said. On the other hand, he heard the reverberation between the walls much louder than usual. He felt both warm and cold simultaneously, and his whole body ached, but especially in the one leg and foot. It was unendurable to either stand or walk. The pain had been bad for several days, this morning he had thought he felt a little better, but already on the way to the church he had noticed that it was only the fever that kept him upright. And now he did not even have the strength to excuse himself, but simply stood outside himself. Everything was white. It was completely white everywhere, it was very strange, and he thought quite a bit about this white. So when the maid came rushing in, he did not really hear what she said, but stood engrossed in his own thoughts.

". . . people outside?" said Lorenzo del Vetro.

"Yes, Your Lordship. A large crowd. Pippo Golaccio has asked them to go away, but they're standing outside the gate and say they want to see a Madonna, whatever they mean by that." She glanced shyly at the painting on the easel.

"She's really quite charming, isn't she?" commented Enzio da Castel-nuovo.

"Now, now," said Lorenzo del Vetro. "She belongs to *my* household. For that matter, how did things go with your little corpse-ravisher that night? Isn't she more suited for a man with your special interests, Master Enzio?"

"She's extremely fine, thank you."

"I'm very glad to hear that. Listen, whatever your name is—"

"Simonetta."

"—tell Pippo that as far as I'm concerned they can stand there the whole day."

"Yes, Your Lordship."

At that moment Fiorello collapsed by the easel. It seemed to him that everything suddenly became totally empty around him and in him, and that he swayed for a moment. Then he lay on the floor, and the floor was warm and rocking like a soothing bath. He did not hear Simonetta complain about his foot and about a sore that had not been cleaned, and he did not hear the doctor's commanding words, but he just barely noticed Lorenzo del Vetro's voice protest: "Fiorello, Fiorellino." And then everything became a deep darkness before they carried him away.

SIX

"Fiorello."

A name. For a long time the darkness around him was red and sore.

"Fiorello."

He lay like that for several days and nights, while someone said his name at regular intervals. It was not a voice he recognized, and still he liked to listen to it, because it reminded him of something. Except the name bothered him somewhat, as the fever attacks came and went. There was something wrong with the name. The dreams were vague and unpleasant, and usually concerned all he had to do. He had to do thousands of errands for his master in the course of a feverish night; he ran and ran, ran through light and darkness, just as a butterfly in shimmering hot sunshine never settles, flies farther, gleaming gold, black as coal. And the whole time he forgot what he was supposed to do, and it was exhausting. He was not really clear about what he saw when he opened his eyes now and then, but he thought he saw Doctor Bevilaqua standing there looking worried once or twice, and also the woman who belonged to the voice. She gave him something to drink, and cooled the infected foot with compresses; his foot was so scalding hot that the compresses dried on his skin almost as quickly as she could apply them.

One night it was especially bad, then she repeated his name constantly, almost as if to give him something to cling to. And it seemed to Fiorello that there was a priest by the bed. But he survived the night. The next morning he was a little better, the fever had gone down somewhat, and he noticed that he was not lying in his own bed, but in a servant's chamber up under the eaves. The window and shutters were open. There was only the bed, a cupboard, and a table in the small room. She sat by the table, asleep, fully clothed, her hair flowing across the tabletop. Outside the window swallows flew back and forth from a nest under the eaves, their shrieks loud and piercing in the morning air. For a while he lay and listened to their voices.

She lifted her head from the table and turned her face toward him.

"Good morning, Simonetta," he said politely.

She rose quickly, brought water to him, supported him while he drank.

"I should—" he began. "Lord Lorenzo is waiting—"

"Later," she said, and stroked his hair. "You almost died last night, Fiorello."

"Oh," he said, drank a little more, and fell asleep.

He lay in bed for more than two weeks after that, while the fever slowly subsided. It had been a serious infection, and the doctor had said that the whole leg should be amputated, but that things had gone so far that Fiorello would not survive the operation anyway, so they had not done it. Simonetta had kept him alive, out of pure obstinacy.

"If you had let me wash your foot the morning you were bleeding, as I asked to, none of this would have happened."

"No," he said. "I didn't have time."

"Uff," she said, "time. Do you think that's something one *has*? It's something one receives."

"No," he replied pensively, "I think it's actually something one loses."

"Fiorello," she said reproachfully, "you're stupid, so why do I like you so much? It annoys me."

"Don't leave," he said.

"I won't," she said.

Lorenzo del Vetro did not come to visit him during the time he lay sick. That both surprised him and did not surprise him. But the girl Simonetta sat there, and she repeated his name. He thought a great deal about the matter of the name, and about time, about whether one received it or lost it. He did not talk much with her otherwise, but she sat there and said his name, and it was both reassuring and a little strange.

"Fiorello."

Although his name was not actually Fiorello; he had another name, a secret name, which only he knew, so secret that he had almost forgotten it. Now, when he was sick, he remembered it, and recalled how he had lost it. Usually, when he was healthy and serving his master, only now and then would he awaken at night with burning cheeks because a voice had said his secret name in a dream, just barely whispered it, softly and tenderly, a voice from the *earlier* time—and then he got up and took large gulps from the brandy jug by the edge of the bed, immediately, with no hesitation, did not dare to keep lying down but stood up and drank, suddenly and deeply, until he grew dizzy and unsteady on his feet. Then he would usually flounder back into bed and sleep soundly, anesthetized, because he had taught himself to never remember *that* voice, that soft woman's voice, from the earlier time, and not *that* name, because it was dangerous, dangerous to remember it, he could lose his self-control and not be in any condition to perform his tasks satisfactorily. That name. Never think about that name.

He had learned this early, yes, actually he had begun learning to erase everything from the earlier time, his old name as well as his true face, his very first day in the service of the del Vetro family; that terrible, clear winter day when she, the other woman, had taken him away from home, away from his father's empty workshop and closed store, away from the childhood rooms with all the familiar objects, his mother's spinning wheel, his father's writing desk, his toys, the laurel wreath that his father had received as a token of respect from the craftsmen's guild—away from everything that had been so alive, and that now was silent and dry, and where the only one left who knew the past of all these things was he himself, Marco.

Marco. Do not remember that name. The name of the only one left who remembered what all these things had been, to whom they had belonged, the only one who remembered all those who had disappeared. Remembered his big brother Pietro on the rocking horse that their father had made, the nice red rocking horse, a big brother who helped him up and watched to make sure he did not fall off even in the wildest gallop, remembered his mother with her handwork, his father who could play the lute so beautifully and carefully, even with his large, thick carpenter hands, remembered—but they were all gone, and now he too was about to disappear into the cold winter day, to be remembered no more, and other children already rode happily on the rocking horse, and a stranger's fingers played new melodies on the old instrument. Other people lived here now, another family, although the last name was the same; and now everything was theirs. That's how it was. The last morning just before he had to leave, he was able to sneak away for a brief moment, to go into the rooms that had been his home; for a few seconds he stood there motionless, as if frozen, as if time stopped for a moment, and remembered everything—a second, a century, it amounted to the same thing. Then she takes him from the room with commotion and scolding, and he has become a century older. The day is as clear and mean as a wolf's gaze. The walls of Florence are like a prison in the distance, ever closer. The moment the wagon enters the city gates, through which he has ridden so many times with the expectation and enjoyment of a visit to the city—the lively streets and the busy people, he feels as if he is going to vomit; now it's as if he is sitting in the executioner's wagon, all life and all colors cut into him, like splinters of glass in the cold air.

And then came the moment when they stood in the del Vetro residence, Palazzo Vetro, his stepmother and he, in the silver hall, and the old duke himself, Luigi del Vetro in his own high personage, looked him over to decide if he was acceptable to serve in such a noble house. It had begun already then, the transformation and eradication, already while the old master critically allowed him to bow and show veneration, questioned him about his schooling and knowledge of Latin, let him recite a couple of verses, read aloud from a book, sing a madrigal—already then Marco had begun to forget.

He forgot his father and mother. So what could be more appropriate than that he also got a new name?

"Marco," old Luigi del Vetro said aloud, tasted the name. "We already have a boy here named Marco. Yes. We do. It would only cause misunderstandings and confusion if we were to have two. Two with the same name, I mean," he added reassuringly, when he saw the woman give an anxious start, uneasy at the thought that perhaps she would have to take the boy home with her again.

"His name is whatever may please Your Grace." She curtsied. The boy hastened to bow.

Luigi del Vetro examined him with small, round banker's eyes. His gaze was black, and hard as agate. He smiled approvingly, stiffly. His mouth—what was it about his mouth?—he didn't move the upper lip, neither when he smiled nor when he spoke, and this made one feel that everything he said was only half meant, that even the smile was only half the truth. This, thought Marco, this is how one gets rich, everything one does is only half.

"*Fiorello*," said Luigi del Vetro, and brightened, "that's an excellent name for someone who has just arrived in the city of flowers. Cheerful and charming. He's still so young, and has the bloom of life ahead of him. And my son Lorenzo, whom he will serve, needs something light and encouraging, a little happiness around him, because he finds the burdens heavy and often grows sad thinking of the responsibility that soon will fall to him, though may it please God to let me see the world and serve our city for some time yet. Don't forget that you're here to give joy and to please your master, will you, Fiorello? Yes, Fiorello is excellent," said Luigi del Vetro, visibly satisfied with his act of christening.

"Yes, Your Grace," said the woman.

"Yes, Your Grace," said Fiorello.

I no longer am named—I am named—I am someone else now, from now on and for always.

And Fiorello forgot his own name, and forgot his own mother.

All this he thought about while he lay ill. He did not think about the altar painting he had delivered, nor about Lorenzo del Vetro's promise not to rest until he had clarified the circumstances around the miraculous painting; furthermore, little by little he stopped thinking about his daily duties and concerns; they slid off him like a cloak, the way the fever slid off him and left an aching weariness as a reminder. But he thought about his mother, whom he had forgotten when he came to Palazzo Vetro. As the days went by, he thought more and more about everything he had forgotten back then.

He forgot her voice, he forgot the small upturned corners of her mouth, and her hands with the deep, nicely curved life line. He forgot the death that had taken her, forgot the last day, her face in the bed when she had looked dimly and wearily at him and his brother, while the attacks of chills came and went. He was still small, only seven years old, and felt cold, even though the room was warm. His big brother put an arm around his shoulders, they went over to her. "I'm dreaming about a big bird," she said, trying to be cheerful. "It's beautiful to look at, but it's so big." Then her mind cleared, she focused her eyes on them. First she held their hands for a while, and her hand was burning hot, she moved her fingers wearily, looked at them, a long time. Then she tore herself loose, could not bear to touch them. She pulled her hands back, tears shone in her eyes, she said their names. For the first time Marco saw that his mother was a person, a young woman, young and beautiful. Then she turned her face away. And the fever came and drew her away.

That way, by forgetting, Fiorello entered into service, as it was called, in the del Vetro household, even though he knew very well that it was not any usual service, but a life, his life, in payment for the economic services the del Vetro house had bestowed in a time of need, when his father and brother were taken away by the condottiere's advancing troops. And the message came that well-known and respected Master Vittorio, whose furniture workshop was known throughout Tuscany for its unique and wonderful work, and his oldest son, would not be set free except by a sky-high ransom, so high that no artisan's family could meet the demand, no matter how wealthy they were. So to whom should one go other than to the workshop's main customer, the del Vetro family, to beg for a large loan with as favorable conditions as possible? Oh, his stepmother had promised everything, if only she could borrow the money, if only she could get her husband back—she forgot to mention the eldest stepson in her haste—the del Vetros could order from the most distinguished furniture maker at cost, no, below cost, for years to come. She came home to the village with a saintly expression, she had gotten the loan, practically speaking she had already saved her husband and a son who wasn't hers; she glowed in the luster of her deed, and let no one doubt whom Master Vittorio could thank for his speedy forthcoming rescue from his wretched imprisonment. Oh, he had done well to marry her in this terrible time of war. But despite the ransom, no life was saved after all. Only the debt remained, and Marco was to be the payment, payment for two dead people. Marco had often wondered what had happened to the ransom money, when his father and brother were found strangled in a ditch only a few days after the money had been paid to the fellows the condottiere had sent to enforce their demand. She, the other woman, had given them the pouch with the costly acquired florins, the entire sum. She had done that. But then, alas, they died anyway, such things happened in this terrible, lawless time. Two bloodless deaths, despite the high ransom; the funeral was beautiful, and the little town had mourned its talented and respected Master Vittorio, carried his portrait through the streets in effigy and honored him as a hero—fallen for the state, fallen for the guild, fallen for freedom. But now the enormous private loan had to be repaid, and how could a poor poverty-stricken widow manage that, now that her lord and husband was dead, and his knives and chisels lay abandoned on the carpenter's bench, and the shavings on the floor had already lost their fresh yellow color and turned as gray as the husband's corpse? How else than by letting her only remaining live stepson, Vittorio's youngest, pay; it was no more than right and reasonable, because who was closer than the boy? It was *his* father and brother the money had gone to, after all—so Marco should pay by going into service, young as he was, in the house that had loaned them the sum; she had enough with her two children from a former marriage whom she had brought with her into her new home. *They* surely could not be required to pay for a father and a brother they were not related to, and besides she was very busy instructing and discussing with the oldest friend in the workshop how to best conduct the business in the future, now that Vittorio was gone. These instructions and deliberations were complicated, and could take the whole night. In short, Marco should pay with a life for a life, or perhaps more correctly: a death for a death. Because Marco died that day, never to return. Although in the beginning Fiorello still remembered the boy he had been, the boy who ran about in the village streets, swam in the river with his brother and the other children, helped his father in the workshop, simply clad, with tousled hair, bare feet, and callused hands. Long after his hair was combed and curled, his hands white and smooth, and his attire elegant and gold and blue, the memory of the other boy remained with him, and the calluses were like small brown pictures in his hands. And he still remembered the songs they had sung, and the wood that had taken beautiful forms beneath his father's knife.

And his own name. Yes, he still had a memory of the name, just inside his ear, like an echo, like a whisper, a tender voice from long ago. For a long time there seemed to be opposition in the very sound when his master, Lorenzo del Vetro, called him by the new name.

"Fiorello. So you're Fiorello."

He met his new master for the first time in Lorenzo del Vetro's workroom. Young del Vetro was completely unlike his father, not only because he was still quite young, but because their facial expressions were different; the old man's face was broad and chiseled, his mouth strong-willed—thin and miserly, yet full of vitality. Young Lorenzo had a narrow, somewhat oblong face, with a weak mouth, even though the lips were as thin as his father's. He had a downcast expression marked by a kind of satiety, and still he gave the impression of being unsatisfied. His eyes were clear and blue. He sat surrounded by many unusual and expensive objects; Fiorello had the impression of being in the study of a scholar, a magus, or a humanist, rather than in a banker's office. There were books in Greek and Latin, there were world maps, hourglasses, and astrolabes, on the walls hung paintings by the new masters with obscure mythological motifs; on the shelves, quicksilver and sulfur lay inert in retorts, on the table lay a skull. Only a few solitary open account books suggested Lorenzo del Vetro's real work. The furniture and panels in the room were of the finest craftsmanship, in oak, cherry, and pearwood, with inlaid ornamentation, borders, and vinelike patterns. On one lengthwise panel the master carpenter had created a masterpiece, a picture made of many different types of wood, in carefully chosen colors, shapes, and shadings, fashioned so skillfully and with a perspective so true to nature that you had the impression you were looking through a half-open window out into a garden where the setting sun tinted everything a reddish gold. Marco had once known this panel well, seen it every day, admired its slow creation throughout a whole year; now Fiorello forgot it, simply looked at it as if he saw it for the first time.

He stood with bowed head while Lorenzo del Vetro rose, walked over to him, examined him thoroughly. He did not know what he could expect, half hoped the young master would not be pleased with him and send him away, away from here, anywhere at all, out to beg on the street, if only he escaped from Palazzo Vetro. Three hours had passed since she brought him here. The old duke had wished him well, and his stepmother had admonished him to be obedient and faithful, and then vanished as lightly as a

fleeting glance. Then he was turned over to the palace's butler, who obse-
quiously examined him from head to toe before bringing him to meet
young Lord Lorenzo. Three hours. It could just as well have been three
months in this palace, which lay brooding like a huge black creature in the
middle of the city, with walls of heavy ashlar blocks and rigid rows of
square windows. Works of art and other treasures graced the great halls,
unmoving, unchanging; looking at them it occurred to him that *time* was
different in here. He did not know where he was or who he was. He sat
outside the door to Lorenzo del Vetro's room for an eternity waiting to be
allowed to enter. Near the door hung a large, strange picture of a happy
feast, out in a forest; he didn't really understand what it portrayed, but a
figure with billy-goat horns was playing the flute, and around him danced
small creatures who resembled children his own age, except they had
billy-goat horns. A wild dance. They laughed a cold, eternal laughter, and
seemed to be having a terribly good time. This painting was perhaps one of
the most beautiful things he had seen in his life, even more beautiful than
his father's work, it was like looking into a shining dreamworld, but still it
put him in a sad mood. He sat looking at it for three months or three seconds. Now he stood before his new master.

"Can you read?" asked Lorenzo del Vetro.

"Yes," swallowed Fiorello. "I can read."

"Then you can read aloud for me. Read . . . this." He handed him an
open book. Fiorello looked down at the book without understanding what
it was about.

"They are poems," said Lorenzo del Vetro kindly. "They should be
read as if they were music."

"I see," said Fiorello. Without understanding any better, he began to
rattle off the words on the page, as fast as he could.

"Stop," said Lorenzo del Vetro. "You don't have to read so fast. Sit
down. Read slowly. Read as if for yourself."

"Yes, Lord Lorenzo," Fiorello said obediently, sat down on a stool, and
began to read again. Lorenzo del Vetro listened to him for a while, then he
took the book away from him.

"I can't understand a word that you're reading," he said, irritated. "You
sound like twittering birds."

"I'm sorry, Your Lordship," said Fiorello, and suddenly got a lump in his throat, because Lorenzo del Vetro had been kind toward him for a little while.

"You need to practice," said Lorenzo del Vetro. "Because I read a great deal, and want to have words around me constantly, but don't want to strain my eyes. What else can you do?"

"I—I don't know."

"Are you good in bed?"

"In bed?"

"Well, it doesn't really matter, that's not my taste. Can you sing?"

"Yes. Yes, Lord Lorenzo."

"Sing, then."

Fiorello sang, the first thing that occurred to him, a little craftsmen's song that Marco had learned from his mother when he was small. Lorenzo del Vetro looked at him with interest, smiled when he came to the refrain, hummed along.

We bring our gifts while the day counts the hours
A house is built in heaven when life is past.

"Very lovely. Charming. You should read the same way too." Fiorello blushed. "You must sing that for me often. Can you play the lute?"

"Yes. A little."

"Good. Practice. Can you fence? Use a knife?"

"No, Your Lordship, I'm too young to have learned that." He looked down. It was still the Marco in him who replied. This was going badly.

"You'll learn, certainly. What do you think about Savonarola?" This was the first time Marco heard the word, he did not know what it meant, but Lorenzo del Vetro's voice darkened when he said it, and now it was Fiorello who answered, amazed at his own words: "It's a terrible thing, Your Lordship. Such things shouldn't be allowed." Lorenzo laughed.

"Oh, you don't think so?"

"Such a thing is a deadly sin, Your Lordship." Lorenzo laughed again.

"Wonderful," he said, "you're amusing." Fiorello did not understand why, but understood that it was a matter of keeping his master in a good humor, so he followed up his luck by letting Fiorello fabricate further stories.

"All sabonarola should be pulled up by the roots and thrown on the manure pile. It's a weed," he asserted. Lorenzo guffawed.

"Better and better."

"Inedible, insensible, intolerable for the farmers. Tough as quack grass, spreads like dandelions."

"Yes!"

"And intolerable for fishermen. The poor fishermen, when they get an abonarolas in their net."

"Couldn't have said it better myself."

"Or the priests, when bandasarola get into their Bibles, it's worse than termites."

"That's absolutely true."

"But really the worst is when you get . . . this . . . sanosenzalenza in your head. It sits like a scorpion in your brain." Lorenzo held his stomach with laughter. "It's nothing to laugh about, Your Lordship," said the boy, amazed at this new Fiorello's progress: "You *never* get rid of it; it's a *very* serious illness."

"You're right, Fiorello. More right than you can imagine. You're entertaining. Someday you must tell my father about sabonarola, it will do his arthritis good. Tell me more truths."

"I can't, Your Lordship," said Fiorello, who could think of nothing more to say. He grimaced regretfully.

"Oh?"

"I've got sabandarola in my throat."

"Priceless!" exclaimed Lorenzo del Vetro. "You're clever. Where do you get that?"

"My mother laughed when I was born, esteemed sir," said Fiorello, which was true.

"Not mine," said Lorenzo del Vetro darkly. "She cursed the day and the hour."

"So you're not happy, Lord Lorenzo?" asked Fiorello, without thinking, because he thought it was strange not to be happy when one had everything.

Lorenzo del Vetro looked at him in surprise. He did not say anything, just scrutinized him intently.

"Something tells me that we'll get along well together, Fiorello," he said at last. "Leave me now, and come back at dinnertime tomorrow; then you can both sing and tell me more about this sad malady—Savona—"

"—raldo, Your Lordship. Yes, Your Lordship. Thank you, Your Lordship."

"I really hope you serve table better than you read."

"I don't know, Your Lordship."

"You don't know, Fiorello?"

"No," said Fiorello. "Fiorello doesn't yet know what he can do, because Fiorello is completely new in the world."

"Oh?"

"Maybe he could make his master laugh, and maybe not, that's not easy to say, because Fiorello has never made anyone laugh before, Your Lordship. Everything is new to him. So maybe he can read too, and, who knows, fence like a swordfish."

"Excellent, Fiorello." He laughed again. "Now be gone."

He bowed himself out the door. That was how Marco began to invent this new Fiorello, and he decided to make him as different as he could, as an amusing, laughing figure from a merry satyr picture, and he was quite satisfied with his invention. Then he stood outside again; the butler was waiting for him, and had obviously listened at the door. He pulled the boy's ear.

"Well," he said, "you thought you were fine fellow just now. Well. Well, well. Not *too* fine, thank you." He pulled him along, down into a noisy, smoke-filled kitchen which was swarming with servants, some in elegant uniforms, others dressed for heavy work, and people laughed and shouted to him when the butler drew him through the kitchen and farther down into the bowels of the palace, through halls and down stairways to what would be his room. "Pay careful attention to where we're going," growled the butler, "because no one can help you if you don't find your way here late at night; we're too many in the house and have too much to do for everyone to know where each person lives, and fellows like you come and go all the time." In a tiny, damp cellar room with a small grated window under the whitewashed ceiling stood two single beds covered with straw; one seemed occupied, because clothes and objects were strewn around it, the other was empty and was covered with fresh straw.

"So," said the butler. "You're lucky, because you get your own bed.

You'll live here with the other boy—Marco. Marco has already been here a couple of years, and will help you understand your duties better." Fiorello nodded, put his bundle on the empty bed, swallowed. "Now, now," said the butler, "don't be so sad. You're lucky, and are going to serve upstairs with the fine folk, and none of them tolerate crybabies, especially not Lord Lorenzo. Take care that you don't end up as a boy in the poultry yard, such things have happened before." Fiorello was wearing his best clothes, but the butler looked at him disapprovingly and said: "We must get rid of those rags, and do it immediately. We must go to the tailor this very day, so you have something that will do for the time being, until the masters decide what will be suitable for you; and we must get that mop of yours clipped before the sun goes down. You look like a haystack. My name is Golaccio, Pippo Golaccio, and I'm the butler here."

"Yes, Signor Golaccio," mumbled Fiorello.

"To tell the truth, you don't seem especially promising, Fiorello. You're too timid one moment and too bold the next."

"Yes, Signor Golaccio."

"Are you always like that? Oh well, we'll see. Do you steal?"

"Steal? No—oh no, Signor Golaccio."

"You're going to be around costly and precious things, Fiorello, and will handle them yourself, and you'll see the masters treat all their valuables as if they were small pebbles at a river's edge, with no value, and then Fiorello might suddenly get ideas in his stupid head, he might think that objects that are treated so nonchalantly don't mean much of anything, even if they are of pure gold, and then Fiorello might think that a couple of jewels more or less won't be noticed, if they should disappear in a small pocket. Do you understand?"

Something made Fiorello look up. And at the same moment Pippo struck his ear so hard it reverberated; he fell down and had to collect himself, but the butler pulled him up by the same ear, without caring how much it hurt.

"But you must never, never think that way. *Never!*" he snarled. "Because then you will *die*. Every single object stands on inventory lists, which are examined and brought up-to-date every week, and every object is acquired with blood, with hard work and sweat, with dearly bought gold, with our city's anguish and woe, indeed, with the work of thousands of people, in many lands and cities. You are just part of the inventory, Fiorello, never forget that, no matter how many compliments the masters may give you some evening when they're in a good mood. You are yourself an art object, like all the other things, a stone on the river's edge, and one day someone can decide to get rid of you; it's just as simple as to obtain you. Do you understand?"

"Yes," sobbed Fiorello.

"Now, now," said Pippo. "How old are you, Fiorello?"

"Eleven years old," said Fiorello.

"You're just a youngster from the country and know less than a kitten still," said Pippo Golaccio. "I hit you in order to knock the first bit of sense into you."

"Yes," said Fiorello.

"Now, now. Stop blubbering. I don't have time to stand here loitering all day."

The tailor measured him quickly and meticulously, brought out bolt after bolt of cloth, from which Pippo Golaccio hurriedly and decisively made his choices. Fiorello noticed the butler's hand when he chose, a half-crooked, slightly imperious index finger, an index finger that was accustomed to getting things the way it wanted. In the time to come, Fiorello learned to know this hand gesture, used by the masters, the highest-ranking servants, and finally also himself. You pointed, and you received, and you were not contradicted. For in the days when Fiorello came to the del Vetro palace, the family's wealth was still so immense, its power so great, that there seemed to be no limit to its vitality and development; it could still compare itself with the foremost families in the city, indeed in the entire country. And the del Vetro influence and fortune expressed itself in this little gesture, it appeared at each shop they visited the first day. They needed only to step inside the door for the salespeople and tradesmen to drop everything they were doing; the moment they caught sight of Pippo Golaccio, they excused themselves from other customers, swarmed around the butler, treated him as if it were *he* who was Palazzo Vetro's master, brought out fabric and shoes, buckles and belts, a dagger, a purse; then Pippo began to point and point: That, that, that pair, not those, not those, those, that, that, not that. Send them to Palazzo Vetro. He pointed the same way while Fiorello was clipped and curled and curried until he was unrecognizable, as scissors and knife flew through the air like silver lightning.

Finally it was evening, and with cold, sore feet and numbed heart Fiorello came back to the palace, where Pippo plopped him on a stool in the kitchen, without a word of praise and with no further farewell ceremonies; he sat there a long time looking at the people running back and forth with pots and pans, listened to their shouts and laughter, without understanding anything. Nobody noticed him as he sat there trying to get warm. When he had heard the bells outside strike once and then strike again, he knew that he was invisible, that he was nobody, not Marco any longer nor really Fiorello yet. He forgot, a little more every minute. He forgot the kitchen at home, where his mother and the maids cooked large pots of soup while he and Pietro ran in and out. He forgot the freshly chopped wood, how it smelled when he carried in large armloads and was praised for how strong he was; he forgot the contented, droning sound of the journeymen and apprentices when they marched into the kitchen at dinnertime, with the master, his father, in the lead, and sat down to eat around the large, well-scoured table; he forgot the laughter, forgot how his mother seated herself at the end of the table, smoothed her apron, and the drone of voices grew silent: "Hello, everyone." "Hello, Signora!" "Today we're having meat soup and salad, and after that, honey cake, cheese, figs, and raisins. Enjoy your meal!" "Thank you, Signora!" And the maids who scurried about serving the meal, and his mother who brought bandages and dressings for the large and small wounds the men got in the workshop; stopped the bleeding with egg white, cleansed scratches with salt water. "You're an angel, Signora! There's no other workshop where people are cared for as well as we are here, with Master Vittorio and you, Signora Marcella!"

"Thank you for *that* bouquet," his mother would say, and pat the journeyman kindly on the head. Laughter. His father laughed happily. That was in the years when the masterpieces began to flow from the workshop, when Master Vittorio found new and sensational ways to use the materials, honed his handicraft, began to form entire pictures with inlays and variously shaded wood, in unusual combinations, with woods of different hardness, which allowed him to create heretofore unseen designs and borders;

indeed, he turned all the furniture into pictures. It was as if the wood and he had become *one* in those years, as if under his fingers the wood melted, pliantly and precisely, just as he wished. He often sang in the workshop during that time, sang the old craftsmen's songs, hummed and droned them, as his swift, sure hand made the chips fly like sparks from the chisel. "Like this," he would explain to the apprentices who stood watching him; "*Like this*," his hands explained more than the words. "*With* the wood, let the wood have some will of its own, don't try to force it too much. It's like with a woman's love, you can't force it to come, don't be too violent, slip in. In the depths, take care to think about what you're doing, don't go too far in at first, make just a suggestion. Maintain the level, maintain the line." And the sons, who helped in the workshop each day, were allowed to practice on the leftover pieces and to discover with their own hands how difficult it was, how easily the wood splintered or split, how easily a crack occurred where even the simplest form was to be inlaid. But for his father it was as easy as a song and, still singing, he marched into the kitchen, kissed his wife, had carved a small figure, a little bird, from a bit of wood, and the bird was so lifelike it seemed as if it were about to take flight when he gently laid it in her hands as in a nest.

"The secret of the art of inlaying," said his father, "lies partially in the glue." He cooked his own glue, different mixtures for different purposes, the best ingredients and eggs from four different birds blended in exact proportions which he alone knew; he went out into the fields and gathered secret herbs, bought only the whitest flour, used only springwater, and guarded the recipe as an alchemist would the philosophers' stone, or as a lover watches over reciprocated love.

Those were the years when the workshop was filled with song each day, and orders streamed in from far and near. His father had to hire more people, he bought the neighboring house, expanded, made plans, invested in property, looked ahead. Every day he put a new bird in his wife's hand, every day she was just as happily surprised by the gift. And journeymen flocked to the workshop in droves, because everyone knew that at Master Vittorio's you were well cared for, you learned a great deal, you were not hit or ridiculed, the food was good and the wages ample, and then of course Master Vittorio had such a lovely wife, and those two loved each other so much that some of the warmth seemed to infect everyone around them, indeed it was as if they all—the journeymen and the maids, the apprentices and assistants—were a wedding gift the couple had received.

All of this Fiorello forgot now as he sat on the stool, invisible, not thinking about himself, a nobody. And he forgot the years that had followed, when the singing stopped and his father stood sullen and brooding at the carpenter's bench, forced himself to work, silent, despairing, without his Marcella; with no one into whose hands he could put a bird; the work no longer flowed so easily from his hand, each work, each masterpiece was forced out by stifled anger and determined effort, evenly, steadily, without joy, in sorrow. But the works were beautiful, indeed, in a strange way perhaps even more beautiful and even more incomprehensible now than before, as if the master wanted to reach for something beyond his grasp, impossible to attain. The number of orders increased. But his mother no longer stood in the kitchen; in the kitchen it was she, the other woman, who now ruled. The brazier's widow.

It wasn't that she was cruel. On the contrary, she was probably like everyone else. A widow in her best years, with two children, from the same city, from the artisan class; what could be more suitable for a widower in the same position? She was pretty, dressed nicely, appeared to take good care of her own children. So six months after his wife's death Master Vittorio dutifully began to get acquainted with the brazier's widow, but first he had to be convinced. Because in the beginning he did not want to do anything, only wanted to sit despondently. In the beginning everything was a mess; the workshop, the house, everything was in disorder. To the brothers, Pietro and Marco, it somehow seemed right that things should be that way; after their mother's funeral, they couldn't really imagine that life could continue. Neither could the journeymen, nor the other people in the house. But as the months went by, and winter came, and the master just sat in the kitchen drinking plum brandy while his tools lay below, people began to wonder a little how this would end. People began to talk, yes, even the furniture-makers' guild was concerned, because during the entire half year since the funeral Vittorio had not been to the meetings, something that was unheard of, in fact was a sin against the guild's very principles and grounds for expulsion. People had overlooked things at first, they had thought Vittorio needed time to get over his loss, after all his marriage had been exceptionally happy, and he had worked very hard the last years, merited the guild's gratitude for his achievements, and might well need a rest. People had made allowances in the whole matter. But now that could no longer continue. Someone had to talk with him.

So it was that the guild master, venerable old Niccolò, had knocked on the door late one December evening, and had sat down with Vittorio in the empty, barren kitchen. The two sons crouched at the top of the kitchen stairs listening and watching, as they had done in the evenings before, after bedtime, while there was still singing and enjoyment and the fire burned until late at night, and their father and mother laid plans, and dreamed, and laughed, laughed the whole evening. The sons listened.

"This can't go on any longer, Vittorio," said the guild master after some introductory sympathy. "You've lost a wonderful wife and your best helper."

Vittorio only nodded heavily above his wine cup, was about to take a swallow, but the guild master stopped him by placing his hand authoritatively over the younger man's.

"But it was God's will," said the guild master solemnly. He laid his hands heavily on the table, somehow put them away from himself, like two heavy tools. "No one knows the day or the hour, Vittorio," he said sternly. "And it's not up to us to ask why or when."

"No, esteemed father and master," said Vittorio, "but if it was God who took her, then God is cruel."

The guild master's lips tightened.

"It doesn't help to blaspheme, son," he said. "Our entire town is proud of you, Vittorio. You're the pride of our guild and have brought high renown to our craft. Some day I hope to see you in my place, as the guild's father and leader."

Vittorio looked at the guild master, said nothing, then lowered his eyes.

"But you can't go on this way," said the guild master. "Your work is waiting below, you're late with your deliveries, you neglect your suppliers, your journeymen are idle, your boys wear mismatched shoes when they go to school in the morning."

"That was God's will," Vittorio began, but the guild master interrupted him sternly.

"No, Vittorio, stop! You mustn't blaspheme. I forbid it."

But Vittorio said: "I've lost my love! My work is without love, and my day is without love. What is a man without love? How can he work, without his love?"

Vittorio and the old man sat for a long time without saying anything. The silence grew across the table.

"But you haven't lost it," the guild master said at last. "It's within you, and you must find it again. You must find it somewhere else than before. You must find it in work and in materials, you must find it in effort and in will. Everything is still just ashes for you, I can understand that, and perhaps everything will always be just ashes for you, Vittorio. But you must try. Remember, you have the boys."

"Yes," said Vittorio. "I know. But they remind me so much of her, of her face and her hands and her voice. They are the bygone years. They are the evening I saw her for the first time, they are the day I promised to dedicate all my work to God—to create more beautiful and noble work than any other carpenter in Tuscany if only I could have the woman I loved; they are the morning when I, a poor carpenter's journeyman, *got* her. And they are all the days that followed. I can hardly stand to look at them, because they remind me of everything that was, and of the fact that once again I'm only a poor carpenter's journeyman."

"But you *got* her, after all, Vittorio. You must keep your promise now, now when it costs you something. You're no journeyman any longer. You must keep on creating your masterpieces. You must nurture love again, in yourself. You must use your will now, put all your effort into your work and into everyday life. Step by step, day by day, one at a time. You'll see, life will go on somehow, and perhaps you'll be happy again, even if there's always a shadow in your heart."

Vittorio nodded, looked straight ahead, looked as if he was going to say, yet again, that he missed her, that he couldn't understand why he had lost her (and how many times had he said that in the past months?), but the guild master forestalled him.

"She's gone and won't come back, Vittorio. You need to find love somewhere else. You need to get the workshop back on its feet, you must activate your workers and your sons, who need you now when they don't have a mother. Yes. All children need a mother."

"Yes," nodded Vittorio, "they miss their mother."

At the top of the stairs, Marco began to cry, softly, so the men downstairs would not hear him. His big brother held his hand.

"And a man needs a wife," continued the guild master, encouraged by his progress. "One who takes care of him and runs the house. Otherwise, if a man lives alone, there's only disorder and drunkenness and whoring. Just look at the monasteries, where men live without wives, they've become absolute bordellos—a disgrace to all Christendom."

"Yes," nodded Vittorio again. "A man needs a woman."

"You should see about getting married again," the guild master suggested. "Find a widow of an appropriate age."

Vittorio gave him an abrupt angry look, so the guild master restrained himself. But then something in the younger man's look changed, and he nodded in resignation.

"Yes," he said, "perhaps you're right, master."

"I *am* right, Vittorio," said the guild master, relieved. "And we've also talked about the matter in the guild."

"The guild, yes," said Vittorio distantly, as if reminded of something he had forgotten.

"You no longer come to the meetings," the guild master said sternly. "Even though in time of need the guild is to be like your own family; yes, like a father and mother for you. Have you forgotten that you swore an oath? But we're not deserting you, we've worried about you and done our best to hold our own against your suppliers, without your knowing, and we've discussed your situation, and I've also talked with the other guild masters in town."

"Perhaps you have someone special in mind, as good mothers and fathers generally do?" Vittorio said bitterly, but the guild master ignored his tone.

"As you know, there's no suitable widow in our own guild. But the braziers' guild has lost one of its brothers; he left a wife and two young children, and the braziers don't know how they will be able to take care of them."

Vittorio said nothing, pondered the guild master's words, looked into his own mind and heart.

"Her name is Antonia," said the guild master. "Maybe you've seen her."

"That's possible."

"She's clever and pretty—even if not as pretty as your Marcella—"

"Oh."

"It's true she hasn't managed as large a household as this, because the brazier had only a few journeymen, and it may well be that she's not as lighthearted and cheerful as your Marcella, but nonetheless: she's good and capable, and not lazy, you can be sure of that."

"When I was young, before I met Marcellina," said Vittorio, "my father, who was a carpenter like me, but a very simple craftsman, wanted to force me to marry a suitable girl from our town, one I didn't love, but who was suitable, one who wasn't lazy. I prevented it only through strong opposition and defiance. I had to leave home, master, leave the town, because I knew if I married her, the suitable one, I'd end up as a poor, average carpenter. I knew I had more ability in me than that, and I sensed, more than I could understand or know, that only the right woman could bring out the best in me, and I *knew*, knew without knowing, that she was waiting for me out there in the world, waiting just for me. I knew that, though I couldn't have said it, if anyone had asked. And full of confidence I shook the dust of my childhood town off my feet, went away, without looking back. Yes. *Without looking back.* And I'd no sooner started with my own shop, than I received an order from a retired squire up in the mountains, not much more than a farmer with a coat of arms, who had a neglected little tower and just one daughter. The house was located in such rough terrain that I almost said 'No thank you.' Besides, I had enough to do. But a dream made me ride up there after all; I dreamed I was in the mountains and found a stream. I awoke from the dream in the middle of the night, because the image was so clear, and the water in the stream was so blue. The next morning as I was sharpening my knife, I cut myself, and wouldn't be able to work for a few days; so I decided I'd go up and see what the squire wanted done. And that same evening, when I saw the tower, I felt very strange, as if I had been there before, as if something was waiting for me. She was standing by the well when I rode into the courtyard, and even before we went inside we had begun to talk together, and to laugh, and I knew that I would take her with me from there, and she knew that I had come to get her, and we were happy because we both knew this, because nothing, not her father nor her mother, not her station nor mine, could stop us. And we didn't stop talking and laughing together until the fever took her six months ago. You see, master, I was young and fearless then. Your words make me feel seventeen years old again. It's *best* for you, it's *suitable* for you to marry a woman you don't love. But I'm no longer seventeen years old, I'm no longer able to oppose your fatherly words and start out, fearless, full of hope, *without looking back*. Because what shall I look *forward* to? One must *believe* that something is waiting out there, that one is going toward something better."

The guild master was silent for a long time. Then he said: "The brazier's widow." He cleared his throat, a little embarrassed. "She's shapely; she can both sew and cook. Her children are nicely dressed, have good, even if somewhat simple, manners; they come from a more modest background. No hunting parties, no land, no money. But well brought up."

Vittorio appeared reluctant, for a moment seemed furious, as if he were going to tell the old man to go to the devil with the whole brazier family.

"The guild needs to be like a mother and a father for you," the guild master said solemnly, "and you need to listen when the guild speaks. You just said it yourself, Vittorio, you're no longer seventeen years old. You're an adult, with responsibility for two sons and a workshop."

Vittorio pulled himself together.

"Perhaps you're right," he said.

"It's your duty as a Christian and as a guild member. The braziers' guild master and I have already talked with her, and she's not unwilling. It would be a great help to her, and she will always be grateful to you. It would be a step up in life for her, if something comes of it, and it's more than she could have counted on in her widowed state. Like a light in a foggy night, those were her words, like a light in a foggy night, she said, when the braziers' guild master and I visited her in connection with this matter. You'll see that love will come by itself, little by little, unnoticeably, the way stars come out in the evening."

"Maybe I'll visit her," said Vittorio.

"Do that, but make up your mind quickly. Because with such things, where good sense speaks and not just the heart, it's best to decide quickly, so the other person isn't hurt."

Vittorio gave him a sorrowful look.

The next day the guild master took Master Vittorio and his sons to visit the brazier's widow. She greeted him shyly, eyes downcast, with a little smile. She was very pretty. He asked her the kind of questions one asks strangers, about the children, about the weather, and about her widowed state. She replied shyly, in monosyllables. She had long, dark hair, pinned up nicely, and a tongue that kept wanting to come out and moisten her lips. When she spoke, she made a small sound, a slight clearing of her throat, before each sentence. Marco could see that this little sound irritated his father, and at the same time he saw how his father stared at her mouth and the tip of her tongue that came out again and again. Now and then she raised her eyes and looked at him, inquiringly, almost a little afraid, as if to discover what he wanted.

"Well, Vittorio," the guild master said encouragingly as they walked toward home, "decide quickly."

But Master Vittorio could not decide quickly, he kept the brazier's widow on tenterhooks for more than half a year. He *could not* decide, he let her wait and wait, until it was almost too late, and so she came to understand, more clearly than necessary, that he felt unwilling, and that this feeling battled with rational considerations. Perhaps this was where all the bad things began. Finally, one January evening the decision was made; Master Vittorio came home after a visit to the brazier's widow, this time with bloodshot eyes and a body as burdensome as a war. He said nothing, went into the courtyard, saddled his horse, and rode away, without saying where. Perhaps he rode far up into the mountains. Perhaps he did not dismount and take the key from the wall, but sat there on his horse and saw the key shining in the moonlight, looked at the locked door. Perhaps that's what happened. He did not return to the village until sometime early the next morning, when the roosters had just begun to crow. He awakened his sons, pulled them out of their beds, and told them, with a smile and a happiness that were not fully believable, told them they were going to get a new mother, a new mother and new siblings, that things were going to be as before, when Marcella was alive, that everything was going to be fine, that they were going to be happy again. Did Marco believe it then? Did he really believe that there would be singing in the workshop again? That the workers would stream happily into the kitchen? Marco did not know. He knew only that his father married someone he didn't love, perhaps in a similar hope that things would be as before, that love would come by itself, slowly, like the stars. Maybe he really hoped that. Because he gave the brazier's widow small and large gifts, as had been his habit with his first wife, he impressed upon his sons and his workers that they must respect and honor her just as highly as they had respected and honored Marcella, he praised her for her housework and her cooking, made sure to tell her she was beautiful, was careful to praise her children as much as his own.

But she noticed it, noticed it in big and little things. She noticed it in the unnoticeable, in the touches and the words, both those which were said and those which were never spoken. And she grew bitter. She had stood beside him in the church with a wreath of flowers in her hair, she had seemed afraid, had gazed up at him pleadingly when he hesitated, hesitated just the slightest moment before he gave his promise. Marco remembered her indescribable expression of simultaneous relief and disappointment when the words finally came, and she gave his father a look that Marco never would forget, not until he had become Fiorello, for in that look he saw unhappiness, and he saw that unhappiness consists of equal parts of love and hate. And Marco remembered the first time, a few days after the wedding, when his father brought her a little bird from the workshop, one made with particular care, and tried to lay it in her hands, but she just took it, looked at it, thanked him superficially, and put it on the shelf before busying herself again with the food. The brothers and the workers looked at each other uneasily. The master was disappointed, but he restrained himself. He tried again the next day, and the day after that. She merely gave the carvings a quick glance. The third bird, a dashing peacock with a tail of shavings that stood straight up in the air, she used as tinder the next morning, something Marco's father didn't see, fortunately. She didn't intend anything bad by that, she just didn't understand. Gradually more and more time elapsed between the birds, weeks could go by between each time he brought one into the kitchen from the workshop. The seventh or eighth time she said, genuinely wondering: "Tell me, master, isn't the workshop busy enough with its orders so that you shouldn't waste time making such pieces of foolishness?" The room grew silent. She laughed nervously. His father calmly put down the bird. Did not say a word.

No, she didn't understand such things. And his father didn't understand her either. So the cold time came, and the silent time, when the exchange of words between his father and stepmother froze like a mountain river in the winter, and everything became hard and silent. His father worked, stifled his anger, was unapproachable. Later the war came.

Fiorello wept.

Someone set a bowl of soup in front of him.

"You must be the new one." Fiorello looked up. His tears must have made him visible again. A boy a little older than he stood before him, elegantly dressed, with long curls and a stylish, ornamented silver dagger at his side.

"I'm Marco," he said encouragingly, as if this was a great and happy piece of news. "Don't sit there feeling sad, because that doesn't help anything; eat a little soup instead, and then you need to sleep."

Fiorello ate obediently, while the other boy kept him company, without saying anything and without letting on that he saw Fiorello was still sobbing a little. He watched Fiorello carefully, as if he wanted to make sure he ate all his soup. Fiorello was grateful for the considerate silence. Then they went to get some sleep.

"You mustn't take it so hard," said Marco kindly as he sat down on the edge of his bed. "It's quite nice to be here in the palace, you see. At least as regards the young master; he's not nearly as gloomy as the old father. Lord Lorenzo gives splendid parties and has lots of fun. Lorenzo isn't bad at all. And you get good food!" He stretched comfortably and pulled off his boots.

"The butler—" Fiorello began.

"Ha, Pippo, the old goat. Don't bother about him. He only puffs himself up and thinks he *is* something. He's just jealous because youngsters like us get a chance to serve the nobility's tables. Don't listen to what he says. Listen to *me* instead." They crawled into bed. "All things considered, you could have landed in a worse place than Palazzo Vetro, Fiorello. Just think.

Out in the world there's war and misery, and here we sit, safe and secure as in Noah's ark, and can eat our fill. And not only that. We get to see the people in high society, experience them, see all their beauty and all the things that surround them. And we can learn all sorts of things. Think about that, and don't feel sad."

"How long have you been here—Marco?" asked Fiorello when the other boy blew out the lamp.

"Oh, it's a long time," said Marco, worldly-wise in the darkness. "A long time."

"How did you come here?"

"Oh, my father was a Greek prince."

"I see," said Fiorello, unable to think of anything else to say.

"Captured in a fight with the Saracens, where we had to defend ourselves. We were two against twenty. But we fought back, and almost a dozen of them lay bloody on the deck when we were taken prisoner."

Fiorello listened to the other Marco's voice.

"I see," he said respectfully.

"My father was decapitated, after being boiled alive, and he had such strength of mind that he didn't scream or lose spirit. But I became a slave in the Saracen king's barbaric court. Only through cleverness and cunning did I succeed in escaping across the desert, but that's a long story I'll tell you another time. After many tribulations I came here, and was taken into service because I knew palace life and know how everything should be done in a palace."

"So you're actually a prince," said Fiorello.

"Actually, yes. But only I and Lord Lorenzo know that, because the others might be envious and start to treat me differently if they found out that I might return to my father's kingdom one day, when I'm old enough and have gathered money for an army to liberate it. Now you know about this too." For a moment there was silence in the darkness. "Don't tell anyone. Then I'll help you figure out things here in the palace."

"I won't," said Fiorello, feeling impressed. "I promise, Marco."

"And you?" asked Marco. Fiorello thought it over.

"My father wasn't a prince," he said shyly.

"No?"

"He was a feudal lord," said Fiorello, "in a large, rich fiefdom, and he was loved by all his subjects. But then the war came. God rest his soul." Marco whistled far into the darkness.

"Did he lose his fiefdom in the war, perhaps?"

"Something like that, yes," said Fiorello.

"You'll probably fit in well here in the palace," said Marco with respect.

And that was how Fiorello's apprenticeship began.

The very next evening he helped Marco during a family dinner with the old duke, the duchess, Lord Lorenzo, and his sister Giulia, as well as a couple of private secretaries. It was a test. Luigi del Vetro gloomily held sway at the head of the table, his wife beside him, while the two children sat so far away that any conversation in an ordinary tone was impossible, everything the family said to each other had to be *announced*. The old father loudly interrogated the children about how they were and how things were going with this and that. Lovely Giulia del Vetro just sat and picked at her food with downcast eyes and an expression of immense boredom and indolence. She replied with well-prepared monosyllables. Fiorello knew that she had recently been widowed, but the sorrow did not appear to trouble her enough to be worth mentioning. To tell the truth, Luigi del Vetro did not seem especially interested in his daughter, and soon began to talk with his son about politics and money. No other subjects were mentioned, and Lorenzo del Vetro murmured his replies to his father without much joy. In any case, most of the conversation went over Fiorello's head, it was all he could do to study and try to understand the servant theater being played around him, as the lackeys and maids made their rounds in a silent, perfectly rehearsed dance, always in the same order; the mistress must be offered the food first, whereupon she would indicate with a nod that her husband should be served first, then she, then Lord Lorenzo, then Giulia del Vetro, and finally the secretaries. The food came and went. Individual platters, sumptuous portions of food, were carried in simply for display—they were not meant to be eaten at all, but were merely shewbread. The duchess, who had sat silent and expressionless throughout the meal, withdrew early, together with her daughter, and only as they disappeared, arm in arm, did one hear something resembling the beginning of normal conversation between them. The men too began speaking together in quieter voices when they seated themselves in front of the fireplace. Fiorello carried in fruit, had to sing a little song at Lord Lorenzo's request, they smiled graciously and lost interest in him. His task for the rest of the evening was to stand ready by the men's chairs, for hours, with all his senses alert to anticipate their wishes as the evening went on. Music was played, and the palace dwarf performed, but was quickly sent out again, because the men had much to discuss. Fiorello would never have thought it could be so tiring to stand still, and when he finally tumbled into bed, his legs ached as though he had run the whole day.

Nearly every evening was spent the same way. Sometimes with guests, other times just the family. During the day it was simpler, because then the two pages were at the beck and call of young Lorenzo, who was far more cheerful when he was alone and, moreover, might decide to have fun— leave the office work and take his pages into the city to do errands, as he called it; mostly it was to see and to be seen, to stand on streets and in marketplaces, sometimes for several hours, talking and discussing with passersby, friends, enemies, women, priests, artists. It was enjoyable, but tiring, because when you were out walking it was hard to keep your attention focused on the real task, which was to assist your master. There were so many colorful things to see, so many things to keep up with. And so much could happen on the street, Marco would say a little nervously; he always wore his silver-ornamented dagger when they went out. At other times they accompanied their master to concerts and art exhibits, or to parties in other homes.

The first few nights, Fiorello cried after going to bed; but one night Marco got up, sat on the edge of the younger boy's bed, and comforted him. He said: "You have to stop crying, Fiorello, otherwise you won't be able to stay here."

"Don't you ever cry?" Fiorello asked his friend.

"That doesn't befit a prince," said Marco proudly. Then he added: "But *if* I happen to cry anyway, well, I'll tell you something clever I've discovered: you must cry with only one eye, the one you turn away. And smile with the other one. You have a nice smile, Fiorello, the masters like it. They put up with your beginner's mistakes and think you're amusing, with all your jokes. I think so too. So why do you cry at night?"

"I don't know."

"Here in the palace you must show only half your face, otherwise you won't last long. And also, it helps to bite your tongue." He lay down in the bed next to Fiorello, and told more about his time as a Greek prince, about fleeing from the Saracens and other exciting adventures, until Fiorello fell asleep.

So Marco became his friend and companion. He practiced bowing and etiquette with him, gave him small pieces of advice and tips about one thing and another, especially about reading aloud. And momentous days would soon follow—moving, fateful days, for those in Palazzo Vetro and for the entire city of Florence. Gradually Fiorello became completely used to being Fiorello, and if on rare occasions a memory about the earlier times came to mind, he dropped it, let it sink into deep water. He was the happy, cheerful Fiorello with all the word games, the perfect page, an adornment for the palace and for his master. He liked Lord Lorenzo, and he had a fortunate way with his master's melancholy, often slightly complaining moods. Together with Marco he served him faithfully from morning till evening. He made raids with Marco through the palace's labyrinths, they spied on the maids, played many rude jokes on the cooks, learned new feats and new songs, thought up more and more ways to cheer the noble family during this hard time. For outside Palazzo Vetro's secure walls things were fermenting, the city was like a vipers' nest. Fiorello and Marco did not understand much of all that happened out in the city. Besides Marco had told him that it didn't pay to try to follow the conversations at the table too carefully, because if that were noticed, people might begin to wonder if they were spying. But when old Luigi del Vetro died the next winter, and his widow shortly afterward, a murmur of uneasy curiosity spread among the servants. For how would things go, when the old man no longer held his protective wings above them?

Lord Lorenzo took over the keys to the money chest. And immediately a fresh breeze seemed to come into the palace; where before one had seen only somber businesspeople and city council members come and go at parties, filled to the brim with their own worth, now young Lorenzo's friends arrived, beaux esprits, scholars, artists, and poets. It was now the large symposia began to take place, and Fiorello enjoyed every minute of them. He enjoyed listening to the conversations, even if he did not always understand what people were talking about, he enjoyed the poetry reading and the music, he enjoyed seeing the painters and sculptors come and go, just *seeing* them. He did not know why. The air seemed to shimmer around them, and Fiorello noticed that he thirsted for this shimmering, needed to have more of it, could not slake his thirst for it. Lorenzo del Vetro held many such gatherings; he arranged theater productions and hunting parties, and constantly ordered new works of art for his ancestral home; in fact he even had plans of expanding the palace, and announced a competition for that, even though the arithmetician strongly admonished him that the palace could not afford it, and most earnestly urged the young master to consolidate his position. There was something fleeting and restless about his numerous ventures, as if he half sensed that it could not last.

It was during these days that Lorenzo del Vetro first became acquainted with the painter Enzio da Castelnuovo, who was then in the process of creating a name for himself. Those two seemed made for each other, the artist and the merchant; with his wisdom and blunt wit the painter immediately became a regular guest at Lord Lorenzo's parties and gatherings. To put his new favorite to the test, Lord Lorenzo commissioned him to paint his current mistress. The girl's name was Veronica, and neither Fiorello nor Marco could bear her, because she was, despite all her charm, a devil when the master was not present. For some reason or other, she hated Lord Lorenzo's two pages from the very first day, and her months with Lord Lorenzo were a trial for Marco and Fiorello. In the morning, when Lord Lorenzo had left his bed, and she was still lying there indolently after the night's visit, it was very risky to stay in the master's rooms to serve her, because she could come up with the most terrible and dangerous things. She mocked their youth, made fun of them for their lowly position, ridiculed their appearance. She requested all sorts of impossible services, and complained about them to her high-ranking lover if they had displeased her in any way, and that was constantly. She threw her shoes at them or destroyed some of Lord Lorenzo's treasures in order to blame one of the pages later. They couldn't understand why she hated them. Perhaps she hated everyone. But she wasn't particularly clever, and complained too often, so perhaps Lord Lorenzo understood what had actually happened and glossed over the matter. Later she tried all sorts of other tricks to get them in trouble. The worst was when she rose from her bed naked and provoked them with movements or touches; Marco and Fiorello made it a matter of principle to never be alone with her, but to go together or, even better, to have a maid with them.

Master Enzio was supposed to paint this little devil, and Master Enzio, who later became so famous for his religious motifs, knew already then that his mastery was not dependent on the character of the motif, not only because his powers of observation were exceptionally well honed but because he had long experience with the tools of illusion. He gave his painting of the beautiful Veronica a mythological base by depicting her as Helen of Troy—an extremely difficult task, since Helen's smile could launch a whole armada, while little Veronica's smile could barely overturn a load of hay. The result was marvelous, and the very small select group that was allowed to look at the painting as it hung in Lord Lorenzo's private quarters long discussed how Master Enzio had created the feeling that the ships very soon would set sail *in them*, when they saw her portrait. Was it due only to the reproduction of the naked young girl's beauty? Or was it that he had made her smile so marvelously while she modeled for him? Lorenzo del Vetro had to admit that the portrait created strong desire in him, even more than the girl herself usually did, and he was uneasy about how the good master had created that inimitable expression in the painted face. What had he *done*, as she sat like that and he painted?

Master Enzio's answer was as short as it was surprising, and Fiorello always remembered it, because he and Marco also thought the painting was considerably more attractive than the subject.

"Triangles, squares, circles!" said Master Enzio.

Lord Lorenzo did not understand.

"She was interesting to use the compass on, I must admit," said the painter. "A naughty little girl. But very geometric. And in the geometry lies the real beauty, it's what makes us experience the beautiful as beautiful. I sketched her a few times, until I knew where the lines converged in her, in her face and in her body. Then I placed her in a right-angled triangle, but in such a way that her shoulders lay in a circle concentric with a point on the hypotenuse, divided according to the golden section from the points of the triangle. The rest was a matter of seeing the light, and of keeping her happy with amusing stories while she sat for me. But without the geometry she would only have looked like a girl in a garment from antiquity—the small garment that she's wearing, I mean."

"Do you mean to say," asked Lorenzo del Vetro with admiration, "that all this beauty is geometrically determined?"

"Yes," said the artist self-confidently. "And I also believe the day will come when the artist won't be satisfied with painting models."

"What else should he paint?"

"Listen, esteemed gentlemen. The painter positions models in postures according to hidden geometric patterns that fit the motif—triangles, rectangles, circles—with the idea that the beauty and harmony of the abstract geometric forms will come through in the visible picture whose limits they help to define. But what if one painted only the triangles? What if one leaped over the woman and instead portrayed only the triangle and the other forms she is created from? Perhaps the day will come when beauty can be expressed in a triangle."

"Do you mean," asked Lorenzo del Vetro in disbelief, and without fully comprehending the painter's strange words, "that my little Veronica's beauty can be summarized in a triangle?"

"Now, now," said the painter with a hearty laugh, "I wouldn't go that far. There are certain additional things, of course. It all depends on which triangle we're talking about!"

A man who could reply like this soon became indispensable, of course, and Lorenzo gave him further commissions; but, unfortunately, he was able to complete only one of them before the stormy events in the city forced him to leave Florence in great haste and seek safer pastures elsewhere. And that one commission was not a painting, not a work of art, but a masked parade to celebrate the coming of spring, for which Master Enzio had designed the costumes and lights, masks and figures, and had planned the entire event in detail. It was a marvelous parade, with motifs from ancient mythology; Apollo and Dionysus each led his own cortege, which then blended in a beautifully choreographed dance in the square in front of Palazzo Vetro, to the music of flute and lute. It was the most beautiful thing Fiorello had ever seen. Standing on the balcony behind his master peering out into the dark evening, he devoured with happy eyes each new figure that appeared in the glow of the Bengal lights and the thousand lamps—lovely dancers, weightless acrobats, gleaming silver costumes, divine masks and terrifying ones. Lord Lorenzo's guests leaned out the windows and acclaimed each new creation with shouts and jubilation, and threw flowers down to the performers, all the while shouting their congratulations to Lord Lorenzo on this triumph in his time as the master of the house, and in the life of the city. Everyone looked forward to the party continuing in a more intimate manner inside Palazzo Vetro's halls after the citizens had been entertained with this magnificent sight.

Far away, on the opposite side of the square, a crowd of spectators stood watching. At first with shouts and jubilation, like the illustrious company leaning from the palace windows, but suddenly the spectators grew strangely quiet and did not reply to the enthusiasm from the other side. A great silence seemed to have come over them, and the lack of an echo made Lord Lorenzo's guests uncertain. They shouted louder, urged the performers to even higher leaps, but the silence had taken root in the dark mass of people on the opposite side. Suddenly a new tone was heard; for a moment Fiorello thought that Master Enzio had added a new musical twist here, but the expressions on his master's and the artist's faces immediately told him this was not the case. Something else had happened. The new tone sounded like humming, a faint undertone to the drums, the flutes, and the shawms, then it grew louder and louder. The crowd sang. Rhythmic, monotonous, and oppressive. At first one could not hear the words, but they gradually penetrated the shrieking festival music.

> *Liber scriptus proferetur,*
> *In quo totum continetur,*
> *Under mundus judicetur . . .*

Lorenzo del Vetro looked worriedly at Master Enzio, threw yet another wreath of flowers to the performers, urged his guests to do likewise; Master Enzio fervently exhorted the musicians, who increased their efforts considerably, and for a while the song was drowned out. But soon it was heard again, like a steady chant, above the orchestra's music, which now threatened to collapse completely.

Ingemisco, tamquam reus:
Culpa rubet vultus meus:
Supplicanti parce, Deus!

At this point the party guests demanded that the guards be called to stop the sabotage, but Lord Lorenzo shook his head; he did not want to challenge the people; after all, he had only wanted to entertain them. Instead Lorenzo gave a sign to accelerate the events and continue the party indoors. The shawms faded away, the drums stopped playing, and the bewildered, somewhat anxious performers hurried through Palazzo Vetro's heavy open gates, to the deafening song from the crowd.

Confutatis maledictis,
Flammis acribus addictis:
Voca me cum benedictis!

The gates banged shut behind the performers, and the window shutters were closed, but for a long time they heard the crowd singing out there, muffled, threatening, and throbbing.

Lacrimosa dies illa!
Qua resurget ex favilla
Judicandus homo reus!

Not until much later did they stop singing, and the party could continue, in a subdued mood. Shortly afterward, the painter Enzio da Castelnuovo left the city; he probably foresaw that his painting of the beautiful Veronica would soon go into a bonfire, and Lorenzo del Vetro did not see him again until they met in Rome several years later, by which time much else had happened.

For this golden age was merely a grace period, and the evenings of beauty in Lord Lorenzo's halls were only a final flight from that which had to come for all the beaux esprits and sybarites who would soon be driven away from Florence—unless they allowed themselves to be reformed and inspired by the black cowl's inflammatory sermons, put away their worldly interests, and returned to the faith. Because the coup was on its way, when the old regime under the house of Medici and all its supporters were driven from Florence, and the del Vetros along with them. In reality the outbreak of quiet in Lord Lorenzo's parade was Savonarola's fault; the root of the frightening silence and the tuning fork for the entreating song was none but he. Fiorello had met the feared monk once, on the street, together with his master.

"Now you'll have a chance to greet your weed, Fiorello." Black cowl. White face. The monk had a little rhythmic twitch in the muscles above his mouth, which made his front teeth show all the time. A friendly smile at Fiorello, a dark look at Lord Lorenzo. Fiorello could not recall exactly what they talked about. But he remembered that his master had greeted the monk courteously, and talked with the holy man in the same way and with the same expression he always had when trying to stay in someone's good graces—friendly, elegant, witty. Halfway. But in contrast to all the others, the monk did not seem to respond in the same halfhearted, half-false, half-uncommitted way. He was not unfriendly. He just appeared to refuse to let himself be drawn into anything, not into the conversation, not into Lorenzo's nor anyone else's luster, but chose to remain standing outside, alone in his dark cowl. Fiorello, who had served his master for over a year and was accustomed to having everyone admire him, or at least fear or respect him, found the monk very strange in this regard. Perhaps the monk was like that in everything, perhaps he did not want to be drawn into any obligations, but chose another way, his own or God's. He stood there utterly calm and heard Lorenzo del Vetro's polite words, and his figure radiated calmness, independence, and incorruptibility. He seemed very strong, and the little tick in his face completely masked the play of his features and made his facial expression difficult to interpret.

Lorenzo del Vetro clearly tried to talk about compromises and solutions with the black-clad man, but in vain. The monk merely responded with simple but firm replies. Unwavering. In the end, Lord Lorenzo gave up.

"Confounded black cowl," he mumbled after they had left the monk with a dignified farewell.

Two months later the black cowl was master in the city, and Lorenzo del Vetro and his household had to flee in great haste. On a couple of occasions people had tried to attack him on the street, but fortunately he had escaped, because he had stopped going out with only the boys in attendance and always took heavily armed guards with him. Now he quickly began putting his house in order, before it was too late. He secretly sent artwork and valuable objects to the south, smuggled out of the city with the firm's other shipments. Fortunately, his father's advisors still held their positions and helped him to save what could be saved.

During these bewildering and hectic days, Marco disappeared. One evening Fiorello had been on duty alone, and when he came to crawl into bed late that night, Marco was not there; his bed was swept clean of straw, and his clothes and other belongings were gone. Fiorello stood for a long time looking around their little room in amazement. He searched in his own bed and everywhere for a sign, a small note or an object from his friend, but the room was empty of Marco. It was as if he had never lived there. Feeling utterly bewildered, Fiorello went to bed. The next morning he awoke with his friend's name on his lips; he thought he had dreamed it all, or perhaps he had dreamed that his friend had returned, but the bed and the room were empty. He dressed uneasily, hurried up to Lord Lorenzo's quarters; the master had to be dressed, be served, Fiorello had incredibly much to do. Already at breakfast the master gave his secret instructions regarding their imminent retreat from the city of flowers; he had no siblings aside from his sister, who, thank God, was in the care of a new husband, an important business connection in Venice; now it was a question of the remaining household, along with the business and capital. Lord Lorenzo spent the entire morning giving instructions. He was pale, and seemed frightened. The cook should not come along, but the butler should. That servant, that servant, but not that one. He announced his decisions tersely and firmly. The lovely Veronica? Stay here. And her painting too. Two arithmeticians would remain to take care of the del Vetro interests, insofar as that was possible, but the private secretary would come along into exile.

"You too, Fiorello."

"Shall I—?" asked Fiorello. "Yes, Your Lordship. Thank you, Your Lordship."

"Don't thank me," said his master curtly.

"And Marco—?" Fiorello dared to asked.

"Marco? Marco isn't coming."

"I see," said Fiorello quietly.

More instructions and commands followed. Fiorello stood there irresolute, then got the idea of bringing a cup of wine to fortify his master; as he handed the glass to Lord Lorenzo he murmured cautiously: "Where is he?"

"Who?"

"Marco," said Fiorello softly. "I would have liked to say good-bye to him."

"Fiorello," said Lorenzo del Vetro, sounding irritated, "you're being impertinent. What curiosity. It doesn't concern you. He's no longer here. He has other things to do."

"I see," said Fiorello quietly, and did not manage to completely hide that his eyes glistened with tears. Lord Lorenzo softened a little.

"You can have his dagger as a memento," he said curtly, took the dagger out of a drawer, and slid it across the table to Fiorello. "There, there, my friend! And now we have more important things to do!"

Fiorello took the dagger, which he knew had been Marco's pride and joy, and fastened it firmly to his own belt with hands that were amazingly calm. It surprised him how calm they were. Marco was never parted from that dagger, at least not if he was going to move about outdoors. As he fastened the beautiful weapon, Fiorello wondered if Marco had endured much pain, if they had tortured him or just cut his throat. And why this had happened. He noticed the tears in his eyes, but bit his tongue. Afterward he never cried again, never so that anyone could see it. As he stood in Lord Lorenzo's quarters among the morning's bustling preparations for their approaching flight, white beams of sunlight fell obliquely into the room; he looked at the rays of light, they were almost blinding, like glowing iron bars that have just come out of the forge, and something rose in him that could have resembled words, resembled a prayer, but which was only as glowing and formless as the light.

Soon afterward they departed, in great secrecy and haste. Only three days' journey to the south, when they had reached their first destination, Perugia, Lord Lorenzo called his servant Fiorello to his room early in the morning; his voice was anxious and perplexed, almost frightened. Fiorello became worried too. By the next morning more blisters had appeared, and before they reached Rome, Lorenzo del Vetro's illness had burst into full bloom.

"What are you thinking about, Fiorello?"

"Nothing, really."

"Well, drink a little water. It's late and you should sleep."

"Yes."

"Do you want more water?"

"Yes."

"Soon you'll be well."

"Maybe."

"Oh yes, you'll be well and can start working again. Then you won't have to lie here and have only me for company."

"Yes."

"There are two of you, do you know that, Fiorello?"

"Yes."

"One who's cheerful and handsome, and then the one who lies here depressed and answers me only in monosyllables even if I bring him fresh water. How can that be?"

"Simonetta?"

"Yes?"

"Why are you so good to me?"

"Because I like to be."

SEVEN

All this Fiorello thought about in the weeks he lay sick, but Lorenzo del Vetro, on the other hand, was a fountain of energy. His newly regained health filled him with uncontrollable happiness, for he had forgotten how it felt to be without pain, and had completely forgotten what it meant to be happy. He threw himself into all the work he had long neglected, and the work no longer hung on him like a wet cape but was done easily; it did not matter if it was dull necessary work—he felt like a schoolboy again, albeit without the dislike of lessons and without the anxiety. And he truly wondered if he had ever been so happy. Life had always been a matter of duty, duty before everything else. When his father had admonished him, the world had grown dark. Night had surrounded him as far back as he could remember. Only books by the old philosophers and poets had given him enjoyment when he was a child, for they had offered a glimpse of light. The pages in the account books and in the heavy folios with inventory lists of merchandise contained a darkness that was almost tangible. Not so much because he had disliked or lacked an aptitude for numbers and columns, but because they frightened him. He had always tried to fight off this fear. When very young he had tried to explain it to his father—that he felt an almost physical discomfort with the thing itself, with the task that awaited him. On hearing his stammering uncertain explanation, his father had shaken his head with mild disdain. What was there to fear? They were *Lorenzo's* businesses, after all. Or were going to be. So what was there to fear?

There is a place in hell called Malebolge which is the repository of all evil. Fraud dwells there. Seducers, flatterers, simoniacs, soothsayers, hypocrites, thieves, fraudulent counselors, counterfeiters. This Lorenzo had from the highest authority, from the *Divine Comedy*, about the human soul. Probably he had suspected this was the case long before his tutor had somewhat dubiously given the book about hell to his inquisitive student (who had already put Virgil and Homer behind him) and allowed him to read it—obviously without understanding what kind of thoughts he thereby nourished in young Lorenzo. Lorenzo already knew all about how things were in Malebolge, and it frightened him. For not even as a twelve-year-old did Lorenzo harbor the slightest belief that this portrayal of a trip into the Underworld was a depiction of the afterlife; on the contrary, he was absolutely certain that Malebolge is a place in the world, in us and around us. And anyone who so much as *touches* account books or does any business will inevitably come to Malebolge while he is still alive. For he must choose, he must make decisions, and it lies in the nature of the matter that he must do it for the sake of his own profit. He must do violence toward his neighbor and toward himself, toward God, Nature, and art. He must flatter and he must lie, spread false rumors and perhaps do even worse things—even fail his table companions, fail his country or his benefactors. And then one is even farther down in hell than in Malebolge, then one is in the Great Well—one is so far down that one can already see Lucifer himself as he lies there chewing like a mountain of evil. From an early age, Lorenzo had seen his father commit all the sins mentioned, without the least scruple. They were part of his métier. And for that matter, no different from what all the others did, in their divided native city. For a long time Lorenzo had harbored the uneasy feeling that something must be terribly wrong with this world and with those who live in it; after reading that book he knew it: Hell is within you. Mankind invents God, and that makes mankind holy. But mankind also invents hell. And this insight made him extremely sad, because he knew that he had no choice. And he knew that even his melancholic despondency qualified him for eternal sojourn in the miry pool, with all those who sorrow in the sweet air that rejoices in the sun, those who bear the thick smoke of pessimism within them—they will mourn through all eternity in the black mire of hell. And of course this knowledge did not exactly make him more cheerful.

Perhaps this was how young Lorenzo had begun to seek the joys of light and air. The joys of the eye, the joys of books and art, the joys of ancient authors and divine figures—all gave him at least some hope that meaning, beauty, goodness, and truth existed beyond this vipers' nest of a city and world. And Lorenzo del Vetro was not alone in entertaining such a hope in Florence and quickly found his way to a circle of like-minded people. But his father, who did not lack taste and generously supported several artists, could be brought to despair by young Lorenzo's passion for art, by the way he squandered his allowance on books and paintings, and by the fact he wasted his precious time in the company of these people. But that's how he was; he couldn't be otherwise. And only with the greatest reluctance could he bring himself to conduct his business affairs.

But now, when his health was restored, Lorenzo del Vetro felt quite a new form of happiness, a *confident happiness*, as if all he knew about hell no longer meant anything. His fear of the practical considerations had disappeared, his paradoxical view of life was gone. His youth suddenly seemed pale and distant, and he really wondered if the illness had lurked in him from birth, been inside him like thick dark smoke from the very day he was born. He was somewhat surprised that this feeling was gone, that he now felt content and composed as he went to his daily duties, and accomplished them without doubts or fear and without being troubled by any thought of the consequences. He also wondered if this was a result of regaining his health, or if regaining his health was just the outer symptom of an inner transformation. And it surprised him that he, who prayed rarely if at all and who did not foster any particular piety, either outwardly or inwardly, but was most attracted by a skeptical philosophical pantheism, should be singled out in this way.

So aside from his many neglected business and political tasks, Lorenzo del Vetro gave the most serious attention to his promise, and devoted his energy primarily to his big new project, namely, researching how the miracle occurred. The work was headquartered in the banquet hall beneath the eyes of the Madonna, who still rested on the easel. Within a week the secretaries had dug through mountains of documents and ledgers from the years in question which could possibly have some connection with the matter. They had gathered all the papers to be found in the church of San Luca al Mare and in the palace cellar, where everything had lain strewn around loose or bound in huge bundles; stacks of letters, ledgers, and brittle individual pages gradually covered the floor in Palazzo Fili's banquet hall as the secretaries searched. Now and then the doctor or Enzio da Castelnuovo participated, and often Lord Lorenzo also sat with all the papers on into the evening. And after several days' searching, the answer was found, in the form of a yellowed letter of receipt written in a somewhat wavering, awkward calligraphy:

For executing an altar painting 9 florines
for the Honorable Luigi del Vetro's
chapel, respectfully received. Girolamo.
14 December A.D. 1450

In other words, the unknown painter, the Madonna's creator, was a certain master named Girolamo. The receipt revealed nothing about him other than this first name, except that the price had been quite high, and the name did not mean anything to Enzio da Castelnuovo when he was summoned that afternoon.

Encouraged by the find they had just made, the secretaries continued looking through the bundles of papers with the good help of Lord Lorenzo himself, and the very same evening they found a letter to Luigi del Vetro from his wife, which mentioned the altar painting commissioned from a master Bonchiodo. Girolamo Bonchiodo. Master Enzio was summoned again, even though it was late at night. Drowsy with sleep, he was shown in to Lord Lorenzo, and this time it dawned on him.

"Bonchiodo," said Master Enzio. "Bonchiodo, Bonchiodo . . . I think," he continued, and peered at the altar painting, "I think during my apprenticeship I heard about a Master Bonchiodo or Bonchiedo from Umbria, who worked up there as a church artist. Mostly in small towns."

"And?" asked Lorenzo excitedly.

"That's really all," said the painter, and yawned. "I never heard that he had done especially outstanding things. He must have died long ago."

Lord Lorenzo gave him a disappointed look.

"But I'm quite sure he had an atelier with apprentices and journeymen," the painter continued, "because in my own apprenticeship . . . wait, how was that? Yes, I'm quite sure that I met a traveling journeyman who had learned gilding with Master Bonchiodo. He was incredibly skilled at applying gilding in the old-fashioned way, but of course he didn't have much use for that."

"What was his name? Is he still alive?"

"Oh," said Master Enzio, "I have no idea if he's alive. He was quite a few years older than I . . . And what his name was?"

"Yes?"

"Oh, yes, what was his name? I met him in Florence, that's certain. But his name?" Enzio da Castelnuovo stood pondering this a long time, looked at the Madonna. "No," he said regretfully. "That was almost fifteen years ago, Lord Lorenzo, and I don't think I met him more than a couple of times, together with other artisans in festive moods. As far as I remember, he was rather rustic and dull. Not a person to talk with. I'm sorry."

Lord Lorenzo looked at the painter with disappointment.

"But," continued Master Enzio shrewdly, "since Your Lordship has offered such a generous reward to the person who can find the answer to the mystery, I will, of course, do my utmost to satisfy Your Lordship, and will ransack my poor memory day and night. And now it is night. Good night." He yawned.

With great dissatisfaction, Lord Lorenzo let the painter leave.

For seven days and seven nights nothing was heard from Master Enzio. Several times Lord Lorenzo was on the point of sending for him again, but restrained himself. The grass doesn't grow faster if one tugs at it. Besides, he had heard that the painter had left on one of his solitary trips away from the city. So Lord Lorenzo turned his attention to other things, and to his work. But he was frequently distracted by the thought of the painting, and went into the hall where the Madonna was. Often he would stand looking at her, feeling his smooth healthy skin with his hand. Now that the blisters were gone, he couldn't seem to remember how they had felt. He tried to call to mind the itching, burning sensation over his whole body, and the disgusting feeling of uncleanness, of poisoning, the feeling that he had a monster inside him that let its venom seep through sore, oozing openings in his body. But he was unable to recall the feeling. Instead he tried to remember the feeling that had gone through him the night he had stood before the altar in San Luca al Mare and looked at the painting, but that wasn't really possible either, because he had been tired and intoxicated. But he remembered very well the feeling he'd had the next morning, a feeling of having slept unusually well. He remembered going over to the window in the morning, and how the light had streamed toward him like a breeze. He looked at the painting of his Madonna. You're mine now. You're mine. You've always been mine, without my knowing it. And I'm going to probe you. I'm going to discover your secret.

Did she have a secret? She sat there on the easel, humbly, her face expressionless, essentially a rural Madonna, with a faint echo of Giotto, simple, proper, and pious. A piece of wood, plaster, and color. Every evening Lorenzo del Vetro stood before his Madonna and looked at her, uncomprehendingly. He did not like the painting, still did not, he would never like it, but he had to go to look at it every evening and every morning. He often thought about the many beautiful paintings he had seen, especially in his native city, which his inner eye could still recall and describe in detail—color, form, motif, composition; yet after having looked at the Madonna nearly a hundred times, often for half an hour at a time, he still could not picture the Madonna in his mind, not her face, not the details. Other than perhaps something about the colors, the gold, the orange fruit, the blue cape. That was strange. It was as if she did not want to reveal it. And often he had to hurry back into the hall to remind himself what she looked like. You're mine, and your secret is mine. I'll wait here until you speak. Now and then, when he had looked at the painting for a long time, so long that the contours began to be erased, he sometimes got the feeling that she was just about to say something. But the feeling always slipped away as soon as he tried to focus his attention on it.

Seven days went by in this way. But on the seventh day, Enzio da Castelnuovo returned from his wanderings and requested a meeting with Lorenzo del Vetro. Lorenzo awaited him impatiently.

"Well," he said, without even greeting him, "I sincerely hope you bring good news, master."

"Esteemed Lord Lorenzo," said the painter with a smile, "I left the city and my work because the weather is beginning to get very warm, and I thought a trip up into the mountains—"

"Get to the point!"

But the painter smiled secretively.

"It pains me greatly," he said, "that Your Lordship Lorenzo won't let me tell him about the many happy and interesting things I experienced on my wanderings, and the girls I met in each village and lay with to my great pleasure. But let me at least tell you that it helped to leave the city, which is beginning to be unbearably hot now—because as soon as I came up into the fresh air, the very first day, the name seemed to appear."

Lord Lorenzo looked at him in dismay.

"And you didn't return immediately?"

"No, no, not the name itself. But the shadow of it," explained the painter, "merely the contours. Up there in the silence I began to think back on the happy days of my youth, and on details from my experiences, things I haven't recalled for many years, people I've scarcely given a thought to, and I began to see him more clearly in my mind, the gilder that is. Began to see him as he sat beside me, wine cup in hand, that time many years ago. It's true he was boorish and a little dull. It's also true that he didn't say anything especially memorable. But he told me about his apprenticeship with this Master Bonchiodo or Bonchiedo. I think the fellow called his master Bonchiedo, and he said that his master was the only one who still taught gilding in the old-fashioned way. I took note that this journeyman possessed such knowledge because, after all, it could be that despite everything one might need a large gilding task done sometime. But the name? I could dimly perceive its contours as I walked, more than I could see the journeyman's face in my mind, because there was something unusual about this name, it was quite an odd name, as far as I could remember. Four syllables."

"Get to the point," said Lord Lorenzo impatiently, but Enzio da Castelnuovo continued pleasantly undisturbed.

"Four syllables which positively leaped across the tongue. That was the first thing I remembered. Gradually I began to hear the ring of the vowels. And then I remembered it, one evening when I was having an especially good time in a tavern: Bassofondo. It hit me while the fiddler was playing and I was dancing with a little—"

"That was his *name*?" asked Lord Lorenzo incredulously.

"Yes, Your Lordship, that was his name, and moreover, it fit his ordinary, rustic manner. Otherwise I would never have remembered it so long afterward. And we should be happy about that, because this country is swarming with painters, and many are namesakes, so if he is still alive, it should at least be *possible* to track down a man with such a name. His first name was Giuseppe, of course. What else, for a peasant like him?"

"Bassofondo," repeated Lord Lorenzo. Then he called for Rizzoli, his secretary.

EIGHT

We will not weary ourselves with descriptions of the months that followed. We will not relate in detail the tremendous effort that Lorenzo del Vetro made to find the simple journeyman Bassofondo, if he was still among the living, since we all know how terribly difficult it can be to find anything at all. For example, keys. But sometimes it can pay to have contacts. Every banker and merchant who served the del Vetro house was now mobilized and asked to search constantly for information about Bassofondo. Every business connection in every city, every spy, every least usurer—in brief, we will not tire the reader; we will not bore anyone and we will not go into detail about this. Just remember that it is often easier to find a nameless person one does not know, than a person one knows by all names. Even several months later, stories were still arriving at Palazzo Fili in Rome, but only about the general living conditions of Master Girolamo from the mountains, who had died more than thirty years ago. One was told what one already knew, that his work had been simple and rustic, that he had worked just a short time in Rome, and that he died unmarried and childless. Beyond this, it seemed as if this unknown master was almost invisible and had lived without scarcely leaving a trace. There was no news about his journeyman.

At the palace, Lorenzo del Vetro's recovery lasted, his skin remained clear and without scabs, and his interests now gradually turned more and more toward other things. Among them, that Master Enzio's pietà was completed and brought both the artist and the donor great renown. Lorenzo moved his Madonna to a less frequented room than the banquet hall, to a chamber next to his bedroom. But he still went in regularly to ponder over her.

A river flows slowly and yet it flows constantly, and it moves its stones slowly and yet the mountain is on its way toward the sea. And thus, slowly, the experience of the wondrous Virgin and the miracle that had befallen Lord Lorenzo glided out of his immediate thinking and became a memory for him. He thought about it, but not every day any longer, and not with the same inquisitive fervor. When he looked at her now, it was as if she were sleeping. And he could not understand what this painting had to do with him. He looked at her with impatience, and it no longer seemed that she had something to tell him. But he *knew* that she did, so he resolutely went and looked at her whenever he had time, but nothing ever happened.

The months went by and became a whole year, winter came and then spring, and the war flared up again, and significant events were brewing in Lorenzo del Vetro's native city.

Fiorello, who had regained his health without divine intervention, again stood at his master's side morning and evening, but Lord Lorenzo did not really need him as before, when he was suffering from his illness. Fiorello still sang for him, and read aloud, albeit more rarely. For there were many things in the city and in the world that demanded his master's attention now that he was completely healthy. Just as a caterpillar is transformed into a butterfly by changing into a chrysalis, so the years of illness had transformed the melancholy, delicate young Lord Lorenzo into a robust adult man with sharpened senses and a healthy appetite for worldly life.

The girl Simonetta was dismissed from service that winter; perhaps Lord Lorenzo had tired of her, perhaps she had displeased him. She was gone, like all the others. Fiorello stood at his master's side and thought about her now and then, but in any case he hadn't seen much of her after he got well. He had a long scar on his foot, where the doctor had cut out the infection with a knife, and where she had applied compresses. When the weather was cold, the scar became red and tender. No, he hadn't seen much of her after he got well—in the corridors and in the kitchen now and then; she had smiled at him a little, and hurried on. He didn't think about her much, actually he didn't think much. He stood there, handed his master clothes and comb and cup and book, pulled off his boots and put on his boots, held his horse for him, pulled off his boots, handed him clothes and gloves; he stood there. He stood there and noticed that some of the fever mood had remained, the same numb feeling of being strangely distant from everything. Or perhaps it was something else. It was too bad that he had never thanked Simonetta properly. He had looked at her while she cared for him, the brown hair, the reflective ridge of her nose; he hadn't told her anything about himself, nor had he asked her who she was or where she came from, and she hadn't said anything of her own accord. Had she said anything at all? Had they talked? And now she was gone, like all the others, and he could hardly remember her anymore, and couldn't recall her face. He had seen her just once since, on the street, outside the palace. But he couldn't see her face in his mind. Just something about her nose and her hair. He stood there, and he read aloud, and he was completely well again, but still a little numb; it was only that the scar was painful now and then. And the winter never ended, but then it ended and the war flared up again, and then early one morning a letter comes to Lord Lorenzo. He is sitting in his office busy with a hundred things, and Fiorello is standing absentmindedly in his corner—nowadays he often stands in his corner absentmindedly, and that displeases his master, Fiorello has noticed that; Lord Lorenzo greatly dislikes having to say the same thing twice, so he really must pull himself together—he stands there, outside everything, this morning, and Lord Lorenzo says something, twice.

"Fiorello! Don't you hear what I'm saying!"

"I'm sorry, Your Lordship." He pulls himself together, seeks desperately for words: "I'm sorry," he merely says.

"Sorry!"

Fiorello manages to produce a smile.

"It's due to," he begins, "my wicked wits, which winter's witches witness in a winter trance."

Lorenzo del Vetro grunts, half satisfied with the poor witticism. Fiorello isn't particularly satisfied with his attempt either, but his master is occupied with something else. He says: "A letter has arrived, Fiorello."

"A love letter, dare one hope, Your Lordship?"

"No, you fool. It's a letter from one of our agents in Padua."

Fiorello is about to create a new witticism, but his master's voice is very quiet, so he restrains himself.

"And I'd almost given up the whole thing."

"Yes, Your Lordship?"

"He's in Padua."

"The agent, Your Lordship?"

"Yes, the agent too, my little friend, thank God. Listen to what he writes. Let's see. Here it is: 'So in its brotherly goodness, the local painters' guild had mercy on the above-mentioned Bassofondo, who is an old man now, and provided for his care with a widow, Signora Bisi, who earns a living by taking paupers into her home.' Let's see . . . 'I hereby report that the said Bassofondo is alive, but often poorly, due to his advanced age . . . not always completely of sound mind, his brain is worm-eaten . . . he does not always remember his own name, and was therefore difficult to track down . . .' Fiorello!"

"Yes, Your Lordship."

"Call Enzio da Castelnuovo. He must go immediately to Padua and talk with the old man. He's exactly the right person to do it."

"Your Lordship, may I remind you: he is not in the city, he has a commission in Naples."

"Ooh. That's true."

"You can send him a letter, Your Lordship."

"No," said Lorenzo del Vetro eagerly, "we have no time to lose. Who can we send instead? The doctor? No. Too little imagination. Verduccio? Out of the question. Rizzoli? No, he's the only one here in the palace who can count. We must go ourselves."

"We, Your Lordship?"

"Yes. We must travel north, leaving tomorrow morning."

"Your Lordship, there's a war."

"Yes," said Lorenzo del Vetro.

"You can't travel, Your Lordship. It's dangerous for you. You're a well-known, wealthy man, and an enemy of the current administration in Florence. You could be taken hostage on the way."

Lorenzo del Vetro gives him a long, pondering look.

"You're right," he says with disappointment. "We must send a letter to Master Enzio."

"Yes, Your Lordship. Shall I ask the secretary to come?"

"Yes. Yes. Do that. Hurry." He rises, goes to the window, looks out at the morning sunlight absentmindedly. Fiorello runs off. But when he comes back with the secretary in tow, Lord Lorenzo has turned around toward the room again. He has raised his forearms halfway and appears decisive and elated.

"I've changed my mind," he says. "You will go, Fiorello."

Fiorello looks at him wide-eyed.

"I, Your Lordship?"

"Yes, Fiorello. It will take too long for a letter to reach Master Enzio, and perhaps it's impossible for him to leave his present responsibilities just like that. Besides, it would take him nearly twice as long to travel north to Padua as it would take from here. So you will go. You'll have an armed escort, of course, so no harm will befall you. And you'll take the direct road to Padua. You leave tomorrow morning." Fiorello turns pale.

"Very well, Your Lordship."

"Don't be so sad! You're my most faithful servant, and one of the chosen few who know the truth of the whole story. Besides, it's time that you do other, more important, tasks for me, rather than just hanging around here all day. That's not good for you. You're no longer a boy now, Fiorello. You've become cross and sullen and impertinent."

"I'm sorry, Your Lordship."

"There you go again! But this is no punishment, Fiorello, it's an extremely important task. It's very important to me that it's done as carefully and precisely as possible, and it can only be done by someone I trust fully and completely."

"Thank you, Your Lordship."

"You must find the home of Signora Bisi, and find this Bassofondo, and if possible get him to tell you everything he can about the altar painting's creation—if he can remember anything about that."

"Yes, Your Lordship."

"Use every means. Art of persuasion, charm, thoughtfulness. Food. Drink. He's probably too old for women. But money. Money hits home for those who will die soon. That's as true for paupers as for popes. I'll write a blank remittance for you, which you can cash with our agent in Padua."

"Yes, Your Lordship. Thank you, Your Lordship."

"Don't be so dispirited, I said. Haven't you had a good life here in my house? Haven't I always treated you well?"

"Yes, Your Lordship. You've always treated me well. Very well. I'm grateful, Your Lordship. This just came so suddenly."

"All right, Fiorello. Take comfort. If you're successful, you'll be richly rewarded, more richly than you could ever imagine; I promised that once, and I keep my promises."

"Yes, Your Lordship."

"I want to know everything."

"I'll do my utmost, Your Lordship."

Before sunrise the next morning Fiorello rode out of the city accompanied by five guards. The guards were already mounted on their horses when Lorenzo del Vetro went down into the courtyard with Fiorello. The guards greeted them dully with early morning surliness, unhappy to leave the city's safety to travel north in days like these. Lord Lorenzo gave them a worried look, nodded to each of them.

"Don't be afraid," he said. But Fiorello, who had been wide awake the whole night, was in an unusual mood this morning. Yesterday, when Lord Lorenzo assigned him the task, he had been frightened out of his wits, but the night had been so strange. He had packed his satchel, prepared his clothes, and polished his boots. Then for a long time he had sat on the edge of his bed. Outside the little window the city night was black as a mine, but the room glowed with a sort of half-light, even though he hadn't lit a lamp. He felt empty and unencumbered. He couldn't sleep, because he kept thinking that dawn would soon come, and he would ride out of the city.

"Lord Lorenzo," he said quietly, and smiled. "When have I ever been afraid?" Perhaps he had never smiled that way at his master before, because Lorenzo gave him an observant, slightly surprised look, as if he did not really recognize his faithful servant.

"Be careful," he said. "Ride straight ahead, take the direct road to Bologna. Don't look to either the right or the left."

Fiorello kept smiling.

Lorenzo del Vetro embraced his servant, helped him mount his horse, and the company rode through the Palazzo Fili gate and disappeared; the gate closed behind them, and Lord Lorenzo was left behind in the deep courtyard. He was completely alone. He stood there for a while before he went up to his quarters.

Then months go by.

Every day Lorenzo del Vetro went to the Madonna in the morning, immediately after he got up. Every morning he stood alone with her, and nothing happened. She was silent, and it was silent within him. Then he left the room and began his daily tasks.

No news arrived from Fiorello, but the accounts of the war gave reason for uneasiness. After two months of waiting, Lorenzo del Vetro sent a letter to his agent in Padua, but received no reply. He sent more letters, without result. Each day the world outside Palazzo Fili's walls was as silent as the Virgin in the painting, and the weeks went by.

In Florence, the monk Savonarola was first hanged and then burned on the 23rd of May. Lorenzo del Vetro was awakened at dawn one morning by his secretary, who told him the news with excited gestures and elation in his voice.

Lorenzo looked at him, thanked him for his good tidings, and sent him away. He sat in bed thinking about the secretary's report, and felt vaguely surprised that he wasn't particularly elated. And since he could no longer sleep, he got up and wandered into the adjoining room to look at the altar painting. It was still before sunrise.

At first everything was the same as always. But when he had looked at the painting for a while, he noticed that something was different, and strange, this morning.

The Madonna *looked* at him. She was awake. She suddenly gave him a look that was completely alive. It lasted only a few seconds, but he could see that it was an ancient look. And at the same time it seemed young. Not smiling, not serious, but young and old. And she *looked*—first at him, but then she moved her eyes, as if making a suggestion, toward the window where the light entered. And Lorenzo del Vetro followed the suggestion, shifted his gaze away from her—even though he knew that he would never again see her *see*. He knew the experience was over the moment he shifted his glance. Nevertheless, he looked away from her, obedient, solemn, almost happy.

Lorenzo del Vetro looked at the oblique beams of light that fell into the room, then turned his entire attention to the sunrise and the increasing light in the eastern sky; the sun itself was still hidden from his view by buildings and walls. He seemed to hear a musical tone from the east, yet somewhere inside him; a loud triumphant *Do!* Apollo is coming, he thought. The sun god is advancing in his triumphal golden chariot; immense, invincible. Gold, he thought, is a quality of the light itself. And suddenly the two things blended together in him—the painting with its intense gold priming and halos, and the invincible increasing gold out there in the east, behind the sunlight itself; after all, it was the same light, just inner and outer, two sides of *the same light*! And suddenly he understood what the artist behind the altar painting really had tried to paint.

He gazed again toward the approaching day; he seemed to sense music for a few more minutes, then the sun had risen high enough, the angle of the rays became less acute, the light whiter, and the day had begun.

When he turned his eyes toward the Madonna again, everything was as it had always been; the look was gone, the eyes were just simple lines, and she no longer saw him.

It took him awhile to pull himself together. The monk is dead, he thought absentmindedly. Much is going to happen.

He left the room and shut the door behind him. And here ends the tale of Lorenzo of the house of del Vetro.

But *we* must continue, we must not lose sight of *our* story, above all we must not lose sight of Fiorello, as he departs on his incredible task. But where is he, after all these months? What has happened to him? We float above the fields, through the landscape, up into Tuscany with spring-green hills and small villages, along the white road, past battle scenes and army units, but where is Fiorello? We will find him, if only we find someone to travel with, for this is dangerous territory; it would be good to go with someone who can take care of us.

There, for example, a small traveling theater group is journeying in the direction of Milan. It's perhaps nothing to brag about as far as companions go, but it's a brave little band of charlatans, *giuliari*, three small wagons; they travel rapidly and only during daylight, men sit on either side of the driver keeping a fearful watch for lansequenets and buccaneers. They are a brave little band indeed, but what shall a poor troupe of artists of illusion do in a time of war that never ends, except travel around as usual and try to earn a living, be on guard, and hope and believe that the next town will open the gates for them? For the Devil is loose in Tuscany; during these years the Devil does his work everywhere he gets a chance, and now he gets a chance everywhere; and not only in the souls of warriors and the hearts of lansequenets, no, even among the scholars, priests, and artists, as well as among the simplest of the simple he finds material for his work. So let us land in one of the charlatans' wagons. There, under the canvas, two young women, scarcely more than girls, one blond and one brunette, are dozing to the rhythm of the wagon; the blonde has her head in the brunette's lap.

But isn't there a man sitting beside them? A well-dressed but conservatively attired man, with books and manuscripts in his satchel, a wandering humanist. Haven't we seen him before? Ah yes, it's the Devil. It's the Devil sitting beside them, and in this warm midmorning hour it's easy to play with those two; suddenly the brunette kisses the blond head in her lap, she awakens. Then they kiss each other, tentatively at first, then passionately, and their dark traveling companion looks on with satisfaction; in reality all three of them are very satisfied. He has been successful; we suspect from his expression that these kisses will mean the ruin of the theater company; because of their newly discovered passions they will plunge themselves and their husbands and all of them into disaster, all because of a little kiss in the shadows under the canvas in a jolting wagon, ah yes, but they just don't know it yet. For the time being they are busy with lips and loins and the wagon's rhythm, careful and tentative; later they lie in each other's lap but in a new way, like Iphis and Ianthe.

"Quid ad haec, Hymenae, venitis sacra, quibus qui ducat abest, ubi nubimus ambae?" quotes their invisible traveling companion contentedly. Then he looks at them, a little uncertain whether they will figure things out: "Mediis sitiemus in undis?" quotes the learned humanist again, half questioningly, but sees there is no reason to worry; pink with blushes, they have found a way to quench their new thirst at once. Then he looks at us.

"Today's women," he declares, "are wiser than those of earlier times, at least if we are to believe written sources from antiquity which have recently have come to light in this marvelous part of the world, to the great detriment of human beings—and to the great assistance of yours truly. Look! Sinnt sie nit schön? Gar holde und gefälliglich!" He obviously falls back into his native tongue when he is really pleased with something. Now he rises halfway, unfolds his cape, prepares to leave the two who are licking each other more and more eagerly there on the bottom of the wagon; between soft billowing loins only curly damp locks of hair are seen, and pleasant half-choked sounds of gaiety whirl in the warm air like birdsong.

"Excuse us," we say, "verzeihet, gnädiger Herr, aber gehet Ihr schön?"

"Ah yes," he says, "I must be on my way at once, everything is already accomplished here, and I've done my part. For that matter, I speak not only mitteldeutsch but almost all European languages."

"But what else is going to happen? Surely they could have discovered this themselves, all on their own and without your intervention?"

"Oh," he says, "you're quite right; it wouldn't have mattered, but they're married—if conjugal life of this sort can be called that—each to her own actor in the troupe; the two sitting with the drivers outside keeping watch—whoops!" One of the women, the blonde, has begun trembling violently, and the cart floor becomes cramped.

"Those two boorish husbands sit out there sensing only peace and lack of danger, Giovanni and Lotto. Giovanni is married to Mona, the blonde, Lotto to Laura, the brunette; however, Lotto also suffers from gonorrhea, the great new scourge of today, and when the blonde, Giovanni's jewel and the love of his life—whoops!" The two have risen to a sitting position, spread their legs, scissor softly toward each other, rustling like silk. "—when Giovanni discovers that the blonde, his Mona, has also contracted this sad illness, after a number of further cicadalike activities of the same sort in the next ten or eleven towns the troupe visits, and moreover *knows* that Lotto is the only carrier of the disease in the troupe, then everything goes to pieces, as you can imagine. Despite his profession, Giovanni doesn't have the fantasy to imagine that *those* two—" He points to the blonde and the brunette. "And *then*, you see—no, really now, that's going too far!" He gives the two pulsing cicadas an irritated glance, folds up his cape, leaves the wagon, and with an airy elegant leap lands at the edge of the road. We follow him, wander a little way along the road with him. "—*then*, you see, then it ends with a *murder*. Giovanni smashes Lotto's skull one wet evening and is hanged in Verona, the other members of the troupe take sides for one or the other, the troupe breaks up, Mona goes to ruin as a prostitute in Venice, and the brunette, Laura, commits suicide by swallowing quicksilver, a beautiful symbolic gesture, to die of a sort of dew like the one she is drinking at this moment; *kurz*—" he flips his hand, elegantly, as if all this were the least of his arts. "My, how time flies. I must be on my way."

And since the Devil is in our region now, and we are all going north this splendid spring day, and furthermore, the Devil seems to be a more locally acquainted guide, with extensive authority, we suggest to our wandering humanist that perhaps we should travel together.

"I don't mind if we do," says our learned friend politely, "but I travel swiftly, ladies and gentlemen."

"That suits us just fine, Messer—yes, what should we call you while we are traveling companions?"

"Oh, that doesn't much matter. Bembo, for example, how would that be?"

"Anyway, Messer Bembo, we're used to traveling swiftly, like the flight of a bird!"

"I see. Well then, fine!"

And see, we are pulled away at once from the poor theater company and its approaching misfortunes, where they fear lansequenets and bandits, while the happy sounds of genuine Tuscany pleasures can still be heard from the wagon; we travel north, pass many travelers, pass troops of soldiers, an ambush, a murder, a besieged city, but Messer Bembo does not stop to rest or practice his handiwork anywhere. Fiorello is nowhere to be seen either. After a while we overtake a dappled brown horse on the road to Siena. Two boys are sitting on it, a little younger than our Fiorello, thirteen or fourteen years old, slim and handsome, with long curls, dressed in the Florentine manner, a young nobleman and his page of nearly the same age; the older boy carries an important letter; they sit close to each other in the saddle, ride calmly through the early summer day, the younger boy, who is sitting behind, leans gracefully toward the boy in front, a picture of beauty and peace. And right here, precisely here, Messer Bembo gets the confounded notion he wants to make a stop, and is there anything we can do about that?

"Look now," he says, "this might be interesting to you." He lands easily and seats himself sideways on the horse's rump, whispers something in their small ears, and immediately they begin to rub against each other as if they have an itch; the younger boy grasps the older one in the groin, the older boy turns around in surprise and looks into the freckled face shining with joy, he digs his spurs into the horse so they can cross the river and there, among the shadowy trees at the river's edge, do it together. And we, we already know from Messer Bembo's naïvely contented expression that this will be their ruin; our humanist's method of operating begins to seem monotonous to us, and not very spectacular; the Devil has no sooner sent them in among the bushes than, confound it all, he wants to take off through the air again; he has done his deed with those two on horseback. But now we're annoyed, now we want to stay and see the consequences.

"Ugh," says the Devil, "so boring. Is that really necessary? Oh very well, if you absolutely must, all right."

And no sooner has the younger of the two come so far that he has begun to suck the other—and he does it very properly, because he has a sister who, although she is only one year older, already has shown him in the most gripping way how it's done, for she often does this and much more with their master—the nobleman's father—as well as with the bishop in the little town where the two of them are servants. She has even learned the Venetian mouthful that quenches every thirst in the shortest time, which happens now too; but then the fateful thing occurs: the older boy has already learned a little about such things from his friends and so forth in abacus school, as well as from some servant girls of his own age, among them the younger boy's aforementioned sister, so for that matter he should be able to control himself for the moment, even if he is young, but now, thanks to Messer Bembo's malediction while they were on horseback, he is suddenly in love! ("Ille etiam Thracum populis fuir auctor amorem in teneros transferre mares citraque iuventam," quotes our traveling companion at this point, and yawns with boredom.) In love! Alas for him, he has forgotten his important task, has forgotten the important letter that his father the prince sent with him; soon the younger boy has sucked him completely stiff and happy again, and he takes the boy, the little page whimpers, for this is quite different than with his sister—still, he valiantly puts up with his predicament, thrusts against his master as best he can, for he too is in love, oh he loves his friend and master, he has him inside, in his mouth and stomach, the mere thought makes him come, despite the painful soreness—then suddenly the dark boots stand beside them, the Swiss lansequenets. The two in the grass have not noticed them, and it is too late; there are many of them, the boys cannot escape, the big, blood-rutting soldiers roar at the sight of the two youngsters and draw their knives simply for the fun of it. ("Now," mumbles the Devil, "follow me. Ego sum tibi funeris auctor.") Good advice is expensive, but the youngest boy begins to plead for his life as he points an accusing index finger at his traveling companion, who grows pale. "He forced me," says the young page in a thin voice, and lowers his eyes.

"Filthy Italians," says one Swiss with disdain, and slits the older boy's throat with no further ado ("Ecce cruor, qui fusus humo signaverat herbas," quotes Messer Bembo); he bleeds to death, the whole time looking at the younger boy, he looks and looks, but the younger boy turns his eyes away, throws himself gratefully at his saviors' feet, smiles devotedly while the other dies without a word.

"Ipse suos gemitus foliis inscribit et AI AI flos habet inscriptum, funestaque littera ducta est," says Messer Bembo, quite moved, as he takes off his hat. (Aren't all his scholastic ways beginning to seem a little hollow?) "Now in return for his life he will have the joy of satisfying the Swiss lansequenet for some months—alas for him, for the Swiss are something quite different from that slender Tuscan youth—until the Swiss gives him as repayment of a debt to a Spaniard, who sells him to a Saracen, who sells him to a Croat mercenary, and so forth for a few more painful months, until finally he too mercifully gets his throat cut when the troops suddenly have to withdraw to the north and leave all their belongings behind, but damn it, you surely don't have to see *all* this," says Messer Bembo irritably, as we leave the forest grove and tread on air again, commend ourselves to Zephyr. "Both boys lose their eternal salvation, of course. In the case of the younger, no explanation should be necessary, but the older has forfeited his salvation too, because his satchel held the letter of safe conduct and the bank remittance that would have saved his father's city, the home of both youths, from the inevitable *sacco*—from plundering—if only the letter had been delivered to the advancing condottiere in time. Instead, he forgot his duty for a moment of scratching; it cost many lives, his father's and mother's and sister's and twenty-seven others', to say nothing of all the material damage, which amounts to thousands of florins, good God, yes. You see—"

"Tell us, is that the only sort of thing you busy yourself with, Messer Bembo?" we ask accusingly.

"What else should keep me busy? Everything else goes so well without my intervention. All the big things. Everyone manages perfectly well on their own. I simply go into the details. The details."

"Yes, we've heard who is in the details."

"Shame on you. One can't edit reality. Well. Look there. At it again." There in a haystack lie a girl and a boy, sleeping close to each other, even though it's late in the day, and at the sight of them the Devil rubs his hands so hard they smell scorched. And we are about to leave this tiresome Messer Bembo, for now he is probably yet once again about to go into details with the two poor people lying asleep in the hay, and it's just too stupid, all of it, who ever heard of such a narrow existence. But then we see that it's Fiorello! Fiorello, in a haystack, far from people and definitely not in Padua, where he should have been long ago! And what has happened to the guards? And who is lying beside him as he lies there snoring?

"Look now," says Messer Bembo with satisfaction, and rubs his hands again, but a little less eagerly this time, only a faint odor of brimstone rises from his fingers as he nears the two sleepers.

"Can't you let them be, esteemed Messer Bembo?"

"Shh," he says. "Now, just look."

The lone horse grazing so peacefully next to the sleepers whinnies uneasily when we approach. But now we've had enough, seriously, this will not do. One tousled head moves in the hay, leans over the sleeping figure.

"What are you doing to me?" whispers the half-asleep boy, as the girl begins kissing him, and the dream he dreamed becomes mouth and moisture.

But now we want an explanation from our traveling companion, for what in the world is the faithful servant Fiorello doing here, in a haystack, together with—

"Yes," nods Messer Bembo meaningfully, "it *is* Simonetta. Wouldn't you know, she followed him, like a second shadow, when he left Palazzo Fili. Stood behind a house corner, waited, and then followed him."

"Surely she didn't run the whole way?"

"Oh no," says our learned traveling companion, "of course not. He lifted her onto the pommel as soon as they got outside the city wall. She suddenly stood in the road ahead of him, simply looked at him, they exchanged a few words, and he took her with him, just like that."

"And the guards?"

"Ah yes, they laughed and found it all very amusing, of course, and sang many droll songs."

"No—not that. Where *are* they?"

"Loyalty," begins Lucifer, "loyalty in these days is a rare and precious commodity on a par with pepper from Malabar, indeed even more precious, for it is rarely enjoyed at aristocrats' tables and even more rarely by a campfire at night in wartime."

"Get to the point."

"My goodness, look!" says Messer Bembo, and points toward the two in the hay. "Look how grown up they are now." But we refuse to be diverted any longer now, we're imperturbable.

"So you mean to say that the guards ran away?"

"No," says Messer Bembo crossly, "these two wisps of hay ran away from *them*, before it was too late. Otherwise they would both have been lying in a ditch long ago with their throats slashed, or something even worse would have befallen them. Robbed of money and chastity; but then, as far as the latter goes, they seem to have stolen sufficiently from each other. The girl heard the guards laying sinister plans by the campfire when they thought the young people were asleep, so she warned the boy, and they stole away with the horse that same night and rode as fast and as far as they could in the opposite direction. As a matter of fact, she saved his life once before too, though I can't imagine why. They wandered aimlessly, and then the war got in the way, one could say, so they had to stay in the mountains and away from all roads for a long time, and here they are

410

now—penniless, hungry, ragged, and lost, but completely alive and in good condition. Just look how they're eating."

"No, no, Professor Bembo, we don't *want* to see, we *don't want to*; we want to go to Padua immediately. And those two in the hay must go there too. It can't end *here*. That's out of the question. *Padua*. Do you hear?"

"Nothing is easier, you'll be there hux flux if you wish; but I'm afraid those two buttercups have to travel at an ordinary speed. But honestly, wouldn't you rather leave them alone and fly somewhere else? To Ceylon in 1939, for example, or to Copenhagen in the sixteenth century, or to a beautiful island in the Baltic in—"

"We want to go to Padua."

"What the—well, well. But those two have to ride at an ordinary pace. And you'll have to wait for them in Padua, and that may take some weeks yet. What will you do in that dull, miserable city in the meantime?"

"That's our concern."

"Well," he sighs, "Padua it will be." He emits a blue spark, and as we speed northward, light as a breeze, we see Fiorello open his eyes, look at Simonetta, rise halfway, smile a little, and the reflection of the hay is golden on their faces.

NINE

The old man laughed, a hoarse cackling laughter that echoed from the cellar's vaulted ceiling.

"Well, well," he said, "well, well. That was a tremendous flood of words. But I don't remember any of all that. I don't even remember who I am, I've become blind, I only want to die."

But the boy said: "Signora Bisi confirmed that you are Giuseppe Bassofondo."

"Does she say that? Well, well. As far as that goes, one name can be just as good as another, and soon I'll be nameless anyway, so it doesn't matter."

"Nevertheless—"

"That was a lot to come from a youngster like you. Yes, Signora Bisi has started to give me food again the last few months, even though I'd already begun to look forward to the grave. Proper food, lentil soup and chicken soup, and not just gruel, after that businessman came here and took a look at me. She was probably afraid that I'd die earlier than planned. Look around here! And smell! Yes, the stink of old age. Fortunately, I've gotten used to it, I'm sure I smell the same myself, and after all, since I'm blind I don't have to see all the miserable old people lying around me here, ah yes—in that respect, I'm well off. Here we die on command, young sir, as soon as it suits the widow, our merciful meal-mother, especially when the annual support payments from the guild or the family begin to run out. And preferably a little earlier, so the old lady gets suitable earnings. One notices that in the end one gets only gruel, and then gradually there is less of even that, and then the grave is next, dark and deep. For you surely don't believe one goes to Paradise?"

"I have authority to—"

"Paradise, young lion. Do you believe in Paradise?"

The old man cleared his throat unpleasantly, spit into the fire.

"It's devilishly cold here," he said with a shiver. "Paradise. So, what do you believe?"

"To be honest, I haven't—" began the boy uncertainly, not really knowing what to reply.

"No, you probably haven't. Nobody believes in Paradise anymore; I don't either. But I *did* believe in it at one time, that's the difference. The difference between the young and people like me. Shall I tell you about Paradise, son?"

But the boy pulled himself together, peered around in the faint light that sifted in through the little window under the ceiling, brought a dirty horse blanket that had been tossed in a corner of the large dark cellar room where all the old people were crowded together, like animals in an ark of death, and gently wrapped the blanket around the old man's shoulders.

"So you are," he said, "the very same Giuseppe Bassofondo, journeyman painter, whom Master Enzio da Castelnuovo remembered had once been apprenticed to Master Girolamo Bonchiodo—"

"Enzio? Enzio. Yes, perhaps I've met him. An unbearable lout. Impossible to talk with. Drank and caroused and threw around all his learning. Talked only about himself. Oh, he was so talented, and he let everyone know it. You couldn't get in a sensible word. He talked and talked, and had a good time with the girls, who fell for him like leaves before a north wind. If things didn't go the way he wanted, he tore apart taverns and inns, and the next day was just as pleased as ever. Talked a blue streak. And all the others talked with him too, because he smelled of money and genius. It might pay to be in good standing with him."

"He spoke of you with great respect, Signore Giuseppe."

"Hah." The old man laughed again, weakly and maliciously. "I really can't imagine that. I think he scarcely noticed me, even less than he noticed all the little girls he devoured. I did help him a few times, that's true. But I stopped talking much with him. He didn't understand much, he was just talented and clever; talent, talent, talent. It flowed from him. No discipline. No inner strength. He could paint everything, and think everything, and so he did that. *Everything*. Instead of *one thing*. It was too easy for him. And now he's a rich and famous master painter, and I didn't even become a master, let alone famous, not to mention the monetary side of the matter, so maybe I should hold my tongue. Yes, he was the most talented of everyone. That he was."

He sat silently for a while. The boy did not say anything either.

"You want to leave," the old man began again. "I can tell that, because one notices such things when one becomes blind. You want to leave, you don't want to be here, and in my mind I can clearly see how you sit holding your nose and longing to be out in the fresh air."

"That's not true."

"Of course it's true. Your voice is thick with nausea at the old man's smell. You aren't even sitting here out of politeness, but out of some sort of strange sense of duty. You want to learn something about a story that isn't yours, and you'll send it on to your noble master—why, I don't understand, and maybe you don't understand it either, but here you sit staring blankly straight ahead and hoping the old man will say something suitable that you can write in your report and be done with it. This isn't your story, son, and it's even less mine, and still we sit here: I, well, because I can't do anything else, but you—you sit here out of duty. Hah. Don't you know that these days duty is no longer to be found, humanity is a wolf against humanity and sees enemy and friend as one and the same, simply another lonesome animal. Confound it, there are no longer any friends to be found, no enemies, no God and no Devil, no meaning and no purpose, no up and no down. Only terror and cynicism. So why are you sitting here, actually?"

"I don't know," the boy said truthfully.

"Bravo," said the old man, "at last, a sensible word from you, after all that ingratiating talk you came in here with. You don't know why you're sitting here, and I don't know why I'm sitting here, and really, does it matter? Can't you just write in the letter to your master that I've gotten soft in the head and can't carry on a conversation? Then we'll both be spared this story that doesn't concern us, and then I can die, after having been given a little extra soup during the months I was waiting for you. The soup wasn't *that* good, actually. It's strange, though, how I regained my appetite for life as soon as I started to eat, and lost it again as soon as I had eaten quite a bit."

"I have instructions to offer you all the gifts and goods you might wish for yourself in your old age—"

"Hah," said the old man. "Wish. Ah yes."

They sat for a while in silence. All of a sudden, from a bundle on one of the bunks along the wall, came a loud, terrible rattling in someone's throat that abruptly died in wheezing, mucous gurgling.

"Listen," said the old man. "He's at it again now. He's dying, you see. Every afternoon about five o'clock. He's done that for three years now. Every single day. A true angel's song."

"Wouldn't it be better for you if I found you lodgings with a more kindhearted hostess—"

"There is no such woman. It would be better for me if you went over to the bellows and cut his throat, once and for all."

"That can be done," said the boy quietly.

"That can be done." The old man spit the words out with disdain. "How brave you are, little boy. Duty before everything. And to stab an old windbag like him, that would certainly be a heroic deed which would benefit your eternal salvation. No, you don't believe in Paradise, that's clear. You only want to get out of here."

The boy did not answer.

"*What are you doing here?*"

"*I want to go with you. I've waited for you. Take me along.*"

"*You can't come along.*"

"I can cook for all of you, and I can help you."

"We're going on an important mission. I can't take you along. You can see me when I come back to Rome."

"You'll never come back to Rome."

"Nonsense. Of course I will."

"You won't come back. I can see that. I can see such things."

"No, you can't."

"You don't know anything about me, who I am, or what I can do."

"Go now."

"You don't know where I come from. I don't even know if you care about me."

"Go now. The guards are looking at us."

"I don't think you care about me."

"Yes I do, but you must go now. We have a long way to travel."

"Why are you so afraid?"

. . .

"Why are you so afraid?"

"I'm not afraid."

"Then take me along."

"Go now. I don't remember any of that anyway. It was just an ordinary painting. It doesn't concern either you or me, or the powerful stranger who sent you."

"Yes," the boy said thoughtfully. "That's true. It doesn't concern me."

"So why don't you leave?"

The boy was quiet for some minutes, because he had traveled a long time to get here, and he had convinced himself to complete the journey.

"I'm leaving," said the boy. "I have nothing to do with this story."

"Besides, you wouldn't understand any of it, and your master wouldn't either. There's no longer anyone who knows how to paint the way my old master did. And how could they? Nothing concerns them anyway. The guilds—the brotherhoods—what's left of them? Support for the poverty-stricken. Hah. Nothing but greed. Where is the brotherhood we swear to uphold?" The old man spit again. "No, it's a strange world. We starve people to death, if we don't rob them. We fight for commissions and intrigue against our brothers. The rulers drive their subjects to starvation and death, the condottieres attack city after city, the scholars read their classic philosophers, the priests whore like snakes or ignite a brimstone glow in the pit of people's hearts. We burn people alive, we fasten them to stake and wheel, we cook them in oil, both the guilty and the innocent, but we paint lovely faces and beautiful perspectives and nicely dissected parts of corpses, and we dig pieces of marble from the ground and admire them and say: Look, how beautiful they are. So noble. So harmonious. Have you ever been at the place of execution and seen what they do?"

The boy did not reply.

"Well?"

"Sometimes. I've traveled through conquered lands to visit you today, Signore Giuseppe. I saw quite a bit."

"You saw quite a bit. Did you want to scream your terror?"

"Yes," said the boy. "I cried at night."

"Did you want to fight? Revenge the dead? Become a soldier?"

Shhh. Shhh. Don't cry. They can't do anything to us. Now, now. Don't cry. Shhh. You mustn't cry. I'm here. There, there. Don't cry. I love you. I'll never leave you. Go ahead and cry. Who are you crying like that for?

"No," said the boy curtly. "I wanted to become an artisan, like my father. Signore Giuseppe, I'm going to leave now."

"Stay a little while. What did you see?"

"We lay hidden in a forest grove and saw a troop of soldiers plunder a village. It was mostly women and children. The men were stripped naked and slaughtered by the river. The women and the children— You're right, Signore Giuseppe, I have nothing to do with this story, it doesn't concern me, I'm going to leave right now."

"Did you want to scratch out your eyes?"

"The strange thing was that it happened so quietly. The soldiers did their deed with no particular antics and the men died with little ado. Another time, in another village—it hadn't even been captured—we saw people burn twelve witches and two witch masters in just one morning. The youngest witch couldn't have been more than thirteen years old. That happened calmly too. We left that village quickly. I'm leaving now. There's someone waiting for me. I have a room." But he kept sitting.

"My master, my dead master, saw all this and even more, but he didn't scratch out his eyes, he didn't scream his terror. He painted. Not beautiful faces and not noble people. But he painted Paradise."

"You're always so quiet. And when you kiss me, it's as if you're telling me a secret. But I don't know what that secret is."

Not all craftsmanship and art can be equal, and science is probably the noblest work of all. But next to science is something which is closely related and which owes its existence to science; this art is practiced with the eye and hand and is called *painting*.

And all science, art, and craftsmanship go back to the day Adam, the first human being, was driven out of Paradise. Lucifer tempted Eve, and Eve tempted Adam, and from that moment they were aware of themselves, of their separation from the rest of the world, and of their own mortality, and could no longer stay in the splendid dream of a garden called Eden, with all its strange and beautiful fruits, flowers, and creatures. For the Lord's wrath was kindled against them, and the Lord set the cherubim with a flaming sword to guard the entrance to Paradise, so people could never find the way back again to this innocent state, but had to plow the ground themselves, watch the weather, build their houses, and spin their wool to yarn; in order to do all this, human beings need knowledge. And from this need all science has come—from this need, and from God's breath, came the little light that lived in Adam and Eve, and which continues to live on in all their sons and is called wisdom and imagination.

And so it was when Adam's first day on Earth began; he made himself a simple farm implement from a tree root, pulled it up from a field for the first time and began to plow his first shallow, uneven furrow. On this day and with this act begins the story of scientists and craftsmen. And the story of art begins here as well, because when Adam made his first furrow through the fertile soil, he discovered that here and there veins of color shone in the clay. The most glorious green, red, yellow, and white. Adam thought it was a miracle that the soil itself could have colors, and that it could be white as a cloud seemed the most remarkable of all. So he gave the colors names, the green he called green earth, the red he called red earth, and the yellow he called ochre, and they are still called this by all painters. But what he called the white, I don't know, for there are so many kinds of white in the earth that shine beautifully at first glance, but which are unusable because they are too oily or turn gray when they dry. And it's still the same as on Adam's first workday; the painter must go out into the fields and find his good colors himself, in the soil and in the rock, and grind and blend them himself, if he wants to achieve the best results on a panel or wall. And Adam scraped the colors he had named out of the veins in the soil and took them home, and smeared them on the wall in his cave; he made seven lines, one for each furrow that, with the sweat of his brow, he had made in the soil that day. And he painted the furrows with the red and brown colors. But with the green earth and ochre he drew the Garden of Eden as he remembered it, with all its trees, and with a piece of coal from the open fire he drew a square for the house he had thought of building by the field. For that is the nature of art, it can show both what is and is visible, and what is not and is invisible, along with all that will be but does not yet exist. For art requires imagination and inventiveness, in addition to a skilled hand and a sharp eye, and its task is to find new things hidden in Nature's forms, grasp them firmly and explain them in such a way that one believes what one previously did not believe existed. And therefore it has as high a status as science, which deals with everything that *is* and is visible, but art goes beyond science. If the painter wants to paint a man who is half horse, half human, he is free to do this, and likewise angels and devils and many other things we normally do not see. And in the gleam of the fire that Eve had lit, the yellow ochre in Adam's first drawing shone even more golden than in the daylight, and the green color of the treetops in Paradise almost seemed to sway in the wind when the flickering glow of the flames struck them, and with this picture Adam and Eve fell into their first sleep on Earth, and dreamed their first dreams, and they dreamed about Paradise, which still lay nearby.

"There is always silence around us wherever we go. Nothing and no one can touch us, because we are protected. We ride through barren land and see people busy at their trades. No place is home and we can sleep wherever we are. And we are

unchanging and always the same and never lose our way, but exist as long as the world endures."

But the next evening a wind came into the cave and swept the colors off the wall like dust. For that is how mankind's first pictures were, they lasted only a single night, and every day had to be painted anew, again and again. Many years passed in this way. But when Cain had killed his brother Abel and went out into the world, one day he grew hungry from wandering, and took some eggs from a partridge nest, crushed them in his hands, and ate them raw, and in the process got white and yellow on his fingers and tunic, and the colors were almost impossible to remove, except by scraping them in sand. And this was how people learned the advantages of keeping birds and of using the eggs' contents as adhesive material. For as everyone knows, the adhesive material in eggs is so strong that it can hold together heavy stone blocks of bridge foundations in torrential rivers for centuries, when all other adhesives would be washed away by the water. In Rome and Florence and Venice and other places, many of the large bridges are glued together with egg. That's how strong the egg is, the soft, fragile egg; it possesses a strange and secretive germinating power, and can transform the formless sun-yellow yoke into birds of all sorts. Regardless of which nest they are hatched in—from an eagle's egg there always comes an eagle, and from a chicken's egg always a yellow chick. The egg knows which form it carries inside. So it's not without reason that the egg is the image of the resurrection, for in the depths of the egg lives a mystery.

Maybe it was Cain, or maybe one of Cain's sons, who saw how the egg's yoke resembled the yellow sun, and got the idea of letting the yoke adhere to a painting's color substances, just as sunlight clings to Nature's colors. This, then, was how our best tempera, our best binder, came into existence. For even if there are many other temperas to be found, egg tempera is the best and finest. And until recently, when a master from Verona brought to our land this new method from the north called oil painting, egg tempera was the only good method for painting on wood panels.

In any case, this is the way Master Girolamo della Valle—who was called Bonchiodo—explained to me how the art of painting began. I was an apprentice with my good master for twelve years, from the age of ten until I reached my legal maturity. I can remember the day my father, who was a carpenter, Giuseppe was his name, took me away from my brothers and sisters and my mother to Master Girolamo, and my childhood ended. It was a warm summer day, we had a long way to travel, and Father, who was normally lively and talkative, said nothing as we trudged along the road. I realized he felt both solemn and moved because, although I was only the second-eldest son, I was the first of his four sons to go out into the world to learn an art. In my family no one had been anything other than ordinary craftsmen, so I too felt proud as we walked along. Father had no doubt long thought that whichever of his sons had the hand most suited to it would be trained as a painter, for he always let us practice drawing small sketches with pencils on unusable pieces of board, and his choice fell on me, because I was the most skillful. And he had saved money to pay a master for the apprenticeship, right from the day he married my mother. It was not a large sum, that's true, and the master was chosen accordingly, for Master Girolamo della Valle, called Bonchiodo, was not among the great masters of the day, and worked outside the large cities, without particular esteem, wealth, or fame. He was known to have a difficult temperament, had a reputation for being both stubborn and old-fashioned, although I learned to know another side of him. As such, he used only his egg tempera long after it became common to use oil as a binder; he said about oil that the smell alone was more than enough for him, and that it was hardly suited to anything other than staining wood. Perhaps he was the last to paint his pictures in the old-fashioned way, methodically and precisely, color by color, with egg on plaster, stubborn and peculiar as he was. But to me, he was a god, for he had taken pity on my father, and the miserable twelve florins my father could offer, and agreed to teach me. And the sun scorched the yellow road as we walked along it, and the crickets chirped, and my father was silent and solemn, and told me to be obedient to my new master, to regard him as a father. At the same time, my father was proud that one of his sons would now set out on the path of becoming a painter, a profession that could bring a humble artisan more honor, riches, and lasting reputation than any other work, and where the service was devoted completely to praising God and His creation, and to explaining divine figures to the common people. And if I'm not terribly mistaken, my father saw something of himself in me as we walked along; perhaps he had wanted to learn the art of painting as a young boy. On the one hand, I was proud and happy, because I felt manly and important, and for weeks had been looked up to among my friends and my brothers, who envied me my good fortune. I had gotten new clothes and, for the first time, proper shoes, and also a gleaming new leather satchel, which could be used both as a traveling bag and as a tool case. My grandfather, who was a saddle maker, had made it for me, from the best pigskin, and my greatest sorrow was that before we left I got a bad spot on it, before it had been made properly oil resistant, because I ran all over town to show it off and stumbled in the mud. I still have that satchel, because it was a good piece of work, and the spot can still be seen through the dark layers of old age which have settled on it. Now I can no longer see with my eyes. But if I touch the bag, I know that the spot can still be seen, and then I remember that day, the last day of my childhood; it doesn't disappear, but is etched into me. For as we walked, the pride and happiness gave way to sorrow and uneasiness, and my mother's weeping still echoed painfully in my ears. The satchel swung and bumped against my thighs, things rattled cheerfully inside it, but with each step I grew sadder and sadder; I was suddenly so strangely alone in the big world.

I must tell you several things about my master. He was a tall man, thin and sinewy. His face had a slightly green tint, like all the green earth he had transformed to the most marvelous skin color during his long workday. He was lonesome and lived alone like a monk. He touched no one, neither women nor men, even though the women were very attracted to him and admired his loneliness and pride. And surely my master saw their beauty, but he never went near them. Maybe he wasn't the greatest painter in the world, at least not as far as status and reputation were concerned. But in the little town where he had his atelier, he was like a god, the most important man in the place. People greeted him respectfully when he took his daily walk down the main street, on his way out into the fields. Because he took a long walk in the morning, every single day, whether he was going to gather coloring materials or not. He wore a big hat. His beard was gray when I came to him; he was already an older man then. But his hair and beard had been gray for a long time, a very long time, since he was quite young, it was said.

He almost never traveled away from the little town. It had been like that a long time, for many, many years. He lost commissions that way, since he was never present to assert himself at the palaces of princes or rich men. But he preferred his little town and the few commissions that came his way nonetheless. They were mostly fresco paintings in small churches and cloisters in the region, and an altar painting here and there. He worked very slowly and methodically. He had few apprentices—we were six or seven altogether. Several left him before their apprenticeships were over—things moved too slowly at his atelier for many young artists—but I stayed. The housekeeping was handled by his sister, an old woman named Teresa. She said very little. Now and then there was an angry outburst from her about some small thing, and then it was over. Master Girolamo was the same. When he wasn't pronouncing his doctrines, he could be silent for days. Then: a snarling outburst about some small thing, a color that cracked, a rotten egg, or about the general decadence of the times. Then just silence and birdsong. Yes, because he kept birds, songbirds. He had a large aviary, where all kinds of colorful small beings flew around. He caught them himself now and then, but usually he bought them from bird catchers he met on his wanderings, before they had choked the small delicacies. The bird catchers thought he was crazy, and gladly sold him their catch, because he was willing to pay them twice what they would have gotten at the marketplace. He often came home with a cheeping satchel. Or he picked up baby birds that had been abandoned in the nest. He cared for them himself, fed them milk and sugar and softened bread crumbs soaked in one of the glazed color dishes; he dipped the finest squirrel-hair paintbrush in the dish and fed them, endlessly patient, day after day, until they could feed themselves. He could spend hours at this. Later he put them in the aviary, where they sang and shone in the sun with all the colors of the rainbow. When the aviary grew too crowded, he let some of the birds go free; that happened quite often. And each morning, before he began working, he went in and sat with the birds and looked at the glistening colors for a long time. He called it washing his eyes. Then he was ready to begin the day's work.

Master Girolamo began my apprenticeship with these words: "Some people come to art because they are drawn to it by an elevated spirit. They come to it without training, are drawn to it because their spirit is noble in itself. From this joy arises the need for a teacher. And they become attached to him, submit to his authority, and go through an apprenticeship in order to reach perfection. Others come to art out of poverty, for the sake of the earnings. But nobility can also be awakened in them. Every morning, Giuseppe, you must put on a garment. This garment is invisible, it's like a secret cloak you wrap around you, no one can see it, but you need to feel it against your skin every single morning, because without it, you'll go to your work naked. This cloak is: love, veneration, obedience, and endurance. Do you understand?"

"Yes," I nodded, even though I didn't understand. But I remember these words because he repeated them so many times, during my years with him he often said exactly the same thing: "You must put on a garment each morning, an invisible cloak."

"And now you'll be allowed to draw," said my master. "That's what you came here for, and that's the most fun, for both children and adults. The art of painting begins with drawing, and anyone who is going to practice this art must draw regularly and copiously, and always find his deepest joy in this work. But first you need to make something to draw on." He took out a boxwood panel, twenty-three centimeters square, clean and even, rubbed and polished with sepia knucklebones such as goldsmiths use when they make casts.

"First you have to grind the bone to powder." He brought out the chewed-off breast and wing bones of an old hen and put them in the fire until they became whiter than ash. Then he showed me the porphyry slab and the smaller stone I would use to grind with. "All the colors and chalk and bone you're going to use must be ground on this porphyry slab," he said. "Your fingers will often be so worn out on this stone that they will almost bleed. Greet it now, because it's yours; I give it to you as a welcoming gift. It's a good stone and you must greet it as a friend each morning, because you won't get rid of it, any more than a hunchback will get rid of his hump and therefore learns to endure it. When you're going to grind colors, you can't cheat; you have to repeat the same movement over and over, often for many hours, and you must learn to let your thoughts fly while you sit there, so you don't get impatient, but not fly too far, because you need to pay attention to what you're doing. Now you must grind these bones for two hours, until they become a fine powder." He showed me the movements. I began grinding. It's really not hard work, but it's monotonous, and wears holes in your skin and causes sore elbows, especially when you aren't used to it. After two hours' work and sore knuckles on my part, he came and looked at the powder and told me to rub for one more hour, the bone powder wasn't fine enough. An hour later he collected it, wrapped it up, took out about a bean's weight and mixed it with saliva. He spread this mash over half of the boxwood panel with his fingers and rubbed it in. Then I was allowed to try. That was how I learned to prime a panel. But I had grown tired and inattentive, and it wasn't until the next day that I was permitted to try to draw on my panel with a small stylus with a silver point. He put me in the courtyard, where there was good light, and placed an apple on the table in front of me.

"Draw," he said, and left.

I drew, and finished quickly. When he returned, he looked disapprovingly at the result, but didn't criticize me, even though I had eaten the apple.

"Do you want to draw some more, or is that enough for today?" he asked.

"More, master," I said.

"You should draw only as long as you have the desire. Just a little to begin with, but a little every day. Later you'll have more endurance."

"More," I said.

"More, more," he said. "*Less.* You must take care that you begin lightly, light as a feather, so you can scarcely see what you're starting to draw. Slowly, little by little, you make the strokes heavier. Take care that the sun always falls on your left. The sun's light, your eye, and your hand will be both rudder and coxswain for you. Then slowly go over the drawing and make the shadows stronger. And don't eat the motif afterward."

That was how he began teaching me. And that was how he taught during all the years I was with him. In the same slow, thorough way I learned all the basics of the art of painting. Grind colors, apply a lime base, stretch the canvas, brush with plaster, scrape and polish the plaster, model in plaster, apply a gold base, gild, polish, mix tempera, apply the base colors, pounce, emboss, accentuate, paint, and varnish. And I learned about wall painting, how one spatters, polishes, ornaments, smoothes, paints al fresco, and finishes al secco. Not one thing at a time, of course, but a little here and there, depending on what tasks my master needed help with in his work.

Above all, there was drawing. A little every day. When I became more skilled, I got permission to draw on paper. I learned to tint paper in a foundation color, let's say green, and that's a laborious task, because you have to grind green earth, a little ochre, and bone powder on the porphyry slab with the clearest springwater for a whole day, from sunrise to sunset, and mix it with fish lime and soften it in a clay pot with two cups of springwater for six hours. Then the mixture has to be cooked over a low fire, skimmed off, and stirred until you see that the lime is completely dissolved. Afterward you strain the mixture twice, and brush it lightly and evenly over the paper you want to color with a large soft brush, back and forth. Five coats is suitable, and the surface must dry between each coat. Often the paper becomes wrinkled or grainy, then the mixture is wrong, and you have to start from the very beginning again. Finally, you go over the paper with a penknife and remove all the granules and unevenness, and then you can draw on it. Your hand trembles the first time you draw with charcoal on paper that has taken such hard work to prepare. You take a dry willow branch and cut it into small pieces, a handsbreadth long. The pieces are shaved to points at both ends, bound together with copper threads, and placed in a clay pot that you take to the baker in the evening when he is finished with his work. You set the pot in the baking oven, with the cover on, and in the morning you have pieces of charcoal that are well charred and nicely black. You can draw on paper with them, and I remember the trembling, happy fear of not doing well with the thick, difficult piece of charcoal when I put it to the paper those first years. It was easier with pieces of lead, for you could erase that with bread crumbs. Later I learned to draw with a pen, which is even more difficult. And I learned to make tracing paper by scraping and polishing kid parchment until it becomes infinitely thin and transparent. And you can put this paper over a picture you want to copy from, in order to study details more closely.

However, we mostly drew from Nature rather than copying finished paintings, because my master insisted that this was the best method. Many of the apprentices who came and went during the years I was there were dissatisfied with this method, they wanted to learn to paint exactly the way the brilliant panels of famous painters were created. But Master Girolamo was adamant.

"Nature," he said, "is the only visible thing, and because it's visible your eye is at home there, because from the time you are an infant, your eye automatically seeks the forms creation displays around us. *See*, then, like a child, but draw like *men!*"

Many left him. But this method suited me, and he was good to me and took good care of me. I turned twelve and fourteen and sixteen years old, and I knew nothing about the world but lived protected, as if in a nest, with my master in the remote little village where he maintained his simple, disciplined existence. Yes, many left him, because they already knew other towns and had stronger heartbeats, and could not endure living like monks for long.

"You should always," my master said, "order your life not as if you were a craftsman but as if you studied theology or philosophy or other wisdom. You should eat and drink in moderation, twice a day at most. And you should choose light, nourishing foods and light wine. Protect your hand and your eye, spare them unnecessary strain. For when your hand begins to tremble like leaves in the wind, you can no longer draw, and you're finished. And the surest way to have a trembling hand and a restless heart is to spend too much time with women. Wait as patiently for the right woman as you patiently wait for your gold orpiment to be ready when you grind it between stones with glass powder; as everyone knows, one can grind this Neapolitan gold, or king's gold as it's also called, for ten years and it will continually improve the longer one grinds it. It's one of the most precious and beautiful colors, and well worth waiting for, as is the right woman, but it's dangerous to get in your mouth, because it contains arsenic and is poisonous, and in that sense resembles the kisses of many women."

He said no more. I remember this admonishment very well because one of the other, somewhat older, apprentices broke into a smile and laughed a little, because the master was probably still waiting for the right woman, which brought on one of Master Girolamo's ill-tempered outbursts; he twisted the depraved apprentice's ear and snarled something unintelligible. But then he let go abruptly, and began to explain about white lead and ink washes or something else that had nothing to do with the previous subject.

I loved my master, that's really the only thing I wanted to say with all this. The first time I succeeded in drawing the apple, and he came back and it lay uneaten on the table, he didn't praise me; he looked at the apple, looked at the drawing, looked at me. He was serious, but his eyes smiled.

"Look," he said. "That's it." He pointed at the drawing. And from that moment on, I was in his power, although it wasn't power but love. Even if he wasn't the greatest artist in the eyes of the world, he was in mine, and in my eyes he could do no wrong, but only what was right and good, and I admired him and loved to watch him paint his panels in his easy, exacting way. It was as if his hands glided, as if he always knew precisely what he wanted and what he should do. I admired his paintings and regarded them as the greatest art in the world, even though they were mostly the same, fixed motifs of saints and Bible scenes. Yet most of all, I loved to watch him when he sketched from Nature, just for a change or to teach us something. Never since then have I seen anyone sketch from life in the same way, or with such sure and unbroken strokes, as Girolamo Bonchiodo della Valle, my apprentice master. And I would have gone through fire for him. From then on, I wanted to do nothing but draw. He lived according to what he preached, piously and quietly, painted his church paintings, gathered his colors in the fields, ate and drank in moderation, and let his wild birds fly away. He always sang when he worked, hummed and sang, always the same calm, gentle craftsmen's song. And I wanted to be exactly like him, because he had become my father. Only once during these years did I leave him and the little town, and that was to attend my biological father's funeral. But my hometown had changed, or maybe it was I who had changed, because the town seemed unfamiliar and no longer had any meaning for me, and my mother and my brothers and sisters seemed like dream images; maybe they didn't fully believe I was real either when I returned as a young man. After that I was always with Master Girolamo. Though of course we went outside the village now and then. Often to draw in Nature, and a few times each year to visit churches elsewhere and to copy. But as I mentioned, he was strict about not wanting us to copy too much, and he especially didn't want us to copy too many masters, but rather to stick to one at a time, over a long period, before copying another. For, as he said, "If you allow yourself to copy one master today and another tomorrow, you'll become a dreamer and a muddle head, filled with enthusiasms that disappear with the wind, for each style will confuse your thinking. You'll try to work in one man's style today and another's tomorrow, and won't grasp either of them. But if you consistently follow one man's way, your mind would have to be very primitive to not get nourishment from that. For if you have practiced drawing from Nature long enough before you begin copying, you will acquire your own individual style, because your hand and your spirit, which are used to always picking flowers, will find it difficult to pick thorns."

But many of the apprentices were dissatisfied; they said that my teacher had no idea how people had begun to paint now in other regions and in the big cities, and that they were rotting from the roots up here in the mountains.

But I, who loved my master, fought with them and got a bloody nose and a black eye. My master came and separated us. He looked at me, and I knew he was disappointed in me, because he pulled me by the hair into the kitchen and over to the trough, and washed my face with stifled anger. I tried to explain that I'd wanted to defend him, but he would hear none of that.

"I don't want to hear such things, and especially not from you," he said. "Nobody needs to be defended here. Maybe they're right, and maybe I'm not a painter of my times but of a bygone era. In my eyes, linseed oil is an abomination that smells awful and is best suited to relieving constipation, or distilling black color, or staining. But it's no good for colors, because it's sanguine and will mix with everything and do violence to the color dish, and it will be easy to cheat, whereas before one had to plan carefully. But maybe I'm wrong. I'll do it in my way. It needs no other defense."

Then he ordered me to go out and ask the others to forgive me. But none of this could change my respect for him, it only strengthened my intention to stay with him for my entire apprenticeship, no matter what the others might think. The fact of the matter was that the previous year we— or more correctly, my master—had received a visit from a painter brother from the north, a truly foreign fellow, with skin light as a cloud and blond hair and those strange pig eyes that people in the north have; a fellow traveling south who had happened to come into our little village and had heard that a guild brother lived here. My master welcomed him hospitably and opened his home to him, as the guild rules and good manners prescribe. The stranger spoke our language quite well, and he and Master Girolamo had much to talk about—for despite his self-inflicted loneliness and isolation, my master was not uninterested in what happened out in the world, but was always eager to hear news, including news about other painters and what they had achieved.

It was this foreign man who showed us for the first time how to make tempera from oil rather than from eggs; it's a very simple process, as everyone knows, but our master had never disclosed it to us, even if he probably knew about it before. You make a little clay oven with a round hole that a clay pot fits into exactly, which keeps the flames from licking up, so you don't risk having the house or the oil catch fire; then put as much linseed oil into the pot as you need and cook half of it away. Even better in fact, cook it in the sun in a bronze pan, but this needs to be when the sun is in the sign of Leo, otherwise the temperature will scarcely be hot enough. When half the oil has cooked away, you can grind color into it in small pewter dishes and mix precisely those you want. And you can thin the mixture with clear oil as much as you wish. The foreign fellow showed us this without my master's knowledge, because he probably thought it strange that our master only taught us to paint in the old, strict, laborious way, while the whole world had adopted the new method more and more.

When my master discovered this, he wasn't angry at the foreign fellow at all, but praised him for having explained to us something he didn't know how to do himself—that was how he expressed it anyway. And it was true that the foreign master could create very finely nuanced paintings with his tempera; his pictures were completely different from everything else we had seen. Especially astonishing were the shadows and depth perception, because he could shade every color from light to dark and into a new color if he wished. Above all, the textiles portrayed in his paintings were excellent. The other apprentices eagerly grasped the new medium he had shown us, but I touched the oil reluctantly, even though today I can't understand why, since maybe I would have become a better painter and had a far brighter career that way, although only God knows the real reason I was unsuccessful. But I was true to my master and wanted to do only those things he fully and completely approved, and I probably sensed that he disliked that the foreign fellow had brought the oil odor into his house. For afterward he never again allowed us to cook oil, except for varnishes and stains, because oil stain is almost as good as white-onion stain and takes far less time to produce in large quantities, even if it doesn't last as long.

Still, he chose to ignore the fact that several of us snuck off to paint in oil secretly, but he himself never used this tempera in his teaching, and this was some of the background for the skirmish I just told you about.

My master kept to his medium, faithful as a monk to his vow of chastity, although in our day the word "monk" is scarcely suited to suggesting notions of either faithfulness or chastity. But at one time it was different. Or at least I choose to believe that.

Then, when I was eighteen and beginning to become a man and get hair on my chin, something happened that brought me closer to my master, in fact much closer than perhaps I'd really have wished. For one doesn't always want to know too well those one admires, not completely in the depths of their souls; often it's better to admire how the glow from deep within them shines through the layers of their minds and temperaments than to dive down into them. Just as a river is not equally pure and without sediment from its source to its mouth, neither is every level in the soul always equally clear; and even the greatest man was once little and the most noble once base. So although what I have to relate about my master is extremely human and understandable, and it was so innocent not even a fly would feel embarrassed by it today, nonetheless, I was painfully affected, yes, shaken at the time. But whether the world has changed since then and is no longer embarrassed by anything at all, or whether the world has always been the same and equally malicious, and it was all just due to my being young and innocent at the time—this I don't know.

My master never spoke of his own past and apprenticeship, but some people in the village believed that he must have come from far away, and that he was not of Italian descent, although he spoke our language perfectly. Others believed he was a monk painter who had run away because, after all, he painted almost exclusively religious things, altar paintings and frescoes; if he couldn't get that type of commission, he just spent the time in his atelier, rather than taking other kinds of assignments, and concentrated instead on teaching us. Yet he never lacked bread or anything else, and so there were also those who believed that he was actually a rich man's son, or a prince in exile, which they thought his noble and kindly manners could indicate (they didn't actually know many princes, you understand), while still others believed that he must have found a treasure on one of his walks, and that he regularly went out to a hole or something to get gold. Once, when I accompanied him on a walk, some farmers we met asked with a sneer if it was true that he *had* found a treasure in the mountains, and if he was on his way there now.

"Yes," replied my master with a smile, "the first time I came here and walked in the mountains I found a treasure, and it was so valuable that it made me stay here with you."

They stared at him openmouthed. But what he meant by this I didn't understand then.

My master went on his lonely walks every forenoon after the morning's work was done. He was incredibly agile for such an old man—he was almost sixty years old—and walked quickly and tirelessly through all types of terrain, and made his way in the mountains like a goat. Heat or rain did not affect him, not even hail or snow. He walked regularly, every day, in all kinds of weather. He seemed to race through the landscape, for often the view or the color vein or the spring he wanted to reach that day lay so far away that he had to walk fast to save time. Even for a youth like me it was hard to keep up with Master Girolamo when he first got going—I should add that the only privilege he openly gave me, his most faithful student, was that now and then he let me come along on the morning walks, which otherwise were his alone. Although perhaps it wasn't really a privilege, but simply because I was good at keeping my mouth shut and didn't speak until he was in the mood for it himself. He greeted all whom he met in a polite and friendly way, was equally courteous to high or lowly, but then hurried on quickly. The same was true this morning. It was a winter morning; it was cold.

We had two errands. We were going to get boiled squirrel tails for brushes in a little hamlet far up in the mountains, and we were going to collect a new supply of green earth, which is the best color for skin tones and for applying gold base; it was the color my master preferred when he worked with gold base, for that's what the old painters had always used when they painted their saint panels. And this could be a further indication that he was a monk painter who had run away, but I never asked him.

This morning there was snow in the air, sharp snow, and I was afraid of wolves. But when I mentioned this, my master smiled and kept walking, and he walked through the wind so fast that it created a hollow in the snowfall behind him, like the wake of a boat, for he was stronger than the wind and more tireless than the snow, and I could follow in his wake, where it was sheltered and safe. Nonetheless, after a while, as the snowstorm got worse, we went astray, and my master suggested that we seek shelter in some goatherds' huts he saw in a grove nearby—low, simple huts they were. We thought they would be empty now in the wintertime, but we were mistaken. For smoke was coming from one of them, and when we opened the door and said hello, we saw a person sitting by the fire who gave a terrible start at our unexpected arrival. My master obligingly put out his empty hands to show that we were friendly and were not carrying weapons, but the person by the fire rose, moved backward anxiously, and huddled against the wall of the little hut. The room was very dark and smoky, and my master slowly bent over and, with a calming gesture, picked up a log and put it on the fire. When it caught flame, we saw that it was a girl who stood there trembling, ragged and repulsive and slovenly, with a dirty face and a foolish expression. Just a goatherd girl, or even poorer. But my master stiffened when he saw her face, and remained hunched over. I couldn't see his face, but I felt that he stared at her a long time. Then he called her by name.

"Maria?" he said softly, and the voice I heard was different from the one he usually used. But I didn't have time to think more about it because the young girl leaped up as if stung by a serpent, crouched, dashed between us, and before we knew what was happening, she had disappeared out into the snowstorm. Master Girolamo lost no time in running after her, but I just stood in the doorway, bewildered, and so I saw them, the girl with flying, greasy, unkempt hair and my master racing after her, amid all the white and gray that flickered past, and it was like a dance, it was like smoke and swirls of broken ice floes in a river, and I heard him shout, as if in a pit, or like a fool. I just stood there.

After a long time he returned, alone.

"I didn't find her," was all he said, in his ordinary voice, but he wasn't like his usual self. "She ran away from me." The weather had improved a little, and I thought we would continue on our way, but my master sat down by the fire and kept sitting there.

"We have to wait for her," he said. "She could freeze to death out there." And he didn't hear how foolish his words sounded, but kept sitting by the hearth and raking the ashes until late in the day, and during that whole long time he didn't look at me, but only into the coals, and I was too shy to say anything. But when the snowstorm grew heavier again outside, I said, "Master, it's getting toward evening." He looked at me; for a moment he was strangely far away and I didn't know him. His gaze was like the coals. But then he seemed to come back, and the next moment he was the same as always, smiled kindly at me and said of course we must go down again. Nevertheless, we barely got down safely, and it was very difficult to follow the path when it got dark, we lost it several times, but at last we were home. Teresa, Master Girolamo's sister, and the other apprentices were out of their minds with worry. But my master laughed and acted just as always toward them, and said they should know better than to think he would be destroyed in the forest and mountains, which he knew like the back of his hand.

"Besides," he said, sending me a strange look, "besides, I had Giuseppe along, faithful Giuseppe, who would always have helped me, because he's my best student."

I flushed with pleasure. Still, I didn't understand him; he usually never gave praise like that, as you've probably realized, and was careful about treating all his apprentices the same. In fact, it was the first time he ever said anything like that to me. But his eyes said more than his mouth.

All the same, he didn't let me come along on more walks when the weather improved, but always found something I needed to do. He was also more impatient about the work in the morning, and left on his walk as soon as he could, earlier than usual. I had to stay home, as I said. We saw no sign of the squirrel tails or the green earth, but he was away a long time, every time. I didn't know, but I was quite certain that he tried to find his way back to the hut where we had sought refuge. When he came home, he was distant and preoccupied, and taught little, and we usually just hung around with nothing to do. We played games. Sometimes he participated, with unexpected zest, but then suddenly might sit with the dice in his hand for a long time, we had to cough or clear our throats to bring him back to the game, and then he had forgotten his previous throw and we had to remind him of the number of dots. He hardly ever looked in my direction.

But one afternoon, when almost two weeks had passed this way, he returned completely calm. He ate well that evening, drank a little too, and went to bed early. The next morning the sun was shining and the snow melted on the sides of the valleys. He went to see the birds as usual, sat there a long time. Then he asked his sister to prepare food for a journey for him and announced to us apprentices that he was going to Rome that very morning to seek a good commission. He could not have amazed us more if he had said that, like the angel he was, he was going to the Underworld, and we must have looked thunderstruck; but he laughed a little and said that he believed he still had some acquaintances in high places in Rome from the old days who would help him. This was the first time he had alluded to anything about his past, and we didn't ask him more either.

Each and every one of us probably doubted our master really would get a commission as he wished, or wondered if he was starting to grow old, and we also discussed this among ourselves; as I've said, he usually didn't seek commissions but waited until he was asked. However, even if we boys talked a great deal about our master's strange decision while he was on his journey, I didn't say a word about what I had experienced with him in the winter storm, nor did I realize then that there was any connection. To be honest, I too doubted that he, an unknown country painter, would get a commission in the big rich city, just like that.

But I didn't know my master well, or didn't fully appreciate his true qualities, because less than four weeks later he returned, happy and content, having been given an important and well-paid commission from a Florentine merchant who had bought a palace in Rome. Master Girolamo was to paint the altar picture for a chapel the Florentine wanted to establish in his neighborhood church. How this had happened, I don't know, but since then I've often thought that the reason my master avoided the world wasn't necessarily because he was awkward in the company of other people, or lacked knowledge or the gift of speaking well, or was unfamiliar with aristocratic customs and manners, because he could be a very charming person if he wished. But he didn't want to be a charming person. At least not outside the village and his small circle of acquaintances. Maybe he had wanted to be charming in an earlier life.

Now he had been to the big city and received a noble commission in a very short time, so he couldn't be lacking in eloquence or powers of persuasion. Or maybe he had received help from his "old acquaintances"— that I don't know, and it doesn't matter. He said nothing more about the commission, and we immediately went back to our tasks, which he guided with renewed eagerness and energy. The weeks passed without his beginning on any painting; spring came and early summer.

Finally I ventured to ask, but he only replied that he had plenty of time, that his spirit was content and resting, and that he would begin the painting soon enough, because he already knew what he was going to do. And he smiled. But it wasn't quite so simple after all. For a few days later he returned again from one of his walks, but not alone; he brought with him a ragged, dirty, shy figure. And I immediately recognized her from our stay in the little hut in the snowy weather. It sometimes happened that my master brought beggars and vagabonds home with him and gave them food and perhaps clothes or shoes, but everyone was very surprised when Master Girolamo asked his sister to prepare a small room for his companion. The girl stood there staring straight ahead stupidly, as if she scarcely understood human speech; she smelled of sheep and soil, and was incredibly dirty. Her hair was one huge tangle, her clothes a patchwork quilt, her feet bare and filthy. There was matter in her eyelashes, snot dripped from her nose; her eyes had a slightly slanted, distant look.

My master's sister, Teresa, who usually held her tongue, put her hands on her hips and demanded to know the meaning of this, and who was this filthy guest.

"I haven't really been able to get her to tell me her name," said my master, "but I've heard from people in the mountain that she's called Ho-Ho, and I think she's a little crazy."

When she heard her name, the girl smiled innocently.

"Ho," she said. "Ho. Hi." And we boys had to laugh. But old Teresa didn't laugh.

"So," she asked, "and what's the idiot going to do here?"

"She has wandered around among goats with her grandmother, and lived by herding goats for first one person and then another. But her grandmother died last winter, and I've taken her down here with me so she won't get utterly ruined among the rough fellows up there, mere child that she is."

But his sister said: "I've never said a single rude word to you about all the strange things you've dragged home with you, Girolamo, birds and rubbish. And I haven't complained about living the way we have for all these years, lonely and far from people. I've given food and clothing to vagabonds and beggars, without mentioning that some little thing or coin disappeared during the hours they were in the house. But I refuse to believe you intend that this girl should live here with us and the apprentices."

"Don't be so sharp, Teresa," said Master Girolamo. "That's my intention, because I'm going to paint her."

At this information Teresa stared at him thunderstruck, opened her mouth to say something, and closed it. Without a word she took Ho-Ho by the hand and drew her into the kitchen, where shortly afterward we heard shrieks and inarticulate protests from the stranger as Teresa prepared a very hot bath in the tub.

The apprentices winked slyly at each other. But our master turned to us, looked at us solemnly, and said: "Giuseppe must begin today to prepare a large poplar panel of the best quality, four by two-and-a-half meters, so that we can begin work within the month. And the rest of you standing there grinning, you can wipe the smirks off your faces immediately and prepare paper and charcoal for sketching. Because we're going to work as we have never worked before, and we're going to work seriously."

I must hasten to add that there was absolutely nothing base or ignoble in my master's treatment of the girl who came into the house; he treated her as respectfully and kindly as any other guest, and did not touch her. He impressed upon us that we should lower our eyes if we came upon her when she was dressing, and that we should be patient with her simple ways, which poor Teresa had the task of improving from the very first day. But that there was some talk and laughter in the village was unavoidable. At the same time, people respected Master Girolamo and probably saw it mostly as an expression of my master's extraordinary oddities.

Still, she was pretty after she had been bathed and currycombed and clipped, with tears and gnashing of teeth. She stood there, red-eyed and sniffling, in one of Teresa's matronly dresses, which was much too big for her, and Teresa exhibited her and was, in fact, quite proud of her work. Her hair proved to be a thick, brown, curly mane, her throat was slim and beautiful, and once the broken nails were trimmed you could see that her hands were long and well formed, like wings. She had poor posture and stood slightly stooped, for one bath is not enough to make a princess out of a pauper. And she kept picking at her eyes, which were red from the dried matter that Teresa had carefully removed. Her teeth were still green, but grew whiter with time as Teresa scrubbed them with salt and finely ground lime.

Teresa was proud of her work, as I said, but at the same time a thoughtful expression came over her as she stood contemplating the newly washed Ho-Ho; her look was musing and a little worried, and she glanced from the girl to her brother as if she had realized something in the steam from the bathwater. She made no further objections or protests about the new inhabitant, never again, but tried to take care of the girl as best she could. But one could see that she was worried, or almost a little sad.

Yes, Ho-Ho was beautiful, we all could see that, and our master forbid us to call her Ho-Ho from now on, or to speak of her by that name, because it wasn't a human name or pet name befitting such a lovely girl. But he didn't know her baptismal name—to be honest, he seriously doubted whether she was even baptized—so he asked her as she stood there wearing her new clothes: "What's your name, girl?"

"Ho. Ho."

"No," he said, "nobody is named Ho-Ho. You must have a name. What did your grandmother call you?"

"H. Ha. Ga."

"I *know* you can talk," he said, "because I heard you talk up in the mountains."

"Can't talk."

"I see. But you must have a name."

"No n-n-name."

So, since it was impossible to find out her real name when she spoke so little, we began to call her Bella, the beautiful one. She quickly learned to respond to that name, and we used this name to call her or greet her from then on, but among ourselves we apprentices still called her Ho-Ho, because we thought she was a bother and couldn't understand why our master had brought this disrupter of peace into the house.

However, my master wasn't satisfied with the clothes Teresa had put on Ho-Ho; he thought they were old-womanish and unsuitable for a young girl, so his sister had to dress the girl again, this time in one of the youngest apprentice's outgrown clothing, until our master could get two dresses and other garments made at the tailor's in the next few weeks.

When she put on trousers her posture improved too, because she wasn't used to wearing a dress, and moved around more freely and easily in men's clothing. And that's how I remember her from those first weeks—like a small, slim, strong animal that had come into the house, that explored every part of the atelier, and that we had to watch carefully so she didn't drink plaster or put her hand into a kettle of unslaked lime. She was a pest and a bother, for although she wasn't allowed to go into the atelier, she took every chance to sneak in there. She showed no interest in the kitchen and Teresa's domain, except when Teresa baked cakes; above all, she wanted to be in the atelier, as if she understood that this was the heart of the house. And she sneaked in, she played with the squirrel-tail hair and the pig bristles, or colored her hands or face with costly cinnabar red, which had to be scrubbed off with shrieks and protests from Ho-Ho's side. She played with the paper and the chalk, and she didn't understand that the quills were anything more than beautiful feathers, and put them in her hair and behind her ears. My master was mildly dismayed at all the mischief she did, but at the same time he didn't take it to heart, he simply gave her a distant look and didn't get angry, for at that time he couldn't be angry with her.

Oddly enough, she never tried to run away; it seemed as if my master had won her trust, just as he had with the birds, but how this had happened, I don't know. She hung around him, and he made small talk, and sometimes she replied in monosyllables, but for the most part she just followed him wherever he went. I probably sensed a prick of jealousy, because I had felt like my master's favorite, but I knew his good heart and knew that he never treated one person differently from another, and never forgot those whom he had let into his heart. His heart was large and without fault, and he would only reproach me and call me childish if I openly showed that I felt hurt.

So I left them in peace and concentrated all my energy and love on preparing my master's large poplar wood panel, which was meticulous, time-consuming work. I cut the panel from dry, oil-free raw timber, removed the branches, plugged the holes with molding wood—that's sawdust in leaf glue—and tin-plated all the nail holes so the rust wouldn't come through the painting. I let the raw timber rest, plugged and polished it again, and then began to brush limewater on the panel, layer after layer, with a large brush made from pig bristles. This limewater isn't strong, but it works like an aperitif on an empty stomach, or a handful of candy or a glass of wine before dinner—it's a way of giving the wood an appetite to absorb the subsequent coats of lime and the plaster base. Afterward I waited until the weather was dry and a fresh, dry wind began to blow from the mountains. Then I covered the panel with strips of the finest old, thin, white linen, which were free of grease and dipped in lime; I spread them across the panel with the palms of my hands so all the unevenness disappeared, and then let the panel dry in the wind for many days.

During this whole time my master was busy preparing himself for his task, and had carved a decorative frame in the panel I had primed and prepared. But above all, he prepared himself by sketching Ho-Ho. It wasn't easy to get her to sit still. The only times I saw him angry at her was when she ran away just a few minutes after he had finally gotten her in the pose he wanted and had settled himself with drawing board, charcoal, paper, and brush. Suddenly she saw a bird or wanted a drink of water, or disappeared for no reason other than that her blood was filled with movement and restlessness. Angry and resigned, my master would throw the piece of charcoal to the ground and watch her fly away. This could happen many times in the course of a day, and the sketching sessions became difficult for both of them. Things improved only when he got the idea of giving her fruit—oranges, apples, and nectarines—which she could eat while she sat there, for she never tired of fruit. The sweetness seemed to calm her for a little while; she sat and ate with an introspective, almost sleepy look and didn't move from the spot as long as there was a fruit remaining on the platter.

That was how he sketched her and learned to know her face and her expressions, and I had never seen him draw in quite that way; whereas he usually was so calm and precise, almost expectant, in his relation to the motif, now he leaned forward eagerly as he worked, drew quickly and intensely, almost passionately. And between drawing sessions I often saw him sit and gaze at her with a moist look, almost as if he were crying. At the end of the morning's work he wouldn't give up, even if she was so full of fruit that the juice ran down her chin and throat; it seemed he could have sat there drawing her until evening. So Teresa intervened and forced him to let her leave. But often he also sketched her when she had fallen asleep in the evening. And a change took place in my master during those days, he became strange and distant and wasn't himself, but sometimes reminded me of the man I saw in him that evening in the goatherd's hut, the first time he saw Ho-Ho.

And he played with her. One day he brought her a lovely doll, which the carpenter had painstakingly made, so she would have her own toy to play with and wouldn't ruin things for the apprentices in the workshop. She could play with that doll for hours, even though she was too old for dolls. But she had never had a doll before, we saw that clearly from the light in her face and eyes when he gave her the doll. Old as he was, he would sit on his haunches or on all fours beside her on the floor playing with her and the doll, devising small dances, singing a little, just like a child. And she laughed, a quick, flickering laughter. The fleeting clouds of laughter blended with my master's deep guffaws, and that's how I will remember that summer, laughter and color and plaster.

By the end of June, I and the others had finished preparing the large panel, as well as three small test panels. I had primed it with roasted plaster, called *gesso grosso*—which comes from Volterra, and is ground and sifted like flour, and mixed with lime—I had spread the warm plaster over the surface, layer by layer, into all my master's carved ornamentation, and had polished the panel until it was smooth as wax. Then I had taken thin plaster, *gesso sottile*, which is the same plaster but slaked in a bucket for an entire month, stirred day and night until the water has, so to speak, rotted away. It becomes soft as silk, and is squeezed in leather until all the water disappears, and is then pressed into cakes. Later the mixture is ground on a porphyry slab and crumbled with lime over heat until it's like a pancake batter. Eight coats are applied to the panel with a broad brush, without giving the coats a chance to dry completely between applications; back and forth, always in the opposite direction of the previous brushstroke, interspersed with coats of lime as needed. All of this preparation, and more, must be done in a single day, for the work can't be interrupted, and the pauses between the coats must be appropriately long, so I remember that we worked until late at night. The panel dried for a week, and then I took a cloth coated with crushed charcoal and rubbed the panel's surface completely black, as my master had taught me. And this is so that later, when the plaster is being shined and polished, one can better see where one has worked, because where the plaster is polished the white becomes visible again, pure and clear as clouds and sky. It's as beautiful as when the day breaks forth from a dark night. And the panel must be polished as smooth as ivory or a child's skin, and finally be buffed with a damp cloth.

All this work was done by the end of June. But my master wasn't finished sketching yet; it seemed as if he had almost forgotten the panel he was to create, but had enough with his daily roving expeditions into the girl's face on paper. However, he finally pulled himself together and began to gather his impressions into a whole. During the sketching phase he had tried a few different poses, now he had to decide on the right one. He tried several positions before he finally felt satisfied with seating her in a rather conventional pose, facing forward, with a bound bundle representing the child in her left arm. But he turned her a little, so that she was sitting at a slight angle, with her right shoulder pivoted away a little from the viewer, and thus it seemed as if she were about to turn toward us. It was very lovely and effective, and when he draped her in the blue cape, her beauty was delicate and gentle, and she no longer resembled the unkempt crazy girl he had brought down from the mountains, but had become something more than herself.

Now began the most difficult time for Ho-Ho, who had to sit in the same pose every single day. But Ho-Ho too felt that she was transformed when she put on the blue cloak; she became quiet and tranquil, and no longer devoured fruit, but sat quite calmly for long periods at a time gazing over my master's shoulder with a deep and inscrutable look; he had set up the large panel in front of her now, and no longer sat down when he worked but stood. She usually just played with the fruit now, she seemed to have had her fill of it. The other apprentices worked at drawing her too, or they helped our master, and something happened to her when she became the center of all this attention; she no longer scampered around, but stayed seated and drew our eyes to her. She had changed in other ways as well, had begun to say hello and thank you, and to speak in simple sentences.

My master took a piece of willow charcoal, fastened it to the end of a rod to create the necessary distance, and began to draw her with light strokes directly on the plaster surface. Only rarely did he use the feather to erase something. This work took three days. Master Girolamo worked quickly and confidently, and Ho-Ho sat still almost the entire time, as if she understood that something solemn was happening. After the third day she was allowed to rest, while my master drew the child. However, he didn't have a mother from the village come with a child, as he otherwise would have done, but drew on his own powers of imagination for all the child's attributes. And during the days he did this he sent all the apprentices away, except for me, because someone had to assist him. And I saw that his face was dark, almost bitter, and that once again his eyes were moist as he tried to draw the child's face. He used the feather more often on the child than when he drew Ho-Ho, and sometimes flung down the piece of charcoal in despair. I had never seen him like that. In the end, the spot where the child's face should have been was completely black with erased charcoal, and we had to carefully polish the plaster again so that he could start over. This time things went better, for he contented himself with a simple sketch of a child's face, and felt he had done well with the expression around the child's eyes and let it be. But he wasn't completely satisfied.

Now he covered the panel and put it away for fourteen days, while he rested. He didn't look at Ho-Ho at all, but walked in the forest alone, to rest his eyes from her and the panel, so that he could look at his motif again with fresh eyes, the way all wise painters do. But Ho-Ho couldn't understand this, and grew restless and wild; she wanted to follow him, and became desperate and cried when he forced her to stay home, because while she had been in our house she had gotten used to having him look at her constantly, and felt empty and sad without his continual attention. Indeed, it was frightful to see the way she clung to him when he returned from his walks in the evening. She threw her arms around him, kissed him, laughed with joy, clung to his clothes, and tried to climb on him. He had to push her away. But she sat in front of him when he ate, she disturbed him when he rested, and she came dragging her doll to play with him. She even put on the blue cloak he draped her in when she posed as his model, but then he got angry. And if she didn't get his attention by good means, she swept her plate onto the floor or broke his wine cup, or poured out some expensive color powder or ruined brushes in the atelier, whimpering all the while with injured rage. In fact, one day he grabbed her as she was pulling the cloth off the unfinished altar painting as it stood in a corner of the atelier; her hands were already in the middle of it, ready to rub out the charcoal drawing so he would have to start from the beginning again. He slapped her cheek, several times, took her by the ear to Teresa, who shook her head and silently received the bundle he flung onto the floor in front of her. Then he locked up the panel and disappeared for three days.

But Ho-Ho was offended, and her restlessness increased, and the second night my master was away she stole into the atelier and climbed up into the loft, where the apprentices slept. Fortunately, I had not yet gone to sleep but was sitting on my bed mending some clothes when she came quietly up the ladder, wearing only a thin shift.

I was still unacquainted with certain sides of love, because I lived utterly and completely as my master prescribed, almost like a monk, without looking at women as anything other than beautiful motifs, so when I saw her I felt mostly annoyance, got out of my bed, and told her that she had no business being up there. But she gave no sign of leaving, just stood there looking at me with big, wide eyes. Her slightly injured expression had been replaced by something resembling the great peacefulness that had come over her while my master sketched the panel; she smiled faintly, and there was a sensuality in her smile and, above all, in her eyes that unsettled me and made me breathe more quickly, for her eyes were like flowing water. It bewildered me, because I didn't understand what was happening. But I pulled myself together and followed her down the narrow ladder, down into the atelier, out into the moonlit courtyard. And it was my firm intention to accompany her into the kitchen and to old Teresa, and to ask our housekeeper to lock her in, if necessary. But Ho-Ho stopped me and stammered: "Bb. Ba. Bad. Bad. Giuseppe is bad."

"No," I said, "you're the one who is bad, Bella."

"No," she said softly. "Bella isn't bad." And she looked at me with the same expression, like flowing water, but now the moon was somehow blended into it, and she came over to me, stood on tiptoe, and leaned against me, with her whole body. We stood like that for a long time. And being unacquainted with such things, I didn't know what to do with my hands, but when she put her mouth against mine, they found the way by themselves. And if there were aspects of love I was not familiar with, little Bella was clearly not without insight in this area, for she had lived her life among goatherds and woodcutters. She drew me, or I pushed her, away from the open courtyard, into the shadows and bushes, then into the aviary where the birds lived, and there, while the drowsy birds stirred uneasily and fluttered over us in the darkness, she took off her shift, and her breasts shone like white stone in the moonlight, and she placed my face against her and let me drink this light. Later she found her way to me, held me with a sure hand, pulled a white stream out of me at once, and another, and yet another, for I was young and excited and inexperienced, but she just smiled and rubbed us both in with the glistening seed, kissed me again and said that Giuseppe was good. To this I could only answer yes, yes, for she was already satisfying me again, this time with the tip of a tongue that was as light as the down we lay on. And so I loved her, and *everything* became as light as down.

I can't understand why I, an old man who smells of death, should bother myself with these memories. And I can no longer fully remember my bitter pangs of conscience from that night, when I sat in the courtyard shivering after Ho-Ho had gone to bed, for now it seems only beautiful and almost innocent. But I know that my heart was happy and unhappy at the same time, and I believe I thought something like this: it was better that she had given herself to me, who loved and respected Master Girolamo, who didn't want to hurt him, and who wouldn't boast to the other apprentices about our nighttime meeting, but silently keep the secret to myself. Still, I was uneasy about what my master would say if he should hear about it, and unhappy; for even though Master Girolamo had never touched the girl, as far as I knew, but always conducted himself toward her like a father or a holy hermit, I knew in my heart that she was something more to him than just the model for his new painting. But what she really meant to him, I could not fathom.

If I swore to myself that night I would never touch her again, my intentions seemed to be blown away when she came to me the next night, and again the following night. I was sick with pangs of conscience and with blazing love, because I was immature, but the fourth night I stood in the courtyard and waited for her, not the reverse. Meanwhile, my master had returned, and was going to begin working again, but she no longer looked at him, as if she were still offended, and that amazed him. But he didn't let it worry him, just contentedly took out the covered panel, looked at it with new eyes, and made corrections. Then he had her resume her pose again, and made further corrections. Now he also drew the background, an orchard with many trees, because he had portrayed her with a fruit in her lap. Finally he declared himself satisfied, took the feather brush and whisked away all the charcoal, so that only very faint lines remained. Afterward he intensified them with fine ink strokes, and heightened the shadings with ink wash and a blunt paintbrush, so that now his picture was fixed on the panel. Then he took a needle and scratched along the edges of everything that would later be gilded—base surfaces, as well as ornaments and drapery details on the figures. Finally, he used modeling plaster to heighten certain parts of the halos and also some of the treetops.

Even without colors it was already a lovely picture, so beautiful it could make you weep. Ho-Ho's slender, graceful neck inclined slightly toward the viewer, her heavy-lidded eyes were filled with sweetness and seemed to half look away; and the aspects of her face and glance that otherwise revealed a somewhat foolish nature, in the master's picture could pass for the Holy Virgin's innocent, yet deep and all-knowing, wisdom. That was how my master transformed Ho-Ho into something other, and more, than Ho-Ho, and it both resembled and did not resemble her, and sometimes I had the impression one saw a completely different girl, while other times I could recognize Ho-Ho, or Bella, by certain characteristics, by all the characteristics I knew so well, by the small well-formed lips, by the conchal curves, or by the long fingers, strong and yet gracefully formed, resting like wings in her lap. Yet it wasn't she, but someone else. And I don't know if I mean the painting or Bella, when I say that she was the most beautiful woman I have ever seen.

Now the gilding began.

I want you to know that gold, which the world's prelates and princes engrave into coins, which merchants and usurers collect in the darkness of locked chests, which the farmer buries in his dark, dirty earthen floor and the thrall greedily hides in sweaty armpits, and for which robbers murder and kings wage war—this gold, which we all desire, owes its real value and its allure to one single thing, a single characteristic, and that is its rare ability to resemble the sunlight. Gold never rusts, never stains, never turns green or black. And therefore gold's true task from time immemorial has been to imitate the holy, to decorate God's altars and crucifixes, or ornament the capes and crowns of the chosen. Gold is imperishable and eternal, and it is the only earthly metal that in itself reflects the divine light, the light that lives out there in the sun's light and within the depths of the soul. Therefore we desire it and commit wrongs in order to steal it; and we thereby degrade the gold, at the same time as we degrade the light within us. We have turned gold into something other than it is. But things were different at one time (for that is what my master taught me); at one time, gold was not respected for its money value, nor as a means of exchange, nor as an expression for *another* value, but exclusively for its own sake. There was a time, my master taught me, when you could not buy anything for gold, but when gold was collected by everyone to ornament human temples and holy pictures, and only in and of itself had any value, which could not be measured in anything but beauty.

That's why ground gold is the most beautiful and the only true background on which to portray a holy picture, and therefore the divine figures are given halos of gold leaf, so they will shine like the sun and remind people in their dark night that morning will come. That's how it was before, but not any longer, and soon there probably won't be anyone who can gild in the old way, because artists no longer make any distinction between holy and profane, between above and below, but paint all figures and themes alike.

The gilding work began in midsummer, and the weather was very dry, so my master didn't use green earth as he normally did, but instead used Armenian red bole; it's a mineral that has been used as a pigment since time immemorial, and is used to give the background a little color, so one can more easily see the effect of the work as it progresses. In a glazed bowl, which must be absolutely clean, the painter whips the white of a chicken egg until the bowl is filled with snowy foam. A cup of pure, cold water is poured over it, and the mixture stands overnight to clarify, from sunset to sunrise. Then the red bole is ground into this egg-white tempera, long and well, and the faintly colored tempera is applied with a soft brush to all the areas that are to be gilded, four layers, which need to dry between each coat. And with each coat one increases the concentration of red bole. Then the panel must be covered well to protect it from dust. We did all this, and I led the work, for in my master's eyes I was the best of his apprentices at gilding. And I would have been happy, for I could already sense that my master's painting would be more beautiful and moving than anything he had created before, but I could not be happy, because I still met her at night. Ho-Ho. Bella. And each night she was the same, she was demanding and giving at the same time, she was hard and soft, and her hands were decisive and capable, almost impersonal. She said hardly anything to me, nor I to her. But she smiled when I eagerly reached for her, and she smiled each time I uncovered myself and she could see how much I desired her. And she laughed when she enticed the silver streams out of me. But one night I told her that I loved her, and then she didn't laugh, but kissed me.

All during the gilding work my master was again very reserved toward her and rarely looked in her direction; and the less he looked at her, the more intense her embraces in the dark became. And I thought she was beautiful and my heart sang when we met, but afterward it grew silent. And I never spoke with her, for after all, what would we talk about? Still, I thought that I loved her.

My master waited for damp weather. And one July morning heavy, black thunderclouds rolled across the mountains, turning the light yellow and blue, and the rain began. We immediately went to work, laid the panel flat across two trestles in the atelier and quickly polished the bole base with scrapers and amethyst stones until it became absolutely smooth, with no lumps or particles, and ready to accept the gold leaf. Every evening my master had prepared egg-white tempera in a dish, in order to be ready if it rained the next morning. This morning he chose a dish with tempera that was three days old, for it's best if the tempera is not completely fresh. He mixed the tempera with water, and then took his costly thin, thin gold leaf from the small chest where it was always under lock and key, and lifted a leaf with a pincers and laid it on top of a card he held in his left hand. With his right hand he dipped the brush in the egg-white mixture and moistened exactly as much of the bole base as he wanted to gild, evenly and precisely. Then he moved his left hand holding the card with the gold leaf toward the moistened area; he let the edge of the gold that extended over the edge touch the moisture. And with a lovely deft movement, light as a puff of wind, he pulled back his hand and the delicate gold leaf fell precisely where he had brushed the tempera; then he immediately began to press down the gold leaf with cotton, using the gentlest pressure possible, for gold tears if you use too much force. This is the most beautiful work to watch and the most difficult handicraft, for the gold leaves are small, and they are light and thin as cobwebs, and you must work lightly and quickly and without mistakes, while constantly alternating among tempera brush, pincers, gold and card, cotton. No one practiced this handicraft better than my master, or with a lovelier result, and he gilded the Virgin's halo himself as one of the other boys assisted him, but I am proud to say that I put the gold around the child's head and on quite a bit of the ornamentation in the frame. The gold leaves must always overlap each other a tiny bit, not too much, not too little, so that with the help of the tempera the gold sticks firmly to what has already been laid. When you have laid three or four leaves and the tempera is still moist, you breathe on the gold, and immediately see the cracks. Then you take a highly polished pillow of smooth, oil-free calfskin, place a piece of gold leaf on it, and, using a fine knife, cut the leaf on the pillow into pieces as tiny as needed to repair the cracks; with a pointed brush you moisten the cracks with egg-white tempera, then lick the end of the brush handle and with it pick up the small gold flakes from the pillow and place them in the cracks. It's tiring, meticulous work; you stand hunched over, often in an uncomfortable position, and you must finish everything in a single day so that you can polish the gold surfaces as quickly as possible. And you must collect every tiny bit of gold that's left over, because it's expensive and nothing must go to waste. So we worked quickly, but I wasn't happy.

Just after midday it stopped raining and the weather became dry and sunny; in fact, it got so dry that my master grew very worried and stopped the work—we had just begun to apply gold on the ornamentation. Now he ordered us to wring out clean linen cloths in cold water and cover all the gilding, and also to cover the panel itself with a clean cloth sprayed with water, and then as quickly as possible we carried the panel down into the wine cellar and set it by the barrels.

The dry weather lasted for ten days, and each evening and morning we went down and moistened the cloths again, and throughout these ten days Master Girolamo was nervous and irritable, and every day he cursed the sun, which he otherwise loved, and his mood affected the rest of us, and no other work got done. Ho-Ho, my Bella, became utterly impossible; she just sat moping in a corner or walked around restlessly and picked leaves off trees and bushes or did other mischief and no longer came to the court-yard late at night. I waited, but she no longer came. During the day she avoided my glance. And I didn't dare to waylay her, because I was afraid to reveal our secret.

But one morning she had been in the aviary and killed a bird with her bare hands, just before Master Girolamo got up. When he came to feed the birds as usual, he found the small bloody heap on the floor, and he shouted, and we all came rushing in. All except Ho-Ho. He stood with the small bundle of feathers in his hand, a poor little siskin it was, and he looked like a boy in despair.

"Look!" he said. "Look." His voice was choked and thick. However, we didn't look at the bird, but mostly at each other, because we felt uneasy. Our master dropped the bird and rushed past us to look for Ho-Ho. He found her in one of her hiding places, and pulled her away, out of the house, while she screamed and carried on and protested in every way, so the whole village must have heard it, and they were gone the entire day.

They didn't return until evening, and their faces were red from the sun, and Master Girolamo said nothing, but was calm. And Ho-Ho smiled happily, because she had my master's attention again. Where they had been, I don't know. She didn't even glance at me. But the next day it rained again, and we could begin to polish. Rather than working with dog's teeth, as is commonly done, we used the best polishing stone.

The stone used to burnish gilding is called bloodstone; it's a hard semi-precious stone. Sapphires or emeralds are even better, of course, or garnets, topazes, and round-ground rubies, but these are expensive and it's too bad if they break, for then they are unusable. So we always used bloodstone, which we had taken to the mill and had ground straight and smooth, two fingers wide. The stones are rounded with emery powder—but not as much as an egg. Then they are fastened to a wooden handle with a brass ferrule, and the handles must be formed so they fit in the palm nicely. Finally you polish the bloodstone on the porphyry slab with crumbled charcoal, so it becomes black as a pupil and gleaming as a diamond. You need several such tools in reserve, for if the stone gets scratched or uneven it can no longer be used, but must be prepared all over again. So these expensive tools are best kept in a soft leather bag, each by itself, and when you are going to burnish you place them against your chest so they will get warm and lose any dampness, because gold is finicky.

We laid the panel on the trestles again, and my master was eager but at the same time calm, almost happy, as if the events with Ho-Ho the day before had rid him of tension, or perhaps it was only that the rain had come. While the rest of us finished the remaining details of the gilding work, he began to burnish. He brushed the gold free of every particle of dust with a squirrel tail, breathed on it, and began to rub it with a bloodstone. Here and there he found some unevenness and applied more gold, which he burnished immediately. Then we burnished the other gold surfaces, and we kept at it the entire day, until the gold had a dark, almost red luster.

The following days my master worked on stamping the halos with dividers, needle, riveting hammer, and bodkin until they had the most beautiful, intricate prick-and-relief pattern. Wherever the bole-colored plaster became visible again, he would later paint other light colors to create an alternating effect between the gold and the colors. But my master did all this detail work himself and didn't let us help him, because he wanted to make sure everything was done perfectly.

Then he began the painting itself, and Ho-Ho was completely happy once more, for she had to pose for him again. And it took time, because painting with egg tempera requires great patience and much planning; the colors must be applied one at a time, in a certain sequence, and therefore the painter needs to have decided most of it in advance and to have made his choice of colors, he can't improvise very much. His inner eye must see the completed painting before he puts brush to panel, he must know exactly where he wants to go and exactly what he must do in order to get there.

The same was true now. And my master set us to grinding fresh colors, Spanish green and malachite green and green earth, arzica yellow and giallorino and realgar yellow, along with glorious saffron yellow—and also cinnabar red, dragon's blood red, and minium red, lead white and San Giovanni white, azure blue and, above all, a costly noble ultramarine blue, the most beautiful color to be found, which my master would use on the Virgin's heavenly cloak, for no color goes better with gold than ultramarine.

Ultramarine is expensive because it is produced from the most precious lapis lazuli, which has only a light sprinkling of pyrites. Lapis lazuli is pounded in a mortar and ground finely on the porphyry slab, with no moisture, until it becomes a blue powder, and then finely sifted. As the oldest apprentice, I was entrusted with the task of making and blending my master's blue colors from this powder, because mixing a panel master's ultramarine is no simple matter. I took six ounces of pine resin, three ounces of mastic, and three ounces of fresh wax, and melted these ingredients into a mush, and strained it over a pound of color powder and kneaded the whole thing with linseed oil until I had a firm dough. The dough has to be kneaded for three days. But extracting color from the dough is even more time-consuming, for you must pour a dish of warm lye over the dough, let the lye turn blue, and then pour another dish, and still another, until the lye no longer absorbs blue from the dough but remains colorless, and the dough can be thrown away. This work with the lye normally takes about three weeks, until in the end there is a long row of such dishes, one for every day, each containing an extracted color of a different intensity. For just think how many different shades of blue are found in an evening sky alone. The first dishes are blue and lovely as violets, the last ones are almost ashen and of little worth. Then you blend the extracts in the dishes together, until you get the number of shades you want, usually three or four, from indigo to light blue, and let the color sink to the bottom in the lye, which gradually becomes colorless. And each day you drip off the colorless lye, until finally the dishes are completely dry at the bottom and you have the shades of blue you want. To give a touch of deep violet to one color, you add a tiny bit of finely ground pregnant scale insects, called scarlet grains because of their red color, together with pulverized brazilwood. The finished color is dried indoors until it is so dry that it can be ground on the porphyry slab again and then mixed with its tempera. I had already begun this patient work several weeks earlier, so the color would be fresh and ready for my master when he started his painting.

My master used only the most excellent newly laid chicken eggs in tempera, and always used just as much yolk as color. And he always worked with great enjoyment, for to paint on panels is worthy of an aristocrat and the most noble aspect of the painter's art. Since the drapery must always be painted first, he began with the cloak, and he used four different shades of ultramarine. First he painted the darkest shades within the folds of the cloak, then worked his way toward the lighter tones in several coats. When these undercoats were finished, he mixed a still lighter shade. Then he applied lead white to the very lightest shade, then the next-lightest shade, and worked down toward the dark shade again, ending with the darkest night-blue within the folds of the cloak. Then the Virgin's cloak was finished.

To paint on a panel is a pure and meticulous task, and you must keep your brushes and colors in good order to avoid making a mistake, for mistakes are difficult to correct or hide, in fact it's almost impossible; a master could immediately see if something had gone wrong during the work on a panel and an attempt had been made to correct it, and such mistakes diminish the panel's nobility and value. Therefore, my master was just as careful, cool, and deliberate in working with his brushes now as he had been passionate in drawing his model with charcoal when still at the sketching stage. He was particularly anxious that this commission should be completed perfectly, so this time he worked alone and didn't let us apprentices take responsibility for any details in the painting, such as the sky or the trees. So we mostly stood and watched him. However, he often preferred to work in isolation, and put us to work at various tasks in the atelier, such as grinding colors or preparing the brushes, or mixing tempera. Or he simply let us leave our duties and wander in the woods and mountains on our own, and all the apprentices rushed off without having to be told twice. However, I was actually more interested in the painting, for more reasons than purely as a craftsman. And one morning I made a pretense of having a stomachache instead of going with the other apprentices, because I knew my master had come to an important point in the work, perhaps the most important, and I wanted to stay and watch. That's what I told myself. But in reality, I was envious of my master, and if jealousy is a kind of stomachache, then I wasn't too far from the truth when I lied.

I stayed in bed until the morning prayer and breakfast were over, and the others had left the house. For a while I lay dozing, but then got up and dressed, and stole down into the loggia to watch Master Girolamo working in the courtyard in the soft, even light under the large white awning he had stretched above himself and his model.

This particular morning he was working on the face; he had applied green earth as the base color the day before, and was now going to begin with the red tones, with cinnabar and lead white. For when the pale green earth color shines through the red tones, it creates the shining, almost transparent quality of human skin, which resembles no other color and mostly reminds us of the heavenly, and which is so difficult to understand and analyze, because it's not one color, but many, many shades and temperatures that work in and over each other. It was a joy to see Master Girolamo work with Ho-Ho's coloring, which he rendered even more golden and even more beautiful than it was in reality. His hands were careful, light as a feather, and at the same time powerful, like the beating of angel wings, as he slowly and meticulously re-created her face on the panel.

How long I stood hidden among the pillars watching them, I don't know. I admired his work and his model, and once again he was God in my eyes, and it was as if no separation really existed between the two figures there in the courtyard, between the man and the girl, the two of them flowed together in my mind, they were like river and sea, two distinct entities but still the same water. The only sound was the faint drone of my master humming his folk tune.

And she sat as quiet as a mouse. So different from in the beginning. Now she was motionless like a flower. And she obediently kept her eyes focused on the spot on the wall where he had placed a cross, so her eyes would not waver the least bit. But her gaze wasn't stiff and tense, it was calm and strangely unreal, as if she could see and yet did not see, as if she saw everything and nothing, and I wondered what she was really thinking, and what her eyes actually took in, and if she understood anything at all about what was happening around her, about why she sat the way she sat, and that she became God's mother. For the times she had posed like that in the morning, when the work session was over she didn't immediately run to the easel to see how the work had progressed, but disappeared to her own activities, or to the kitchen to eat, or ran over to my master to beg for candy or to get him to play with her. If she saw the painting before it was covered, she cast an indifferent and slightly uncomprehending look at it, as if she couldn't really see what it was, or that it resembled anything at all. It seemed that it could just as well have been confusing clumps of color as far as she was concerned, meaningless lines, a meadow of poppies. She didn't understand, and didn't care that she didn't understand. No, I had never seen her understand that there was any connection between her and the painting that was created, and I don't even know if she understood what a painting *was*. But she sat, and she was beautiful as she sat there, and she had changed during the months she had been in the house, she resembled herself less and less, and more and more resembled the picture my master was painting.

And then it happened. Master Girolamo was just lining her lips, with fine carmine red color, when he put down the pointed brush, took a step backward, looked at the painting, looked at her. Then he took off his painter's smock and his shirt, for it was hot and he had been working for several hours; his chest glistened with sweat. He looked at her. I could not see his gaze, but I saw that she met it with her own. Then he went over to her and knelt at her feet, halfway up on the podium where he had set her chair, and he put his white-haired head in her lap, closed his eyes, lay completely still. She looked down at him a little uncertainly, shifted her gaze for the first time, lay a hand on his head, and began to stroke his hair, carefully, rhythmically.

That was all. Nothing was said and nothing more happened. I don't know why it shook me so much nevertheless. He lay there looking extremely tired, and for the first time I saw that he was a very old man. And for the first time I saw pain in his features. She carefully stroked his hair as she shifted her gaze back to the chalk cross and continued staring straight ahead in the direction he had asked her to look when she posed—the same way a bird can be paralyzed by a chalk mark if you press its beak against it. It was almost as if she didn't understand that he lay there, or as if this were the most natural thing in the world. That was all. Still, I was shaken, in fact I trembled to the roots of my soul at the sight, because I had never seen my master's face like that.

Suddenly her gaze rested on me; I felt it more than I saw it. I sensed the light from her eyes against the skin of my face; she had discovered me standing there. And she didn't stop caressing Master Girolamo's hair, but just smiled at me. And it was a smile I can't explain, for it was both triumphant and innocent, filled with ignorance and at the same time with knowing promises and enticements. It was like honey. I couldn't understand it. Sick with emotion I stole out of the courtyard, out of the house, away. Because I had wanted to tear his head out of her lap with all my might.

I thought then that my master had never touched her, but just lay like that with his head in her lap, and that this was enough for him, yes, perhaps greater and sweeter than if he really had embraced her. But I couldn't understand why. And I can't say I was surprised when she suddenly stood before me late the same evening, and pulled me into the supply room and did it with me there, more insatiably beautiful than ever, and as wordless and remote as ever. But I wasn't happy, for despite my youth I understood that she was something quite different, and far more, for my master than for me, even if I couldn't understand *what* she was for him; and I didn't want to hurt my master, who had only been good toward me and whom I loved more than a father. But she told me I was good, good. And I loved her. For the first time I longed to leave my master's atelier, longed to take her with me, run away with her, find another city and another place, where I probably imagined that we would always be together and be happy and otherwise not do much, because one is foolish when one is young, and one dreams when one is young, although not only in that unfortunate period of life, as you will see.

But my master, Girolamo Bonchiodo della Valle, completed his painting slowly and leisurely, with the utmost attentiveness, the noblest artistic presence, and the greatest mastery of his craft. And I swear that he never created a finer work, for the painting was sublime, beautiful as a misty meadow and lonesome as the morning star. I don't know if he continued to lay his head in her lap when he paused in his work, because I never again went to watch him paint her alone. But my Bella came to me now and then, and my heart was unhappy and happy, and I almost stopped eating completely, and longed both to be with her and to be away from her, for this was love.

At the very end, Master Girolamo put light in her eyes and hair and placed gold ornamentation on her cloak by laying the finest gold leaf on a moist stain with his ring finger—always and only his ring finger, which is the most sensitive of all five fingers. Then he put the painting away, well covered. For it's best is to wait with the varnishing as long as possible, preferably a whole year, if the deadline for the commission allows that, for the colors are very ungrateful and lose their freshness if you varnish them immediately; whereas, strangely enough, they seem fresher and lighter if you let them age and be transformed before applying the varnish.

But before the painting was covered and put away, we gathered in the courtyard to look at it, and old Teresa was there too, and Ho-Ho, my Bella. Master Girolamo did not say much, just stood at a distance from the painting and let us praise it and comment on it. Standing there in his white shirt, he breathed lightly and deeply and looked like a young person, and he was happy.

When we had looked to our complete satisfaction (although how could one look to complete satisfaction at such a beautiful work?), my master took a couple of steps forward, fell to his knees, and worshiped the painting for the first time, and we all knelt with him, except Ho-Ho, who kept standing and didn't understand much. Then my master thanked God for His mercy (he always did this when a work was finished), and on his knees he praised the Lord, the One, whose mercy had allowed him to complete yet another work. But after having said his simple prayer of gratitude as usual, this time he had something more on his heart.

"I thank you, Lord. Thine alone is the honor. From Thee come beauty and love, and they return to Thee. And he who once lost beauty and love should not despair, for they will return to him if he is faithful and endures, for they always rested in Thee and were never lost, but exist forever and ever. Because nothing that exists is ever lost, but rests like a child in its mother's lap." He stopped, swallowed. He gave us a serious look.

"And by Thy grace I have found them again, and I pray for your mercy when six months from today I intend to marry the woman who is here with us, and who has given a face to the Virgin in the picture I have painted to the honor of God. Amen." He rose, went over to Ho-Ho, and took her hand.

For a moment there wasn't a sound. No one else rose. No one looked at him or at anyone else. Only Bella seemed unaffected, uncomprehending. I heard a deep sigh from old Teresa, as if she was about to say something. But then my master prayed the Paternoster, and we hurried to join in the prayer.

But later I ran off and was gone until the evening. And I don't know where I ran or how I was, but despair was like a hunger in me. And I shouted within myself, shouted into my own being, that this must never,

never happen. It will never happen. Instead I'll poison him by putting real-gar yellow in his food.

This isn't my story, I began by saying. I lied. Yes, it is mine. But it's also another man's story, a man I can say only good things about, and who, God knows, was a finer human being and had a nobler soul than other people, and was a greater artist than any I've had the misfortune to meet since, all of whom have disappointed me, because in my eyes none of them measured up to him, my master.

Yes, this is his story too, and it is his secret; and I don't know if there in his heaven he will forgive me for not protecting it and taking it with me to the grave, which is not far away but is already opening its jaws for my bones. But let me say this much: late the same evening, when I came back to the house, tired and dirty, and stole into the kitchen to find something to eat, Master Girolamo was sitting there with his sister, and they didn't notice me, and she spoke to him differently than usual, and I heard her say: "Dear brother, dear brother. But she *isn't* Maria."

"She is," said my master quietly.

"Oh, dear brother," said Teresa carefully. "Maria is dead."

"No," said my master. "She's alive and is here with me now."

"Girolamo, it's almost fifty years ago."

"It was yesterday."

"Look at your hands. Look at the wrinkled old man's skin."

"I see my hands, that's all."

"Then look at *me*. An old woman, that's all that's left of me. I almost believe I've disguised myself when I look in the mirror in the morning."

"Then stop looking in the mirror."

"She *isn't* Maria. Maria was intelligent, she could read and write, and you could talk with her. You talked and talked with her, it never ended; you could have still been talking with her."

"I do that. I've always done that."

"You're lonesome."

"No, I'm not lonesome."

"You've lived like a monk all these years, surrounded only by mountains and trees. You're lonely."

"No," said Master Girolamo, "I was lonely in the cities. Lonely until I came here, and found loneliness. Loneliness is a friend, but it's a powerful friend, whom one must listen to if one is to benefit from the friendship. Loneliness is the treasure I found when I came here and went up into the mountains for the first time, because I was completely empty inside, and it was just as empty around me as it was within me. And then I understood that I could no longer be in the cities, that the cities would kill me, because there I couldn't really listen to the loneliness that had become my lasting fate. For deep within the silence, in the uttermost emptiness, lives a voice, and I could hear it again when I came up here. If one can't hear it, the loneliness is unbearable, and the emptiness is merely an anxiety. Some people become poor from loneliness; I became rich."

"Girolamo, she's a child, and you're an old man."

"Who cares."

"She's half crazy. She hardly understands what one says to her."

"But she has a good heart."

"She has a wild heart. She'll make you unhappy."

"She makes me happy."

"She doesn't even know what marriage *is*."

"She knows who *I* am. She's the only one who has always known, who has always known me."

"She *isn't* Maria. She just resembles her. She'll make you unhappy."

"She tells me that I'm good."

"You don't know her. She'll run away."

"Then I'll run after her."

"That would be a lovely sight. You're blind."

"I've regained my sight."

"You should have remained with the monks. Stayed there with your master in the monastery and painted, from youth to old age. You should never have met her."

"Do you know what, Teresa? It's very hard to worship. It's very easy to take someone's life, for example; it becomes easier and easier each time one does it, I've heard. You need only go to the place of execution to see how easy it is. It's an everyday thing, which happens constantly and without much ado. Those who are killed scream a little perhaps, but they end up like all the others, because the executioner practices his craft, completes his task. As does the soldier and as does the murderer. One is surprised at how simple it is to let somebody die, and finally one isn't even surprised any longer. But to worship, Teresa, that's difficult. It gets more and more difficult. Finally one has to leave the monastery. Leave the cathedral, leave the holy books, leave the faith."

"That's blasphemy."

"No. I'm following my path. It led me away from the monastery, to Maria; it led me through the realm of the dead, it led me here. And finally it led me to the young woman sleeping in there. She who resembles. Resembles so much it makes me ache. Now I have painted and worshiped what I've always wanted to paint and worship, painted the face that has always seen me, and that I thought I'd never see again, far less portray."

"She'll be your fate."

"She is my fate, and always has been."

They said no more to each other. I stole out quietly, and went to bed hungry. But I will say no more about the details in my master's story which I learned much later, because that is his story and not mine. That is his youth, his love. I think one only has the right to tell about his *own* youth. I've done that. It was tiring.

❧

The boy sat silently for a long time, with his head in his hands.

"But—" he began, "but what happened? What happened later?"

"He married her, just as he had said. In all simplicity, on the varnishing day, six months later. Two years afterward, he died peacefully."

"But—you?"

"I stayed with him until my apprenticeship was completed, a few months after the wedding. Then I left as quickly as possible. I never touched the girl again."

"You loved her?"

"Yes. I loved her. I truly loved her. Even if I didn't understand her, nor she me. But I loved her. And I never touched her afterward, but bore the sorrow like a cloak, an invisible cloak that I put on each morning before I went to my daily work. I thought then that I understood what my master had meant with his words about the invisible cloak. And I thought I would find the same peace as he. But I never found it. And I didn't grow through the loss and sorrow, but became smaller, because I didn't have my master's strength of soul. Or perhaps my loss was not as great as the one he suffered and it never became my destiny. Perhaps it wasn't a remarkable sacrifice, even if it felt heavy at the time. I was young. I got over it. I believe I did. I worked with gilding. I'm only a simple craftsman. I have no destiny."

"And the girl—Ho-Ho?"

"Maria. She bore the name Maria in the wedding, because no one knew her baptismal name. And she brought him trials and tribulations, the short time it lasted. Turned the house upside down. She was unfaithful to him with two of the apprentices. She had done that from the time she came into the house. In my time too. I just didn't know it; I thought I was the only one. So my noble behavior had made no difference to anyone except myself, my sacrifice hadn't protected my master from pain at all. Yet I'm glad he never experienced pain caused by me, because I loved him more than any of his other apprentices did, and I know he appreciated me and would have been very hurt if I had disappointed him. But he didn't get angry at her when he discovered it, and didn't beat her. She knew no better, and he forgave her. Instead he sent the apprentices away, and completely stopped painting for the rest of his life. But by then I had gone out into the world."

"Was she with him when he died?"

"She ran away a year after the wedding. Suddenly she wasn't there, had gone off into the woods at night, without taking anything with her. Maybe she had just wandered away, with no particular intentions. She was just gone, and took nothing with her. My master didn't seem to be unhappy, but he died lonely."

"Lonely." The boy had buried his head in his arms.

"I imagine him humming. The little folk song he always sang when he worked." The old man hummed a few notes. The boy looked up.

"I know that song too," the boy said in amazement. "My mother used to sing it to me."

"It's an old song, son," said Giuseppe Bassofondo. "All craftsmen sing it, and have always sung it. So if you heard it lying in the cradle, then you come from craftsman stock. But let me end here: after my master died he was carried in procession, under his guild's insignia, to rest in the village church, where he is buried under the floor in the choir, which he himself had painted. May God bless him and give him peace, may the Holy Virgin's hand touch him like the wing of a bird, and give him life and hope on Judgment Day."

The old man sat looking straight ahead, the light flickered over his hands, he smiled sadly, wearily. Then he closed his eyes.

"Go now," he said. It was barely a whisper. He opened his eyes for a moment: "Go now. And thank you."

The boy was about to say something, but the old man shook his head.

"I hope things go well for you," he said. "And don't forget me, or my master."

Fiorello took off his cape, the blue wool cape Lord Lorenzo had given him for the journey; he spread it over the old man so he would not be cold, drew it up to his chin. The old man had already closed his eyes, he was asleep. Fiorello slipped out quietly, walked up the stairs, came out into the street.

❦

Fiorello sat at the table in the room at the inn for a long time, while Simonetta slept. She was still tired after the journey. He chewed on the pen for a while, then he wrote to his master that the trip had been fruitless, that although it was true the old man, Giuseppe Bassofondo, still had certain vague memories about Master Girolamo Bonchiodo's atelier, unfortunately he could not remember the Madonna as a work of any particular worth, nor any of the circumstances surrounding its creation, and that one would therefore presume there was no longer anyone still alive who could provide further details about how the altar painting came to be. He continued scribbling elaborate polite regrets like this for a few more minutes, while he thought about what else he should write.

Fiorello put down the pen and just sat there a while, as the day rapidly came to an end in the streets, and life and sounds grew quieter. Simonetta lay asleep, stretched across the bed on her stomach with her head between her arms. She slept softly and quietly. They had traveled far to get here. I know nothing about her, thought Fiorello. And yet, I think I know more about her than anyone.

Next, Fiorello wrote that he most respectfully asked to be discharged, since he was nearly grown, and now desired to learn a proper craft. He had found a favorable opportunity here in Padua, he lied, which he could hardly refuse. Simonetta got out of bed, stretched, brushed the hair from her face. She looked at him, laughed quietly.

He pondered for a moment. Carpentry, he wrote, with a crooked smile. I don't know anything about her. I must ask her. It's best to begin asking in good time. It's important that everything is in good time.

From the depths of my heart I thank Your Lordship for the good years I have worked for you, and for the many good memories. I remain sincerely, Your Lordship's most faithful—

She stood by his chair, behind him, put her arms around him. He put the pen down. My beloved, he thought, my home.

Outside

PART

FOUR

ONE

INTERLUDE IN THE UNDERWORLD

· · ·

dic, cara raritas,
dic, rara Caritas,
*ubi nunc habitas?**

CARMINA BURANA, 131.1

darkness fell quickly. The sun went down over the wet, warm jungle; it was May and the monsoons would soon begin. A thin layer of condensation seemed to cling to every metal object, to the theodolite and the leveling rod, to the machines, to the tools, to the rifle barrels. He flung off his pith helmet and sat down in the deck chair on the veranda overlooking the pond. His khaki suit was covered with moisture, sweat, and stone dust, and his face was grimy. Large clusters of insects already swarmed in the air around him. Dragonflies flew across the water in the brief colorful twilight—enormous creatures, devil's darning needles, Satan's steeds, horse stingers, mosquito hawks—in every mineral color, always in mineral colors, malachite green, garnet red, cinnabar red, syenite navy blue; the birds of prey among insects, hovering horizontally in the damp air with their compound eyes with thirty thousand lenses and three ocelli to help see in the dark, watching in every direction for prey to capture in flight. Or for human eyes to stitch shut. The evening chorus of ungodly animal sounds rose in the forest, and he shouted for help.

*tell me, beloved rarity,
tell me, rare love
where are you now?

"Boy!"

"Yes, sir?" Caspar stood before him in spotless white. Caspar wasn't his native first name, but it was possible to pronounce.

The insects, he indicated with a movement of his head. Caspar covered the windows with mosquito netting, lit the lamp. The insects immediately began to thrash angrily against the netting.

"A bitter gin, that's a good boy. Thank you."

"On the double, sir."

"Chop-chop," he called after the servant gloomily; usually there was much humor in their relationship, considering the circumstances.

The drink appeared before him.

"A terrible day, Caspar. No luck. We had a major, regrettable accident."

"I'm sorry, sir."

"And the weather will be the end of us. Damned humid."

"It's the season, sir."

"Godless land, boy, verflucht noch mal."

"Yes, sir."

"Godless people."

"A great many interesting gods, sir."

"Another one, Caspar. A double."

"Very good, sir. Shall you be waiting up for Mr. Andersen?"

"Possibly, if he's not too late getting home from town. Make it less bitter this time, mind you."

His servant left, returned with a new glass. Sitting on the veranda for a while, he noticed how the stiff drink on an empty stomach seeped into him and made his whole body sickeningly sweet somehow. Godless place. Godless people. Godless insects. He could no longer stand to hear the furious buzzing sound as they tried to get through the netting, and extinguished the lamp. He sat in darkness. His assistant had at least seen the sunset in the city, the sly fellow, had regaled himself with friendly British bureaucrats and a sunset over the open sea. He should have gone to the city himself, and left the other man here with the problems.

The roof fell in again, he said to himself. Hellish ground to work in. Two dead wops again today. Andersen would have panicked, like the last time. This afternoon it had been the wops' own fault. Maybe. They needed to be careful, so they didn't have more trouble. They were close to success now, he could sense it. He felt in the breast pocket of his shirt; then carefully opened the packet and sat with the mineral in his hands. He was dirty and should have bathed before he sat down. He did not want to light the lamp again, so he contented himself with the flame of his cigarette lighter. It could have happened today, it could have. He saw the small fragments in the piece of stone, in the yellow gleam they became colorless; they looked promising. It could be the main vein they had struck today, before the accident occurred.

"Boy!" White clothing glimmered in the shadows. Caspar's voice was there immediately.

"Sir?" He must have been standing as he always did, patiently, in the darkness just inside the door, waiting.

"Dasselbe noch einmal."

"Yaworl, sir."

"Your German pronunciation still leaves a great deal to be desired."

"Unfortunately, very few German gentlemen in the area here, sir."

"Alagana pengal eppolothum makkal viruppamilai. That's because Germans don't like pretty girls." Caspar grinned, cheered by hearing his own language.

"Nanparkal eppolothum nanparkalai iya enru kuruvathilai. Very kind of you, sahib."

"Another double, Caspar. Encore!"

It stood before him.

"Shall you be needing the girl tonight, sir?" He said it straightforwardly, as if it concerned a sleeping pill.

"You're a godless people, Caspar, that's all I can say."

"We have low conceptions of what's proper," Caspar said kindly. "That's well known."

"Moreover, I don't *need* her; that's not what we're doing."

"No, sir." Outside the netting on the window, the fireflies were flying, like floating scraps of gold leaf.

Here I sit, he thought, stranded in the kingdom of Serendip, away from the war and everything. Ten thousand pounds sterling, he thought. Ten thousand pounds more, then he would have something to start with.

He thought about screaming men and burning huts; they had made an example of many people before the previous monsoon, after the bad accident and the mutiny. He remembered the smell and the flies above all, but only one of the blackening faces. However, he remembered that one face very well. But that was in the distant past. It was no longer necessary now. They had needed to do it less and less frequently. The last time was over a month ago. Even the girl didn't seem to think about it anymore. It was as if she had forgotten everything, forgotten her dead father, her beaten brother. She really didn't remember it. She smiled at him, spread her legs willingly and lovingly, opened herself like an orchid, like a sea anemone. For her, there seemed to be no connection between the person and his actions. He was one thing, his deeds something else. Or maybe the seed he spurted into her was an injection of forgetfulness. Afterward he always felt sick, but he didn't beat her; not anymore. Here I lie, he would say to himself, a man in the prime of life. A widower. What in the world am I doing here? I'm acting like a monster.

You must clothe yourself in the dragon's armor in order to understand it, someone had said.

Who had said that?

Fifteen thousand pounds more?

He sat alone in the dark again and felt how far away he was from home. Maybe it was the alcohol. And he felt that he was falling, that he had never stopped falling, falling backward, that he was still falling, like a stone, into the pitch-black darkness.

TWO

Maybe the whole story was just a fairy tale. And the fairy tale could perhaps begin something like this:

Once upon a time, long, long ago, there was a miner—or to put it more correctly, a mining engineer—and perhaps not so long ago either? But he was a miner now, and he loved the mountain, had loved it since childhood; loved its druse cavities and syenite veins, its harsh black hornblende, its shining mica, thin as a leaf, and its peaceful, rigid wave patterns once created by cataclysmic continental movements. He loved its metals and its crystal deposits, and he loved the fossils in the layers of sediment. Already as a young boy his room was filled with fossils he had gathered himself in a limestone field by the sea. No fantastic examples, but quite a good amateur collection—odd extinct forms, graptolites, brachiopods, chain corals, slipper corals, horn corals, cylindrical and curved squid shells (*Orthoceras* and ammonites), which appealed to his sense of the dramatic in nature, and the inevitable. Take just the trilobite—a species with a rich history of development through several geological periods; he had collected at least twenty different examples, and a whole box of trilobite fragments. At one time, in the Cambrian period, the land was covered by ocean, and the trilobites went to work immediately, through the entire Cambrian and into the Ordovician period and on toward the Silurian. During two hundred million years the little sea creature created an endless number of inferior species and variants, over ten thousand; then it ended with the little sea dung beetle (he knew perfectly well it wasn't a dung beetle, but the shape resembled one). Two hundred million years. While the land sank and rose, and seas came and went, while the continents slowly slid back and forth across the earth's crust, while the Baltic and Canadian plates pulled away from each other and later met and shoved bedrock up into the light. The trilobite quietly moved around in the shallow Cambrian sea and busied itself with its own concerns. How long could such a creature live? A few months? A few years? They sloughed their skin, like crayfish, and ate small organisms in the slime. One of the trilobites in his collection, the most beautiful, had rolled itself into a pretty ball. Had it defended itself? Was it afraid? It is dead and buried in the ooze, is disintegrating, the hollow space in the mass is filled with other sediment, petrifies, and then five hundred million years pass, while the sea rises and falls, while the continental plates crash together and press mountains high into the air, while ten-meter-tall horsetail plants and giant ferns and club moss trees as tall as a ten-story house grow in large, wet, birdless forests, the petrified trilobite lies there. While lizards wander on the earth and disappear again, while volcanoes erupt in Skagerrak and the little four-toed horse gallops along the beaches, while the ice settles and scrapes mountains to gravel, time after time, while someone chops with a flint ax, the cast of the frightened little trilobite lies there. Until a young boy with a hammer finds it in a stone. It has waited for him. It lies like an egg in his hand.

He had gone around with his hammer like that, and he was perhaps eleven years old the first time he thought about how old the world is. The curled-up trilobite fossil lay in its bed of cotton in the typesetter's case he used for his collection—it looked almost as if it were alive.

This human species to which he belonged, this noble ultimate consequence of everything—of the brachiopods and graptolites, the lizards and horses with all their different numbers of toes—which now hit a stone or two with a hammer, or sent some ships to war or to the bottom of the sea, or built pyramids and temples, cathedrals and churches, or held a popular vote for or against national prohibition of alcohol. Yes, what should one think? What difference did it make, one way or another? Someday an ocean will come and cover us with slime. Time is long, and the sun is old.

Had he thought like that? Probably not. But when as a fifteen-year-old he mustered the courage to go and see his father in the library, he was certain he was right. His father was a little worried, both about what his wife would say and what effect it would have in the small town when the company owner's eldest son didn't want to set a good example for the county's other young people and be confirmed (it was sure to raise quite an uproar), but he completely respected his son's wish. The boy was bright, thought clearly, and rarely said anything without a basis for it. Hadn't he encouraged his son's scientific interest himself? Hadn't he seen the direction in which the new times were headed? Wasn't this exactly what he had predicted? But at the same time, he didn't want to be an irresponsible father.

"I assume this is a question of conscience for you?" he said sternly. And the son replied: "No. But Earth wasn't created six thousand years ago."

"It wasn't?"

"No, Father. That's a geological fact." His father had to smile.

"And what does this have to do with your confirmation?"

"I'm not quite sure."

"So! You don't know?"

"It's just that—"

"Out with it!"

"It seems to me that the belief is founded on unsound reasoning when based on the notion that the world was created by God six thousand years ago, period. I can't confess to believing in such a religion."

His father was satisfied.

"So you can't hold this belief even partially, aside from the matter of creation?"

"No," said the son. "I don't believe any of it. I don't see God's hand in creation, I see only processes. And, in the larger perspective, I don't see what's supposedly so wonderful about human beings as a species either. The species come and go."

"Those are big words from a young man," said his father, but did not ridicule him. "And the Messiah?"

The son did not answer, just looked down in shame. No, no, thought his father, that was a stupid question. Instead he said: "There are many great men who have believed in God, without being fools." The son looked straight ahead, past his father, past the old clock and out through the window, out into the garden, which was in full bloom.

"I'd prefer not to do it," he said then. "It would be just playacting if I stood at the altar and played the hypocrite."

"That's all right," said his father. "You won't have to. Your mother will take it hard. But don't worry. I'll bear the brunt. I'll suggest that we have a family celebration anyway, so you can still get confirmation presents. What do you say?"

"I—that's very kind, but—I'd rather not do that either. Wouldn't it be a little artificial? Can't I get out of that, Father?"

His father was very proud. Besides, he knew the boy did not enjoy obligatory family events much—just like himself, for that matter.

"We'll see," he said. "Your mother may insist, and you'll have to go along with that."

"Yes, Father."

"This matter of geology—it's really something you're interested in?"

"Yes, Father."

"That will be your major field of study, then."

"I hope so."

"You really should study business and economics, and perhaps agriculture. You're going to take over here one day."

"I can study that at the same time," the son said eagerly.

"I agree," said the father. "It's much more important that you get what you can from a scientific field. The country is changing, and we must be equipped to create value in new areas. Besides, one learns systematic thinking better through scientific study than by taking only business courses; most people in that field seem utterly crazy."

The son made no reply. But was happy. And there *was* a family party. His father gave him a reflection goniometer, much too expensive, for examining crystals. His father was proud and wanted to show it. And the goniometer was quickly put to use during his high-school years; he gradually left the fossils and began to seriously study minerals and rock species. Just as he had avoided the confirmation playacting, he deftly and systematically avoided everything else that smacked of pretense and false sentiment.

What did the grown-ups quarrel about anyway? What did his fellow high-school students talk about so intensely? He avoided it, paid no attention to it, for no sense of greatness came over him when he listened to it, no enthusiasm, no truth. Whereas the rock crystals' angles and proportions—*they* were true. So true he could get shivers down his spine when his gaze into the ocular suddenly focused on this pure expression of the world's enduring concepts. They were *concrete* ideas, they were *visible*. *They* worked, always. Why fight about words, when there was so much undiscovered *truth* in the world? What were words? Continental plates shift back and forth, the world is shaken by earthquakes, by upheavals, by everything that comes and goes. True joy, real enthusiasm, is as unchangeable as the innate properties of minerals. He never gave a thought to the idea that he should take over after his father. Didn't he have brothers? As for him, he thought, he would forever be satisfied with a field hammer in one hand and a geological map in the other, along with a few sandwiches in the pocket of his windbreaker. And his father calmly accepted that his eldest son disappeared to Minnesund to search for beryls for a whole summer, or that he sat with his nose in thick books day in and day out. True, the trip to Minnesund resulted in a pretty necklace for his mother, but aside from that, he wasn't of much practical use. But his father didn't worry, for he held the old belief that a person who can count can also do all sorts of other things if necessary. Moreover, he *had* other sons after all, fine sons, so if the eldest son should decide to devote his life to the mysteries of rock species, it wasn't a serious sacrifice. Because he was proud of the boy, he saw his son's happiness with the subject and enthusiasm for learning; besides, he belonged to the rational school and seriously meant what he had said about what was needed to build the country.

So the son became a mineralogist, and later a mining engineer. Perhaps what happened to him was a fairy tale, all of it, or perhaps it was the flare of a small organism, a flash of lightning in the millions of years. Just look at him, as he leaves home that snowy morning, lost in his own thoughts, like a happy Professor Ruminator.

THREE

It had snowed all night, thickly and quietly, like a white whisper from heaven. It was still snowing when the engineer left home in the darkness about six o'clock in the morning, but now as very fine precipitation, no longer as heavy swirls of thick flakes. He was a rather young man, tall and erect, but not athletic. The wolf-skin fur coat he wore as protection against the cold did not really suit him, he did not yet have either the ability or the figure to really *strut* in it, the way one should in order to look right in such a luxurious article of clothing. Instead, when he began walking in there, it seemed to take awhile before the fur too began to move and follow along. Nevertheless he was quite elegant, with tousled blond hair beneath the fur hat and pale blue, slightly dreamy eyes beneath a forehead that was still white with sleep. But he was completely awake, because he loved snowy weather. This January morning in 1937 he was twenty-five years old and he was going to his work, his *own* work, his first *position*—the fur coat was, for that matter, a slightly too elegant good-luck gift from a slightly too proud father.

He had begun his work up here in the old mining town several months ago, when the winter and the snow that would come were still just a thought among the red-and-golden autumn trees. And when he saw the little town for the first time, he had decided it was the right place to meet this winter, his first as a free and independent man. Despite his scientific education, at that time he was one of those people who act purely out of feeling and not from forethought. It had been like that with geology too, his *enthusiasm* had taken him by the hand when he found his first rock crystal as a boy—a decision method that he, as a good realist, could not explain or defend, but which nevertheless had made him take the position at the mine here, even though he had gotten a better offer someplace in the north. But when he came here and saw the little town in the autumn, he was sure he was right and did not want to be anywhere else. He saw the little house they would get, he and Karin, and he imagined how Vesla would ride on his shoulders, and how they would go far up into the hills and mountains together as soon as she got bigger and could enjoy it.

The ground had been bare during a raw, disagreeable period of mild weather that lasted until Christmas, but now the snow had finally come and he delighted in it as he walked. The days between Christmas and New Year's had been dark, cold, very sleepy. Today he was properly awake, awake and warm. That was not due to the wolf-skin fur coat, it was the snow, because snow makes one warm.

Sleds and cars made deep, blue tracks in the white carpets that had been streets. When horses plodded past him, he heard their hooves only as faint thuds against the soft snow. They lifted their hooves higher than usual, and moisture rose from their heads and flanks. They seemed almost not to touch the ground as they approached, and each time they lifted their hooves their horseshoes glistened. Like airy beings, like snorting cloud phantoms, they danced and glided through the falling snow.

It was not a thick, wet snowfall, and the air was quite chilly. The grains that sifted down in the sparsely lighted streets were individual crystals: delicate, perfect. Several times he stopped and studied them in the glow of a streetlight as they fell on his coat; he examined them with the same elated interest as when he was a boy. The crystals stuck to the fur: unique, beautiful. There really is no word, he thought, to describe crystalline classifications, other than purely abstract concepts. Rhombus. Tetrahedron. Octahedron. So the crystals also are a representation of something totally abstract and unseen, of adherence to laws we don't understand completely. A *tree* one can understand and immediately describe, so it comes alive for us. A house too. Perhaps even a face, if one is skillful. But a crystal can't be described; it's an expression for, and reproduction of, a principle, a force that lies behind the other visible things that *can* be described, a principle that can only be described with the help of principles. Look at them shining there, he thought, in lovely ramifications on my fur coat, they almost remind one of graptolite colonies or certain coral formations (strange, how life in its simplest forms imitates minerals). They lie there for a moment, barely sticking to the long wolf hairs, before they melt in the warmth of my face and turn into water, ordinary water.

They are the water's secret principle.

It's strange that an abstract principle can still be so beautiful, even if it can't be portrayed.

He had to smile a little at himself as he stood there with his nose on the sleeve of his coat. If people see me now, he thought, they will think I'm crazy. A grown man, an engineer at that, staring at snow crystals; people don't do such things. But the funny thing is, I have papers to show that I'm permitted to be crazy. You could say that I'm *warranted* to do that. It is, so to speak, *expected* of me that I should stand and stare at snow crystals. In any case, at crystals. I'm certainly fortunate to have those papers.

As he walked farther he continued to fantasize about a poetic resemblance that had struck him back in his student days, when just for fun he made comparisons between the endless variations in the shape of snow crystals (no two are alike; that's the little bit most people know about snow crystals, this fascinating, but oh so fleeting, subject). Anyway, the resemblance between snow crystals on the one hand and plankton's many beautiful forms on the other hand. The ocean's snow, he had thought poetically, and probably was careful not to express such a thought too openly. For at that time, when the future mineralogist had not yet received his passport to madness and fantasy, he always obediently turns back to the mysteries of the magma. To tell the truth, the reason he sits there, with the magma, at the institute, is in order to get such a document, and none of the students have time for comparative phenomenology or similar disciplines. The country must be developed. Mines must be dug, tunnels blasted, projected railroads built. Useful new minerals and vital substances must be found. So a childish fascination with the beauty of snow crystals and plankton becomes as meaningless as the beauty of the geode cavities where the quartz reveals itself in the rock like a sealed, shimmering, lilac secret, or as unimportant as the monumental beauty of giant's kettles that gravel, water, and ice have hollowed out in a mountain, as only Nature's true giants can: gravel, ice, and water. During a student fieldwork project in connection with a new road to the north, they had come upon a truly monumental giant's kettle, six meters deep and polished so absolutely perfectly that the soft veins in the red granite were visible; the erratic boulders still lay at the bottom. He had lowered himself into it, admired it, worshiped it, let his hands glide along the smooth walls. It was icy cold down there, and he could see his breath even though it was the middle of July; it's cold in the giant's kettle. There wasn't a single patch of moss growing on the walls, they were too smooth. Granite measures 7.5 on the hardness scale, it's one of the hardest rock species we know, and yet water and ice had managed to do what people must use dynamite for. "Gutta cavat lapidem, non vi, sed saepe cadendo"—the drop hollows out the stone, not with force, but by falling often. But one doesn't have time for Latin quotations when there are examinations to take in magma, a country to build, a tunnel to blast. He had gone down into the mountain, down into the kettle's cavity, several times during pauses in the work; he had dreamed about the giant's kettle lying in his sleeping bag in the tent at night. The fourth day he had gone along to blow it up with explosives. He did not feel well in the weeks that followed, but a country must be built. A giant's kettle, created by giant drops, is just as incidental to building the country as the folktale about the giant and the kettle once was; if the giant's kettle lies in the way of the new road, then it must be blasted away. But he had discovered it, had been the first to go down into it, and he felt as if he had blasted away a secret in his own mind, even if he was not the one who filled the bore holes or detonated the charge.

"Gutta cavat lapidem"—that wasn't just Latin, it was improper as well, he thought with a smile. It was Ovid who had written that, the old Roman swine, before Caesar Augustus sent him into exile for immorality. Publius Ovidus Naso, with his long nose, which he stuck into all sorts of things that were none of his business, and for which he was expelled from the country. The words came from Book I of *Ars Amatoria*, or *The Art of Love*, a work that the young man had studied very thoroughly the last year of his studies, for urgent reasons.

He smiled, licked the crystal water from his sleeve, and started up the long hill to the mine shaft. Coming down the hill toward him were men from the night shift on their way home. They raised their caps to him wearily. Some of them. He gave a fur-clad greeting in return.

It was a matter of dripping for a long time, said Ovid. And he had dripped and dripped, because Karin had been hard as gneiss. Now she was asleep down in their little house, with Vesla held tightly in the crook of her arm; Vesla had awakened and started crying about four o'clock again last night, and he had walked the floor with her for over an hour until she calmed down, and then he had put her to bed with her mother. As for himself, he had been fresh and wide awake, and had sat down to read by the kitchen table for the scant hour that was left before he had to go.

He was very, very happy.

This morning he hung up his fur coat in the office as usual, put on his work clothes and helmet, was issued a lamp and backpack as usual, and began the descent in the hoist to level 175, the Fortuna drift. It was nice and warm down in the mountain, cozy, and suddenly very quiet. The change from the winter cold made him start sweating even before he had reached the lunchroom, where a couple of foremen were drinking coffee; foreman Knudsen on the morning shift and one of the old fellows, foreman Hoel from the night shift.

" 'Mornin', sir."

"Good morning."

"Coffee?"

"Yes, thanks."

Most of the men liked the absentminded, bespectacled young engineer; he made no distinctions among them, seemed equally absentminded with everyone. And he never thought himself too good to sit down and have a cup of coffee. He seated himself on the hard wooden bench beside them in the little hollow that was the lunchroom.

"Are you goin' to the old Ulrik drift again today?"

"Yes," said the engineer. "Here are the maps." He spread out the yellowed papers for the men, who examined them with the air of experts. "I've already mapped five hundred meters in. It looks good."

"Uff," said foreman Knudsen. "You've gotta be careful when you go in there."

"Yes," said the engineer. "I'm always careful."

" 'Cuz this paper ain't worth the ink it's written with," Knudsen continued.

"Oh."

"It looks so nice on paper. But I'll tell you one thing, I was in there pokin' around once, and it was like a Swiss cheese."

"Hmm," said the engineer. "I'll be careful."

"Is there deposits in there?" asked Hoel, who had said nothing until now.

"That's what we're going to find out," said the engineer. "We have to search now."

They gave him a serious look.

"We need to explore all possibilities," said the engineer, equally serious. "That's why we need to map the old mine first. Unfortunately, I'm not sure how far in it goes. Maybe there are veins farther in. We'll take samples when we've mapped the lode more precisely. We may find a continuation of the Ulrik vein in there somewhere, if we're lucky."

"I don't believe none of this," said Hoel. "They wouldn't of given 'em up, if they'd been profitable. I think the Ulrik goes up higher, up there."

"*You* can't know that," Knudsen objected.

"I just have a feelin'."

"Well, I don't know," said the engineer, which was true. "It's possible it goes upward. It's also possible the Ulrik is completely exhausted. But remember that today we've got methods of investigation that didn't exist a hundred and fifty years ago."

"They gave 'em up way long before that," said Hoel. "There's nothin' in there, that's what I think. I heard they went in farther just in case they struck somethin' more."

"That ain't necessarily true," said Knudsen.

"There are several passages in there," said the engineer, "where the Ulrik meets the old shafts from the earliest days."

"Take a cat to go in there without light," said Hoel.

"A Swiss cheese," Knudsen repeated. "They didn't go in wide before, like they do now. They dug around and forward and up and down like rats, depending on their whim, no system. There's drift paths all over, and lots more crosscuts than on this here paper."

"It's not exactly easy to make sense of it," the engineer admitted. "But that's why I need to go in there." And as he reminded himself of this, he drained his coffee cup in one gulp. "Well, men, I've got to get going. Sleep well today."

"Thanks."

He walked farther in and down toward the barricaded drift, lit his lantern, and checked to make sure he had his hammer, chisel, measuring tape, and notebook in his overall pockets so he wouldn't have to go back that long way. The mine was swarming with life at this hour, and he kept having to leap aside for wagons and other traffic. At the 180 level, by the old drift, a dark, untrafficked side passage branched off, and he entered it. The barrier was twenty meters farther in, and here the Ulrik drift began its way inward.

This was his first important task, to map the Ulrik drift and the adjacent parts of the old mine, and he was happy doing it. The whole day, from early morning until late at night, he roved around deep within the mountain, with his lantern as his only company, and tried to get an overview of what might be hidden in there. He was never afraid. He was where he belonged, after all, inside the mountain, and he regularly found interesting indications. Then he stopped, took notes eagerly, marked his position on the map, and continued. He had a headlamp and hand lantern, and a flashlight in reserve besides. As he walked along, slowly, he let his gaze glide up and down the walls and roofs of the tunnels, he observed the mountain's passages and branchings, searched for traces of veins. Sometimes the map was imprecise, but he was always careful. Besides, he went slowly, in order to absorb everything. He never looked at his watch, because the silence in here and the sight of the glittering minerals and traces of ore made him happy, put him almost in a trance; he was *in* all of it, *saw* the mountain. It was so peaceful, nothing could reach him. He had plenty of time to think. If he got hungry, he sat down calmly on the stump of an old beam and ate his sandwiches; he had a thermos in his backpack. No sound was to be heard, other than perhaps a little dripping water. But otherwise it was silent, a silence one never can experience on the earth's surface, the absolute absence of sound. If he stopped walking, he heard his breathing, his beating heart, his body's small and large sounds. If he turned his hearing outward: nothing. The mountain rose dead and motionless around him.

And still he knew that forces dwelled in it, slow forces, movements, pressures, and tensions that were simply there, that were so slow that centimeters had to be figured in thousands of years. If he thought this thought, it struck him that the mountain nevertheless had a sound, some sort of deep tone, far within the silence. Although not a *tone*; what he sensed was actually the pause *between* the vibrations in this slow, slow sound. *Once* during the weeks in the old mine he had heard a large stone loosen and thunder down somewhere behind him; that was that, he thought, *one* vibration. Maybe it will be a year until the next time. Or maybe it was just the beginning of a vibration, just the oscillating prewave.

Also this morning the silence put him in a happy mood. He made his way in toward the place he had marked the day before, examined the map, looked at the compass, and began to go farther in. He was not afraid of getting lost. The few times he had gone astray in his work he had laid a rope behind him, like a second Theseus in the labyrinth, and quickly found his way back. It was just a matter of keeping a cool head and orienting yourself. He had always had a good sense of direction. And he was not afraid, moreover, because it was only a mountain after all.

As he walked farther in, the drift became narrower, and there were also a number of crosscuts. He went very slowly and carefully, seven or eight steps at a time, stopped and shone a light for a corresponding stretch ahead before he began to walk again. At each stretch he shone his light up and down the walls to see if there was anything interesting. He checked the map continually. It took a long time to make his way inward like this, but he did not get tired.

When he had gone in surely half a kilometer, he stopped. It was evident from the echo and the ventilation that the space expanded above him now, and he shone a light upward.

An enticing gleam of silver glittered up there.

Then he dropped his lantern on the ground and it went out.

He swore, groped along the ground in the light from his headlamp, found the lantern, fiddled with it a bit, got it lit. He shone it upward again.

All he could see was gleaming black bedrock everywhere.

But he *had* seen the silver. He shone the lantern upward once more, let the beam of light search for the roof that sloped up in the direction he was going; he turned, took a few steps here and there to see if the angle might make a difference, but did not see any silver.

Confound it, he thought. It *was* there. He took a few more steps in different directions, shone the light systematically along the roof, took still another step backward. Then the ground disappeared from under him, and for a moment he floated, floated without feeling. In that brief moment it seemed to him that he knew everything, and it annoyed him that he had taken a false step, he realized during these tenths of a second that he was falling, that he had stepped into a drift that wasn't on the map. Or maybe it was there; the passage was wide and maybe he hadn't looked carefully enough, he had dropped the map and the lantern when he fell so he couldn't look anyway, besides he was falling, so it didn't matter if the drift was on the map or not. In any case, he was in the drift now, in the air, and he realized it was deep, and he was strangely annoyed that he was going to die.

Ammm. He lay there. It was completely dark all around him. Perhaps he was unconscious for some moments, or a whole hour, but it was dark nonetheless. It didn't matter much whether he had his eyes open or not, but he knew that he was awake and that his eyes were open. He lay there. His back felt numb and painful from the fall. So he was lying on his back. So he was alive. But his headlamp and lantern were gone, and something warm under the back of his head told him that he was probably bleeding. But here he lay. A substratum held up his head, back, and buttocks, but his limbs, his arms and legs, hung straight down and seemed very heavy. He lay there in the darkness and tried to understand how he was lying. He supposed that the swaying, unpleasant feeling was dizziness, and that everything would have sailed up and down like seasickness had it not been too dark to use his eyes. Despite the swaying feeling in his whole body, he took the chance of moving his right arm, groped around carefully, down and to the side, but found only emptiness. At that moment he nearly lost his balance and almost rolled off the substratum his back rested on, so he reached in toward the substratum, held fast. He heard a rattling sound as something fell, gravel or sand, then everything was silent. He thought: I must lie very, very still now. He should have a flashlight in his right back pocket, and he tried to carefully ease his right hand under his buttocks without losing his balance, in order to find the light and take it out. He was probably lying on a projecting beam, because he could feel the form of the beam along his thighs and arms. He tightened his knees and thighs against the beam and lifted his buttocks a tiny bit, carefully, for the beam (if it *was* a beam) was too thick for him to be able to grip around it with his left arm; he raised himself slowly, without losing his balance, and with his right hand reached under himself, in the right back pocket, found the loop on the flashlight, pulled it out with his thumb. It hung on his right thumb, and he lowered his buttocks again to the substratum, to the beam.

At the same time he heard a rattle of broken glass under him and he knew the light was broken and wouldn't work. Even so, he fumbled feverishly with it in the dark until he found the switch, pushed it up. No light. He pushed it down again, shook the light, pushed it up. Broken flashlight glass sprinkled over his right hand, the shards trickled over the back of his hand and disappeared without a sound.

It must be very far down below him.

He fiddled with the flashlight for a while, then gave up. He felt toward the broken glass with his index finger, felt that the bulb was broken and that only the socket remained. He held the flashlight in his right hand, which hung down into nothing, as did his left arm and both legs. Had he fallen far? Five meters? Ten? How far down was it? He thought for a moment, then he let the flashlight fall, fall into the pitch blackness that was below him. He let it go, and all was silent. All was silent and silent, a thousand and one, thousand and two, thousand and three, all was silent, thousand and five. He stopped counting. Then he heard the flashlight hit the bottom of the drift, faintly, from deep down.

It was at least a hundred and fifty meters down to the next level. He had fallen, how far he did not know, but hardly more than four or five meters. Maybe less. He lay on a projecting beam; he had been lucky. He had no idea how far out from the drift wall he lay. One meter, maybe two. How far out did the beam stretch? Impossible to know. Didn't it stop just above his head? Maybe. Maybe there was an upward path right by his feet, along the drift wall, maybe not. It was impossible to find out, because it was pitch dark the whole time. Good heavens, how dark it was. And absolutely quiet. He heard his own breathing and his own heartbeat. If he turned his hearing outward, everything was absolutely silent. He had walked many hundred meters into an old drift, and there was no one nearby. No one would miss him for many hours. His back was extremely painful. He must have fallen quite a distance. He must lie very, very still, during all the hours it would take for anyone to miss him, sound the alarm, discuss the situation, enter the labyrinth of the Ulrik drift, and perhaps find him. What time was it actually? Nine in the morning? Ten? No one would miss him before five o'clock at the earliest. In other words, seven or eight hours. He closed his eyes. Did he close his eyes? Seven hours. He had to lie absolutely motionless, without going to sleep and without shifting his balance, because the beam on which he lay was narrow. He had to stay awake.

"Help!" he shouted. The shout died away immediately, without an echo. "Help! Help!"

Below him he felt the depths as a faint shiver in his limbs, which hung like a tangled mass of seaweed, downward. Above him he felt the ventilation from the drift somewhere up there. The mountain was silent.

"Help!" He shouted so loudly his lungs ached. "Aaah! Help!"

Just be calm now. Calm. This doesn't help. It doesn't help to shout. You have to lie still for seven, maybe eight hours. Maybe even longer. You're tired. You're in pain. But you must not move. The small of your back aches. But you must not move. Body, lie still. Yes. But eight hours—

It was dark. The coffee had tasted good. Lie still.

You who in life's morning stand
think about life's nighttime too.
Mid gladness think of sadness, and
think that death will capture you.
E'en the lovely rose, my friend,
withers someday in the end.
Fidelionkongkongkongkei
fidelionkongkongkongkei.

A Trondheim student song, a parody of a broadsheet ballad. What was it called? "Martin in the Locomotive," that was it. It had at least thirty verses and was incredibly funny. If only he could remember more than the first verse. But he hadn't been one who often took part in student singing and fun.

You who in life's morning stand
think about life's nighttime too.

No. That was the first verse.

Martin in the locomotive stood—

No.

An eternal sense of shame
Martin Pedersen hath tied
to the railroad's noble name
by the wretched way he died.
You're here today, rosy and red
then gone tomorrow, bloody and dead.

No. That wasn't right. Not right, and furthermore, not especially cheerful either.

Fidelionkongkongkongkei,
fidelionkongko-ongkongkei.

Hmm. The refrain was pretty good.

For the last time in his life
Martin stands on his own feet.

Maybe he ought to find something else to sing. Another song from student days.

Under Italy's blue sky
among vast mountain tops am I,

looking upward—oh so far!—
to my shining, lucky star.
Never will I forget, Italy my home.

That was better. More cheerful, somehow. Good Lord, how many verses would he have to sing before eight hours had passed?

Never will I forget, Italy my home.

He closed his eyes. Did he close his eyes? The glow of a pink lampshade on a night table, girlish and pretty, and a bed as soft as a cumulus cloud, with a duvet as airy as a ptarmigan's breast. After a Saturday at the student center, after a musical revue and a dance, it was quiet. Just the light and the duvet, just the soft mattress and a girl's hair in his nose. Did all girls smell as sweet? He trembled with happiness, he trembled with elated fear—

Don't fall now.

—he trembled with elated fear and happiness when he felt her skin, dear God, her skin that he had desired for weeks and months, like a silky soft shock against his own. He was completely naked and rubbed his trembling body against her.

"Shh," she said. "Shh."

He tried to throw himself on her, but she just stroked his shoulders and neck and made him relax, made him lie on his back, relax.

"Why are you so active, Willy?"

"Am—am I active, do you think?"

"Mmm."

Caramba. Mid gladness think of sadness. He closed his eyes in shame.

She laughed softly, he heard the duvet rustle, then she lay on top of him and he felt her breath against the hollow of his throat, fragrant as autumn leaves.

"There's no need to be so active, is there, Willy?"

No.

"You're nice," she said.

"If I'm active," he began, and cleared his throat, "it's because—because I—"

"Shh," she said. "I've been longing for you too. Just look." She sat up, astride him, the duvet fell off her and he saw all of her. Everything was pink and red in this light, even her hair, although she was blond. Her eyes were narrowed, she smiled sweetly at him, moved back and forth a little, he grew warm inside, from his groin and upward, a soft red warmth.

"I—I love you so much," he whispered; he didn't know if she could hear it, he whispered so softly. But there were indications that she had heard. She leaned forward slightly, raised herself a little, kissed him, and he slid into her.

It was soft and gentle and not difficult at all.

She moved, he just lay there. At first her movements were slow, then faster, her breasts were pink and swayed in rhythm to the movement; dear God, he thought, this will go too fast, her breasts were the most beautiful things he had ever seen, and because they were so beautiful everything would—he had to keep his thoughts focused on something, *all mammals have milk glands*, he thought feverishly, *and these are a vital necessity for them*. Oh, dear God. Now he went still farther into her, now she leaned forward so her breasts lay against his chest, dear God, now, fortunately, she straightened her back again, and he saw them once more, *therefore milk glands must have been created in the most ancient past*, he silently quoted further, while he shut his eyes and tried to pretend nothing was happening, *and we cannot know anything definitive about their development* . . . Oh, dear God. What was she doing? He had to open his eyes after all. Now she raised herself even higher, pulled her knees under her, impaled herself while she arched her body backward. Karin. She had been hard as gneiss, but she was no longer hard, she was soft, soft as water and fertile ooze, he had her now, she had let him in, they had walked home together, just the two of them, on a evening filled with autumn leaves and rain, finally alone, finally alone, she had taken his hand and held it tight the whole time from when they crossed the river, he had kissed her by a wrought-iron fence, and she had held his hand, his trembling hand. I've longed for you so much, he had whispered; you're nice, do you know that, she had whispered. Then they were at her home, and she had let him in, into the soft bed and the pink light, her breasts stuck straight up and she laughed while everything tightened and softened around him. He clenched his teeth.

Most supporters of the theory of evolution believe that mammals are descended from a type of pouch animal, and if this is the case, milk glands must have originally developed in the fetus pouch. All of a sudden, she was absolutely motionless above him, like a drawn bow bent backward, then she bent in the opposite direction, fell on top of him again, lay still. It had gone well. She breathed heavily, her back was damp and cool with sweat. He had managed to do it. *In accordance with prevailing laws of specialization, the glands in a certain area of the pouch had to be more highly developed than the rest, and they would then form breasts, but initially without nipples, as we see with the platypus at the beginning of the mammal phylum. How the glands became more especially developed than others over time, whether it was partially compensation for growth, the result of use, or natural selection—I will not attempt to determine.*

Neither will I, he thought.

He was calm now. He had managed to do it. She raised her head, looked straight at him, observed him contentedly.

"You're good," she breathed.

Bless Charles Darwin.

"It's just natural selection," he murmured cockily.

"I want more," she whispered.

"But—your parents."

"They won't be home before tomorrow."

"Oh."

Hammm. Don't go to sleep. Don't go to sleep. Then you'll never see her again, not if you go to sleep, then you'll roll off.

"You who in life's morning stand, think of Italy my home!"

He shouted it, this time so loudly it echoed in the drift, and then everything was quiet again. He had awakened himself. But then she was there in the darkness again.

"More," she said. "I know you can."

"Yes," he whispered.

"Don't wait this time," she said.

He closed his eyes for a second, then she had turned them, they had turned themselves, he saw her face under him and the movement began again, hard, sweet, soft. He let go of all thoughts of the origin of the species, and as he shouted from enjoyment and from a year of repressed desire, he was very soon completely inside the mystery of his own origin.

"Just look how it's sucking."

"Don't call her *it*, Willy."

"But, my sweet, it is an *it*. The demonstrative pronoun in the Norwegian language."

"You're such a pedant, sometimes." But she wasn't annoyed, merely pretended to be.

"Besides, it's just like a little monkey. *She* is."

"Do you think so?"

"A pretty little monkey. She has your eyes."

"It's probably a bit early to say that."

"No, she has your eyes, Karin."

She made no reply, raised her back carefully so the baby didn't lose her breast.

"Are you worn out? Do you have any pain?"

"No. I'm fine."

"Did you know that kangaroos have their larynges way up in their noses so they won't be choked by their mother's milk as babies? It's terribly practical, but that's why kangaroos are mute."

"Oh, Wilhelm, you talk so romantically. Isn't she beautiful?"

"Yes," he said. "You're both beautiful. I'm so proud of you. Well, hello. A little burp, eh. Ooops, a little more. Ish, what a mess you make."

"She doesn't have her larynx in her nose, you know."

"Thanks, I can hear that. My goodness, what a voice. Does she cry like that all the time?"

"Yes."

"I see. Will it be many years before she stops doing that?"

"Yes, Willy. Six or seven years, at least. You'll just have to get used to it."

"I suppose it's not so bad when you get used to it."

"Are you happy?"

"Yes, Karin. I've never been so happy."

"Me neither. Shh. There, there, little one. Mommy is here. Mommy and Daddy. Mommy and Daddy are always here."

The baby found the breast again.

He looked at Karin's face; it was a little long and irregular, not really pretty but so strangely full of everything. She was the prettiest woman he knew. She was even prettier now than the first time he saw her, and even then she had been the prettiest woman he had ever seen. If only she had been here now, here in the darkness with him, then she could have sung. She could do things like that. She could play both the piano and the violin, and was also a good dancer (which he wasn't—he danced the same four steps regardless of whether they played a fox-trot or a tango); she knew the words to all sorts of songs and everything else it was fun to know. They weren't at all alike. He was a rationalist and scientist, she was—like that. Maybe that was why he fell so deeply in love with her when she stood before him in the doorway of his student apartment that winter Sunday morning with her knapsack dangling from one shoulder, looked at him cheerfully out of gray eyes and said that she was an envoy, an envoy from his friend Finn, and that they were going skiing now; if he would please come along, Finn and a couple of other friends were waiting down in the street. He looked at her, did not understand, rubbed the sleep out of his eyes. Skiing? Yes, in Bymarka. His whole body trembled while he dressed and packed his knapsack, faster than had ever been done in the entire history of Norway he was sure, just so he would have the pleasure of walking down the stairs with this girl, the most beautiful girl he had ever seen, who stood shifting from one foot to the other at the threshold of his door and scratched her neck under the lining of her windbreaker.

The rest of the day he just followed behind her in her ski tracks and looked at the small of her back and her elbows.

She painted and drew and dreamed of being an actress, things like that. She wrote. As for himself, he went around with his samples of rock hardness in his bag and wasn't able to say a single word when she was nearby. He just looked at her. She probably noticed that he looked at her. But for one thing, she was already keeping company with a lieutenant from Kristiansund, and for another, they never talked to each other. He became mute when it was just the two of them. She thought he was dull. They had a nice, friendly relationship, in a way. That bothered him. But he held firmly to the thought of her, did not give up, waylaid her after meetings and parties, stood outside her door in the morning, went to see productions and hear concerts, read poetry and novels, developed a new vocabulary. But unfortunately, it made little impression on her when he tried to stammer his newly acquired points of view and hard-won insights. I see, she said.

The others said she was stuck-up. Probably she was. It could appear that way.

The turning point came in late summer, when finally one Sunday morning it occurred to him that maybe he should try to talk with her about something *he* knew, so he put one of the beryls he had found at Minnesund in his pocket and mustered the courage to knock at the house where she lived and ask if perhaps Miss Karin was at home. She was.

The next Sunday she wanted to go along into the fields to find green stones like that. They didn't find any, but he gave a nice little lecture while they walked. She looked at him with interest. He got the impression that it wasn't what he *said* so much as the *way* he said it. On the way home she let him hold her hand. Drip, drip. The lieutenant on maneuvers, Willy lying in ambush with roses one Saturday evening—in the most friendly way, of course, since she was alone again, and wasn't her sweetheart on maneuvers quite often? Drip, drip. Then he discovered that he could do the same with other things too, just as with the stones, he could talk about himself and his own interests in the same way, about his own thoughts, tell about the giant's kettle, tell about the house he had grown up in, tell about his father and mother and brothers, tell about the sea there in the south, about the park around the house, and she listened. Hand in hand.

"She's smiling at me, Karin."

"That's probably just a gas pain."

"Now you're the one who's pedantic. Look! She's smiling."

"Mmm. You're right. She's smiling."

"Has she smiled at *you* before?"

"Lots of times."

"Well anyway, now she's smiling at *Daddy*."

"Do you know that I thought you were so nice, right from the beginning, Willy?"

He was silent.

"You're the nicest person I know," she said seriously.

Amm! Hammm! No, no. Don't tip over. Awake. I'm awake. How long had he lain there? He was afraid. Would anyone come? Had he lain there long? He didn't think he had lain there more than maybe half an hour, and already he was aching and stiff and kept slipping in and out of drowsiness. That was dangerous. He thought about Vesla.

———

Was someone coming now?

Was that voices he heard? Yes, far away, like an echo, he thought he heard men's voices.

"Here!" he shouted at the top of his lungs. "Here! Help! Help!"

He stopped shouting, the echo of his voice died away, he listened up into the darkness. Had he been mistaken? It was utterly quiet for a moment. But then he heard it again, there *were* voices, they came nearer, he heard footsteps, the heavy tread of mine workers resounded somewhere in the drift above him, he shouted again, shouted for help.

"Halloo!" he heard a deep voice from overhead. "Halloo there!"

Another man's voice, not quite so deep, joined in.

"Halloo!" The steps came nearer. Now he saw a light. Oh thank God, light. Flickering light approached somewhere up there, light and footsteps, voices, people.

"Is there a man over the edge?" shouted the deepest voice. The light was just at the edge now, three or four meters above him, two lights, two flickering lights. He couldn't see those who shouted, but he could dimly perceive movement in the light.

"Yes!" he screamed. "Here! Man over the edge!"

"Be calm. Just lie there quietly! We'll get help!"

Now he heard more voices in the drift up there, a whole chorus of miners' voices, and could just barely make out the words.

"Man over the edge here—man over the edge—get help! Get help!"

The message was shouted along the passage up there.

"Lie quietly," said the more high-pitched voice. "Just lie quietly, and we'll get help."

"Thank you!" said the engineer.

"It's a narrow projecting beam. Just lie completely quiet until they come with a rope."

"It's—it's good you came with light."

"Hurry up!" the same voice shouted out toward the others. Footsteps running, voices hurrying each other. Silence.

Now there were just the two above him. They must have come in to look for him. He must have been lying there a long time.

"Don't worry. We'll stay and give you light until they come with help," said the deeper voice.

"Yes," said the other voice. "You can count on that."

Thank you, the engineer said to himself, reassured. It was so good to see the light from their lanterns, warm and softly flickering. And they kept saying reassuring little things to him, until all at once their voices disappeared, suddenly it was silent above him.

"Hello!" he shouted up into the beam of light. "Are you there?"

"Everything will be fine now, friend," said the one voice.

Then the light died away.

The light died away and once again he lay in pitch darkness.

He shouted. Shouted and shouted, but clung fast to the beam, he shouted and clawed his fingers firmly into the wood. The minutes went by. The light did not reappear. And he knew that this was the worst thing that had ever happened to him. He shouted. He cried out. And once again he saw light above him, but different—steady, cool, blue; he heard steps, and now white light from a couple of lanterns shone down on him. This time he saw faces too, he recognized Knudsen.

"What th' devil! Mr. Bolt!"

"Get me up!" he shouted.

"Rope!" someone shouted. "Hurry, goddamn it! And more men!"

FOUR

When they had hoisted him up, strong hands placed him on a stretcher, and then they slowly carried him out, out toward the light. Knudsen walked beside the stretcher and shone the light.

"Why did you leave? Goddamm it!" he shouted.

"Leave?"

"You were there, you had discovered me and were shining the light. Then you left again and let me lie there."

Knudsen gave him a baffled look.

"I think the engineer got hit on the head," he said.

"Hit!" shouted the engineer. "Believe me, I'm ready to hit *you*!"

"They never should of let anybody go messin' around in here alone, young fella," said a voice.

"Hmm," growled another. "No excuse for it."

The engineer listened to the voices, listened very carefully, but did not recognize any of them as the *first* voices he had heard above him in there.

"Which of you was it?" he shouted.

"Now, now," said Knudsen. "We're gonna be out soon. He's had a shock, poor guy."

The engineer was about to shout something, but held his tongue; he could glimpse the light now, they would soon be out of the darkness.

"Look!" said Knudsen. It grew light. They had come out into the side passage, the one the engineer had set off from a few hours earlier, through the opening to the Ulrik drift.

They put down the stretcher to catch their breath.

"This is where me and Bjørnsrud heard a shout from in there. We was standin' right here takin' a leak," said Knudsen.

"Here?" said one of the stretcher bearers in disbelief.

"Yep," said Knudsen. Then his voice grew quiet, as if he understood the significance of what he had said. "Right here it was."

"Not a chance," said one of the others. "We went in there almost a kilometer."

"But we *heard* him, didn't we, Bjørnsrud?"

"That's right," said Bjørnsrud. "*Man over the edge!* somebody shouted from in there."

"Did you shout that, Bolt?"

"I don't know," said the engineer, half rising on the stretcher.

"Anyway, there was somethin' strange about it," said Knudsen. "When I think about it. I thought there was *several* guys shoutin' in there."

"That's right," nodded Bjørnsrud. "We just followed the voices. Then we discovered it was only the engineer."

The men looked at Bolt, looked at each other.

"There were others," said Bolt. "They came and shone a light and told me to lie still until they got help. Then they left again, and then you came."

They were all silent for a while. Knudsen thought it over.

"It's an old drift," was all he said. "Lucky we got that warning from in there."

He looked at the engineer.

"Otherwise you would of been lyin' there a long time before anybody came lookin' for you." His words were spoken solemnly. He smiled at the engineer.

"You were lucky," agreed the engineer.

"Mmm," said Bjørnsrud. "Warnings like that happen sometimes," he said, his voice quite ordinary. "Lots of odd things in the mountain." But he too had a solemn look on his face.

The men straightened their backs simultaneously, lifted the stretcher again.

"Strange story," said one of the stretcher bearers.

Nothing more was said about the matter, not then or later. He came up into the daylight, out of the darkness, and was driven to the hospital, where Karin already awaited him with Vesla in her arms. Karin came running toward them when they carried him in.

❧

And I, poor useless devil, have to go on living! I! *Is there any MEANING in that? What good was that whole underworld circus, when I go on living?*

FIVE

The insects still swarmed outside. He sat sleeping heavily in his chair. He had probably been weeping, but you couldn't see that in the moist heat. He has probably been weeping again, the servant said to himself as he carefully covered the man with a thin lap robe and cleared away all the glasses. He should be put to bed, thought the servant; but the native wasn't strong enough to lift him alone.

"He's probably been weeping again," Caspar said when Mr. Andersen returned from town. And Andersen went to his friend and traveling companion, gently lifted him out of the chair, put him over his shoulder, carried him into the bedroom, laid him on the bed. Caspar spread a coverlet over him.

"Is it always his wife he's thinking about, when he's like this, sahib?"

"Yes. It's always his wife. And his daughter."

"Very unfortunate for him, sir."

"Yes." They glanced at the night table, where there was a photograph of a young woman with a child in her arms.

"A shame," said the tall man in a tropical suit. "I think he was originally a good person, before he lost them."

The old man still lay in his coffin and saw all this which no one else can see. It was very strange, and at the same time very natural. He smiled a little in the darkness, which was as buoyant as undulating water. He had to smile at himself a little. Many, many things have happened through the generations, he thought, in order that the two of us should meet. Many things have happened so that we should lose each other. Isn't that what she's thinking? Isn't that what I'm thinking? There's a connection; it's well hidden, but it's there; it can be searched out by one who no longer has limbs or loins to drag around. Much still remains.

Isn't that what I think? What does she think?

I thought I was lonely, and would always be so. Then once again a flutter of wings came into my life. *Everything*, he thought (and it was strange), *she will have everything, all my sorrow, all my silver, all that is.*

Everything I can remember, and I can remember almost *everything*.

The swallows take flight, and morning rises in the sky. Lea enters the church, the notes vibrate between her legs, into her, into stone walls and coffin lid, into flower fragrance and sunlight.

Life is a bird. And you are the branch that sways back and forth.